RIVER OF REMORSE

HEART ISLAND SANCTUARY SERIES

By

AnnaLeigh Skye

Inner Muse Publishing LLC

COPYRIGHT

River of Remorse by AnnaLeigh Skye

First Edition (2022)

Published by Inner Muse Publishing LLC
Hallstead, Pa 18822

Cover by Corinne Preston
ISBN: 978-1-957903-06-4(paperback)

This book is dedicated to

Tania Fodor Jenkins
I wouldn't have survived my teens without you by my side. I know we're both an acquired taste, but I love you just the way you are…. Your fierce support and eternal love are a gift. Your beautiful brain, brutal honesty, and quirkiness make you absolutely perfect and I wouldn't change a thing about you—except for the amount of time I get to spend with you. I love you forever and a day!

CONTENT WARNING

Dear Readers,

This book is intended for mature audiences over the age of eighteen. There are graphic scenes depicting steamy romance, violence and sexual violence that may be uncomfortable for some readers. Reader discretion is advised.

RESOURCES

If you need help or know of someone else who does, please contact

National Human Trafficking Resource Hotline -US

call 211 or text your zip code to 891211

or call
1-888-373-7888

CHAPTER ONE

Others Would Treasure You...

Rhyanna Cairn pulled her long, honey-blond hair over her shoulder and quickly braided it. When she finished, the thick braid brushed her waist. She looked at herself in the mirror, wondering what exactly it was that drew Kyran Tyde to her. Large, emerald eyes looked back at her skeptically. A smattering of freckles dusted her nose and cheeks, standing out against her pale skin. High cheekbones in her heart-shaped face narrowed down to a pointy chin. Her skin was clear and burned easy in the summer. To her eyes, she seemed average—at best. Her shoulders were wide, and her hips matched. What did she have that would keep the most handsome man she had ever known—and a prince of the Court of Tears—by her side?

Rhyanna waited centuries for the man destiny had promised her, and recently, she thought she had finally found him. Kyran was handsome, standing nearly a foot taller than her five-foot-eight. His height and muscular build made her feel petite and dainty, something she had never been. Blond hair fell to his shoulders, highlighted from the time he spent working outdoors. Cerulean blue eyes changed with his moods and gazed at her with love and longing. Large, strong hands caressed her with a gentleness that belied his size. The man was perfect, she loved him, and recently, they found out that he was betrothed against his will to someone

1

else. A water element, he returned to the home of his Elemental Clan, known as the Court of Tears, to try and settle the matter.

The news devastated her, and she was still reeling from it. Kyran made her happy, and he awoke the untouched woman in her. If he couldn't resolve this issue, she would never know what they might have been together. It was too depressing of a thought to dwell on for long.

"Get over it, ye idgit," she thought to herself. "Ye've not the time nor the energy to keep dwelling on a man ye can't have." Even though she said the words with conviction, her heart still ached from his loss. She missed the evening strolls they had taken and the way he made her feel like every moment they spent together was a gift. Rhy had never felt so cherished before.

She left her suite of rooms in the Gothic structure known as the Heart Island Sanctuary and headed downstairs. As she stepped into the foyer, a whirlwind of activity in the form of a five-year-old boy came barreling towards her.

"Auntie Rheee," Landon screeched, "can you please look at my rat later? Mrs. O'Hare hurt him with her broom." He batted his eyes at her. "I know you can make him all better."

Holy Mother of all, how was she going to treat a damn rat? The look of hope in his pale eyes begged her to help his little friend. She adored the lad and knew she wouldn't be able to say no. "Aye, laddie, I would be happy to look at him after dinner. Have Uncle Fergus come with you to help contain the little beastie, please."

His smile brightened up her day as he threw his arms around her middle, hugging her tightly. "Thank you. I knew you could save him for me." Without another word, he went racing down the hall, most likely headed for the kitchen to steal a pocketful of cookies.

Landon's appearance reminded her there was always hope. His father, Ronan Pathfinder, and Madylyn SkyDancer were separated for centuries before being reunited this spring. Landon, a son Ronan had been unaware of, joined them, and Maddy was expecting a child this winter. Their family proved that most any obstacle could be overcome.

A real smile on her face now, she stepped outside and walked down the path to her apothecary shoppe and clinic. The sun shining brightly overhead warmed her from the inside out as she walked—mayhap it healed a little bit of her broken heart. Kyran promised her when he left that he would fix this, and she needed to believe that somehow he would.

Feeling better than she had since Kyran left, she gave some love to the calico cat, who had claimed her as her own. She met Rhy outside the door, waiting for her morning meal. Rubbing up against her, she twined around Rhy's ankles as she purred. "Hello, my darling, I should give ye a name, but ye haven't earned one yet." She took some kibble out of a container and fed the colorful beastie.

Rhyanna entered her shoppe, casting witch light into the lanterns by the door, the large hearth, and the chandelier hanging in the middle of the room. Warm, golden light flooded the room, chasing the shadows and the cool air away. She filled the large, cast-iron kettle with water from the hand pump in her sink and returned it to the hook over the hearth.

A large maple box with tiny drawers held ingredients for teas, and she quickly created a strong black morning brew with a hint of bergamot. Filling a metal ball, she set it in a porcelain teapot and focused on breakfast while she waited for the water to boil.

Hearing movement in the back room she used as a clinic, she smiled and put on a skillet to make scrambled eggs for her charges. She scrambled a dozen eggs, then crumbled some thyme and parsley from the bunches of herbs hanging from a metal rack on the wall. She sliced thick slices of sourdough bread and toasted them while the eggs simmered.

The door between the shoppe and the clinic opened, and a shy face peered out. Hailey Gallagher hesitated before she walked into the shoppe, her eyes carefully looking around the room to see if Rhyanna was alone.

Rhy smiled at her trying to reassure her. "C'mon in lass. Breakfast will be ready in a few minutes. Are the others up and ready?"

Hailey shook her head and said in a voice that was barely an octave over a whisper, "Grace is training with Danny, and Genny is still sleeping." The hesitant lass was still a shell of the young woman she had once been, but her cheeks were filling in, her bruises were nearly healed, and she was surrounded by people who loved her. Hopefully, time would help with the rest. Rhyanna had become very close to the young woman during the time she spent taking care of her. Hailey reminded her of one of her sisters.

Rhy and her fellow Wardens rescued Hailey, Genny, and Grace from a human trafficking ring. Nearly dead, horribly beaten, and abused, they nearly drowned, as the ship the girls were shackled in had gone aground off Grindstone Island. Six other young women drowned before the wardens arrived, and Hailey had nearly joined their numbers. Weeks had passed since they brought the girls to Rhyanna's clinic at the Sanctuary on Heart Island, but the young women had a long way to go processing and recovering from the trauma they experienced.

Grace, the oldest, was learning self-defense. She worked daily with Danyka, honing her fighting skills so that she would never feel vulnerable again. Genny's father sold her into the lifestyle, and she was terrified that if she returned home, he would do so again. She was knowledgeable about healing, so Rhyanna offered her an apprenticeship to keep her safe.

Hailey's Uncle Roarke was part of the crew that rescued the girls. He immediately contacted her parents, and they soon joined her on the island where she was recuperating. Today, she would return home, and Rhyanna could sense her trepidation.

"Join me for a cuppa, lass?" Rhyanna asked. Hailey nodded, and Rhy set two places on the table with porcelain cups and plates, placing a generous portion of eggs on each of the plates and adding the buttered toast.

Hailey joined her and sipped her tea after adding cream and sugar to it. Rhyanna could sense her unease, so she reached out telepathically to communicate with her, knowing that she hesitated to speak aloud, making Rhy wonder what kind of punishments were administered for talking.

"*Are you afraid of going home, lass?*" Rhy asked on their internal link knowing this was a more comfortable way of communicating for Hailey.

"*A bit,*" she admitted. "*How do I ever go back to the world I used to live in? No one will ever see me the same again. I will always be the girl who vanished, and I am sure the rumors have started already about what I went through.*" Her eyes welled up. "*I don't want to talk about it with anyone. EVER,*" she thought vehemently. "*They will never understand the things I did just to survive, the things I hate myself for doing. I should have just let myself die.*"

"*Please don't ever think that, Hailey,*" Rhyanna said gently as she reached out and covered her hand with her own. "*We all have a purpose, each and every one of us. Every step of our journey leads us to where we are supposed to be. Those steps are rarely easy, and many of us seem to have more struggles than others, but every day that ye wake up and take a breath, is a day that there is hope that it's going to be a better day. Never forget that. Ye have a wonderful network of people who love ye and desperately want to help ye if ye'll allow them to. Don't shut them all out, lass. It will only lead to more pain for everyone involved.*"

Hailey looked at Rhyanna silently for a long time. "*Ye've been very kind to all of us, and I am grateful for your advice. I wish I could stay here with you.*"

Rhyanna's heart ached for the sorrow and uncertainty she could sense radiating from her. "*I know ye do, lass, and ye are welcome to return for a visit anytime ye wish.*" She reached up and tapped the side of her temple. "*Ye may also contact me by our link any time, lass. Day or night. I will be here for ye.*"

"*I know now why my Uncle Roarke favors you, Mistress,*" she said. "*You don't see it, but I know him, and few earn his respect or his attention. You've earned both.*"

"*Sadly, Hailey, I am already spoken for,*" Rhyanna said with a smile, hoping she truly was.

"Thank you for your kindness and your compassion, Mistress Rhyanna," she said aloud as she stood to hug her. Rhyanna squeezed her tightly, sending strength and courage into her frail body. It was the first time Hailey had allowed Rhyanna to hug her.

The door opened, and her Uncle Roarke walked in. "Are you ready, sweet pea?" he asked, looking down on her. Roarke was a big man. Six-and-a-half feet of ruggedly handsome man with broad shoulders, a narrow waist, and an easy smile. His blond hair hit the middle of his back, and his dark brown eyes were warm and welcoming as they sought hers. Hailey walked over to him and allowed him to put an arm around her narrow shoulders. "Yer ma and pa are outside waiting, lass. Go on. I'll be right out." He opened the door for her before turning to Rhyanna.

"Again, I am in your debt, Rhyanna," he said solemnly. "You have helped us all, not just Hailey, and we will never forget your kindness or how hard you worked to save our girls."

His sincerity was heartfelt, and his gaze lingered on Rhyanna with just a hint of something more. She didn't examine it too closely because she didn't need any more confusion or instability in her life. A light blush stained her cheeks at his praise.

"I was happy to be able to help them," she said. "I only wish I could have done more to heal the wounds we don't see. They are the hardest ones to recover from."

"You're right about that," he sighed. "She has a long road ahead of her."

"Aye, she does. Ye might want to let her family know that she communicates easier if she doesn't have to speak aloud. I'm sure there is a good reason for it, but she'll be more receptive on her private links with each of you." She looked down, her eyebrows nearly touching as she tried to put words to her next thoughts.

"Speak plainly, Mistress Rhyanna. Don't overthink what you want to say," he said with a gentle smile.

"It's going to be a long time until she feels like herself again. If she becomes overwhelmed returning home, she is welcome to come back and stay here, or in the Sanctuary, for as long as she needs to. I am sure we could find her a position, so it doesn't feel like charity to her. Ye ken?"

"Aye, Mistress, I do. If she has trouble readjusting, I will contact you myself." He ran a hand through his hair. "Thank you for the offer. We appreciate it more than you realize."

"Ye've no need to be so formal with me, Roarke. 'Rhyanna or Rhy' is just fine." She smiled at him before asking, "Will ye be leaving with them?"

"Ready to be rid of me already, are you?"

"Nye," she laughed. "I've just gotten used to ye being around."

"Aye, I will be escorting them home." He smiled warmly at her. "I'll be back this evening, though." The warmth fled as his eyes grew colder, and he said, "I fully intend to help the sanctuary hunt down the men responsible for this and find Rosella."

Rhyanna watched him. His aura was screaming red with rage, and she could feel the need for vengeance pouring out of him. His sister Rosella was abducted a month ago, and they had found very little clues to help locate her. The women they rescued provided additional pieces of the puzzle, but not near enough to locate her.

"We'll need all the help we can get, Roarke. We're covering a large area and short-staffed as it is, with the Romani patrols focusing more on the river."

Roarke nodded. "I'll be happy to help. A good day to you then, Rhyanna; I'll see you soon." He turned for the door, then impulsively turned back and hugged her tightly. "Hailey was lucky to have you," he whispered into her ear before stepping back and looking at her wistfully as his hand cupped her face. "We all are."

Rhyanna blushed with the way his eyes held hers. She'd never had a suitor until destiny dropped two men into her path over the past few months. Unfortunately, she only loved one of them.

"Kyran better appreciate your worth," he said as he released her, "because there are others who would treasure you." His eyes held hers for a long moment before he turned and walked out the door.

Rhyanna's heart raced as his bedroom eyes bored into hers, promising nights of pleasure. Vengeance wasn't the only emotion her empathic side read from him. Roarke was attracted to her and holding back, only out of respect for her and the man she loved.

CHAPTER TWO

Frustrated

Kyran Tyde dressed carefully for his audience with the king and queen of the Water Court. A turquoise silk button-down intensified his cerulean eyes. He wore a black double-breasted brocade vest fastened with pewter clasps. Dark trousers and knee-high, black leather boots with similar accents on the wide cuffs finished the ensemble.

He combed his shoulder-length blond hair back from his face, tying it in a low tail, and called it good. His reflection in the mirror reminded him that he was still under-dressed by court standards.

"Sir, this will help," his personal valet, Myles, said as he held out a jacket. Kyran stretched out his arms and slipped on the long, black velvet jacket with matching pewter buttons. Wide cuffs finished the sleeves, and a high neckline suited him.

Myles bowed. "Dashing, sir. Is there anything else I might have the privilege to do for you today?"

"Thank you, but no," Kyran said with a smile. "I appreciate your help, but I need some time to myself."

Myles nodded, and as he headed for the door, he offered Kyran some advice. "Keep your temper in check, Prince Kyran. It won't help you once you step through those doors."

His eyes locked with Kyran's before he continued, "If there is any way in which I might offer assistance, I hope you will consult me. I wish you the best of luck. You don't deserve to be forced into a betrothal with a stranger. I hope you get the answer you need." He closed the door without a sound on his way out.

Myles had been his valet since he was a teen. The man was polite and discreet, two things that were low in supply at court these days. Kyran thought of him like an eccentric uncle. Myles's cryptic advice surprised him, and he let out a long-winded sigh while tugging at the buttons around his neck.

He was suffocating, not just in the outfit but in this cesspool in general. Trapped at court against his will was his own private hell. The formality, the petty bullshit, and the ass-kissing wasn't his style. The leash holding back his seldom seen but very explosive temper was fraying fast.

Kyran looked in the mirror once again and realized he no longer associated himself as a member of this court. How was it possible that he felt like an imposter in the environment that raised him? Once proud to call the palace his home, he no longer recognized it as the place he had grown up in. He and his siblings roamed the halls of this palace freely, supported by his loving parents and the Water Clan's community within its walls. Kind faces and friends abounded. The Court of Tears was a safe, welcoming place to reside or work in. They treated their staff well, and they were well-known for their hospitality.

With water as his primary element, he should have been more at home here on the Atlantic Ocean than anywhere else on this half of the continent. Water elements found solace near any body of water, but the body of water closest to their clan always brought them the most peace. Heavily influenced by others' emotions, hormones, and subconscious feelings, the ocean helped them to transmute any negative energy into something much more tranquil.

The Court of Tears, the highest Elemental Court for all of the Water Clans on the Atlantic coast, should have offered him peace. The halls he walked down today no longer resembled the ones of his childhood. Instead, this place felt like a prison. Fear swamped his senses until he was drowning in the unhappiness and unease from the staff and courtiers alike. How had his father's court become so tainted and sadistic?

Courtiers stalked him in the halls like fresh meat, even though they knew he hadn't slept with anyone at court in centuries. What had once been a proud, beautiful place to seek an audience was currently the evil queen's playground, and Kyran was tired of feeling like her prey.

Water Clans on the eastern seaboard fell under the jurisdiction of the Court of Tears—King Varan and Queen Merial. The king was Kyran's father, and the queen, his stepmother. Kyran's mother, the former Queen Yareli, left court and the king a century ago after finding out about his infidelity with Meriel. The king at the time was indifferent to her devastation, which led to the dissolution of their relationship.

The Court of Tears was based on the feudal system. A formal court and caste system still existed. The court expected all of its members to be amenable to its decisions. Rarely did they issue decrees that were unfair or unreasonable.

When Meriel became queen, she ruled with fear and suspicion as her advisors. Vexed by the inability to control Varan's five children, she used her power and authority to make their lives difficult.

As the king's health deteriorated, she continued to rule without mercy. Courtiers vied for their monarch's attention in court policy or the bedroom. Lately, the only opportunities that seemed to arise were to join either the king's formal harem or the queen's sadistic one.

The previous queen, Yareli, earned the love of her people. Generous with her time and her resources on the people's behalf, they sought to show their appreciation.

Queen Merial, on the other hand, longed for her peoples' favor, but she didn't want to do anything to earn their devotion or their respect. If they wouldn't shower her with the attention she thought she deserved, she would shower them with fear and suspicion. She turned loyal friends against each other and rejoiced in destroying happy couples.

The king quickly grew tired of his new queen, missing Yareli more every day. Meriel would never be Yareli, and her presence was a constant reminder of his mistake and how much his infidelity cost him. In addition to the loss of the woman he loved, the relationship with his children deteriorated after their parents' separation. His sons no longer respected him, and he rarely saw his only daughter. He chose separate chambers—away from his new queen—soon after their pledging ceremony. Rumors abounded that his strange behavior was due to the loss of his true love.

After witnessing his parents' failed marriage, Kyran wasn't sure that he believed in love. Tired of wasting centuries with one-night stands, he'd remained celibate for the past century. He thought he was content with his situation, but then he met Rhyanna.

The moment he laid eyes on her, he fell in love with the sweet, compassionate, earth mage. Rhyanna was a warden and a healer at the Heart Island Sanctuary, where he was currently stationed. She was everything he had ever dreamed about and so much more. In addition to her sweet disposition, she was an impressive healer and sexy as hell. His little nymph possessed one hell of a temper if he made her unhappy. He had done it once and was doing his best not to piss her off again. It took a hell of a lot to get her there, but holy hell, once she did, she was explosive—and even sexier, if he was being honest.

For the first time in his life, he took the time to get to know a woman. His body instantly responded to her physically, but he pursued her slowly—

slower than she wanted at times. It was important to him not to rush their relationship. He wanted to properly court her—she had never experienced that, and she deserved to. Hell, he had never been with anyone long enough to consider a courtship before.

Kyran fell more in love with her every time they were together. Their relationship started with evening walks after dinner. She showed him the island while they talked and laughed. Working together added a layer of respect and awe at her healing gifts. Her loyalty to her fellow wardens was admirable, but more importantly, she took his breath away every time he was near her.

They were on the eve of consummating their relationship when this fiasco occurred, preventing them from fully becoming lovers.

A Pledging Ceremony for Madylyn SkyDancer, Heart Island's Head Mistress, and Ronan Pathfinder, a warden who was the island's Stable Master, had taken place. The entire island attended the feast after the ceremony and was well into their cups when guards from the Court of Tears arrived on Heart Island, insisting Kyran return at once to court. The king and queen had betrothed him to a princess from the Fire Court, a woman he had never even heard mention.

If they denied his petition, and he refused to obey his king and accept this betrothal, he would most likely be banished from the Court of Tears for the remainder of his life, or he could be incarcerated until he agreed. Was he willing to lose his family over this? He'd thought of nothing but this conundrum for the past few days. The answer was a resounding "yes" because she was his future.

"Is everything all right, Kyran?" Rhyanna asked on their private link. *"You seem agitated, me laird."* A sense of peace rolled through him from her, settling his nerves and making him miss her more.

Kyran sighed as he rubbed his hand over his heart. They entwined a piece of each of their heart chakras, allowing her to sense his distress even from a distance. She hadn't spoken to him since he left, and he couldn't blame her after the shock and devastation the announcement had caused them both. She had requested time to think, so he gave her the space she requested and hadn't attempted to contact her. But he missed their constant connection, and it devastated him when their only way to communicate at a distance was on hold. He was grateful that she finally reached out to him.

"Rhyanna, my lady, I have missed you."

Silence met his statement, so he decided not to push his luck. *"I'm fine, my lady. A little nervous, perhaps. Court is about to begin, and I feel like a young boy, begging for a treat. I shouldn't have to beg to spend my life with the woman who makes me happy."*

"Nye," she agreed. *"Ye shouldn't have to."* She hesitated, and he waited patiently for her to continue. *"I'm sorry I've been shutting ye out since ye left. I'se afraid to get me hopes up and be disappointed again...but I miss ye, Kyran. I long to hear yer voice throughout the day on our link. Will I be able to see ye anytime soon?"*

"I'll do my best, but always remember that I love you, Rhy, and I can't wait to spend the rest of my life proving that to you."

"I love ye, too, me laird."

For the first time that day, a smile crossed his face. She only used that term when they were being intimate. He missed their nights of teasing. *"May I contact you tonight?"* he asked hopefully. Even if it wasn't in person, they could spend time together and share pleasure through the telepathic bridge they had built.

"I would like that very much, Kyran," she said, and through that bridge, he could feel her longing and her anticipation for the night to come.

"I watch the sunset while I take my evening bath, if it's convenient for ye, me laird."

"I'll make sure it's convenient, my lady." His body reacted to the mere thought of her naked in the tub. *"Thank you, Rhy, for finally reaching out. I have been lost without the ability to sense you. Please, don't shut me out again."*

"I'm sorry, but I needed the time to process our new situation. It wasn't easy on me either. I, too, have been adrift without ye in me life. Until tonight..."

"Until tonight." He sent his love and longing through their line, then added a heavy dose of lust to make her spend the rest of the day anticipating their night together.

Anxious to return to Rhyanna as soon as they settled this insanity and dissolved the contract, he paced. A pledge ceremony was in his future, but she was the only one he would accept as his life partner.

The king and queen heard petitions from their people once a week. He waited impatiently for a court date that would allow him to challenge the quickly approaching betrothal. He arrived a week ago and missed Court by a day. Today was finally his chance to get out of this ridiculous forced betrothal.

Even though the king was Kyran's father, Kyran received the same treatment as any other member of his clan, as did his brothers Kenn, Kano, and Kai, and his only sister, Klaree, who still lived with his mother as they all had their first century. His brothers lived at court, enjoying the benefits and advantages of being princes. They were indifferent—for the most part—to the intrigues going on around them. He truly hoped it was because they were ignorant of them, and not because they didn't give a shit about their peoples' suffering. Kyran was the oldest and had long ago outgrown their playground. He petitioned for the Heart Island assignment to get away from court and his father's steady decline. Now, he just wanted to get this settled and go back to the Sanctuary and to the woman he loved, Rhyanna.

The first set of bells rang, indicating Court would be in session in a quarter of an hour. Kyran steeled himself to plead his case and fight for the life he wanted. He simply refused to accept the one planned for him with a complete stranger. With a quick prayer to his grandsire Neptune, and to the Earth Mother for her assistance, he prepared himself to face his future—whatever it might be.

CHAPTER THREE

Landon

Landon ran through the main floor, heading for the kitchens. Mrs. O'Hare just left the building, and his window to sneak a few cookies was rapidly closing. He never knew how long she would be gone—might be hours or merely minutes.

Cautiously, he stepped into the dark kitchen. He smiled; the dark meant the room was empty, but he knew his way around it well enough that he didn't need any light. He spied the massive glass jar with the matching lid sitting on the walnut countertop. Moving quickly, he crossed the room and quietly lifted the lid off with his right hand. With his left, he stuck a cookie in his mouth and two more in his pants pocket. Carefully, he placed the lid back on the jar, cringing as it clacked together.

A noise from the other end of the long room startled him, and he almost dropped his cookie. Something moved in the dark pantry behind him. Heart racing, he turned and sprinted for the door. He'd nearly reached it when voices coming down the hall stopped him in his tracks.

Maddy would be disappointed that he was eating sweets before dinner, so he made a mad dash and slid under a metal prep table. He scooched all the way to the back before two of the scullery lads wandered in. They moved past him and headed for the pantry in the back. Crab crawling carefully out so he didn't bump the table, he made his escape into the hall. Whew! He looked both ways and, with no one coming, headed left for the back door leading to the gardens.

The sun was still high as he headed into the formal gardens. His nose crinkled at the sickly-sweet smell from all the flowers. He didn't understand why girls liked them so much. They smelled funny and made him sneeze.

13

A flagstone path was his quickest way to bypass the stables and his father. He liked Ronan, but he liked exploring new areas of the island more, especially on such a nice day. He would have preferred to take a horse with him on his adventure but doubted he'd be allowed without a chaperone. Maybe one of the hellhounds would have liked to go for a walk with him? Second thoughts came quickly as he remembered his Grandfather Cheveyo's warning about tanning his hide if he ever caught him in there without an adult. Cheveyo had never laid a hand on him, but Landon believed he would follow through on this specific threat.

Reassessing his options, he headed for the dragon cave. Isabella and Alejandro were the two dragons living at the sanctuary. Isabella was pale blue and green in color, while Alejandro was black with dark blue on his neck and belly. He loved the dragons, and they tolerated his visits.

His dark head was barely visible as he raced through a hayfield bordering the forest. The rows of hay swayed as he moved through them like a large serpent winding from side to side. He plucked a piece and stuck it in his mouth like he remembered Ronan doing. He chewed on it, then spit it out, wiping his lips with the back of his hand. He didn't know why men did that when it tasted disgusting.

A pasture was fenced off near the river. He crawled under the split rail fence and ran through the sheep, goats, and young beefers stocked for use by the draconian pair. The goats were used to him coming by and ran with him as he chased the lambs. His high-pitched laughter rang out as he nearly caught one. Tripping on a root, they gained quite a lead, and he slowed to a walk, realizing he'd lost his prey.

The pasture sat on a bluff above the river. He could hear the waves crashing below. A footpath followed the edge of the bluff down to a cave forty feet above the water. Landon carefully made his way down the path until he stood in the entrance to the cave. Remembering his manners, he reached up and pulled a string that was attached to bells. He waited as patiently as he was able to at five until a voice in his head said, *"You may enter, little Ronan."*

"Thank you, Isabella." he said. "How many are there now?" He wasn't as good at using his inner switchboard, so he spoke aloud to her.

"Thirteen, little man. Would you like to see them?"

"Fergus says thirteen is lucky, but I don't know what for, and Mrs. O'Hare calls thirteen a baker's dozen, but I thought a dozen was only twelve. Do you think it's a lucky number?"

"Well, it sure isn't a baker's dozen, now, is it?" she snorted, and tiny curls of smoke rose from her nostrils then floated away in rings through the entrance, fading on the wind.

Landon loved when she blew smoke rings for him. It wasn't intentionally for his benefit, but he enjoyed it anyway. His face lit up as he gazed up at her. He took a step closer and reached up to stroke her head as she leaned down to him. His small hand stroked gently down over her nose. "You're one of my best friends," he told her solemnly. "I don't have very many. My rat ran away after Mrs. O'Hare threatened to kill him."

"How could he have left a sweet child like you?" she asked with what might have been a chuckle. Her whole body shook gently as he petted her.

"I dunno. I was trying to get him a snack, and she went crazy hitting him with a broom and threatening me with no more cookies."

"I doubt a little threat stopped you, did it? How many did you bring today?"

"I took one for me, and then I brought two for you." He pulled them out of his pocket. The journey here reduced them to pieces, but he laid them carefully on a stone in front of her. "Maybe they will help with the cravings you were talking about last time. They help Maddy when she gets them."

"Mayhap. I was thinking more in the line of trout, but mayhap these will help." Her golden eyes looked at the man child, and she couldn't help the equivalent of a smile. *"Would you like to see them?"*

"Please, can I? Please..." He bounced up and down like a broken spring.

"Do you remember the rules, little Ronan?"

"I has to be quiet," he ticked off the rules on his fingers as he spoke, starting with his forefinger, "no touching, and I can't ask Alejandro questions, or he might eat me."

"You are correct. Now come quietly, and I will show you."

The small boy followed the enormous creature down a long, dark tunnel. He kept his hand on her side as she moved slow enough for him to keep up. Every time he visited her, they went to a different location. He would never be able to find his way in the maze of caves on his own.

A cool breeze rushed past him, and he knew they were close. Isabella gave a small sigh, and flames lit up the room in front of him. Alejandro curled his massive body into a tight ball on the hay piled high beneath him. His tail encircled a round nest. Inside were thirteen iridescent eggs in shimmering, pale blues and greens and a few dark blue and black mixed in. The eggs were nearly as big as Landon, and every now and then, something pushed against the shell, testing its boundaries.

"They're beautiful," he whispered, remembering his rules. He gazed up at her in awe. "Will there be any more?"

"No, this is all of them."

He moved closer in small increments. Alejandro saw him and hissed. Landon was fairly sure he didn't like him much. He worried at times that if

Isabella wasn't looking, the male might make a snack out of him. A small nod acknowledged the male's dominance in their situation.

Close enough to reach out and touch, the boy watched in awe as Isabella used her snout to roll each egg and breath on them. Before he came to the sanctuary, he'd never seen a dragon before, let alone touched one or fed them cookies.

"How long until they hatch?"

"That's up to them, Landon. They need to make their way out of the shells on their own, or they won't be strong enough to survive. We can't help them, but it should be soon. Come, it's time to go."

Landon hated to leave. He wanted to be there when the eggs hatched but knew better than to push his luck. Alejandro might ban him, and then he wouldn't be able to visit anymore. He couldn't afford to lose any more of his friends.

They reached the entrance, and he could've sworn she was chuckling behind him. *"I can't imagine Madylyn objecting to a kitten, can you?"*

His eyes widened, and he bounced again in excitement. "No, ma'am, she wouldn't," he said excitedly.

"When you get to the top of the path, go to the right. I think there's a black and white one that's been abandoned. You'll hear her crying. She'll need a bath; she smells a little strong. Tell Maddy that Fergus should be able to help with that if she's upset at all."

She was definitely laughing, but he wasn't sure why. "Thanks, Isabella. I promise I'll take real good care of her, and I'll bring her back for visits."

"Thank you, but that's not necessary."

Landon ran off with a wave. As he crested the hill, he heard some pitiful mewling. He found his black kitty digging in the ground, eating bugs. He sat down and waited for her to come to him like Cheveyo had taught him with the ponies. The pitiful little thing crawled into his lap and fell asleep. His nose scrunched up because she did need a bath. It reminded him of something he had smelled before, but he couldn't place it.

He tucked the wee thing into his shirt and hurried home, trying not to wake her. The stables were on his right as he headed up the path, eager to show Maddy what Isabella had sent her.

Ronan was outside and smiled when he saw Landon heading his way. He reached down to ruffle his hair then reared back with his hand over his nose. "Landon, what have you been into today?"

"Visited the dragons and did some exploring."

"Did you play with any new animals?"

"Naw, I ran with the goats and lambs, saw the dragon eggs, and then Isabella gave me a new kitty to bring home to Maddy. She said Maddy'd let me keep it. Ferg might have to help though; she needs a bath."

Ronan's eyes widened. "Where is your kitty now?" he asked, afraid of what the answer might be.

"Here, look." He reached into his shirt and pulled the sleepy creature out. "Want to hold her?

Ronan heard Cheveyo chuckling as he exited the barn behind him. "Actually, I think your grandfather wants to hold her first."

Cheveyo cursed softly behind him, and Ronan knew paybacks would be a bitch.

"FERGUS, you are needed immediately at the stables," Ronan sent on his internal switchboard to the fire mage.

"I'm right behind ye," the scrawny giant said. "HOLY SHITE!" He scrambled backwards as his hands tangled in his wild red hair. "What the feck do you think I am going to be able to do with that?"

Landon looked up at him, surprised at his language. "Isabella said you could help give her a bath."

"She's evil," he said, glaring at Ronan. "Ye all are."

"C'mon, buddy, you got to have something up your sleeve. Maddy will have a fit if we take it in like that."

"Please, Uncle Ferg." Landon batted his eyes as they welled up. "My rat ran away yesterday, and I don't have any friends left."

"That's not true, laddie," he said, shaking his head. "We're friends, ain't we?"

"It's not the same."

Fergus looked up at Ronan and said under his breath, "Ye fecking owe me big for this one, Ronan."

Forming shields around his entire body, and double shields on his hands, he reached for the offensive creature. As quickly as he could, he magically descented the little guy. "Lucky fer ye, I've had to do this before for a lass's familiar." He stood and turned to Ronan. "Yer givin her a bath. I've done me part."

"Let's go, buddy," Ronan said to Landon. "We need a tub, some soap, and a whole lot of luck to explain this to Maddy."

"Isabella said it's a gift, so she can't send her back, and look how pitiful she is. I'll take good care of her. I promise."

"God help us," Ronan said as they headed for the barn to find a tub and some strong soap. "If we can't get the smell off of us, we all might be sleeping in the barn before the night's over."

CHAPTER FOUR

Never Gonna Happen

Kyran left his suite and navigated the familiar hallways to the throne room. Courtier's flirted as he walked by, and he ignored them, staring straight ahead. A final left turn led him to the throne room, where the king listened to petitions. As he turned the corner, he nearly missed a step at the sight of the harem lined up along the final corridor on either side. Beautiful women and men, nearly nude, kneeled with their hands behind their back and eyes straight ahead. The absurdity of it, here of all places, caused him to look more closely.

It appeared every race and every fetish was on display as well. Leather straps covered small sections of skin on some, while others were outfitted with various animal tails and ears…What the fuck? He was by no means a prude, but this was what every visiting dignitary and petitioner experienced anytime they approached the ruling monarchs. It was ridiculous and ensured their court would never be taken seriously by any visiting diplomats or any of the elemental clans. His temper flared as he reached the end of the line in front of the gilded doors.

Jaw clenched, he entered and stood to the left with his hands clasped behind his back, fifth in the line of petitioners. Waiting, he tried not to think about the people outside. He couldn't afford to be distracted from the reason he was here today; his future depended on it. But familiar faces were in that lineup, and he knew damn well they weren't there willingly.

A deep breath helped calm him, and he went over his petition in his mind as his eyes traced the intricately patterned walls. He tried to calm his anxiety. Surely, his father would understand his feelings as he'd felt the same way towards his mother at one time. Not long ago, his father would have fully supported him. Today, Kyran had no idea what to expect.

He watched the proceedings with the cases before him, and his heart beat faster as he observed the curt manner in which the rulings were coming down. None of them were favorable for the petitioner.

Kyran was his father's mirror in both appearance and temperament. The man, who raised him to respect the importance and authority of his position as the head of the clan and the responsibilities that came with that position, seemed distracted and bored, traits completely out of character for him in formal court.

It was a struggle for Kyran to comprehend the changes as he silently watched the proceedings. The queen was handing down all the rulings, and he knew that didn't bode well for him.

His turn finally arrived. Kyran stepped forward and dropped to one knee as was customary, with his head bowed, prepared to remain there until summoned to rise.

"Kyran, what a pleasant surprise," the king said in a bored voice. "What pray tell, have you done, that you would need to petition us for anything, my arrogant, seldom-seen son?"

Groaning inwardly, he stared at the floor. His father was in a mood, and not a good one. From the corner of his eye, he watched the king picking at imaginary lint on his ocean-blue silk sleeve and knew he was lucky to gain an audience.

The queen watched him from the chair to his right. She was a beautiful woman, there was no denying that, but her beauty was skin deep and disguised a sadistic, evil interior. Platinum blond hair fell over her breasts in soft waves. Pale skin was the backdrop for large, innocent-looking gray eyes and ruby red lips. A tall frame supported a much too thin body with small breasts and no ass worth mentioning. She wasn't the type of woman Kyran would have looked at twice, but many men found her entrancing.

His stepmother smirked at him from her throne, well aware that she held all the power. They had never gotten along, especially after she tried to seduce him less than a month after marrying his father. Repulsed by her behavior from the beginning, he knew she was responsible for the deterioration of the court that his family successfully ruled for centuries.

"Your highnesses, I am most grateful for the audience you are granting me." Kyran kept his head bowed and waited for permission to rise. His father left him there for another ten minutes as he chatted with the queen and other members of the court. Finally remembering his kneeling son, he turned back to him and gestured for him to rise.

"What is it you want, Kyran?" he finally deigned to ask as he covered a yawn.

"First, I wanted to thank you for my appointment to the Heart Island Sanctuary. I am enjoying the opportunity to represent my court and my family in that region."

His father nodded, pleased by the level of gratitude prior to his groveling.

"I'd also like to ask your permission to marry a fellow warden I fell in love with there." He decided to move ahead with his agenda, completely ignoring the reason they dragged him back to court.

"Tell me of this woman who has finally caught my eldest son's heart. It has been quite a while since I have seen you this..." he paused, struggling for a word to describe Kyran.

"Happy?" Kyran suggested trying to speed things up a bit.

"Desperate?" Queen Meriel supplied with a sickly smile at Kyran as she motioned to have her husband's jeweled goblet refilled. She looked him up and down, and Kyran felt the lust rolling off her. "Pity, we've already struck a deal with the Fire Clans for your hand in marriage." She smirked at him as she watched his hatred race across his face. "But you already know that, Kyran."

"I did not agree to the betrothal," Kyran growled at her, "and I will not be part of an arranged marriage."

Queen Meriel laughed outright at his audacity. She reached out, took King Varan's hand and said, "Oh, my heart, your children never fail to amuse. He honestly thinks that he has a choice in the matter." Meriel's eyes glittered dangerously, and her tone changed to ice as she continued. "Your marriage will restore trade agreements with the Fire Clans that our people desperately need. You don't get the right to be selfish this time, Kyran. Love matches are rare and seldom a luxury the nobility are allowed."

Kyran tamped down the rage rolling through him, knowing how easily they both would sense it. He ignored the queen, a woman he despised, and turned to his father.

"Your majesty, I come to you as your son, beseeching you to intercede on my behalf. You married for love once. Have you forgotten what it was like to pledge yourself to the person who holds your heart? Do you recall what it felt like to find a woman who feels the same way and is willing to love, honor, and cherish you with all that she is? A woman who would never betray or cheat on you. Can you even begin to remember what that was like?" Kyran knew he was taking a chance playing on his father's past relationship with Kyran's mother, but he honestly believed Varan always regretted losing his first wife.

His father watched him from his throne, and if Kyran hadn't known him better, he would have thought he was drunk or using drugs. Vacant eyes stared out at him as if he were a stranger. Kyran fully expected a reprimand after his disrespect to the queen, but the king barely registered the insult.

Bringing up his mother should have made the man angry at the very least, but he seemed indifferent to the son standing in front of him.

"Father?" Kyran addressed him again, hoping for some sign that the man was aware of his surroundings. "King Varan!" he said in a commanding voice and still received no response. Furious and worried, he turned to the queen asking, "What's wrong with him?" His hands clenched at his sides. "What have you done to him?" Rumors reached him while he was away that the king's health and mind were deteriorating quickly, and Kyran had his suspicions as to why, or rather, who was to blame.

"Nothing," Meriel said as she stood and walked down the stairs towards him. With an elegant movement of her hand, she dismissed the courtiers and scribes who were awaiting the conclusion of his petition. "For the official record," she said as they looked at her in surprise, "Kyran's petition is denied until the king says otherwise."

An evil smile crossed her face as the door closed behind them. She stepped off the dais and circled around Kyran. Long, pointed fingernails brushed lightly over his shoulder and down his arm, trying to entice him. "He's getting older, Kyran. I just think it's catching up with him." She giggled then. "It's exhausting trying to keep up with me in bed."

A shiver shuddered through him as he found her touch repulsive. Any chance of a civil relationship with his stepmother evaporated the first time she slid into his bed in the middle of the night. He almost killed her when he woke to find her draped over him. Meriel was on her honeymoon, had just destroyed his parents' relationship, and was still delusional enough to think he would ruin his relationship with his father by fucking her. Fisting her hair, he dragged her out of his bed, then made her crawl on her knees to the door before he flung her into the hall. Wanting no misunderstandings, he made sure the entire wing heard him tell her to stay the fuck away from him and out of his suite before he told his father what a whore she was.

Rumors of her unwanted sexual conquests abounded. Meriel was bound and determined to enjoy all the Tyde men. Kyran wanted no part of it and avoided her at all costs. Unfortunately, his other siblings hadn't been as smart or lucky.

"Father," Kyran called, trying once again to get him to consider calling off the betrothal. He waited for an answer, and when none was forthcoming, he took a chance and looked away from the predator circling him. His father had fallen asleep on his throne. It was just another piece of the puzzle that didn't fit.

King Varan had been a well-loved monarch, respected by his court and by the other clans. Varan's opinion held value, and his company was sought out by friends and family alike. A fair ruler, whose people loved him,

21

changed when he remarried, and a new queen stood at his side. His behavior tonight stunned and concerned Kyran.

Queen Meriel continued circling him as he appealed to his father. He felt her hands slip around his waist, her right one dropping lower to reach for his cock until he wrapped his large hand around the bones of her wrist and squeezed. "You have three seconds to take your hands off me before I break it," he growled.

Meriel laughed behind him with her breasts pressing in against his back. She gasped, in pain or pleasure, he wasn't sure, as his hand tightened painfully around her wrist. She wisely released him, giggling as she walked away. "You know, I can make this betrothal go away. Don't you?"

"For what price?" he snarled at her.

"Give me a weekend to have you—any way I want you. I'll stop wondering if all the rumors about you as a lover are true, then I'll move on, and someone new will catch my eye. If I can't convince you, I may have to find someone new, someone younger and more handsome—maybe, someone like Kai," she said in a veiled threat.

Kai was his youngest brother, who was inexperienced and very naive. He looked like an angel with the build of a gladiator. His older brothers taught him all they could about evading the bitch, but Kyran knew how determined Meriel could be.

Meriel eye fucked him as she walked in front of him, her eyes locking on his. He knew she could see and feel how much he hated her because he didn't bother to hide his emotions.

"What are the terms?" he grudgingly asked. The ammunition would come in handy to prove to his father what a backstabbing bitch she was and how badly his court was suffering because of her.

Queen Meriel paused, surprised that he asked because previously, his answer had always been a resounding no. "You would spend a weekend in my bed with your cock or your tongue between my thighs." A long, lacquered nail tapped at her lips as she paused to reconsider. "On second thought, I'll have them anywhere I want them. You'll perform any act I request, be it to me or one of my pets. You'll appear to enjoy the time you spend with me; I want you all in if you agree." Her finger again tapped at her ruby-stained lips. "I would own you for two days. Your body will be my toy to thoroughly enjoy or break if I should choose." She gave him a moment to consider the offer. "In exchange, I will release you from the betrothal, leave your youngest sibling alone, and none will be the wiser." An evil little grin quirked across her lips. "Especially, that little hedge witch you've been playing with." Taking a seat on the stairs to the dais, she spread her legs wide, then pulled her skirt up to her thighs, giving him a glimpse of what she thought he was missing. "If I can't play with you, I'll make damn sure she can't either."

"How do I know you will honor our agreement?" Kyran asked, disgusted with the whole mess.

"You have my word. That ought to be enough," she said, picking at her nails, bored. "Don't think for too long. Kai will be home soon. The offer is rescinded upon his arrival." She leaned back on her elbows, stretching, showing him more than he ever wanted to see.

"I'll consider the offer. To clarify, a Saturday and Sunday with you, a one-time event, and no further harassment of my siblings."

A laugh burst from her. "I didn't say that, Kyran. Don't push your luck. Friday night through Sunday, once, and this offer was for Kai. If you want to offer for Kenn and Kano, too, we'll have to renegotiate."

Kyran turned away from her before he reached out and killed her. The urge was so strong he could taste her blood in his mouth and imagine it painting the throne room walls. His father snored behind them, and Kyran was determined to find out how she was manipulating him. Exiting the room, he slammed the door so hard on his way out that a picture fell off the wall. His boots crunched through the glass as he stormed off. He reached out to all his siblings on their telepathic internal links. "Meet me at the Rusty Tap on Friday for breakfast. It's important."

Hesitating at the corner, he turned back to look closely at the kneeling members of the queen's harem. Walking slowly back towards the gilded doors, he memorized every face on his right, then turned and started on the left. His eyes widened as he found friends he'd known for years. As he cataloged the kneeling members of court, he realized Meriel must have put on this particular display just for him. There were half a dozen women he had bedded and three guards he learned to fight with and considered good friends.

As Kyran stood in front of the man he once considered his best friend, he tipped the man's face up to see his eyes. The rage and humiliation swirling in them and throughout his aura settled it for Kyran. On a private link they had formed as boys, Kyran spoke to him. *"Dashiel, I need you to answer one question truthfully for me. Blink twice if you understand."* Kyran waited for confirmation. *"Do you belong to her or to me? You know of whom I speak."*

Dashiel's expression never changed, but Kyran heard him loud and clear. *"I hate that cunt. If you get me the fuck out of this nightmare, you have my loyalty until the day I die, my lord. I swear it on my life."*

Kyran felt the muscles in Dash's face clench in loathing. Hating himself for what he was about to do, he caressed the man's face watching the fury cross it as he played his part.

23

"I'll hold you to that Dashiel. If you betray me, our bond will see you dead beside me. Do you understand the binding of which I refer to?"

"I do, my lord, and I will agree to it without hesitation. I would like the chance to regain my honor and my self-respect."

"This bond will tie you to me now and forever. You will be the first of many whom I will try and gather to our cause to retake our court from the evil infiltrating it. Last chance, are you sure?"

"Just fucking do it, Kyr, so I can get off my fucking knees."

Kyran tried not to chuckle, glad to see Dash's spirit was still intact. Silently he tied a piece of the man's spirit with his own, using a spell his grandsire Neptune taught him well. It guaranteed loyalty and honesty better than anything else could. *"I need you to trust me and go along with this next part."*

Kyran's hand continued stroking the man's face while they communicated. His thumb dropped to the man's lips, and he stroked them as the doors opened, and the queen exited the room.

"Are his lips as soft as they look?" he asked Meriel as she paused next to him.

She looked at him in surprise. "What about your little hedge witch, Kryan? Is she aware of your preferences? Never heard anyone mention your interest in men," she asked with a laugh. "Can I watch?"

"What happens at court, stays at court. Isn't that the way it's always been?" Kyran said as he looked over his shoulder at her. "Sorry, but I haven't agreed to your terms...yet." He left his answer open to the possibility that she might get the outcome she wanted after all.

"Glad to see you sampling the merchandise, Kyran. Not sure when court will be in session again, might as well enjoy yourself," she threatened with a smile as she sauntered away.

His grip had tightened painfully on Dash's face. Dash played the part perfectly, never flinching. "Guess, I'm about to find out," he said as he grabbed the leather collar and jerked it to get the man to stand and follow him. Not trusting anyone anymore and needing to make this believable, he also grabbed the collars of two women he'd never been with and dragged the three of them behind him as he returned to his room.

Kyran knew the rumor mill would be working double time, and he just needed to make sure Rhyanna never walked these corridors to hear them. If playing the game was the only way to win his freedom and protect his family, then by all the gods of the seas, he could play it with the best of them. He would participate in this charade even if it broke his fucking heart and lost him the only woman he'd ever loved.

There was more at stake than his personal happiness, and for the first time in his life, he chose to put his people first. If Varan wouldn't man up and save his court, then the job fell to Kyran, next in line to the throne. His people deserved better than what their court was currently offering them. They deserved to live and work in an atmosphere free of fear and sexual harassment.

His heart raced as he thought of Rhyanna and the betrayals she would never understand or forgive. Then he thought about his brothers. The possibility that she could influence Kai in any way made him sick. Kai was the best of the Tyde men, possessing a gentleness that Meriel would intentionally destroy. Kenn and Kano were old enough and devious enough to stay out of her reach. There had to be another option to save them all because touching that woman sexually was never gonna fucking happen.

CHAPTER FIVE

What Could Have Been

Rhyanna remade the beds her patients had used. She gathered the dirty linens and placed them in a large wicker basket. It was one of many baskets she had woven over the years. She lit a lavender sage smudge stick and cleansed each area, then swept and mopped the floors.

When she had everything ready for future occupants, she stood back and made sure nothing was amiss. It seemed so empty without her young patients.

Rhyanna's eyes filled as she realized how much she was going to miss Hailey. She stayed with her longer than Grace or Genny, the other two girls who the wardens rescued on the same day. Hailey was a sweet young woman who had gone through a horrific ordeal.

Rhyanna healed her physical wounds the best that she was able to over the past few weeks. The emotional trauma was something Hailey would have to find a way to face on her own. Rhyanna recommended a woman near them who was good at healing the inner demons she would face.

A wide maple rocking chair in the corner of the room beckoned her. Pulling her knees up to her chest, she rested her chin on them as she wrapped her skirt behind her calves. Rhy closed her eyes as the loneliness in the building seeped into her. She wouldn't have wished any of those girls to have gone through the horrors they experienced, but she would miss the sound of someone else's voice in this room.

She closed her eyes as tears leaked out and slipped down her cheeks. Some of them were for the other women, and some of them were for her own broken heart that she hadn't allowed herself the time to grieve.

Rhyanna waited a lifetime for destiny to send the man of her dreams to her, and by God, he was more than she'd been capable of dreaming—a handsome man, blond of hair, and blue of eye. His body was perfectly chiseled to match the angular planes of his face. He treated her with respect and care, and she wanted to dedicate her life and her body to him.

Destiny can be a funny thing at times, not quite as fickle as fate, but a mite more contradictory, one might say. Destiny encouraged her to wait for her man, and wait, she had. He finally found her, they fell in love, and when, finally, they were ready to physically celebrate their love, they found out he belonged to another without his knowledge or permission. So, now, once again, Rhyanna waited on destiny to decide her fate with Kyran Tyde, a prince of The Court of Tears, and the only man she'd ever loved.

Rhy asked him to give her space, and he reluctantly respected her request. She wanted to reach out to him so many times but didn't, wanting him to have the time he needed to settle the betrothal on his own. Sensing his unease today, she reached out, wanting to give him strength. It was in her nature to be compassionate, even when she was upset with someone. The conversation with him through their link, and the love and longing he sent back to her, made her miss him so much, but she couldn't help wondering if they would ever be free of his court entanglements.

As she cried, finally allowing the pain and heartache she kept holding in the release it required, she closed the lover's bridge she and Kyran formed. Surrounding it with a cushion of air dulled the emotions passing through it. Their bridge would alert him to extreme emotions, and she didn't want to worry him.

She was sobbing so hard that she failed to hear the door open and shut in the shop. Strong arms surprised her when she felt herself lifted, and she started to struggle until she realized it was Roarke who held her. His eyes captured hers, and the compassion in them started the waterworks all over again. He sat down in the chair with her on his lap and just held her. She sat sideways across his legs. He tucked her head under his chin and rocked her while she cried, rubbing her back all the while.

He began humming while he comforted her, an old song she remembered from her youth. The bards often sung it—a tale of a man and woman destined to love yet never come together. He sang softly, his voice deep and melodious as he soothed her aching soul. Her tears slowed, and the hiccupping breaths eventually stopped, but still, he held her as if there was nowhere else he needed to be. Before she realized it, the heat of him beneath her and the safety and care he was offering her lulled her into a deep, dreamless sleep.

Roarke continued to rock Rhyanna even after she faded off. Even as his legs went numb and common sense warned him that he should set her on one of the beds, he continued to sing and hold her. His eyes memorized her features as she slept. It was the first opportunity he'd had to watch her without an audience or jealous beau glaring at him. Her long blond hair fell to her waist and was naturally curly. Her features were delicate, her skin flawless and pale except for the dark smudges under her eyes. He wondered if they appeared due to her late nights with her young patients or because of Kyran's absence.

Roarke never wanted a committed relationship. He was never home long enough, and life as a sailor suited him—a girl in every port and sometimes two. Looking at Rhyanna he wondered, though. He wondered if he had met her before Kyran, would she have given him a chance? Would he have been smart enough to see her worth? Would he have been capable of making her happy and been able to offer her the permanence she longed for?

Rhyanna mumbled in her sleep. Her head burrowed in closer under his neck, and her ass ground into his pelvis as she tried to find a comfortable spot. His body responded instantly, his pants growing much too tight. He groaned inwardly, deciding it was time to put her down before she awoke and misread his reaction to her movements. He stood easily with her in his arms and walked over to one of the beds.

Roarke set her down gently, reluctantly releasing her luscious body. Her scent surrounded him, and her hair still clung to his arms. He covered her with a light blanket and watched her for a moment longer, wishing he was the one she wanted and wondering what it might be like to come home to a woman of worth. Rhyanna possessed a silent strength, a heart of gold, and a body that he was afraid would haunt his dreams in the weeks to come. He hoped Kyran truly appreciated her and was able to fix the mess he was in because Rhyanna deserved nothing but the best. If Kyran was unable to provide it, Roarke just might step in and fill that position.

CHAPTER SIX

Dash

Kyran headed down the hall with his evening's entertainment in tow. A headache was forming behind his eyes, and his stomach turned at what he was about to do, but he needed something to keep his mind off the insanity he was trapped in, and he needed to find more allies.

If he couldn't save himself, maybe he could save someone else that he cared for. They reached his suite, and he was surprised to find a pair of the court's guards outside.

"What is the meaning of this?" he demanded.

"Prince Kyran," the one on the right said, "as befits your position, Queen Meriel has assigned us as your private guards for your protection. We will be by your side for the duration of your stay in the palace."

"Don't trust the fuckers, Kyr. They're her spies, both of them," Dash said.

"No, shit," Kyran replied as a muscle in his cheek ticked.

"It is not necessary for you to be by my side. You will not enter my suite for any reason, do you understand me?" Kyran's glare stopped the one on the right from speaking, but the one on the left was clueless.

"The queen prefers us in her bedchamber while she is…distracted. At times she prefers for us to join her. She thought…"

"First off, I'm not the fucking queen, so don't presume to know anything about my preferences." He dropped the leashes holding the evening's entertainment and grabbed the man by his neck. Kyran swung him around until his back hit the wall opposite his doorway. "Second, you both will remain here, on this side of the hallway. Neither of you will speak to me unless I've spoken to you. Third, the only people allowed to enter my suite are Myles, and Dashiel, who is about to become my lustful companion for

29

the coming weeks." He jabbed a finger into the man's chest for emphasis. "Last but not least, I don't want nor need you to join me for my entertainment. I will never be so distracted as to be unaware of my surroundings, and there is no place for you in my form of entertainment. Please be sure to thank Meriel for her concern."

He turned and yanked the leashes hard making all three of his charges stumble. The women's hands went to their necks, trying to lessen the bite of the metal on their necks. Dashiel, on the other hand, gave a sensual moan, and his eyes were half-lidded as they looked at Kyran with longing.

Kyran wanted to vomit. He wasn't the only one good at acting, but this time he wasn't sure if it was an act or not. Guess there was only one way to find out.

The first guard had joined the second on the far side of the hall. They both looked at Kyran warily, unsure of what to expect from the prince, who was acting nothing like the calm easy-going man they had both known over the years. He acted like he was walking a fine line between insanity and fury, and they were bound to get caught in the crossfire.

Kyran entered his room, slamming the doors behind him. Dash kept watching him with hungry eyes, and the women didn't know what to anticipate.

Kyran sat in a leather chair by the fireplace. The fire had been lit earlier, and a bed of coals glowed, craving more fuel. "Dashiel, add wood to the fire," he said in a loud commanding voice. "I want it warm in here."

As Dash knelt next to him to do his bidding. Kyran spoke to him alone. *"I should have asked if you had a preference in the women I chose since you are going to have to fuck them. Do you?"*

Dash's hand paused for a moment, then he continued adding kindling to the coals in front of him. *"You chose well, my lord. The brunette is the woman I'm in love with, and the blond is her sister. I swear on my life that you can trust my woman, Elise. I haven't known Amiel as long, but I'm pretty sure she is solid."*

"'Pretty sure,' can get any of us killed," Kyran said. *"Until we know for sure, we use extreme caution in front of her. Does she know about your relationship with her sister?"*

"No, not to my knowledge. We understand the dangers of showing affection to anyone. Meriel uses it as a weapon, and more often than not, someone ends up dead or missing. There's never a happy ending in the harem; just a reason to cause us more pain."

"How did you end up here?"

"I said 'no' to her majesty. The next day I woke up collared in the dungeon. Been here ever since. I've learned to play the game well enough to stay alive. I didn't know how much longer I could do it...until I met Elise. Now it's all I can do just to get a glimpse of her throughout my day. On the rare occasion we are in the same room, we do as much as we can get away with, but we've never been able to be truly together."

Kyran nodded thoughtfully. He needed to make the guards believe he was still capable of the level of immorality this court was steeped in.

Dash finished stoking the fire, then stood with his hands behind his back, waiting for Kyran's directives.

"Place the other chair across from the doors for me and prop the doors open so our guests can watch the show."

Kyran stood and approached the blond woman. "What's your name?"

She looked surprised that he cared but answered in a soft voice, "Amiel, my lord."

Kyran stroked her face, feeling absolutely nothing sexually towards her at all. "I want you to give my apologies to the guards for my behavior. Can you do that?"

"Yes, my lord."

"Then I want you to get on your knees in front of them, and I want you to touch yourself slowly. Will you do that for me?"

She looked at him hesitantly. "Yes, my lord, if it pleases my lord. How long do you want me to stay out there?"

His hand continued stroking her face gently as his eyes locked on hers. "I want you to very slowly make yourself come, any way you enjoy. I want the guards to watch you pleasure yourself. I want their eyes glued to you with every stroke of your clit and every time your fingers dip inside. I want them to want you so badly they can't remember their own names. Are you up to the challenge, knowing that they will not be allowed to touch you?"

Her eyes were locked on his, and the mild compulsion he was spinning around her with his words settled into her mind making her want to do exactly as he said. "Go on, show them how you like to be touched so that I can watch you from my chair. I want them to forget they are supposed to be protecting me."

Amiel made her way out to the surprised guards. Dash stood at the foot of the bed with his hands behind his back, looking bored and waiting for his instructions. Elise knelt beside him nervously with her eyes straight ahead, ignoring Kyran as much as possible.

"Elise, I want you to lay on your back on my bed with your knees bent and spread wide open."

A sad look crossed her face, and she tried not to look at Dash as she turned towards the bed and followed his instructions, but Kyran knew that Dash could feel her reluctance to have Kyran touch her in front of him.

"Take your cock out and stroke yourself until you're hard," Kyran said to Dash. *"Before you go getting pissed off at me, you need to know that you are the only one who will be touching her tonight, but we need to make this believable, so work with me."*

Dashiel's eyes flew to Kyran's, and the surprise and relief in them tore at him. No one should ever have to endure what this couple was going through.

"I want you to get her ready for me so that I can fuck her. I want her dripping, do whatever you need to, but make her come before I get there."

Dash gave him a look of immense gratitude as he stepped towards the bed. His eyes traveled gently over the woman he loved as he prepared to touch her for the first time. Her eyes filled with relief and love as she gazed up at him.

Kyran could see that from where he sat. Needing to play his part in this charade, he sat in the chair where the guards could see him and pulled his pants open. Taking himself in hand, he stroked his flaccid penis, finding no inspiration or desire in the room. He could see Amiel in the hallway as her body shuddered through her first orgasm. The guards were rubbing their cocks through their uniforms as they watched her exclusively.

He turned his head towards Dash and saw him taste his woman for the first time. His hands tightened on her inner thighs as she trembled in anticipation.

Kyran closed his eyes and remembered the night of the melding when Rhyanna came to him seeking relief. She sought more than relief, but he had hesitated to give it to her, causing a misunderstanding between them that nearly cost him her love.

The thought of her did what nothing in this sensually charged room could, and his body responded to his touch. He buffered their line, not wanting to wake her nor explain this situation to her. Stroking himself until he was throbbing and desperate for relief, he stood and walked towards the door with his thick swollen cock standing at attention for the guards to witness.

"Amiel," he said in a voice harsh with need, "come. I think you're ready for me now."

Her eyes were sad as she stood and walked towards him. The guards watched her ass as it swayed with each step.

Kyran let her come to him, then he turned to the guards who watched her with hungry eyes. "I hope my apology was sufficient."

A chorus of "Yes, my lord," followed him as he shut the door on them, leaving them uncomfortable.

Kyran walked Amiel over to the settee. He laid her back and opened her thighs. "I want you to touch yourself again so that I can watch this time, and as you get turned on, I want you to moan loudly. When you come, you will scream my name in pleasure. Then you will curl up and sleep soundly until I wake you, do you understand?"

"Yes, my lord," she said as her hand reached between her legs again. She moaned immediately. "Won't you take me, my lord?"

"Close your eyes, Amiel, and listen to the sound of my voice," Kyran chanted in a soft sleepy voice. "Every time your fingers dip inside of you, that is my cock sliding in and out of you. If anyone asks you tomorrow how our evening was, you will tell them it was the best night of your life, and I was the best lover you've ever had. I fucked you all night, and you hope that I choose you again. Will you remember that?"

"Yes," she moaned loudly before she came, screaming his name. Her body shuddered as she curled up on her side, looking at him with sleepy eyes. "Thank you, my lord, for the unexpected evening and the respite, you have my gratitude..." her voice faded off as her body responded to his command.

Elise was sobbing in pleasure behind him as Dash teased her body on the bed. Kyran closed his eyes, imaging that he had Rhyanna laid out on his bed doing to her what Dash was about to do to Elise.

Feeling like a voyeur, he walked into his bathroom and started the water for a bath. Kyran stripped and settled into the hot water . His hand went to his cock, and he continued his fantasy of having Rhyanna wrapped around it instead of his hand. His hand tightened as he moved it up and down his shaft seeking momentary relief. As his body responded to the thought of her, he sent Dash a final command.

"Make love to your woman. Make her yours. Take your time. I'm going to soak in the tub."

"Kyran, thank you for this gift. I will treasure tonight like no other."

Kyran didn't respond, wanting him to take his pleasure without an audience. The hot water soothed his muscles and his mood as he rested his head against the high back. He missed Rhyanna, and he was starting to wonder if they would ever get the opportunity for him to make love to her. The longer he remained at court, the harder it was to believe that he would ever get out of his personal hell. His eyes closed as his exhausted mind relaxed. He didn't have the energy to worry about it anymore tonight. Tomorrow, he would find more allies, come up with a plan and try to find a way to save them all without losing the woman he loved. Right now, he had a date to keep with the woman he was missing, and he intended to give her his complete attention.

CHAPTER SEVEN

Copper Tub

Rhyanna awoke in the faint light of the setting sun. Confused, she looked around for a moment. She never slept in the clinic unless a patient needed supervision, and she'd just made all the beds, so why was she lying on one? She sat up, trying to remember what happened before her unexpected nap.

Hailey left. Rhy cleaned the room and then curled up in the rocker. She folded the blanket that was covering her and returned it to the end of the bed. As she set it down, she got a whiff of a man's scent, helping her memories to come rushing back in. She'd finally given in and had her crying jag. She never heard him enter, but Roarke appeared and just held her, asking no questions. He simply gave her comfort without any strings attached. Few men would have been so considerate.

Roarke constantly surprised her. Devastatingly handsome, though a little rough around the edges, mixed with a sexy sense of mystery, he was kind and compassionate when least expected. Rhyanna suspected he was attracted to her. She closed her eyes, trying to imagine Roarke as more than a coworker. Then she tried to imagine kissing or touching him. Again, nothing.

Switching tactics, she pictured Kyran's face, and instantly her body came to life thinking of him. He was the same height as Roarke, but with light eyes instead of dark. Otherwise, they were similar in features and could have passed for brothers, but only one of them made her heart and her blood sing.

She was grateful Roarke appeared when he did—grateful for the shoulder to cry on and the sense of caring he exhibited. She knew

34

instinctively that she could count on him if she ever needed anything, and for that, she would always be grateful.

She closed the door to the treatment room and wandered into her shop. The fire in the hearth had burned down to embers. She knelt down, watching the fire drakes dance in the heat. She enjoyed their performance for a while as she looked for a sign, a vision, anything that might help her understand the challenges she was facing but found none. Frustrated, she pulled a light wrap around her shoulders and closed the apothecary down for the evening.

Restless, Rhyanna wandered the grounds enjoying the late spring flowers and the way the earth was changing from its dull winter tan and browns into the late spring vibrant greens. The Strawberry Moon would soon be on them. The river would slowly heat up, and the fields would flourish with foliage. As an earth element, the season that produced the Earth Mother's finest gifts for healing and nourishment was her favorite. The cycle of death and rebirth in her garden was a constant reminder of the possibilities in each season of one's life. Nothing remained the same. New growth would always appear, light would always chase away the dark, and one need only hold onto hope to survive the winter.

Her steps faltered as she finished that thought, realizing she had just found the answer she was seeking. Her turbulent emotions caused by Kyran's departure were only temporary. Rhyanna believed he would receive an imminent release from his betrothal, and then, they would finally be able to spend time as a couple, getting to know each other better in every way.

Rhy missed their evening walks. He always held her hand as they meandered, gently stroking her fingers as if an afterthought. She became so sensitive to him that just his slight brush of his fingers against hers would make her body clench in need. Kyran wanted to take things slowly and court her properly, and she respected his approach. Rhyanna was grateful for his consideration and patience with her inexperience.

As time passed, she grew restless, and her body was making its demands known. She woke in the middle of the night with her knees pressed tightly together as her center throbbed after the dreams she had of them finally coming together. In the darkest hours, she reached down and gave herself the release she needed, wondering if she woke Kyran through the lover's bridge they created.

A lover's bridge provided a committed couple a place to meet on the ethereal plane when they were separated geographically. They could meet while in a trance or sleeping and communicate or "see" each other while there. They formed a lover's bridge recently, allowing them to communicate telepathically, as well as experience each other's emotions. It wasn't the same as being together physically, but it was a close second. The distance they were separated dulled the sensation, but they were still able to sense each other's emotions, especially the extreme ones.   Anger, fear, disappointment, desire, and even orgasms easily telegraphed through their bridge.

Early on, Rhyanna found a way to wrap her emotions in currents of air so that Kyran wouldn't know what she was feeling if she didn't want him to. It was a red flag to him that something WAS indeed wrong when she dropped off his grid. She'd since learned to control her emotions better so as not to concern him.   It was difficult enough for him being separated without wondering what was going on that he couldn't be here to help her with.

One of the benefits of their bridge was that they could share pleasure across the distance using it.   If the link was open, he could sense her touching herself as well as the slow build up to an orgasm.   Their link heightened his ability to feel her need and her touch and sense the final crashing wave as her body went over the edge.   Not only could he give her an orgasm, but he could experience it through her as well.   Their recent separation should have had them finding creative ways to enjoy each other from a distance, but instead, Rhy had asked for space to cope with him leaving. The gentleman that he was, he had granted her wish.

Today was the first time Rhy had reached out to him since he left. Earlier, she sensed his distress, and the compassionate side in her couldn't let him flounder without reaching out to show him support.   At first, she second-guessed her decision until she felt how much he was missing her. She agreed to meet him through their bridge this evening.

As intense as their sessions at a distance were in the past, Rhyanna could only imagine how he would make her feel when they finally made love together in person.   Thinking about their evening date, she headed back to her suite.   She didn't know what he was currently doing, but she knew what she was about to start with or without him.

Her center throbbed with need as she walked up the long flight of stairs to the second floor.   Her face flushed as each step rubbed her thighs together in a delightful way.   By the time she reached the corridor leading to her rooms, the flush descended to her chest.   She reached out with her mind and started filling the large copper tub that sat in the corner of her room. Windows graced two sides of the room—one where the sun would be setting momentarily, and the other where the moon would soon be rising.

She entered her suite, locking the door behind her.   She ripped off her peasant shirt and started working on the laces of her corset.   Her breasts thanked her as she released them from the unforgiving contraption.

Reaching up, she massaged them as she looked down at the creases left on her skin from the corset.   She watched a slight flush moving across the pale skin as she kneaded them gently with her hands, enjoying not only the freedom from her clothes but the sensations racing through her body. As she scraped her nails over her nipples, electrical shocks ran down her abdomen ending in that sweet spot at the apex of her legs. The small nodule started to throb in time with the pressure she applied to her breasts. She arched back as her breath came in short gasps. Her body was close to the edge when she pulled her nipples taut, pinching them hard enough to nearly make her come. Her soft pants filled the room like the clouds of steam rising from the bathtub in the corner.

Wanting to wait for Kyran to join her, she reluctantly released her nipples and walked unsteadily to her wardrobe to retrieve a robe. As she pulled the door open, her eyes went immediately to the burgundy silk dress she wore for Madylyn's Pledging Ceremony. She reached out, fingering the beautiful material. It was the first time she'd ever felt sultry, like she could have any man she wanted, and more importantly, the one she wanted.

What seemed a lifetime ago was only a few short weeks. Everything changed so much for her the night Kyran was taken by the court guard. She knew not when he would be given leave to come back home or if he ever was going to be allowed to resume his life.

Rhyanna retrieved a short robe and headed for the tub. After dropping her clothes in a basket, she pulled her waist-length locks up into a messy knot on top of her head. Testing the water, she sighed at the perfect temperature and stepped in. Copper was her favorite choice for a bathtub because it held the heat for a long time. She settled herself against the high metal back and stretched her legs out in front of her.

A glass jar sat on the shelf beside her, filled with rare pink salt. She scooped out a handful, then picked up a small amber bottle with a dropper on top and squeezed out seven drops into the pile of salt in her hand. The combination of lemon and lavender assaulted her senses as she dropped it under the running water. The lavender soothed her soul while the lemon invigorated her body.

Crystals lined the sills of the huge windows on either side of her. They soothed her while she bathed. The moonlight shone down on them, cleansing the beautiful stones and imbuing them with the full moon's healing power. Rhyanna also used them to set her intentions for emotional healing and patience through her current situation.

Picking up a bar of soap she'd recently made in the same scent, she lathered up her hands and traced them down her neck and over her hypersensitive breasts. She closed her eyes, remembering Maddy and Ronan's big day, and focused on the way Kyran looked at her in her silk dress. She could still see the flames of desire and the promise of pure pleasure scorching her from across the room. Unfortunately, their night was interrupted, and Kyran was forced to leave, leaving them both disappointed.

She rolled her soapy hands over her nipples and sighed as that exquisite feeling started below again. She looked out the window on her right as the full moon rose slowly above the tree line, shining directly through the glass onto her

The light was off in the bathroom, so the moonlight falling on her added to the sensual overload. She caught her lower lip between her teeth as she tried to breathe through the slow build up in her sensitized core.

Closing her eyes, she ripped the link she shared with Kyran wide open and sent him all her pent-up desire and frustration arrowing right towards him. Smiling, she felt the instant response on his end come hurling back at her, and she gasped at his magnified desire, hiding a healthy bit of rage.

"Starting without me, my lady?" he asked. She could feel the humor rolling through him and sense his cock thickening in his pants as he spoke to her. *"Give me a moment to prepare, so that I may properly join you,"* he begged.

"Better hurry up," she laughed, *"before I continue without ye."*

"Rhy..." he said in warning, then groaned as he felt her rub her soapy hands over her breasts again then progress slowly down over her abdomen. *"Dammit, woman, wait for me!"*

She smiled as she felt his urgency. She giggled at him, knowing that he would feel her laughter coming through. Her hands rolled up around her breasts again, and she groaned. Her knees came together as she throbbed. She knew it wouldn't take her long once she reached down and

"RHY, don't you dare," he threatened.

"Or what?" she challenged, then gasped as she sensed what felt like his fingers stroking her nipples. *"What kind of trickery is this?"* she demanded. *"And why haven't ye done it afore."*

"I was holding out, hoping to give you something to look forward to. I never thought it would take this long for me to return, and I wanted to find a way to make you truly feel like I was there with you."

"Well, na," she said, *"show me what ye've got then, me Laird of the Water."*

She felt a deep chuckle rolling through him and missed him terribly.

Sensing her change in mood, he spoke in a commanding voice. *"Place your hands on the sides of the tub, my lady."*

Rhyanna did as he directed, not wanting to tease him any longer. Her body ached because he had her so keyed up. She wanted to let him play as much as she wanted an orgasm. His form of play always benefited her tremendously. She closed her eyes and drifted on a sea of anticipation mixed with a smidge of desperation.

She moaned as tendrils of water lifted from the tub and traced over her jawline before moving, ever so slowly, down to her nipples. She arched her body out of the tub, wanting greater surface area for him to touch. The pressure settled on her breasts swirling around each and increasing her need of him. *"Kyran,"* she groaned.

She felt the intense desire running through him and knew exactly how sensitive the tip of his penis was becoming and how swollen the shaft was. She felt his hand reach down, and he stroked himself a half dozen times.

"No fair," she cried out. *"I can't return the favor."* Her hands clenched the tub, trying to keep herself in place as ordered. It was getting harder to do as her breathing became shallow and her chest heaved.

"You're doing a damn good job of teasing me," he said, *"don't you ever doubt that."*

His cock was throbbing harder and his hand stroking faster, and she whimpered, overwhelmed by their combined desire. The stream of water he was using to tease her grew larger and moved down over her belly. With her eyes closed, she could have sworn it was his hand that lay on her, not merely the pressure from the water squeezing her hip.

"Open your legs for me, Rhy."

She complied, opening them partway. Her legs trembled with the anticipation.

"Wider, love," he requested. *"Let them fall against the sides of the tub for me, please."*

"Stop being so damned polite, Kyran, and get on with it already," she growled at him.

That deep, dark, sensual chuckle came through once again, warming her even more inside. *"Patience, love, patience."*

"I am running out of that particular skill, ye bloody bastard. Do something," she demanded. Her right hand released the side of the tub, and she trailed it down her belly until she was tracing her pubic line. She stopped suddenly as she realized all movement had ceased. *"Kyran,"* she said, not sure if she was threatening or pleading.

"Hands back on the edge first," he said softly, like he had all the patience and time in the world.

Rhyanna smirked and sent him an image of her on her knees before him, reaching for his cock. She laughed out loud as his hand moved faster, and his cock twitched in his palm as his nerve endings lit up, ready to join her when he finally let her have her orgasm.

He wiped the smirk off her face with a thick stream of water rushing between her legs and pummeling her clit. She moaned loudly then resorted to begging as he kept moving the stream. He also managed to produce a second stream that massaged the outside of her labia, pushing her lips slightly apart, giving him better access to her clit.

Her head thrashed against the back of the metal tub as her orgasm hovered, and she swore under her breath as he doused both streams of water and waited for her to come back down to earth again.

"KYRAN!" her voice exploded in his head as she sent him more graphic images of her choking his cock with her hand while opening her mouth and displaying razor-sharp teeth.

"What the hell!" he screamed, the image and sensation as real as the images and feelings he was sending to her. Even as he yelled, his desire and need for her increased dramatically. He loved her fiery temper when she was riled and the fact that she wasn't afraid to ask for what she wanted.

"If you're not going to finish this..."

"Lie back, my lady," he whispered. *"I promise, no more teasing."*

She did as he requested, but her back was arching out of the tub as soon as he touched her again. This time the pressure was harder and the water warmer. Her orgasm stopped teetering on the edge and executed a swan dive over a cliff, falling hard and fast as lights exploded behind her closed eyelids. *"Yes, yes, yes, oh sweet mother, yes,"* she chanted repeatedly.

Her body writhed in the water, sloshing it over the side as the pleasure rolled over her, taking her under and coming back for round two. He continued his assault even as she tried to close her legs against it. This time, the water wrapped around her thighs tightly, holding her open as another stream pummeled her throbbing clit once again. The second orgasm raced through stronger and more powerful, starting in her toes, and rippling up through her legs and across her abdomen. Her abdominal muscles seized over and over with each wave assaulting her senses until she lie there, finally having had enough.

Her legs were shaking, and she struggled to pull them together, trying to absorb the overwhelming sensations. *"No more, please, by the mother, no more, Kyran, it's too much,"* she whimpered as he pulled back. The tendrils stroked her arms and legs gently, bringing her back into the present. Her body was exhausted, and her limbs shook in the chilly water.

Even though she could have happily rolled down in the water and slept in its embrace, not caring if she could breathe or not, she was finally aware enough to sense his body's arousal, and it bordered on discomfort.

"Tell me how to please ye," she whispered through their line, as she visualized reaching out and stroking him firmly with her hand. As she projected the visual, she wondered what she would do with him if she were there.

"Anything you do will please me, Rhy. I am so goddamn close that anything you imagine will get me off. There's nothing you can possibly do that will disappoint me." Kyran paused and decided clarity might be necessary. *"Anything except biting it off."* He chuckled, but it faded as she sent an image to him.

Rhy imagined kneeling in front of him. She'd seen his cock aroused before. Grateful for her perfect memory, she remembered the length and girth of him as well as the ridge around the head and the purplish veins running down the sides. She leaned forward and grabbed a hold of him, laughing at his growl of pleasure. Then she lowered her head and slowly extended her tongue. Softly, she traced the vein that she was so fascinated with.

She felt his moan of pleasure through their link and took more of him into her mouth. She circled her hand tightly around him and paid attention to his reactions. His body vibrated through their link, so she figured that she had to be doing something right. She increased her suction and moved her hand faster. His orgasm raced through him, tearing down all his defenses and giving her a rare peek into his heart.

Kyran loved her, without a doubt—that came through first and foremost. He missed her desperately, but he knew he needed to finish his mission here so that they could be free of his court.

Her heart sang as she read his feelings for her.

Slowly, they caught their breath. *"I'm getting out,"* Rhy said. *"I'm freezing."* She toweled off, quickly donned her robe, and headed for her bed. As she curled up beneath her heavy covers, she could feel him softly on the edges of her conscious mind.

"Sleep well, my lady," he gently whispered to her across the distance of their *bridge.*

"Good night, me laird," she sent back as her eyes grew too heavy to keep open. *"I miss ye."*

"And I, you," he said. "Sweet dreams," he murmured as he felt her drift off. *"'Til we meet again, my love."*

Kyran gently disconnected from their link, leaving her to dream as she would without him distracting from her rest. He sent up a brief prayer that his exile would be short-lived because he didn't know how much longer he would be able to live without her in his life, without her in his bed.

A small part of him worried that, even though they still experienced pleasure together and could communicate throughout the day, his little nymph would grow tired of waiting for him to return. Insecurity was an unfamiliar feeling to him. He worried she might cut him loose so that she could move on to someone real, someone stable, someone available without the family drama that he brought. Someone like Roarke...the thought enraged him, so he reined it in, knowing that his jealousy would be the quickest way to lose her.

Kyran closed his eyes, letting go of his angst and trusting that what they'd built was strong enough to help them make it through their separation. He drifted off to nightmares of the alternative. A life without her.

CHAPTER EIGHT

What in the Ever Loving !@#$

Madylyn SkyDancer, Mistress of Heart Island Sanctuary, looked up from her desk as a knock sounded on her door. Her frown turned into a smile seeing her son, Landon, standing there. Landon had only been with them for a few weeks, but she felt like she had given birth to this handsome young man. He was the spitting image of his father, Ronan Pathfinder, the man Madylyn recently pledged her life to. Ronan hadn't known Landon existed until the day Madylyn did, and in the few short weeks he'd been with them, he had become an integral part of their life and their world.

At five, he was tall for his age—no surprise with the height of the Pathfinder men. Ronan taught him to knock before entering her office because it was her place of work. Today was the first time he remembered to do so.

"Well, good morning, sweetheart. Please, come in. I see you finally made your way to breakfast," she said with a smile. The evidence of his breakfast smeared his cheeks and the front of his clean shirt. Raspberry jelly, from the looks of it, and ketchup. "What can I do for you, Landon?"

Landon walked in and stood in front of her with his head down and his hands in his pockets. He shuffled his feet—a tell if there ever was one. Madylyn was pretty sure he had done something he shouldn't have, and the staff sent him to her to confess. He pulled a dirty hand out of his pocket and wiped his nose with the back of it, adding a wet smear to go with the raspberry jam.

"I..." he faded off, mumbling the rest so that she couldn't hear him.

"I didn't quite catch that, honey, a little louder, please," she said calmly, trying not to laugh out loud. This wasn't his first trip to her office, just his

43

first of many today. She tried really hard to keep a straight face, but it was a struggle.

"I let my pet rat loose in the kitchen !" he yelled.

"Again? Did you do it intentionally?" she asked, trying to breathe calmly. A freaking rat. Sweet Mother, please help her raise a little boy. The one she was carrying damn well better be a little girl, she thought. Rhy better not have that wrong.

"No," he said grumpily. "I just sat him down to get him a snack. He was hungry because he was afraid to come back yesterday. He ran across Mrs. O'Hare's foot. She grabbed the broom and tried to kill him with it. She was yellin'; I was yellin'. We might have knocked over some stuff with me rescuin' him and all," he said glumly.

"Did you help her clean it up?"

"I tried," his voice quivered. "But she banned me from the kitchen." He sniffled and his eyes filled with tears. "She said I'se ain't g-g-gonna get any more cookies from her if I brings him in again." His little shoulders shook. "He n the new kitty are the only friends I'se got here."

Her heart broke hearing him describe his relationship with the rodents. She stood up and went to him, then bent down and scooped him up, hugging him tightly. "No, they are not," she said softly, kissing the side of his neck. "I'm your friend, too."

"Not the same." He sniffled into her hair. "You have to like me," he said, crying louder. "I wanna go home," he whimpered.

"Hush," she whispered, her heart breaking for him and for his father if he heard him say he wanted to leave. Ronan loved being his father and was just really getting to know the boy. She was trying to think of any boys his age on the island when it came to her. "Want to go on an adventure?" she asked him excitedly.

"Where to?" he asked, still sullen.

"You'll get to ride a horse," she said, trying to entice him and cheer him up.

"Do I get to pick which one?"

"That will be up to Ronan, sweetie," she said, setting him back down. He wasn't comfortable yet calling him any version of dad, and that was all right for now. "Why don't you go wash your face and change your shirt while I set everything up."

She smiled as he ran out the door excitedly. Then, she bent over and laughed out loud. To have seen the look on Mrs. O'Hare's face. Damn, that would have been worth it. Mrs. O'Hare ran Madylyn's household at the Sanctuary. You did not want to get on her bad side and being banned from her sweets was not getting on her good side.

"Claire, would your boys be up for meeting a new friend this afternoon?" she sent a quick message on her internal switchboard to a friend of hers on the west side of the island. She had three boys of her own around Landon's age, and they always had a bunch of cousins nearby, too. Landon needed kids his own age to run, play and get dirty with. She would arrange play dates for them over the next few weeks.

"Would be wonderful to see you, Maddy, and the boys would love to meet your Landon. Anytime this afternoon would be wonderful."

Maddy smiled, pleased that it worked out for today. She poured a cup of tea, wishing it were coffee, then returned to her desk to finish going through her correspondences.

Quickly, she separated her correspondence into three piles. A formal letter from the Court of Tears caught her eye immediately. Grabbing a hand-carved maple letter opener with raised maple leaves running along the flat surface, she broke the wax seal with the imprint of a weeping woman, the formal seal of the Court of Tears.

Madylyn always thought their seal was a morbid, though accurate, depiction of their court because they were known far and wide for the devastation they had recently created among the hearts of their people.

She unfolded the heavy parchment, hopeful they would honor her request to return Kyran Tyde. Using his service contract as an excuse to return him to the Sanctuary, she hoped he would be able to finish out the last two years on Heart Island.

It was a last-ditch effort to get Kyran back before he was forced into an arranged marriage that he had no knowledge of. He was in love with Rhyanna, and she with him, so Maddy was doing everything she could to try and help resolve the distance between them.

The Court of Tears was always a slippery slope to negotiate. They controlled all the waters, freshwater and salt, on the east coast. The Heart Island Sanctuary was one of thousands of small islands on the St. Lawrence River. A good relationship between the Court and Sanctuary was imperative to her community.

Madylyn was fairly sure Queen Meriel orchestrated this whole fiasco. It was one more way for the queen to flaunt her power and position to the other courts and sanctuaries under her jurisdiction.

She scanned through it quickly, exhaled, and said, "You've got to be fucking kidding me," a little more forcibly than she intended to. Just to be sure, she wasn't interpreting it incorrectly, she reread it once again.

Queen Merial and King Varan thank you for the correspondence they have received regarding Kyran Tyde, a favorite son of the Court. We appreciate your concern and your request.

Unfortunately, we regret to inform your Sanctuary that it is our belief that Kyran will best serve his Court and his monarchs by being present at Court. He will also serve his people by marrying Princess Elyana of the Great Lakes Fire clan to seal a trade compact with them. This compact benefits both courts greatly. A formal betrothal has been in place for years. This should have prevented Kyran from entering into any relationship with the intention of anything more than a casual dalliance.

Rumors of his relationship with one of your wardens has reached us. Kyran is more than welcome to keep the lower-ranked woman for a mistress, if he should choose to do so. She will never become anything more than that as long as he remains pledged to Elyana. There is a place in our Court for people of her rank. However, it is not sitting by the side of a prince of the Court.

If she would like to remain near him, she is welcome to join our Court. We are always looking for kitchen wenches and laundresses. Your only necessary response to this missive would be to request a low-level position for her. Of course, room and board are provided, and she will have her choice of suitors amongst the working class if she chooses not to join the King's Harem.

If she prefers to remain Kyran's mistress, be aware that she will also be available to any of the princes or high-ranking members of the nobility as well. The women who make this choice are aware that exclusivity is not an option. She will be required to be marked in a manner which allows all to know of her availability and eagerness to please on command.

At this time, we do not see Kyran ever returning to your Sanctuary, but we will be happy to send his younger brother, Kai, to take his place. Our decision is final. We appreciate you respecting that how we determine to best use our assets is none of your concern, or frankly, your business.

Have a blessed day.

King Varan and Queen Merial

Madylyn's entire body vibrated with anger. She was so upset that she picked up a paperweight from the desk and turned to throw it at her wall. She needed the satisfaction of breaking something before she spontaneously combusted. The weight left her hand, but it never hit anything. In her rage, she failed to see Fergus Embers, Heart Island's Fire Mage, walking through the door and into the trajectory of her launch.

The gangly red-haired giant easily caught the weight and returned it to the top of her desk. "What vexes thee, me lovely Madylyn?" he asked as she sputtered, trying to produce a reply. "Cat got yer tongue?" he couldn't resist asking as she still was trying to speak through the rage rolling through her. "I don't think I've seen ye this mad since the day Ronan arrived," he said, chuckling.

Maddy glared at him before launching the letter from the Court of Tears at him. "See if you're still smirking after you're done reading this," she snarled at him. She watched his eyes flare as he quickly read the missive.

"The mother fuckers all but call her a whore, and are still stuck in a fucking feudal system that's been extinct since the 1600s. Generous they were offering her work in the kitchens, the laundry, or on her fucking knees." Maddy paced the room, livid.

Fergus's pale skin flamed an angry red right along with hers. "Feckers," he snarled, "how dare they treat her this way." He took a deep breath, trying to see past his mad. His fire drakes were running up and down his arms and through his flame-colored hair, soaking up the negative energy and rage radiating from him. A couple of the blue and red ones looked at Maddy and almost launched themselves at her until she turned and hissed at them.

"Maddy," he said, trying to calm down, "listen to me, darling." He approached her, trying to get her attention. "Ye need to calm down, lass. Ye can't be getting all upset like this in yer condition, now can ye?"

He saw the shock and then the guilt race across her face as her right hand automatically rubbed her slightly swollen belly. "Yer fine, lass. Just sit down and breathe for me, can ye, please?"

He looked up, and his attention turned to young Landon standing in the doorway, afraid and unsure.

"Landon, me laddie, come on in. No lingering in the hall now," Fergus entreated with a smile. He could tell that their outburst upset him.

Landon walked in tentatively to Maddy. "Are you ok, Maddy?" he asked softly while twisting his hands together in front of him.

"I am sorry, honey, if you heard me yelling," Madylyn said, as she took his hands in hers. "I didn't mean to scare you," she said, now on the verge of crying.

"You said a bad word," he said, his eyes too large in his face. "Two of 'em."

"You caught me, honey." He made her smile as she confessed to her crimes. "I'll try to do better in the future, all right?"

"Okay," he said, as he reached out to hug her and tried to pat her back awkwardly. He turned to look at Fergus somberly. "Ronan says that we shouldn't talk that way in front of women. It's for men only."

Fergus rubbed a hand over his face, trying to hide his grin as the wee lad corrected him. He nodded, trying to look properly contrite, not trusting himself to speak.

"He did, did he?" Maddy asked, again trying to hide a grin. "When you grow into a man, make sure you remember that lesson."

Madylyn stood up, taking his small hand in hers to ground her. "Fergus, we'll speak later. I have an appointment with this young man for the next few hours. I'll see you tonight then?"

"Aye, Maddy, ye will, and I will look into this supposed trade compact before I return to ye," he said as he walked out ahead of them. "I've friends in high places in the Fire Court as well. She's messed with the wrong people this time; I promise you that."

"Excellent." Madylyn walked out the door with Landon, her head still reeling from the response. If they thought they could intimidate her, they had made a grave mistake. Madylyn SkyDancer was a force to be reckoned with. She hoped the Court of Tears was ready for the gale-force shit storm she was about to rain down on them.

CHAPTER NINE

Have Faith

Rhyanna reached into a long trough filled with water and pulled out a handful of reeds soaking there. The rest of her supplies lay on a table within reach. She settled on a stool outside of her apothecary shoppe so that she could take advantage of the beautiful day. Sturdy oval reeds served as the frame of the piece she was creating, and she carefully anchored them in place. She reached for a piece of the wet reed and worked it tightly around the frame, snugging it down tight to the bottom. When she finished, she gathered up another reed repeating the process until she once again tamped it down tightly.

Her mind wandered as her hands worked competently from muscle memory. Over, under, over, under. Snug, tamp, move on to the next piece. A smile lit up her face as the large piece began to take shape. This was one of the largest hand-woven baskets she'd ever attempted, and honestly, she wasn't sure if it was going to work out for what she intended. The pattern she was creating came from a dream the night before. She was excited to try it out.

Rhy continued working, humming as she worked, weaving the reed in and out easily, as she'd done since she was a young girl. Her aunt was an expert weaver, and Rhyanna learned by watching her for hours. When she turned nine, weaving baskets became her responsibility. Her father sold them at the local outdoor market while her mother offered her services as a healer. With six siblings younger than Rhyanna, it was a small way she could help her struggling family. After the first week, she had woven with rags covering the blisters on her hands until the blisters became callouses. She learned to ignore the pain until her skin toughened up. Eventually, her designs became much sought-after works of art.

Her parents didn't care what she wove; as long as it had a purpose, they were able to sell it. With a flair for colors and textures, they gave her the freedom to create her own works of art, not just utilitarian pieces. Embellishments and colors were added as they appealed to her, and she enjoyed the craft because it allowed her a creative outlet. Rhyanna wanted the things she created to be durable and beautiful. This became her mission until her path forked and led her in the direction of healing when she reached her teens.

Nowadays, she wove for the joy of it and the peace it brought her. She created gifts out of her creations— meaningful, beautiful, and practical works of art. As she wove, she hummed her favorite songs from her youth—pretty little melodies that she also used to weave her intentions into the pieces. She wove lasting love, protection, and healing into her creations.

Rhy picked up the piece she was working on and eyed it critically. This piece was special and needed to be sturdy and safe. She carefully made sure all the rough edges were on the outside of the basket. She attached a length of a small round birch branch on the outside, weaving around it so that she could eventually loop a leather strap through the gap to create a handle. The piece was coming along beautifully, exactly as she had dreamt it would be. Her eyes closed as she remembered it.

She stood in a doorway watching Ronan and Madylyn in their suite smiling and cooing over their newborn. Their beautiful little girl was sleeping soundly in the basket Rhyanna was making. The basket sat on a sturdy stand next to their bed. The couple was so incredibly happy together. Their relationship had taken a long detour, and they deserved the joy they finally found together.

The dream changed, and she saw a young girl using the basket for her dolls to lie in. Then once again, time traveled forward as a young woman used it to gather herbs alongside Rhyanna in the field. This was when the leather strap would be needed. Rhyanna smiled as she watched her, knowing this child would play a significant role in all their lives.

Sighing, she returned to the present. Satisfied, Rhy continued weaving this basket for her best friend and for the child she would soon have. She wove it for the young woman who would bless all of them with her existence, and she wove it for herself to bring peace to her anxious soul. More so, she created it for the sheer joy of making something beautiful out of nothing more than old pieces of dried reeds and marsh grasses that most would have thrown out or burned.

Her mind wandered to Maddy and Ronan and how everything worked out for them in the end. She tried to find hope in their story, even as hers felt so bleak. The ache in her chest from missing Kyran grew stronger every day, and she wondered if their story would be as blessed as theirs was. As her fingers wove without even thinking about it, she sighed and dug her bare feet into the ground trying to connect with the earth and settle her soul.

"Have faith my child. All shall be well." The Earth Mother's voice whispered through her head. Rhy's sorrow eased, and she threw her cares to the wind because she could no longer carry the pain by herself. They were never alone on their journey, and today she was grateful for that reminder.

CHAPTER TEN

Rosella Diaries-Third Entry

Rosella brushed her long, strawberry-blond hair, preparing for bed. The soft waves fell to her waist. Finished, she loosely braided it over her right shoulder and looked at her reflection in the vanity. Her hazel eyes seemed too big in her pale face, and the innocence they had sported only months ago had vanished.

The past two months had cost her the luxury of childhood and the comforts of home. Manfri, the man she loved, had been cruelly murdered in front of her, and she now found herself adrift in a world she didn't understand. She was trapped on a large ship with no way to run or to seek help. A flesh monger by the name of Pearl and her lackey, Jonah, seemed to be in charge.

Unwilling to trust anyone, she kept to herself and tried not to draw any undue attention. Her future was bleak as she was trained to be auctioned off in the coming months to the highest bidder. Her virginity was the only thing of value she possessed in this world, and the fact that it would be given to a stranger without her consent galled her. Rosella was a Gallagher, and Gallagher's didn't go down without a fight. Rosella had fought, kicked, and caused as much damage as she had taken trying to escape. Now, she fought in a different way. Learning and acquiescing, she sought an advantage, an ally, or any way out of this hellhole she resided in.

Her maid, Shaelyn, passed behind her. "If there's nothing else ye need, milady, I'll be turning in na."

Rosella tried to match Shaelyn's smile, but failing, she nodded at her in the mirror. "I'm all set. G'night."

Shaelyn scurried over to her pallet in the corner near the door and settled in for the night. Her breathing slowed quickly, and soft snores soon filled the room. The sound made Rosella sigh in relief. Finally, peace from the incessant chatterbox. The girl meant well, but she didn't know when to stop.

She stood and wandered the length of the large room she occupied. A bank of windows drew her as she tried to figure out where on the St. Lawrence they were. Her brother, Roarke, was a ship captain, and she had often traveled the length of the river with him. Nothing seemed familiar anymore, and she struggled to maintain hope that she would ever be found. Leaning her head against the cool glass, she reached out once again on her familial links, trying to communicate telepathically with someone—anyone. Finding nothing she could use, she gave up and headed for bed.

Her guard, Braden, was seated on the floor in front of the door. She wasn't sure if he was there to protect her or to keep her from escaping. Unlike Shaelyn, he only spoke when spoken to. Rosella had rarely done so, having no need to connect with someone who was keeping her from leaving this place.

Rosella climbed into the high bed and settled into her comfortable nest of down and velvet covers. She pulled a pillow in front of her, and as her eyes grew tired, she slipped into the place in her mind where she recorded her ordeal. With a photographic memory, she remembered every word she committed to the pages of her mental diary. She visualized untying the strings and opening the leather ship captains journal. Picking up a metal calligraphy pen, she dipped it in a bottle of ink and began to write.

Dear Diary,

Days have passed since my last entry, and I am grateful for a room to myself with a window so that I may judge the passage of time.

To clarify, I have a room, which I share with a chatterbox of a maid, Shaelyn, and my personal guard Braden. I suppose I should be grateful it is only the three of us.

Braden is the tall, brooding type with dark hair and the palest blue eyes I've ever seen. He rarely looks at me, and then only if I force him to acknowledge me in the way of a question that needs answering. I realize he is not here to be my friend, and I doubt I would trust him if he seemed to be.

I feel the same way towards Shaelyn. She talks a lot, but fortunately, she doesn't encourage me to contribute to the conversation. I just listen and nod when it seems appropriate, even though I tune out the drone of words coming from her mouth.

The first night after my bath, I was allowed a brief period to rest, which surprisingly I did soundly. Somehow, I felt safe in that room with Braden by the door. As I faded off, I felt his eyes on me and managed to pry mine open once more. His eyes held mine for a moment, and the compassion and sorrow in them for me was staggering. As I drifted off, I couldn't help but wonder, what horrors awaited me in the coming days.

After my recovery period, they led me, once again, to the large room that was a combination dining room and formal parlor. I sat amongst the other waifs eating a meal fit for a king. I heeded the warnings of many of the girls about eating lightly after my 'confinement,' as they all referred to my imprisonment.

My stomach protested at the second bite of meat, so I stuck to small bits of bread, fresh fruit, and more of the broth.

It was strangely normal sitting there amongst all those young women. We might have been a group of students at university or a family gathering for a Sunday meal. The whole scene was surreal, with laughter and smiles from most of the girls.

I watched discreetly, trying to memorize faces and look for any possible allies amongst the group. There were a handful that looked as lost as I felt, but the others were comfortable and seemed happy in their lifestyle.

Pearl sat at the head of the table in an intricately carved captain's chair. High-backed in polished walnut, it matched the one at the other end that was twice the size of hers. Jonah joined us late and ate his meal while looking longingly at the other end of the table.

I long to have someone to talk with, if even for a few moments of the day, but I don't dare share anything deeply personal.

Surprisingly, I was allowed to sleep in the next day until the mid-day meal. Shaelyn was my updated version of the rooster that crowed under my window every morning before dawn. Mornings are no different with her. She is eternally cheerful and chatty. I don't think I've mentioned that I, on the other hand, wake up sullen and cranky. This hasn't changed.

After my morning ablutions, I was ushered to the dining room, where light fare awaited. Warm hot cross buns, fresh fruit, and various cheeses were offered. T'was quieter than the previous evening, and some of the young women didn't make an appearance. I wondered if it was optional, or possible, to take meals in my room. I quizzed Shaelyn on it later, and she told me that it was a privilege I was a long way from earning.

A dozen of us walked through the maze of hallways to a moderate-sized room with chairs lining all four walls. We each found a chair with our name on it and waited patiently for our next lesson until Pearl arrived. Our guards wandered off to their own meal. That was a small relief. Braden wouldn't have to see me humiliate myself once again.

Pearl arrived in style as always. A long emerald gown trailed behind her as she entered. She was beautiful in such a unique way that I could understand Jonah's infatuation with her. A long sheet of straight black hair usually fell to her hips. Today, the silk strands were tightly braided and pinned up. Her large eyes were so dark you couldn't see her pupils. If eyes were the windows to the soul, I figured it was a warning that she didn't have one. A double row of lashes made her eyes look like she had lined them with a kohl pencil, adding to the sensual heat she cast with her gaze.

A petite woman, it would be easy to mistake her size for weakness, but weak was one thing that woman is most definitely not. Jonah might appear to be her protector, but I had no doubt that she was a weapon on her own.

She walked into the center of the room, followed by a dozen men of varying heights, weights, colors, and builds. They were unique, each of them, except for the fact that they were all nude and sporting an erection. I realized my next lesson was waiting for me in one of them.

Some of the other girls giggled next to me, pointing, and comparing the men's attributes. The men stood in a circle in the middle of the room, staring straight ahead, emotionless. I felt the heat in my cheeks, embarrassed for them and for myself. I looked down at my hands, not sure where I should be looking, but knowing for damn sure I didn't want to be staring at them like a piece of meat.

"Silence." Pearl spoke softly, but her voice was like a slap, and all sound ceased. She walked around the room, assessing us. I was still looking at my hands when she stopped in front of me.

I was unable to stop myself from flinching when her hand lifted my face to meet her gaze. She smiled sweetly at me. "I trust you slept well, Ella?"

I nodded. "Yes, ma'am."

"Good. Your days will be busy, and your nights long, so it's best you get used to the change in your sleep patterns."

She released me, much to my relief. I didn't want to have any attention drawn to me. Moving like a predator, she continued around the room, speaking to every girl, politely inquiring about them as if she genuinely cared. It made me nauseous watching her.

Lost in my thoughts, I didn't realize that she had returned to me until her hand stroked down my hair. "Ella may be the newest sister to join us, but she is not that far behind in her training than the rest of you. Some of you have been working on this for weeks and still struggle. She performed better with Saul than any one of you could have managed. Even filthy, she had the grace to look elegant, even as she believed she was debasing herself in front of us."

Her hand continued to stroke my hair, making goosebumps rise over my entire body. I struggled to comprehend what she was saying, too afraid of what was next. As the fact that she was complimenting me sank in, I felt a ridiculous amount of pleasure that I had done something right. I didn't want to be here, and I sure as hell didn't want to sell my body or my soul to survive this, even though I knew that was a requirement. It sickened me that her praise instantly pleased me, and I was terrified I would lose myself in the attempt to garner more of her good graces.

"Because you did so well on your first attempt, you will go last today." I let out a visible sigh of relief until she continued, "Watch and learn, listen to the feedback the others get, and when it comes to your turn, I expect you will give another outstanding performance."

She turned from me and headed towards a tall woman with dark red hair. "Gemma, you may pick first."

Gemma looked up, dismayed to be first. She walked around the men and made her choice. Her subject was short and stocky with ebony skin. She took his hand and led him to her chair. Resuming her seat, she took his cock and pulled him closer to her using her hand to guide him. Taking her time, she familiarized herself with his cock and balls. She rolled them gently between her fingers, squeezing lightly. Her hand grasped him firmly, finding a rhythm and stroking him exuberantly. When a drop of precum appeared on the tip, she pushed him back slightly and lowered herself to her knees.

She grimaced as she bent down and licked it off before stroking him with her tongue. She took him in her mouth, bobbing up and down quickly. Her cheeks hollowed as she added suction.

Terrified, disgusted, and embarrassingly fascinated, I watched her expressions and body language, as well as the man she was trying to please. She radiated disgust and an eagerness to get it over with. He clenched his fists tightly. I wasn't sure if that was evidence of his pleasure or his willingness to get it over with as well. My answer came quickly as he grabbed the back of her head and thrust quickly in and out of her mouth as deeply as he could.

Most surprising of all was the fact that once he took over, Gemma's face relaxed. She allowed him to control her head as he took his pleasure. Ella could see the struggle Gemma was having swallowing all of him, but her relaxed pose made it much easier than fighting the inevitable. With a grunt, he stilled, emptying himself into her.

Gemma's hand kept playing with his balls as he finished. When his body ceased shuddering, she released him and licked her lips. "Thank you," she said softly before resuming her seat.

Pearl came forward, and the man took a step back. "Thank you, Deacon, for consenting to join us today."

He stared straight ahead as he said, "You're welcome, ma'am." His voice was melodic and reminded Ella of the islands her mother's family came from.

"If you don't mind," Pearl encouraged, "Gemma would appreciate your critique of her technique so that she might do better next time."

"Happy to, ma'am," he said with a wide smile. His teeth were strong and straight and a blinding white against the ebony of his skin. He was a handsome man. "First off, thank you, Miss Gemma, for the gift you just gave me. I really enjoyed what you did, and this is just my personal preference, mind you, not anything you did wrong. I would have liked it if you had stroked me slower in the beginning, giving a chance for my body to enjoy it longer." He rubbed his hand over his bald head and continued, "The only other thing I would advise is to be careful with your teeth when you are sucking. A little bit can be pleasurable, but too much deflates the mood and is painful." He looked at Pearl, who nodded.

"Thank you, Deacon, for your honesty. I am sure that Gemma will take your suggestions to heart and do better next time, won't you?" she asked.

"Yes, ma'am. My apologies, Deacon, for any discomfort I may have caused you."

"Accepted, little lady.

Pearl smiled at them both. "Deacon, you may go enjoy the rest of your day."

Gemma settled back in her chair somberly, knowing Pearl wasn't pleased with her.

I watched this process over and over until my turn came. I paid attention to the critiques and watched intently, wanting to get my turn over with, with minimal complaints.

When my turn arrived, only one man remained, saving me from making another poor choice. A tall blond, his penis wasn't particularly long, but he made up for it in girth. I stroked him softly at first, then firmly feeling him grow larger in my soft hands. When his body released that first drop of milky white fluid, I did as all the others had and dropped to my knees. Taking my time stroking and licking him, I ignored everyone else in the room and focused purely on the task before me. It was my mission to please the beautiful blond man with the thick cock.

I played with him until I could sense the tension rising in his body. Then, I slowly took him in my mouth. He wouldn't cut off my airway like Saul had, but it was a struggle to open wide enough for all of him. Cringing, I thought of Gemma as my teeth dragged a time or two, causing him to hiss and tighten his hand in my hair. When he pulled my head back, my eyes met his, and I realized that the sound he'd made was one of pure pleasure.

I wanted to close my eyes and let him just finish, but I couldn't do it. I had to witness the pleasure he took from me. If Pearl was going to prostitute me out, I needed to look them in the eye, daring them to forget me after I touched them because I would never forget their faces. Someday there would be a reckoning, but until that day, I would remember them, saving their faces and names as a reminder of one more day that I survived.

"Please introduce yourself and give your report," Pearl said with a smile.

"Caden at yer service, ma'am." His smile made his eyes light up, and he looked down at me with affection. "Hard to believe yer new at this, Ella, but my critique won't follow the rest. Ye nicked me twice, but I tend to like a bit of pain with my pleasure, so that's not a complaint for me. Ye could've squeezed me tighter in the beginning, too, but that's a matter of personal preference. Thank ye, darling." His hand cupped my face before he turned to Pearl, waiting for her permission to leave.

She nodded then looked back at me as he walked out the door. "What have you learned today through your observations and your performance Ella?"

I thought about her question carefully, approaching it like I would a subject in school. "No two men are alike; each has different preferences and needs. We need to find a way to figure out what brings them pleasure and what doesn't."

Pearl smiled down at me, pleased. "Exactly. And next time, you will learn how to read the man you're touching—how to pay attention to the cues and signals he unknowingly gives you. Good job, ladies. Head on out for lunch, and then take a two-hour break before our evening lessons."

We stood to leave. I was near the end of the line when Gemma approached me. "How did you figure out all of that your first lesson?" she asked, genuinely interested.

"I just watched all of you. I paid attention to their body language and facial cues." I shrugged, not sure how to explain it to her. "Is this what every lesson is about?"

"Nye, just the morning ones. We learn a lot of other things that have nothing to do with men." She looped her arm through mine as we walked down the hall. *"If you have any questions, don't be afraid to ask me."* Her voice dropped barely above a whisper. *"You can't trust everyone. Be careful who you confide in."*

I smiled at her, wanting to trust her, but her warning left me feeling ill at ease. *Can I believe her or is she just trying to get close to me for Pearl? I don't know. The only one I know I can rely on is myself, and I intend to keep it that way.*

Until next time,

Rosella

CHAPTER ELEVEN

Warden's Council

Madylyn walked into her office to find it full of her fellow wardens. An unusually somber group, they waited for her to take her place behind her mahogany desk. Ronan, her partner, sat on the window seat of the bay window behind her. Tall with dark hair and light eyes, he smiled as she walked into the room, and her heart relaxed just knowing he was here.

A leather couch held Danyka, a petite woman with short black hair, big blue eyes, pixie-like features, and deadly reflexes. She preferred leather pants, corsets, or vests to work and play in. Her tiny stature belied the fact that she was the deadliest warrior of Madylyn's wardens. The sanctuary counted on her tracking skills, and her partner counted on her having his back. A member of the Air Clan, she was smart, beautiful, and feisty as hell, but an acquired taste for some. An accomplished shape-shifter, you could often find her soaring far above them in her favorite form, a peregrine falcon, patrolling their borders from the sky.

Her partner, Jameson Vance, sat next to her. A member of the local Earth Clan, his family raised horses on Wellesley Island. He was six feet of solid muscle, barrel-chested with a narrow waist and thick thighs. His straight hair was pulled back and banded every two inches with strips of pale leather that contrasted with the rich chestnut brown that hung to his waist. Indigenous ancestors gave him his bronze coloring and angular features. Jamey, as they called him, was their rock. He possessed the best personality, kindest heart, and softest shoulder to cry on. The men loved partying with him, and the women—well, they just loved him.

He and Danyka rescued magical creatures and captured dangerous ones released during the Earth Mother's Retribution. Occasionally, creatures they were unable to rehabilitate, sadly, had to be put down. It was their job to keep the locals safe from the things that went bump in the night. Though they tried their best to not harm anything, they didn't always get the outcome they wanted.

A lanky red-haired character who answered to Fergus Emberz walked in and plopped down next to Jameson. He was their Fire Mage and a complete fashion catastrophe. Today he blessed them with pale-yellow leggings and a bright red and black flannel. Knee-high leather moccasins were strapped to his legs just shy of his knees. Tiny metal bells hung from the laces, announcing his presence as he walked. His red hair was in tiny braids all over his head, as was his long rust-colored beard. Braided into both were tiny yellow beads that matched his pants. A wide belt wrapped around his waist with various tools of his trade attached. Sighing contentedly, he leaned back and settled in.

Fire drakes of all colors raced back and forth over his skin, absorbing his energy. The tiny serpentine figures danced between his fingers, and when aggravated, they had been known to cause damage to those nearby. Barely three inches in length, they were flashes of color barely noticed because of their size and speed and often mistaken for flashes of light. Their size was proportionate to the amount of energy they siphoned off, and they could become much larger. They thrived on the darker negative emotions of frustration, disappointment, and their favorite, rage.

Rhyanna entered and sat on the settee across from them. Absently, she braided her long blond hair over one shoulder as her emerald eyes took in the somber mood. As their healer and a strong empath, she picked up on the underlying currents in any large group she was around. For this reason, she tended to avoid crowds, especially if drinking was involved. But these people were her family, and she loved spending time with them, even when the reason they gathered today was heartbreaking and horrifying.

Following her into the room was Roarke Gallagher. New to their group, he was ruggedly handsome—tall, thickly muscled with shoulder-length dirty blond hair and eyes of chocolate brown. A local ship captain, he joined the wardens to search for his missing sister and his niece, Hailey. They rescued his niece, but there was still no sign of his sister. He joined Rhyanna on the settee, smiling at her as he sat.

Madylyn looked around at her friends, her co-wardens, and her partner. "I'll start with what I've learned since our last meeting, and we'll go from there."

Her eyes met each of theirs as she started to speak. "I've been in contact with districts up and down the eastern seaboard and as far as the Great Lakes. The majority of them are not seeing the increase in missing cases that we are on the St. Lawrence." Groans of frustration were heard around the room. "However," she continued, "the ones having a spike in cases are within a hundred-mile radius of the river. We believe they are using the river as means of quick transport to get the abducted women out of our area. There is an increase in the number of sightings of larger vessels traveling at night without any lights and strange crews wandering through the local ports." Madylyn gestured to the tall stacks of files in four piles on the left side of her desk.

"I've been granted access to all the records of those who have gone missing over the past five years. I want all of you to look at them. Search for patterns or any links between locations. Having a broader region to compare might make it easier for us to figure out what they are trolling for amongst our people."

Her hands clenched as she glanced around the room. "These animals are preying on not just our young men and women, but all ages. It needs to stop, and we need to find a way to protect our people on and off the river. Rhyanna, what have you learned from the girls you were taking care of?"

"From what I ken, only two of 'em weren't taken directly off the river. One woman was abducted off the streets in broad daylight, and the third sold to support her mam's drug habit. Grace was abducted in a similar way to Rosella. All of the girls woke naked, drugged, and chained in small cells. They were barely fed the first week they were in captivity. Weak, dehydrated and desperate by the time they were released from their isolation, they'd have done anything jest to stay alive."

Rhy was aware of Roarke sitting next to her as she spoke. His face blanched as she continued her report. Reaching out to Maddy privately, she asked, *"Should I continue with him present?"*

Maddy raised an eyebrow at her and looked at Roarke, also noting the way he was clenching his jaw in rage.

Roarke caught the undercurrent of their communication and spoke out loud. "Please don't sugar coat anything just because I'm here. I have a pretty good understanding of what they went through and what Rosella might still be going through."

Rhyanna nodded and continued. "From what I gathered, they were bathed, then examined by a healer to determine their value and look for diseases. After a light meal, they slept 'til night. After a period of training, their captors lined them up on the deck and auctioned them off like animals." She paused, taking a breath before continuing with her information.

"Virgins were saved for last. Bidding wars would go on for quite some time over them. The younger, the better. Male or female, it didna matter. There is a market for both. The auctioneer fitted them with collars and placed them on a leash for their owners to claim. Needless to say, they went through hell," she said, reaching over, taking Roarke's hand, and squeezing tight. He clung to it like a lifeline.

Danyka cleared her throat before speaking. "From what I heard, the better they were at their 'job,' the nicer they were treated and the better the accommodations. If you adjusted well, you could work your way up to fancier yachts, pleasure boats, riverboat brothels, better drugs or food, and less vile things required of you."

She was pale as she spoke and needed a moment to continue. "Those who were too traumatized, or who refused to adjust, were heavily drugged and given to the larger ocean-bound ships to be placed in their own private brothels, their 'stables' on board. The girls on those ships never last long. They're used and abused by the harshest of men repeatedly, day after day. Eventually, when they're finally broken physically or emotionally beyond repair, they're tossed overboard like refuse. Their loved ones will never know what became of them."

"Grace spent the longest amount of time in captivity. She said they never stayed in one place for long. Every night, they docked somewhere different. She grew up on the river and had a good idea of how far they traveled daily, but it was never consistent enough for her to track. The girls transferred to different vessels every other week. It kept them confused and off-balance."

Madylyn sighed as Rhy and Danny finished their reports. "Now that we understand the what and why of it, we need to find the who and where. We need to find the puppet master pulling the strings. Someone has the power and clout to get away with this. I want to find out who it is." She turned to Danyka and Jameson. "Any luck on the islands you checked out?"

Jameson shook his head. "The islands are being used, but they are also local party stops for kids. We could tell someone docked there with a large crew from the refuse left behind. It's hard to say because it could have been a bunch of local kids hanging out. No evidence on any of the abandoned islands indicated anything more than a gathering had occurred. I don't think these people are stupid enough to leave evidence of their passing. They've had years to perfect their illegal activities, and they aren't going to be careless about it. That's how they have stayed under our notice for this long. I think the only reason we found that ship on Grindstone is that they didn't have time to come back and properly dispose of it before we got there."

"That makes sense," Maddy said. "Fergus, any luck in locating the illegal gaming ships or finding out who signed off on the manifest?"

"Negative on that. I've got me some feelers out with men I trust. It's a fine line we walk asking about this kind of thing, Maddy, without ending up dead. Like Jamey said, they've done this fer a long time, and they've precautions in place to avoid the law finding and taking 'em down. They may be evil shites, but they ain't fecking stupid. That's why they've gotten away with it for this long." They may be greedy, but they're not sloppy. More missing brings more attention and more patrols on the river. They either need a good plan in place or plenty of crooked local officials willing to take bribes to look the other way."

Ferg shook his head disgustedly. "I'd put money on the fact that this goes all the way to the top of the food chain. There's no fecking way it's this big without someone funding it or covering it up for 'em."

Absently, he played with the bells in his beard before continuing. "The harbormaster who signed off on the scuttled yacht was found floating in his harbor two days after we found the ship. They ain't leaving any witnesses for us to trace back to 'em."

"Goddamn it," Madylyn cursed before looking at Roarke. "Have the locals given you anything helpful?"

He shook his head. "Nothing concrete. But I can tell you, they're afraid. They sense something is going down, and they want no part in it. They are doing everything possible to stay out of it. After dark, you hardly meet anyone alone on the docks anymore, even the men."

Roarke hesitated to share the next part because Maddy was the local law. He ran his hand through his hair and gave it up. "I've discretely offered rewards for any information that can be found through my contacts on the docks."

Maddy raised an eyebrow at him. "Are you admitting to bribing local officials?"

Roarke met her eyes without blinking, "I'm saying I am offering rewards to *anyone* with information. Take that as you will." His voice was sharp as he finished.

Maddy nodded at him, accepting his methods. She watched her crew, grateful to have such a dedicated group of people by her side. "Anyone else have anything to add?" she asked.

Nothing was said until Maddy opened her mouth to dismiss them, and a deep voice from the doorway startled them. "I would like to weigh in, if that's all right with you, Mistress SkyDancer."

Rhyanna looked up, startled to hear Kyran's voice. She couldn't believe she hadn't sensed his approach. She wasn't the only one who'd learned to block their telepathic bridge. Her eyes flew to his, happy to find him standing there. His eyes locked on her—more specifically on her hand grasping Roarke's. Blushing, she yanked her hand away even though she did nothing but offer the man comfort. The jealous rage Kyran was radiating came through telepathically and in the glare as his eyes latched onto hers.

Madylyn watched the emotions playing out between the two of them. She also sensed Rhyanna's discomfort and sought to break the tension.

"Kyran, please take a seat. We would be grateful for anything you can add to our meeting."

He walked into the room, followed by a young man with similar features but taller by half a foot. "Thank you. First, I would like to introduce my youngest brother, Kai." Kyran took an empty seat in front of Madylyn with his back to Rhyanna while Kai remained standing, leaning against the doorway. "I've spoken with several of the harbormasters between here and Quebec. There have been multiple sightings of vessels slipping through late at night, all running without lights. It hasn't gone unnoticed, even though they are making a hell of an effort to stay hidden. The only sign of their passing is changes in the water. Men who've spent their lives on the river know the currents like the back of their hand. These ships may pass silently and invisibly, but they can't stop the water from parting in front of them. Must be one hell of a mage on board to keep them hidden from sight, but they don't have a strong enough water mage to control the water."

"One old-timer I spoke with thought he was losing his mind as he watched the water part in front of him. He picked up a rock and threw it at the empty space, watching as it bounced back at him. Repeating it numerous times, he was able to gauge the size of the ship. It was an ocean liner and fully loaded at that. It was a clear night, and he could tell how far down it disturbed the water. The tough son of a bitch followed them for miles to see how long they would stay undercover. There are some low population areas where he thought they might drop the shield, but they kept it up the whole way."

"I knew dark mages were involved somehow," Fergus said. "Fecking hell, if they are powerful enough to hide something that size for that long of a distance, yer going to need some heavier firepower than I've got available. I'm damn good and not shy about saying so, but I think they're a helluva lot more powerful, or else there are a lot more of them working together."

"The patrols of rivermaids and men are aware and watching for similar discrepancies. They have mages amongst them that can sense if magic is coming into play. They will determine what kind and their strength," Kyran said with a glance at Fergus. "They will contact you if they find anything."

Fergus nodded in agreement. "If I know where they've been, I can look for any residual magic and try to identify the mage who created it. We each have a unique magical signature, and if it's someone I've encountered before, I'll recognize them."

"How quickly do you need to check out the scene to be able to trace the mage?" Kyran asked.

"No later than twenty-four to thirty-six hours. After that, it will have dissipated too much to be of any value."

"I'll make it happen," Kyran said.

"Anyone have anything else to add?" Myranda asked once more.

When no one spoke this time, she said, "We're done here as far as I am concerned. We'll continue gathering intel and building a case. Roarke, Jameson, and Kyran, as you have time over the next week, I'd like you all to look at the reports that came in and see if there is something we're missing. Look for correlations between the people taken, the locations, time of day, et cetera. You three are the most familiar with our section of the St. Lawrence." She smiled at their newest addition and added, "Kai, welcome to the Heart Island Sanctuary. I am sure Kyran will fill you in and help you get settled."

"Thank you," Kai said in a voice that seemed much too deep to go with his age.

They stood up and slowly dispersed. Roarke reached out and squeezed Rhyanna's hand. "Are you all right?" he asked softly.

She nodded, looking at him guiltily. "Thank ye, Roarke, but I'm fine."

"You weren't doing anything wrong; you understand that, don't you?"

"Aye, I ken."

Roarke released her hand and stood to see Kyran watching their exchange. He glanced down at Rhyanna, and she was blushing guiltily as she glanced at Kyran. The poor woman didn't have a deceitful bone in her body. It would have been comical if he hadn't seen how heartbroken she'd been over Kyran.

Roarke turned away from her and approached Kyran offering him a hand, which at the moment, he wasn't sure Kyran would take. Kyran looked him in the eye for a long time before accepting it and shaking. "Good to see you again, Kyran. I know Rhyanna is happy to have you back, too." He made a point of mentioning her to calm the jealousy he saw running through Kyran's eyes.

"Thank you," Kyran said. "It's good to be back." He glanced towards Rhyanna. "If you'll excuse me," he said to Roarke, walking away.

Rhyanna watched the exchange between Roarke and Kyran and was torn between staying or leaving. She'd never been a coward, but guilt plagued her over yesterday's meltdown in his arms and her simple act of compassion today. The tension between the two men was palpable, and she always avoided conflict at all costs. If the mood radiating through their link was anything to go by, Kyran's emotional state was unsettled at best.

He approached her slowly and as apprehensive as she might have been initially, the closer he came to her, the more she felt something else beneath his green streak.

Rhy smiled at him in relief as she was overwhelmed with his pleasure at seeing her. The heat radiating from him surrounded her, making her feel adored and, more importantly, missed.

"My lady," he said huskily, "will you honor me with a walk?"

The heat in his gaze scorched her as she smiled up at him. "Aye, me laird, it would be my pleasure," she said in a soft voice. She reached for the arm he held out, but Fergus intercepted them.

"Sorry, Rhy, darling," he said, trying to placate the threat in her eyes. "It's imperative that I speak with him for a wee bit. I promise to send him right along."

Her eyes flashed dangerously at him. "Ye damn well better," she said in disbelief. "I haven't seen him in over a week, and I'm not in the mood to share Ferg. Make it quick," she snapped.

"I wouldna ask, lass, if it wasna important," Fergus said with an apologetic pat on her shoulder."

Contrite, she said, "Very well then." She looked longingly at Kyran.

Not caring who was watching, Kyran leaned down and kissed her softly before whispering in her ear, "I'll find you when we're through, my lady."

Rhyanna gave him a smile that lit up her face, then left the room on a cloud of anticipation.

CHAPTER TWELVE

Riot Act

Kyran met Kai by the door. "I have to meet with Maddy privately, and then I *need* some time with Rhyanna before they drag me back. Can you distract my guards for a few hours?"

Kai smirked at him. "So, I'm guessing the voluptuous blond is the one causing all the trouble and the reason we haven't seen you in months?"

Kyran grinned. "She is, and I'd much rather spend time with her than my younger brothers any day. Can you help me out?"

"I got your back. Kicked the captain's ass in cards last week, and he still owes me. I'll keep them entertained for a while." His face fell as he looked around at the strange environment. "Kyran, why are you leaving me here?"

"Things are about to take a turn at court when I return. I don't want you anywhere near that place or that evil bitch running it."

"So, you think I'm a liability and unable to take care of myself?" He sounded disappointed and hurt.

"I don't think that at all, Kai. I know your valor in battle. She's already tried to use you against me, and I don't want her to drag you into this insanity. She can't touch you here, and I need to know you're safe. I honestly think you will like it here if you give it a chance. I would love to have my favorite brother collaborating with me when I return, and I will be back."

"You'll send for me if I can help in any way?"

"Count on it. You're helping me already by watching over the woman I love. I wouldn't put it past Meriel to try and use her, too. I'm trusting you with Rhyanna. I didn't ask either of your brothers to come here because I know you will treat her with the respect and honor she deserves."

Kai placed his right hand over his heart. "I will treat her as my sister and protect her with my life."

Kyran clapped him on the shoulder. "I knew you would, and that's why you are the one I chose. You have more honor than Kenn and Kano combined." They both chuckled at that. "Go, distract them for me, and let me spend some time reminding Rhyanna why she's waiting for me."

Kai held up his hand, not wanting to hear anymore.

Fergus waited until everyone left, then walked to the door, closed, and locked it. Rejoining Maddy, Ronan, and Kyran, he glared at Kyran and said, "Ye mind telling us what the feck is happening at yer bloody court?" His face mottled with red patches as he restrained himself from striking the man.

"I'm not exactly sure what you're referring to, Fergus," Kyran said with a frown.

Maddy picked up a letter off her desk and handed it to him. They all witnessed his expressions changing from confusion to shock and finally outrage.

"Well, guess he wasn't aware of how much she was worth to his court, was he?" Madylyn said to Fergus.

Kyran handed back the missive clenching his fists at his side, trying not to hit something, anything to release the fury running through him. "You have my sincerest apologies for the manner in which they are treating her."

"My concern, Kyran," Maddy said coldly, "is this how you see her? Is she just one more piece of ass in your court's harem that you're going to be willing to share with anyone else walking down the hall? Your brothers? Your father, for that matter, is well known for his promiscuity. Maybe it will be with the other lords and ladies who attend your lovely monarchs that you'll want to share her with." She stood in front of him, challenging him as she said, "Is that truly all you're looking for in Rhyanna? Because I promise you, she will burn the fucking place down before she submits to that for any man."

"Maddy..." Ronan said, standing to move between them as he saw the storm rolling in from the south. "I think that's enough." He reached for her arm, pulling her behind him as Kyran exploded.

His voice cracked like the thunder overhead. "Have you lost your fucking minds? You should know me well enough by now to know that I love and cherish her. I'll never share her, and I sure the fuck won't be allowing anyone else to touch her and survive." He paced like a caged animal looking for an outlet for his rage. "It's bad enough the queen's propositioned me, but demeaning Rhyanna in such a manner...I'll kill her."

"Now, I wouldn't be recommending that, laddie, Fergus said as he clasped him on the shoulder from behind.

Not expecting his touch, Kyran turned so quickly that Madylyn barely tracked him as he grabbed Fergus by the throat and pinned him against the wall before Fergus had any time to react.

"Don't fucking touch me," Kyran snarled in his face. "I'm not in the mood."

"Release me before ye sorely regret it," Fergus said much too calmly. His amber eyes were backlit with a hellish light turning them near to gold. His fire drakes snarled as they raced up and down Kyran's hands, leaving scorched skin in their wake as they grew, feeding on his rage. Kyran's water sprites fought back just as aggressively, dousing them.

Kyran took a deep breath, gave a slow blink, and slowly released Fergus. He backed up two steps before pivoting around. "Forgive me, Madylyn. My behavior is inexcusable. I will never allow anything to happen to Rhy. The Court of Tears is a den of lies and deceit, and it already colors my perception after only weeks there. I see enemies in every corner and hear deception in every word."

"I can only imagine how frustrating this whole situation must be for you, and I understand your anger," Maddy said. "We are here for both of you. Please remember that the next time you put your hands on one of my wardens in anger. Next time, I will let Fergus unleash his temper on you." She smiled wickedly at him. "I promise you will not enjoy that." She walked back to her desk and sat down. "So, did you accept the evil queen's proposition?"

"Gods, NO!" he said. He grimaced at the thought of it before laughing. "You've got her title right, I'll give you that." He dropped to a chair in disgust. "Has Rhyanna read that?" he asked, pointing to the missive disgustedly and hoping desperately that she hadn't.

"No, I wouldn't hurt her that way," Madylyn said. "The four of us are the only ones who know about it, and we'll keep it that way, under my orders." She put her head in her hands, suddenly tired. "Rhy detests court life, and this will only make everything worse when she makes an appearance in a few weeks." She saw the fatigue and frustration on Kyran's face and sympathized with him. "Have you spoken to your father?"

"I've tried. It was useless. He's not acting like himself. The queen is running the show from what I can see, and I've been unable to get him alone to speak with him."

"Do you still have any friends or allies at court?" Fergus asked as he sat opposite him.

"A few. I'm not sure who to trust. Loyalties change rapidly amongst the nobles. I've been keeping mainly to myself to stay away from the courtiers and the queen's spies."

"I think, laddie, ye need to make yourself a bit more available. You just need someone you can trust by your side." Fergus grinned.

"You volunteering?" Kyran asked, laughing. "They'll eat you alive."

"No, lad, they won't," Fergus said, dead serious. "Won't be the first den of inequity I've been to, nor the last." He stood, stretching his lanky frame. "If nothing else, I'll be a distraction for the court and keep her Wickedness occupied, giving ye a much-needed break."

"Thank you, Fergus. It's more than I deserve after earlier."

"Yer welcome. Your thanks will come in the form of making sure I get the hell out of there in one piece."

"I'll do my best." Kyran looked at Madylyn. "Would you be willing to consider my brother Kai as a temporary replacement? He would be a good fit here, and it would be safer for him away from court right now."

"Yes, Kyran. If you think he's qualified, I would be happy to provide him a safe haven."

"He is. He's young, but he's brilliant and very knowledgeable about our river's ecosystems. Make sure your agreement gives you exclusive rights for a specified period, or she may try to pull this bullshit again," he advised.

"I will," Madylyn said as she stood and moved towards Ronan. "Your little one is hungry." She turned back to the other two men saying, "If you will excuse us, I need to visit the kitchen, and I believe you, Kyran, have a woman waiting on you."

He smiled at her eager, to go and join his woman. "I'll take my leave. Thank you for showing me what arrived. I will see to it upon my return."

Madylyn shook her head. "No, I'd prefer you don't. Keep them wondering about the wild card Rhyanna is."

Fergus laughed. "They'll never see the lass coming, and they won't be ready for her when she gets there."

"Precisely," Maddy said as her stomach growled, and she opened the door to leave. "That's one hornet nest they don't want to kick." She shook her head ruefully. "It's a rare thing for her to lose her temper, but it's a thing of beauty in its intensity. Ye'll not want to get on her bad side, Kyran, trust me on that."

"I think I've already had a little preview of that, and I aim to not let it happen again," he said, following them down the stairs. "Ferg said it perfectly after the melding, 'she was fecking terrifying.'" But damn, she was stunning in her rage." He laughed out loud. "Might be worth it once in a while to get on her bad side."

"Aye, lad, nothing like make-up sex," Fergus said with a chuckle.

They joined him in his laughter as they went their separate ways. Kyran headed for the front door, looking forward to the brief amount of time he would have with her. Anger wasn't on the agenda for today, but pleasure was. He walked faster, knowing where she went and anxious to join her.

CHAPTER THIRTEEN

Our Lake

Rhyanna left Madylyn's office and headed outdoors. She stepped into the bright sunshine, blinking against the light blinding her. A right took her off the main path, and she hiked uphill towards the lake in the center of the island. The conflicting feelings racing through her distracted her from the beautiful day.

Surprise and shock assaulted her when she'd gazed into Kyran's angry eyes as he stood in the doorway. The shock was followed quickly by guilt for holding Roarke's hand. The guilt transformed into anger for making her feel guilty about offering someone comfort in the first place.

The pleasant surprise she felt at the sight of him was doused by the jealousy coursing through their bridge. Hurt followed quickly behind all of her other changing emotions when he intentionally sat with his back to her, even though a chair was available to her right.

Kyran partially redeemed himself when they finished, and he kissed her. She realized that he may have needed the time to compose himself, but the ups and downs in so short a span frustrated her. This was her first relationship, but they seldom were at odds about anything important.

The only time they had an issue was when Maddy triggered a Melding Cycle, increasing sexual pheromones for everyone, and Kyran elected to put Rhy to sleep rather than make love to her for the first time during a highly charged pheromonal event. She quickly dissuaded him from thinking he would ever challenge her free will again, and then they were separated before their relationship could go any further.

Today was the first time she'd set eyes on him in weeks, and it wasn't how she envisioned their reunion. She felt fury rolling through him and wondered what the meeting with Maddy was about.

Reaching the lake, she took a deep breath to calm her racing heart while kicking off her shoes and sinking her toes into the calming feel of the earth below her. She spread her arms and turned her palms face up. Her inner chatter slowed, and the anxiety she was feeling seeped away as the ground absorbed and transformed it into a gentler form of energy.

The wind blew through her hair as she tipped her face up to the sun and basked in the powerful energy radiating onto her face and hands. The sound of the water gently lapping at the shore in front of her calmed her inner turmoil.

Rhy stood there for a long time before she sensed someone coming up behind her. She remained there, refusing to make the first move. Lowering her arms, she settled her spirit firmly back into her body. Her eyes opened, and she caught his reflection in the water before her.

The sight of him always took her breath away. He was so handsome and imposing, standing there larger than life with his shoulder-length blond hair blowing softly around his face as his eyes captured hers.

Rhyanna turned towards him at the same time he took a step forward. His hands clasped her head, and his lips crashed into hers in a bruising, missed-you-so-much, claiming kiss. Rhyanna moaned as she melted against him. Her arms came up around his neck and her body fused against him. The heat between them escalated as their tongues twined, vying for control and their hands roamed, trying to touch as much as they could.

Groaning, Kyran pulled back, just far enough to look into her eyes. "I knew you would return to our lake. I've missed you, my lady," he whispered. He dotted small kisses over her eyes as he said, "the look of you," before moving down to the tip of her nose, "the smell of you," then lower to her lips again, but gentler this time, "the taste of you." He leaned down, burying his head in the side of her neck, "and for the love of the gods, the feel of you under my hands and my lips." His hands grasped below her hips, and he lifted her up against him so that they were at eye level as he kissed her again.

Rhyanna had forgotten how good his enormous hands felt on her. Always self-conscious about her size, he made her feel tiny, wanted, and incredibly sexy. On their own, her legs made their way around his hips, and he sucked in a breath as her warm core scorched the front of him by sliding against his swollen cock. He rubbed against her with only the thin material of her skirt and his pants between them.

Carefully, he went to his knees with her still clinging to him. He laid her back on the soft, warm ground and positioned himself on his arms over her as he rocked slowly against her core. Her breath caught as he pulled her skirt up around her hips. His eyes locked with hers, waiting to see if she wanted him to stop. When she lifted her hips so that he could remove her panties, he knew she wanted more. His hands caressed her thighs as he pulled them down her legs and over her naked feet. He knelt there and took his time looking at the paradise between her legs. Her breathing was shallow, her breasts rising and falling rapidly. His hands moved under her shirt and fondled her generous breasts overflowing from the top of her corset. He rolled and tugged her nipples gently as she writhed beneath him. Abandoning her breasts for tastier places, he pushed her thighs apart and softly blew against her moist folds. She glistened in the sun, and he just gazed at her, memorizing the delicate folds that made up her inner world.

Looking up, he caught her watching. Her lower lip was between her teeth, and her eyes were begging him not to stop. "I've always regretted not tasting you the last time I had the opportunity, my lady," he said as she whimpered in anticipation.

His hands stroked her thighs, and he smiled at the goosebumps he saw rising on them. She twitched nervously, and he settled down between her legs. His shoulders spread her thighs as wide as they would go before he brushed little kisses up her inner thighs, still taking his time. As he reached the top of her thigh, he changed from kisses to little nips that had her squirming beneath him. He brushed a finger up through the center of her, gently manipulating the little pearl nestled there. She bucked hard beneath him. He knew she was close, but he was going to take his time savoring their time together because he didn't know when he would get the opportunity to see her again, and he wasn't about to rush this.

He dipped his finger in her juices, dragging them up and soaking her so that his fingers would glide easily over her sensitive spot. Leaning down, he used his tongue and traced her from the bottom of her slit up to the top where he latched onto her while sucking gently.

"Kyran, yes, yes, yes..." she chanted beneath him. "Please don't stop, please don't stop," she begged him as she grabbed his hair, holding him in place.

He pulled back long enough to say, "Not a chance, my lady. I remembered the smell of you, but I've fantasized about what you must taste like, and I'm not leaving until I've had my fill." He dove back down and licked her again, this time using his tongue to penetrate her virginal body. He groaned at how tight and wet she was and at how desperately his cock wanted into that tight sweet spot.

Today, however, wasn't about what he wanted or needed; it was about what he could give to her. Their joint session through their bridge the other night was fucking amazing, but not as good as her soft body in his hands or the taste of her on his tongue.

She was whimpering beneath him. "Please, Kyran, I need..." her head thrashed back and forth as her body accepted the onslaught of his lips and tongue. He knew what she needed, even if she didn't yet know what to ask for.

He smiled against her as he said, "Say it for me, Rhy. You want me to make you come?"

"Yes, please, Kyran, make me come," she begged, squirming for him to go back to where he belonged.

He chuckled darkly and then settled in once more. He lapped at her and sucked on her clit until he knew she couldn't take much more. When she reached that point, he very gently slid his forefinger into her sheath until he felt the barrier stopping him. Her hips thrust against his hand. He pulled it out and added another, closing his eyes at the feel of her body choking his fingers. Her hips were pumping wildly against his hand, and the chanting started again, although this time he couldn't understand the language she was speaking. He latched onto her clit and kept his thrusts shallow as he pumped slower, making her inner walls much more sensitive.

"Kyrannnn, she keened as she came apart in his hands and on his tongue. He felt the ripples going through her abdomen and up and down her thighs as she continued rocking against his hand. He stopped, letting her come down softly as he rubbed his five o'clock shadow against her inner thighs and placed gentle kisses against them. She was still panting when he rose above her, watching her flushed face and her chest heaving still for air.

Her sex sleepy eyes opened and looked at him in surprise. "T'was," she stopped, licking her lips, "better than I'se ever could possibly 'ave imagined."

He chuckled arrogantly, knowing he was good at what he did and realizing that he wasn't anywhere near finished making her come. He leaned up and kissed her lightly on the mouth, letting her taste herself on his lips. He kissed her softly at first and then more aggressively as he slowly started stroking the fingers still in her, in and out again.

She sucked in a breath as he slowly finger fucked her, this time watching her eyes as he built the tension in her body and added the sensation of his weight covering her body to the equation.

Rhy rocked against him without shame, seeking relief again. He continued kissing her as his thumb started bumping into her clit every time he rocked his fingers into her. Her hips tried to move with him, but his body over hers hindered her movements.

Kyran kept her on the edge, wanting her to feel every nuance of him making her come this time. Her inability to rush him was part of that process.

Her body tensed up around him as her channel flooded his fingers. He swallowed her screams this time while she chased her pleasure and finally fell over the edge upon finding it. Tears leaked from her eyes, overwhelmed by the intensity of her orgasm. He kissed her until every little spasm around his fingers faded and her breathing slowed down to almost normal. She cleared her throat not knowing if she could speak after that. "I never knew it could be so..." she struggled to find the right words, "so much," she finally settled on. "T'was much stronger than anything I've ever experienced before." Her hand came up to caress his cheek. "Thank you, me laird, for sharing this new experience with me."

"You're most welcome, my lady, but" he leaned down, kissing her once more, "I want to watch you do that once more."

"Nooo," she whimpered as his fingers started up slowly again. The gentle glide of them in and out twice was all it took for her over-sensitized body to come apart once more. Her legs clamped shut around his hand, and he moved off her hips so that she could ride it out this time, following it for as long as she chose to.

Kyran kissed her softly and sweetly as he slid his fingers out of her body, watching her whole-body twitch as he did so. He nuzzled her neck gently as she ran her fingers through his hair. "'Tis what it will be like with you inside of me?" she asked, as her hips pushed against him unconsciously.

He chuckled at her as he straightened her clothes. "I think it will be similar, although I am quite a bit bigger than my fingers, so it should feel fuller and might be more intense when you come, choking my cock in the process." Helping her to her feet, he brushed the grass from her skirt.

"Where are me panties? I can't go back like this," she said shocked.

"Aye, ye can," he said, kissing her again. "You will be so sensitive that you just might get to do that again on our trip back as your legs rub together."

"Nye," she said, horrified, "I willna. Someone might hear me screaming."

He pulled her close and whispered in her ear, "I think some might already have."

"Don't ye dare say that," she said, blushing scarlet. "I won'ts be able to face them."

"Rhyanna, my love," he said laughing at her, "I guarantee you that this island has heard a lot of pleasurable screaming. We're not the first to have done so."

She buried her face in his chest and groaned, thinking of the melding cycle that encompassed the island not a month ago.

He pushed her hair back and kissed her on the forehead. "Next time you hold another man's hand, I want you to remember what my hands are capable of on and in your body."

For all his arrogance, he missed the look that crossed her face as his words sank in. It was a mistake he would soon regret.

Rhyanna pulled her hand from his and looked at the ground, processing what he had just said. He turned and looked at her, his brows meeting in confusion.

"What vexes thee, my lady?" he asked, still oblivious to his mistake.

"Ye just ruined what was one of the best moments of me life. Yer telling me ye only pleasured me because ye were jealous that I was holding Roarke's hand?" Rhyanna rarely lost her temper, and she was working up to it now. "Was all this nothing more than ye pissing on yer territory to ye?"

Kyran immediately regretted his choice of words when he saw the emerald flames in her eyes. "Rhy, honey, I didn't mean it that way," he said, trying to backtrack and fix this before it completely derailed. He took a step towards her, trying to soothe her.

Her hand up and her flashing eyes prevented him from coming closer. "Roarke is heartbroken over his sister, who, in case ye've forgotten, has been abducted and is probably being violated as we speak. He was hearing some pretty fecking harsh things from the others afore ye appeared, and I took his hand as a show of friendship and compassion, ye arrogant ass." She paced away from him, full on pissed off now. She turned back and pointed at him indignantly.

"Two days ago, that man sat and held me while I wept over YE. He never said a word, never touched me inappropriately, never did anything unacceptable to me, but be there for me while me heart broke over missing ye."

Kyran ran his hand over his face, feeling like a total ass. "I'm sorry, Rhyanna. It's been exceedingly difficult being away from you, knowing that he was near. Our relationship is so new, and I am struggling with the fact that I can sense how much he is attracted to you."

"Ye think I'm not struggling then?" she asked him. "Aye, it's new for both of us. It's brand fecking new fer me as I have never had any relationship with a man." She paced again before turning and giving him another piece of her mind. "However, yer reputation as a man whore has been brought to me attention many times by others, not realizing that I care for thee." She glared at him as she took another breath to continue ripping him a new one. "Yet, I have never once doubted yer intentions or that ye were being faithful to me." She stood waiting, and when he said nothing, she continued her rant. "I think I've earned the same courtesy from thee, and if ye can't trust me, Kyran, then what the feck are we doing here?"

Kyran had the decency to look ashamed by his actions. "Again, love, I'm sorry. You're right, you didn't deserve for me to treat you that way, and I admit I was wrong. Being back in that atmosphere makes me question everything I know and do. I had to wait weeks to see my father, and when I finally got to see him, he fell asleep and left me with his whore of a wife, who suggested we could fix this if only I would spend a weekend in her bed. The entire court is steeped in infidelity and wantonness, and the only thing I want is to return to you. Forgive me for letting my experience there make me doubt your intentions."

Rhyanna watched him for several painfully long minutes, which made him think he'd gone too far. Her eyes never left his as she searched his soul, judging his intentions. Finally, her features relaxed, and she took a few steps towards him. He met her partway and framed her face in his hands.

"I know you are true to me, and I do trust you, Rhy. I need you to believe that."

She nodded as he spoke. "Good, because if Roarke comes between us, it's not because of anything he's done or that we will do together. If he comes between us, it will be because of the way yer acting. I would never do that to ye."

"Message received," he said taking his chances and leaning down for a light kiss. "I'm glad he offered you comfort when I couldn't be here to do so."

Rhy wasn't sure how much she believed that, but she let it go. "Did she really have the gall to proposition ye?" she asked, her eyes blazing.

"Aye, and not just to service her, but anyone else she chose for the weekend," he said disgustedly.

"What did ye tell her?"

Once again, he looked distinctly uncomfortable. He held tightly to her hands so that she didn't run off on him. "You have to understand; she told me that if I turned her down, she would pursue my brother, Kai, who is too inexperienced to play her games. You met him today, Rhy."

"Ye didn't answer me question, Kyran," she said bluntly. "What was yer reply."

"I am trying to buy some time, Rhyanna," he said desperately, knowing he was on the verge of losing her. "I told her that I would consider her offer and get back to her. I just needed enough time to remove him from her grasp."

Rhyanna paled as she absorbed what he just said. Then she surprised him by laughing hysterically. "Ye have a queen propositioning ye—no, maneuvering ye into her bed, and yer jealous at me openly holding a man's hand with half a dozen other people in the room." She laughed harder, holding her sides. "Ye really don't see the irony in it?"

"All right, I'm not going to ever live that down, am I?" he asked as he took her hand, and they resumed their walk back to the Sanctuary.

"Nope! How long can ye stay?" she asked somberly as she saw the guards representing the Court of Tears waiting outside.

"I have to leave now," he said. "I was lucky Kai convinced them to give me a bit of time alone with you."

Her hand tightened on his. "Ye've my word to wait on ye Kyran. I want yer's that if anything changes on yer end, ye'll have the decency to come to me first."

"You have it, Rhyanna, and you've my promise that nothing will change my intentions or feelings for you." He kissed her thoroughly, his hands framing her face as he took his time and softly showed her how much she meant to him. "You are much too precious to me, my lady."

He pulled away, but not before she saw the regret and longing in his eyes change to concern. He released her reluctantly before turning and walking away from her without looking back.

Rhyanna experienced a strong premonition that their relationship would never be the same again once he returned to court. She stifled a sob.

A shadow fell over her, and she looked up to see Kai standing in front of her. His eyes were paler than Kyran's, but his features resembled him in many ways. The concern on his face made her realize that tears were streaming unchecked down her face. She wiped her cheeks, embarrassed for him to see her like this.

His deep voice took her off guard when he gently said, "I know I am a poor substitute for my brother, Mistress Rhyanna, but I would very much like the opportunity to get to know the only woman who has ever claimed Kyran's heart. Would you care to walk with me, lady?"

His manners were perfect and so much like his brothers that Rhy felt an instant affinity to the young man. "Aye, Kai, I would like that as well. I know so very little about him; perhaps ye can help me to understand him a bit more. I need every advantage I can get."

"No, my lady, you don't," he said. "You've already won his heart, now we need to help him win his freedom so that you can keep it."

His eyes were so serious, but then he smiled at her, and his face lit up like the sun above her. This young man was a small consolation to her heart. He was a part of Kyran's world, and with the Mother's blessing, he would be a part of her world in the future as well. She could find the rainbow through the clouds of their relationship because she refused to contemplate that her heart was nothing more than a pawn in a game destiny was playing.

CHAPTER FOURTEEN

Formal Request

Madylyn read the directive before her in disbelief. It arrived by special courier moments earlier, from the High Elemental Court. The High Court ruled over all the elemental courts and the sanctuaries throughout their world and was the final say in disputes.

Greetings Mistress SkyDancer,

We anticipate that this message finds you well. After receiving your inquiry, we have our law guardians combing through their records for missing people per your request. We will convey any additional files or information obtained that might be helpful.

As to your request for the return of Kyran Tyde to complete his contract, we defer to the Court of Tears's decision in how they choose to assist your sanctuary. Citizens residing under the Court of Tears expect to serve their court in any means deemed necessary. We were informed that a replacement has been agreed upon by both of you, and we consider the matter closed.

However, the Court of Tears has made a formal request for your healer's assistance immediately. Mistress Cairn's knowledge is needed to assist the court's physician in treating the king. The court anticipates her arrival before noon tomorrow. Please make sure that she is available and willing to treat his highness.

Mistress Cairn is permitted to travel with one escort. The court has formally requested that she refrain from any attempt at contacting Kyran Tyde while she is in attendance. They ask that she and the rest of the sanctuary members respect that he is no longer a part of your team or your world. His impending Pledge Ceremony negates any relationships he might have had prior to returning to court.

We fully support the court's requests and know that you will personally tend to the matter, making sure the proper arrangements are made and their requests respected.

Respectfully,

Stewart Fitch
Elemental High Court Secretary

Madylyn covered her face and tried not to scream in frustration after re-reading the post. She had appealed to the Court to try and bring Kyran back under the refuge of the sanctuary, and she failed. In addition to her failure, she now had to tell Rhy that she had to do the one thing she abhorred more than any other—respond to a formal invitation to treat a monarch at court. Rhy was going to lose her seldom seen temper, and Maddy couldn't blame her in the least.

Not only did she have to go to court, a place she despised, but she would be near Kyran and unable to spend time with him or talk to him. It wasn't just mean; it was vindictive. Queen Meriel was slapping back at Madylyn for going above her head to the High Court. Now, Rhy would suffer because of it. With no way to avoid it, she contacted Rhy.

"Rhy, are you with patients at the moment?"

"Nye, jest doing a wee bit of gardening. What can I do for ye, Maddy?"

"Would you come see me, please? I need to discuss something with you."

There was a brief hesitation on the other end before Rhy answered, "Is everything all right, Maddy?" The concern came through their line.

"I'm fine. I'll explain everything when you arrive."

"Let me git cleaned up and I'll head over."

"All right. Thank you, Rhy."

Maddy stood and paced, waiting for her to arrive, but not looking forward to this conversation because she doubted it would end well. She was frustrated, and she was angry because she had backed herself into a corner, and there was no way for her to fix it.

"Maddy?" Ronan's concern was obvious. *"What's wrong, darling?"*

"I'm fine, just frustrated. I'll tell you about it later. No need to worry," she said, trying to calm herself before he made an appearance. Rhyanna walked through the door, and Maddy sent him a quick, *"I've got to go. I'll talk to you tonight."*

Maddy smiled at Rhyanna, but she knew it came across strained. After a quick hug, where she might have held her just a little bit too tightly, she indicated the chairs and took one opposite the earth mage.

"What's wrong, lass," Rhy asked with a frown. "I know ye better than ye know yerself, and I ken something is amiss. The fact that I'm the only warden here means it's to do with me, so out with it."

Maddy gave a soft laugh. "I never can hide anything from you, Rhy." She reached out and took Rhy's hands, having a tough time looking her in the eye.

"I reached out to the Elemental High Court to see if they could help us with the situation with Kyran."

"I'm thinking it didna go well from the way ye is acting."

Maddy shook her head. "They've elected to stand by the Court of Tears's decision and stay out of a problem brewing between us." She took a deep breath before continuing. "They've also made a formal request involving you, Rhy. I can't turn them down, even though I wish I could on your behalf."

Rhy squeezed her hand tightly. "Out with it, Maddy. Taking longer ain't about to change anything. We'll deal with whatever 'tis. I'm na about to run shrieking from the room."

Maddy laughed as she looked at her, but it was a harsh sound in the quiet room. "Your presence has been formally requested to treat King Varan at the Court of Tears. You are allowed one escort but under no circumstances are you to contact Kyran while you are at court."

Maddy watched the shock and then horror transform into disbelief before spawning one seriously pissed-off woman.

"Jest so I'm clear, they are ordering me to appear in that den of wickedness with hardly more than a maid and thinking they can dictate who I can or canna speak with?"

She yanked her hands from Maddy's as she glowered down at her. "Yer right to be concerned, Madylyn. Those feckers don't know who they are dealing with now, do they? I hate being at court, as ye well ken, but I would have accepted had they only asked me directly. Then, they implement a formal fecking decree banning me from Kyran." She paced a few steps from where they sat before spinning around. "Is the king even incapacitated? Do we have any idea what's wrong with him? Am I allowed to speak with their healer? What the feck does she think she's proving by doing this?"

The questions fell quickly, and Maddy let her rant, knowing she wasn't looking for answers, just getting it out of her system. Maddy watched the whirlwind of distress in front of her, letting it run its course. She knew the patterns of Rhyanna's moods, and this was about to blow the other way when she realized exactly what she was about to embark on.

As if Rhyanna heard her thoughts, she suddenly deflated. She reclaimed her seat and slumped defeatedly in it. "I canna go there, Maddy, ye know I canna." Her voice cracked and was so much like the devastated young girl she'd first met; it broke her heart.

Rhyanna had arrived at wardens' training the same week Maddy began. She came from a forced stint in a European court. The place had been a nightmare for her. Her family was tormented by the rulers in charge at the time. Her parents and one of her sisters were nearly killed, and a young Rhy was a witness to it all. They all had their pasts to deal with, but Danny and Rhy had more internal trauma than the rest.

The thought of going to any court without the protections of her fellow wardens by her side caused Rhy immense distress, unlike any Maddy had ever seen her experience.

Maddy was just as frustrated at the thinly veiled request for help as she was in the queen's disrespect of her authority over the sanctuary and her wardens, but she would deal with her later.

"I'm sorry, Rhy, truly, I am."

"Can he na come here?" Rhy asked in a pitiful voice.

"Not, when the High Elemental Court has already told them you will arrive tomorrow, Rhy."

With a resigned sigh, Rhy sat up straighter, drawing on the inner strength that always aided her as a healer in the midst of battle. When she raised her head and looked at Madylyn, her eyes were clear and determined to do her job. "Who will be escorting me into me own personal hell?"

"Lily will go as your personal attendant; they won't be able to refuse you a maid. She will keep me appraised of the situation and will let me know if you require assistance. Fergus will join you by the evening meal. You won't be alone unless you must attend the king immediately, but I doubt Meriel wants this over with quickly. You represent the Heart Island Sanctuary and go to the Court of Tears with my full support and the protection of this sanctuary behind you."

"I hope that'll be enough, Maddy," Rhyanna said as she stood to leave.

"If anything happens to you, Rhy, I will destroy the Court of Tears with or without the backing of the High Court. We all will."

Rhy gave her a sad smile that didn't reach her eyes. "Aye, I ken ye will, but by then, it will be too late, na won't it. Whatever threat might be awaiting me will have already been executed." She walked for the door forgoing the usual goodbyes she gave Maddy. "I best git packed."

"Lily has already started. I sent some things up I thought might be better suited for court. You can choose the ones you prefer."

"Doesna matter what I wear because none of them would have been something I ever would have chosen." She headed out the door without another word.

Madylyn sat there feeling horrible at what she was consigning Rhy to. Somehow Meriel knew Rhy's weaknesses and was already playing on them. Who knew how bad it would be when she arrived tomorrow? At times like this, Madylyn hated being the Head Mistress and wanted only to be Rhy's best friend, not the woman sending her into hell.

All Maddy could hope for was for Rhy to arrive, do her best, and return as quickly as possible. Her greatest fear was if Meriel pushed Rhy too badly, Rhy would destroy their court before Maddy had a chance to portal to her.

Rhy possessed more power than anyone looking at her would ever anticipate. Beneath their sweet lil hedge witch lie a woman with the power of the Earth Mother behind her and the entire planet beneath her at her command. Blessed Mother help them if she ever felt the need to tap into it to defend herself because the Court of Tears might not be the only thing she destroyed.

CHAPTER FIFTEEN

Court of Tears

Rhyanna looked at her reflection in the full-length mirror. She didn't recognize herself in the outfit Maddy chose for her formal introduction to the Court of Tears. A long-fitted brocade skirt and jacket with tails in emerald green matched her eyes. A cream-colored silk camisole molded to her breasts, and a large black obsidian pendant nestled in her generous cleavage. Obsidian was the only part of the outfit that was her choice. She picked it for protection and for showing her the truth in situations because truth would be in short supply where she was heading.

A green fascinator hat sat jauntily on the left side of her head, attached to her perfectly coiffed updo. Her thick blond curls were tamed by Lily, Madylyn's ward. Lily created an elaborate updo, adding the emerald-colored hat with a partial lace veil to compliment her outfit. She wore black leather gloves and Victorian boots that were currently pinching her toes as she stood, delaying the inevitable.

Rhyanna rarely dressed so formally, and she was already missing her long, flowing cotton skirts and peasant blouses. Madylyn assured her that the Court of Tears was always a formal affair trapped in their version of a feudal system. She would need the outfits Maddy chose for her as armor for her visit. Rhyanna detested being in any of the courts but knowing Kyran was here took a little bit of her anxiety away, even if she wasn't allowed to approach him directly. Her only hope was that she would see him in passing, and he would come to her. She was willing to do anything for the opportunity to spend time with him, even if it meant working around the High Court's decree.

The portal door opened, and she stepped into it alone. Lily and Fergus would meet her later. It was important that she arrive confidently on her own. She struggled to find that confidence. Choosing her destination, she took a deep breath, trying to settle the nervousness unsettling her stomach. "Ye are no longer that pitiful little peasant girl ye were hundreds of years ago. Yer a strong, confident, accomplished woman, a representative of the Heart Island Sanctuary, and a Warden of the High Elemental Court. Yer more than capable of dealing with anything the Court of Tears throws at ye," she chanted to herself. She released her breath and triggered the portal to transport her to her desired location. Relaxing into the feeling of weightlessness, it only took a moment before the portal door opened, and Rhyanna stepped out into the bright sunshine and the smell of the ocean. A strong southern wind blew across her face, teasing her with the few tendrils it tugged loose.

The Court of Tears was located in the northern Atlantic on a remote island in the Labrador Sea. Rhyanna's breath caught as she stepped out and stood in awe at the magnificent castle sprawled before her. White marble gleamed in the sun, nearly blinding her. Round towers accented each corner with teal-colored banners flying from the top. The castle was set on an island, and the portal was on the mainland of the Labrador Peninsula. A wooden drawbridge connected the two land masses, offering access and protection if needed. Rhyanna took in the details of the palace as she waited for the guards who were approaching on foot. Stained glass windows with brilliant scenes of the ocean were like eyes peering at her across the waves.

A dark-haired man approached her from the left. "Welcome, my lady, to the Court of Tears. I take it from your expression that you have never been here before?"

"Nye, 'tis me first visit." She sighed, finding a bit of peace in the outdoors. "It's beautiful though, ain't it?"

"Aye, it is," he agreed. "We would like to escort you to the keep if you would do us the honor," he said with a warm, genuine smile. His gray eyes were kind and helped her to relax just a little.

"I would like that," Rhyanna said as she smiled back at him. "What is yer name, sir?"

"You may call me Tristan, my lady, if it pleases you, or Master of the Guard—whichever you are more comfortable with."

He held out an arm for her to take. "Leave your bags. My men will have them brought to your chamber."

Rhyanna put her arm in his and tried to take in all the details of the magnificent building. They crossed the draw bridge then walked up the bridle path to the main entrance, where she could see the gold leaf in place on the cornices of the foyer. Carved reliefs of Neptune and his court flanked either side of the double doors. The doors opened, and as they walked in, the footmen bowed deeply to her. Rhyanna blushed, uncomfortable with such treatment.

She had been born into feudal Europe to a family that existed well below the poverty level. Her ma was a wonderful healer and eventually earned a position at court. The respect she earned as one of the finest helped raise her family a slight degree above those living on the streets.

"Queen Meriel has requested that you attend her immediately upon your arrival," Tristan said, leading her down the wide hallway.

"I thought I'd be given a moment to settle in first," Rhyanna said as her stomach knotted at the thought of dealing with that woman on her own.

"My instructions were clear, my lady. My apologies if it distresses you." He squeezed her hand where it rested on his elbow.

Rhyanna tried not to snort in disbelief and failed miserably. She felt Tristan chuckle through their contact as they turned right and walked down a long hallway.

Servants scurried down the hall and, in a few doorways, scantily dressed men and women knelt. Their eyes stared straight ahead, and in the center of their foreheads was a colored gem in a diamond-shaped setting.

Numerous turns later, she could tell they were coming closer to the higher-ranking nobles by the well-dressed couples and courtesans lounging in rooms and talking in the halls. Rhyanna tried to pay attention to the turns they had taken, but it was difficult not to feel out of her element as every set of eyes watched her like fresh prey. Her corset felt too tight, and her breathing was shallow as she struggled to keep up with Tristan's long strides.

A snide laugh came from her right, and Rhy heard the woman's voice as they passed. Prince Kyran chose me, Elise, and Dash last night to join him in his chambers." The shocked gasps surrounding her caused Rhyanna to pay more attention to her words than where she was walking.

"He's better than everyone says he is. I spent all night with him. At least he's not one of the selfish nobles. He made sure I had as much pleasure as I could handle. I hope I get the opportunity to do it again sometime soon." Sighs of longing and requests for more details faded away as Rhyanna and Tristan continued walking.

Rhyanna stumbled as she replayed the words in her mind over and over, wondering why she was waiting for this man when she obviously meant so little to him.

Tristan steadied her. "Are you all right, Mistress Rhyanna?"

Rhyanna leaned on him heavily for a moment then gathered her strength to answer. "I'm fine. Thank ye fer asking, Tristan." She took a deep breath, determined not to cry. She wouldn't shed a tear for that man here.

"May, I give you some advice, mistress?" he asked in a soft voice.

"Aye, I'll take any advice I can git to survive this day."

"Don't listen to the hallway gossip. It's rarely accurate."

Rhyanna's eyes flew to his knowing ones, realizing her relationship with Kyran wasn't a secret here. And why should it be? This man was offering her a kindness, and she managed a small smile, trying to remember his words as they passed another group of gossiping women.

"It's difficult fer me to understand the lifestyle here," she said, confused.

"Please don't repeat this, but I have a tough time understanding it myself lately. This isn't the court I longed to serve in as a young man, and at times I wonder how much longer I'll be willing to serve in it."

"Why don't ye leave then?"

"One doesn't leave Queen Meriel without permission, mistress, or one ends up on their knees with a gemstone announcing the queen's displeasure." His voice dropped to a whisper. "Or the queen targets someone you love to keep you in line."

"I'm truly sorry that ye have to live like this."

"I've always wanted to serve my court in any capacity that I was able to. I only hope that my being here protects my king for a little while longer."

Tristan looked at Rhyanna with a sad smile as they reached the end of the hall.

"Ready?" he asked her.

"I'm as ready as I'll ever be," she said in a lost voice and nodded.

Tristan knocked on the door and waited for the command to enter. He reached for the latch and pulled the door open. His eyes still on hers, he bowed and extended his arm, announcing in a loud voice, "Mistress Rhyanna Cairn, Your Majesty."

CHAPTER SIXTEEN

What Have I Done to Deserve This?

Madylyn entered her office, furious once again by the second missive she'd just received from the Court of Tears. The cocky bitch thanked her for sending Rhyanna to join in the court's harem and guaranteed they would have her broken in and up to speed within the week.

Sending for Fergus, she sent a scathing reply to the queen.

Queen Meriel,

Rhyanna Cairn, our mistress of healing, was sent there as my emissary because of an imperial command from the Elemental High Court to assist King Varan. This was done as a courtesy to the Court of Tears.

Mistress Cairn comes to you with my blessing and the hopes of a swift recovery for the king. I reiterate, she is at court as a healer and only a healer. This is in no way an acceptance of your earlier offer.

To further clarify, you will leave her to herself, and she shall remain untouched and unspoiled for the length of her visit. Should these terms be disregarded and any harm befall Rhyanna in any way, you will deal with me directly, and I promise you that the full wrath of the Elemental Courts will be brought down upon your house swiftly and without mercy.

Abusing a Warden of the Court is a punishable offense by the High Elemental Court. In the event that you ignore these guidelines, you can anticipate swift and severe justice. Your best interests lie in treating her with the utmost respect and care that you should show to any visiting dignitary. Please, do not think to challenge me on this.

Rhyanna is a valuable member of my court and shall be treated as such by all in attendance at the Court of Tears.

I am also sending Ferguson Emberz, High Mage of the Northeast, to act as her escort. He will be provided adjoining rooms to Rhyanna and will also be afforded the respect expected for a mage of his standing.

Full reports will be sent forth to the ruling courts over your house upon their return. We have the right and the duty to report any improprieties or human rights violations my emissaries might witness during their time at the Court of Tears.

I thank you in advance for your immediate attention to this matter. I expect a reply, in person, from King Varan himself to answer to the correspondences we have received thus far. He will be expected at our portal a week hence at noon to join us for the midday meal. The king may bring two guards and his sons, Kyran and Kai, who may serve as his advisors while he is here. He will be provided lodging for a week while we discuss the state of his court and the health and safety of our shared river.

You, Queen Meriel, on the other hand are not welcome to join him on this visit. If you do arrive, your lodgings will be on the mainland in the best inn they offer. You can see to those arrangements yourself. Your behavior of late makes it clear that you are not welcome on any property that the Sanctuary has claimed.

As always, I'd like to say it's been a pleasure, but we both know how far from the truth that actually is."

Sincerely,

Madylyn Skydancer
Mistress of Heart Island Sanctuary
Warden of the Court

Madylyn finished the letter. She addressed an envelope, sealed it with her midnight blue wax, and used her rose seal to securely close the flap. The midnight blue rose stared up at her, still warm, glossy, and damp to the touch. She let the wax cool before she handed the letter to the courier, who arrived while she penned the missive. She put it into his hand along with one she had first written to the king, sending the invitation regarding the urgent matter they needed to discuss.

James, one of her most trusted couriers, waited patiently. He was well known at all the courts and loyal only to her. Madylyn stood facing him. "These missives must be placed directly into the hands of the king and queen. I prefer you give the king's to him discreetly without the queen's knowledge. Wait for his reply, and then an hour or so later, you may give the queen hers." She paused, looking at him seriously. "These are of dire importance. Do you have any questions, James?"

"No, me lady," he said, shaking his head. "The king gets his privately and before the queen receives hers, and she receives hers after I get an answer from the king."

"Perfect," Maddy said. "Do you think you will have a problem getting him alone?"

"Not at all, ma'am." He chuckled. "Me knows where the king goes for his sport, and me knows hows to get in behind hims, me do."

"Wonderful. Remember, discreetly with both of them."

"Aye, Miss Madylyn."

"Off with you then. Safe travels and return, James."

"Thank you, me lady."

James stepped out as Ronan entered. He pulled her close, hugging her. "What's wrong, Maddy?" he asked after brushing his lips against her forehead.

Madylyn clung to him for a moment. "I never should have sent her there," she whispered, burying her head in his chest. "It's not safe for her there. The queen has all but promised to take advantage of her, and with Meriel, that would mean physically and sexually."

"Can't you recall her?" Ronan asked, puzzled.

"Not this quickly, but I wish I could. She's outright threatened to add her to their harem." She pinched her nose at the headache forming between her eyes. "Of all of us, Rhyanna is the least able to handle the kind of threats this court will throw at her."

"Why did you send her then?"

"I received a command from the High Court I was unable to refuse. Also, because Kyran believes his father is drugged or poisoned by his behavior, and Rhyanna is the best able to confirm or deny these accusations."

"How can we help her?" he asked, leading her to a chair and settling with her on his lap.

"I'm sending Fergus." She sighed heavily. "He is the best to feel out the underlying level of bullshit at court and cut straight to the heart of the matter. The lasses love him, and anything he needs to know, he can find out easily from them, so this won't quite feel like a punishment to him. He is an equal opportunity ladies' man," she said. "More importantly, he thinks of Rhy as a sister and will protect her with his life. If they cause her harm, he will make anything I was afraid she'd do look like child's play.

She snuggled into him as he kissed her softly. His right hand, as it often did lately, lifted her shirt and stroked her belly. He was fascinated with her changing body. The hormone fluctuations made it hard for them to keep their hands off each other. She moaned as his hand started to wander, and

91

then was rudely jolted out of her pleasure when a disgusted snort filled the room.

"Fer fecks sake, Ronan, ye've got a fecking room. Maddy, love, I can't unsee that." Fergus groaned as he faced away from them as they readjusted her clothing. "Ye fecking called me here; ye knew I was coming."

"Relax, Ferg, not like you haven't seen a woman or two before." Ronan chuckled.

"Or three," Maddy said as she walked back around her desk, her cheeks scarlet.

"Yes, I have, but dammit, I was joining them, not being tortured having to watch them."

"You could've knocked before you came in."

"The blasted door was open, ye edjit." He tossed himself into a chair across from her desk and opposite the one they had just occupied.

"Well, I'll make it up to you, Ferg. How about I send you to an all you can eat and fuck buffet?"

"Come again, lass?" he said, his brows meeting in his confusion.

Maddy laughed and then proceeded. "You've won an all-expense trip to the cesspool known as the Court of Tears."

"What've I done wrong to deserve this?" he asked sullenly.

"Ye've not done anything, Ferg. Rhyanna is there alone and needs your protection. Unfortunately, I am not able to go myself, or I would just so I could bitch slap that woman."

"Whoa, slow your roll, lass. What's going on?" he asked, instantly alert by her vehemence.

Madylyn handed him the missive she'd received from Queen Meriel that morning. "I responded to her initial missive and thought the matter settled. I was mistaken. Trust none, Kyran included for now." She shook her head sadly. "Returning to court hasn't been good for him or for them." Her eyes filled in sympathy for her best friend. "Protect her, Fergus, and for God's sake, protect yourself. He's concerned that they are drugging or poisoning the king."

Maddy shook her finger at him. "For the sake of all the gods, don't you dare return with a case of the pox, or Danny and Rhy will never let you live it down."

Fergus laughed raucously. "Ye of so little faith. I know what I'se about Madylyn. Give me a wee bit of credit, won't ye, lass?" He headed for the door and then looked back, all mirth having fled. "If there are any limitations on what I am allowed to do to keep us safe, Maddy girl, speak now, or I won't be responsible for the hell and havoc I unleash."

Maddy leaned forward, placing both of her hands on the desk supporting her. Her eyes met his fiercely. "If those fuckers have hurt her, Ferguson

Emberz," she snarled in a voice he didn't recognize, "save the innocents you can and burn the fucking palace to the ground. You ken?"

"I ken, lass. And will we have the full support of the elemental world behind us if I do?"

"You trust me to worry about that. Damian is at the High Court as we speak, and he will procure the clearance for us to do anything necessary to take Queen Meriel down if it's unavoidable. I will make sure the Sanctuary, and you personally, are not held responsible for anything done under my authority. I will personally take the blame for any backlash that might come our way. You have my word."

"That's good enough for me, lass." He strode for the door, saying, "I'll be there within the hour." He closed the door behind him as he left. "In case you want to pick up where you left off," he yelled as the door locked behind him.

Ronan walked toward her, intending to do just that to distract her from this situation. As he pulled her against him, a knock on the door had him cursing softly in disgust,

Maddy leaned her head against his chest laughing. "Guess it's just not meant to be this afternoon."

"Maddy, are ye in there?" a little voice hollered from the other side. "You gotta see what I jest found."

"God, help me," she whispered, "what do you think he found us this time?"

Ronan laughed. "Frog, snake..."

"Roadkill, rat..."

"Are you in there, Maddy?" His little fists hammered on the other side of the door loudly.

"Let him in, Ronan." She laughed as she took a seat. "We can face it together."

Ronan opened the door to Landon and desperately tried not to laugh. The little man had fallen or washed up in a mud puddle and was standing there smiling as happy as could be at the treasure he held before him.

"Look what I found," he said proudly as he swung an old pocket watch back and forth between his hands.

Maddy jumped up and ran for the child, nearly knocking Ronan over in the process. "Isn't that lovely," she stuttered, reaching for the swinging watch quickly as he jerked it back from her. "May I please hold it so I can look at the details closely?" she asked desperately. Her eyes were wide, and her hand trembled as she reached for the dull metal.

Ronan watched her, confused at her terror over the object. *What's wrong, Maddy?*

She looked up at him, horrified. *"I just need for him not to move it anymore and to gently hand it to one of us."*

Landon watched her, finally understanding the look on her face was anything but happy. His little face fell. "I'm sorry, Maddy, I didn't know this was yours. I found it in the dirt outside." He held the timepiece out to her, and as she reached for the muddy item, it fell. She froze the watch in midair along with Landon.

She looked at Ronan desperately. "I need you to step back, love, because if that watch opens as it's falling, I don't know where or when I will end up, and you need to stay here with him. He can't lose another parent, Ronan." She smiled sadly at him. "I love you both so much, and you need to know that if something happens to me, I promise you, I will return to you, no matter how long it might take. I will find my way back to you. Tell Fergus when he returns what happened, and he can help send me something to help me find my way home."

"Maddy," Ronan said, his voice almost breaking, "I can't lose you again."

"Let's hope it doesn't come to that, Ronan." She moved forward and put her hand around the watch. "But please step back for me." She waited for him to do what she asked, and then she unfroze Landon and the watch. Her hand clasped the watch firmly, and she let out a low, slow breath of relief.

Maddy stood on shaky legs, then walked over to her desk. She unlocked a hidden drawer before placing the watch inside and adding a magical lock to the physical one. She looked back to find Ronan hugging the child fiercely. Joining them, she knelt next to Landon and clasped him to her tightly.

"I'm sorry," he said softly. "I didn't know I couldn't touch the watch."

"Hush, honey," she said, running her hands over his hair before pulling away far enough to see him. "You did nothing wrong. You found something very important that has been lost for an awfully long time."

His eyes lit up with the praise she gave him. "Why can't I keep my treasure then?" he asked as his brows met in confusion.

"I wish you could keep the watch, sweetie, but that watch belonged to a time traveler, and if you are not careful with how you use it, you might wind up in a time and place where we couldn't come and get you, and we wouldn't want to ever lose you. We love you very much."

Landon smiled brightly at her, then he moved closer, giving her Eskimo kisses. "I love you too, Maddy." He looked longingly at her desk. "Maybe when I am older?"

"Maybe," she said. "For now, we'll put it somewhere protected and safe so no one else gets lost either. Fergus will magick the drawer so no one can touch the watch, including you."

"Ok," he said, disappointed. "I just thought it was pretty. I was going to give it to you anyway."

"Well, now you have. You have given me an especially important gift. I'm incredibly grateful for the watch, Landon. You can treasure hunt as much as you want if you promise to show me what you find before you open anything and before you show anyone else." She held out her hand. "Do we have a deal?"

"Deal," he said, taking her hand and shaking it firmly, something he'd recently learned. Her heart sang, and she hugged him again. "Maybe we can find you a watch similar to that if you like."

"Can we really?" he looked up at Ronan, who was still pale from the thought of losing him. "Will you come help me pick one out, Daddy?" he asked, jumping up and down.

Ronan's eyes met Maddy's. They beamed at her, full of pride. It was the first time Landon had called him "Daddy," and it pleased him immensely.

He picked him up, putting him on his hip. "You betcha." Maddy stepped in close to him on his other side. He hugged both tightly, grateful to still be able to reach out and touch them both.

"And no treasure hunting," he said, waiting as Landon's face fell in disappointment, "unless you take me with you!"

"I know jest where we need to try next. There's this puddle behind the stables full of peepers and salamanders. It's deep." He stretched his hands apart, top to bottom. "I could swim in it."

Maddy groaned at the thought, but Ronan leaned down and kissed her. "Better hope Rhy's right and this one is a girl," he said, rubbing her belly."

He smiled as she laughed. Squeezing the child tighter, he tickled Landon's ribs as his son shrieked in laughter, and Maddy giggled warm against his side. His heart overflowed with joy as he thanked all the gods that he'd long ago forsaken for not taking either of them from him. Like Fergus voiced earlier, he couldn't help but wonder what he could have possibly done to deserve this.

CHAPTER SEVENTEEN

Acceptance of My Terms

Tristan patted Rhyanna's hand in support, bowed, then quietly left her there in the lion's den.

Rhyanna walked into an opulent sitting room, trying to keep her expression neutral as she approached the beautiful, long-limbed woman reclining against the arm of a dark teal settee.

Long white-blond hair with soft waves cascaded over the edge, nearly touching the floor. Queen Meriel wore a gossamer gown of turquoise, attached at both shoulders with enormous pearl pins. The gown gathered under her heavy bosoms in an empire waist. One leg was bent as she reclined against the back of the settee and the other on the floor with her knee turned out. The gown split down the middle from the waist. The position the queen reclined in pulled the fabric open at her navel. As Rhyanna walked farther into the room, she noticed an artist with an easel. The queen was having her portrait done—a risqué portrait at that.

Rhyanna couldn't help but glance at the work in progress as she passed by to see that he, indeed, was doing a detailed account of every visible inch of her majesty. Rhyanna's face turned redder as her gaze landed on the woman in front of her. This woman, who held all their fates in her hands, smiled at her in a way that made Rhy's skin crawl. She wanted to flee this place as quickly as possible. Finally remembering where she was, she dropped quickly into a deep curtsy and waited for the queen to acknowledge her.

"I wondered if you would remember your place at court," the queen reprimanded her. "Rise so that I may inspect the reason for my eldest son's contrary mood," Queen Meriel snapped at her with no hint of civility.

Standing quickly, Rhyanna did as she was commanded and waited for further instructions.

Queen Meriel circled the air with her finger before uttering, "Turn."

Again, Rhyanna did it without thinking, even though her inner self balked at the way she was being treated. A small burst of anger woke inside of her, making her want to lash out verbally, but she restrained herself, knowing full well it would do her no good and only make the situation worse.

"Well, as far as I can see, you're rather thick through the hips and thighs. I can't imagine him being turned on by that for long." Her laugh was harsh, like ice breaking in a puddle on a late fall day. "Looks can be deceiving. You must have one hell of a magic mouth or pussy."

With a flick of her wrist, she dismissed the artist. She turned, fully facing Rhyanna as she spread her knees wide and pulled her gown open fully before resting her arms across the back of the settee. "So, let's see which it is." She snapped the fingers of her right hand and pointed at the floor. Her harsh laughter rang out, echoing off the walls of her chamber at the outrage on Rhyanna's face. Her painted-on smile faded as she said, "I don't have all day, little peasant girl."

Rhyanna stood there for a moment, stunned at the insult and the command the woman had just given her. If Meriel thought she was going to do that, she had another thing coming. Rhy would rather rot in the dungeon than touch any part of her with a ten-foot pole. Sucking in a deep breath to calm her racing heart and still the rage rolling through her, she ignored the summons. She turned and sat in a chair behind her, gripping the arms so tightly that she expected the wood to snap beneath her hands.

Locking eyes with the depraved queen, Rhy ignored the digs into her status at court and internally reminded herself who she was and where she'd come from.

"Yer correct, yer majesty, I was born a lowly peasant girl, and me hips might be a might on the wide side." She gave her a saccharin smile as she desperately tried not to ruin the relationship between the Court of Tears and the Heart Island Sanctuary, but it was getting harder to do.

"Contrary to yer mistaken belief, I be a high-ranking member of the Elemental Court, and I'se forced to come here through their summons as a healer and not as another one of yer nasty lil playthings." Rhyanna stood and turned to leave. "I've made an appearance as ye've requested. Now, if ye'll direct me to yer healers so that I may confer with them, I'll see to the king, whom I was told needs me assistance. I'll be more than happy to treat him and leave yer lovely palace, which I'm sure will make both of us happy in the long run."

Rhyanna took two steps for the door before she heard raucous laughter from behind her. "Stay, Rhyanna Cairn. Please, stay. It's been a long time since I've been so entertained."

Rhyanna turned and looked at her suspiciously. "Are ye done with the games, now then?" she asked with an arched brow.

"No games, lass, just a mere test of your mettle." Meriel laughed again. "You did well, although for a moment there, I thought you were going to spontaneously combust."

Rhyanna took her seat cautiously, not trusting the woman at all. "I don't care fer yer little test, milady. It was beneath ye."

"I don't know about that. The fact that you set foot in my court tells me that ye've accepted the terms I set forth to Mistress SkyDancer and to Kyran."

"I beg yer pardon, milady? I don't ken what yer speaking of." Rhyanna said as her brow creased in confusion.

Queen Meriel tipped her head as if studying Rhyanna like some strange exotic creature. "You truly don't know, do you, child?"

Rhyanna looked up at her sharply. "Nye, I've no idea of what ye speak. I doubt yer much older than I be, so no need to be calling me 'child,' Yer Majesty."

The queen giggled—giggled for God's sake. "Well, darling, let me rectify that right now. I sent a missive to Mistress SkyDancer a week ago. In it, you were allowed the privilege of attending my court on one condition."

She paused, enjoying the confusion and horror that was mounting on Rhyanna's face. "Kyran will be marrying into the Fire Clan. It's a done deal. That is going to happen no matter how much you or he dislikes it. The best thing that you can do now is learn to accept it and hope that you can work your way up to his level."

Her smile widened at the disappointment and confusion that flashed through Rhy's eyes. "I understand that you wouldn't want to be parted from one another, so I reached out to the mistress of Heart Island and told her that you were more than welcome to join him here as one of my courtesans."

She laughed as all the color drained out of Rhy's face. "Becoming one of my courtesans would give you, with my permission, of course, the ability to become his mistress whenever he was in residence at court. When he leaves, you would be absorbed into the royal family's harem. One of his brothers might fancy you; you never know. You will be branded with a jewel on your forehead. The jewel's color indicates the status you have achieved within the court. In addition to Kyran, you would be available for any noble his rank or higher. At any time, you could be required to drop to your knees and pleasure your betters, male or female. Your appearance here today constitutes your acceptance of my terms. Perhaps my initial request makes more sense to you now, child."

Rhyanna sat there, dumbfounded. Her usual swift, snarky comebacks were lost as she processed the ridiculousness of the queen's statement.

"Close your mouth, love. It's unattractive."

Rhyanna snapped her jaw closed, irritated that she let it drop at the insanity proposed to her.

Queen Meriel smiled broadly as she looked down her nose at Rhy. "I so look forward to teaching you the proper etiquette for my harem." She giggled once again. "I look even more forward to breaking you of your feisty manner and the way you speak to your betters. I'm sure you're a stranger to obedience, and I will enjoy every moment of your punishments, much more, I dare say, than you will."

Queen Meriel stood and sauntered over to Rhyanna. She caressed the side of Rhyanna's face before threading her fingers through the delicate hair at the base of her neck to keep her still. Dense, dark elemental power flowed over her, slithering into her pores and overwhelming her senses. The weight of it slowly pinned Rhy's arms to her side and her legs against her chair. Meriel was a strong water element with a heavy dose of black magic intertwined with her own. Her energy left a heavy, oily feel behind as if it were contaminated.

Using her grip on Rhy's neck, she tipped her head back, forcing Rhy to look at her. Meriel smiled at her as she trailed a finger over her cheek and across her lips. "You are beautiful lass, in your own lower-class way."

Rhyanna sat there, horrified to be trapped within her own body with no way to defend herself. She tried to fight the oppression that lay over her like a weighted blanket. As her eyes met Meriel's, she pulled her strength inward and coaxed it into a tight dense ball of anger and rage, feeding it more of the same as Meriel tightened her grip on her hair, causing unwanted tears of fury to form in her eyes.

Queen Meriel watched her for a long time, waiting patiently for her to realize she was powerless. When she was sure that Rhy was truly immobilized, Meriel leaned down and kissed her softly on the lips, her eyes never leaving hers. Using her teeth, she captured Rhy's bottom lip and bit softly, drawing a bead of blood. Her tongue came out and licked it away. "I break in all of the new courtesans, and today is your lucky day."

Rhy was so focused on not looking away from her, or showing fear, that she failed to notice where the queen's other hand disappeared to. Soft caresses between her knees and along her inner thighs quickly brought her up to speed. Horrified, she tried to close her legs and prevent entry but was unable to do so. As difficult as it was for her to try and force them closed, they opened easily under the queen's touch.

"Since the magic obviously isn't in your tongue, it must be down here then, isn't it?" She smiled as she once again bit down on Rhy's lip, pulling it painfully out as her fingers found their way towards Rhy's entrance. Running a finger along her panty line, she purred, "Oh, I do love the au natural approach you are keeping up. Too many women prefer to look like little girls. I like women to be like the Earth Mother intended them."

Rhyanna was still paralyzed from the queen's powers and from the sheer panic she was beginning to feel. Not knowing what else to do or who to reach out to for help, she ripped open her link to Kyran and let him sense her discomfort and fear.

Kyran responded immediately. *"Rhyanna? My lady, what's wrong? Where are you?"*

Rhyanna was mortified to have him find her this way, but she was more terrified of what the evil woman would do to her if she didn't reach out for help. *"Queen's chambers."* She hesitated, unsure of how much she should say, then finally sobbed, *"Please tell me yer here. Hurry! Help me, Kyran."*

Meriel's hands were still touching her inappropriately, removing her panties as she continued tormenting her. The gentleness of her touch was a sharp contrast to the hate in her eyes as she watched Rhyanna's every reaction.

"I've wanted Kyran since before I wed his father. He only wants you. I wonder if he would be up to a trade, and I wonder if you would be woman enough to let him make that trade. His body in mine, instead of mine inside of yours? I'll make sure you stay and watch so that you can see what it will take to please a man from Neptune's line. If he's anything like his father—and for the record, that man is the best fuck I've ever had—you will never be enough for Kyran just as I was never enough for the king."

Her breath caressed Rhy's lips as she continued taunting her. "I'm not trying to be cruel, my little healer, just stating a fact you will soon have to face. Better now than once he's taken your precious virginity along with all your hopes and dreams of destiny's kiss."

Meriel giggled again. "Didn't think I knew about that, did you, child?" she said, continuing to torment her. She settled on her knees between Rhyanna's legs, then turned and spoke to someone outside of Rhy's vision. "Prepare the large brown one for me quickly, and give me a clear crystal."

While she waited, she pushed Rhyanna's skirt up to her hips, giving her a complete view of her lower body.

Tears of humiliation burned in her eyes, but she willed them back with everything she possessed, refusing to shed them in front of the queen. Her spark was turning into an inferno as she continued feeding it her battered emotions.

Rhyanna was horrified. How dare the queen treat her in such a manner? How dare she take advantage of an ambassador of the Elemental Court? The ball of power expanding in her heart chakra was nearing maximum strength and getting difficult for her to control. Rhy was waiting for the moment when Meriel would be most vulnerable because she would destroy this woman before she ever let her violate her or mark her as hers, even if it was the last thing she ever did. Rhy would make sure that Meriel never had the power or ability to touch anyone beneath her ever again, even if Rhy had to destroy herself to accomplish it.

Movement from the corner of her eye distracted her, and she watched a young maid come forward. Rhy's empathic side sensed the fear the dark-haired girl tried to hide as she hurried to please the queen. She looked at her with such compassion that Rhy wondered what else Meriel intended to surprise her with. As her maid, the young woman would have seen the queen at her worst. If she was afraid, then Rhy was fecking terrified.

Rhyanna forced herself to look at what the maid was carrying, and if she could have gasped or shrieked, she would have as loudly as possible. Her body strained against the invisible forces restraining her as the young woman neared Meriel. In her right hand, she carried a large phallic-shaped piece of black marble. The glossy stone glistened in the light because it was generously oiled in preparation for the queen to assault her with it. In her left hand dangled a clear quartz crystal cut into a diamond shape.

As Rhy's eyes tracked the girl, she noticed a similar stone embedded in her forehead. They were the same except for the color. The maid's stone was a brilliant green.

"Hurry up, you useless chit," Meriel snapped at her before snatching the items from her hands. "Return to your position until I call for you."

"Yes, mistress," she whimpered, running around the bed and dropping to her knees with her forehead on the floor.

Rhyanna's breathing was ragged as she watched Meriel fondling the black marble. It had to be at least ten inches long and three or more inches wide. It was bigger than any erect man Rhy had ever seen—Kyran included.

Meriel glanced up, smiling at the fear in her eyes. "You thought you were so much better and so far above our ways here, didn't you, my little hedge witch?"

Meriel stroked the piece of stone. "When I am done with you, my little peasant girl, you will have no problem taking a man anywhere in your body. No, when I finish with you, will be able to take two or three at a time comfortably."

Her soulless eyes looked into Rhyanna's eyes, enjoying her terror and completely missing the rage building behind it. "Honestly, child, you'll be thanking me a week from now for breaking you in. I'll be gentler than any man ever will be." The ice in her gaze belied her intentions. She would enjoy causing Rhy as much pain and humiliation as she could.

Meriel set the marble down and reached for the crystal. She tipped Rhy's head back and looked her in the eyes as she placed it in the center of her forehead.

Rhy gasped as the queen placed her hand on top of the gem and began the process of adhering it to her skin. Tendrils of power raced through her body, evaluating her strengths and weaknesses, leaving her feeling hollowed out and violated at the energetic level as the pain of the gem embedding itself into her skin made her nauseous. She glared at Meriel, refusing to give her any more of her fear. Tears ran down her cheeks from the agony, and her helplessness infuriated her.

Rhy saw the moment Meriel thought she'd won. The queen removed her hand, ready to move on to round two, while Rhyanna hurled all her emotional energy into a powerful external burst, shattering the gem and sending Meriel and her god-awful toys across the room, pinning her against the wall. Freed from the queens' powers, Rhy stalked toward the helpless queen.

Rhy's hair flew around her head in a tangled mass as her eyes glowed with pure vengeance. She was an earth element and proud to be one of the calmest elements as a rule. Today, she embraced her secondary element and pulled a massive ball of fire into her hand, letting it grow in intensity. The damage it would create would be catastrophic, most likely killing the queen. A part of the healer in her grieved because, for the first time in her life, Rhyanna would have gladly taken a life without remorse. She was a healer, and healing was all she'd ever wanted to do. Tonight, she didn't care which energy she embraced. Dark or light, it didn't matter; all she knew was that she couldn't allow Meriel to ever do that to someone who couldn't fight back.

Rhyanna looked into Meriel's eyes as she approached her, wanting her aim to be true. She threw her hands toward the queen, releasing all her energy with it at the same moment she heard Kyran's voice behind her. "Rhyanna, for the sake of the Goddess, NO!" The next thing she knew, a heavy body slammed into hers, taking her to the floor.

"NYE," she howled like a wounded animal. "Don't ye dare protect her from me. Ye've no idea what she planned to do to me. I won't have it, so step aside, and leave me be." She clawed and screamed at the man pinning her down.

He laid over top of her, grabbing her arms and pinning them above her head. "Rhyanna, look at me." His voice purred in her ear. "You know I'll never hurt you. The only reason I stopped you, is that I would have been signing your death warrant if I allowed you to harm her." Her body shuddered under his with sobs of frustration. He released her hands and framed her face. I'm here, my lady. Hush now, I've got you, lass." He gathered her in his arms then turned to leave.

"This is far from over, Kyran," Meriel said in a raspy voice behind him. "Don't you dare walk out on me; we are not done bargaining for her release."

Kyran stopped and looked over his shoulder at her. He let all his loathing and hatred come through his eyes. "You touch her again, and I'll kill you myself. She doesn't exist in your world. She is an innocent, a guest of this court, and I can promise you that when Madylyn knows how you treated her, and I guarantee you she will know, she will tear you apart and this court with it. You've messed with the wrong team, and I can't wait to see you pay for it." He glared at her for a long moment, letting her see the truth in his eyes.

"I am taking her out of here. You will not stop me, nor will your guards, or I'll destroy you myself. She is untouchable. Do you understand me?" His voice thundered, shaking the windows in their panes. For a moment, he thought Meriel might have actually paled at his displeasure. He waited for her nod of acceptance before turning his back on her and leaving her chambers. Kyran needed to get out of there before changing his mind and killing her where she stood.

CHAPTER EIGHTEEN

Eyes on Me

Jameson sat nursing a beer, one too many, truth be told. Fergus had declined the offer to join them tonight. He'd been quiet lately—moody even. Danny was running the pool table like she did most nights.

Jamey watched the pretty little barmaid, Carsyn, waiting tables. She was a petite blond with long, thick, curly hair and chestnut-brown eyes. They hooked up occasionally, neither of them looking for anything serious. They hadn't been together in a while, and he was drunk enough that it seemed like a good idea.

The fact that Danny headed out back about fifteen minutes ago with a stranger might have weighed in on his decision. He was falling more in love with Danny by the day, but he didn't judge her choices, and until he could sense something solid between them, he wasn't going to abstain from enjoying himself either.

Carsyn stopped by his barstool and winked. "I've got twenty minutes. You interested tonight, handsome?"

Jameson gave a slow, sexy smile and stood up, rearranging his leathers as he did. They were getting tighter by the minute, anticipating what her mouth was capable of. "Aye, where to, lass?"

"Out back, it be dark enough," she said, grabbing his hand and leading him to the door.

Jamey tried not to wonder how many others she brought out back on her breaks. He didn't have nor want the right to know. There was no commitment between them—just pure pleasure.

Carsyn walked outside and pulled him closer to the corner of the building.

He reached down and kissed her, his right-hand fisting into all that thick hair at the nape of her neck.

She moaned, writhing against him. "What's your pleasure tonight, Jamey?" she asked. His other hand framed the side of her face, and his thumb swept over her lower lip.

"How about we start with you on your knees."

Smiling, she pulled her skirt up and settled on her knees, reaching up to untie the laces of his breeches. Her hands ghosted over his thighs before he felt the cool night air hit his raging cock. A purr of feminine appreciation rumbled through her as she took him out and wrapped her hands around him, loving the girth of him. She stroked him slowly, watching his hooded eyes fixed on her and the way his head kicked back against the building.

His hand was still playing with the long length of her hair, and he couldn't help twisting it around his fist, trying to encourage her sweet little mouth to open for him.

"Patience, love," she laughed. "You know I like to play."

"I think the word you're looking for is tease." He moaned as her rhythm increased.

"Yet, you always seem to enjoy it," she said, leaning into him, her breath caressing the top of him.

Jamey closed his eyes, giving in to the sensations overtaking him. The softness of her hands, the smell of her perfume, the anticipation of her tongue…and, oh, thank you, gods, there it was, the warmth of her mouth. She had taken just the tip of him in and was expertly running her tongue around the edge, flattening it on the underside and adding a tiny bit of suction. He tried unsuccessfully to keep his hips from moving towards her, and she laughed throatily around him when he failed.

She took more of him, and he blocked out nearly everything around him, rubbing her head as she pleasured him. "Take more," he begged as she tagged him in warning with her teeth.

Carsyn retreated, releasing him once more into the chilly air. "No, love, I want to make this last. You'll need to beg more than that."

Jamey had fisted her hair, and now he pulled it taught, pulling her head back, knowing that she liked the bite of pain it produced. He gently pulled her closer, and she allowed it. Wrapping both hands around him again and using a twisting motion as she ran her fists up and down nearly made him whimper. Thank God for the wall, or he would've ended up on his ass. Once again, she leaned into him using only her tongue.

Hearing a gasp, his head whipped to the left, focusing on the far end of the building. Danyka was bent over at the waist with her hands on the wall for balance as her flavor of the night was pumping slowly into her.

Carsyn, finally deep throating him, brought his attention back full and front to the woman who was currently doing magical things to his cock.

Danny growled in frustration as the man behind her grabbed her hips tighter and increased his thrusting. She moaned as he damn near hit that magical spot inside of her—the one that was so fucking elusive, they rarely found it. His hands reached around to palm her breasts, and she slapped him off. "I said no touching except my hips," she growled at him. She wanted him to fuck her, not grope her.

The door opened, but she paid little attention to it. Never shy about her body, she honestly didn't care if anyone saw her or not. She knew what she wanted and wasn't afraid to take it. A couple at the other end was laughing, and her head jerked up as she recognized it was Jamey with the bar wench. She looked over at him, surprised. He rarely indulged anymore; he'd been acting celibate of late. The light from the door backlit the couple, and even though she knew she should look away, she couldn't.

Jameson leaned back against the wall with Carsyn on her knees before him. Danny couldn't stop herself from watching as Carsyn took his cock out and played with him.

No surprise there; Danny had seen him full and proud during the melding, and Jamey had been blessed by the gods in that department. But then again, everything about Jamey was damn near perfect. His looks, his manners, his pecs, his smile...

WHAT. THE. FUCK. She had never thought of him like that before.

Unable to stop watching, she enjoyed the show while Mr. In-A-Hurry continued to go at it behind her. "You almost there?" he asked, winded, and she could sense the desperation in his voice.

"No where's near," she replied cattily, not wanting to move. He stopped trying to catch his breath as he leaned over her.

"Let me touch you," he implored, "I swear it will make it better for you." His hand started to move towards her clit until she spoke.

"If you want to lose that hand, keep on going," she growled menacingly. "Try me fucker." She moved slowly back against him. "Be grateful I gave you this much."

"Your loss," he said nastily as he started thrusting violently against her.

Danny didn't care; hard and fast was normally fine with her. However, she didn't want to lose the view she had, so she stood up with him still inside of her and twisted at the waist to look him in the eye. She gazed into them as she moved closer like she was going to kiss him. "You're nowhere near ready to cum, lad. Are you?" she compelled him gently. "You can go all night until I give you permission to cum, can't you?"

"Yes, ma'am," he muttered as his urge to cum faded. He couldn't help wondering where the urge went as moments before, his balls were ready to explode. "I'll fuck you until you tell me to stop, and however you want it, fast or slow."

"Slow it down a bit," she replied, still drawing him in with her eyes. "Focus on the way your cock glides into me with every stroke."

She released his gaze, and he set out on the mission she gave him, moaning behind her as he appreciated every second he was in her body. She rarely compelled anyone, but he was irritating her tonight, and she was tired of the chit-chat.

Danyka rotated back towards the wall and bent over once again, hoping to help him find that magical zone. She looked back at Jamey and found his eyes locked on her. They were still half-closed, and she could tell the bar wench had swallowed most of him and was making him forget his name. His hips were thrusting slowly as he pumped in and out of her mouth. As Danny gazed at him, she realized he was matching the rhythm the man behind her was setting. Her breasts felt heavy watching him, and her breath was coming in pants. She rarely got this turned on, and never by watching someone else get blown.

Jameson heard Danny compel the man behind her. He received a little magical buzz on their line when she did it. Holy fuck, she looked hot, especially when she turned back around, braced against the wall, and arched her back. But what almost made him blow his load was when she turned, looked him in the eye, and didn't turn away. He knew she could see him, and that didn't bother him. He was enjoying himself too much to care. She, unfortunately, didn't seem to be having the same experience.

He hesitated for a second. They never reached out to each other on personal issues, but he was just drunk enough to not care. *"Are you getting anything out of that?"* he asked her telepathically.

Her eyes widened the moment she received his message.

"No, not really, but I was hopeful in the beginning," she sent back with a chuckle.

He tried not to laugh aloud. Carsyn might not appreciate it, and, God, she was working extra hard trying to finish him off, but he didn't want to, not yet. He was enjoying this strange game they were playing. *"Why do it?"* he asked her.

"Helps chase the demons away," she said so softly he almost missed it. *"Best way at night to deal with them."*

Whoa. He knew little about her past, but if this is what she used for therapy, then it had to be pretty fucking bad. *"Do you ever enjoy it?"* he asked. Like it was any of his fucking business.

She looked at him for a long time before she answered, wondering why he cared about her sex life.

He wasn't sure she was going to fill him in, and he was on the verge of apologizing.

But then she whispered, *"If I am drunk enough, if he's big enough, if the moon's full enough…who knows what it takes to trigger me."* She stopped suddenly, looking lost in thought before she sent back, *"Just another part of me that's broken, that's all."*

She must be drunk too, he thought, sharing this much, although she didn't look it.

"How about you? Are you enjoying that?" She nodded towards the woman below him, trying for all she was worth to please him, and figured her jaw must be killing her by now.

"Fucking yes," he said both internally and aloud as he rolled his hips forward, pushing his cock down Carsyn's throat with deep thrusts. He looked over at Danny and lost some part of his ever-loving mind when he asked, *"You want to come along for the ride when I cum?"*

Danny loved the look of pure male pleasure taking over Jamey's features. In a moment of lunacy, she wished she was the one on her knees making him look like that. The thought created heat in her groin and made her moan. *"What will I get out of it?"*

"You will have the unique perspective of what it's like for most men, Jamey sent to her. *"And then I'll let you watch when I make her come so you'll know what you should you be getting out of your flavor of the day,"* he said, nodding towards the man behind her.

He moaned again, his hips picking up a wicked rhythm that, Goddess bless her, Carsyn kept up with without missing a beat. *"Why won't you let him touch you?"* he couldn't help but ask.

"Because if he touched me, I would kill him," Danny said without a hint of humor. *"Better hurry up. Her break must be about finished, and if you aren't going to be a selfish lover, you got some ground to cover."* She heard him chuckle, although it quickly turned into a rumbled throaty moan that she could hear all the way down here. *"Alright, for shits and giggles, show me some alpha male magic."*

Jamey fought the urge to laugh again. He loved her mouth and the snarkiness that came out of it. Their internal link lit up for him, and he relaxed the hold he normally kept on it, allowing more than thoughts to come through their line. He allowed his physical sensations and the pending orgasm building in his balls to transfer through to her.

He heard her gasp and looked over and saw her cheeks flush and then sucked in his own gasp as she reached up and palmed her breasts. Hot. As. Hell.

Jameson refocused on the woman in front of him, feeling a bit guilty that he'd briefly abandoned her, albeit only in his mind. His body was enjoying every second of her hot wet mouth. *"You ready?"* he asked her as he reached down with his hand and cupped the side of her face. She nodded around him. He felt his cock swell as he grabbed her head and pounded into her mouth.

Experience told him she could take it without him hurting her or her hurting him. She relaxed her throat, and he slid further down into her exquisite heat. He was so close, but he couldn't quite let go. That never happened. He looked over once again at Danny, watching her speed pick up and her eyes start to glaze as they locked on his. *"Touch yourself, Danny. Reach down and make yourself come with me,"* he implored, wanting her to come with him.

"I can't," she wailed in his head. *"I've never been able to."* She squeezed her breasts harder as she looked at him. *"I can tell how badly you need to, Jamey."* Her voice in his head was panting. *"Let me at least experience your pleasure."*

"As the lady wishes." Jamey moaned as he kept his eyes on her, yet still managed to make the woman on her knees feel like he was present. His hand kept stroking her face as his speed increased. He moaned again, and then he grabbed her head, holding it still as he spilled his seed down her greedy throat.

"Holy fuck." He staggered a bit, then leaned back against the wall, half sitting on it to keep himself up. "Give me a moment, lass, and I will take care of you."

Danyka could barely keep herself on her feet as she felt the physical release that Jameson shared with her. She staggered back against the man behind her. "Harder," she ordered.

Jamey could see Danny was desperately chasing something she most likely wouldn't find. He found himself wanting to help her claim her orgasm.

"I pleased you?" Carsyn asked him coyly, knowing damn well she had.

"Aye," he smiled down at her and gave her his full attention. He pulled his breeches up, laced them loosely, then reached down to gather the lass to him. "Ye pleased me very much." He leaned down and kissed her briefly, tasting himself on her lips. He smiled wickedly at her. "Your turn. Pull your skirts up around your hips now."

Carsyn shivered in anticipation as she quickly did as he said. She knew someone would come looking for her soon, but she needed this. She looked up at him through thick lashes and reached out to stroke the cock that he'd just put away semi-hard. *"I was hoping I might enjoy this in me again this time."*

"Sorry, lass," he lied. "I don't have it in me tonight, but I'll not leave you wanting." He knew the real reason he didn't want his cock in her was that after tonight, there was only have one woman that he wanted to put it into. Right now, she had another man filling her.

Danyka kept her eyes on their exchange as her body coiled tighter and tighter. She might make it after all. Unable to keep her eyes off Jameson, she waited until the lass pulled her skirt up around her waist, and Jamey dropped to his knees.

Jamey moved so he was on the other edge of the corner. This way, she could still watch him, and he could see her. A rare pang of jealousy swept over her. Danny didn't want him to touch Carsyn; she didn't want him touching anyone. However, she did think that she just might want him to touch her.

"Still there, Hellion?" he sent to Danyka.

Her eyes grew wide as she didn't expect him to continue their game. *"Aye, I'm still here,"* she whispered back, her voice raspy with need.

"Let's see if I can make you both come," Jamey sent her with a wink. With her falcon vision, he knew that she could see as clearly as if he were standing right next to her. *"Slow your stud down. You're going to want slow and steady for this, and he looks like he might pass out soon."*

"Good luck with that," she said mirthlessly. *"Just worry about your blond there; no need to impress me."*

Their link opened wider, and she could feel him run his hands from Carsyn's ankles slowly up to her knees. The sensation was so real, she almost dropped to her knees. *"What the fuck?"* she sent to him breathlessly. *"Why does it feel like your hand is on my thighs?"*

Jamey smiled wickedly at her as he kissed the outside of Carsyn's leg *"Did I never mention that I'm empathic and can channel not only what I'm feeling but also what someone else is? You're not the only one with mind magic, Hellion."*

She sensed his amusement before hearing, *"Hang on, love."* He sent the last part to Danyka telepathically and to Carsyn verbally.

Still running his hands up and down Carsyn's legs, he spread them wider and leaned forward, rubbing his five o'clock shadow on the inside of her right thigh. Using his heavily muscled shoulders, he pushed her knees wider, and his hands ghosted up her thighs, sending shivers through both women.

"Jameson," Danyka whimpered, sounding panicky. *"I don't know if I can do this."*

"Aye, lass, you can if you choose to." He waited, desperately wanting to do this with both women. Carsyn would be easy, but he found himself wanting

to take Danyka over the edge with her. *"Just keep your eyes on me."* He waited, wondering if she would slam the door on their link.

Carsyn was writhing in his grasp. "Roll your skirts up higher, love; keep them out of my way," he whispered to her as his left hand lifted her right leg and placed it over his shoulder. Her pretty, little, blond curls dripped in anticipation. His right hand still played along her leg, and he brought his fingers up to graze over the crease in her leg and across the front of her curls. "Please, Jamey, don't make me wait all night," she begged, trying to bring her core in line with his mouth.

He leaned down and nipped the edge of her lip just enough to make her gasp. "Patience, lass, I'll not be rushed." He rubbed his face on her inner thigh as he looked over it at Danny. The man behind her was slowly pumping in and out. Her face flushed, and her eyes were wild-looking. He smiled, loving her reaction.

"Still with me, Danny?" he couldn't help but tease.

"Aye," she said breathlessly, *"but if this is all you've got…"*

"Nice try, darling, but I won't be rushed by either of you."

He focused on the beautiful body in front of him, kissing his way up towards her center. He took his right hand and stroked through her middle, slowly, loving how her body was weeping for him. His hand was soaked. He dragged his forefinger up the center of her until he brushed lightly against her clit. Carsyn bucked against him, sobbing for more.

"Danny," he whispered, opening the link more and sending more of Carsyn's sensations through to her.

"What?" she gasped. Her body was writhing against the man behind her.

"I want you to follow my instructions to the letter," he said wickedly.

"Why?" she asked, irritated. *"What instructions?"*

He could see her glare from here, and it amused him as much as it aroused him.

"Put your finger in your mouth."

Danny glared at him like he was daft. *"What for?"*

"Because, if you don't listen to me," he said solemnly, *"I'll stop until you do."*

"You wouldn't," she challenged

"Wouldn't I?" he countered. He pulled back from Carsyn and looked up at her hooded eyes begging for release. "Are you sure you want more?"

"Stop teasing me," Carsyn snapped, thrusting her hips forward. "I'm running out of time."

Jamey looked over at Danny in the shadows and saw her put her finger in her mouth. *"Take it out and slowly slide it down the front of you."* He smiled as she all but glared at him.

"Touch yourself and keep the rhythm I am setting with her," he commanded.

He swiped through Carsyn's wet core before applying gentle pressure to her clit with his thumb. He rocked it back and forth while he slowly slid his forefinger into her.

Carsyn moaned greedily. "MORE, Jameson," she pleaded. "Faster."

He slid his finger in and out a few more times while stimulating Carsyn's clit. His eyes were locked on Danny, and her hand was down the front of her. Her head kicked back, and her eyes were almost closed. *"Look at me, Danny,"* he commanded. *"I want to see you when you come."*

"I won't," she sobbed in his head.

"You will," he countered.

Another finger slid into Carsyn while he increased his speed. He made sure Danyka experienced Carsyn's physical pleasure through their link as he stimulated the spot at the upper side of her channel. He heard Danny gasping loudly as he pulled out and added a third, all the while gently rubbing Carsyn's clit.

"Stay with me, Danny. Touch yourself in time with me and tell him to hold still so you can ride him in time with my fingers. You can control how slow or fast his cock is going into you."

Jamey gazed at her longingly as she turned and gave her boy toy new instructions. Danny promised him she was almost finished with him and that he could cum as soon as she got off. *"Ride him slow and steady,"* he encouraged, showing her what he had in mind. *"Now be ready to pick up the pace."*

He started to lean into Carsyn but then looked Danyka straight in the eye. *"Lean forward on your other hand. You're going to need it to support you after we're done here."*

His wicked fingers kept up a steady rhythm as he leaned forward and latched onto Carsyn with his lips, sucking her clit into his mouth and rolling it with his tongue. Her hips started their own rhythm, and he kept pumping in time. He sucked harder as he sensed her impending orgasm.

Jamey sent a command to Danyka. *"I want you to tell me what you are feeling on your end."*

Her words were choppy as she struggled to communicate while her body was on the verge of exploding. *"I can sense the tremors running up and down her legs and the way her stomach is seizing."* She gasped, still sliding on and off the cock behind her. *"I'm close. Oh, sweet Mother, you don't understand how rare it is that I'm this fucking close."* Her voice was rising in a panic. *"Dammit, Jamey, do something."*

Smiling against Carsyn, he continued to suckle her clit while she rode his hand. Just as she was ready to fall off the edge, he bit her clit lightly, and she screamed out her pleasure against him. He wiped his face on her thigh as he looked over and witnessed Danyka sobbing with pleasure. The man behind her was finally cumming, even though it sounded painful from here.

Jamey continued stroking Carsyn gently, bringing her down as she wrapped her upper body around him, sobbing in pleasure. He pulled his fingers out of her and kissed her on her inner thigh, rubbing his face against her gently. She finally sat up and tried to pull herself together. Jamey lowered her leg. "Will yer legs hold ye, lass?"

"Aye, Jamey" she whispered. He set them back on the ground and then held her, rubbing her back. She reached down and kissed him gently. "Thank you for that and for all the times we've shared," she whispered to him with a sad smile. "I've enjoyed them."

She started to walk away and then looked back at him with a hurt expression. "Jamey, as much as I've enjoyed our time together, my name isn't Danny." She waited for him to say something, anything. When he sat there mutely, he could see the knowledge in her eyes. She realized he hadn't been totally present for their encounter. Without another word, she turned and went inside.

He hadn't meant to make her feel used. They both found their pleasure, but he still felt like a shit.

Jamey wiped his face on the side of his sleeve, still smelling her on him, then turned to look at Danny, but the shadows held nothing. She'd fled. He wasn't surprised, but that didn't stop him from being disappointed. They had just shared the best experience of his life, and he knew from now on, there would be no other women touching him. There was only one woman he wanted, and now, he just needed to convince her to give him a chance.

CHAPTER NINETEEN

Little Late for that Now, Ain't It?

Kyran strode from the room with Rhyanna in his arms. She clung to his neck, crying. Her tears soaked his shirt, stoking his rage at her assault. Her breath hitched, and he pulled her closer, kissing the side of her head. He'd longed to have her in his arms, but this sure the fuck wasn't how he had planned it. He was furious at what she'd been forced to endure and afraid to open his mouth and have her misinterpret his temper.

Rhyanna was in shock, her body shook, and she was cold now that the adrenaline had worn off. Aware of the symptoms, she cuddled closer to Kyran's warmth. She was still trying to comprehend what had happened.

As horrifying as the meeting was, what bothered her most right now was that her best friend Madylyn seemed to have sent her blindly into this hell hole without any warning. Grasping onto that thought, she was more hurt by her closest friend's betrayal than by the near assault.

A moment later, her internal link to Maddy flared to life.

"Rhy, are you all right? I can sense your rage and pain from here. Do you need me to join you? What can I do to help?"

"Little late for that now, ain't it?" Rhy snapped back, unable to pretend she wasn't pissed off. *"Ye might 'ave mentioned that my appearance here would constitute a nonverbal agreement to be her whore."*

"She didn't," Maddy gasped, the shock coming through and the fury right behind it. *"She had no right! I clarified the arrangements of your arrival with a missive I returned to her.*

"Aye," Rhy said, snidely. *"She did, and damn near branded and assaulted me in the process. Helluva first time that would have been, na wouldn't it?"*

Maddy's stunned silence said it all. Her rage coming through their shared bond surrounded Rhyanna, and instead of making her feel better, it made her feel worse.

"Ye didn't trust me enough to tell me, Maddy," she said, her voice rising as she remembered. *"I lost control, and if Kyran hadn't arrived when he did, I'd 'ave killed her, and he would be returning me body to ye after they executed me tonight for attacking a monarch. All because ye couldn't tell me what ye was sending me in to? Did ye think I would've backed out? Do ye truly think so little of me?"* Her questions kept coming, leaving Maddy no room to answer.

"Rhy," Maddy said softly, regretfully, *"I didn't tell you because you've been so upset with Kyran gone. I didn't want to stress you more than you already were. I wanted to get you in and out as quickly as possible, then bring you home. It had nothing to do with trust, love. I'm furious with the way she spoke of you and the insinuations she made about you joining their harem. I told her you were to be treated with nothing but the utmost respect and dignity as befitted a member of any sanctuary."* She stopped, trying to find a way to make this right.

"Ye'd have been more infuriated if ye'd seen what she'd been about to do to me." Rhy sighed inwardly, knowing it hadn't been intentional. *"I'll take yer word that ye'll never send me in blind in an attempt to protect me again, Maddy."*

"On my honor, Rhyanna," she said in a voice dripping with remorse. *"I am truly sorry."* Maddy paused, not sure what else to say. *"I'll be there in an hour to deal with this."*

"Nye, ye won't." Rhy snapped back. *"Ye had faith in me to come; ye'll stay put and let me finish playing out this farce first. I need to get to the king before I can return."*

"Can you keep your temper in check?"

"Fine time to worry about that now, ain't it?" she snapped again, not willing to let her off too easily.

"Ferg will be arriving within the hour. Him joining you was planned long before this, lass."

"Send copies of the missives with him. I want to know exactly what they said."

"Done," Maddy said contritely. *"I'm sorry, Rhy. In the future, I won't try to protect you because I know you are more than capable of taking care of yourself."*

"I'll hold ye to that, ye ken I will." She ended the conversation and started paying attention to where they were in the court so she could find her way out if necessary.

Kyran continued walking briskly with her in his arms as if she weighed nothing. The tension in his body beneath her left no doubt as to how angry he was.

The courtiers they passed watched them with thinly veiled curiosity, wondering what upset her so. Her empathic side picked up on their curiosity, their compassion for her, and their relief that it hadn't been their turn.

If Rhyanna guessed correctly, it would be all over court before dinner tonight, and she honestly didn't give a shite. Let them gossip. She'd survived worse. Their snide remarks and looks were the least of her worries. She had to survive the day and still find a way to see the king.

He turned a corner in a corridor she recognized from her arrival earlier. They passed more courtiers, and then she sat up straighter as two women dressed in mere scraps of fabric around their busts and hips dropped to their knees as Kyran passed. Her rage reignited as she realized that this was to have been her fate. It would be a frigid day in hell before she would drop to her knees to perform for any man "better" than her.

Kyran carried her easily without breaking a sweat or losing his breath. Any other time, she would have enjoyed the ride in his arms, but she found herself irritated with him as much as she had been with Madylyn.

Why did everyone feel the need to protect and coddle her? Yes, she was a virgin, but she wasn't a blooming fecking idiot. Over-familiar hands and court games were something she learned to defend herself from long ago. Rhyanna wasn't intimidated by the sex that went on at court, it was a part of the lifestyle, but it was a part in which she didn't participate—yet. Then again, she'd never encountered a court as debauched as this one either.

Tired and emotionally wrung out, she leaned her head against Kyran's shoulder, finally allowing her body to relax a little and her hands to release the death grip she had around his neck. He looked down at her, and the concern in his eyes diminished a mite of her anger towards him. Snuggling into him, she let the heat of him warm her cold, tired body.

Kyran carried her in silence. The corridors were busy this time of day, and he wanted privacy before they spoke. A locked door wasn't enough; he wanted a suite he'd personally warded from prying eyes and ears.

His heart was still racing from the call she sent him. Her plea had cut through him, laced with her terror and impotence. Arriving at the queen's private suites, he blasted through the door and two of her guards outside of it. He didn't have the time for explanations, and he could feel the tempest Rhy was about to let loose inside of the queens' chambers. His intervention saved both women's lives.

Kyran didn't blame Rhyanna for attacking Meriel, but he was terrified of the repercussions the evil bitch would demand.

Rhyanna had been glowing when he entered. She'd been terrifying and more beautiful than he'd ever seen her. Gone was the sweet young woman he was courting. In her place was the Goddess of War, who made every masculine part of his body stand up and take note.

He loved the gentle side of her but seeing her in action made him want to pick a fight with her just so that he could see her with her hair flying and eyes blazing at him like that before they made up.

116

Kyran felt her settle as he reached her suite. He opened the door and entered, reluctant to put her down. He sat against the headboard in her bed, holding her tightly, never wanting to let her go. He pulled a throw around them and relaxed for a moment, just holding her.

With his eyes closed, he reached out energetically, and calling on strands of air and water, he soundproofed her suite of rooms and both rooms on either side of her. He would be occupying the one on the right, and he would put someone he trusted in the left one.

His fear transformed into anger as he thought about what he nearly lost because of her appearance at court.

Unfortunately for him, Rhyanna was empathic enough to notice the moment his fury overcame his concern. She looked up at him with her gorgeous, emerald eyes flashing, and he thought he might just get his wish to piss her off sooner than he wanted.

CHAPTER TWENTY

Daughter of Daphne

Meriel lay in a heap on her sitting room floor. Her young maid stood on wobbly feet and made her way over to her. Trying to be of assistance, she reached for her queen.

"Get the fuck out!" Meriel screamed at her, needing to be alone and lick her wounds.

The young girl scampered out the door like a scalded puppy as Meriel crawled on her knees to the hand-carved four-poster bed. Using the bedpost carved to represent the sea, she hauled herself up off the floor.

Blood trickled steadily from a gash on the side of her head. Warm and sticky, it ran down her face until it dripped off her chin and onto the floor. A deep laugh bubbled out of her as she remembered the look of fury on the little hedge witch's face.

Meriel didn't think she had it in her to fight back, but it had been worth pushing her to react. She wouldn't have gone through with assaulting her. No, she would've saved that privilege for one of the meanest fuckers in her guard who liked to break new girls in. She owed him a reward for disposing of a recent problem in her kingdom. The test had been to see how powerful the healer was when riled up. Meriel was surprised and a tad bit impressed if she allowed herself to admit it. Rarely bested, the healer did some damage, and Meriel hoped it didn't scar.

Wincing, she reached up and felt the jagged cut on her hairline where her head connected with the wall. She really needed to remember to thank Kyran for showing up when he did. Maybe she'd send him a fruit basket. If she didn't desperately want the handsome fucker in her bed, she would make sure to poison the fruit first, but she wasn't done tormenting the man. Plans with his name on them were already in motion, and she fully intended to see them come to fruition.

Steadier, she stood and staggered for her vanity. Bending over to pick up her toppled chair made her head hurt like a bitch, but she finally managed to stand it back up so she could collapse on it. Needing to inspect how badly the little hedge witch damaged her, she chuckled ruefully as she took in the triple mirror's cracks spider webbing out from the center mirror in what seemed like an intentional design.

Dozens of reflections stared back at her, mocking her that a peaceful little healer had done so much damage to a mage of her power. Not finding a shard large enough to peer into, she yanked her hand mirror from the drawer and examined her head wound with a scowl.

A long gash ran from her right temple down to her chin, nearly peeling the skin from the side of her face. That was going to be a pain in the ass to have stitched. Good thing pain turned her on then, wasn't it? At least it didn't look like she would have to shave her head. That would have pissed her off to the point she would have taken Rhyanna Cairn's head for restitution, thereby creating a diplomatic problem with the Elemental High Court. Looks like Kyran really should get that fruit basket...he'd saved her life twice.

A dark chuckle emerged when she remembered the fury running through the woman when Kyran thwarted her. The queen knew he was going to have his balls handed to him when he got the healer back to her room. Damn, Meriel thought, little Miss Rhyanna Cairn would have been fun to torment, but there was always next time.

Deftly braiding the long, platinum length of her hair into a thick rope that fell down her back, she wet a cloth and began to clean the blood from her face. She removed the makeup she wore as she went, and there, in the shattered views, she let her glamor drop for a moment. With a thought, she locked the door, not wanting to be interrupted as she assessed her current situation.

Decades had passed since she last dropped the glamor. She couldn't imagine how it was possible for any woman to forget her true face, but Meriel had. Lost in the part she was playing, she had transitioned out of her youth wearing a glamor, and she rarely released the magic keeping her in this form.

This version of her wore chestnut hair and hazel eyes. Her cheeks were a little plumper, and a scattering of freckles ran across her nose. A beauty mark perched above the right-hand side of her lips, and she had a cute, pert nose.

119

The real Meriel wasn't a hag, but she wasn't the kind of woman a king would have glanced at twice—a problem necessitating the long-term glamor. And if it cost a small piece of her soul…it was well worth it. She chose the farthest thing from the common, dark hair, exotic dark eyes, and gorgeous caramel skin of Queen Yareli as she could imagine.

Long sheets of pale, platinum hair and soft gray eyes made her seem vulnerable. Tall and wispy versus curvy and petite, Meriel was Yareli's polar opposite. Varan had been struck by her uniqueness, and once she caught him looking at her out of the corner of his eye, she set about learning the royal family's routines.

Yareli always tucked her youngest children in and spent time with the older ones before retiring. While she did that, Varan enjoyed a nightcap or two beside the fire while waiting for her. Meriel made sure she was the one to bring his drinks for a week or so, and he was always polite, dismissing her immediately after setting the tray on the table by his chair.

Varan never suspected she began dosing his beverages a little at a time. At the end of the first week, he was nearly asleep before finishing the first glass. By the second week, he was craving what she was bringing him and desperate for more.

One night, he spoke to her, and she kept him chatting long enough for him to drink the second stronger one as well. The opium hit him hard, and he was staggering when she helped him to bed. Varan was completely unaware by the time she undressed him and then herself. Straddling his hips when Yareli entered their suite, Meriel gave a good show of riding the king and pretending the queen hadn't just walked in.

In a stupor, Varan turned towards the door, glazed eyes watching the horror on his wife's face. Unfortunately, his drugged mental state made it impossible for him to respond to Yareli's distress in any way.

Yareli waited for no explanations or excuses, turning on her heel and exiting their chambers. Had she taken the time to throw the usurper out of her bed, she would've found Varan an unwilling participant beneath Meriel, having absolutely no interest in the woman slithering against his limp cock.

Varan was devastated by losing the woman he adored, knowing she would never forgive him. His beautiful Yareli only asked him for one stipulation when they married—his vow of fidelity—and he had just trampled on that along with her heart.

Once the queen abandoned him, Meriel faked a pregnancy to keep the man tied to her. Varan made her his new queen with very little encouragement after Yareli dissolved their union. The truth would never leave Meriel's lips, but they had never been intimate. He believed they had at least once, and that was all she needed him to believe to gain a throne.

Varan may have made her his queen, but he never shared a bed with her again. She was nothing to him but a reminder of all he lost. He thought to take solace in their child to love, but her loss of the imaginary child killed all his hopes of something positive coming out of this situation.

Trapped with this woman, he chose separate quarters and kept the rooms he once shared with the love of his life, leaving Meriel to her own devices. No longer having any interest in his court or his boys due to his newfound addiction, he was clueless to the state of affairs in his court for decades.

Meriel gazed into her shattered reflections, looking for some part of the young girl she had once been before she set out on vengeance. There, in the center where the glass was the most shattered, she found her. Gazing back at her was the woman who abandoned her centuries ago.

Not sure if she was pleasantly surprised to see her again or horrified by the reminder, she found her mother's visage peering back. This was the first time she noticed the resemblance. Hard to believe she had forgotten what her facial structure looked like or how she naturally smiled. Minutes passed while she took the time cataloging her features and deciding she hated the fact that this is what she had morphed into from her youth. Her mother's mirror was the last thing she'd ever wanted to be.

The woman who birthed her was weak and pitiful, and Meriel didn't want to resemble her. With a whispered word of enchantment, her new self-settled back in comfortably like a threadbare sweater one snuggled into in the deep of winter. The woman looking back at her now was empowered and took what she wanted. And what Meriel wanted most was the ruin of the Tyde family.

Neptune was Varan's father, and Varan was his only son. The Tyde line would die out with his children—if Meriel had anything to say about it—and she fully intended to see them all dead or sterile. Her sole mission was to make their lives miserable before the final strike.

Morale at court was at an all-time low as Meriel worked her way through the Court of Tears like a worm through a perfect apple. Shiny and full of color, summer sweetness with a hint of tart—the fruit drew the pests that would work their way through, tainting the fruit from the inside out. Turning one family member against another and brother against brother fulfilled her deepest fantasies of revenge.

Meriel would leave the Court of Tears in ruin, make sure Varan lost his crown, and see to it that his children despised him. When she was through with the Tyde family, she would make sure they knew their grandsire, Neptune, was to blame. Then, her work here completed, she would find new sport.

Her mother, Daphne, became infatuated with Neptune when Meriel was a wee lass. Daphne was a daughter of The Court of Summer Seas, and she had fallen for Neptune one summer while he visited.

Never promising her anything but a good time, he made her feel special and worthy the way he doted on her all summer. When the time came for him to take his leave, Daphne was convinced he would take her with him. When he came to say goodbye that morning, she was inconsolable, on her knees, begging him not to leave her.

Neptune reminded her of her duty to her daughter and how much her family didn't approve of their summer fling. Daphne was willing to throw it all away, but Neptune wouldn't allow it. He forbade her to come with him, trying to let her down gently, but the woman was beside herself. Eventually, he gave up and left her sobbing on the damp sand, shaking his head as he left and muttering under his breath about never again having anything more than a one-night stand.

Meriel watched the theatrics, wondering if they were going on a trip. Confused, she witnessed her mother's humiliation as she cried and pleaded with the handsome man, trying to change his mind. This one moment from her childhood became her strongest memory and the motivation for her overachieving goal of destroying a demigod's world.

For a month, her mother did nothing but weep by the tide line, waiting for the God of the Sea to return to her, proclaiming his love. She forgot she had a daughter who needed to be fed and bathed. Meriel survived by living on the kindness of others and by gathering the edibles the sea provided that she used to help her mother gather before she lost her mind.

Daphne ceased eating and drinking in her final week. Delirious, she kissed Meriel goodbye, telling her that she needed to find Neptune because he was waiting for her—calling to her. Meriel had no tears left to shed and no reason to beg her to stay. This woman wasn't her mother because her real mother loved her, and this woman was selfish and uncaring.

With the sun in her eyes, the little girl bore witness as the woman who brought her into this world waded into the ocean, confident that Neptune would come for her and take her to his underwater court to join him. The foolish woman never gazed back to wave at her daughter, too concerned with a man who never loved her.

Meriel saw an enormous wave knock Daphne down, and weak, she never emerged from the water again. Meriel waited for days, hoping she would return with Neptune for her, and when she finally ran out of food and was tired of scavenging, she made her way to the road leading to the castle.

A pitiful child wandered the road, begging for food. Some fed her, some clothed her, others used her. Never staying with any family long, she made her way to the home of her grandparents, who took one look at her and knew what had become of their daughter.

Daphne was their foolish daughter, and nothing more was expected of Meriel, but Meriel was smart, and she was wily. She took every lesson they taught her and banked that information, learning everything she could possibly need to exile a queen, gain a king, and rule a court.

"I fucking did it," she said to her mother's reflection in the center, unchanging, even with the glamor back in place. "No one's tried to stop me, and no one will stand in my way now. With the allies I have gained, I will ruin this kingdom exactly like I intended to do all along."

A touch of crazy was in her eyes as she grinned into the shattered glass, the motion pulling her torn skin painfully. Her reflections grinned back at her, but the one in the middle gazed on somberly, wanting to discourage her game, wanting to warn her not to get ahead of herself, and more than anything else, wanting to make sure she didn't lose everything in her quest for revenge.

CHAPTER TWENTY-ONE

Damaged and Broken

Danyka pulled her pants up and dismissed the man she'd just used. She glanced over and saw Jameson sweetly kiss the pretty lass he shared the corner with. The scene tugged at her in places she didn't allow herself to go. Places deep inside of her longed for soft and sweet, longed for a man she could bed more than once, and for someone she trusted enough to fall asleep with. That man was never meant to be hers.

Jamey was a ruggedly handsome man who possessed the biggest heart and the kindest soul of anyone she'd ever known. He deserved someone sweet and kind who could reciprocate what he was able to offer. Danny had no right feeling anything for him. They were partners.

It was never smart to become involved with someone you worked with, especially someone you counted on having your back. So, what in all the hells was she playing at tonight? She prayed to any of the gods listening, even though she really didn't believe in them, to let him forget about tonight and go on as before.

She raced back to the portal, wanting to leave before he caught up with her. Her body was so sensitive from the massive orgasm he coaxed out of her that the feel of her leather pants rubbing between her legs made her moan.

No one ever made her come like he just did. She had a full-body, toe-curling, angels-singing, big O. The irony of the whole thing was she would probably never experience another. It was a stupid drunk challenge. An original one, though. And he never laid a hand on her...what the fuck was that superpower he used on her?

So if that's all this was—a stupid drunk challenge—why was she feeling so damn hollow and lonely. Danny paused for a moment with her hand over her heart. She felt like she'd just lost her best friend. Jameson was one of her closest friends. True that. He always treated her like one of the guys.

Danny stumbled forward, quickly moving again, desperate to race back to her room and the bottle hidden beneath her bed.

And why, for fucks sake, did she feel like she was going to cry. The best sex of her life—she wanted to ride the high of the experience—yet she felt broken, like she gave something precious away.

As he gently kissed Carsyn, Danyka wondered what it would be like for him to kiss her, to touch her, to fall asleep holding her. More importantly, what would it be like for him to love her?

Danny stepped into the portal, catching her reflection in the transparent door, and goddamn her if she didn't have tears rolling down her face. The door started to close when a hand shot through and stopped it, and to her complete horror, Jameson stepped in.

He stepped right into her, pinning her against the wall. He took one look at her and pulled her into his arms, and for the first time in decades, she allowed someone to just hold her. "I'm so sorry, Danny," he whispered, his head in her neck as he held her small frame against his chest. "I never thought what we did would affect you this way, or I never would have goaded you into joining me."

Listening to him apologize for one of the most beautiful moments of her life made her feel worse, and she sobbed harder. Somehow, he managed to hold her and work the portal because as her knees started to buckle, he easily picked her up and walked out of the portal into one of Heart island's many gardens. He walked with her in his arms until he reached a bench, and then he sat and cradled her against him. She curled up smaller against him, not wanting to have to explain her reaction to him. He rocked her gently against him while humming an old ballad.

Jameson was devastated to find her with tears rolling down her face. What the hell caused that? Not knowing what to say or do, he did what he did best and tried to comfort her. The sobbing was worse, and she curled up on his lap like a tortured child. "I've got you, Hellion. Let it out." He sensed that whatever broke loose inside of her didn't only have to do with tonight.

His big arms held her to him while one of them rubbed circles on her back. She'd wondered what it would be like for him to hold her, and look at that, there he was. Irony. Again. Her sobs subsided to light hiccupping breaths she struggled to bring under control. The tears kept coming, but they were slowing down. She should say something, but where did she start?

"I'm sorry," he said again.

"DON'T!" she said vehemently. Danny pulled back to look at him. She used her hands to wipe her face and wiped her nose on the sleeve of her shirt. She spoke again, softly this time. "Please don't apologize for one of the most beautiful moments of my life, Jamey. Please don't regret what we did. I don't." She watched the confusion on his face.

"If it was so beautiful, why are you so upset, Danny?"

"You showed me something beautiful, something I didn't think I deserved." She tried to move from his lap, but he pulled her back against him as if he knew once she stood, she would run from him. "You couldn't possibly understand." She looked away from him again.

Jameson watched her trying to run away from him and what they experienced together. He needed to understand what triggered this so he didn't make the same mistake again. He reached down and placed his large palms on either side of her face lifting her face to meet his eyes. "You're right. I don't understand." He hesitated while his thumbs gently wiped the tears starting up again. "But I truly want to." His big, chocolate-brown eyes remained locked on her baby blues while she processed his request.

"Why?" she asked brokenly. "Why do you care if I am having an emotional breakdown.?"

"When you're hurting, Hellion," he whispered, "I'm hurting too. Let me help carry this burden for you."

"I can't," she sobbed. "If I tell you all the horrible things that have been done to me and that I've done, you'll never look at me the same way again." Danny sobbed openly. "I couldn't stand for you to look at me like I am damaged and broken." She tried to pull her head from his hands, but he wouldn't let her. "And I am damaged and broken, Jamey. There's no other way to say it. I'm fucked up beyond repair, and I will never respond like most women physically, sexually, or emotionally."

He never flinched watching her outburst, and he never let go. "We're all damaged to some degree, Danny. It's how much we allow the damaged part to take over that makes the difference. We all have demons and faults. I'm not afraid of your demons, Danny. Bring them out and let them play. They don't scare me."

She laughed then hysterically. "I'm not afraid I'll scare you off, Jamey. I'm afraid I'll disgust you, and you won't be able to look at me with anything but pity or revulsion."

Danny alternated between sobbing and laughing hysterically, and still, he held her like he cared and looked at her like she was worth something. "I'll never have a man look at me or touch me like you did to her tonight. Until tonight, I never wanted anyone to, but watching you with Carsyn, I wondered what that would be like."

"I'm still here, Danny, and I'm not going anywhere." He saw the despair in her eyes, and it killed him. He gently leaned his head against hers, then rubbed his nose along hers. "Let me in and tell me what you think is so horrible." He stroked her face gently with his fingers. "When I look at you, Danyka, the only thing I see is courage and an unending strength. You'll always be my fierce warrior, Hellion."

"Fuck it," she thought. He was like a dog with a bone and wouldn't let it go. "You really want to know?" she asked, her voice changing as ice seeped into it. "I'll tell you, and then you'll comprehend what I'm truly worth." She looked at him one last time before closing her eyes and beginning to speak.

"Did you know Maddy found me when I was twelve, months after my mother sold me to a brothel specializing in children?" She opened her eyes to see him shaking his head as the color drained from his face.

"She rescued me from a cold, dark cell in a club for sexual degenerates." His eyes flared, but no other emotion crossed his face. "I'd been there for about three months, I think. It's hard to say because I lost track of time." She sniffled lightly, and her voice lost some of the edge as she remembered her childhood. "I'd been raped repeatedly since the day I arrived. Usually, three or four times a day." His body tensed with rage beneath her. "I became numb to the abuse. I stopped fighting after the first week. If I didn't fight, they didn't hurt me as badly, and it was over quicker." She smiled sadly, staring off into a place he couldn't go.

"This brothel specialized in high-priced clients who enjoyed children. Once they fucked me a few times, they always wanted someone younger and less 'soiled,' as they called it. Someone pure. Virgins were always better. They got off on their fear as much as the pain they caused, breaking them for the first time.

"My owner was a crafty bastard. He brought in a powerful spirit mage who owed him a favor and could perform 'miracles,' as he called it. This man would come in and temporarily change my hair and eye color, heal my bruises. Make me pretty again." She reached up and ran her hand over her short dark hair. "My blond hair was long and beautiful." She laughed sadly. "It was kind of like Carsyn's, thick with slight waves. It was the one part of my appearance I was vain about. Well, as vain as you could be at twelve. I cut my hair after I escaped and changed the color because I never wanted anyone to use it to cause me pain again.

"I liked the mage because he would take away the pain for a little while. He brought me food and sweets." Her eyes were glazed as they wandered through scenes in her mind. "When he started changing my appearance and healing me, my owner came in one night with a challenge for him. He wanted him to repair my hymen. You couldn't pretend to be a virgin without one. And the men who paid the most would demand proof of my purity before purchasing me."

Danny leaned into him as she continued talking, her head resting against his heart. The steady, solid beat soothed her, and his hand started rubbing her back again. She could feel how tense he was and sense the rage pouring off him, but he continued to hold her ever so gently. "That night he agreed to try." She sighed softly as she remembered. "The mage looked at me with the saddest eyes as they tied me to a table. I often wondered what they must have threatened him with to make him agree to do what they asked. I knew he lost a piece of his soul every time he healed me." She shuddered as she remembered that night. "After the first time I was raped, I learned to tune the act out. Hurts most the first time, you know."

"So that night, he healed me, and my owner raped me immediately to see if it worked. Then he made him repeat the process so he could take me again. He stood there, stroking his cock, waiting, keeping himself hard each time in between. He even let a few of the guards have me. Most never broke in a virgin, and here was a free opportunity. So he healed me, and they each got a chance to break me. They were only allowed a few strokes. This was an experiment, after all. My owner wanted to see how many times I could handle being broken in one night. Every single time was torture because every time he healed me made it harder for them to break through my barrier. They took multiple turns until I finally passed out." Her soft voice was detached as she spoke of her abuse as if someone else had experienced the nightmare.

"Convinced that I was his 'lil gold mine' and that he could earn more from me this way, he auctioned me off multiple times under different disguises and different names. Some of my buyers were kind until the time came to make me theirs. They always took me in the missionary position so that they could see how much pain they were inflicting. Then, they would attempt to train me to please them. I failed at that part; I wasn't obedient or grateful for their attention, and they quickly grew bored with me. When they finally did, I was sold back to the brothel for other purposes. The first night back, I was always given to the lower classes and gang-raped for the rest of the night as punishment for being returned."

Danyka's voice broke as she finally looked up at him. "I prayed for death so many times, but the gods didn't listen to me." A soft sigh emerged. "Then I changed my prayer, and I prayed for vengeance..." A sad smile crossed her face. "The blessed Mother sent me Maddy, my avenging angel."

Jameson didn't know what to say. His head tried to process the horror, and his heart shattered for her. She possessed such strength and deserved so much better than what this world had shown her so far. His face was locked in a mask of neutrality, hoping the shock and horror he felt inside wasn't showing on his face.

"So you see, Jamey, you can't fix me, and you can't put me back together again because I've been broken too many times to care. But you gave me a gift tonight. I may never have that again, and I thank you for the experience. Thank you for making me feel like a woman wanted. Thank you for comforting me like someone who is loved."

She pulled his hands away, stood, and stepped away from him. "And thank you for forgetting all about this conversation. I love you too much to let you remember all my heartache," she said sorrowfully. She reached down and held his face between her hands, kissing him lightly on the lips before looking into his eyes.

"Don't," he started to say, but she'd already sucked him in to the compulsion to forget everything she said and to forget their night together.

"You didn't see me tonight, Jamey. I left the bar before you got there. When you see me tomorrow, you won't remember seeing me or talking to me tonight."

At least she could remember and hold the memory tight, taking it out and remembering tonight when she needed something beautiful to help her through.

She ran her hands over his hair and caressed his face as tears ran silently down hers again. "You are such a wonderful man, Jamey, and someday, someone will be so lucky to call you theirs. Another time and place, that someone might have been me, but I'm cursed to not know happiness or joy. Born under an unlucky aspect, I suppose."

She looked into his eyes and reminded him once again, "Tonight never happened. We got drunk and went our separate ways. Tomorrow will be like any other day between us." She brushed her lips lightly against his once more before she walked away, tossing a casual "G'night, Jameson" over her shoulder.

CHAPTER TWENTY-TWO

We're Bound to Fail

Kyran held Rhyanna tightly as they sat on her bed. As he held her, her emotions fluctuated between shock and rage. Rage would be a hell of a lot easier for him to deal with than her tears. She tried to pull away from him, and he ignored it, pulling her closer still. "Rhy, give me a moment to hold you, please," he whispered. "I need it as much as you do."

Rhyanna shoved him back, and he got his wish to see her in full action. Her eyes blazed at him with pure fury. "How dare ye stop me! Do ye ken what she was about to do to me, Kyran?" This time when she pushed, he let her go. She stood and slapped at his chest again as her eyes shot sparks at him. "Or did ye manage to completely miss her on the verge of raping me?"

Kyran grabbed her shoulders and shook her as his entire body vibrated with fury. "What did you say?"

"Do I typically go around tossing people across the room for no reason?" She yanked herself from his grasp, not wanting to be touched by anyone.

"She had me pinned down, her elemental power overwhelming me senses while her hands touched me inappropriately. Right before ye walked in, she was preparing for the main event. She'd finished burning one of those jewels into me forehead and was going to shove a huge fecking marble cock into me. Meriel likes to break in her new girls to prepare us to be assaulted by multiple men at the same time in the week to come."

She backed away from him, trying to catch a breath. Her fingers ran over the diamond-shaped red mark on her forehead as she tried not to look at him because she was so pissed.

"Do ye have any idea how violated and filthy I feel right now? And ye jest walked in and protected her." A hysterical laugh escaped her. He tried to pull her close again until she shrieked, "Release me!"

Kyran let her go, shaken by her tirade. Astonished by what she experienced and what she nearly did in retaliation, he said, "Rhy, you have to know I would never have let her hurt you."

Rhyanna turned to glare at him, but the tears finally overflowed and tracked down her face, ruining the effect. "YE. WEREN'T. THERE," she yelled, punctuating the words with her finger drilling into his chest. "Ye couldn't have stopped her if ye wanted to. She has power like I've never experienced. It's dark, and it's evil, and it's growing every time she feeds on someone else's pain and suffering. I'm no coward, but I don't feel safe here, and if I remain here under the same roof as her..." A deep, shuddering breath escaped her. "If I do, I'm afraid I'll kill her." Her shoulders drooped as the tears came heavier, horrified that she could house such violent emotions.

Kyran stood there at a loss as to what to do or say. He'd known Meriel was blatantly cruel to members of the court but not to visiting dignitaries. "I'll deal with her," he said, his fists clenching.

"How, Kyran?" she asked in a devastated voice, lifting her palms up into the air. "How will ye fix this when ye don't even have access to yer father?" Her expression was defeated as she glared at him. "I've figured out in less than a day that she runs this place, not him. Ye can't really have any delusions about that, do ye?" Her shoulders slumped as she walked over to a wingback chair and plopped down. She wiped her face with her hands, hating to appear weak. Turning sideways, she pulled her knees to her chest and clutched them to her. She faced away from him. Her head rested on the wing behind her as she stared out the French doors into the raging sea. "Ye should go. I'm sure there is something far more important that needs yer attention right now. I'd like to be alone. Fergus should be here soon."

A single tear escaped and rolled down her cheek, hovering on her jawline. Her sorrow reached across the room and wrapped him in her misery, even though that wasn't her intention. Kyran's senses picked up on her emotions, and they battered against his instinct to hold her and promise all would be well. But how could he promise that to her? She was right; his destiny was so far out of his hands that he no longer knew what control, if any, he had here. He saw her pulling farther away emotionally from him by the minute. Their bridge was locked down, and she let no hint of her internal chaos escape through their link.

Rhyanna was so damn good at hiding herself from him. The lover's bridge he asked her to create weeks ago had backfired more than once on him now. His heart ached at the thought of losing her. With heavy steps, he crossed the room slowly to her, noting that she refused to look at him anymore. He knelt in front of the chair, and still, she gazed sightlessly out the window. Her sorrow matched the color of the sky outside. He paused for a moment as he realized the storm was reflecting his inner turmoil.

Reaching out, he grasped both arms of the chair to prevent himself from picking her up and setting her in his lap so that he could just hold her. Kyran craved her touch, needing to reassure them both. He didn't touch her because he didn't think the attempt would be welcome at this point, and he was trying not to piss her off again.

"My lady," he whispered on their link, *"please don't shut me out. I know you are angry and hurting, and I realize I am the cause of much of this, but please, don't shut me out. You may not see my wounds as easily as I see yours, but the time I spend here does more damage to my heart and soul than I ever wanted you to see."*

Finally, she turned to him as another tear rolled down, joining the first, on the verge of teetering over her chin. *"Isn't that the whole point of a lover's bridge, Kyran?"* she asked as her shimmering emerald orbs sucked him in. *"Isn't that the point of linking at all? If it's not, then it damn well should be. Ye see me pain, ye share in it, ye help me carry it, and ye help me lick me wounds when I need to. Should it not also be me place to help ye with yers? Won't ye give me yer pain, yer frustration, yer hurt, and yer anger to share? Am I so damn fragile that ye'll na trust me with it?"*

She waited for an answer, letting that sink in. *"If ye can't or ye won't, then what are we doing here? Because we're bound to fail if we can't be honest with each other, and there's nothing more honest than sharing one's inner struggle. My link may be closed right now because I can't begin to process me emotions, but I verbalized them to ye. Ye ken what I'm feeling right now, even if ye don't like it."*

Rhyanna witnessed his struggle to understand what she was saying. The knowledge that they were balanced on a precipice that would make or break them hung heavily between them. Sorrow and pain flashed through his stormy blue eyes, and she wondered if he would reach out to her with something. If he couldn't give her all of it, then something at least.

A brief flash of pain, then resignation shone through before those gorgeous eyes shuttered and once again locked her out. A third tear leaked out in disappointment as the realization hit her that he was letting her go.

Kyran looked at her, memorizing every facet of her face, every angel-kissed freckle on her nose. He noted the color and curl of her hair where it lay against her face and tumbled above her head. He took a deep breath, pulling the scent of her into his soul as he reached out and gently wiped away the hovering piece of her heart. He leaned in and kissed her softly on the lips, lingering for a moment with his head against her forehead, unwilling and nearly unable to leave her.

"I'm sorry, my lady, to have caused you such sorrow. It was only ever my intention to love and cherish you for the rest of my days. You deserve so much more than I can possibly

offer you right now, and I've no guarantee of my circumstances changing any time soon. Please forgive me for the pain I've caused you, and others have caused you on my behalf. I never wanted you to have to endure this place, and you have done so for me. I will not see it destroy you because of me. You must know that you take my heart with you when you leave, and it will only ever belong to you. I will find a way to dissolve the bridge you so abhor."

Kyran took a deep breath before standing. He stood, looking down at her for a long time.

Rhyanna knew he was leaving her. She sat there with her heart shattered and her mind desperately trying to think of ways to make him see that they could survive this if they did it together.

"Please don't do this, Kyran. Please don't give up on us jest yet. Jest let me in love; that's all I need. I don't care about the bridge. I've proved more than once I can get around it if I choose to. Today, that bridge brought ye to me aid."

Nothing changed as she sent that message to him. Other than his jaw clenching and the muscles in his face tightening, his eyes were still shuttered as if another conversation were taking place. Looking at him, she knew that his heart and soul were no longer available to her. His eyes were locked with hers, but she couldn't reach him. After a long time, he turned and headed for the door.

Her voice cut through the air like a whip striking him across his back as he reached for the handle. "Never took ye to be a coward, Kyran. The first time you sat and soothed my wounded heart, ye confessed to being nothing more than a man whore to give me the option to back out. I knew that about ye, and I admired yer sense of honor for telling me and trusted that ye would be faithful to me. What could be so fecking horrible that ye can't even face me with the truth. What could be so much worse than everything else that's happened today that it's worth letting me walk out of yer life forever?"

She paused, her voice breaking as she tried to cling to the mad. "Ye made me feel treasured, and ye made all the centuries that I waited for ye seem worth it." Her breath hitched. "Ye couldn't have felt for me what ye claimed if ye can walk out that door right now and leave me feeling disillusioned, unattractive, and unwanted." Her words were raw, cruel, and honest.

Kyran remained facing the door as the rage he'd been choking on finally let loose. He hauled off and punched the wall beside the door repeatedly until a gaping hole formed. Then he turned and strode back to her in long strides, his fury at their entire situation a palpable thing. Blood dripped from the knuckles of his right hand, littering the floor with the evidence of his internal turmoil.

Reaching her chair, he reached down and turned her towards him before grasping her forearms and pulling her to stand before him. "You want the truth, lass? Well, here it is. It isn't fucking pretty, and this won't change a fucking thing because I'm still going to walk out that door without you when I'm done. I won't leave you wondering. I won't worry about hurting your feelings. I won't give a fuck if you hate me when I am done because if this is what it takes to get you the fuck off this island, so be it."

He shook her before pulling her closer. His head bent closer to hers, and she recoiled back at the fury radiating out at her. "Your so goddamn stubborn and never know when to stop. You have to know what I didn't want to share? Well, you've got your wish, one last gift from me." He laughed ruefully. "Now, have fun with the images this will bring."

Rhyanna had never been afraid of him, not once. The Kyran standing before her right now terrified her in ways she never would've thought him capable of. His glacial eyes captured her frightened ones and refused to back down.

"I didn't want you to know, lass, that the only fucking way you're getting out of here is I've just agreed to spend a weekend with the queen and anyone she decides to include, male or female. We will spend the weekend fucking and sucking and doing whatever she commands. I might do them, or they might do me, and I will stand there and take the abuse like a fucking man to keep you and my younger brothers safe." He paused, watching the shock wash over her face as his truth sank in.

He grinned humorlessly. "I will whore myself out to a woman whose throat I would rather slit, but I'll do what I have to. I'll fuck her senseless any and every way I can, and then I'll do any of her courtiers who are in favor. I will grin and bear it and act like I've had the best sex of my life." He laughed wryly before continuing. "And when she orders her biggest and meanest motherfuckers to line up to fuck me—because that's what it's gonna take for you to leave here with your virginity intact—I will pretend to enjoy myself more than I did with her by asking for more because none of this will count if I just go through the motions."

Rhyanna sobbed aloud, but he continued without mercy. "I will drink excessively and use whatever drugs I can put my hands on to remain hard and to try not to see your face over theirs or call out your name because if I don't forget you completely, I get to repeat everything again the following weekend. And do you know what?" He shook her once again. "I would do what she wants every fucking weekend for the rest of my life if it's what it takes to protect those I love from her grasp. I willingly give up the one thing I love more than life to do this because I can't stand the thought of you knowing what I'm about to do. But worse than that, I can't stomach the thought of lying to you about her intentions either." He laughed harshly.

"To answer your earlier question, yes, by the end of the night, I will truly understand how violated and filthy you felt."

He finished his tirade on her wounded gasp, taking no pleasure in breaking her once again. He pulled her against him and kissed her possessively, taking what he'd wanted to take gently earlier. He ground his lips against hers and invaded her mouth with his tongue rougher than he'd ever kissed her before. He pulled away, resting his forehead against hers long enough to say, "You're the most beautiful woman inside and out that I have ever known. Don't you dare ever doubt your worth." His lips found hers once more. His hands still held her arms fiercely, and he was sure she would bruise tomorrow, but right now he didn't give a shit. She forced this confession from him, and now he was going to take one small thing for himself. He pulled away suddenly, dropping her arms like she had scorched him. "If you'll excuse me, my lady, I must go prepare myself to become her entertainment."

He walked away, lobbing one last remark over his shoulder. "Safe travels on your way home, my lady. I'm off to fuck you out of my system before I give the performance of my lifetime." His dead eyes met hers one last time before he turned and left her room, slamming the door so hard on his way out that a painting of wildflowers hit the floor.

Rhyanna stood there, horrified and sick to her very core. Somehow, she managed to unlock the French doors and stumble down to the beach until her feet were submerged in the rough surf. With her feet connecting her to the earth, she released a primal scream she hoped the sound of the crashing waves covered. She waded out into the cold waves, letting the water embrace her like a mother would a child as she sobbed all her sorrow out for both of them. Rhy never would have imagined what Kyran finally shared with her, and now it was all she could think about.

Somehow, she needed to find a way to stop Queen Meriel from ruining any more lives. Right now, she needed to ground herself, grieve, and then pull herself together so she could function well enough to do her job and tend to the king of this fucked up kingdom. If he was anything like the queen, may the Earth Mother have mercy because Rhyanna Cairn wouldn't be able to find any.

CHAPTER TWENTY-THREE

Rosella Diaries
Fourth Entry

Rosella slept fitfully, dreaming about the night she had been abducted once again. One moment she and her beau, Manfri, had been laughing and talking about their future, and the next, she watched a man murder him before he knocked her unconscious. When she awoke in chains, her world had changed forever.

There were times that she barely remembered his smile or the way his unruly black hair fell over his left eye. But sleep offered her no quarter as it often reminded her of the first man she had loved in graphic detail. She heard his voice and his laugh and felt his arms around her as they floated on the river, dreaming about a future that was never meant to be theirs. She whimpered as her dreams circled back to their last night together, and she thrashed, tangled in her sheets as she tried to escape the path before her.

Braden sat cross-legged against the door, dozing lightly. One of many Romani guards on this ship, he needed little sleep. He was able to take what he needed in snatches of time while the women were busy with their lessons or when other guards abounded. Able to rest his mind and his body with his eyes wide open, he rarely needed more than a few hours to completely rest.

His half-mast eyes opened as Ella whimpered in her sleep. His eyes drifted to her thrashing form, and he allowed himself to observe her more closely. She was a beautiful lass with thick, strawberry-blond hair that he longed to stroke a hand down. Her eyes were beautiful, though haunted, as was her smile. Slow in coming but worth the wait, he watched discreetly throughout the day, hoping to watch it light up her face.

Ella, as he knew her, sobbed in her sleep, muttering the name Manfri as she did most nights. Braden figured it must have been the man she had loved prior to her captivity. The more she thrashed, the tighter the sheets constricted her movement. He saw her breathing change as she hyperventilated in her nightmare.

Concerned, he stood silently and went to her. He could have woken Shaelyn, probably should have, but the selfish part of him wanted to have an excuse to touch her, even if only for a moment. Approaching the bed, he noticed the flush on her cheeks and on her chest where her nightshirt had come open. The length of it was wrapped around her hips, showing an indecent amount of her legs. His eyes lingered on them as they tried to kick free of the covers. Long and shapely, they nearly nailed him in the balls as she moved even more violently against her restraints.

He sat on the edge of the bed and reached out to run his fingers over her brow, trying to soothe her. For a moment, all activity ceased until he removed his touch. Fascinated by her response to him, he repeated the action until he was certain that it was he who soothed her. A funny sensation settled in his chest, confusing him. He felt a strong urge to protect her, and the thought horrified him. There was nothing he could do to protect her or to save either of them. Their fates had been decided the day they stepped aboard this vessel, and nothing would change that.

Braden stood up, acknowledging his actions for the foolishness they were. He turned to leave when her whimper stopped him. Glancing down, he found her sorrowful hazel gaze on him.

"Don't go…" she said in a whisper.

His eyes locked on hers and the anguish in them pulled at his heart. He sat on the edge of the bed, keeping a respectable distance. "I'm sorry for what you've endured, my lady," he said in a deep, melodic voice.

Her hazel eyes filled at the simple acknowledgment of her predicament. "Why would you care about my plight?" she asked numbly.

Unable to stop himself, he reached out and pushed the disheveled hair out of her face before softly cupping her cheek. Dropping the guard he kept up with everyone else, he sighed sadly and said, "We are all prisoners here. Some of us will be sold or used as you will be; others of us are here to prevent someone we love from being taken in the same manner. We provide a service that makes sure our families are protected and paid well."

He paused, reflecting as his thumb stroked her cheek. "It was not my choice to be here either. My family traded my future for the protection of my four younger sisters. I don't like it, but I would do it again to protect them."

Braden removed his hand and reached for the sheet wrapped around her legs. She stiffened beneath him. "If you will allow me, my lady, I will untangle you so that you might sleep better." He looked at her, waiting for an answer.

Ella watched him warily. His pale eyes were kind, and his hands gentle. She believed his story, but she trusted no one here. With a nod, she granted him permission to touch her. As he quickly removed the fabric binding her tightly, she gasped as his fingers accidentally brushed against her calf. The sensation that ran through her body startled her, so she pulled away quickly.

Sensing her unease and intimately aware of the electrical connection between the two of them, he quickly covered her back up and began to stand when her hand gripped his tightly.

"Please," she whispered, "would you please stay with me for a moment until I fall back asleep?"

Her eyes begged him, and he was unable to refuse her. "Aye, for a few moments, I will stay." His thumb rubbed against the back of her hand. "Sleep safely, my lady. Nothing shall harm you while I am here."

Still clinging to him, Ella's eyes grew heavy as she pulled up the image of her diary in her mind and quickly wrote a new entry.

Dear Diary,

This shall be a quick entry as I am sleepy. I am confused. After one of my many recurring nightmares I have had of Manfri, I awoke to find Braden sitting next to me with such a compassionate look on his face that it nearly broke me.

I am unused to kindness in this place and know not what to think of it. I want to respond in kind, but don't trust him fully yet.

He has granted me a boon and remained by my side as I drift off. His presence grounds me as he guards me, and I find myself pleased to have him near. While untangling me from the sheets, his fingers grazed my leg, and I felt things such as I have never experienced, not even with Manfri.

These sensations confuse me and have no place in this world...

I am drifting off again.

Until next time,

Rosella

Braden sat there until, eventually, she drifted off once more. Attuned to the sounds of the room, he noticed the silence coming from the pallet near the door. Not wanting trouble for either of them, he stood and left Ella and went to check on Shaelyn.

She was curled up in a ball with her blankets up to her chin. Her eyes were closed, but he knew from her breathing that she was awake. Braden squatted next to her and waited for her to acknowledge him.

With a resigned sigh, her emerald eyes popped open, and she looked at him solemnly. "'Tis not a good idea to get attached, Braden, and you ken that," she admonished.

He laughed softly. Shaelyn had arrived to work the same time he had, and they were friends. "I'm not getting attached, lass. She had a nightmare I woke her from. 'Twas all."

"Ye've never woken me from a nightmare like that."

"That's because you sleep like the dead and snore like a sailor, lass. Nothing troubles you when you sleep."

She laughed with him, then rolled to her side, facing the wall. "G'night, Braden."

"G'night, Shae."

On silent feet, he reclaimed his position in front of the door and closed his eyes. The inability to see did not dim the memory of her hair sliding through his fingers or the soft skin of her calf. Nor did it dim the sound of the shocked gasp escaping her lips as he'd stroked her leg. Stifling a groan, he leaned his head back against the door, slowed his breathing, and let his mind drift. Even trying to ignore her, he couldn't stop his eyes from tracing her sleeping form across the room and wondering what it would be like to curl up with her.

CHAPTER TWENTY-FOUR

Voice of Reason

Fergus packed a bag of his most conservative outfits and headed for the portal. His fire drakes raced around his neck, feeding on the uneasiness creeping up on him.

He stepped out of the portal, surprised to find four guards awaiting him. A tall, middle-aged man held out a hand to him. "Master Emberz, the Court of Tears welcomes you. I'm Tristan, the Master of the Guard. If there's anything you need during your stay, please don't hesitate to ask for me."

"Appreciate it," Fergus said. He tugged at the stiff collar of the starched white button-down choking him as he followed the man across the bridge. "Did Mistress Cairn arrive safely?"

"She did. I met her myself and escorted her to Queen Meriel's chambers as directed."

Fergus's head whipped to the side, his shocked gaze meeting Tristan's. "I was under the impression we both would be meeting her this evening," he said with a hint of irritation.

"I can't answer that for you, sir. I just do as I'm asked and keep my questions to a minimum. Ensures job security."

"And the king," Fergus asked, "how does he fare?"

Tristan's jovial facade cracked as he hesitated to answer. "As far as I'm aware, his highness is doing well."

"Then what the feck are we doing here?" Fergus thought. "You been with the king's guard for long?"

"Most of my life," Tristan said. "My father was the previous Master of the Guard, and his father before him."

"King Varan must do well by you to earn that kind of loyalty."

"Aye, he always has…" he trailed off, catching himself before he said something he shouldn't.

"And, the queen," Fergus said softly, "has she earned as much of your loyalty?"

Tristan's looked at him suspiciously before giving him a safe answer. "My loyalty has always been to the Court of Tears, and that's where it shall remain until I take my last breath."

"Yer dedication is admirable," Fergus said as they stopped in front of a set of double doors.

"Your rooms, sir. Mistress Rhyanna's are to the right."

"Thank ye, Tristan."

Fergus shut the door, grateful to be alone for a moment. Flinging himself into a large leather chair, he plopped his doeskin boots on the ottoman and closed his eyes. It had been a long fecking day already. No two ways about it. His meeting with Maddy and his worry about Rhyanna had eaten away at him all afternoon.

He didn't know what had gone wrong after her arrival, but he knew the lass was devastated. Centering himself, he imagined a large barrier of white light surrounding him. He pulled energy into it and protected his aura from the tainted energy he could already feel running through this court. Around the white forcefield, he imagined a pink one layering over top. This one would help repel the emotional onslaught he was about to face when he walked through the door adjoining their suites.

Rhyanna was the heart of their Sanctuary. She was always there for everyone else, asking nothing in return. Today was her first taste of the heartbreak she was about to experience if they didn't find a way to change the outcome. Fergus had no intention of leaving her here to deal with it herself. He was going to be there to support and help the lass as she dealt with this shit show.

Taking a dozen deep breaths in and out, he prepared himself for the evening he was about to have. He needed to help straighten out Rhyanna's mood and get them both successfully through dinner with a deranged king and an evil queen.

He made his way to the adjoining door and knocked lightly on it. Silence greeted him, and he thought she was either ignoring him or sleeping it off. Quietly, he opened the door to be greeted by the late gray of the afternoon fading away to the shadows of night. Casting a dim light in her hearth, he stepped in and found her huddled in the middle of the bed sleeping. She was pale, and tears stained her cheeks, ripping out his heart for her. Anger ran through him as he wondered what the fuck happened to her. His rage was also aimed at the one man here who should be by her side right now, trying to make it better.

Fergus sat on the edge next to her. "Rhyanna, love," he said so softly it could have been the whisper of the breeze coming through the slightly opened window. "Lass, it's Ferg," he whispered to her as his hand ran over the top of her head and down over her long hair.

She blinked once, a slow, confused where-am-I look at the world she was waking to. Rolling to her back, she ran her hands over her face, rubbing her eyes. He was sure they were gritty from all the crying she had obviously done. Opening her eyes fully, she looked around the room as her memories of the day come rushing back. She turned towards the door, finding Ferg still sitting next to her.

Her eyes met his and knew he realized something was wrong. "Why are ye here?" she whispered.

"I thought ye might need a friend, lass," he said gently. His hand continued stroking her hair, soothing her battered soul

Finally, she nodded in agreement. "Oh, Ferg, I'm a fecking mess." The waterworks started up once again, and he reached for her. She threw her arms around his neck and clung to him while she sobbed her heart out in his arms. She recognized his telepathic touch as he reached out to her on their link.

"Lass, if ye can't talk about it, can you please show me what happened?" He rubbed her back while he communicated with her. *"I won't judge anything I see; I just need to know what we're dealing with in this cesspool."*

Still clinging to him, she nodded.

"Start with yer arrival and visit to the queen," he said, encouraging her to focus on something other than her sorrow. As the scene replayed through their minds, his body vibrated with rage at Meriel's behavior towards Rhy.

"No, she couldn't be fecking stupid enough to do that to ye?" he said aloud, pulling away to see her expression.

"Aye, Ferg, she didn't care about repercussions. She was horrible, and I would have killed her if Kyran hadn't walked in and stopped me."

"So, Kyran was yer knight in shining armor?" He waited for her answering nod. "Then why are ye still crying, lass?"

Rhyanna bowed her head against his chest, not wanting him to read her in the eerie way that he had. She took a deep, shuddering breath. "He left me, Ferg. He's finished with me."

"What the feck are ye talking about, lass?" he asked, shocked by her statement. He shook his head at her "Yer not going to convince me he doesn't love ye, lass, fer I ken he does. The sun rises and sets on ye in his world."

"It might have once," she said, her voice breaking as she tried to stave off the tears once again. "But I think right now I'm too much work with everything else he has to deal with."

He took her hand, gently stroking her skin with his thumb. "I ken this must be deeply personal, lass, but there are so many things afoot in this fecking place. I need to ask..." He cleared his throat and sighed, hating that he had to pry. Finally looking back at her, he asked her softly, "Will ye show me what happened between the two of ye today?"

Rhyanna shook her head violently while trying to pull her hand out of his. Her eyes filled once again as she looked at him. "Please, Ferg, don't ask that of me. It was painfully embarrassing for both of us, and jest horrifying what he will be going through."

"That's exactly why ye need to show me, lass," he encouraged with a soft smile. "If somethings afoot, I may be able to help ye." He paused before adding, "Help ye both." He might be pissed at Kyran right now on Rhy's behalf, but he was still trying to give him the benefit of the doubt. Fergus wasn't as sure as Rhy seemed to be that this was over for either of them. "Do ye trust me, lass?"

"Aye, Fergus, I've always trusted ye with everything. Everything except dressing yerself." She found a smile—a sad one at that. "Yer right, this is deeply personal and hard to put all of my insecurities out there for anyone to view."

"I understand what ye are saying, Rhy, truly, I do," he said, his voice dripping with sincerity. "I jest need to understand where his mind and heart were. I promise this will only be between us." He chuckled. "Pinky swear."

Rhyanna couldn't laugh even though normally she would have. She laid her head down on his chest and sighed heavily. "I'm trusting ye, Ferg. Don't let me down."

Fergus clasped her tightly to him with his chin resting on her head as he rocked her slowly. He closed his eyes and appealed to her inner self once again.

"Let me in, lass," he said softly. Her barricades opened enough for him to enter her inner world. "Take me to yer last conversation with Kyran."

Rhyanna remembered every detail of their last conversation. Every word he said, every expression that crossed his face, and every nasty fact he threw at her. She gave them all to Ferg, then she offered up all the guilt, hurt, and insecurities she'd acquired since then. She gave him all the regrets that she hadn't made love to him properly. Then she showed him the self-defeating parts of her that never believed she was good enough for Kyran coming back out to play.

Fergus insisted on knowing, so like Kyran had done to her, she ripped her heart open and handed the shredded pieces to him—the good, the bad, and the ugly, along with the shame, the blame, and the raw, aching pain that was clawing deep inside of her. She gift wrapped the whole mess for him and threw it at him psychically.

Fergus took the onslaught of emotions from her. He accepted them from her, then examined the scenes causing her such pain. He pulled them from her heart chakra and sent soothing healing energy back into her. He replaced the shame and the blame with positive energy and clarity. Taking on her guilt and her pain, he replaced them with compassion and fortitude.

She tried to throw away all the love she possessed for Kyran. She boxed her feelings up neatly and tossed the whole lot to him. He protected her wounded hopes with a cushion of air, dulling the hurt and surrounding it with love. Someday soon, he knew she would regret tossing all her feelings aside so easily.

As he processed her pain, his heart broke for them both. He knew the sacrifice the man was trying to make for her. Kyran was sending her away to protect her, and whether Rhyanna realized that initially, Ferg was going to make sure she knew why before they left. If she wanted to end their relationship, that was her choice, but Ferg was going to make damn sure she looked at the facts first.

"He threw me away, Ferg, like I meant nothing," she rasped out. "He headed out to find someone else to sleep with when he could have been with me."

"Do ye honestly think ye were receptive to him in that way when he left?" he asked her.

"No, but he didn't need to tell me he was running right off into someone else's bed."

"Come here, lass," he said as he turned her towards him. His forehead rested against hers as he said, "Let's look at this one more time from my viewing perspective. Pay particular attention to the look in his eyes as he sends ye away from this place. Those aren't the actions of a man who doesn't care. Just the opposite, in fact. They're the action of a man who is trying to save ye and his siblings from harm."

"Why was he so damn cruel about it?"

"He knew that if he was kind about it, ye'd never leave him here—ye'd fight to stay by his side, even watch him wed someone else, much to yer detriment."

He watched the light come on in her eyes as comprehension broke through the haze of hurt. "He loves ye too much to let ye waste yer life on something he may not be able to give ye."

"By accepting Meriel's offer, he knows he'll lose me."

"Ye need to remember that he's accepting her offer to save yer life and the lives of his siblings regardless of the pain and humiliation he will suffer through."

Ferg gave her a moment to process his words. "I can damn well guarantee ye that she'll delight in not only having him, but in humiliating him repeatedly. She'll also make sure that the entire court knows that he finally acquiesced to her."

His eyes blazed into hers, forcing her to comprehend the sacrifice the man was making on her behalf. "Add all of that on top of knowing how much he hurt ye and how much pain he's experiencing knowing he's lost ye. He doesn't think he has anything left to lose." Ferg laughed ruefully. "I'd admire the man if I didn't think it would end up pissing ye off sorely." His crooked smile teased her. "I'd hate to be cursed with a case of the pox from me favorite wench."

Rhy sniffled then managed a half-smile, not ready to laugh yet. "What now?" she asked, looking at him expectantly. She was waiting for him to work his magic and tell her what the next steps should be because she was too emotionally exhausted to see them clearly.

"First step, love," he said, "is to get ye cleaned up. We can't go saving yer relationship with ye looking like this."

He dodged the hand that came up to cuff his head and jumped off the bed. "Get a move on, lass. Dinner's at seven, and we dare not be late. The king gets cranky when he's hungry."

Rhyanna stood up and trudged to the en suite facilities hoping to at least wash her face and fix her hair. That was all she had time for, and she hoped it would be good enough for dinner. Crossing her fingers, she sent a prayer to the Goddess for strength and the Earth Mother for balance, asking for the two qualities she needed most, and praying they would hear her and answer her prayers.

CHAPTER TWENTY-FIVE

Compromise

Rhyanna took one last look in the mirror before walking out. She left her hair down, and Lily arrived in time to fix her ruined makeup. God bless her, she never asked what happened, just set about putting it to rights.

She quickly stepped into a strapless, emerald, silk evening gown with a sweetheart neckline and a corseted back. She looked down at her exposed decolletage. Her breasts were barely contained. She wished she had a scarf or shawl to put around her shoulders. Her arms were the one area she always felt insecure about. She pulled the front of the gown up, praying everything would remain in place for the evening.

"Turn me lady," Lily said, holding out a piece of jewelry for her to wear. Rhyanna fingered the teardrop pendant she received as a gift from Kyran. Tears threatened, but so did Lily's ire if she started weeping again. Wearing it was easier than explaining why she didn't want to. Placing the large gem around her neck, she prayed that it would give her courage and protection in this place. Her fingers clasped the large emerald as if it held magical properties to ward off evil. It nestled perfectly between her neck and her bosom.

Lily turned her so that she could see the full effect in the mirror before she left. The silk flowed around her beautifully, hugging her generous curves and accenting her small waist. A partial updo left long curls framing her face and cascading over her shoulders and down her back to her waist. The honey-blond curls were perfectly shaped and arranged around her shoulders as if she indeed did have a scarf. Smiling at Lily, she said, "It's perfect."

Lily smiled, pleased that her work was appreciated. "I'll take me leave now, me lady," she said, curtsying as she did.

"Ye may," Rhyanna responded. "Ye ken all that's not necessary with me, don't ye, lass?"

"Aye," she said. "I do, but easier to remember to do it all the time than forget in front of the court."

"Ye've a point, lass." Rhyanna sent her off with a smile. "Go and enjoy yer evening, but be careful, lass."

"I will, me lady." She reached for the door as a knock sounded on it.

Rhyanna turned away to gather her shoes. "Let him in. I'm expecting him," she said, expecting Fergus at any moment.

She heard the door open and close as she leaned over to put on her shoes. "I'm almost ready, Ferg. Just give me a moment." She stood back up and gasped, startled at the man who stood in front of her. Her heart skipped in her chest. Speechless for a moment, she just stared at him. Their eyes locked, and the hunger and remorse she saw in his gaze spoke volumes. Finally, she found her voice and softly asked, "Why are ye here?"

Kyran stood before her, dressed in a long, black, split-tail jacket over black leather breeches and boots. His wet hair was slicked back from his face, accenting his strong features. An emerald silk shirt peeked out from under his long jacket, matching her dress perfectly. His eyes were on her, memorizing every inch of her. He cleared his throat as he looked at her, then put his hands into his pockets awkwardly.

"Fergus said I was needed to escort you to dinner." His eyes roamed over her. "You look absolutely beautiful, as always, Rhyanna." His expression clouded over. "But my lady, for all that's holy, why are you still here?" he asked, exasperated.

"Ye should know me well enough by now to ken I don't scare easily, and I don't make a habit of running away from something that intimidates me or hurts those I care about."

Their eyes never left each other. As they gazed into each other's souls, they somehow managed to move close enough to touch. She reached up and pushed back a piece of his hair that had fallen over his brow. "Did you manage to feck me out of yer system before the big night?" she asked, proud of herself for her voice not breaking as she tried to lighten the mood.

He closed his eyes and groaned, having the decency to look ashamed of his own words. When he opened them again, he said, "You must know, I didn't mean most of what I said earlier. I just want you safely out of here. You don't realize how bad this place can become. You've only been given a taste of how dishonorable and immoral the Court of Tears really is.

"It's become a den of lies, deceit, and deadly intrigues, each one more complicated and more diabolical than the last. It's the last place I would ever want you to be." He took her hand. "I wanted you safely away from here." His other hand gently cupped the side of her face. "Even if it meant I had to make you hate me to do it."

"I don't think I could ever hate you, Kyran. I was hurt, I won't lie. You hurt me badly and preyed on all my insecurities. It will take me a long time to build my confidence back up when it comes to men."

She moved away from his touch. "Ye meant what ye said about offering yerself up as a sacrifice fer me, didn't ye?" Her eyes locked on his, and when he remained silent, she took a step back. "If nothing else, can't we simply be honest with each other, Kyran?" Her shoulders drooped in frustration as she retreated further. "Ye gave me yer worst this afternoon, and I'm still here, aren't I? Please, jest talk to me. Fergus and I are here to help if ye'll let us."

"Why are you still here, Rhy?" he asked. His voice was hoarse, and when she met his eyes, she could feel his desperate need to understand why she stayed.

"Fergus helped me understand what ye were doing this afternoon. I was too close to it, too hurt and angry to see what ye were doing fer me—fer us." She stepped back into his personal space. "Do ye really need me to say it, Kyran?" She watched his expression, and when the pain in his eyes returned and he nodded, she reached up and took his face in both of her hands.

"It wasn't fair of me to blame ye fer what happened this morning. The blame lies solidly in Meriel's lap. I closed myself off from ye because I am in an environment I hate being in. I don't know the rules, so I can't even compete with them in this game. Being a virgin makes it even worse when everything about the culture at the Court of Tears revolves around sex."

He opened his mouth to speak, but she placed her fingers over his lips and hushed him. "Please let me finish, Kyran. If this is the last time I see ye or the last time we speak, I don't ever want ye to wonder about today or tonight and my motivation in being here."

She waited until he nodded before continuing. "I was angry, hurt, and confused earlier. I'm not now. I've had time to process the day, and all I can tell ye is what I know as truth." Her hands traced the sides of his face as his arms found their way around her, caressing her back.

"I love ye, Kyran, don't ye ever doubt me heart. I understand why ye offered yerself up to her, and though I hate the thought of her hands on ye or ye inside of her, I understand ye feel ye've no options to protect yer family." She reached up and lightly kissed him. His eyes widened in wonder that she could still care for him after the way he treated her earlier. "I need ye to answer a question fer me, Kyran, and I need to have yer honest answer. Will ye give me that?"

"Always, Rhyanna. I've never lied to you."

"Were ye with anyone since ye left me earlier today? Did ye get me out of yer system?" she asked, barely able to breathe waiting for his answer. If he said yes, she was going to teleport herself right out of this room.

A shadow passed through his eyes, but he shook his head vehemently. "No, Rhy, I swear to you, I wasn't with anyone after I left. I'll always be honest with you. I'll admit I thought about it when I left, furious, hurt, and knowing I would submit myself to her soon. It crossed my mind to seek pleasure elsewhere. I thought you would never speak to me again, but I was physically ill over it when I reached my room."

"Will ye do something fer me then?" she asked. Her voice was so soft he barely heard her request.

"Anything, Rhy, you've only to ask," he said as he turned his head to kiss the palm resting on his face.

"After dinner. Tonight." She stammered, uncomfortable with asking for what she wanted.

"Just tell me, my lady, tell me what I can do to make this better."

Rhyanna stared at him for a long time before answering. She could still hear Meriel's voice in her head, *"I wonder if you would be woman enough to let him make that trade."* Her comment circled in Rhy's head repeatedly after Ferg helped her understand what was at stake. The whole time she was getting ready, she kept asking herself that question. Now, she needed to make a choice she could live with. She brushed her lips against his one last time before answering him.

"Be with me tonight. Stay with me. Love me and let me learn how to love ye. Hold me as I fall asleep, and wake me with kisses come morrow. Give me tonight, Kyran, to be yers, and tomorrow ye can go to her with me blessing, as long as ye have an official writ stating it's a onetime thing, never to be repeated."

Kyran's eyes widened in shock, and she watched the gray storm clouds rolling back through them. "I would accept the gift of a night with you gladly, my lady." He bent down and kissed her soft and sweet.

"I don't know how to respond to the rest." He pulled away from her and paced. "How can you ever want me again after I'm with her...with them?"

"If she had succeeded in raping me this morning, or someone else had, would ye no longer want me?"

"That's different, Rhyanna," he said sharply. "It wouldn't be your fault."

"How, pray, is it different? This isn't yer choice. If I am taken without me consent and ye are forced into giving consent to protect those ye love..." She moved in front of him, lacing her fingers with his.

"The time ye spend with her will mean nothing to me if it obtains all yer siblings' safety for life from that predator. Ye accepted her terms, and ye'll follow through. If ye don't accept her offer, I will offer myself to her in yer stead for the same arrangement of safety with ye included in the deal."

His hand nearly crushed hers as his other one grabbed the base of her neck. "The hell you will, Rhy, this is my problem to deal with, my family to save. Don't even say those words. These walls have ears, and if you even utter them outside of this room, it will be considered a verbal contract, and there will be no going back. Do not do this; I will accept." He leaned his forehead against hers and pulled her tight. "I don't deserve you, my lady, but I swear to try and earn the right to be by your side every day for the rest of my life."

"Yer family may one day be mine, Kyran, so you do what ye need to with my blessing. When it's over, return to me, and I will cleanse your body and mind of the evil that's touched you. Ye'll let me hold ye through the night, and, eventually, we'll erase every horrible memory by making beautiful new ones to replace them."

He lifted her face to his and searched her eyes, trying to clearly see her true feelings on this. "You've no doubts about this, my lady?"

"That's my request. Can ye do that? Can ye give me tonight and return to me afterward, no matter how bad it was?" Her fingers tightened on his. "If ye can't, I don't ken how we're ever going to make this work. Ye'll never leave here, and I'll never return to this place as long as she sits on the throne."

"Aye, Rhyanna, I can do that. You have my word. I'll find a way to remove her from this court and return it to a place we can be proud of, on one condition."

"Name it."

"You never ask me anything about the time I spend with that woman. Not one detail about what I will be forced to endure."

"I accept yer terms."

His lips met hers in a kiss, sealing their compact. A promise of their future, and the strength to survive anything thrown at them. The kiss transformed, and that same kiss turned up the heat and gave them both a glimpse of the pleasure they would find later tonight.

Now, all they had to do was to navigate a formal dinner safely. They both should have known nothing would be that easy

CHAPTER TWENTY-SIX

Fury

Jameson sat there still as a statue as he watched her walk away. He dutifully called out a drunken "Night, Danny." When she was far enough away, he whispered, "I love you, too." A single tear escaped down his cheek before he embraced the rage he had been struggling to contain while she told him about her childhood.

He'd never been susceptible to compulsion. Few could successfully make him forget anything, and Danny gave him enough notice for what she was attempting to do that he had time to reinforce his inner walls, keeping her from tampering with his memories.

His head dropped into his hands as he tried to process what she shared. Holy hell. What do you even say to someone who's gone through that? Nothing. Because nothing you say will make a damn bit of difference. Nothing takes it away, and nothing makes it all better. He sighed, closing his eyes and remembering the way her tiny but deadly hands stroked his face and how soft her lips felt against his. Her past didn't matter to him, but how would he ever convince her of it.

Jamey stood and paced, wanting to kill something, no someone. He wanted to find every one of those sick fucks and castrate them before he tortured and killed them. He leaned back and let his inner beast roar his frustration, not caring who heard. She would be far enough away by now. He needed to find a way to vent and release the rage he was feeling before Danny realized she hadn't compelled him.

He debated who to reach out to for help in dealing with what he now knew. Closing his eyes, he reached out to Maddy.

"I need to talk to you, Maddy."

"Now?" her sleepy voice questioned, surprised at the suppressed rage underlying his words.

"If at all possible, bring Ronan with you."

"Where?"

"Wellesley. The gazebo on the dock will be empty this time of night."

"We'll be there in thirty. Do I need to bring anyone else?"

"No." He hesitated before adding, *"Danny told me how you found her."*

"Oh, Jamey." The sorrow and pain in her voice confirmed all his worst fears. *"We're on our way."*

"This is just between the three of us."

"Of course. She wouldn't be happy to find us talking about her past, but you need to know what you are facing for the two of you to move forward."

"That's the only reason I am dragging you out of bed, Maddy."

"On our way."

Jameson headed for the portal, trying to see past the fury he felt for what had happened to Danyka and his frustration for what he couldn't fix.

CHAPTER TWENTY-SEVEN

Saccharin Smiles and Women's Wiles

Kyran and Rhyanna entered the dining room behind a dozen other couples. Rhyanna glanced around for Fergus and was unable to locate the man. She figured he would stand out at court in his outlandish outfits, but she found no sign of him. She turned to ask Kyran if he could see over the other couples in front of her when his deep voice came from behind her.

"Rhyanna, lass, you look exquisite," he purred as she turned towards him. She was startled by how handsome he was tonight. He wore a full black watch kilt with black boots and accessories. His wild red hair was slicked back neatly into a que at the back of his neck. His beard was neatly trimmed, and he seemed brawnier than usual.

"Fergus, look how handsomely ye clean up, lad." She smiled and hugged him affectionately. "I almost didn't recognize ye."

He hugged her tightly while sending a message silently to her. *"Things alright with the two of ye, lass?"*

"Aye, Ferg, they are. And this is the only time I will ever thank ye fer meddling, but thank ye, love, with all my heart. Thank ye for sending him to me."

"Yer most welcome, darling. I hated seeing ye hurting. It's plain to see how the two of ye feel about each other. Glad it sorted itself out."

"It will soon, Ferg. Soon."

He raised a quizzical eyebrow at her, but let it go, sending one last afterthought. *"If it doesn't, ye make sure and let me know. I'll help ye roast his balls this time."*

She pulled away laughing as Kyran reclaimed her by his side. "Do I want to know what that was all about?"

"Nye," she said with a smile, leaning into his arm around her waist. She liked the possessive way he held her but was surprised he was showing it here. Concerned, she took a step away.

He raised a brow in question, hating the distance between them.

"Might be smart to not be so affectionate here. She's walking towards us."

"Agreed, my apologies." He turned a huge smile on the queen as she joined them but shared one last thought with her. *"I just can't help myself. When you're next to me, I instinctively want to reach out and touch you."*

Rhyanna stifled a smile, pleased by his admission. She felt like they had come a long way today, and she was trying to relax and get through this meal.

As they made their way to the table, Rhyanna's nervousness increased as she noticed the seating arrangements. It appeared Kyran would be across from her instead of next to her. She tightened her grip on his arm and his eyes met hers, concerned.

"What is it, my lady?"

"I thought we'd be seated together. I'm just nervous about being on my own."

"I'm right across from you, and Ferg will be next to me." He smiled down at her. "If you need anything, you just use our bridge, my lady, and I will make our excuses to leave."

She gave him a cheeky look and asked, *"Can't ye make them for us now? I'm eager for ye to finally bed me."*

He groaned inwardly as he sent back, *"Rhyanna, how will I ever sit through this meal comfortably?"*

"Hopefully ye won't; it will motivate ye to get us out of here much sooner."

Kyran pulled out her chair for her, then walked around the table to his seat. He pulled his chair out to sit, and as his hips touched his chair, the queen piped up from the head of the table, "Kyran, come. I've saved ye a seat with yer family. Come, join us," she said as her eyes challenged him to refuse her. She patted the seat next to her, making sure he was out of Rhyanna's view. He gazed longingly at Rhyanna as he said, "Of course, Your Majesty."

As he moved to join her, Meriel sent Rhyanna a wicked little smile, and her voice popped into Rhyanna's head on the community line. *"Ye can never compete in this arena, little girl. Why don't ye go home and cry to Mommy Madylyn. She can threaten to spank me all she wants, but what she doesn't understand is that she doesn't scare me. I thrive in chaos and look forward to the challenge she has issued. Hmm, all this uproar over you. I don't understand the attraction, and honestly, I've tried."*

Rhyanna's face lost all color as she met Meriel's eyes without fear. It took a tremendous effort to keep her emotions neutral and cushion her links to Fergus and to Kyran. As hard as she tried to ignore the barb, she couldn't stop herself from sending a reply. *"Not surprising, Your Majesty. How can one of yer caliber of evil comprehend kindness, compassion, or basic human decency? It exists outside the limited scope of your twisted imagination."*

Anger flashed quickly across the queen's face, but just as quickly, it was masked under the honey-sweet smile she kept plastered on her face every time she gaped at Kyran.

Ferg's voice whispered through her head in warning. *"Rhy, honey, don't go poking at any bears, love. I ken she's baiting you, but ye needs ignore her taunts and just keep smiling at me like yer having the time of yer life."*

Rhyanna sent him the requested smile, true as could be, in gratitude for what he was trying to do for her. *"I'm so very grateful yer here, Ferg. Have I told ye that?"*

"Ye jest did, lass. And pleased, I am, to be by yer side as well. Yer looking lovely tonight, Mistress Rhyanna."

"Aw, Ferg, stop."

"King Varan," the butler announced as the king wandered into the dining hall. The entire table stood as one and bowed or curtsied deeply to their ruling monarch. Fergus and Rhyanna watched him closely. He seemed to have a tough time walking in a straight line. His eyes were rheumy, and his face paler than the white tablecloth in front of them. His dirty blond hair was limp and lifeless around his face, and he hadn't bothered to shave in days, evidenced by the patchy growth on his face.

"Sit." King Varan motioned to them all. He sat at the head of the table with the queen on his left and Kyran next to her. A hefty swig of his wine signaled for the meal to begin. He spoke briefly to the woman on his right, an elderly woman who held a high-level position in court. They laughed over a comment he made, and she leaned closer to him to better hear what he was saying.

Rhyanna continued to subtly watch him throughout the evening, looking for signs of what was causing his illness. She studied everyone at the table, wondering if it could be someone other than the queen who had something to gain by harming him.

Carefully sipping at her wine, she picked at her meal. It was truly lovely, and any other time, she would have taken the time to enjoy it. Today, she managed to only keep down a few small bites. Rainbow trout stuffed with herbs and wild rice made the rounds, followed by pork roasted with apples and raisins, then quail stuffed with honeyed pears were offered. The meats were accompanied by roasted vegetables and heavily seasoned mushrooms simmered in red wine. Rhy tried to smile and made polite conversation with the women on either side of her as the night went by painfully slow.

Rhyanna finished all she could force herself to eat when she realized the table had grown silent. Her gaze went to Ferg in a panic as she realized the king had spoken to her. "I'm sorry, Yer Highness, would ye please repeat the question? I'm afraid I didn't hear thee." She bowed as deeply as she was able to in her chair. She dared not glance at Kyran because she could feel his concern radiating through her and figured Meriel would be tittering over her discomfort.

"Of course, my lady," he said kindly with a smile. At that moment, he was so much like an older version of his son, she couldn't help but return the smile with a genuine one of her own.

"Careful, lass." Ferg's voice rattled through her head. *"He's a womanizer, and ye're one fine lookin' woman, Rhy. Never forget that."*

As she met the monarch's eyes, something in his demeanor changed. His eyes followed her like a predator scenting prey. Grateful for Ferg's warning, she toned down the smile and waited for the question.

"Rumors of your healing abilities and the Heart Island Sanctuary have reached me for some time, my lady. We're honored to have you join us for a visit. May your stay be pleasant, and your worries be none."

"A little late for that," Rhy thought, but she nodded her head as she met his gaze, answering honestly. "Apart from some inconveniences when I first arrived, I'm enjoying the splendor of yer court, Yer Majesty."

"I do hope you will partake of its many opportunities for pleasure, my lady. Indulge all your fantasies and your desires while you're here. If you have any issues, please come to me directly, my lady, so I may personally see to your comfort."

King Varan's eyes darkened with desire when he spoke to her as if none of the others existed. His innuendos clearly implied the help he was offering. She couldn't see Kyran, but she could feel the barely contained rage he had for her.

Uncomfortable, Rhy nodded and hoped he would move on, forgetting her. She picked up her wine and took a small sip, watching her alcohol intake while in this den of iniquity.

Dessert arrived looking wonderfully decadent, yet the fluffy chocolate mousse and fresh raspberries tasted like ashes in her mouth.

Rhyanna thought she'd made it through the night unscathed until the bubble-headed woman to her right turned to her and clapped her hands together. "I finally remembered where I know you from, lass. Well, not you, per se, but your name." She giggled loudly, drawing attention from the head of the table once again.

"Why, this morning, while I was in Prince Kyran's bed going down on him, he called me by your name—twice. It's a beautiful name but rare. I'd never heard it before, so I know that's where it was from. Anyways, later, when he was pounding away behind me, he was growling it like he wasn't sure if he wanted to fuck you or hate you."

Her laugh was grating as she continued, oblivious to the distress she was causing. "He kept saying he was going to fuck ye out of his system once and for all." She reached over and touched Rhyanna's arm, mock whispering to her. "I must confess," she whispered lower now, "I've been with the old man, and the apple doesn't fall far from the tree. I don't understand what the history is between the two of you, but I can honestly say he was the best lay I've ever had. I'll take him if you're done with him."

With a saccharin smile plastered to her lips, Rhy turned to the woman and said, "He's all yers, me lady. I believe I've had my fill."

The words barely left her mouth when tears threatened to unleash. Kyran's voice rang through her head. *"Rhyanna, don't! Please, my lady, don't do this until we have a chance to talk."*

Ferg popped online, weighing in once more. *"Lass, don't be doing something ye'll soon regret. There's been enough of that in this day already."*

Rhyanna couldn't look at either of them. Her gaze was molded to the beautiful flowers adorning the table in front of her. Late spring blooms in vibrant colors mocked her in the center. How could something so beautiful, something she had always found such joy in, now only represent the end of something else equally as beautiful? This was the image that would remain in her mind long after she left this horrid place. It was the image of goodbye.

Rhyanna refused to look at Ferg because she couldn't take any more excuses. She couldn't look at Kyran, or her heart would overrule her senses. And goddess help her, she didn't dare look at the queen's smug smile, or she would be too damn tempted to leap across the table and slap it off her heavily painted face.

Rhy's inner switchboard buzzed from two lines simultaneously. Ferg and Kyran both weighed in with the same word. *"LIES!"* Fergus shouted at her. *"LOOK AT ME, LASS."*

Then Kyran came through with, *"I swear on my mother's life, I was with no one after I saw you this morning."*

Rhyanna couldn't help but ask. *"Were you with someone before you saw me this morning, Kyran?"* she inquired, receiving no response. She wanted to look at him and see the truth on his face, but still, her view of him was blocked. *"I think I deserve an answer, my lord. Have you been fecking the lovely women of this court since your return?"* she spoke much too calmly. *"I overheard a pretty little blonde bragging about you in the halls. She had an orgy with ye, Dashiel, and I believe Elise."*

157

"My lady, can we please talk about this later when we meet?" he asked somberly.

"It's a fairly straightforward question, Kyran. A yes or no will suffice," she said tartly. *"Did you feck this woman today, last week, or anytime over the last month?"*

"It's not as straightforward as they would have you believe, my lady," he sent back stiffly. *"But if you must know, I awoke this morning in a dream state to that whore sucking my cock and my body on the verge of release. Her hair was down and covering her face, and half asleep, I mistook her for you. I didn't fuck her. She was fucking me, and when she turned and got on her hands and knees, I thought I was still dreaming as I took her from behind, calling your name."*

He paused for a moment before continuing. *"The second she opened her mouth to speak, I knew it was not you, and I was so ashamed of what I had done that I threw her out of my room, a room she had no business being in to begin with. I did not invite her nor encourage her to seek me out. You must believe me. You're the only woman I want to be with and the only one who has been on my mind constantly."*

Rhyanna closed her eyes and took a ragged breath. Her fingernails were drawing blood in her palms as she squeezed them shut as tightly as possible.

Fergus chose to pipe in once more. *"He's telling the truth, lass. As much as it hurts, as wrong as the whole fecking thing is, he's not lying to you."*

"No, Ferg, he's not lying to me at the moment, but the sins of omission are the ones that always topple kingdoms. Are they not?"

She took a deep breath as she pondered what to say to make him understand the level of devastation she was feeling.

"How many others are there that he has deemed unimportant for my pretty little mind to worry over? Trust is everything to me, and as long as he remains here, we will never have it. We both know who wins in this ultimatum, and truly, I don't blame him. Family is everything, and he should see to their health and protection. My love can't compete with that. I'll lose my mind wondering where he is and who he's doing if he remains in this place. And my heart," a wave of grief battered him on their line, *"my heart can't take being broken and glued back together over and over and over. I can't do this right now. I'm leaving."*

Ferg's line went eerily silent as he pulled back, not knowing what to say. She looked across the table at his solemn face, and his eyes seemed to ask her, *"What do you want me to do, lass?"* She shook her head no at him. She wanted nothing from him at the moment.

The queen turned to speak to someone else, and Rhy finally had direct sight of Kyran. His face was drawn, and his eyes begged her to understand, begged her to forgive him.

"Kyran, the opportunity to tell me about this came before dinner when we laid all our cards on the table. Ye must know that. Ye were going to come feck me tonight after having been in that woman this morning, and ye honestly thought I'd be all right with that? Do ye know me at all?" she projected all her disappointment and hurt into her message.

Abruptly, she stood and curtsied deeply to the king and queen. "My sincerest apologies, Yer Majesties. There is an urgent matter on Heart Island that needs attending. Me Laird, I beg yer leave, so that I may gather my things and return. It's a serious matter, and I must not delay. Please excuse me, Yer Majesty." Her last plea she sent directly to the king, batting her eyes for a moment to help get his sympathy.

"Of course, Mistress Rhyanna. You must promise to come back as soon as you are able to," he said, standing and coming to her side. He leaned down and kissed the top of her hand. "I would like to get to know you better, my lady," he whispered as she withdrew herself from his touch.

"I'm incredibly grateful yer so understanding, Me Laird. My apologies to your guests for the disruption. I'll be on my way."

Without another look back, she left the room, walking slowly, the picture of imperial calm. As soon as she was out of sight of the dining room, she lifted her dress, removed her sandals, and started running down the hall leading to her suite. She was leaving tonight, with or without Fergus. Her heart couldn't take any more pain today. She had almost reached her room when she heard Kyran shouting her name.

"Rhyanna, please don't leave. Please talk to me," he yelled as he approached her quickly from the opposite end of the hall.

He looked like hell, and Rhy knew if she stayed, she would give in. Unfortunately for him, she felt like she'd given in more than enough for one day. She turned and eyed the distance to the door of her room as he closed in on her and then did the only thing, she could think of to survive having her heart broken twice in one day.

As Kyran neared with his hand reaching out to grab her arm, she gazed at him sadly and said, "Goodbye Kyran," with tears running down her face and her raw emotions on display for him to see. As his fingers desperately tried to reach her, she disappeared right from under him.

Rhyanna teleported to the portal and tried to find the location she needed on the map through bleary eyes. Reaching for the first thing she recognized, she made her way back to the mainland, once again alone and disenchanted.

CHAPTER TWENTY-EIGHT

Wellesley

Jameson paced the gazebo, waiting for Maddy and Ronan to arrive. His mind was still struggling to come to terms with the horrors Danny had shared from her past.

Part of him was grateful she'd finally confided in him because it helped explain a lot of her behavior. The nightmares, the heavy drinking, the endless parade of men, and the distance she kept everyone at, it all made sense now. Completely horrifying, tragic fucking sense.

Jamey closed his eyes, still able to feel her in his arms. Her scent lingered. She smelled like thunderstorms and cloves, sweet and spicy with unpredictable heat and a splash of danger mixed in. His shoulder was still damp where her tears soaked his shirt, and he wished he were still cradling her, making her feel safe from the horrors of her past.

His mind couldn't help but relive every word she uttered, every bit of pain and torture she'd survived. Jamey couldn't begin to imagine the hell Danny had been exposed to at such an early age or how she had managed to come out of it and become the warrior she was today.

Terrifying at times, yes, she could be, but she was also one of the most loyal, dedicated, and competent partners he'd ever had the privilege of working with. They had been together for decades, and he couldn't imagine trusting anyone else to have his back.

Jamey knew she needed him to forget about tonight, but that would be like forgetting her name. Never gonna happen. What he could do, though, was pretend she'd successfully compelled him to set her mind at ease and return to business as usual. He fucking hated doing that.

Roaring his pain into the night, he hauled off and pounded his fist into the thick wall of the gazebo, doing nothing more than shredding his knuckles. But damn, it felt good and took away part of the fury building up inside. His fingers elongated as claws emerged from the tips. His eyesight sharpened, and he knew his eyes were glowing with the unholy light that accompanied a change. Tendons relaxed, and joints loosened, his body ready to allow him to shift into his other form.

This form, he kept muzzled and tightly leashed at all times because it wasn't safe to be around him when he shifted. He lost all sense of his surroundings, and even the people he loved had a tough time reigning him in. This was the reason Jameson always kept his emotions tightly under control. Terrible things happened when he let his inner beast loose.

Jamey moved to the railing, listening to the crashing waves below and waited for Maddy and Ronan's arrival while trying to hold onto his humanity. A slight shudder in the basement announced the portal was in use. Footsteps on the stairs behind him alerted him to their presence.

He continued facing the water, willing it to soothe his ragged emotions and racing heart. If only the waves could carry away the horror stories he had heard. His claws grasped the rail in front of him, the wood creaking with the strain he put on it.

Madylyn crossed the room cautiously, sensing how close he was to a shift from the energy he emitted. Ronan put an arm around her middle, halting her before stepping in front of her. He'd worked with dangerous animals long enough to recognize what was in front of him.

"What kind of shifter is he, Maddy?" he asked, not wanting to draw Jamey's attention to them.

"Grizzly."

"Fuck me," he sent back, assessing the exits as she once again moved around him.

"Ronan, he will never harm me, even in this form."

"Not willing to take that chance," he snapped, *"with either of you."*

She turned to him and framed his face with her hands before kissing him softly. *"Trust me on this, my love. I would never jeopardize our child."* She pulled away but not before adding, *"Don't make me freeze you in place."*

"You wouldn't!"

"Wouldn't I?" she asked with a cocky glance over her shoulder.

Ignoring him completely and focusing on the shifter in front of her who was hanging on by a thread, she proceeded with caution. "Jameson," she said softly, "You asked us to come here and talk to you about Danny?"

A deep pain-filled growl filled the night, scattering the pigeons roosting in the rafters.

Maddy moved two steps closer. "I know you care for her, Jamey. We all do." Another step took her closer as she tried to ignore Ronan's concern flooding her.

"Maddy, be careful," Ronan said. She was proud of him for not trying to tell her what to do even though the intent came through in his tone.

Jameson's claws dug into the railing he clutched, shredding the wood. His head lowered as she came closer.

"You remember me, Jamey, and you don't want to hurt me. We need to talk about Danny. I need you to come back to us. You hear and recognize my voice. Fight the change and come back to me. You can't help her like this."

Maddy stood to his right even with him. As Ronan inched closer, she reached out and laid her hand on top of Jamey's partially shifted one, soothing him. Ignoring Ronan's concern screaming through their link, she kept on talking to him.

"Danny's special. She's beautiful, funny, tough, and terribly insecure." Her hand tucked into his as his claws retracted, and the fur faded away as if it had never been there.

"Danny needs someone strong enough to hold her tight and not let her run away when things are difficult. She needs a man who cares enough to work through her issues and loves her more because of what she endured. She needs someone like you, Jamey—someone who already loves her exactly as she is today, and who won't let the horror, guilt, or the shame of her past come between you. Are you strong enough to be that man?"

Jameson finally turned towards her then. The tendons were standing out in his jaw from the tightly leashed control he had over his grizzly, but his whiskey-colored eyes were still backlit with an amber glow. He didn't speak, and his eyes didn't change, but his hand closed around hers tightly, clinging to the lifeline she offered.

"I know you're the man she needs. I'm also aware that she'll fight it every step of the way by thinking she's not good enough for you and that you deserve someone more pristine."

"That's utter horse shit," he finally managed to choke out. "She's perfect exactly as she is."

"She is, isn't she?" Maddy said, smiling up at him. "Take it slow, but don't let her pull away from you." She laughed. "She'll try, and she'll challenge you at every step."

"I look forward to it," he said with a sad smile. "What are her triggers?" he asked, his voice breaking as his hand tightened painfully on hers.

"How much did she tell you?"

"Danny said that she was sold, by her mother, for fucks sake." He pulled away as the violence threatened to return. "I know that she was repeatedly assaulted." He closed his eyes, physically ill knowing what they had done to her.

"As bad as you think it is, Jamey," tears fell as Maddy remembered the devastated child she had found, "it's worse."

"Why does she think it's not safe for her facing someone?" he wondered aloud. "The only way she'll have sex is with men behind her. She's said more than once, 'It's not safe.'"

Maddy shuddered at the memory she was about to share. "The only thing I can imagine is the way I found her."

Ronan joined them then, sliding his arms around her from behind, offering comfort. She gratefully leaned against him as she prepared herself to tell the rest of the story.

"Danny was chained in the basement of a high-priced brothel, servicing sexual deviants who preferred children. She was in the middle of a cell with her arms chained above her head while two men assaulted her at the same time." She shuddered, remembering it.

"I could hear her screaming from upstairs, and by the time I reached her, she had taken matters into her own hands. This tiny, pitiful, damaged child ripped out the throat of the man facing her. The spray of his blood soaked the front of her as her blood ran down her legs from the brutality of the assault. As his partner tried to pry her off him, she clung tighter. When she finally released him, he was dead."

"Good. I was wondering how many of the fuckers would be left for me to kill," Jameson snarled.

"I executed the other one," she said without an ounce of remorse. "The owners were long gone when we arrived—tipped off somehow that we were coming. I gave Danny a choice, and she chose to join us and never look back." Her chest filled with pride. "And she never has."

"Her nightmares?"

"That is the only time she revisits the horrors she lived through. Rhyanna gives her something to help with the night terrors, but it only works if she takes it, hasn't drunk too much, and isn't exhausted.

"Her father?"

"Died the winter before, leaving her mam with half a dozen starving kids and very little options. Danny was one of those options to try to save the others."

"Did she save them?" he asked bitterly. "Was her sacrifice worth it?"

"I'm not sure. I thought at one point she may have looked for them, but she never told me if she found them."

Jameson ran his hands through his hair before letting out a shuddering breath. "I love her, Maddy."

"I know you do, honey."

"I don't want to be a casual fling for her. I want it all, and now I am terrified of pushing her away or triggering something that she can't get past emotionally or sexually."

"It won't be easy. I can guarantee you that. What you need to ask yourself is this; is she worth the commitment it will take, the mistakes you both will make, her doing and saying things you abhor, and her doing everything in her power to make you give up on her?"

"Absolutely."

"Can you forgive her if she falls back on past behaviors? Can you still love her when she wants nothing to do with you? Can you tolerate her trying to compel you repeatedly to forget and to move on from her, or using other men to disgust you? Because I can assure you, that's what she will do to chase you away."

"I'm more resilient than she realizes." He laughed ruefully. "And more stubborn than she can begin to imagine."

"She's lucky to be the one you love, Jamey." Maddy sighed as she looked at the moonlight on the rough waves. "We will all help you any way that we can, but the emotional and psychological battle you face will not be easy."

"Bring it on," he said with a hint of that growl back in his voice. "When have you ever known me to back down from a fight?"

A hint of a smile crossed her face. "Never. You have my blessing, Jamey, not that you need it. You also need to consider whether you will be able to continue working as partners. Will your personal life interfere with your safety on missions? Will it be too much of a distraction?"

Maddy held up a hand as he took a breath to answer. "You have a lot to think about, and I don't want an answer today. You have a long road ahead of you, but if it endangers our team, I will ask you both to pair up with someone else."

"Fair enough," he said, understanding where she was coming from. "You have my word; I will come to you if we can't work together."

"I'm counting on it."

He looked over her shoulder at Ronan. "Thank you for bringing her and for not attacking me when you were within your rights to do so."

"Thank you for pulling your shit together and not making me," Ronan said. "For what it's worth, I have first-hand knowledge about being held against your will and forced to do things you could never imagine just to stay alive. Be patient with her and be kind. Remind her that you aren't afraid of her demons. They won't chase you away. Be. There. Consistently. Even when it gets hard and you're not sure if you want to anymore. Don't give up on her." He pulled Maddy closer and softly kissed her neck. "I promise it will be worth it."

Jameson nodded at him, understanding. Ronan and Maddy had their own tortured past, and if ever there was a lesson in patience, their love story was it. Maddy hadn't wanted to give him another chance, but Ronan hadn't given up. He stuck it out, getting Maddy to listen to him and finally trust him again. Expecting a child, they couldn't be happier now if they tried.

"Sorry for dragging you both out in the middle of the night."

"Don't you dare apologize." Maddy stepped away from Ronan and hugged Jamey tightly. "I've been waiting for the two of you to get this show started."

Jameson chuckled. "That obvious, are we?"

"Only to those of us who can't help but see."

"Everyone but Danny and I then," he said with a chuckle.

"Well, not everyone.... G'night, Jamey."

"Night, Maddy." He nodded at Ronan. "Thank you."

Ronan returned his nod, offering his hand. As they shook, he offered one last piece of advice. "Sometimes, the best thing you can do to help them is to give them some space. Don't make her feel cornered. She'll come back around after a while; just give her the time she needs to settle."

"You're right. I need to treat her like a skittish foal," Jamey laughed ruefully, "and forget that she ever told me anything at all. That's going to be a tough one."

"It will be," Ronan agreed, "but she's worth it."

Jamey watched the couple depart and drew courage from their story. Separated for centuries, they found peace, forgiveness, and hope in each other after nothing but anger and ashes survived their separation. If they could find the happiness they did, he knew that he and Danny could also find it. The family they were now, with Ronan's son, Landon, and a child of their own on the way, was a fine example of the family he wanted with his hellion. He wanted a future surrounded by friends and family and someone to look forward to coming home to at the end of the day. He craved a home filled with love and laughter, and someday, sons and daughters. Now he just needed to find a way to convince Danny that the future they could create was worth taking a chance on.

CHAPTER TWENTY-NINE

Will This Fecking Day Ever End?

Rhyanna stepped out of the portal in Clayton to a fine mist. "Jest great," she yelled at the overcast sky. "Will this fecking day ever end?"

In her bare feet, she walked to town in her silk dress. Too exhausted from teleporting and too emotional from this nightmare of a day, Rhy couldn't even bother to try to use her magic to keep herself dry.

By the time she reached the Rusty Tap, her dress was clinging indecently to her body, and her makeup was running down her face. Her hair hung limply, and indeed, she looked and felt like something the cat had dragged in.

She entered the tavern and limped to the bar, grateful that Carsyn was working. Her feet left muddy footprints on the floor with splotches of blood mixed into the mess.

She took the towel Carsyn handed her and tried to clean up her face. As Carsyn raised an eyebrow in question, Rhy raised a hand to stop her. "Jest don't even fecking ask." She could see Carsyn was trying not to smile. "Lass, get me three fingers of top-shelf whiskey on the rocks, please, and leave the bottle. Is me tab still good here, or has Fergus drunk it all up?"

Carsyn smiled and chuckled as she poured her drink. "Bottoms up, Rhy. Looks to me like ye need it." She picked up the bottle to return it when Rhy snapped her fingers at her, pointed her finger at the bottle, and then down at the bar. She managed this while tossing the entire glass down.

"Ye've got that right." She stood, taking the bottle with her. "Make sure an give yerself a generous tip, Syn. I've always liked ye, lass."

"Thank ye, Rhy."

Rhy waved over her shoulder at her and took the bottle to stand in front of the hearth and dry her dress out. The damn thing clung to her like a second skin, and she had already gotten one too many inappropriate glances from the resident drunks. With her back to the fire so she could watch those around her, she almost missed Roarke walking in and heading for the private chamber in the back. Curious, she watched him, his body language telling her all she needed to know about what he was doing. Whatever it was, was either personal or illegal.

Roarke did a double-take as he noticed her by the fire. Curious, he walked over to check on her. "Lass, what are ye doing here by yerself and at this time of night? Jameson and Danny have already left, and there's been no sighting tonight of Fergus."

He eyed the men left in the bar. "You shouldn't be out here alone, especially in that." He pointed at the dripping dress still molded to her. Her nipples were tight and visible through the fabric, and damned if she couldn't help but smile when his glance stopped there for a second.

Groaning, he took off his jacket and handed it to her. At her confused look, he reached for the bottle. "May I have this for a moment, Rhyanna?"

"Of course, Roarke, I wanted ye to have a drink with me." Her voice was slurring, and her stability was questionable. She leaned toward him and whispered. "Am I keeping ye from yer business out back?"

He looked at her sharply and said curtly. "I've no business out back, mistress. Ye must be mistaken."

His sharp tone made her snap her eyes to his, and in them, she saw the warning he gave her as he held out his long leather duster for her to don before returning her bottle.

"Of course, I am. Before you leave, Roarke, find me and join me for a drink."

He nodded before heading to the bar and motioning to Carsyn. "Keep yer eye on her for me, won't ye please?" he asked with a wink and left her an extra tip on the bar.

"Already am," she said, tucking the bill into her corset.

"By giving her a bottle?" he asked, laughing.

"Fire will keep her in here. The bottle will keep her from wandering too far."

"I applaud your strategy." He chuckled. "I'll make sure she gets back to the island when I leave."

"Glad to hear it," Carsyn said as she turned to another customer flagging her down.

"It will be my pleasure," he said under his breath. He returned to Rhyanna and said, "If you need anything before I return, Rhy, talk to Carsyn. You understand?"

167

"Aye, captain, she said, slurring her words. "I'll be waiting right here for ye, love!" she hollered when he was halfway across the room.

Roarke gave her a half-wave as he chuckled and continued on his way. He was almost to the back door when he heard her holler.

"And thanks for the bloody jacket, too!"

Shaking his head, he moved on, hoping she didn't find unwanted trouble before he returned. Somehow, he doubted her ability to stay out of it in the condition she was in. He couldn't help but wonder what had made her turn to alcohol, and how much of it had to do with Kyran?

CHAPTER THIRTY

Door to the Dark World

After leaving Carsyn with instructions to watch Rhyanna, Roarke made his way to the back of the building. Near the back entrance was another door that only opened to those who knew the password.

Roarke spoke the magic words and was allowed entrance. Walking quickly with a hand on the dagger at his side, he entered a dank tunnel leading to a platform and a steep staircase outside. The ancient metal stairway creaked in protest as he descended. He often wondered if it would collapse under him on one of his late-night trips down it.

At the bottom, he stepped onto the long, wooden boardwalk with a narrow lane of doors on the right that offered entrance to the hidden world of dark deals and forbidden pleasures. Roarke had rarely entered this place before Rosella's disappearance, but lately, he'd become a regular in this hidden world.

He'd put the word out on the street that rewards would be forthcoming for information about the darker inner circles dealing in the flesh trade. With the right contacts and a lot of discretion, one might purchase any form of pleasure one wanted. Men, women, children of both sexes, multiple partners, freaks of nature, bondage, submission, and role-playing, there was a door for all of it.

With the proper bribes, no questions were asked, nor authorities called in response to the screams ringing through the thin walls along the lane.

In addition to one's personal pleasure for the evening, one might also find the option to purchase the same types of pleasure on a more permanent basis. Mistresses were set up in their own homes. Slaves were sold to live in

169

cages of basements if they were lucky. Rumors of sacrificial offerings were hinted at. Drugs of any kind, poisons, thugs for hire, mercenaries for contract killings, small security squads who didn't hesitate to maim or kill, and more important than the things and people for sale, were the network of spies available for hire. Information was king, and reliable information was worth a king's ransom.

This hellhole was where Roarke slowly made himself at home even though his skin crawled every time he made the rounds. He became a regular at the underground taverns and ingratiated himself with the flesh peddlers by paying for high-class whores. Then he turned around and paid the whores to keep their mouths shut about the fact that the only sport he sought with them was the information they provided him.

He made it clear to the lovely ladies of the night that he would pay them twice what their pimps charged as long as they kept their mouths shut and spoke of it to none.

Roarke suffered through a few blow jobs until he found women he felt were worth trusting and who trusted him not to be local enforcers for their pimps. He made it worth more than they ever imagined, and they relayed information to him on his weekly visits.

Tonight, he was going to visit Raelyn, a curvaceous brunette with an old European dialect. Raelyn was a safe bet; she kept her mouth shut and was willing to rent out her room as easily as the space between her legs. She was one of the few he believed was clean enough to touch him on the rare occasion he felt the need. She was high-end and did things with her tongue that made him forget his name.

On one drunken occasion, he allowed Raelyn to please him, and then he returned the favor, a bonus for the high-priced whore. Since that night, she always tried to entice him back into her bed. Her attempts failed miserably as Roarke's fondness for the ladies of the night faded as his interest in a certain healer peaked. He knew he stood no chance, but he preferred to keep himself clean in the unlikely event the fates smiled down on him.

Through Raelyn, he found a connection to the network he believed was responsible for kidnapping girls on the river and for convincing young runaways they would find safer, easier work on a floating brothel.

The wayward girls didn't realize, though, a floating brothel was no different from a permanent one, save for the fact you were trapped on it with no ability to walk away. They escaped one hellhole for an iron prison with nowhere to go but down—down to the ship's stables, or down to a watery grave if you tried to escape.

Roarke knocked on Raelyn's door and waited for her to answer. He heard voices inside and assumed she was finishing up with a client. The voices rose, and he became concerned for her welfare until the door finally opened.

Raelyn stood, blocking the inner sanctuary of her bower. She faced Roarke, and he saw a bruise taking form on her right cheekbone. He stepped closer and reached out to trace it gently.

"This just happen?" he asked in a whisper.

"It's nothing. I've dealt with worse," she said. Her lips smiled, but her eyes were terrified as she spoke loudly. "Tonight's not a suitable time for me. I'm no longer on the market, sir. Trample off, darling."

Roarke sidled closer and slipped an arm around her. He threaded his fingers through hers as he nuzzled her neck and whispered in her ear, "You have company?" Softer, he added, "Squeeze my hand once for yes and twice for no."

One squeeze.

"Your pimp?" he asked as his hand roamed over her back, and he sucked on her neck like a drunk customer trying to change her mind.

Two this time.

"Someone who scares you more than him?"

One firm grasp

"Is he suspicious of what we've been doing?"

One squeeze, harder this time.

"Listen, Sugar, I'd love to let ye in, but I'se already gots me a handful to take care of right now. Ye move along now. Try Cherry two doors down. She's not as good as me, mind ye, but she's clean, and she'll give ye a good ride."

"Can I come back later?" he whispered, looking into her eyes and seeing the flash of panic there.

Two squeezes.

"I'm sorry, love, my services have been purchased by a higher bidder, and I'm no longer available. If ye return, my security team might not take too kindly to it. So ye best stay away from now on."

Roarke tried not to let his frustration show, as she was obviously terrified of someone. He leaned in once more. "I promise I'll help you, love, if you would only ask. You know how to reach me. Send word if I can do anything."

He saw the gratitude race through her eyes as he listed drunkenly against her. "One last kiss, lass, afore ye kick me to the curb," he slurred thickly.

She bent down and kissed him thoroughly, whispering, "I am so sorry, Roarke. Check out back before you leave."

"Get on with ye now, and make sure ye tell Cherry I sent ye her way, and she owes me one," she said in a loud voice, dismissing him publicly.

Deciphering her cryptic message, he staggered two doors down. The door shook under the weight of his fist as he pounded on it. A gorgeous petite redhead opened the door, and Roarke was pleased to see one of the girls he'd met through Raelynn in the past. She and Raelynn were close, and he trusted her to help him.

"Must be my lucky day," she said as she grabbed his shirt with two fists and pulled him inside.

"You remember me?" Roarke asked, suddenly sober.

"Sure do, handsome," the redhead said as she twirled a long lock of her hair.

"Raelynn said you might be willing to help me out and that you owed her one."

Her countenance changed, and the bubble-headed bimbo was gone, replaced by a woman of action. "What do you need?"

"She told me to look out back before I leave. Can you get me out there without being seen?"

"Sure can," she said, "come with me." She took him through the sitting room and down a hall that led past a bathroom complete with a soaking tub, a bedroom fit for a queen, and a small kitchen. A back door led out of the kitchen into a dark alley.

Roarke stopped before heading out. He turned and handed her a wad of cash, which she started to refuse.

"Listen to me," he commanded, "they will be following up on my visit. You show them what I paid you, and you will be safe." He pulled off several larger bills. "Split this with Raelynn and tell her to let me know if she needs anything. I didn't intend to bring harm to her doorstep, but I am afraid that is exactly what I have done."

"Thank you, Roarke," she said in a husky voice, "from both of us. You just made it so we both can escape from this hell hole." Tears shimmered in her eyes as she raised on her tiptoes and kissed his cheek.

"Find me on the south side of the pier if you need anything, either of you, you hear?"

She nodded as he stepped out the back door and watched her close it behind him.

He was supposed to meet an informant in Raelynn's chamber who witnessed one of the yachts recently anchored offshore. The ship was being emptied for emergency repairs while the occupants sought shelter on the adjacent beach.

The informant would arrive at midnight on his rounds of the dark docks. Going by the name of Samson, he worked both sides of the network, taking all he could from one without hurting his chances on the other.

Roarke peered at his watch and saw midnight was only minutes away. He turned to the right and kept to the shadows as he made his way back to Raelynn's back door. He stepped into an alcove to avoid the light when he felt a dagger poking at his kidney. An arm came around his neck, holding him still.

Roarke raised both hands to show he wasn't armed. The arm around his neck loosened and pushed him away

Roarke spun around to find a man with ebony skin who towered over him by a foot. His hair was tightly braided into thin rows with colorful blue beads woven throughout. As Roarke met his gaze, he realized the beads matched his startling pale blue eyes The contrast between his eyes and his skin turned an average man into a uniquely handsome one.

"Samson?" he asked.

The man nodded, his gaze following Roarke's every move.

"Roarke Gallagher," he said. "I believe you may have some information for me."

"Whatchya offering for it?" the man thundered at him. His voice vibrated like the depths of hell.

"Name your price, sir," Roarke said, his voice vibrating with sincerity.

Samson was a quiet man, an observer. His skills were honed to listen and evaluate the information he happened upon. The second part of his skill was finding the right buyer for the information he possessed.

Samson sensed the desperation of the man in front of him. The smell of concern and fear of the unknown polluted the surrounding air. Samson had heard whispers about a Gallagher on the search for his sister. This man would give him anything he wanted, but there was only one thing he was interested in.

"I wants me freedom, and I wants away from here." He watched Roarke carefully. "I wants a job on your ship, and double what you pay yer men."

"What makes you think I'll do that?"

"I've information on yer sister, and I'm worth every penny in more ways than the whores can ever be to ye."

Roarke looked at him dubiously. He couldn't afford to let any information go by, but he wasn't sure he trusted this man either.

"How do I know I can trust you?"

"You don't," he said in a voice ringing with honesty, "but I promise to do everything I can to help get yer sister back," he ran a hand through his long thin braids before adding, "because the bastards have my sister, too."

Roarke held out a hand. "Welcome aboard, Samson. And you better not be fucking with me. If you are, I will toss you overboard for chum in the deepest parts of the ocean."

Samson chuckled a deep rich sound. "Fair enough, Captain. Buy me a drink."

They wandered off, and Roarke couldn't help but wonder what the fuck he'd just gotten himself into.

CHAPTER THIRTY-ONE

The Wine, the Beer, and Much More Whiskey

Rhyanna watched Roarke walk away and wondered why she couldn't fall in love with him. He'd shown an interest in her, but she'd already considered herself Kyran's at that point.

Roarke was handsome, friendlier, and he traveled. She sighed, thinking of the exotic points of call he must visit. Following that line further, she started thinking of all the exotic women he must visit also, and there went her brief fantasy.

Warmed and drier from the fire and his jacket, she took a sip and looked around for any of the regulars. Odd. Tonight, she didn't find many familiar faces.

Stepping down off the ledge in front of the hearth, she tried to catch her balance and almost managed it. As she stepped off the six-inch stone, she landed on one of the deeper cuts on her foot, Wincing, she pulled it back up, which caused the fiasco that occurred next.

Losing her balance, she stumbled into the table beside her. It was one with men who had been eyeing her clinging attire...or lack thereof. She caught the shoulder of the sailor, who turned and snarled at her, while the one next to him pulled her down into his lap.

"What ave we here, Nelson?" he asked as his other hand tried to relieve her of her bottle.

"Methinks we've been given a gift on this miserable eve, me has." This, from the surly one with a balding head and rotten teeth. Cystic acne covered his face and looked painful as well as nasty.

Rhyanna might have been tipsy, but she had her wits about her just enough to hang onto the bottle.

"Begging yer pardon, sirs, I don't mean to interrupt yer games," she said politely.

"Yer not interrupting nothing worth doing lass," the one holding her said with a sneer. "Ye've jest brought us better sport." He laughed darkly, and his friend joined in.

Rhyanna's senses were sending up all kinds of warning signals, and even tipsy, she had the sense to listen.

The man whose lap she landed on had quick hands. Both had somehow managed to get under the jacket and were dangerously close to her breasts.

Shifting slightly, she positioned the bottle snugly against his groin, effectively capturing his family jewels in a damaging vice. To get his attention, she leaned her weight down on the bottle while giving him innocent eyes. "Problem is, sir," she slurred into his ear, "I'm nobody's sport, so yer gonna wanna be removing yer hands from me bosoms before ye sacrifice a body part. Ye ken?"

His eyes were wide and pissed off as he looked at her. "I ken, milady. Jest having some fun is all."

"Do I look like I'm having fun right now?" she asked as her eyes glittered maniacally at him.

"No, ma'am," he said, lifting his hands in a placating manner.

Standing awkwardly, she walked off, but not before turning back and saying, "Me apologies again for disrupting ye fine gentlemen."

She moved away towards one of the fine chairs that sat in front of the fire. Roarke's duster dragged the floor on her petite frame, and she absently thought about how dirty she was making it. She lifted the bottle and took another healthy sip.

"*Atta girl,*" her inner voice cheered as the alcohol woke her dark side up. "*Ye need to fecking lighten up. Pull up a chair and finish that fine swill yer holding.*"

Rhyanna sat, pulling her legs up under her and wrapping the jacket tightly around her front. She was swimming in it, and not just the length. Like Kyran, Roarke was a big man.

"*Bet he's big everywhere,*" naughty Rhy continued.

Rhyanna ignored her and kept cataloging his assets.

"*And what an ass it is,*" naughty Rhy cackled. She only came out to play when Rhyanna drank hard liquor, which is why she didn't very often. Alcohol turned off every one of her filters and let naughty Rhy loose.

Back to the man at hand. She giggled at the thought. Roarke was a dirty blond with bottomless, deep, dark, chocolate bedroom eyes. He entranced her with his kindness, his smiles, and his sincere hugs. Ye gad's, the man had dimples that made ye blush. Thinking about him warmed her inside. Or maybe t'was the whiskey.

"Yeah, right, blame it on the whiskey. It's called desire ye twit."

Rhyanna thought about the two men who had recently shown her attention. She'd been single for so long that it was odd to have so much attention now. Roarke had only been a friend and a fellow warden. Honestly, she hadn't thought much about him until recently when his niece, Hailey, kept telling her he had feelings for her.

"Yeah, feelings all right. All feels between his hips if ye ask me. And since ye did ask, I'd ride those feels like a fecking carnival pony…up…down…up."

"Piss off, Rhyanna hissed, and then realized those sitting closest to her were looking at her strangely. She smiled crookedly at them and raised her bottle in salute. "Carsyn," she hollered. "A round fer the house on me." Carsyn nodded, and the strangers staring at her moments before like she was crazy raised their glasses to her instead. She joined them, but this time when she drank, t'was more to shut the evil bitch up.

Roarke had been there for her when she'd broken down missing Kyran. His compassion and kindness while he held her had surprised her. Never once did he try taking advantage of her or bad-mouthing Kyran.

"Well, somebody ought to bad mouth Kyran, the fecker."

Ignoring her inner voice, Rhy pulled the duster close, inhaling Roarke's masculine scent. He smelled like fresh air and the sea with a whiff of clove cigarettes and whiskey. She snuggled into the security she found wrapped up in Roarke's essence.

"Ye really should unwrap him first so he can properly wrap around ye."

That was what Roarke made her feel, she decided—warm and secure, protected and taken care of. He also made her feel wanted and sexy without ever having touched her improperly. She was fairly certain if she had been with him during Maddy and Ronan's Melding, he would have never turned her down.

Blearily, she looked around at her surroundings. It had been such a long day, and such a bad one, that Rhyanna allowed herself the luxury of curling up in the common room of a tavern, nursing a bottle and comparing her two potential lovers. She giggled, thinking how ludicrous it seemed.

Kyran offered her safety by holding her too tight. His jealousy was a surprise to her as he had only ever been kind and sweet since she had met him. She sensed it came as a surprise to him as well. Steeped in the horrors of his court, she understood where he was coming from for some of it, but she had never given him a reason not to trust her.

Rhy couldn't tolerate the fact that he hadn't told her about the woman he had bedded just this morning. She wouldn't have been happy to hear about it, no two ways about that, but she wasn't known for making hasty decisions, especially important ones when angry, and there were ways to have found the truth of what truly happened. The whole situation was just the icing on the shit-cake of a day she had experienced, and her patience had long since fled.

Her nose brushed against the collar again, and the scent of Roarke was stronger. She moaned softly as she rubbed her face against it. Surrounded by the sensory overload, courtesy of Roarke, she turned her attention to Kyran and tried to remember how he made her feel and what she thought she was in love with.

Kyran was handsome, without a doubt. She didn't blame the women at the Court of Tears for wanting a piece of him. Six-and-a-half feet of solid man, she was tiny next to him. Another blond, she thought with a giggle, but Kyran's was thick, shoulder-length, and pale. She loved running her hands through his hair.

His eyes, though, yes, they were what stole her heart. Uniquely expressive, moody, and changeable, they captured her soul. His crystal blue gaze was calm and cool like the Caribbean on good days, but when he was angry, she could swear storm clouds rolled through, making them swirl with the dark gray rolling across them.

"Always loved storms, we did. Fitting ye find a man who can create them...just think what angry sex could be like..."

Clenching the bottle tighter so she didn't speak aloud again, she agreed that it might be fun sometime to see what happened after the clouds came.

"I'll probably never have the chance to know," she whispered sadly to herself, remembering the look of devastation and hurt on his face as she teleported as fast as possible away from him.

Her inner switchboard buzzed. Kyran was calling again. She debated answering, but her inner beast reminded her she was still furious.

"Don't answer the bastard. Let him sweat it out for a while."

Tears threatened as he tried to reach out to her again. It made her heart hurt to think of him, of them. So, she ignored his pleas. Tonight, she wanted to stop feeling and stop hurting for a wee bit. Was it too fecking much to ask? As he was the one causing such upheaval in her life, she decided that she'd turn him off for a bit.

Their relationship wasn't always like this. When they first met, she knew the second she laid eyes on him that he was her destiny.

"Lust will do that to ye."

Kyran made her feel like the most beautiful woman he had ever seen. She felt cherished and honored with his formal court manners and his kindness.

Cherished had transformed into overprotective. Destiny was derailed with a betrothal that he had no control over, and worst of all, lately, he treated her like a doll that was much too fragile to play with. He'd overridden her decisions about their sexual relationship, and she was still waiting for him to claim her.

"*Let's be honest, girlie, therein lies the majority of yer problem,*" Inner Rhy chimed in. "*Yer sexually frustrated and waiting fer him to fix the problem. Mayhap it's time fer ye to take matters into yer own hands and get the ball rolling!*"

As Rhyanna sat there musing, Roarke finally came out of the back. His face was pale, and he looked pissed off enough to kill someone as he slammed through the door leading out into the night.

Rhyanna sensed his anger and, more importantly, his sorrow. She might be a trainwreck herself, but she could still go after him and see if she might help ease his emotional state.

"*Ease him, that's right. Might jest be able to ease him right out of his breeches.*"

Groaning in frustration at her inner demon, she made her way unsteadily to her feet and hobbled out after him. Misery, loving company, and all that horse shite.

CHAPTER THIRTY-TWO

Why Did I Do That?

Danny left Jameson as quickly as humanly possible. She struggled to forget the dazed, hurt look he gave her the moment before she compelled him to forget everything she had said.

As soon as she'd gotten far enough away from him, she stripped and shifted into her peregrine form. Unable to run away from the thoughts tormenting her, she took to the dark sky and rode the air currents, seeking peace. She didn't find any.

Their encounter after the portal still unnerved her. Danny could still smell Jameson's scent on her as she glided. The unique combination of pine and leather that she always associated with him comforted and tormented her at the same time. His distinctive scent wrapped around her, infusing his essence into her pores, encouraging her to seek him out and finally give in to the sexual energy that was arcing between them lately. Her falcon shrieked her frustration.

The comfort she found as his arms tucked her in tight to his chest made her long to fall asleep with him wrapped around her. The murmur of his voice soothing her with a song continued playing on a loop in her mind. The rasp of his stubble against her cheek had increased her awareness of the virile male beneath her before the thought of him remembering the truths she'd shared with him horrified her.

Jameson was a wonderful man, and he deserved a woman who would mirror his qualities, not diminish them with a sordid past. Danny had been the equivalent of a high-priced whore by the age of twelve, and though it wasn't her choice, the fact remained. Men paid for and used her body repeatedly. In her mind, there was no difference, just semantics.

No, she hadn't been willing. She was friendly with many of the whores on the docks, and most of them didn't start out willing either. Fate, circumstance, or that evil bitch destiny had taken a steaming shit on all of them, leaving behind broken dreams and limited options to feed themselves or their children watching and waiting in the shadows for the few coins their Mam might make for the evening.

Danny held no judgment on the women's choice of profession or the lack of choice as it most often was, but she was eternally grateful for the day Madylyn saved her life and offered her new choices. She'd grabbed those opportunities with both hands and ran with them as fast and as far as she could. She became a deadly weapon in her own right, determined to never again be at the whim of a man who decided he would take her by the sheer advantage of size or will.

Madylyn and Rhyanna knew about the hell she'd survived, and she suspected Fergus might as well, the prophetic bastard. He never spoke of it, nor did he look down on her in any way. Beyond the three of them, no one knew about her past. She'd never been ashamed of her past until she recently found herself considering Jameson as more than her partner.

Soaring in ever-widening circles, she stayed above the night hunters and kept her eyes and ears tuned in for the rush of movement on the air currents around her. A protection spell surrounded her like a bubble, and a mild electrical current emanated from her, discouraging larger nocturnal birds of prey from attacking. Danny was faster in this form than any of them, but she wasn't in the mood for a chase.

The stars beckoned before her, and for a moment, she wished that she could fly toward them and away from the pain in her chest every time she thought about him. When she allowed herself to think about Jamey, her heart hurt because, in the deepest darkest corners of her heart, she hid her most vulnerable truth. Protected behind chained doors, she kept her heart's greatest wish. It was a secret and a secret she didn't even share with Maddy or Rhy. She kept it for herself because she knew she would never get her wish, and on the very off-chance she did, she would never have the courage to accept the offer if he extended it.

Danyka's secret was that she loved Jameson, and she wanted one night to know what it would be like to be loved by him. One night would be enough to hold her for a lifetime because she was bound to fuck it up within about twenty-four hours. She watched him with Carsyn twice, and both times made her want him with a ferociousness that confused her. She was never territorial with any man she spent a night with, but Jamey would be different. Tonight, she found herself with the irrational urge to gut Carsyn for allowing Jamey to bring her pleasure.

The thing was, she liked Carsyn. She'd never considered herself the jealous type, but holy fuck, the rage that rolled through her as Jamey set his mouth to Carsyn tonight almost overrode the amazing fucking orgasm he gave to both of them. The overload of jealousy, followed swiftly by guilt and then shame to have allowed it to go that far, nearly ruined the whole thing. Then, if all that emotional bullshit wasn't enough, she had started crying. Crying, for fucks sake. Tears falling at alarming rates, snot streaming, breath hiccupping. WHAT. THE. FUCK.

Danny didn't do jealous because she never gave a shit about who she fucked, and she didn't do guilt because it was a useless emotion. Commit to action, pay the consequence, and don't be a pussy if it turns tits up. Shame was something she left behind after her childhood because she couldn't allow herself to backtrack, and she sure as fuck didn't do crying anymore.

But she had cried. Deep heart wrenching, soul-gutting cries were wrenched out of her chest as she ran for the portal, wanting to avoid the inevitable pillow talk Jamey would most likely demand. She loved Jameson as her friend, her partner, and her fellow barfly, but Danny didn't want to deal with him in a post-coital haze when she couldn't figure out what was wrong with her.

She'd stepped into the portal, eternally grateful to have made it without him catching up to her. The gratitude was short-lived as his arm snuck in, stopping the doors from closing and the portal from activating. The horror on his face as he looked at her said it all. What they had done was a mistake. One of the most beautiful, sensual moments of her life was nothing more than regret in his eyes as he looked at her tear-streaked face.

"FUCK!" she shouted silently as she remembered. Her current form shrieked in protest with her.

She wavered in flight, and the slight tremor reminded her to stay focused or get the hell out of the sky. If she couldn't maintain her form, she would fall and splat on the ground below before she had time to shift again. Shifting required complete focus at all times when inhabiting another form. It was the first lesson she taught her students and one she needed to remember right now herself.

She glided back down to the cliff where her clothes lay strewn on the rocks. Landing softly, she allowed her body to remember the feel of her human form. She embraced the long sinewy form of muscles and the solidity of her bones encompassed by her protective outer skin. The energy around her shimmered as her body transformed into her human form, and she shivered in the night air. The wind blew her long bangs over her forehead. Her eyes closed as they pulsed for a moment. When she opened them, her vision returned to normal, although normal for her was twice the sight any man would ever have.

The cliff she had launched herself from overlooked the Saint Lawrence. On her hands and knees, she looked at her reflection on the mirrored surface of the river below. The night was still, and she could see her haunted eyes looking back at her. "Why did I do that," she asked her reflection. "Why did I take a chance on everything we have?" Her reflection watched her somberly but offered nothing in return. "What am I supposed to do when I see him again? How am I supposed to act?"

The eyes watching her blurred, and Danyka realized with horror that they were filling up again. She shoved herself into her breeches so quickly that she took skin off in places. Wincing, she snatched up her leather tank and crisscrossed the straps under her bosoms and then around her waist before slamming her feet into well-worn boots.

Standing, she took one last look in the depths below her and gasped when she saw a different set of eyes staring back this time. Now, they were cold, detached, and back to looking like the heartless bitch men often accused her of being.

Danyka turned away, ready to head back to her rooms and the private stash of bourbon she kept for the rare occasion when she wanted to tie one on quick. Tonight qualified as one of those occasions. As her feet hit the path, a disembodied laugh came from behind her. The hair stood up on her arms as a voice from behind asked her a question.

"Why don't you try acting like a woman worthy of being loved by a man like Jameson and stop running away from the feelings you have. Stop being a coward and hiding behind your compulsions, your past, and all the fucked-up things you have done since then. Be brave enough to face them. He deserves that much from you. Daughter, he loves all of you. Jamey knows about the ugliness you harbor, and he doesn't care. Acknowledge your feelings and see what possibilities await the two of you."

The voice stopped, and Danny froze in place, stunned speechless by the message she'd just received. She knew she didn't imagine it, and it wasn't on her internal line, so that left only one other place it could have come from. In deference, she kept her opinions to herself and listened, repeating the message thrice to herself so that she would remember it come morn. Finding the courage to move again, she took another step.

"Or you can run with your tail between your legs and fuck your way through the coming years with a barrage of unworthy, unsuitable men. You'll spend your lonely nights always wondering what might have been and seeing his face every time someone else touches you."

Danny's breath came quickly. Short bursts of fog escaped her lungs, puffing out into the cool night air as the Earth Mother ripped her a new one. You couldn't argue with your creator when she decided you needed a heart-to-heart.

"You've more courage, little Danyka, than a battalion of men and more spirit, too. Make your choice wisely, child, because he deserves a woman with courage and spirit. He's a good, kind man, and if you don't want him, I'll find him someone who will appreciate him for the wonderful man he is, but she'll never be you, and then there will be three of you miserable instead of just one."

A shudder ran through Danny as the last of the message sank in. She felt cold seeping into her bones at the thought that she might have run out of options in her quest for freedom and her desire to protect him from her past. When she tried to imagine him with someone else, a fiery rage burned away the cold and gave her something to focus on.

Unfortunately, ultimatums were something that never worked well for her. Danny wouldn't be forced into a decision by anyone, and that sure as hell included the deity who'd just handed her ass to her. She took it all with a grain of salt and stowed it away to chew on later because she refused to be coerced into dealing with this shit show tonight. It had been a long day already, and she'd had enough.

CHAPTER THIRTY-THREE

This Isn't A Good Idea

Rhyanna watched Roarke leave the building, furious. Worried about him, she managed to make it out the door without falling on her face or losing her bottle.

The tavern sat on the water's edge, and a boardwalk meandered along the waterfront to a small park. Weaving her way down the boardwalk, she stopped and tried to locate him. The night had finally cleared. With open skies, the temperature dropped, and an almost full moon made an appearance, lighting her way. The wind tossed her hair in her face as she tried to see where he had gone. Finally, she saw movement ahead of her. Sitting on a park bench in the distance, she could see his profile. He was bent over with his elbows on his knees and his head in his hands.

Shivering in the cool night air, she pulled his duster tightly around her. Approaching slowly, she joined him on the bench and sat silently next to him, waiting for him to speak. Time passed, and still, nothing.

The whiskey bottle was half empty when she put it to her lips. Taking another healthy chug, she wiped her lips on the back of her hand before offering him the bottle.

Without looking at her, he reached out and took the bottle from her, drinking half of what was left before returning it to her. "Want to talk about what's wrong?" he asked.

"Nope," she replied, watching the dark waves break in front of her as she pulled her knees to her chest. "Ye?"

"Nope."

They maintained the silence as they finished the bottle, passing it back and forth between them. When he handed it back to her empty, she tipped the bottle up to see if she could get a drop or two he might have missed, but she was out of luck.

"I just missed her," he said so softly she almost missed that he had spoken.

"Come again?" she asked, tilting her head as she looked at him.

"We nearly had information on Rosella," he said, leaning his head back against the seat. "My new ally, Samson, thought he had a lead. Some men were bragging in a tavern in Clayton last night about a new girl their dark mistress had recently acquired. He discretely watched them because he thought they might know where the girls are being held. He made a quick trip outside to relieve himself, keeping the door in his view the entire time. No one left the building from either exit. When he reentered, the men had disappeared, and the barkeep and drunks had no recollection of them being there only moments before "

Roarke gave a wry laugh. "Half empty whiskey glasses were still on the table, and tips for the barmaid." He turned his head and looked at her. "Working men don't waste whiskey, Rhy. They work too hard to earn their wages, and they enjoy every last drop." Scrubbing his hands over his face, he sighed defeatedly. "Strangest thing was no one saw them leave. They vanished, and no one remembers any details about them except for Samson because he stepped outside. There is dark magic at work here that I am struggling to compete with. I'm always one step behind them."

"Roarke, I'm so sorry," she said, instantly sobering up considerably.

"The sailor who was bragging claimed to work on a ship with a new girl. He called her Ella but described her perfectly." He choked off a curse as he continued. "He claimed to have helped break her in, was her first for oral sex." His fists clenched at his side, making the muscles in his forearm stand out vividly. "I would've killed him without a thought if I'd heard him say that."

Rage and frustration swam through his dark eyes as he looked at her. "She was within my grasp, and I fucking lost her again." His voice broke. "How do I live with that, Rhy? How do I go back to my family and tell them I failed again?" Roarke choked on what he needed to say the most. "How?" He cleared his throat against the lump that was stuck there. "Aw, fuck, how do I face her someday knowing I could have brought her home, and I let her slip through my fingers?"

Tears streamed down Rhy's face as she listened to his tormented voice. She said nothing, knowing he needed to get this out, needed to confide in someone.

A sob tore out of his chest. "It's taking me fucking weeks to learn this much, and I can guarantee you they won't be so sloppy next time. Their security will be tighter, and it will cost us to take them down. I don't mean money; I mean lives."

Rhyanna sat there silently, not knowing what to say. There was nothing she could say to make this easier for him. She watched as his head returned to his hands, and he tried to hide the emotion that was drowning him. She might not have the words that would make this easier, but the empath in her couldn't sit by and feel his pain without sharing the anguish with him, trying to ease his conscience.

Standing, she moved in front of him and then dropped to her knees between his legs. She reached up and wrapped her hands around his wrists as she leaned her head against his. He tried to pull away from her, but she clung to his arms.

"Don't, Rhy. This isn't a good idea for either of us tonight."

"Did ye na offer me comfort not a fortnight ago, Roarke? Did ye na sit and hold me with no expectations except to be there for a friend in need? That's what I be offering ye, a friend to talk to, an ear to vent to, and a body to hold if ye wish to hold me. Please don't push me away. After the day I've had, please, jest let me do some good."

He raised his head and lowered his arms to look at her. "This isn't a good idea, lass," he repeated as his hands pushed her hair back and framed her face. "I'm not thinking straight, and judging by the state of yer bottle, neither are you."

"I'm plum out of good ideas, Roarke, and I'm too damn tired to try and come up with anymore."

"I care for you, lass."

"I care for ye, as well."

"I consider Kyran a friend."

"I'm not sure what I consider him tonight, but here, he's not, and he damn sure ought to be."

She moved closer, leaning her head against his and sliding her smooth cheek against the roughness of his. "Just let me hold ye, Roarke," she whispered against his skin, "like ye held me, and we'll call it good." She moved her arms around his neck and tucked her head against his shoulder as he pulled her flush against him.

This close to him, she felt the fears and the rage he was trying to hold back, and she feared they would drown in it, it was so heartbreakingly raw. She hugged him tighter, and as she stroked the back of his head, she said in a soothing voice, "Let it go, Roarke. Ye need to let it go." Her hands caressed the back of his head, stroking his hair as she spoke. "Ye won't be able to move forward and help her if ye can't get over this. We've all failed someone we love at one time or another, but it's our willingness to keep trying to make it better that allows us to hope and separates us from those who fail by giving up."

Roarke's hands banded around her back and squeezed her lightly as he picked her up off her knees and onto his lap. Her knees naturally slid around his hips while he held her. There was nothing sexual about it as he clung to her and let go. There was nothing inappropriate and nothing to fear from his touch. They were just two lost souls comforting each other on a cold, sad night. Her tears mixed with his as she sympathized with him and cried for the disappointments she had suffered over the past twenty-four hours as well.

Rhy poured calming energy into him, and their embrace transformed into something else. She pulled back and wiped his face dry and then leaned down to kiss his eyes and his damp cheeks. "There na, ye got that out of yer system, and tomorrow, ye'll better be able to focus on what needs be done. Ye'll find her again, I know it, Roarke, I truly do."

Her lips were but a breath away from his, and her sorrowful eyes were on his. She witnessed the raw need he had for her, the hunger, and the desperation to erase the pain they both were feeling.

Both hands dug into her waist as if he couldn't decide whether he should pull her closer or push her away from him. Whatever his mind was wrestling with didn't prevent his body from moving forward and pressing his chest closer to hers. His eyes shifted to her lips and then back to her eyes. Her breath hitched, and whatever he saw gave him the courage to lean down and take her lips in a desperate kiss. He moaned against her lips as he wrapped his arms tighter around her.

Rhyanna kissed him back equally as committed. She had only ever been kissed by Kyran, but Roarke knew what he was about, taking over and leading her through it. She felt the moisture pool between her legs, and when his fingers grazed the side of her breasts, she felt the heat building in her core.

Moving frantically against each other, his hands moved to her hips, gathering the fabric and sliding it up so he could stroke her legs. It was her turn to moan, and as she did so, she said his name.

Suddenly, Roarke pushed her away. His breathing was ragged, and his eyes were lust-filled pools. "This isn't right, Rhyanna," he said, holding her at arm's length away.

Hurt and confused to be rejected yet again, she just stared at him stupidly. His cock was beneath her, and she could feel the size of him, and it was worth mentioning, the man was well-built. She couldn't help sliding against him once again, wanting to finish this.

Roarke sucked in a pained breath. "You're not ready for this, lass," he said, "and I don't want to lose you as a friend because of a mistake we make while you're drunk."

"I'm not nearly as drunk as ye might think, laddie." She purred trying to move closer to him.

"I think Kyran and I could be friends," he said as he pushed her off of him, "and I don't think you're ready to move on to someone else." He smiled sadly at her. "For the first time in my life, I've found someone I could see as more than a friend with benefits. You're special, Rhyanna, and you deserve more than what I'm offering tonight."

"Buttt..." she sputtered, unable to grasp the fact that another man was saying no to her.

"Lass," he said softly as his hands framed her face, "you just called me by his name, so no matter what's got you in a mood tonight, I'm telling you from experience, you're not ready for this."

"Who gives a feck if I jest called ye by his name?" she asked, getting angry once again. Was she destined to constantly be refused?

"I just fucking might," came a low growl behind them.

Rhyanna gasped, and Roarke let out a curse before setting her away from him. He knew where this was headed, and she needed to be safely out of the way.

"Hello, Kyran," he said, standing and ready to take whatever the man was about to hand out.

"What the fuck are you doing?" Kyran directed at Rhyanna.

"Jest following your example and trying to feck you out of my system," she threw back at him.

"You know I didn't mean what I said, nor follow through on it," he shouted, moving towards her.

Roarke moved towards him with his hands outstretched. "Kyran, this isn't a good time for either of you to really discuss this. She damn near finished a bottle of whiskey before you got here." He half chuckled. " Only reason she didn't is because she shared the last bit with me."

Kyran looked at him, and his eyes narrowed as if he wanted to charge at the man. His hands clenched at his side and his body tensed, remembering how Rhyanna had been straddling him when he arrived.

Roarke rolled his eyes at him. "You need to take a swing at me to get over this?" he asked, resigned to it. "Or would you rather move on to fixing whatever the fuck you've done to mess up your relationship?"

He shoved his hands in his pockets "Out of respect for you, I will apologize for tonight, but if you fuck this up and let her go or lose her, I'm giving you fair warning; I will be courting her. So I highly recommend that you figure this the fuck out."

A muscle ticked in his jaw as Kyran stood fuming for a few more moments before slowly releasing his tense hands. "I've got no grievance with you, Roarke. I arrived in time to hear you try and dissuade the situation. This time, I'll overlook it. I agree, the potential for a worthwhile friendship does exist." He shook his hands out. "Should it happen again, you'll have to excuse me if I kick the ever-loving shit out of you for touching, no less kissing my woman."

Roarke laughed at him. "You'll try Kyran, but don't be surprised if this scrapper gets a few good licks in along the way. Don't go pissing your woman off, and she won't come looking for me."

Rhyanna finally spoke up. "I'm fecking standing right here, you two arrogant feckers." She pointed a finger at Kyran and, in an ear-splitting voice, screeched, "Ye've got a lot of fecking nerve thinking ye can jest show up and get yer knickers in a twist after what ye fecking pulled today."

Kyran's face turned red, but before addressing her, he turned to Roarke and spoke. "If you will excuse us, we've much to sort out before the night is through."

"Roarke, ye don't need to go," Rhyanna pleaded, not sure she wanted to face Kyran alone right now.

Ignoring Kyran, Roarke walked over to her and framed her face. His eyes searched hers. "I'll stay if you want me to, lass. But my heart tells me I need to let you see this through one way or the other. Fix it or fuck it—figure this out. You need to make a decision without me here."

She clung to his shirt before leaning her head against his chest. "Yer right," she whispered.

He looked down at her and kissed her on the forehead. Looking up and seeing the fury washing over Kyran again, he couldn't help but reach down and kiss her gently on her lips before saying, "You're a beautiful, sensual, and magical woman, Rhy. Don't let anyone ever make you feel like less."

Rhy met his gaze watching the longing in his eyes and the resolution that she wasn't meant for him. "I'm sorry I put ye in this position, Roarke."

"You didn't put me in any position, lass." He smiled sadly. "You offered me comfort when I needed it, and I'm grateful for what you did." He released her and walked around her. As he approached Kyran, he stopped and met his glare. They were of an equal height. Roarke may have outweighed him by thirty, but Kyran was also a son of a demigod. The animosity Kyran was radiating at him was almost comical.

"Take me out of the equation, and you figure out what the fuck you're doing. She deserves better than you've been giving her, and she deserves a commitment or her freedom." Roarke saw Kyran's eyes flare with the threat of violence, but he kept on goading him. "You man enough to let her go if you're still fucking trapped into an arranged marriage? Or are you going to keep her on the side, fading away waiting for you to finally make her yours?"

He witnessed Kyran winding up even tighter, his face turning an unattractive shade of red. "She deserves better, and you fucking know it. Family aside, court aside, be a fucking man and make a choice." Roarke had moved closer with every statement, and they were now toe to toe. Right up in his face, he delivered the final kick. "But then again, you pretty court boys, the queen's little play toys, never did have the fucking balls to make a decision that wasn't self-serving, did you?"

Finally, there it was, the match that would spark the fire. Kyran swung out and hit him. His head snapped back as Kyran broke his nose, and Roarke embraced the pain, letting it drown out the self-sabotaging feelings he had been trapped in. Another one caught him on the side of the jaw, and he felt some of his teeth loosen as his mouth filled with blood. He spat it out on the sidewalk while rubbing his jaw. Never losing his footing, he straightened back up and faced Kyran's wrath while Rhyanna screamed in the background.

Roarke chuckled darkly. "My work here is done. Go deal with your woman, Kyran. Now I know you won't lay a hand on her because you took it out on me."

Kyran looked at him in confusion, then in understanding. "You're fucked in the head, Roarke. I never would have hurt her. You just wanted someone to make you bleed tonight, didn't you?" He laughed darkly. "I was happy to oblige, my man." He pushed by him. "If you'll excuse me, I have a relationship to salvage."

Roarke walked off, not even looking back as he heard Rhyanna screeching at Kyran. He wished them the best no matter the outcome. He genuinely liked the two of them as individuals, yet he wasn't joking when he told Kyran he would pick up the slack if he messed up again.

Kyran stalked towards Rhyanna, the true reason for his ire. "What the fuck are you doing? Why haven't you answered me, and why did you run off? I could have explained."

"That's just it, Kyran. Ye always have a fecking explanation, and they're always good."

He stood in front of her as she reached out and pounded her little fists down on his chest.

"Are you playing me for a fool? Do ye ken so little about me that you think what you did this morning would mean nothing to me because it meant nothing to ye?"

Rhyanna punctuated each of her words with a fist to his chest. When her hits produced no response, she glared up at him and slapped him across the face. "Answer me, damn ye." Slapping him harder, trying to prompt a response from him, she repeated, "Answer me!"

Kyran growled at her as he grabbed her swinging arms. His cheek throbbed, and surprisingly, as pissed off as he was, his cock started throbbing, too, as it always did in her proximity.

Pulling her up against him, he held her arms pinned behind her back. Her back was arched, and her hips pressed against his as her breasts thrust against his chest. His breathing was ragged as he leaned over and yelled back at her. "Goddamn it, Rhyanna, you mean everything to me, and I fucking hate that I have put you through so much. I knew the situation would devastate you, and I was trying to prevent hurting you, not protect myself. I knew you would try and find a way to forgive me, it's in your makeup to do so, but I didn't want you to doubt yourself once again by comparing yourself to that whore."

He shook her as he held her pinned against him. "I would never trifle with you or lead you on, and I have been nothing but as honest as I am able." He drew in a ragged breath.

"What does that even fecking mean? 'Honest as I am able,' only tells me you are lying or holding something back. What am I supposed to think? Release me, damn it."

"It means, it's not safe to tell you more. That's what it fucking means. It means that I need you to trust me and not run off getting drunk and throwing yourself at whoever the fuck's available when I can't be here." He witnessed her eyes widen at his words and sensed her intention before her knee connected with his family jewels. While deflecting her knee, she somehow managed to head butt him, causing his nose to bleed. He released her immediately as his eyes stung and blood poured down his chin.

"Are you seriously going to lecture me on keeping me hands to meself? This is fecking absurd, this whole fecking situation. I'm done with this and done with ye."

Kyran wiped his nose on his shirt as she ranted at him and tried to walk around him.

"Let me by, Kyran," she said much too calmly. "We be in no shape to have this conversation tonight, and I really don't like ye at all right now." She shoved him, trying to walk by him, when he grabbed her arm and pulled her back. Feeling spiteful and mean, she threw out a barb that would come back to haunt her. "Mayhap I should take yer father up on what he was offering tonight. At least I'll have no fecking delusions about what I'd be getting myself into.

"You're right, Rhyanna. This isn't the time for us to talk, but there is time for me to make you forget his lips ever touched yours before you leave, and maybe I'll give you a little taste of how the king would have treated you tonight when you accepted his offer."

"Kyran, don't..." she managed to say before his lips came crashing down on hers, making her forget what they were fighting about, forget Roarke, and forget where they were.

CHAPTER THIRTY-FOUR

King Varan's Unexpected Arrival

Madylyn waded through the paperwork at her desk after returning from Wellesley Island. Worried about Jameson, she had been unable to sleep. Deciding to catch up on the work piling up on her desk, she enjoyed a mug of cocoa—the only caffeine Rhy would let her indulge in until the baby arrived.

Additional reports were making their way to her from districts and sanctuaries farther west of them. One of the reports came from the great lakes many miles away. They all were disturbingly similar to the missing in her area.

The human trafficking ring they were looking for appeared much larger and more far-reaching than any of them originally anticipated. She scrubbed her hands over her face as she tried to come to terms with the scope of what they were dealing with. Her hands tangled in her loose bun, pulling strands loose.

Why hadn't she seen that this existed before now? She was tormented by the fact that she had missed the signs for so long. These thoughts haunted her daily as they searched for clues, trying to find the people backing this deplorable form of human slavery.

A butterfly kissed the inside of her slowly expanding waistline. A smile crossed her face as she felt the very first evidence of the life growing inside of her. "Hey there, wee one. About time you said 'Hello.'"

A wee lass would be joining them in early winter, the mother willing. Madylyn's family was rapidly growing. When she accepted Ronan as her life partner mere weeks ago, she also gained a five-year-old son he had known nothing about. The same day that Landon arrived, Rhy gave her the news that she was expecting a child of their own.

This year had been full of so many blessings for them. They helped override the tragedies and horrors it had also brought them. The responsibility of raising these two little souls made her desperate to make the banks of the St. Lawrence River safe for them to grow up on.

Excited to share the moment with Ronan, she was about to reach out to him when an urgent message from the Romani River Patrol arrived first.

"Mistress SkyDancer, we have an urgent matter rapidly approaching the docks."

"What is the problem this time of night," she asked in an exhausted tone.

"Were you expecting an official visit from the Court of Tears this evening?"

Maddy stood up abruptly, looking down at the casual comfortable clothes she currently wore. They were not fit to meet a king in.

"No, I was not. I had requested a meeting, but it was never confirmed." Maddy's blood pressure rose as she imagined who had arrived. *"Please remind the queen as to the clear terms of the letter I sent her. She is not welcome to stay on Sanctuary ground."*

"If only it was that simple, mistress."

"Well, please explain what makes it so complicated."

"Well, ma'am, it's not the queen but the king, and he outranks all of us."

"Not quite, but I'll be right there."

Maddy glanced down again at what she had worn to meet Jamey and sighed. She quickly tidied her hair and headed for the door. If the king decided to arrive without notice, he would have to take her as she was. It would appear more of a snub to leave him waiting at the dock for another hour.

Heading for the door, she sent messages to all the wardens on the island. *"I need anyone who is available to meet me at the docks. A royal entourage has arrived with no warning. Come as you are; let's not make King Varan wait."*

Maddy didn't wait for answers as she headed for the stables. She smiled as Ronan made his way out with her massive beast, Levyathan, saddled and another horse for himself. He gave her a quick boost onto the destrier and mounted his horse.

Levyathan snorted as they headed out before communicating with her. *"You're getting fat. Must be the parasite you're carrying."*

"Parasite—how could you call my child that?"

"Trust me, it will suck the life right out of you. I've seen what my two spawns have done to Sabbath."

Maddy laughed. *"You're just jealous that Sabbath doesn't have time for you anymore."*

He jerked his head as she spoke, and Maddy realized the other half of the problem. *"You don't think I'll have any time for you either, do you, my friend. Well, I promise that won't happen. I'll need to ride to keep my sanity."*

"You better! The youngling of Ronan's visits often; I might consider letting him ride me when he is less breakable."

The thought of Landon on Levyathan made her woozy. *"Yes, let's give him another decade, please."*

Fergus and Danyka led their mounts out and joined them in the courtyard. Maddy smiled at her team and felt pride well up in her chest.

"No Rhy?" Fergus asked her. "Or Jamey?"

"Jameson is not here tonight," Maddy said with no further information. "Did you leave her at court by herself?" Her voice rose at the thought of Rhy on her own in that hell hole.

"Nye, I wouldna do that, and ye damn well ken it, Maddy." He gave her a disgusted look. "She took off after Kyran made a mess of things. Can't say that I blame her. I expected to find her when I got back. She's not answering me. Any of the rest of ye heard from her?"

As everyone shook their heads no, Maddy said, "If she's hurting, she'll want time to herself. She'll need time to lick her wounds, and we'll give her tonight before I hunt her down."

"Let's hope she sleeps it off and doesn't drink it off," Danyka said with a grin.

"Blessed Mother, yes," Maddy said. "But if she doesn't, we'll be there to hold her hair back, won't we?" She raised an eyebrow at Danny as she said it.

"Damn skippy, we will. God knows she's put me back together more times than I can count. I'll check on her later tonight."

"Let's get going. I've made him wait longer than necessary to prove a point."

Maddy cast balls of soft blue witch light into the lanterns lining the path as they headed for the docks. The trip was quick this time of night, with little foot traffic to watch out for. As they headed down the final hill, she couldn't miss the enormous barge at the docks with dozens of retainers.

Maddy paled as she realized the mess she would be in with Mrs. O'Hare if she arrived unannounced with this many guests.

"Mrs. O'Hare, I am in dire need of your swift assistance."

"What is it, lass? What can I do for you this time of night?"

"First, you can accept my apologies for the mess this evening is about to become. King Varan has arrived with at least two dozen courtiers. If you can manage to have their accommodations ready when we arrive, it will go a long way towards making us appear less incompetent. This isn't exactly how I'd hoped to receive him."

"Think nothing more of it," her housekeeper said soothingly. *"I'll put the word out and have every available body readied to help me pull this off. Thankfully, most of the rooms in the west wing are vacant and ready for nothing more than fresh linens. The suite for his highness, I'll tend to meself."*

"Thank you, Mrs. O'Hare. I will make sure the staff is properly compensated for their late assistance."

The group dismounted, and Maddy led them towards the traveling throne. The barge was decked out in turquoise and white silk curtains surrounding the perimeter. The curtains on the side facing the docks were pulled back and restrained by long ropes of white pearls.

Court attendants abounded in their colorful livery as they attempted to anticipate their monarch's needs before he even realized what they were. Persian rugs and overstuffed silk cushions were scattered across the floor, interspersed with velvet chaise lounges. Pale white witch light lit the sconces on the walls, and small floor lamps were scattered in an effort to provide dim lighting across the scene.

Madylyn searched for King Varan but was unable to locate him. Along the back wall, a dozen members of the party were scantily dressed. Male and female, they waited on their knees, hands clasped behind their backs and eyes staring vacantly forward. Each wore a gem in the center of their forehead. The gems were similar in size, although slightly different in shape and color. Looking closer, Maddy realized that they designated ranks amongst the men and women.

Fury ran through her as she imagined this fate being forced on Rhyanna had Queen Meriel succeeded with her assault earlier today. The members of the court and the staff watched her groups approach subtly as they waited for introductions.

The hell with that, Maddy thought. They had arrived unannounced to her home and were showing complete disrespect to her station and the people who stood with her. Fuming, she stalked to the front of the barge and looked for the king's steward.

Unable to find him, she approached a page. "Where may I find King Varan?"

He looked down his nose at her disdainfully. "I'm not sure I know, and if I did, I sure as hell wouldn't be telling the likes of you."

The arrogant ass made the mistake of beginning to turn his back on her when Maddy lost her temper. She froze him in place before moving in front of him once more. Her eyes bored into his, and she let him see her power and her authority without saying a word. His eyes darted nervously to his left, answering her unspoken question. Maddy smirked at him and said, "Be a good lap dog, and wait here for me." She left him there, unable to move, and could feel the palpable fear radiating from him. No doubt, it wasn't her he was afraid of, but his master's wrath once he realized the slight he had given her.

Madylyn wandered into the crowd with her fellow wardens following behind her. As she stepped onto the flotilla, her senses were overwhelmed by the lust rolling off the attendees. She moved deeper onto the barge and saw a large four-poster bed to her left with an assortment of occupants pleasuring each other. King Varan was the only one fully clothed. The men and women on either side of the massive bed left nothing to the imagination with their public orgy.

The king's stare was vacant as he peered at her, confirming their suspicions that he was drugged or ill. Maddy circled to the right-hand side of the bed, trying to attract his attention. He blinked at the movement, and his eyes followed her until she stood near the head of the bed. Ronan, Danyka, and Fergus waited at the foot of the bed in a formal stance, protecting and supporting her.

"King Varan, we are honored that you have chosen to join us for a few days. Rooms are available for you and your..." Maddy waved a hand, indicating the others on the flotilla, "retainers. At your leisure, please make your way up the hill to the Sanctuary where you may partake of our hospitality. A late meal is being prepared as we speak."

The king watched her warily but never moved nor made a sound. Maddy clenched her teeth, trying not to snap at the man. He might be royalty, but as a warden of the court and headmistress of this sanctuary, her rank was nearly equal to his, and his behavior was beyond inappropriate.

"Stay calm, darling," Fergus said, feeling the anger radiating off her. *"Something is very amiss on board this vessel."*

"I'm very aware. Make sure no communication of any form is able to come or go while they are here. We are going to lock down the island during their visit until we can figure out what the hell is going on. If we can figure out what is affecting him and bring the old Varan back, we might have a chance of helping Kyran out of that damn betrothal."

"Need to do something quickly, Madylyn. Rhy's had about all she can take, and I'd hate to see her give up on this. Kyran's good for her."

"I agree. Do you sense anything magically affecting him?"

"Aye, lass, he's got a double whammy on him. He's definitely drugged, and hopefully it's not toxic, but this isn't the king I've dealt with at any point in recent history. Dark magic is magnifying the physical effects he's experiencing."

"KING VARAN!" Maddy said, adding a little bite to the command and a mild compulsion to make him answer her.

The only response she received was his head as it turned towards her voice. His eyes flared in annoyance. Reaching down, he fisted the hair of the woman next to him, stopping her head from descending once more on the engorged cock in her hand.

"Leave me," he said in a voice that sounded rusty from disuse. He pulled the sheet up over his waist as bodies left the bed. Varan looked around in confusion while running a hand through his hair. His eyes were glassy, and Maddy wouldn't be surprised to hear that he had a migraine from the looks of him. He glanced at the men at the end of his bed, then back at her and said, "Who the fuck are you to interrupt me in my bedchamber?" His words were thick and slurred.

Maddy donned her headmistress attitude and responded, "You, King Varan, have landed your floating brothel at the Heart Island Sanctuary— without notice, I might add. You are more than welcome to stay at the Sanctuary this evening with your retinue, or you may remain here freezing your balls off. The choice is yours.

"While you are here, you will address me as Mistress SkyDancer and my fellow wardens as Master Pathfinder, Master Emberz, or Mistress Danyka." She glared at him disgustedly. "When you remember your manners, your rank, and a change of clothes, you may request an audience with me. Until then, get your ship in order because, sir, if it continues to run like this, I have to wonder how much longer you will remain at the helm." Her eyes bored into his, letting him know that she meant every word that she said. "Goodnight, sire. May tomorrow find you in better straits."

Madylyn turned away, vibrating in anger. The man was a fool, and she knew exactly who was running the Court of Tears, and it wasn't the king. Furious with herself for sending Rhyanna there without an escort, she dashed away the angry tears that were cascading down her face when she reached Levyathan.

Ronan boosted her up without a word, sensing that she needed time to herself before he intervened.

Maddy kicked the horse into a gallop, wanting to ride the attitude out of her system before she took the mood back to her family or her bedroom. Ronan didn't deserve to have it taken out on him. She adored him and knew he would have done so for her without a second thought, but he shouldn't have to. He rode up beside her, keeping her company without a word, and she loved him even more.

Rhyanna deserved better than what the Court of Tears had shown her, and Madylyn wouldn't allow anyone else to treat her in the way Queen Meriel had done over the past few days.

The king sorely misjudged her if he thought she was going to tolerate his poor excuse of a court. She didn't answer to the clan courts; she answered to the Elemental High Court, and she was about to remind him of that. If

Varan didn't fix the shit show his court was becoming, she would take him before the High Court.

By the Earth Mother's grace, she would demand a reckoning and a cleaning out of the trash that was residing there now for Rhyanna and for the rest of the Water Clan, who didn't have anyone willing to fight for them.

That should have been Varan's job, and in Maddy's opinion, he'd failed his people. The queen was a menace to her people and the Tyde family. Something needed to change, and she was going to do everything she could to see better days return to the people who resided in the court's shadow.

The Court of Tears was the court of emotions, namely, love. It was in desperate need of a change, and Maddy hoped they could help Varan and his sons become what their people needed—a ruler who actually gave a shit.

CHAPTER THIRTY-FIVE

Lessons

Kyran grasped Rhyann's head firmly in his hands as he continued with the bruising kiss. When he expected her to cry out and pull away, her fingers dug into his shirt, pulling him closer. Their lips sought dominance, and his won. He bit her bottom lip, drawing blood and a whimper from her, but he didn't stop. Finally, she was in his arms. She wasn't hitting him nor walking away, and for the moment, that's where he wanted her to remain.

His hands tangled in her hair as he pulled it, stretching her neck away from him. His lips moved down the column of her throat, sucking and nipping, leaving little bruises on both sides. His hips ground against her as the sounds he extracted from her made his cock surge even harder.

Dropping to his knees, he dragged her with him, wincing when she cried out as her knees hit the ground. He was too far gone with anger, jealousy, and lust to be gentle. If she was so desperate to be fucked, who was he to continue denying her? Needing the smell of Roarke off her, he pushed the leather duster from her shoulders and tossed it to the side. Pulling her breasts out of the corseted top, he set to sucking on her nipples. Grazing his teeth over the tips until they nearly met through her flesh, he smiled as she gasped.

Again, he waited for her to stop him, but when her hands grasped his head and pulled him closer, he laughed darkly. His little nymph liked it rough. Maybe she would have fit in at court better than he expected. While his teeth all but took the skin off the tip of her right nipple, his right hand gave her the same experience on the left. His thumb and forefinger pinched and pulled until he knew she had to be experiencing pain. He released her breast to look at her face, and her eyes dared him to continue.

The pretty flush staining her cheeks and her chest confirmed how turned on she was. His hands gathered her dress to her hips, and his hands sought the sides of her panties. With a vicious wrench, he tore them from her body.

Kyran's lips returned viciously to hers and his hand buried in her hair, cupping her neck. He came up for air, glaring at her. "Is this what you want, my lady? Is this what you have been so desperately holding out for? Because tonight, after all the bullshit today has thrown at me, this is all that I can offer you. This is what you would have gotten from a stranger who looked like me. You make sure you won't have any regrets come tomorrow because if we continue down this path, I guarantee I won't look back on it with anything except the pure pleasure I'm going to take in fucking you senseless."

He was breathing hard as he spat out one more opportunity for her to back down. "You think you're ready to take on the king of the Court of Tears? I seriously doubt you can handle me in full swing, let alone the bastard who fathered me," Kyran sneered as he spoke.

Flames sparked in her eyes at his challenge, and she glared right back at him, daring him to continue. Rhyanna knew he was once again trying to frighten her off. Well, feck that. She was tired of him treating her like a fecking fragile doll. Fully capable of handling anything he thought he could dish out, she hated that this was the only way for her to prove it to him. Tired of this see-saw they seemed to be on, she decided to take something for herself for a change. If he hadn't interrupted them earlier, she would have had Roarke balls deep in her by now.

"I be waiting, Kyran. Show me what ye've got. That way I'll have something to compare yer father with when I return to court tomorrow." She bucked against him. "C'mon, be a man, and take what ye've wanted from me since the beginning." She threw herself at him once more. "Take out that huge fecking cock everyone in the palace is talking about and feck me with it."

Her inner voice was getting louder as her temper flared, telling her she wasn't pretty enough or sexy enough. It cackled in delight, waiting for her be rejected once again.

"Whatchya think, lassie? He must have a reason for continuously turning ye away. We ken he's no fecking monk."

Ignoring the inner chatter, her eyes locked with his, and beneath the rage and the jealousy, she saw how much her behavior was hurting him, but she couldn't make herself stop. Fecking whiskey—this was why she rarely drank more than a glass or two of wine. She climbed onto his lap and dug her hands into his hair, returning the pain he had inflicted on her scalp earlier.

He blinked, the only indication of the discomfort she was dishing out. "What's the matter, me laird? Are ye truly afraid of touching me? Don't trust yerself right na?" When he continued looking at her silently, waiting for her next move, she threw the one barb she knew would set him into action. "I be sure Roarke hasn't gone far na, and he be more than willing to pick up yer slack. He might've found another partner by na, but I be willing to try new things," she finished with a giggle as she finally witnessed the familiar storm clouds rolling through his eyes, and thunder sounded in the distance.

Part of her sighed in relief, knowing he would finally give her something. Anything would be a welcome distraction—better than this hole in her fecking chest. Her heart had become an empty, gnawing place that was consuming her from the inside out, making her doubt her feelings and every decision she'd made about their relationship.

Kyran felt something break inside, and it terrified him but not enough to stop him from reaching out and pulling her against him with one hand while the other unlaced his breeches. "I'll give you exactly what you think you want, Rhyanna, exactly what you deserve right now, and I don't give two fucks about how much pleasure you do or don't receive." He met her eyes one last time, praying she would back down because he knew if he let loose, they were over. Completely and irrevocably over. For a moment, he tried to reach her through their bridge, but she still had him blocked, and the only emotion radiating to him from it was hurt and rage.

Kyran's eyes were locked with hers, trying to find some way to redeem their relationship. He saw little flames dancing in her emerald eyes like he had in Ferg's at times. A minor fire element was running rampant right now, encouraging her outburst.

Rhy leaned forward and kissed him. This time she left her own bite, harder than his had been. Blood dripped down his chin, and he chuckled as he wiped it away with the back of his hand, then fucking grinned at her wildly as she taunted him.

"I still be waiting."

"As you wish, my lady," he said in a dark, fathomless voice.

He slammed her to the ground, not caring that her back was sure to be bruised by morning. As he pulled her dress up over her hips and spread her thighs with his knees, she sat up and grasped his head in her hands, jerking his face to hers. He hoped that she had finally found some sanity until he looked in her eyes once again.

Fury flashed in them. "Not like this Kyran, no fecking way. Ye take me on me hands and knees like ye did her." She watched, without remorse, the regret that crossed his face, but she kept going.

"Then the next time some whore services ye without yer permission, ye'll fecking ken what I shoulda looked like spread out in front of ye. Ye'll ken what the shape of me ass would have looked like and how the curve of me waist fit into yer hands. Ye'll see the way me hair woulda fallen around me, and how I woulda sounded as ye pleasured me."

She witnessed the moment the pain fled, replaced by his own fury and a grim determination. "Ye'll take me like that or not at all. Every time ye feck a woman in that position, I want to make sure yer thinking of me because it will never fecking happen again. Ye'll have a visual reminder of what your omission cost ye. I could've gotten past what happened with time, especially after being in that hell hole—I'd have understood. But after everything we shared, why the feck didn't ye tell me?" She threw her hands up as he started to speak. "Ye know what, I don't fecking care, just feck me."

Eyes locked on his, she climbed off him. Still watching him, she turned away from him and looked over her shoulder so he was still in her line of sight.

From this angle, she saw that his pants were half unlaced, and the swollen head of his cock jutted over his waistband, thick and pulsing. The size of him alone should have slowed her down, but her hurt pride and lots of liquid courage refused to let her back down. She reached down and pulled the dress out from under her knees and raised it up over her hips as far as the corseted back would allow her. His ragged breathing confirmed the effect she was having on him, and she reveled in it. Spreading her knees, she bent down, her head cushioned to the side on the damp ground and her blond curls spread out around her.

The sight of her body displayed and waiting for him made him react on a visceral level. Anything remotely intelligent, caring, or decent left in him fled the scene. He had repeatedly tried to give her a way out. With both of their emotions out of control, angry sex should not have been her initiation into love-making any more than a melding should have been.

Rhyanna was acting like they were over anyways, so why should he worry about the aftermath? After the taunts about Roarke, anything civilized had vacated his mind, and he was acting on pure adrenaline and animal instinct. The sight of her pussy glistening at him set him in motion.

Slowly, he finished unlacing his breeches, eyes never leaving hers. He saw them widen in shock and a bit of fear as he pulled the breeches down over his hips. His cock stood up long, thick, and throbbing like a bitch. He closed his hand around it, barely able to make his fingers meet.

He'd suspected the queen had slipped an aphrodisiac into his drink at dinner, and now he knew for sure. He was a big man on his own, but this bordered on ridiculous. He heard her breathing change and watched an ounce of fear make an appearance. Committed now, he knew she would not back down. So. Fucking. Be. It.

Finally, he moved behind her. His hands ran over her plump cheeks, and a shiver ran through her. He wasn't sure if it was in anticipation or in fear. Again, his conscience had deserted him. With his arms, he knocked her knees wider apart, giving him plenty of room and hoisting her into a better position for him to access her. He considered seeing if she was ready for him and then figured, "Fuck it," when she continued glaring at him.

"You made it crystal clear to me, Rhyanna, that you think you're teaching me a lesson."

He stroked his painfully hard cock against her entrance, surprised to find that she was indeed wet. Wondering if it was because of him or Roarke, he growled. He positioned himself to breach her but stopped to pull off his shirt. Leaning over her back, he sensed the heat and the nervousness rolling off her. Leaning down beside her ear so he could watch every expression that crossed her face, he felt her body start to tremble violently beneath him, anticipating his next move. The head of his cock had barely entered her as he had moved to cage her in. He reached down and threaded his fingers through hers, spreading her arms forward as if she were on a rack.

"Now, it's my turn to teach you one, lass. You don't keep pushing a man when he's at his lowest and think you can reign him back in once you've let his inner beast loose. Mine's at the gate and ready to play, and I guarantee you will feel me every time you take a step tomorrow and probably the day after."

His fingers tightened on hers, and his body pushed harder against her, making her suck in a breath at the pressure his cock was putting on her entrance. Rhy squirmed a bit, not knowing whether to move closer or pull away as he went on punishing her with his words.

"Every man who fucks you after me will be a disappointment, and as much as it's your beautiful body you want me to remember every time I am in someone else, it will always be my body that you hunger for when someone else is inside of you. I will mark you tonight, Rhyanna. I will brand myself in you in places you can't begin to wash away. I will be so deep inside your body and your mind that you won't know where you end and I begin. So remember tonight the next time you want to play games with me." He pulled back and then inched in more. "I've spent my whole life playing these kinds of games, and I play to win. Every. Fucking. Time."

His legs shoved hers wider than she thought was possible, and when she realized that there was no stopping this train, regret finally made an appearance. As his hands trapped her and his breath caressed the side of her face, his head was buried in her neck, preventing her from shaking her head no, and her pride was too far gone to allow her to speak it.

As Kyran pulled back and gained purchase with his knees, she panicked and tried to move away from him, but his hands and body kept her caged firmly in place. He slammed fully into her without any warning. Pain ripped through her body as he more than filled her. Without waiting for her to adjust, he pulled back out and slammed into her violently again. Her body moved from the force of his thrust, but his cock remained in place. She whimpered, and tears rolled down the side of her face unchecked as she struggled not to sob. His forehead was still in the base of her neck, and she wondered if it was intentional, so he wouldn't see her tears.

Kyran rose over her, and with the next thrust, he growled at her. "I never wanted to fuck you like any of those whores." His body thrust into her again. "But you insisted, so I will show you exactly what part of them they get from me." Again, his hips met hers. "I give them nothing of myself, except my body." His speed increased. "Like a well-oiled machine, I can fuck all night long, and I make sure they enjoy it, or I would be dishonoring my court." Harder and faster, he pummeled into her. "I was raised on sex and lies." Over and over, he moved, finding her end painfully with each thrust. "You were the one pure thing I had found."

He released her hands so that he could grasp her hip with one of his. Using the other, he reached down and pinned her by the nape of her neck, once again effectively caging her and gaining more leverage. "I wanted to know what it was like to learn to love someone and to make love." Even harder, he slammed into her as his disappointment and devastation echoed through his actions.

Rhyanna sobbed openly as her body cramped from the violence he was subjecting her to. But even worse than the pain she was physically experiencing was the pain his words brought her.

The litany continued with every stroke. "I wanted nothing more than to cherish you, Rhyanna." His hips never missed a stroke. "I wanted to love you and shower you with the respect you deserved." He went faster, shouting at her now as he continued to take her violently. "Then you threaten to fuck a man who is one of the few I consider a friend if I didn't give in to you." Harder and harder, his balls slapped against her body, punishing her for her threats. "What kind of a man am I if I don't give you what you want? If I don't take what you offer? Isn't that what you've implied?" He stopped speaking as he continued pounding into her ruthlessly.

Kyran's cock swelled as he took out his frustration on the woman beneath him, enraged that this was how they had finally come together. Over and over, he sought the end of her, enjoying the little gasps that evolved from her sobs. He tuned out the sobs, fresh out of compassion for the situation they were in. Even as he tuned them out, he realized her body was making room for him and lubricating him as well. She might just find some pleasure out of this with no help from him.

His cock was screaming for release, but the drugs in his system refused to allow it. It throbbed and grew the longer he stroked in and out of her sweet little chamber. He reached down and pulled her legs even further apart, clasping her inner thighs. Releasing her head allowed her back to round some. This changed the angle enough for her to start moaning. Rhyanna's pussy was starting to flutter around him, and as much as he should have slowed and celebrated her body joining the party, he couldn't. Picking up speed again, he chased his own orgasm, the sweet agonizing pleasure bordering on pain. As her body started to milk him, he reached around and tweaked her nipples, making her buck beneath him.

His balls pulled up tight to his body as he continued taking it out on her pussy and found his voice once again. "I hate that this is how I made you come for the first time with me inside of you. You need to know that. This is not how I ever would have imagined we would be." He moaned as he finally neared his release. "Even if you never allow me to touch you again, Rhy," he choked out as his voice came in short bursts, "I will always remember," he rode her some more, "how fucking amazing you feel wrapped around me." His hands still stroked her breasts as he chanted, "You're so fucking wet and tight." His voice cut off when his body finally erupted. "Fucking you is like finding heaven, Rhy." He growled as he collapsed, blanketing her body as she screamed his name. They knelt there together with his arms wrapped around her middle as they both struggled to breathe.

He hated to move, not knowing what was going to happen next. Rhy wasn't pulling away, nor was she coming closer. Finally releasing a long sigh, he slid his semi-hard cock out of her. He leaned back onto his ankles as she sank to the ground and curled up in a ball in front of him. She pulled her knees to her chest and started rocking herself slowly while tears spilled silently down her face.

Kyran was nauseous watching her. He should have never allowed it to come to this. He tried to reach out to her, and though she said nothing, she recoiled from his touch. He knew when he slammed into her with that first stroke that nothing would be the same between them again, and yet he hadn't stopped. This was the consequence of his actions, and he would have the rest of his life to spend regretting tonight and mourning her loss in his life.

He stood, reaching down to lace his breeches back up, and stopped as the moonlight showed the evidence of her first-time glistening on him still.

He found his shirt and blindly pulled it on. He stood and looked down at her, knowing she wouldn't allow him to touch her. "Do you need me to call someone for you, my lady?" he asked her gruffly.

Rhyanna shook her head violently and listened to him stumble away. The sound of him vomiting not far from where she lay was an indication of her disappointing performance.

She pulled her knees closer as her womb contracted in sharp spasms and the fog of alcohol lifted from her mind. Kyran had unleashed his inner monster, and she had no one to blame but herself. Tears ran down the side of her face as she realized he must hate her right now.

CHAPTER THIRTY-SIX

Mama What Do I Do?

Jameson stood on the dock for a long time before deciding where he needed to go. His emotions were raw, and he wasn't ready to head back to the Sanctuary, but he couldn't go home smelling like this. His parent's horse farm was a short walk from where he stood, and even though he hadn't fully shifted, the animals would scent the grizzly on him as soon as he came near.

He pulled his shirt over his head and kicked off his boots before stepping out of his breeches. Cringing, he jumped into the river, knowing it was going to be ball-shriveling cold. He came up sputtering and gasping for the air he lost as the cold settled into his bones.

Quickly, he yanked his pants and shirt off the dock and rinsed them out as well. He climbed out, shivering, then dried himself and his clothing as quickly as possible with minute amounts of his elemental powers. As he dressed, he added a warming spell to the clothes to combat the cool night air.

Heading north, he embraced the peace the night offered. The familiar sounds soothed his raw edges as he walked. Raccoons chittered conversationally by the riverbank, and an owl hooted a warning nearby.

He replayed the evening's highs and lows and tried to sort through his turbulent emotions regarding the revelations Danyka shared with him earlier.

Jamey suspected she'd had a difficult past, but she never mentioned any of it. She never talked about any family, and he assumed they had passed on. The Sanctuary was the only home she ever mentioned, and Maddy and Rhy were like sisters to her.

He was in love with her, had been for a while now. A month ago, he finally stopped lying to himself about it. Any scenario he imagined with the two of them wouldn't be easy, but she was worth the challenge if he could convince her to give him a chance. What he didn't know how to do was be around her now and act like nothing had changed.

Jamey made a right at the fork in the road and vaulted over a steel gate barring the lane. The horses neighed at him from the pastures on either side as he walked by. An ornery one stomped his foot in warning. The porch light beckoned, and a dim light glowed in the kitchen. It warmed away the cold that was settling into his soul following this evening's revelations. He felt the tension seep away as he followed the lane to his childhood home.

A large wooden structure stood before him made of rough-cut logs and love. Six generations ago, his grandparents built this house. The families living in it made it a home. Jameson and his two brothers were born and raised here. His father hoped one day one of his boys would settle here and continue to work the family farm.

Two other houses stood an equal distance away, separated by large pastures. They were far enough for privacy yet close enough in case of emergency. Jamey's uncles and their families lived in them.

Jamey looked at the homes steeped in tradition and love and realized how lucky he had been to grow up here. He'd been surrounded and protected by those who loved him. He tried and failed to produce even one scenario that would have made any of them think they had no options left but to sell a child into hell.

The front door opened, and his mother stood there waiting with a cup of coffee in each hand. "You coming in, love, or are we settling on the porch?"

"Porch," he said as he walked over and took the mugs from her. He set them on a small table between two wooden chairs before reaching around and hugging his mother tightly. She hugged him back just as fiercely, sensing the chaos in his soul. He felt her unraveling the knots she found in his aura and cutting the auric cords threatening to overwhelm him.

Feeling lighter already, he released her and looked down into her wise, amber eyes. Her head barely reached mid-chest on him, and her frame was small, but her grip was fierce, and her strength was something he could always rely on.

His mother always sensed when something was off with her children. She always allowed her boys to seek her out in their own way or time when they were troubled, and they often did.

Jamey's way had always been late nights or early mornings. After all these years, he was still surprised to find her waiting with fresh coffee or cocoa to greet him when he needed counsel. No matter how hard they tried to hide their problems from her, she always knew.

His mother was a beautiful woman with straight, black hair falling to her hips. Her skin was a sun-kissed bronze from the hours she spent working in the sun taking care of the animals and her gardens. High cheekbones framed a delicate face. Her unlined skin made her seem closer in age to her boys than she was because the centuries she had lived had been kind to her. Her whiskey-colored eyes mirrored his as she smiled at him, welcoming him home.

Kateri Vance was blessed with three strapping boys, but you would never think they had emerged from her small frame. They all had their father's height and brawn, but Jameson inherited her delicate features, making him a very handsome man.

She reached up and framed his face. "I've missed you, Jamey. We haven't seen you in a while." Her words were kind with no censure intended.

"I've missed you too, Mama," he said, placing an arm around her shoulders and hugging her again. He led her to a chair then picked up his mug. They sat quietly while he drank his coffee and silently searched for a way to broach the subject that was tormenting him.

"They'll be up soon," he said, anticipating his younger brothers barreling down the stairs to fight over breakfast.

"I can never feed them enough." She laughed. "I think the two of them are worse than when I had all three of you underfoot."

Jamey laughed. "They're nearly my height, and I think Tobias may be taller than me when he's done growing."

Jamey usually returned home with stories of Fergus and Danyka's antics. He loved sharing the missions they went on and the people they helped with his family. His brothers wanted to be wardens when they were old enough and looked forward to hearing about his recent adventures. Tobias would be attending the summer session coming up, and Jamey would have the opportunity to spend more time with him while he at Heart Island.

His family always made room for one more, and their house was a revolving door for people who were down on their luck and needed a boost to get back up. Jamey often brought strays home with him—those who needed the comfort of a place off the grid, hard work, and people who gave a shit about them. Many of them found permanent work and a home on this farm.

Silence loomed between them, a rare occurrence. Kateri sat quietly, waiting for him to begin. Even if she couldn't sense his distress, his silence would have communicated it loudly to her.

He cleared his throat as he set his mug down. With his elbows on his knees, he interlaced his fingers and studied his hands. He clenched them as he tried to figure out where to start.

"It's Danny," he began. "I'm in love with her, and I don't know what to do about it."

His mother gave him a soft, knowing smile. "I wondered how long it would take you to come to that conclusion."

He sat back, meeting her eyes. "You knew." A statement, not a question. "Of course, you did. A shame you couldn't have shared that information with me and saved me some time."

"You needed to figure out what your heart was telling you. That wasn't my job. I could see it every time you looked at her. Your life changes when you find the woman you love, and it should." She raised an eyebrow at him. "You've had time to date and play—commitment-free—and there is nothing wrong with that," she said, "but I see your heart Jameson, and your heart belongs to her. It was obvious the first time I saw the two of you together. You just haven't trusted yourself enough to chase after her."

"That's not it, Mama," he said respectfully, "not all of it anyway. I've loved being her partner, always have. She's my best friend, and I didn't want to do anything to jeopardize the relationship we have. If this doesn't work, I don't just lose a lover; I lose a partner and a friend."

"I respect that, honey," she said, "but you'll always wonder what could have been if you never take that chance. How much longer are you going to be able to watch her with other men and not resent it? Eventually, your working relationship will be affected whether you pursue her or not."

"I understand what you are saying, I truly do," he said, "but I found out something tonight that changes everything and makes it even more difficult to move forward with her."

"You can tell me anything, honey." She reached over and placed a hand on his shoulder. "Anything you tell me will stay between the two of us, and I won't ever tell her."

He nodded as he ran his hands over his face, then looked up at her with tormented eyes. "Danny thinks the world of you and Da. It would destroy her to find out you knew. She would never come here again."

The severity of his claim made her sit back and take a deep breath. "You know I will never share what's spoken between us on this porch, Jameson Vance. Nothing you tell me about her will make me think any less of that woman. Please, share with me, so we can face this together and figure out how to help you both move forward." She reached out and rubbed a hand down his back.

Jamey pinched the bridge of his nose as he stared at the decking beneath his feet. "I've never heard anything about her past, her childhood, or family. She doesn't talk about them, and I've never pushed her."

His lip crooked up as he looked at his mother. "She's always been like a skittish foal, afraid of touch. A free spirit, she needs to run or soar unencumbered. It's one of the main reasons I never looked too closely at the ties my heart was forming to her. I doubted she would ever be able to settle down with any one man, and I didn't want to put myself through the heartache or disappointment. I've been a coward on that front."

"You're not a coward, Jamey. You're cautious. You'll find a significant difference between the two."

"Doesn't matter much now," he said, disagreeing. He struggled to give voice to the horrors Danny experienced. Clearing his throat once more, he spoke without looking at her.

"We had..." Ah, hell. How could he explain to his mother the joint sexual experience they shared? "We had an intimate moment tonight, and afterward, she ran off."

His breath caught as he continued, "When I found her, she was devastated. She told me that she's damaged and broken because her mother sold her to a brothel that catered to pedophiles when she was twelve." He heard her gasp but continued before he was unable to. "She was raped repeatedly, sometimes by more than one man, before Maddy rescued her."

His tormented eyes glanced at her and saw the horror and compassion on her face. "Danny has a lot of issues—triggers if you will—with men, and understandably so. She needs someone who can look past all of that and all her self-destructing behaviors because of her past. She still has night terrors. That's why she drinks so much and why she will probably never allow a man to ever get close to her emotionally or sexually for more than just the rudimentary act."

He stood and paced for a moment, leaning against the beam next to the stairs leading off the porch. He looked up at the sky littered with stars, trying to decide if they represented all the possibilities the two of them could have together or all the potential pitfalls they would face if they went down this road.

His mother sat silently behind him, processing what he'd told her. Jamey scented her tears and sensed her sorrow for the young woman she already loved.

This time, she was the one to clear her throat. "I can tell you one thing, Jamey. If there was ever a man with the patience and the compassion to heal someone who is hurting, it's you. You were always the best of us when it came to the skittish foals. Treat her like one. Give her the care and the space she needs and be there when she is ready to come to you for more. Leave the door open for the potential for more and sweeten the deal just by being the wonderful, loving, caring man that you are."

The question you need to answer, Jamey, is this. Can you let go of your anger over her past to make room for all the love she is going to need? She's going to require everything you've got to believe in the possibility of a future with you." Kateri stood and walked over to him. "She's the reason you nearly changed tonight, isn't she?"

Ashamed, he nodded. "I haven't lost control like that since I was a boy." His body trembled at the memory. "I could have injured someone tonight because the men I wanted to go find and kill are already dead."

"You didn't lose control, though, did you?" She rubbed his back in a slow, soothing pattern. "Did she see how upset you were after she confessed her past to you?"

"No. That's the best part of this whole messed up night. She compelled me to forget and then walked away. I had no choice but to pretend that it worked. She doesn't realize that I remember what she told me, and if I tell her, nothing will be the same between us again."

Silence lay thick between them as he gathered his thoughts.

"I contacted Maddy. She and Ronan met me at the dock, and she confirmed everything." He growled aloud, a bit of his inner beast showing again. "I love her." His eyes begged her for an answer, or at the very least for advice. "Mama, what do I do?

Kateri looked at her eldest son, and her heart broke for the pain she could sense coming off him and for the defeated look in his eyes. She wrapped her arms around him and whispered, "Honey, I can't tell you what the right thing to do is in this situation. The only advice I can give you is to keep loving her with everything you've got. Let her know that you will always be there for her, no matter how she lashes out. Show her that her past doesn't matter and that she is worthy of being loved." She sighed before adding, "We love her too, Jamey, and if there's anything we can do to help, we will."

Jamey put his arm over her shoulders, grateful for the loving home his mother had always provided for all her boys. He was close to both of his parents, and after hearing Danyka's horror story, even more grateful for the blessing of his childhood.

They stood there watching the sun rise over the hill in front of them. Jamey let the promise of a new day be his guiding light as he braced himself to move forward into the darkness he needed to pull Danyka out of. He needed to find a way to show her how much he loved her without scaring her away. Good thing he loved a challenge.

CHAPTER THIRTY-SEVEN

Even Though You're an Asshole

Kyran staggered away, horrified and disgusted by what had transpired in the park. He barely made it a few hundred yards when he bent over and wretched until he was dry heaving. His body rejected his behavior as much as his mind did. As he stood there doubled over with his arms around his middle and spittle dripping off his chin, he wondered how it had all gone so horribly wrong.

His intention had been to find Rhy and usher her safely home before she made a mistake she might regret in the morning. He knew how intoxicated she was before he even reached her. Their link made it clear that she was under the influence and incapable of making coherent decisions.

"Banner. Fucking. Job," his inner asshole chimed in. Not only had she made a mistake, but he helped her make it, and they were already regretting it.

He stood, wiping his mouth with his hand and hoping he could make it back without heaving again. His mind raced back over the events, and he cringed at his reaction to Roarke and the way he had allowed Rhyanna to verbally push him to lose control. He was a grown man, goddammit, and he'd never lost control sexually or taken a woman as violently as he had just taken her. He groaned as he remembered the blood staining his cock. He knew she had been pure, and instead of being gentle the way he had always intended, he had used his immensely swollen cock like a battering ram forcing his way into her.

The image of her lying on the ground curled up and sobbing, unable to look at him, flashed repeatedly through his mind. She had been terrified of him, and he knew there was no way she would ever trust him again.

215

He continued moving towards the portal listlessly as the memories of her body under his hands and the sensation of her smothering his cock had him groaning out loud. She was beautiful, ethereal, and so very sensual. He wished he had spent more time on her mouth; it might have calmed the beast she had awoken and helped him to regain control.

Images kept rolling through his mind, fresh, raw, and so very real it was if he was still touching her. He could see the curve of her neck under his hand, the tuck of her waist as he grasped her hips and dragged her on and off him. The silkiness of her curls and the taste of her skin under his lips made him rub his fingertips together and run his tongue over his lips, trying to catch any lingering taste of her.

Reaching down and palming himself, he could still see the heart shape of her ass and feel her plump cheeks against his thighs as his balls slapped against her.

"You're a goddamn fool, Kyran," a voice came at him from the right. "Doing what you did to her, you don't fucking deserve her, and I won't stand by and watch you hurt her again. You hear me, friend?" That last one came out sounding more like a threat than a warning.

"You don't understand what you came upon, Roarke," Kyran said sadly. "There's more to it than mere appearances."

"I know enough from the eyeful I got before you finished and from listening to her sobbing as she curled up into a ball and begged me not to touch her. That was before she disappeared right in front of my eyes," Roarke said as he moved closer with each accusation. "Where the fuck did she go?"

Kyran hung his head, exhausted and defeated. "She teleported, probably back to the Sanctuary, and I gave her nothing more than what she asked for." His excuse sounded weak, and by the way Roarke looked at him disgustedly, he knew it was exactly that, an excuse for inexcusable behavior. "I have nothing further to say about the incident to you. When she is ready to receive me, Rhyanna and I need to speak, and we will sort the whole ugly thing out."

"Well, you got one part of that right, asshole." Roarke glared at him as he walked into his personal space. "It was fucking ugly and not the way to treat a woman you claim to care about." He shoved at Kyran, knocking him back and almost off his feet.

"Don't fucking touch me," Kyran growled, moving towards Roarke with his fists clenched tightly at his side.

Roarke was in the midst of one of the shittiest days of his life, and he needed a way to take the edge off. Kyran had broken his nose earlier; how bad could it fucking get? His head snapped back as Kyran swung and barely missed him.

Roarke swung low towards his kidneys. If Kyran wanted to fight dirty, Roarke excelled at it. You didn't grow up on the docks and not know how to defend yourself and fight dirty. You didn't make money for losing, and when you were paired against those who were starving on the streets, you needed to fight like your life depended on it. A win meant the difference between a full belly and going to bed hungry in his leaner years.

Roarke held him close while connecting on Kyran's right side. Kyran swung an uppercut and connected hard. Roarke would have been impressed if he hadn't been trying to stay upright while his head cleared. He staggered back and managed a few deep breaths before Kyran closed in on him again.

Surprising Kyran by putting him on the defense, Roarke pummeled his face until his left eye was swelling shut and his upper lip split. Kyran, in turn, managed to pummel his nose again, and it was all Roarke could do to see out of his streaming eyes. Thank God for the alcohol running through his system, numbing most of the pain. Exhausted, they both stumbled together and landed on the ground, sprawled next to each other.

Gasping, they both lay there, trying to breathe and not choke on their own blood. Kyran threw his forearm over his forehead. He watched the night above and wondered when this day had turned sideways and kept fucking him in the ass. "I love her, Roarke," he said simply.

Roarke shut his eyes against the pain in his chest as Kyran was finally honest about his feelings. "I suspected so earlier when you broke my nose." He cleared his throat before continuing. "I'm surprised, though."

"Enlighten me," Kyran said, too tired to fish for more.

"You took her awfully brutally for someone you loved."

"She begged me to fuck her and basically called me a coward if I didn't follow through." He coughed while clenching his ribcage. He thought Roarke might have cracked a rib or two. "Oh, and let's not forget she threatened to go join you in a threesome and then take my father up on his offer to bed her if I couldn't be bothered. Yeah, that's what you missed when you took off, and it's what led up to what you obviously witnessed, Peeping fucking Tom."

"Public space, asshole," Roarke said, chuckling softly. "Use some discretion next time if you don't want anyone to watch." He turned his head and looked at Kyran with a raised brow. "A threesome?" He laughed harder until his sides hurt.

"What the fuck are you laughing at?" Kyran managed to kick him in the side hard enough to cause him to yelp.

"Motherfucker," Roarke shouted in pain before he started giggling. Giggling, for fucks sake. "Man, she's got you by the short hairs." He laughed harder. "She knew exactly what buttons to push to make you do exactly what she's wanted for weeks now."

Despite the situation, they both chuckled. "Fuck Me," Kyran said. "I've been trying to be a gentleman the whole time, and she maneuvered me like a pro." His laughter died off. "You think she'll forgive me?"

"I think she will. She loves you, even though you are an asshole." He hesitated, opened his mouth to speak, then closed it again.

"WHAT?" Kyran asked, tired, hurting, and in no mood to play guessing games.

"Will she be all right?" Roarke asked. "Tonight? She seemed pretty devastated."

"She will. I promise. I'm sensing a lot of guilt and shame, but not any major physical pain."

"Good thing, or I would have to kick your ass again."

"Again?" Kyran said, "I think we're at a draw."

"You going to her?"

"Not tonight. I don't think she'd welcome me." He sat up and groaned. "I want to. But I think I need to give her tonight to sleep on it and pray she will see me sometime soon." He glanced at Roarke and couldn't fucking believe he was going to ask for his opinion.

"What do you think I should do?" Kyran asked. This was the first time in his life that he was at a loss when it came to a woman. He shook his head. He couldn't believe he was asking his competition for advice.

"Better get on your knees, boy, Roarke muttered as he pulled himself onto his feet. He offered a hand to Kyran. "You're going to need to do a lot of groveling before you're on your knees for anything else anytime soon."

"As much as I hate to admit you might be right, I have my doubts that she'll ever forgive me. I'm terrified that I'll have to live with the knowledge that I earned her trust and her love, and now I may have lost them both. I don't know if I can stand to live without her."

"Maybe you should try and check on her tonight, then. I don't think she's one to hold much of a grudge, but time may not be your friend this time."

"Wish me luck," Kyran said.

"You fucking kidding me? I hope she kicks the shit out of you before she tosses you out. Then it will be my turn to show her what a real man has to offer," Roarke said as he started to walk away.

"Should've fucking killed you," he heard Kyran mutter.

"Yeah, brother, you should've if you could've," he chuckled darkly. "But you couldn't, and even if you could, where would the fun be in that?"

CHAPTER THIRTY-EIGHT

Stay

Roarke and Kyran parted ways. Kyran, he supposed, was going to find Rhyanna and try to salvage any part of their relationship that he was able to. Roarke liked Kyran, and he adored Rhyanna. They had the potential to be a wonderful couple. He hoped Kyran could fix the mess they were in now.

His mind wandered back to what he had witnessed between them after his original confrontation with Kyran.

He'd walked away from the shit show behind him after allowing Kyran to punch him. He spat out another mouthful of blood as his nose continued to bleed heavily. Chuckling darkly to himself, he wondered if he should thank Kyran for helping pull him out of his stupor.

With the first blow to his face, his disappointment and frustration cleared, and he knew what the next stage of his plan was to find Rosella. He'd allowed himself to be ruled by fear and frustration for a brief period, but now he knew where he was headed.

He'd walked about half a mile before his conscience turned him back around, and he headed towards the arguing couple he'd just left. His concern was for Rhyanna. He'd never seen Kyran so enraged, and he hoped the man would have the sense to keep his hands to himself before he thought of touching her in anger.

Reaching the corner where he could see the bench they had sat on earlier, he was surprised to hear them still yelling at each other while on their knees facing each other. Unable to look away, he heard her goad him into taking her as she faced away from him and presented herself to Kyran.

"Holy fuck," he muttered as he stood there stunned—and to be completely honest—highly turned on as Kyran positioned himself behind her. He saw the battle rage still on his face, and he knew he should step in, but he couldn't think straight as his cock swelled watching them.

Rhyanna looked beautiful, spread out like a dark offering, and as he witnessed Kyran slamming himself into her with no foreplay, he came back to his senses, sickened that he was turned on by this.

Roarke heard Kyran's body slamming into Rhy's and every word that he growled at her, still enraged. Rhyanna's sobs increased in length and volume. Roarke wondered if it was from actual pain or the shame that she had pushed this normally levelheaded man into this situation.

Ashamed of himself for standing there uselessly, he moved forward to prevent him from doing any more damage when her sobs changed into moans of pleasure. He saw Kyran begin to stroke her shuddering body as he chased his release, taking her with him.

Quietly walking away, he was swamped with equal parts of desire and disappointment. It would be a long time before he got the vision of her luscious body and tear-streaked face out of his head, and even longer until his heart let go of the first woman he thought he might be able to love. He was glad for them, truly, he was, but he couldn't pretend that he hadn't wanted her as well.

After the second run-in with Kyran that left them both bloodied and limping, he headed for the red-light district and turned down the second street on the left—Moonstone Way, named after the brothel owner who had built an establishment years ago. Amelya Moonstone opened a brothel that catered to the working-class men on the docks. Her girls were clean, and she insisted that they be treated with respect. The establishment was reputable and, more importantly, discreet.

Wiping his face with the back of his sleeve, he noticed his nose was drying up quickly. Wasn't the first time it had been broken, and he doubted it would be the last. Stopping at the bar for a bottle of top-shelf whiskey, he headed for the back room where Amelya's office and private suite were located.

Knocking thrice so that she knew he was a friend, he waited for her acknowledgment.

"Enter," came her soft voice from inside.

Roarke entered, closing the door and locking it behind him. Amelya stood before him in nothing more than a black velvet corset and some minuscule panties in black silk. She had one leg propped on a stool as she rolled a single lace stocking up her leg to mid-thigh. She tied the stocking with a pink satin ribbon. The pink was glaringly obvious against all the black she wore. She ignored him as she did the other side as well. Standing, she repositioned her breasts in the corset until they were damn near overflowing from the top.

Finally glancing his way, she gave him a once over from the blood drying on his face to the massive hard on he was sporting.

"Why 'ello, Roarke," she purred as she headed towards a clothing armoire. She pulled out a short, black, satin robe and faced him after donning it. Her long, honey-colored curls flowed thickly down her back to her waist.

This was the first time he had ever seen her hair down, and he was struck by how closely the color and texture resembled Rhyanna's. Looking over her generous curves as if for the first time, he realized how closely she resembled her in almost every way. The only thing missing was the small smattering of freckles dusted over Rhyanna's cheeks.

"What an I do for ye laddie?" she asked, coming over to him and tossing a damp rag at him.

Their relationship had always revolved around business. Roarke helped her out of a sticky situation long ago, and in return, she helped provide him with information from the docks and the dark world.

As if she sensed a change in the air, she came closer and stood, looking up into his eyes for an awfully long time before running her long-manicured nails lightly over his chest.

Roarke recognized the desire in her eyes, and it matched the hunger gnawing inside of him. The raging fire in his blood and in his throbbing cock desperately needed an outlet. He'd ignored his body's needs since his sister's disappearance.

Amelya ran the cat house, but she had long ago given up the life herself. He'd never even heard rumors of her being with anyone since he'd met her.

He reached out and grabbed her hips, pulling her flush against him. His hand snaked up into her curls at the nape of her neck, and he tipped her head back, pulling her hair tightly. "How do you feel about expanding the boundaries of our arrangement, Mistress Amelya?" he asked as he pushed his hips against hers.

"I like you, Roarke, I always 'ave," she purred as she rubbed against him in return. "But I don't usually mix business and pleasure."

She moaned as he slid a knee between her thighs and stroked her core firmly. She sighed and rubbed against him harder.

"This has nothing to do with business and everything to do with pleasure," he muttered as his lips took hers fast and furious. "If you want me to leave, speak now," he growled as he kissed her.

"Stay," she said decisively as she wrapped her arms around his neck.

He picked her up by the ass and rubbed himself harder against her core as her legs found their way around his hips.

"I don't have gentle in me tonight," he said between nips at her lips.

"I don't recall asking fer gentle," she growled and nipped him back.

He laughed and found his way to her bed, realizing she was just what his bruised heart needed. No strings, just some good, old–fashioned, mutual pleasure. He rolled her onto her stomach and pulled her hips up so that her heart-shaped ass was at the right height for what he needed.

He stripped off his torn and bloody clothes, then stood there fisting his cock as he looked at the beauty before him. With her hair falling like a halo around her, she turned her head and looked at him expectantly.

"Getting right to the main course, are we?" she asked in a husky voice.

"Only for round one, darling. Then we're going to start over, and I'm going to take you very slowly."

Her smile and her gasp as he positioned himself behind her was what his wounded ego needed. Pulling her legs farther apart and lifting her hips, he slammed into her and proceeded to act out the scene he had witnessed earlier. There was more than one way to get over the woman he would never have, and there was nothing wrong with taking his pleasure with the next best thing.

"Harder, Roarke," she whispered as he slammed into her again.

"Whatever the lady wants," he said as he leaned over and kissed her softly on the back of the neck.

"She wants more…"

He proceeded to give her exactly what she wanted, repeatedly, throughout the night and into the next morning. As they caught their breath with their limbs entwined, he found a sense of peace he hadn't experienced in months.

"Thank you, darling," he said as he drifted off.

"No, Roarke," she said with a sigh, "'tis I who should be thanking ye."

He smiled against her temple and then slept deeply for the first time since Rosella had been taken, with Amelya's hands combing through his damp hair and her lips whispering over his skin.

CHAPTER THIRTY-NINE

Shame and Blame

Rhyanna landed, still curled in a ball on the floor of her bedroom. Her emotional state altered her intended location, and she missed the bed by three feet. She blocked all her telepathic links to anyone in the sanctuary as she lay sobbing for what she caused and what she lost due to her drunken antics.

As she lay on the floor, she could still feel the strength of his hands covering hers as he interlaced their fingers. She remembered the moment she realized he was going to take her, and he wasn't going to be gentle.

His cock barely breached her opening before it dawned on her that he was much larger than anticipated. She only had a moment to be afraid before he thrust through her barrier without a hint of foreplay. The pain was white-hot and explosive, and for a second, she couldn't breathe. A second was all she was given before he pulled out and started slamming into her viscously over and over again. His cock tore through her body, battering her inner walls, while the contempt in his tone as he fucked her ripped her heart to shreds, causing her greater pain.

Kyran was a man who had never been anything but gentle and kind to her. Rhy never would have believed that she could have provoked him to take her virginity the way that he had. Remembering her taunts, she groaned and honestly couldn't blame him for proving his point to her over and over, thrust after painful thrust. There had been no love visible in their encounter or the aftermath.

Squeezing her thighs together tightly, she tried to forget how much pain there was every time he slammed into her. Her body cringed as she reviewed their encounter scene by scene. When he finally released her hands and repositioned her, it was even worse. The instant pain of his first thrust didn't last long, but the way the length of him kept slamming into the end of her canal was brutal, and her womb started contracting in painful bursts. As if that wasn't bad enough, the girth of him at his base was so wide that he tore her entrance. Each additional thrust rubbed against the minute tears, irritating them even more.

She tried not to cry, not wanting to admit her discomfort after she begged him for this. The majority of her sobs were from his verbal attack, not his physical one. He talked to her with such utter loathing that her heart seized up in anguish when she realized he had given up and was fucking her like someone he wouldn't even remember whence done.

Rhy knew she'd lost him as he took her like a common court whore, giving her exactly what she demanded and nothing more, having no consideration for her regrets or her pain.

Even knowing that this was her choice, she felt cheap and used. The fact that her body started enjoying his ministrations, as harsh and cruel as they were, made her feel even more despicable. As his cock swelled inside of her, he'd released her hands and changed the angle once again. Her body stirred in pleasure and surprise that there was something enjoyable at the end of the overwhelming pain and humiliation. Her channel lubricated, helping him glide in and out easier, bruising her less as he moved within her. As he thrust faster, the head of him bumped a place inside of her that made her nerves light up, and instead of sobbing, she found herself moaning every time he brushed against it. Her hips moved with him, meeting his thrusts, and when he finally came apart inside of her, her body seized around him, milking his cock as her limbs trembled with the full-body pleasure she received.

For a moment after he finished, he leaned against her, and she thought he might not despise her, but then he stood without a word and walked away to pick up his shirt. He dressed and re-laced his breeches before turning back to her and asking if he should contact someone. She held up her hand to keep him back, too ashamed by her behavior and terrified of seeing the loathing in his eyes and hearing the scorn in his voice. He left her then, and she was sure she heard him retching, mortifying her even more.

She lay curled up on the carpet, rocking back and forth, wondering how in the hell she was ever going to salvage what they once had together or her dignity. Her behavior today was so far from her norm that she was terrified he would no longer want anything to do with her.

For the first time since they met, she knew fear. She was afraid that he was lost to her forever and that he would never look at her like he once had—like she was someone special, treasured, and loved.

As the alcohol burned out of her system, she experienced pure terror that she had taken something irreplaceable and shattered it beyond recognition. How could she face him again after this? Would her heart be able to stand his disdain and disappointment? She would be devastated if he looked at her with the cold, dismissive stare she saw for the first time tonight.

She wasn't afraid of the storms raging in his eyes; she liked the heat and welcomed the challenge. The cold scared her, though. His indifference and the lack of anything left between them was what she was terrified to face.

With her mind, she started the water pouring into the copper tub, keeping the temperature on the hot side to soothe the aches out of her battered body and heart. She picked herself up off the floor and caught her image in the full-length mirror hanging on her door.

Walking closer to her reflection, she traced the bruises on her neck from his love bites. The edges of his fingers were becoming visible where they gripped her neck from behind. The bosom of her dress was ripped from when she had fallen to her knees. Her hair was tangled and had bits of dirt and old leaves tangled into her curls.

Looking like something the cat dragged in, she reached behind her and loosened the corset back on her dress to remove the damaged fabric from her body. She balled the outfit up and threw it in the trash behind her, never wanting to see it again. When she turned back once more, her eyes continued tracing the evidence of the ways he had loved her.

Loved? No, that word had nothing to do with what they had done. Love hadn't been involved in any way or form. He fucked her, pure and simple. That's what she asked for, and that's what he gave her. She wanted him to take her like he had taken the courtier earlier in the day, and he showed her just how much it meant. Nothing. A release. Simple, unadulterated sex. No feelings, no remorse, and no messy emotions afterward. A quick meaningless fuck is what she had reduced them to.

Her eyes continued to overflow as her hands traced the marks her eyes had already mapped out. Her sobs stopped as if her throat had closed, unable to voice the anguish she was experiencing. She traced her waist where he held her tight as he plowed into her repeatedly, chasing his release. Then they moved lower to her hips where, again, bruises were forming.

As her eyes traced her dark blond pubic hair, she noticed moisture still trapped in her curls, evidence of her arousal arriving late to the scene and his seed still dripping out of her. Curious, she ran her finger through the mess and brought it to her nose, wondering how they smelled together. Musky with a hint of wild. Sliding her finger into her mouth, she tasted the saltiness of his seed and a hint of copper from him battering through her barrier.

As she finally met her eyes in the mirror, she noted the innocence lost and the haunted loneliness she was terrified would be her future.

She shut the water off with a thought and stared at the sorrow trailing down her face and knew squarely where to put the blame. She closed her eyes, shutting out the evidence of losing her mind and her temper. Reaching out with her power, she extinguished the light to stop seeing the reminder of her mistakes in the mirror.

Rhyanna sensed someone coming down the hall and prayed they wouldn't be looking for her. She froze as a light knock sounded on her door.

Panicked, she stood frozen and naked, not wanting to see any of the other wardens right now. She needed time to put her defenses back into place and to be able to plaster a smile on her face when she still wanted to scream. Praying they would go away, she remained silent until she sensed him.

She knew who was at the door the moment her bridge lit up with his presence. Heart racing and unsure of what to do, she was about to reach for a robe when Kyran spoke so softly she thought she was imagining it.

"Rhyanna," he said, pausing before adding, "please, let me in." His voice was gravelly and destroyed.

She waited, heart in her throat, not sure she was able to face the shame and guilt racing towards her once more like a tidal wave ready to drag her under.

"My lady, please..." he begged softly. "Just talk to me."

That was all she needed to hear. "My lady" was the term he always used as an endearment because he liked to think of her as his. The tears fell faster as the realization that he wasn't done with her finally registered. Hope lifted its battered head inside of her, looking for the light.

Without another thought for her nudity, she opened her door. He stood as he had the first time she had seen him in the foyer—his arm leaning against the frame, his head resting against it, and blood dripping onto the floor.

He had been looking down until she answered the door, and his eyes flew up to meet hers. His regret and concern floored her. He looked her over from head to toe before speaking again. "My lady, I'm so sorry. Can you ever forgive me?"

CHAPTER FORTY

Rosella Diaries
Fifth Entry

Rosella's days had flown by. When Pearl had first purchased her, she anticipated being whored out rather quickly. Pearl's training process surprised and impressed her. She looked at each woman in her care as a gem that she wanted to polish until she made it sparkle and shine, awaiting the proper fitting to set it in.

Afternoons were filled with tutors in etiquette, voice, music, and art. Pearl supplied high-end escorts—as she liked to call them—when she was finished with the girls. Rosella wasn't sure if she was happy that her mind was as much of a consideration as her ability to sexually please a man. She was anticipating a rather rudimentary first night, not having to entertain them with her singing or playing the piano.

The madam took the time to get to know her charges, having one of them dine with her privately for the noon meal. Their mistress wanted to ascertain how they were settling in, and she tried to learn about their lives before captivity. Rosella believed she did this to have more leverage over them. Today was Rosella's turn to dine with her, and she wasn't looking forward to the event.

Her mornings were still filled with learning how to provide proper oral pleasure to a man. Most days had been like her first day amongst the girls. Perform—critique—try to curry favor with your performance, repeat. Today's lesson looked to be a bit different.

There would be no personal choices today. The girls learned quickly who came the quickest, with the men rotating through their days, and often picked the easier ones to manage. Pearl was giving them a challenge today.

A dozen men were lined up against a wall with a number written on their chests. Many of them, Rosella didn't recognize. Her heart beat faster when she realized that Braden was lined up as well. He refused to look at anyone, staring straight ahead. Each girl pulled a piece of paper out of a hat with a corresponding number. Instructed to kneel at the foot of the man they had drawn, Rosella watched as the numbers dwindled, men were claimed, and Braden was still available. There were only two numbers left when her turn to pick arrived. Pray as she might that she did not choose him—she did.

Cheeks burning, she settled on her knees in front of him. The men's cocks were flaccid, although, through her peripheral vision, she noticed some of them stirring with anticipation.

Pearl stood at the end of the line closest to the door. She handed a cobalt blue jar to the first girl in the line, a petite blond with gorgeous emerald eyes. She opened the jar and waited for further instructions.

"Using your first two fingers, swipe a dollop of cream from the jar and apply it to your specimen." She always referred to the men in a clinical way. The little blond did as asked and passed the cream down the row.

When the jar arrived in Rosella's hands, she understood the cream's purpose by watching the men quickly swelling to obscene sizes. Their cocks looked painful to her. She looked up at Braden as she reached for him and whispered, "I'm sorry," as she applied the cream. He continued staring straight ahead. Except for a tightening of his lips together, he let no other sign of discomfort cross his face. The other men's discomfort was evident by their pained expressions as they tried not to touch themselves.

Before her eyes, his flaccid member grew, and her eyes grew wide at the sight. She'd performed on assorted sizes of men, but holy shit, this bordered on ridiculous. Not only did the man have girth, but the length of him was at least three to four inches more than she had taken on before. The comment Pearl made to her when she chose Saul on her first night of captivity came back to haunt her. *"Braden would have taken half an hour to come, and your jaw would be aching by now."* Oh Goddess, she hoped not. Breath catching, she wasn't sure she was up to the task.

"You ladies have been given the opportunity to learn how to properly perform oral sex at your own pace. So far, you have been in control of most of your experiences. The participants have allowed you control by holding back their instincts and enjoying your performances without assisting you in any way. This will not be the case with most of the men you service.

She wandered down the line with all eyes on her until she stood near Rosella. "Today, you will learn to give up control of the situation. You will need to relax your mouths and your throats to better take the man before you while he forces you to pleasure him. If you damage them with your teeth, you will be punished for it, and none of you would want to have to use Saul for a week to appreciate the men I offer you here. Do you?"

Every girl on their knees shook their head, looking at Ella in sympathy. Most of them would have chosen Braden the first night. But when Rosella had looked in Braden's eyes, she knew he didn't enjoy being used any more than she enjoyed performing. So, she chose a disgusting smelly man over him and had no regrets over her choice. Here they were once again, and she didn't have the ability to make a different choice this time. He knew this as well, but it didn't make the situation any better.

Pearl's voice snapped her back to the moment. "Today, you will allow them to fuck your mouths any way they choose, and it will be a much different experience. For some of you, it may be difficult to keep up, to breathe, and to trust them not to harm you. But I give you my word, they will do no permanent damage."

Her fingers traced over Rosella's shoulders as she leaned down and said, "You've got a challenge there; let's see how you manage it."

Pearl made her way back to the door. "If you look down, you will find two large rings on the floor. I need you to reach down and grab one in each hand. You will not use your hands in this exercise." She gazed down the row, meeting each girl's eyes. "Your lesson today is in submission—it is in relaxing and allowing this to happen. Someday you will realize the power you possess even in this lifestyle. Power can be achieved by becoming proficient at making your partner happy. Remember there is power in being a woman when you learn to exert your femininity."

The men at the beginning of the row were shuffling their feet uncomfortably and trying not to thrust their hips. Their swollen members glistened from the cream and from the drops presenting themselves on the head of their cocks.

Braden was fully erect, and when she looked up at him this time, the naked desire in his eyes as she caught his gaze made her warm and wet inside. No other man would have made her body respond, but this man had been kind to her when she least expected it, and he'd never been cruel to her. He'd offered her comfort when she needed it from a nightmare. Offering him some relief seemed the least she could do.

Pearl waited, and the pause was pregnant with lust and a hint of fear from some of the girls. As the girls tightened their grips on the rings, she said, "Begin."

The first three men grabbed their respective girls by the hair and thrust their cocks into their mouths without preamble. Rosella only knew this from their fractured gasps. Fear began to creep in as the other men followed suit. Tears were rolling down the face of the girl to her left as her subject pounded into her face, ignoring her muffled sobs.

Rosella's frightened eyes turned to Braden as he reached down and cupped her face. His finger ran over her lower lip, opening her mouth for him. She blindly obeyed as she looked into his hooded eyes gazing down at her. His dark hair framed his face, and he let out a moan as she parted her lips for the thick head easing towards her. He held his cock in his hand and stroked her lips with the soft skin, watching with a gasp as she licked the drops off his head.

Braden studied Ella's expressions. He didn't miss the fear that came over her face as the other men took Pearl at her word and fucked their girls without mercy. She had told them any way they wanted, and he chose to take it slow and enjoy the process, hoping not to traumatize her along the way. The man beside him was also taking his time, so Braden didn't think he would draw unnecessary attention to Ella.

When he cupped her face, the gratitude he found reflected in those beautiful orbs fucking slayed him. He didn't want to do this to Ella. Scratch that; he didn't want to do this with her being forced to participate. He'd begun to fantasize about her more than was healthy for either of them.

The cream Ella had applied to his cock burned for a second, then made him swell to obscene proportions. He knew she was going to struggle to keep up—most women did—and as the oils in the cream settled into his system, he knew he would only be able to take it slowly for a little bit longer.

He pushed the hair off her face and whispered, "I'm sorry." She looked up at him with those gorgeous, haunted eyes and blinked in understanding. His cock slid through her glistening lips easily, and he found a gentle rhythm, giving her part of his length that she managed with ease. He closed his eyes, enjoying his fantasy coming to life, and imagined her reaching up and cupping his balls and stroking the rest of his length in her soft palm. A growl of pleasure erupted from his lips.

Ella was grateful for the reprieve he had given her to begin with. He took his time and let her acclimate to the size of him by only giving her half of his length to start. She observed him as he used her mouth for his pleasure. The sight of his dark hair damp with sweat against his face, his eyes nearly closed, and his teeth clenched as he growled in pleasure made her experience something in the pit of her stomach she had never known before. She was flushed and damp between her legs. When he stroked a thumb across her cheekbone and whispered, "Can you take more of me?" She gave a short nod because, in truth, she wanted to witness this man losing control because of her. Ella wanted to be the reason he came undone, and she wanted to do it well.

Braden noticed the flush covering her face and the top of her breasts and recognized the flare of desire in her eyes from the little bit of experience he'd had with women who were willing. The fact that she didn't look at him with revulsion turned the heat up another notch. When he asked her if she was able to take more, and she nodded, he nearly came right then.

Taking her at her word, he slowed his thrusts, and on the next push in, he gave her more of his cock, watching as she struggled to swallow only three-quarters of what he had to offer. Her eyes were wide on him, and he reached down with both hands and massaged her jaw, tipping her head back as he kept up a slow, steady pace.

Holy fuck was she beautiful swallowing him like that. He kept his eyes on her face, looking for any signs of distress, and when she seemed comfortable, he picked up speed as sweat dripped off his face onto her breasts. He wanted this to last, but his testicles had already pulled up, and the cum boiling in his balls was ready to explode.

Ella wasn't quite sure how she managed to take as much as she did. Pearl's advice kept going through her mind about relaxing, and she did. Gift-wrapping her trust and handing it to Braden because she believed he wouldn't do anything intentionally to hurt her, she tipped her head further back, allowing him to thrust deeper.

"I'm fucking close, Ella," he said in a throaty moan. "Are you ready to take all of me, now?" His eyes searched hers for any fears and doubts. "I will call attention to us if I take it too easy on you," he said in a whisper.

Ella knew what he needed and what was required of her to successfully complete her deed. Grateful for what he was trying to do but understanding his dilemma, she nodded as much as she could around his thick cock.

The sound of moans of completion and thighs slapping against faces surrounded them, but the only thing she heard was the mere whisper of the words he had been saying to her. At times, she wondered if she was merely hearing them in her head or making them up, but his hand on her face so gently cured her of her delusions.

"Oh, fuck," Braden ground out as his right hand fisted her long hair, winding it around his hand, and his other still stroked her face. "Ready?" he growled at her, and barely waiting for her response, he pushed the rest of his cock down her throat until her nose was buried in the curly hair covering his groin. "I'm fucking sorry, but you're so fucking good at this."

Ella began to panic as she fought to breathe when he found a fast and furious rhythm, his cock pounding down her throat. As she fought the urge to fight or bite him, both hands clamped down on the sides of her head, and his voice whispered through her again, "Look at me, Ella." Her eyes snapped to his as his desire peaked. His lips pulled back in a grimace she thought was pleasure, even though it looked almost painful. Goddess help her, she liked the power she had over him and understood now what Pearl meant. She relaxed her mouth even more, allowing her jaw to unhinge further as he pumped furiously into her.

Braden was having the best sexual experience of his life. No one had ever been able to deep-throat all of him—not in his personal life, and not any of the women who used him for training purposes. The tension in her face and terror in her eyes called to his need to protect her. When he let go of her hair and grabbed both sides of her face, stroking her skin, he knew the moment that she gave him her complete trust. The selfish part of him never wanted this to end, and the other part of him wanted to cum quickly to put her out of her misery.

Everyone else in the room had finished, and they now had an audience. He knew if he took it too easy on her, she would be punished, and he didn't want that for her. When she finally gave in, he buried himself in her over and over, never looking away from her eyes as she took him down like a pro. Two tears rolled down her face, and his thumbs wiped them away as he finally exploded down her throat, watching as she swallowed everything he gave her.

Eyes filling and throat burning, Ella wasn't sure she could finish this without passing out. A moment of fear returned when she thought of having to touch Saul again. When her tears escaped, and he gently wiped them away, she was so grateful she picked his number today. As he trembled before her and finally spilled himself down her throat, she swallowed, taking every drop he offered. Continuing the suction, she enjoyed seeing the shudders running through his body. One last stroke of his thumb against her cheek, and he gently disengaged from her, then stepped back against the wall. His eyes were once more straight ahead and distant as if they hadn't just completed the most intimate of acts.

Applause around her snapped her out of her disappointment. Ella's eyes snapped up to Pearl's as she stood before her. "Well done, Ella!" She stroked a hand down Ella's hair and looked at the rest of her girls. "Some of you were comfortable with the lack of control, although many of you struggled. Ella had the biggest mouthful," she paused until the giggles calmed down, "and she did it with grace and ease.

"A big thank you to today's participants." Each of the girls said a dutiful "thank you" to the man they had serviced. After a mumbled "you're welcome," they turned as a group and left. "You ladies did so well today. You've earned an afternoon off. Enjoy it as you will."

Pearl turned to Ella. "I'm sorry, but I will have to reschedule our lunch for next week. I need to be away for a few days. You're adapting well. I know this hasn't been an easy transition for you, but I'm proud of you."

Rosella gave her a sweet smile, even though inside she was relieved by the reprieve of her company. "Thank you, Mistress," she said, bowing her head.

Pearl's hand cupped her chin, raising it so she met her eyes. "I sense something incredibly special within you, Ella. When I'm done with you, you will be something unique and sought after. Someday, you will thank me for the doors I will open for you."

Rosella doubted it but dutifully said, "Thank you again, Mistress."

Grateful to get off her knees, she stood and followed the other girls out the door. She chatted amiably with Gemma as she ate a light meal. Nervous about seeing Braden once more, she didn't eat much.

Braden was waiting for her when she finished. His face was void of emotion, and he was looking straight ahead as usual, as if nothing had happened since he dropped her off this morning. Rosella wasn't sure how to act or what to say to the man. He acted like she was a stranger once again.

Since the night he had untangled her from the sheets, they had been a little friendlier towards each other. She was even making more of an attempt to befriend Shaelyn. This was her new world for the unforeseeable future, so she figured she might as well make the most of it and forge some allies.

Braden strode next to her, not knowing what to say to the woman who had just rocked his world. He'd begun to enjoy her company and lighten up around her, but he wasn't sure if she would hate him for forcing her to take all of him the way he had this morning.

Opening the door into her suite, he followed her in. Shaelyn stood ready to help in whatever way Ella needed her. "Yer back early, mistress. What can I get for ye?"

"We've got the afternoon off. Would you mind fetching me a pot of hot tea with cream and sugar and some of their shortbread cookies, please? Then I want you to take the afternoon off to do something you want to do."

The shock on Shaelyn's face floored her. Rosella was ashamed of the way she'd been treating her.

"I not be sure if I should be doing that, milady," Shaelyn said as her face paled.

"Have you made any friends while on board?"

"Aye, a few of the other maids and deck hands." A blush crept up her face at the second half of her statement.

Rosella smiled, knowing she could use that to her advantage. "We were all given the afternoon off; perhaps some of them were as well. You don't have to, but if you would like to, please take some time for yourself after you bring me the tea. I'm going to read and take a nap. I won't need you until it's time to get ready for the evening meal."

Shaelyn gave her a brilliant smile. "Thank ye, me lady. Would be nice to get out of this room for a change and have the fresh air on me face." She curtsied and headed for the door. "I be right back with the tea."

The second she left, Braden made his way to her. He grabbed her face and stared into her eyes, the concern in his face evident, surprising her. "I'm so sorry if I scared you or hurt you, Ella. It was never my intention."

"You didn't, Braden. Not at all," she whispered, staring back at him. "I was surprised to find you there."

"I avoid those assignments as often as I can."

"I didn't know you had a choice."

"Most of the guards think of it like it's one of the benefits of this job. I prefer my women willing," he said as he released her.

He searched her eyes because there was a moment or two when he thought she might have enjoyed what she was doing.

They broke apart when they heard the doorknob jiggle. Braden went to open it to help Shaelyn. She breezed in with a stainless steel tea set loaded with shortbread, fresh fruit, and chocolates.

"My goodness, where did you find all of this?" Ella asked her.

"Jest have to know who to ask," Shaelyn said, blushing from the praise.

"Ye sure ye don't need me, me lady?"

"No, absolutely not. Please take your time and enjoy your afternoon off."

"I will, but I promise to return before the evening meal to help ye dress."

"That will be perfect." Ella gave her a bright smile as she left them once again.

After a few moments, Braden peered out the door to make sure she was gone.

"So, you were saying you prefer your women willing?" Rosella asked, picking up their conversation.

"I do, and had you been my woman, I would have kissed you afterwards to thank you for one of the best experiences of my life, then I would have given you the same amount of pleasure."

"You jest!"

He moved closer to her. "Never. I say what I mean."

"Always?"

"Always."

"So, you wanted to kiss me?"

"Truth be told, I still do."

He was so close to her, the heat radiating from his body warming her. She wanted his arms wrapped around her, giving her the illusion of safety, the way he had earlier when he cupped her face. "What's stopping you?" she asked boldly, not knowing why she was flirting with this man.

"If I kiss you, it will be because we both want it, and you're still getting over the man you loved. It's too soon. I don't want to be the man you distracted yourself with to cover up the pain."

Tears welled in her eyes at the thought of Manfri and the near betrayal she had just encouraged. "I'm sorry, you mustn't think very much of me."

"You're wrong about that. I think a hell of a lot of you," he took a breath, "and about you. But we can't afford to think down those lines when there are no happy endings waiting for us." He cupped her face and traced his thumb over her lips. "If we got caught giving in to this, at the very least, they would kill me. Pearl would give you to the men in steerage to play with. I've seen it happen, and I won't put you through that, no matter how much I'm attracted to you."

Rosella appreciated his honesty and concern for her. She turned and kissed his palm, then took a step back from him. "I understand what you're saying, and I'm grateful to you for being gentle with me earlier. Most of the other men weren't, but you made it easy on me. I won't forget your kindness."

Surprising her, he leaned down and kissed her on the forehead, and before he thought better of it, he whispered in her ear. "You're welcome. Thank you for not hating me for it."

She gave him her first genuine smile. "Would you like some tea?"

"I would, my lady."

She fixed him a plate, then settled on the settee with a book. She only managed to turn the pages twice because all she could think about was the statement he made earlier, *"I would have given you the same amount of pleasure."* The gravel in his voice when he said those words made parts of her body perk up that she'd never been aware of, and Ella was struggling to keep her eyes off him.

A few moments later, when she failed to do so, her breath caught as their eyes met. He gazed across the room at her with raw desire. A blink later, and the moment was gone, and she wondered if it had ever been there to begin with.

The book fell from her hands, and she ignored it. Turning inward, she pulled up her diary, wanting to record today.

Dear Diary,

My usual morning training session came as a bit of a surprise today. Our lesson was to let go of control and allow our bodies to relax. Easier said than one might think.

Partners were chosen by luck of the draw, and as luck would have it, I chose Braden. To say I was mortified is quite the understatement. We have become civil with each other. Not quite friends, but no longer strangers either.

We used an aphrodisiac cream to prepare the men and prepare them it did. Painfully erect and larger than usual, they were given the ability to take us as forcefully as they chose to.

I was blessed by my choice today, for even though Braden was larger than any other there, he exhibited a decency and kindness that was commendable.

Going slower than most, he helped me to acclimate to his size before choking me with it. He also took longer than anyone else, and by the end, I was struggling to complete the task I'd been given. His patience and kindness helped me find the courage to finish gracefully.

My only surprise in the event was the awareness that I enjoyed the power I have to give him pleasure. I loved that I held the key to making that proud man come undone.

Braden told me later that he wanted to kiss me afterwards and that he'd thought about me, but there was no future in deluding ourselves.

I am loathe to say that I like the man. His gentleness appeals to me, and I begin to look forward to the times our eyes meet. After seeing them filled with desire, I wonder what other emotions I can provoke from him. The Goddess knows that he provokes enough from me. His heat-filled glances make me warm inside, and I find my mind drifting to him.

We were given a reprieve for the afternoon, so I shall spend it resting and reading a book while he looks on from across the room. My ever-present well-endowed shadow....

Disgusted with her thoughts, she tried to find something to distract her. Rosella turned towards the wall of windows and observed the gulls on the deck. The last thing she needed to worry about was an attraction to a man when all she wanted to do was escape this place and never look back. Rosella envied the bird's freedom and reminded herself, when she found an opportunity to leave, she didn't want anything that would make her take a second glance back from reclaiming her freedom.

CHAPTER FORTY-ONE

Forgive Me

Kyran stood in the doorway, waiting for her answer. She couldn't look away from him, and her eyes traced the new bruises on his face and the devastation stamped across his features. Struggling to find her voice, she finally managed to get out, "Can ye forgive me?" Her voice hitched, and she wasn't sure who moved first; all she knew was that she was in his arms, sobbing.

His arms banded around her naked hips as he picked her up, while hers wrapped around his neck. *"May I come in?"*

He waited for her nod and then walked through the door, kicking it shut behind him. Without a word, he strode into her bathroom, casting soft witch light into the nearby fireplace. Setting her down for a moment while searching her shelves for what he wanted, he gathered lavender bath salts and heavily dosed the steaming water.

Pulling his shirt over his head, he tossed it to the floor before kicking off his boots and stripping his breeches down. Nude, he met her gaze as his hands framed her face. *"I just want to care for you. Please let me."* His eyes were tormented as they stared into her tear-filled ones.

They looked at each other for a long time, having a silent conversation full of apologies and both begging for another chance. Rhy moved first. She turned away from him and stepped into the copper tub, settling in the middle, leaving plenty of room for him behind her. Her arms banded protectively around her knees as she scooted further ahead in the massive tub. She laid her cheek on her knees as she looked at him with swollen, damp eyes, not wanting to let him out of her sight—afraid he might not really be there.

Kyran observed her silently. She looked so little and lost in the tub, waiting for him. How could he have been so rough with her? She deserved gentle and sweet. If she ever allowed him the honor of bedding her again, that is how he would love her.

Grabbing towels and washcloths off the bench nearby, he moved them closer. Stepping in, he settled behind her with his long legs wrapped around her. She sat waiting, and he sensed her uncertainty on their bridge. She didn't know where they stood, and neither did he. He reached out and gently pulled her back against him.

"Tip your head back, love." He continued to communicate telepathically, not wanting to lose the intimacy it provided. He waited until she complied, then used a pitcher on the shelf next to the tub to wet her long hair. The ends of it were tangled around his cock enticingly, but the only intention he had right now was to take care of her—to right his wrong. He lathered and rinsed her hair while she sat silently.

Rhyanna sat tensely while he gently washed and moisturized her hair. Picking up a wide-toothed comb from the nearby shelf, he gently detangled the long strands. The silence was both soothing and nerve-wracking. She was terrified of the conversation they still needed to have.

Kyran separated her hair into three neat sections and efficiently braided it loosely to keep it out of his way. Draping it over her shoulder, he picked up the cloth and lathered it with her favorite soap. He knew it was her favorite because she always smelled like lemons and lavender. Starting at her neck, he gently washed her, taking care where the love bites and bruises were appearing, and grimacing as he found each bruise. Working his way down slowly, he washed her back, noting the marks that were forming from when they had first hit the ground. Lathering his hands, he gently reached around her and washed her front. His hands gently stroked her throat and then moved to her breasts, quickly and effectively cleaning her. When he finished, he used the pitcher to rinse the soap off.

Kyran's eyes traced over her bruised skin, ashamed that he had been so rough. He gently pulled her back against him. With her head against his chest, he leaned down and gently kissed the side of her neck that was bruised the most. When he finished, he turned her head the other way and repeated the gesture. His hands remained on her hips the entire time. Not soothing nor enticing.

"Please stand for me, my lady," he said softly.

She looked back over her shoulder at him in confusion but did as he asked. The water sluiced over her hips and legs as he looked at her in the soft light and lost the capacity to breathe. She was exquisite standing in front of him, back straight, proud and trembling.

Kyran resumed his ministrations with the cloth from her hips down her thighs and calves. Once again, his lips followed, softly soothing the hurts as he went. When he had finished, he had one more request. "Face me please, my lady." She still trembled, and he wasn't sure if it was from the cold or fear, or both. He wasn't sure she would comply until she took a deep breath and slowly turned. Her hands came out to grasp his shoulders to keep her balance as she moved.

Her breasts were at eye level, and he had only to tip his lips up and he could have sucked gently on them, but that wasn't what this was about. Rhyanna looked straight ahead, and it concerned him that she wouldn't look at him.

He started working on her front as he drained the tub and started refilling it with clean, warm water. He rinsed off her hips and legs before his lips took their time tracing the bruises on her waist and lower. He stopped with his face right in front of the juncture of her thighs. He started to pick her leg up to change her position when her hands clamped down tightly on his shoulders. He looked up into her startled gaze as his hand ran up and down her calf soothingly.

"I'm going to move your legs to the outside of my thighs, Rhy, so you have a wider stance. That is all, love." He noted the confusion on her face and tried to reassure her. "I promise, lass, I won't hurt you. This will help with the discomfort, I swear."

Rhyanna locked eyes with him for a long time, trying to sense on their link what he was up to. So far, he had been nothing but kind and considerate, but she wasn't sure she was ready to resume where they had left off for a while. Curious to see where he was going with this, she complied, widening her stance and clinging to the high sides.

She gasped as his unshaved face rubbed the inside of her thighs. His lips followed, kissing their way up the right and then the left side until he stopped at her core. Not sure they should continue, she started to pull away until he placed both of his hands under her ass cheeks supporting her.

"Kyran?" she asked, shocked and needing to slow this down. "What are ye about?"

"Demigods of the water courts have a healing enzyme in their saliva. Mine isn't as potent as those who have stronger doses of the gods' blood running through them, but it will help heal the discomfort you are experiencing if you will permit me." His eyes held only compassion and guilt as he entreated her to let him do this.

She sensed his sincerity to help and nothing else from him. She wasn't sure she could be so clinical about it, though. Just the thought of his mouth down there made her wet, and she knew he would be able to tell. So be it. Her curiosity and discomfort got the best of her. With a slight nod, she allowed him to pull her to his mouth.

Kyran was relieved she would allow him to touch her like this. He had his doubts that she would ever trust him again after his earlier behavior. His lips skimmed up her thighs once more, until he wedged his shoulders between her thighs, and his hands supported her ass. He gently swiped his tongue across her labia, familiarizing her with his touch. His thumbs came into play carefully pulling her folds open so that the next swipe went up the center of her, making her gasp and try to pull away.

"Shhhh, love," he whispered on their bridge as she hissed in a breath. *"I know it stings, but I promise this will help."* His tongue went back to work, slowly licking her. As he came closer to her entrance, he couldn't help tasting the sweetness of her arousal, and he noted how she was starting to move with him, too. Her hips were coming forward, rocking onto his tongue as he plied her gently. The next time she rocked towards him, he speared her with his tongue, sinking it as far inside of her as he could go.

Rhyanna gasped at the indecency of his tongue inside of her and then moaned at how good it felt. Her body was spiraling itself up to the pleasure that she knew she could find if she allowed herself to relax and enjoy it, but she wasn't sure this was the right time.

"Let me make you come, my lady," he pleaded. "It will help you relax, and you will sleep better after." His tongue never ceased plunging slowly in and out while he awaited her answer.

Her hands moved to his head and anchored in his hair. Her breath was coming quickly, and as she directed him forward again, she answered, "Give me this, Kyran. Please."

He smiled against her center as his tongue continued penetrating her gently. His right hand moved towards her front and found her clit swollen and needy. She did notice the pain was nearly gone and then noticed very little else as he rubbed her clit in time with the strokes of his tongue. Her back bowed as her body shattered apart. His knees raised behind her for support and were all that kept her from drowning in pleasure. Her thighs clasped around his head and hand as his tongue kept right on going, giving her body multiple orgasms before gently bringing her down.

As she sobbed her release and her legs gave out, he gently lowered her into the water. She wrapped herself around him tightly as the aftershocks still ran through her body. Her head rested on his left shoulder with her arms loosely around his neck. She'd straddled him as she sank into the water, her core nestled against his groin, and it was all he could do to keep his body from responding. Unsure if further advances would be welcome, he was more than content to hold her. He just wanted to help with the healing and tend to her needs.

Kyran slid them down deeper into the hot water to keep her from getting chilled. His feet didn't reach the end of the tub, and he was not a small man. "I love this tub," he said as his arms rubbed up and down her back under the water.

"Me too," she said, nestling against him. "I've been wanting to get ye in it for a while na."

They laid in silence, neither of them sure how to broach the event that had landed them in the tub. Finally, Rhy couldn't stand it any longer, and without meeting his eyes, she reached out and asked, *"Is it possible fer ye to forgive me, me laird, for me behavior earlier?"* Her request was laced with sorrow, fear, and a longing to fix this as her fingers traced nervous patterns on his chest.

He said nothing for a long while, yet his hands kept on stroking her back. As he felt a teardrop hit his chest, he tipped her head up to meet her eyes. "It is I, my lady, who needs to be begging for your forgiveness. I have been a coward, afraid to ask because I'm fearful of your answer."

Her emerald gaze locked with his, and beneath all the sorrow, he found hope and, more importantly, love. "I acted like a common whore and forced ye to take actions ye did not want to, to maintain yer honor, and I couldn't be sorrier for all of it, Kyran, ye must know that."

"There was nothing honorable about the way I treated you tonight. This is not an excuse, but I was drugged at dinner, and my head and my cock were not thinking as they should be." He pushed the stray hairs that escaped from her braid out of her eyes. "I have never been a jealous man, and I am not proud of those feelings. If you don't want to be with me, I completely understand. The way I took you earlier was unforgiveable." He clamped his hand over her mouth before she could speak. "But I truly hope you do forgive me, my lady, because I'm lost without you."

"It's not what I wanted at all for us either, Kyran. Fecking whiskey."

His cerulean blues crinkled with laughter at that, and he spoke. "Ah, love, there is nothing common about you." He caught her hand when she swatted at him. "Blaming the bottle, my lady?" He chuckled beneath her. "Is that all I must do to pick a fight with you? Set you to drinking?"

"Only hard liquor. I'm not to be trusted, especially with whiskey. I can be a mean drunk, and me filters no longer exist. Rarely has this happened in the past. I don't like who I become."

Kyran quickly sobered as he listened to her. "I need to also ask your forgiveness for causing you to seek the release you found in drinking then, too, don't I?"

"Ye didn't force me," she said fiercely, and then sadly added, "I couldn't think when I returned—couldn't face coming back here alone. I didn't want to answer questions or deal with anyone, so I went to the bar. Showed up looking like a drowned rat, too." She tucked her head back into his neck. "It was a coward's way to deal with everything, and I'm not usually one." She sighed. "I didn't think today would ever fecking end."

"Aye, it was a day from hell," he said as his hands stroked her back. The ups and downs since this morning have been hard on us both, and I have never let a wee nymph goad me into doing something that I didn't want to before." He reached down and kissed the top of her head softly. Serious again, he asked, "Will you forgive me?"

"I do, but what about yer betrothal?" she asked softly.

"I've already procured a position for Kai here and an offer of protection from Madylyn. The other two are old enough to know what they are dealing with. I will request Political Asylum for myself also, and we will deal with the court as we must. I won't lose you over this, and I've wasted enough time already."

Rhy sat up straighter framing his face with her small hands. "Speak plainly, Kyran. I'll have no more misunderstanding between us and no more secrets either. We share everything, or we share nothing. It's the only way we'll ever work, ye must fully understand that, or we're wasting each other's time."

His hands framed her face, and as they gazed intently at each other he said, "I love you, Rhyanna. I want to spend the rest of my life with you, create a home, and a family together if you want it. I don't want to be parted again, and if you will agree to be mine, I vow to do everything in my power to make you happy, to always share my troubles with you, and to give you nothing but honesty." He sighed heavily. "I will also learn to reign in my jealousy."

She giggled at the last part. "I love ye, Kyran. I want ye in me life and in me bed. I want to learn to please ye and to tease ye," she added saucily, loving the sensation of him chuckling beneath her. "More importantly, I want to be the safe place fer ye to come home to. A place fer ye to lay your troubles down and find peace afore ye needs return to that nightmare from which ye came."

Rhy's eyes never left his as she continued, "I trust ye to return, if need be, but only if ye promise to share everything. Every tart that hits on ye, every time the queen flirts. All of it. Ye need to learn to trust me to handle them as ye can trust me to manage Roarke. I may be a mite more direct, but I be capable of taking care of meself, and now that I know what I be walking into, I won't be taken by surprise again. I need ye to have faith in us that we are strong enough together whether we are here or apart. Our bond is strong enough to take anything they throw at us. If ye don't believe that, then we'll never survive." She stopped when his lips captured hers.

"I accept your terms, my lady, all of them."

"And I accept yers, me laird, and I promise to never again give ye a reason to be jealous."

He released the water and set her on her feet. He stepped from the tub, wrapping a towel around his waist. Grabbing a bath sheet for her, he wrapped her in it as he removed her from the tub. Setting her on the floor, he vigorously rubbed her dry before pulling her against him again.

"May I stay with you tonight, Rhy?" he asked as he feathered kisses over her face. "I just need to hold you."

"Aye, ye may." She kissed him gently. "Now, take me to bed before I catch cold."

Kyran lifted her easily, and as she wrapped her legs around him, he kissed her sweetly. He made his way to the bed, depositing her in the middle before ridding himself of his towel and joining her.

As she yawned, he wrapped himself around her, loving the way her head tucked under his chin and her ass against his groin. They couldn't get any closer unless he was inside of her, and that wasn't going to happen tonight. If she wanted him in the morning, he would make love to her properly. Sweetly, gently. But right now, he just wanted her to feel safe and secure in their promises to each other.

As she fell asleep, he held her tightly with the taste of her still on his tongue, the warmth of her in his arms, and the scent of her wrapping around him. He prayed to all the water deities he could think of to find a way out of the nightmare he had found himself in because he was afraid that when it came to the Court of Tears, nothing was ever that easy, and he wasn't ready to break a promise to her. Not when everything was finally back on track.

Burying his head in her hair, he slept, but his dreams were restless. He dreamed of taking her roughly again, and then he dreamed that his father was taking her and making him watch. The last thing he remembered was that they were all dead and he was standing in the middle of the Royal chambers with blood splattering his face and hands and Rhyanna lying unmoving at his feet, her dead eyes accusing him of not saving them, not saving her. He woke in a cold sweat, trembling as he pulled her closer to fend off the evil dreams while praying that was all they were. Just dreams.

CHAPTER FORTY-TWO

Bro Code

Kyran awoke with Rhyanna tucked in against his side. Her long hair was tangled around his arms and waist, teasing his already hard cock. He gently brushed the hair away from her face, taking the time to study her delicate features while she slept soundly.

His fingers traced her cheekbones before trailing over her jawline to the small dimple in her chin. She scrunched up her nose, moving her face away from his hand, then snuggled in tighter to his side.

Kyran suppressed a chuckle. He desperately wanted to wake her slowly and sensuously, showing her all the things that were possible between them in a better way than he had initiated her last night. He noted the dark smudges under her eyes, and guilt quickly chased away the desire and peace he found with her by his side.

Last night would be one of his biggest regrets until the day he died. He wondered how she was so easily able to forgive him. He didn't deserve such a sweet, compassionate soul paired with his rare but explosive temper. The memory of her temper the day before made him smile and rethink that. Mayhap, they were perfectly paired.

Gently he eased out from next to her. She sighed softly, and her hand followed him, reaching for him in the wide bed. The blanket was gathered around her hips. With a tug, he untangled it and gently pulled it up over her shoulders, tracing her skin with his fingers as he went. She smiled in her sleep as she curled up tighter. Leaning over, he kissed her forehead before turning to dress.

He was pulling on his boots when his brother Kai reached out to him.

"Kyr, where the fuck are you, man?" His tone was irritated. *"Been looking for you all night. We need to talk, and NOW."*

Kyran ran his hand over his face, groaning. With everything that happened last night, he forgot that he was supposed to meet all his brothers at the Rusty Tap for breakfast.

"Sorry, I'm on my way. Be there in ten. Everyone there?"

"Everyone, but you, asshole. You got us out of bed at this obscene hour and didn't show. Not cool, man."

"All right, I'm coming. Order me a trencher of potatoes, steak, mushrooms, and peppers with four eggs, over easy, on it. I'm leaving now."

"Move your ass, or I'll eat yours, too," Kai said.

Kyran knew he wasn't joking. The youngest of his brothers was still growing, and they all had bets if he'd stop at six-eight. He was the biggest and the brawniest of them all, but he was also the gentlest and kindest unless you required him to meet you at the ass crack of dawn and didn't show. Made him a little bit testy.

He found paper on her desk and left a quick note for Rhy on the pillow next to her. Committing the image of her to memory, he left her there, sleeping in the middle of her bed, snuggled into his pillow. Damn, he wanted to stay, but she wasn't the only one he needed to protect, and this meeting needed to happen today. It wasn't easy gathering all of them together away from court without someone noticing.

Needing the fastest transport, he used the portal. He exited at the end of the dock near the Rusty Tap. He walked in and spied his siblings in the small alcove in the back that offered privacy and a door to close if necessary.

A pretty little barmaid set his trencher down, and Kai glared at him as he stole the first bite.

Kyran pushed Kai into the corner as he took a seat on the narrow bench. It groaned under their combined weight. Neptune's line tended to breed massive men and small dainty women. Varan's boys fit that description, with the smallest of them hitting six-four and weighing two-fifty. Kano was across from him and Kenn was on the inside.

"So, what the fuck's so important that I had to watch the fucking sun rise?" Kenn asked, managing to throw his favorite word into that sentence twice.

"Varan," Kyran said as he shoveled food into his mouth, starving. He refused to call him father when his behavior lately showed little to no concern for his offspring. "Damn, this is good."

"Yeah, it is." They all agreed simultaneously, nodding their heads and filling their mouths.

"What about the bastard?" Kano asked. "He add some new playthings to his harem? Do we need to smooth over everyone else's hurt fucking feelings? Fine with me. Frees up more for the rest of us."

Kyran and his brothers were all named after water of some sort. Kai's name meant sea in Hawaiian, Kenn's meant bright water, and Kano was named after the Japanese God of Water. Their mother should have named him after the God of expletives.

"That is so wrong man," Kai said disgustedly. "I don't want anything that man has touched." A full-body shiver ran through him. He was the youngest and least experienced, but most particular of the four brothers when it came to women. "I've got standards. You should consider that yourself."

"I have fucking standards," Kano argued. "They have to be breathing, fair to middling to look at, and not have a fucking dick attached to them. I'd say those are damn good standards."

Kai shook his head in disgust.

Kenn shook his head while rubbing his bloodshot eyes. The only brunette amongst Varan's offspring, his dark coloring came from their mother's side. His eyes were as dark brown as his hair, and he had a double set of eyelashes that made him look exotic. Women loved his eyes, and he had to do very little to find company.

Kyran could smell last night's bender on him. Lately, he was drunk more than not, and Kyran needed to talk to him alone and figure out what the hell was up before he took off again. Kenn was reclusive, and when he didn't want to be found, it was damn near impossible.

"Listen up, assholes. You," Kenn pointed at Kano, "need to start treating women with a little bit of respect. Show yourself some while you're at it."

His eyes trapped Kai as his next target. "You, younger brother, don't have enough experience to judge any of us on where we choose to stick our dicks." Kai's blush made him move on to Kyran. "And you, fucktard, called a meeting at this ungodly hour and were fucking late. Get on with it so I can go the fuck back to bed. I'm nearly fucking blind from the sunlight."

"No big surprise. You haven't seen it in months," Kyran said.

Kenn glared at him, his dark eyes smoldering. "You asking me something or trying to tell me something, older brother?"

"We'll dive into that later," Kyran said with a smile, but his eyes bored into his brother's, letting him know that a reckoning was coming.

"Can't hardly wait," he ground out.

"Good, me neither," Kyran said.

The table was suddenly silent. They all knew Kenn had a problem, but none of them had been willing to poke that bear. Kyran wondered if they would stick around for the show or request the recap from him later.

"Sorry to disturb your beauty sleep, but we need to talk about Varan," Kyran said.

"Again, what about him?" Kenn repeated.

"What's wrong with him, is more the question," Kyran said. "I think he's being drugged. He fell asleep during petitions last week, wouldn't even agree to see me privately, and he's not acting right."

"What, he's more of an asshole than usual because he won't let you have your little blond healer? I'll take care of her for you when you marry into the Fire Clan, big brother," Kano said with a lascivious grin.

Kyran moved so quickly they never saw it coming. He was over the table, lifting Kano by the throat and pinning him to the wall by his neck. His brother was turning purple as the dishes he'd dislodged hit the floor.

"Don't you even think of disrespecting her or deign to speak of her. She is nothing but pure, sweet, and compassionate. That's something you've never known and will never appreciate."

Kano clawed at Kyran's hands, trying to catch a breath. Kyran noticed the barmaid heading towards them with a broom, so he released Kano before she arrived.

He turned on her with a huge smile. "So sorry, mistress, for the mess. Please, let me take care of it. He reached for the broom."

She shook her head. "No trouble at all." She nodded at Kano still trying to draw air. "He gonna be all right?"

"Yes, ma'am," Kryan said with an aw-shucks grin. "He choked on his coffee."

"I see. And ye were just helping him then?"

"Yes, ma'am. That's what older brothers are for."

"Say no more, I understand the bro code. Got five brothers meself." She quickly cleaned up the mess on the floor and the dishes from the table. "Can I bring you anything else?"

Kenn lifted a hand. "A whiskey and make it a double."

She raised an eyebrow, then nodded and went to fetch it.

Kyran peered at him, but Kenn growled, "Don't say a fucking word," before anyone could comment on his day drinking.

Kano's eyes had stopped streaming, but they glared at Kyran, promising retribution.

"Yes, Rhyanna's part of the problem," he said, looking directly at Kano and answering his earlier question. "I love her, and I want to belong only to her."

As they shook their heads, he continued. "I know that is a foreign concept to all of you. It's not like I didn't do my share of sleeping around over the centuries. Trust me when I say it eventually grows old."

They laughed outright at that until Kano piped up, "Maybe we'll have to try something pure and sweet while you're gone to see what all the fuss is about."

Kyran's face turned red, and Kai reached over, pinning him to the back of the seat with an arm across his chest. "You just had to open your mouth and say something, didn't you, asshole?"

"I ever see you near her, I'll fucking kill you," Kyran said, and his tone let them all know that he meant it.

His hand formed a fist, and he was about to let one fly when Kenn reached over and bitch-slapped him across the face, diverting his attention. "Since when did any of us let a piece of ass come between brothers?" He waited for an answer and was greeted with stony silence. "I'll tell you when—fucking NEVER."

Kano opened his mouth, and Kenn elbowed him. "Shut UP!" Looking over at Kyran, he said, "You obviously care about her deeply, and we will all respect that." He stomped on Kano's foot as he started to mumble something. "We will ALL," he glared at Kano, "help you keep your girl. What can we do?"

He smiled at the bartender when she brought his shot, chugged it, signaled for another, and continued. "The day I have to be the voice of fucking reason is a cold day in Hell, so pull your shit together, and tell us what's going on so we can get the hell out of here before I request the goddamn bottle."

Kyran ran his hands through his hair, trying to calm down. His emotions for Rhyanna were so out of the norm for him. "I knew the moment she opened the door that she was my destiny. She's beautiful, smart, sassy, and innocent in many ways."

Kano gave a naughty chuckle and spoke. "Now I understand. He found himself a virgin, boys, and wants to keep her all to himself." He put his hands out in a placating manner. "Just stating a fact, Kyran. Explains all the possessive bullshit. Not like I haven't had your sloppy seconds before."

Kyran groaned at the asshole. "Doesn't matter whether she was a virgin or not, it wouldn't change how I feel about her. I need to escape this fucking betrothal before I lose her. Can't you understand? I've found someone worth keeping, and I don't want to mess that up."

"Why don't you run?" Kai asked.

"Meriel threatened the rest of you, especially you, Kai," he said, hating to tell him that.

His middle brothers sat up straighter at that. All bullshit aside, Kai was the baby, and they had done everything they could to keep him out of her grasp.

"Kano and I can fend for ourselves," Kenn said, suddenly sober. He glanced at Kano, who nodded.

"I've been staying off her radar for years. I make sure she knows I like things she doesn't. It helps," Kano said. "I'm in control, or I don't play."

"Don't worry about me," Kai started to say before all three of them weighed in.

"Shut up," they said in unison.

"She will never touch you," Kyran said in a tone Kai had never heard him use before. "I will kill her before I ever allow that to happen."

"And if he doesn't succeed," Kano added, "we will."

Kenn nodded in agreement.

"Here's what we need to do." Kenn surprised them by saying, "I have a plan."

"Wait," Kyran said as he put a sound barrier of air in place. "Go on."

They gathered round and listened, then smiled at the plan he laid out.

Kyran, for the first time in weeks, felt hope stirring and sent up a prayer to Neptune that it wasn't premature.

CHAPTER FORTY-THREE

A Powerful Ally

Rhyanna was torn from her dreams by the late morning sun filtering in through her window. She'd fallen asleep in Kyran's arms, and every time she moved, he'd pulled her tightly against him, then buried his head in her hair.

A smile crossed her face as she remembered the warmth of him behind her, his saltwater scent surrounding her, and the feel of his cock hardening against her. Even though they hadn't made love again, she liked that he responded to her as easily as she did to him.

A slow stretch reminded her of the events leading up to her now sore muscles, and her smile dimmed. The night nearly ended in disaster after her drunken taunts finally gave her what she thought she wanted. The pain they caused each other because of her behavior made her curl up in a ball of shame. The blame for the way they came together lay squarely with her. Alcohol might have started her roll, but she goaded him mercilessly and didn't blame him for his behavior. Kyran repeatedly tried to defuse the situation, and she refused to back down.

"Thank you, Mother, for sending him back to me and for teaching me a valuable lesson in humility," she said in a whisper before adding, "and for reminding me that whiskey is not me friend."

She rolled towards his side, sadly noticing that his warmth had fled. Her hand traced the pillow he had lain on, then her eyes fell on a piece of a paper that lay on top of it.

"My lady,

Thank you for loving me enough to give me another chance. I will spend the rest of my life doing everything I can to make up for my behavior last night.

Miss you already.

Kyran

Tears filled her eyes as she pulled his pillow closer, burying her face in the smell of him lingering on the material. Missing him too, she reached out to him. *"When will I see ye again, me laird?"*

The warmth of his emotions flooded her as he replied, *"As soon as I am able, my lady. I am hoping to join you in a few days if all goes as planned."*

"I look forward to yer return."

"Not as much as I anticipate our reunion. I didn't want to leave you this morning, but I promised to meet my brothers and didn't want to wake you when I left. You were so tantalizing lying there."

"Wish I had woken with ye next to me. Me bed is a mite too empty without you in it. Mayhap ye can stay longer next time."

"I would like that, Rhyanna, more than you know. I've got to go before I turn around and head back to join you. I'm trying to resolve this once and for all. I will talk to you tonight."

"Until tonight."

As their link became dormant, she felt lost without his active presence on it. Well, the best way to conquer her melancholy was to get her arse up and moving. A groan escaped her as she sat up, and her aches and pains reminded her once again that she would be feeling them for a few days. She would think twice the next time naughty Rhy wanted to play.

Making her way to the bathroom, she filled the tub as she moved slowly around the small room, gathering supplies. Heavily dosing the steaming water with bath salts and essential oils to help her sore muscles, she lowered herself in slowly, cringing as she adjusted to the hot water. She quickly braided her hair and tossed it over the back of the tub to keep it dry.

Her eyes closed as her muscles relaxed, and the herbs and salts did their job relaxing her from head to toe. The aroma soothed the last of her jitters about last night and quieted a piece of her soul that she hadn't realized was still worried about the repercussions of her drunk and disorderly evening.

As the tension evaporated, her active mind searched for solutions to their problem with Kyran's pending betrothal. The king and queen would be of no help at this stage. She didn't trust Meriel any further than she could throw her, and Varan was oblivious to his son's affection for her. Oblivious or uncaring, Rhy wasn't sure which, but the result was the same.

Rhy heard rumors while at court that the king wasn't acting like himself. She thought back to her meeting with him last night. Varan was besotted with her, but she doubted it meant she was special. Many women gained his attention, yet very few were able to keep it for long.

Rhy picked up a cloth and soaped it as she considered the predicament they were in. As she rubbed the lather over her body, she tried to think of anyone who would have the power and would care enough to step in on their behalf. They needed someone with enough clout to question the betrothal without making the situation worse. They needed allies.

As she contemplated potential allies, Maddy popped up on her line. *"Rhy, when you have a chance, King Varan is waiting outside your clinic. I'm certain he is being drugged by his behavior."*

Rhyanna groaned, thinking about the handsy older version of Kyran. It wasn't what she had been hoping to do today, but she might as well get it over with.

"Well, he can damn well wait until I'm dressed and have something to eat. Relay that for me, Maddy, won't ye."

"I will, Rhy. If you are free this evening, would you stop by?"

Rhy noticed the cautious tone Maddy was using with her and knew she was treading softly after Rhy's angry words yesterday. After everything else that happened yesterday, she'd nearly forgotten about how hurt she was by her best friend. *"Open a bottle of wine after dinner, and I'll join you. I'll drink yer share, too."*

"You better enjoy every drop for me," Maddy said, and Rhy noticed the humor and relief in her voice that they were back on good terms.

Dressing quickly, she headed downstairs, grabbing a croissant and some cheese before leaving and walking to her clinic. She took her time as she contemplated how to deal with King Varan after his attention last night.

Had it just been last night? So many emotional scenes had played out for her in the past twenty-four hours that it seemed surreal to be feeling so hopeful. Deciding it was better than the hopelessness that had preceded it, she slowed as she caught sight of the Court of Tear's retinue lined up outside her apothecary shoppe and clinic.

Gaily dressed courtiers and attendants crowded the path to her door. Colorful silks and satins adorned them as well as jewels that were ridiculously out of place on this island. Many of those in attendance stared down their noses at her simple outfit.

Rhy was dressed casually in a peasant skirt and blouse, with her hair neatly in a long braid over her shoulder. This was what she typically spent most days in. Comfortable and practical were two of the requirements she had for any article of clothing in her wardrobe.

Snickers followed in her wake as the crowd parted to let her through. She heard their catty remarks and chose to ignore them. The bimbo that had been seated next to her at dinner batted her eyes in sympathy as she took in her attire.

Disgusted by them all and irritated at them for deflating her good mood, she searched for the king but didn't find him in the crowd. As she reached her front stoop, her door was ajar, and that pushed her from disgusted into full-on pissed off. It was always locked when she wasn't in attendance. There were medicaments inside that could be harmful if used improperly. Incorrect dosages could be deadly in the wrong hands.

As she took the last step up to enter, she overheard the bimbo say in a fake whisper, "The poor dear, I'm sure she is just devastated at losing the prince's attention. But look at the way she is dressed; is it any wonder? If she doesn't take any more pride in her appearance than that, she won't keep any man's attention for long."

And there it was, the spark to catch the tinder of her raggedly controlled anger. Turning mid-step, she faced the crowd of imbeciles.

"Yer right, me lady, to yer eyes, I be dressed poorly. You wouldn't begin to understand why because I doubt ye've worked a day in yer life. I help people every single day, and some of that is messy and bloody, so it doesna make sense fer me to wear silks and satins. Do I have them? Of course, I do. I jest don't feel the need to impress any of ye by wearing them. The people who matter in me life don't expect me to be sitting around doing nothing but looking pretty like ye seem to do all day."

She took in the crowd gathered and continued. "I run a business and heal those who've need of it. If any of ye have need of me services, yer welcome to stay. Form a line and wait quietly. Otherwise, I'll kindly ask ye to wait somewhere else. I've other patients arriving."

She turned back around but then glanced over her shoulder at the court bimbo again. "Me lady, from what I saw at court, a case of the pox is making the rounds, and ye might want to have that spot on yer face checked afore ye leave." It was petty of her, but she couldn't help it.

The woman's face lost all color as she slapped her hand over the pimple Rhy had acknowledged. The crowd surrounding her took a step back, not wanting to catch the sexually transmitted disease by close proximity.

"And the rest of ye best be on yer way elsewhere," she said in a testy tone before turning her back on them and slamming the door behind her.

Striding past King Varan without a word, she went to the hearth, starting the fire with a thought, and putting the cast-iron kettle over the flames. Soft witch light already burned in the lamps and the overhead candelabra.

Two guards flanked the king. The captain, Tristan, she met upon her arrival at court. The other one was young and shifted nervously. King

Varan seemed irritated to be kept waiting and then ignored her when she did arrive.

Facing the trio, she addressed the two unnecessary people in the room. "Out with ye both. Me business is with the king, and I'll attend him and him alone."

The young guard blanched, and an angry flush stained Tristan's cheeks. "My lady," he said in a patronizing tone, "the king is never left alone. It's for his safety."

"Really, na?" She stood in front of Varan and closely examined his appearance, taking note of his sunken eyes, sallow skin, and the patchy rash on the side of his neck. She took his hand and examined his nail beds.

Rhy studied Tristan and nodded at his partner. "He leaves; I'll not budge on that." She gave him a sharp stare. "Lead him out and disperse with that ridiculous crowd, and you may reenter."

Tristan turned to Varan, waiting for direction. The king gave a nod and he left with the threat of, "I'll be right back, sire," tossed quickly over his shoulder.

Rhy turned quickly to King Varan and framed his face with her hands. "Do ye trust Tristan, yer majesty?"

Varan tried to yank his head away and peered at her suspiciously. "Like a brother, I do."

She held on tightly, letting him see the sincerity in her eyes. "Be sure, yer majesty. Yer life may depend on it."

His eyes searched hers, and finding nothing but honesty and concern there, he nodded. He searched her energy for any form of deception, and though his senses were sluggish, he found none.

"Can we quickly form a simple link before he returns?"

"Aye, we shall."

Rhyanna felt a gentle probe into her mind. She allowed him limited access to her inner workings, sending him a simple link in the form of a piece of ivy that led to him. He took it and wove a piece of turquoise coral with the ivy, and they formed a simple mode of communication. They completed it a moment before Tristan rejoined them.

"Would ye gentlemen like a spot of tea?" she asked as she gathered her tea tray and the accoutrements that went with it. She made a simple blend of black cherry and cinnamon then set the pot on the table. "Tristan, will ye pour a cup for the three of us whilst I gather some herbs to help him?"

She gathered activated charcoal tablets and some herbs to help with the detox that would be necessary to rid the king of the toxins she suspected. They drank their tea as they waited for Rhy to finish.

"Sire, I need to do a more thorough examination in my clinic, with yer permission, of course."

He stood to follow her, and Tristan followed like a faithful hound.

"Please command him to stay here so that I may speak frankly with you."

"We met last night, my lady, did we not? I was enamored by your beauty and disappointed when you had to leave so early. I am grateful to have more time to spend with you, alone. Tristan, wait for me here."

"Aye, me laird, we did." She looked down bashfully as she took his hand with a smile, and he led her into the back room.

Once inside, she pulled him to the last bed and sat him down. She placed her palms on top of his head and drifted to the auric plane, trying to find the cause of his decline. Quickly, she cataloged the damage to his organs and his mind.

His hands on her waist, pulling her closer, snapped her out of her clinical assessment. They continued traveling, one heading for her bosoms and the other towards her arse.

Her irritation at the man made no room for him being a king. She threaded her fingers into his hair and yanked his head back viciously. His startled eyes met hers, and the beginnings of a smile played on his lips. "You like it rough, my lady?" he asked, pulling her in tighter.

"Remove yer hands from me, immediately. I am na one of yer empty-headed little playthings, and I never will be. If ye choose to ignore me help, ye may leave, and I wash my hands of yer fate, but if ye want to live more than the next few minutes, ye'll listen to me and stop fecking around."

Varan searched her eyes and saw the deadly intent at the same moment he registered her surgical scalpel against his throat. "You dare to threaten a monarch?"

"I dare to defend myself against an egotistical arsehole, yes, Yer Highness, I do." She glared at him, never breaking a sweat or moving an inch. "I been sewing up men for centuries, which, I assure ye, has taught me the quickest ways to take 'em apart. Now, what's it gonna be?"

He smiled lazily at her, and for a moment, she floundered, seeing an older version of Kyran playing with her. His hands dropped from her body before he raised them placatingly in front of him.

"The man you're in love with, lass, I hope he's worthy of ye."

"I believe he is, as long as he is nothing like this version of ye."

His brows drew together in confusion as he viewed her through different eyes. He examined her aura as she had done to him, quickly sobering. "Which one of my sons have you formed a bridge with?"

Rhyanna gasped and stepped back, shocked by his ability to read her so easily in his confused state. His power when he was healthy would be a force to reckon with. She sighed heavily as she answered. "Matters not, me laird. He is not meant fer me. Appears destiny has other plans fer him."

"Horseshit!" he snapped. "The only part destiny could have in their lives is one that I would have insisted upon. I've never interfered in my children's personal lives. If one of them fancied you, lass, I would have wholeheartedly supported it."

"But, Yer Majesty, ye've done jest the opposite. Because of the drugs in yer system, yer easily maneuvered and unable to think fer yerself. Yer sons and yer court are suffering heavily fer it."

His rheumy eyes watched her distrustfully. "Mistress, enough hints at it. What do you claim ails me?"

"Yer being heavily drugged, me laird, with opiates. They make ye confused, lethargic, loathe to eat. Ye've lost weight recently, I'd wager." She waited for his nod of confirmation. "It takes more alcohol to affect ye than before. Ye may have some issues with impotency or a low libido and constipation. Your liver is sluggish, and yer heart's been affected. If ye don't cleanse yer body, ye will na live another year."

King Varan gaped at her prognosis. "How is this possible? How could I not know?"

"I'm sure that it's been introduced in yer food or yer drink gradually, so ye've built up a tolerance of sorts. Now, it's wearing down yer organs damn near to the point of failure. Particularly yer liver, which tells me ye are very fond of a full cup. Added to the drugs, they're taxing yer system near to failing."

"You don't pull any punches, lass, do you?"

"I don't see the point, Yer Majesty. I can help ye, or I can send ye on yer way. That's all I have the power to do."

"Will, you help me, Mistress Rhyanna?" he asked with a heavy sigh. "I never wanted to disappoint my people or my family. Can you help me fix this?"

Rhyanna reached out and took his hand in hers, giving it a quick squeeze. "Aye, sire, I can and happy to do so, I am. Ye jest need to trust me, and ye need to be rid of yer retinue for the time being. Keep Tristan by yer side, if need be, but the others must go until we can figure out who is harming ye." She reached up and touched his face gently, trying not to compare him to his son. "I'll help ye, Yer Majesty. Let's hope for all our sakes that it's in time to help others as well."

"Thank you, Mistress Rhyanna. And please call me Varan. No need to be so formal when you're soon to be family." He reached for her hands, clasping them tightly in his own. "He is lucky to have found you, my lady. I had lost hope that any woman would interest him for life."

"We shall see how this all plays out, sire...Varan." She caught herself stumbling on the man's name. She released his hands and walked towards the shoppe. "I'll have Tristan come in, and ye can explain to him yer decisions."

As she reached for the doorknob, his voice came to her softly. "You didn't tell me which one of my sons you were in love with, my lady."

Her voice caught as she answered him. "Nye, me laird, I did not. When ye are well, ye may ask me again." Then she left him sitting alone to ponder his situation and what he could do about it.

Tristan entered and approached his liege. "My lord," he said gravely, "how may I be of service?"

King Varan peered at the captain of his guard and one of his closest friends and asked, "That wee lass tells me I have not been myself for quite some time. She said my sons and my court are suffering. Is she telling me the truth?"

Tristan's face blanched as he registered the king's first lucid words in the past few years. "Aye, my lord, she is."

Shadows whipped across the king's cerulean eyes, a storm threatening to let loose. "Why haven't you, my trusted friend, been the one to tell me this?" his voice thundered, and the walls of the small clinic shook with his wrath.

Tristan dropped to one knee. "I tried, my lord, many times, but you couldn't hear me with the queen whispering in your ears." His head dropped, but not before the sorrow on his face caught the king's eye.

Varan reached out and clasped a hand on the man's shoulder. "Speak freely; it's imperative I hear what you need to say."

Tristan looked at him with tormented eyes. "Queen Meriel is behind it all, my lord. She's threatened to place my wife and daughters in the harem or send them off on a slave ship if I act against her. I was threatened with this if I tried to sway you in any further way. It didn't matter because you wouldn't listen to me anyway. I chose to stay by your side, trying to minimize the damage that I could, Your Majesty."

Varan was sick, listening to the man's words. "You have my sincerest apologies for what you have been through and what your family is going through. If you will vow to help me overcome this, you will have the gratitude of your king and a boon to ask of me in the future."

"I only want you well, sire. I want my liege and my friend returned better than ever."

Varan squeezed the man's shoulder. "Rise, Tristan. Now we need to figure out what to do with them." He waved his hand loosely at the door, indicating the entourage waiting outside. "We can't send them back, or she'll know something is amiss. What do you recommend?"

"We could send them on an island scavenger hunt, with large rewards offered to the winners. I'm sure Mistress SkyDancer can help create some entertainment for the lords and ladies for a few days."

Varan smiled. "Sounds like enough to keep them busy and vying for my attention. Arrange it."

Tristan smiled as he made his way to the front. "Good to have you back, Your Majesty."

"I'm not there yet, but I plan to be. It will be good to feel like myself again. Please send Mistress Rhyanna in as you leave."

Rhyanna entered with a tray. She gave him some dark capsules and the glass of water. "Bottoms up."

Varan took them, then drank the tea she offered him. "How long will it take to remove this from my system?"

"Depends on how motivated you are."

His eyes locked on hers as he said, "As quickly as possible. I have a court to redeem myself with and some trash to remove."

Varan took Rhy's hand. "My lady, you have my apologies for any harm I've caused or any inappropriate remarks I may have made last night." His eyes traced her face, and she felt his energy gently probing her.

Rhy gave him a genuine smile. "Thank ye, Yer Majesty. I accept yer apologies."

"I'll offer Kyran those same apologies when next I see him."

Rhyanna raised a brow at him.

"I would know my eldest son's energy anywhere. Will you please tell me what's keeping you apart, my soon to be daughter?"

Rhy's face blanched. "If nothing changes, Yer Majesty, 'twill not be I who becomes your daughter, but another. You've brokered a betrothal with the Great Lakes Fire Clan with Kyran as the intended."

Varan stood shakily, towering over her. He framed her face with his hands and kissed her forehead. "I will fix this, Mistress Rhyanna. You have my word." He released her and asked, "What do we need to do to remove this from my system?"

"Drink as much of this tea as you can stomach, then lie down, and I'll work on you. This process will not be fun, and it'll be messy, but this will work if yer committed to the process. Do not accept anything to eat or drink from anyone but Mistress Madylyn, Mrs. O'Hare, or meself in the coming days."

He drained the cup with a grimace and poured another. With two in him, he laid on the exam table and allowed her to place her hands on his head. With a long exhale, he said, "Do your worst, mistress, and let's be done with this as soon as possible."

"As you wish, sire," she said as she closed her eyes and observed the muddy colors of his aura. The toxicity she was about to delve into made her nauseous, but she persisted, wanting to help the man and knowing that Varan was her only hope of salvaging her relationship with Kyran. She would do anything she could to ensure the future destiny had promised her. Destiny had sent her a powerful ally, and she intended to fully utilize the gift she'd found on her doorstep.

CHAPTER FORTY-FOUR

Kenn

The brothers stood and headed for the door. Kano and Kenn were in the front, with Kyran and Kai bringing up the rear. Eyes followed them as they moved past, but they ignored them. They were used to being watched as princes of the Court of Tears and as eye candy on the queen's to-do list.

A few of the women flirted, and Kano gave it right back, while Kai stared ahead, softly blushing. Kyran ignored them, having no interest in anyone but Rhyanna.

Kenn met the curious women head-on, and something in his eyes made most of the spectators look away. A touch of crazy or a hint of mean told them he wouldn't be an easy conquest nor a pleasant one. One harsh-looking woman at the bar met his eyes brazenly, recognizing a kindred soul in him. Kenn looked her over appreciatively as she played with a leather collar around her neck, and one corner of his lip curled into a half-smile and an invitation. He turned, intending to follow through, until Kyran grabbed his arm, stopping him.

Kenn glanced over his shoulder with a nasty sneer until he saw the pleading on his brother's face.

Kyran released him and said, "Can I please have five minutes of your time, and then you're free to go. I need information, and you're the only one I can ask."

Still irritated but intrigued, he followed him back to the booth.

Kyran sat on the edge of the bench, facing him as he stood. He ran his hands through his hair, struggling to speak.

Kenn was losing patience, and he was concerned. Kyran was always on the top of his game, and he didn't hesitate to say what was on his mind.

"Out with it. What the hell is bugging you?" he asked. "Is this about my drinking?" He quirked an eyebrow, expecting a confrontation about his recent dive into a bottle.

"No," Kyran said as his eyes met Kenn's, "not today anyway." His hands clenched where they rested on his knees. He cleared his throat and finally spoke.

"Why does she leave you alone?" he asked softly. "Why doesn't she torment you like she does the rest of us?"

"You sure you want to go down the dark path of my sex life, brother?" Kenn asked in a voice full of surprise. "You might not like what you learn."

"I don't give a shit what you're into, little brother. I need to find a way to take the targets off Rhyanna and Kai."

Kenn took a seat while his eyes moved to the woman watching him from the bar. "She leaves me alone because she likes to inflict pain, not receive it. A sadist at heart, she loves sex, but she gets off easier while terrorizing people. It's becoming harder for her to find her high, and it takes much more damage to her victims for her to find an orgasm, ensuring they don't want to repeat the performance—if they survive."

He rubbed his hand over his face, never anticipating this conversation. "Meriel thrives on draining the innocence out of people. She sees that in Kai, and she wants to drain him of his joy. She wants you because you refuse her. She creates minions. Think of them as her children who crave the same. She appears less evil when they go off the rails. Pain mixed with pleasure is becoming the norm in her harem. Look at the backs of her guards, and you'll find trails of scars from her flogger."

"And she leaves you alone because...?"

"We're alike in some ways; I'll admit that to a point. I enjoy causing my partners pain...but only because they get off from the exquisite sting of a flogger or a whip and request my brand of sex. I would be considered a Dom more than a true sadist. I pull more pleasure than they have ever experienced out of them in the process. I provide a safe place for them to act out their fantasies. If they become overwhelmed, we stop, and I give them a softer version without leaving them wanting or making them feel like they disappointed me."

"Do they disappoint you if they can't take what you want to give them?"

"Not at all because their ultimate pleasure is my goal. Sometimes I need to back down for a bit, let them relax, and regain control over any emotions the session might bring up. Most times, they need someone to listen to them and hear their inner pain before they beg me to work them back up and take them farther than we originally anticipated."

"Damn, that's a hell of a way to find pleasure." He raised his hands up, stopping the fight he could see brewing in Kenn's eyes. "Not my preference, but no judgment on yours."

"I appreciate that," Kenn said. "Think of my presence as therapy for many of them. Some have Daddy issues, others have a compulsion to please, and then there are some who simply love the sting of a whip. The pain borders on pleasure for them."

Kyran cocked an eyebrow at him and couldn't help but ask, "What do you get out of all this?"

Kenn laughed low and dark. "I get off right along with them, sometimes in them or on them. The closer they get to the release they need to find physically or emotionally, the harder I get working them up to find the pinnacle they need to cross to fall over. The longer it takes for them to reach it makes my impending pleasure border on pain, and that's what makes the process work for me. The longer I need to make them work for a release, the harder I'm working to find one, too." His eyes glowed as he talked about his sexual preferences.

Kyran shook his head, trying to absorb the psychology of pain and pleasure together. "All the more power to you. Sounds like you have to work a hell of a lot harder to get laid than the rest of us just blowing a load. No wonder you're exhausted all the time."

Kenn laughed. "Getting back to Meriel. She has no use for me because she can't break me. As sadistic and ruthless as she is, she can't defeat me because I embrace the pain. The sting of her lash and the feel of blood running down my back and thighs makes me harder and makes her madder. She leaves her partners in shreds physically and emotionally. When she passes them in the hall, and they tremble remembering what she did to them, it's her version of foreplay."

Kyran nodded thoughtfully. "Did she make you this way?"

Kenn laughed aloud at that. "No, man, I had my predilections long before she started sniffing around. Sometimes I wonder if I fed into hers." His laughter died, and he was quickly sober as his fists clenched. "She can never touch Kai; she would destroy him. He's too good of a person to become the train wreck I am."

"Ain't nothing wrong with you, brother, as long as your partners are willing." Kyran locked eyes with him and asked, "Are they?"

Kenn nodded as his eyes heated. "Of course, they are. I would never force somebody into my lifestyle."

"Then stop hiding who you are from us. The others aren't going to give a shit what or who you prefer to do behind closed doors as long as you aren't touching anyone underage."

"I never said I was bisexual," Kenn said as the color fled from his face.

"You didn't have to," Kyran said as he stood. "The woman at the end of the bar isn't the only one you've been checking out this morning. You've been eye-fucking the guy covered with tats playing darts just as much."

"How long have you known?" Kenn asked in a whisper as he cleared his throat.

"Almost as long as you have. There's no shame in what you want. Own your sexuality, bring it out into the light, and fucking embrace who you really are." He put a hand on his brother's shoulder and squeezed in support. "Hiding your true self is the reason your drinking, isn't it?"

Kenn nodded. "I've been terrified you all would find out. Kano is..."

"He's an asshole. There's no excuse for him. Yeah, he might rib you some, but once you kick the shit out of him, he'll leave you alone. Kai doesn't care."

"Wait," he said, his eyes widening, and his breath coming in short gasps. "You all know?"

"Yeah, and it's okay, little brother. No one cares who you're fucking or how you fuck them as long as it's consensual and they aren't minors."

Kenn's eyes showed shock but, more importantly, relief. He set his head down on his arms for a moment, trying to gather himself.

Kyran slapped him on the back. "Gotta go, but you can thank me."

"What the fuck for? Seeing the sunrise?" Kenn snapped as he glanced up, instantly back to his usual self.

"For getting you up early enough that you might be able to enjoy both of them before noon if you pull your shit together."

Kenn laughed then, a real one for the first time in a long time. Kyran had missed hearing him sound happy.

"Maybe, you'll be less miserable when you climb out of the fucking closet."

"Don't count on it, bro." Kenn smirked as he stood. "The miserable prick persona is part of why they flock to me."

Kyran smiled and left him there, looking more relaxed and comfortable in his skin than ever before. He'd been afraid of having this conversation but was glad he had finally grabbed the bull by the proverbial horns. He glanced back as he opened the door.

Kenn was talking to the guy playing darts and motioning the woman over to join them.

Kyran hoped eventually Kenn would find someone to make him happy; that's all he'd ever wanted for any of his brothers.

CHAPTER FOURTY FIVE

Enemies in Our Midst

Queen Meriel stalked through the halls, a dangerous predator seeking prey. Servants dropped to their knees, their eyes on the floor, praying she wouldn't notice them. Courtesans also knelt, but they did so with their knees spread and their heads held high, eyes staring straight ahead, hoping to be noticed and recruited for an evening with the queen.

The queen ignored them all, not interested in sport at the moment. She had a meeting in the lower levels of the hall that was of much more importance than an afternoon dalliance in her bed chambers.

Her personal guard followed in her wake. These were the men and women whom she trusted not only with her life, but with all the skeletons in her closet. If her misdeeds were ever found out, she would take all of them with her when she left kicking and screaming. Their blood oaths to her were imbued with dark powers that prevented them from betraying her in any way. Others had tried, and the throne room had been covered in their entrails when they tried to alert the king to her unholy behavior.

Meriel took the last flight of stairs, descending into the bowels of the castle and to the waterways that ran beneath it. Small vessels used the waterways under the cover of night to apprehend and disappear with enemies of the court—or rather, enemies of the queen. Dozens of citizens had simply disappeared since she gained the throne.

The stairs ended on a rough, wooden dock, the platform of which was in desperate need of repairs. The ancient slats were splintering in places and completely missing in others. The dark was breached by small torches, lining the walls at uneven intervals. The ever-present wind caused the light to dip and dive, nearly giving out at times, making the trip across the rickety platform even more of an adventure.

The queen's entourage reached the bottom and waited behind her. The silence was broken by the slapping of the waves upon the dock and the nervous shifting of her guards as they searched for hidden dangers to their monarch.

A faint light appeared in the distance as a small skiff approached. Securing the vessel, a middle-aged man stepped out and waited for permission to approach.

"Wait here," the queen said to her guards.

"Your Majesty?" Fintan, the master of her personal guard, questioned, concern evident in his tone.

"I gave you an order," Meriel said as she turned the full force of her agitated gaze on the man. "Are we going to have a problem?"

"No, Your Majesty." He bowed, hoping to curb her irritation.

With a disgusted flick of her hand, she dismissed him and moved forward.

Fairfax McAllister met her halfway. He was a spindly man. Streaked with gray, his dark hair was slicked back and greasy. Hollow cheeks made his flat onyx eyes even more pronounced over a nose that had been broken more than once. His smile showcased a mouthful of rotting teeth as he gave her a wide grin.

"Yer Majesty, it is truly an honor to see you again," he said as he removed his cap and bowed so far down he nearly unbalanced himself. "How may I be of service?"

"Stand up before you tip over," Meriel said in disgust. "We don't need to fish you out of the swill now do we?"

Regaining his balance, he hunched over as if anticipating a blow. He wrung his cap between his arthritic hands and peered up at the woman who stood half a foot taller. "How might I be of service to thee?"

Meriel laughed at the greed in his eyes. She wasn't sure if he were more turned on by the amount of money he stood to make or the thought that she would debase herself with the likes of something like him. She didn't have many standards, but she did have some, and she didn't settle for ugly men when she could have damn near any man she wanted.

"I have someone I want taken off the grid. Do you understand me?"

His beady, dark eyes watched her carefully, weighing her request. "Taken of the grid permanently, milady, or just removed from the local grid?" He wasn't about to agree to an execution without being very well compensated for it.

"I want her removed from the local grid. She's a healer and might benefit you on one of your ships. Not bad to look at either—your stables would benefit from her as well." Meriel gave a wicked smile. "But I want your guarantee she begins life on board with one of your roughest, most vicious men. She has little if no experience, and I want her broken in by someone who won't give a shit about what shape they leave her in when they're finished. I want her to suffer. Is that clear enough?"

"Forgive me for second-guessing ye, milady. Wouldn't ye prefer if she were sold to the gambling dens or the traveling bordellos? Ye could make a pretty penny from her."

"Absolutely not." Her eyes bore into his. "I'm willing to pay you very well to make sure her life is abject misery. I don't want her pampered or primped over. I want her used and abused. If you're incapable of the job, I'll find someone else."

"NO! Milady, I will happily take care of this situation for thee." He twisted his hat even tighter. "Where will I locate this woman ye despise so?"

"Heart Island Sanctuary," the queen said with a sneer. "It must happen within a fortnight. Can you accomplish this?"

McAllister's face blanched. "I'm not welcome in the area, milady. The whore running the place banned me."

"I'll pay three times the usual price."

His eyes bulged as he anticipated the gold he would earn. "Four times, and ye've got a deal." He watched her shrewdly. He knew if she wanted it badly enough, he could name his price.

"Done." She turned away, her voice fading as she gained distance. "If you fail to live up to your part of the bargain, Fairfax, YOU will no longer be on the grid. Are we clear?"

"Yes, Yer Majesty." He turned away, wondering what the hell he'd just gotten himself into. His greed would be the death of him one of these days. But until that day, he planned to make as much as he could. There was always a use for the bottom feeders in the world, and he happened to be one of the best skimming the bottom.

CHAPTER FORTY-SIX

Something to Look Forward to...

Rhyanna entered the foyer of the sanctuary, drooping from exhaustion. She'd spent hours helping King Varan purge the drugs from his system. This process would normally take a week or more, but the king was adamant about working through as quickly as possible so that he could try and fix the damage that was being done in his absence.

Rhy finally called an end to their work because she couldn't take on any more. Her body and her mind were exhausted, and she would be no good to anyone if she didn't take a break. She was also concerned with detoxing him too quickly and causing other issues.

The king vomited until he was dry heaving. His body was alternating between fever and chills, rambling incoherently in anguish for the pain that he had caused.

She left him with Tristan for the evening, promising to check in on him throughout the night. Rhy forbade him to tell the king about any more of the atrocities that had been conducted during his mental incapacitation. It wasn't helping the situation, and there would be plenty of time to assess the damage later.

She stumbled to the kitchen, her body needing fuel, even though she was nauseous from taking on some of Varan's side effects. Listening to what her body needed versus what it wanted, she perused the leftovers in the cold box and settled on some broth and steamed vegetables she thought she could keep down. Finding a fresh loaf of bread in the breadbox, she took the heel and slathered it in butter, adding it to a carved wooden tray.

Reaching for a bottle of wine, she remembered Maddy promised to have her favorite chilling for her. She took her meal with her and faced the daunting staircase to the second floor. Reaching the second floor successfully, she moved slowly toward Maddy's office. Peering in, she said, "Am I too late to join ye tonight, Maddy?"

"Never, Rhy." Maddy left her desk and met her on the sofa in the middle of the room. A bottle of wine chilled in a bucket in the center of a trestle table. Rhy settled on the sofa across from her as Maddy poured her a healthy glass. She handed it to her and was startled at the shadows under her eyes and the hollows beneath her cheekbones. "Honey, I hate to say this, but you look horrible."

Rhy managed a nod as she took a healthy swig of local red. "I feel it, too. I ken Varan wants the poison gone so that his mind will clear, but he's pushing too hard, and I fear the long-term effects if he doesn't allow his body time to heal as he goes. I couldna take any more tonight, so I gave him a restorative with a nip of something to make him sleep for a few hours. Na I need a nip to keep me going."

Maddy chuckled. "He can be a bit much. Have a nip for me, too."

"Aye," she agreed, taking a sip. "But there are times he'll look at me, and I see an older version of Kyran looking back at me, and I wonder what he was like prior to the current queen."

"I knew him, then," Maddy recalled as she took a sip of her tea—a poor substitute for the wine she really wanted. "He was a kind man and a fair ruler by all accounts. Queen Yareli and his children meant everything to him. I still don't understand how he was willing to lose his family over Meriel." Her nose scrunched up in disgust as she said it. "She's nothing but a piece of power-hungry trash."

"That she is," Rhy agreed in between bites of her meal. "And much kinder put than I'dve done." She took a bite of her bread, enjoying the crunchy exterior and soft, squishy inside. "I'm beginning to wonder what else the queen had a hand in. I don't believe he betrayed his wife willingly, not from the spells I'm unraveling from his aura. There's some serious dark magic surrounding him, and I am navigating it as slowly as I can. I fear triggering a subliminal suggestion that may be lethal or cause him to become violent. I could use Fergus's help tomorrow if he's available."

"Not tomorrow, he isn't." Maddy said. "He'll be gone for at least another day or two."

Rhy knew better than to ask for more details. Maddy always shared what she was able to with all of them. If she wasn't being forthcoming, there would be good reason for it.

Maddy set her cup down and fidgeted with the ring on her finger. She twirled the silver band as she tried to find the words to express her horror at what Rhy had gone through at court yesterday. "Rhy, I can't begin to say how sorry I am for what you experienced yesterday. There is no excuse on my part. I didn't believe she would summon you before Fergus arrived, and I thought I made our position clear on why you were attending."

"Maddy, stop," Rhy said.

"You were right; I never should have let you go in blind. I should have made you aware that there was a target on your back before you set foot on that island." Tears filled her eyes as she thought of what could have so easily happened if Rhy's elemental magic had been weaker. "You could have been…"

"Shush, na, love," she said, taking Maddy's hand. "I wasna, and that's what matters. I was furious when we spoke yesterday, but not at ye. I was angry at the whole damn place, the situation, and this fecking mess Kyran and I are in. I shouldna have taken it out on ye."

Rhy squeezed her hand, changing the subject. "How've ye been feeling with the wee little one? Has she made herself known yet?"

Maddy's face lit up with excitement. "Aye, she kicked for the first time this morning. Just a little movement, a flutter, but I felt it!"

"And where's your handsome man this evening while I am taking up all of your time?"

"I wanted to spend time with you, Rhy. It's been too long since we just chatted about something but work." She smiled lazily as her mind went to the man she loved. "He's settling Landon down for the night. It takes some doing; he doesn't like to admit the day is finished."

"He's an exuberant lad, that he is." Rhy giggled. "Any more exotic pets?"

Maddy rolled her eyes. "Thank the Mother, no," she said. "I think a rat and a skunk for best friends is enough for now, don't you?"

"Yes, it is," Rhy said with a chuckle as she stood. "If ye'll excuse me, me head is pounding, and I can barely keep my eyes open. I need to check on Varan in a few hours, so I'm going to catch a wee bit of sleep before then."

Maddy stood and hugged her. "Thank you for visiting with me. I've missed this."

"Me, too." Rhy headed for the door with one last thought for the evening. "Might the next time we gather be with all our friends and family. Seems lonely here with half of them gone."

"Aye, it is. Gives us something to look forward to—a full house and happier days.

CHAPTER FORTY-SEVEN

Take One for Your Kingdom

Kyran stepped out of the portal and into a shit storm. The Court Guard circled around him, leaving him no option but to follow along or get stabbed in the back.

"Tristan!" he called loudly, demanding to talk with the Captain of the Guard.

Tristan's second in command, Satish, a weaselly, little man turned to face Kyran. "'e's not on the island, and I be currently in command, so that'd be me ye need to grovel to, ye lil shite."

Kyran wanted to punch the arrogant little fuck, but he knew it wouldn't help the situation.

"Anyone want to tell me why I am being detained?" he snarled at the crowd, meeting some of the guards' eyes as he asked. Some of these men had been friends of his for many years. They couldn't meet his eyes.

Satish shoved him back, saying, "Ye left without Yer Majesty's permission." An evil smile crossed his pointed face. "Ye've also a commitment to uphold. Hope yer lil whore was worth the tumble because the next forty-eight hours will be hell."

Kyran struggled to keep his breakfast down, having completely forgotten about the agreement he made with Meriel for Rhyanna's safe passage. The past few days had been so unsettled that he hadn't even contemplated his payment coming due. Mentally tallying up the days, he swore under his breath. This was the weekend he committed to. Now, how the fuck was he going to get out of this situation?

"Move along, arsehole. We've got an evening to prepare for." Satish looked him over with a malicious grin that made Kyran's skin crawl.

Kyran reached out to Fergus telepathically. *"Please tell Rhyanna that I won't be in touch for a while. It can't be helped, and I think my ability to use our bridge will be muted. I don't want her to think I've left her willingly, Ferg. Please."*

Ferg replied, sounding like Kyran had interrupted something. *"Don't ken what mess ye got yerself caught up in now, lad, but ye best not be breaking that lass's heart again. Ye hear?"*

"Nothing new, my friend. An obligation to fulfill that I'd hoped to be free from. Don't tell Rhy; it will only upset her to know and not be able to tend to me afterwards."

"That obligation have something to do with yer stepmother?"

"Yes."

"Crickey! Yer in it deep, lad, aintchya?"

"Up to my eyeballs and sinking fast."

"Feck, Kyran. I can't come directly. I've a lead to follow, and don't ken when we'll find another as good as this one."

"No, worries. She won't kill me, just humiliate me. I can survive that. When this is over, I'll never come back here again."

"Still don't make it right, lad."

"Ain't a damn thing about the last month been right, Ferg. Eyes on the prize."

"Rhyanna's going to roast yer balls when she realizes what yer doing."

"We'll be all right. We discussed the possibility of this before she left court. This isn't playing out the way I'd hoped, but it can't be helped now. Tell her I love her and to hold tight, Ferg, if you will."

"Aye, lad, I will."

His line was silent for a moment, but Kyran knew he was still there.

"Whatever it is, Ferg, spit it out," Kyran said tersely.

"Don't show any fear or pain, lad. That's why she enjoys this so much. She craves yer negative emotions like the NightMares do. It's a compulsion for her to try and push ye past yer limits, and she will do everything she can to humiliate ye. No doubt about that. Ye've challenged her often enough and made her wait decades fer this.

She'll take her pound of flesh and let others do the same." A brief pause filled the line before he communicated again. *"No fun in humiliating ye if she thinks yer enjoying it. Ye see where I'm headed?"*

"Thanks for the pep talk, Ferg. I think you missed your calling because that doesn't help me a fucking bit," Kyran said with a hint of a chuckle. *"And as much as it makes me want to puke, I understand."*

Fergus's laughter came through their link. *"Aye, it's good to laugh while ye still can."* The mood sobered considerably as he left him with one last thought. *"Now, go take one for yer kingdom and yer woman."*

Kyran stumbled as he trudged after Satish. The man laughed and elbowed him in the side painfully, enjoying every bite of pain he gave the prince.

"Bring me the chains," Satish said with an evil grin. "Don't want him calling fer a rescue, now do we boys?" Laughter surrounded Kyran as he stood, gasping for the breath the blow had robbed him of.

In his mind, he raced to the bridge he shared with Rhyanna, needing some way to give her a clue as to what was going on. The blue light in the lanterns caught his eye, and he had an idea. This was a longshot, but worth a try.

"Here we go," Satish said as he took a set of chains forged from titanium from the soldier in front of him. He snapped the cuffs around his wrists and the spiked collar around his neck. The spikes were on the inside of the collar, putting mild pressure on Kyran's neck. He knew they could become deadly if enough pressure was applied. He reached again for the bridge and Rhy and felt desolate at the emptiness waiting for him. He would be unable to communicate with anyone until the damn thing was removed.

Satish grabbed the leash dangling from the collar and took great satisfaction in yanking him nearly off his feet. Kyran stumbled but remained standing and glared down at the little man with contempt. Soon the tables would be turned, and there would be repercussions for every slight. A reckoning would soon be upon them, and he intended to tally up this weekend's insults and pay them back in kind.

CHAPTER FORTY-EIGHT

No One's Lapdog

Kano fisted the brunette's hair tightly as she sucked his cock. He stood in the middle of his room with her on her knees while he watched the performance in the mirrored doors of his closet.

He didn't consider himself a narcissist, but he couldn't deny that he loved watching multiple images of her deep throating him—of any woman performing that act. His right hand fisted her hair tightly until she released him with a popping sound from her mouth. Tears were pooling in her eyes from the pressure he was exerting.

"You still think you're up to playing in my league, little girl?"

The tears were still there, but she glared at him through them. She nodded, albeit reluctantly.

"If you've had enough, get the fuck out of here, otherwise bend over the chair in front of the fireplace."

She swallowed noticeably, then shakily climbed to her feet and positioned herself over the chair, spreading her legs wide for him.

Kano ran his hand through the short curls on top of his head before rubbing the shaved side. The stubble soothed him as he ran his hands over it. He was so sick of the women in the court's harem. Every one of them thought that by banging one of the princes, they were bagging a future. They should know he was a losing bet by now because he rarely fucked any of them twice. He never kissed them or bothered to ask their names. Honestly, he just didn't give a shit and wasn't about to make the effort to remember them.

The ground rules were covered before they entered his suite. No talking, no kissing, and stay the fuck off his bed. The last thing he wanted was the smell of some skank he picked for his afternoon fuck.

Neptune only knew who else she'd been with before him today. Thank God he always wore a fucking condom. Always. No little bastards looking like him were going to be running around the palace in his lifetime. He refused to subject a child to the lifestyle he had grown up in.

He made her wait a few more moments while he decided if he really wanted to bother or not. He needed sex and lots of it. His libido, like most of the males in his line, was off the chart. The physical release he craved was necessary to survive the day.

Looking down, he found his cock was still in the mood, even if his head wasn't. Hating to waste it, he joined the brunette, vaguely wondering if she was getting lightheaded from bending over for so long.

"Last chance to escape," he said as he gripped her hips and lifted her feet off the ground to meet his height. When no sound exited her lips, he slammed into her with no preamble. Thrusting as hard as possible, he chased his orgasm so he could get her the fuck out of here because he was already bored.

Light gasps came from the woman as he found a brutal rhythm and kept it. His fingerprints would be visible on her for days, and she would be sore every time she took a step, but in return, she could claim she fucked one of the princes, and her standing in the court harem would rise. Her availability would be restricted to only the higher nobles, and the gemstone on her forehead would change from dark green to a light blue, acknowledging her accomplishments.

Kano preferred the middle ranks of the harem. Too low, and not enough experience. Too high, and too much ambition. He didn't like the newbies because he was afraid of breaking them. The consorts who made it to the upper tiers were looking for a noble to rescue them and take them away. Kano wasn't anyone's fucking hero.

Varan's line was eagerly sought after due to their endurance and high virility. Courtiers propositioned him a dozen times a day as he walked the palace halls.

This woman chose to be here, knowing his rules, so he pounded violently into her, without any guilt. Most women got off when he did. He wasn't sure this one would. Closing his eyes, he tried to get lost in the feel of her wrapped around him, and for the first time ever, he struggled to cum. Frustrated, his speed picked up as he continued using her, trying to finish, when a knock came on his door.

"My lord, I've a message from the queen," his personal valet, Charles, said.

"Enter," Kano gasped, never slowing down for a second.

Charles entered, not surprised to find him fucking another member of the harem. "Would you like me to read it, Prince Kano?"

"I'm waiting," he groaned. Finally, his balls were tightening up, and he could feel the cum rising. Setting her feet on the ground, he kicked her legs farther apart and grasped her shoulders as he thrust deep a few more times before finally emptying himself.

Charles opened the missive and read it aloud. "Your presence is required in the queen's chambers at once for a special mission representing the court. You'll be leaving immediately, so come prepared to do so."

"You can't accuse her of being wordy, now, can you?"

"No, my lord, she is quite succinct."

Kano pulled out and left the woman gasping as he entered his bathroom to dispose of the condom.

Walking back into his chambers, he saw she had dressed herself and was heading for the door. Her face was pale, and she didn't bother looking at him as she left. Worked for him.

Kano sat on the edge of his bed while he grabbed a cigarette from the nightstand. Lighting up, he inhaled deeply, embracing the burn all the way to his lungs and the way the nicotine hit his system. Falling back onto the thickly covered mattress, he closed his eyes, seeking a moment's peace.

"Anything else I need to know before I attend the royal whore?"

Charles tried not to smile. Kano knew there was no love lost between him and the ruling monarch, so it was safe to speak freely. Charles had worked for the Tyde family since Kano was a boy—nearly making him family.

"Not that I am aware of, my lord. I've heard rumors of escorting a princess back to court, but nothing beyond that."

"Lucky me, another princess to parade around like all the other high-class whores they turn out to be. Better pull out the full monkey suit and make it look good."

"Aye, sir. I believe the court colors are a wise choice."

"Well, she can wait on me. I'm taking a shower so that I look my best to represent my court. Do I need to pack a bag, or are we returning tonight?"

"I believe you will be gone a few nights, my lord."

"Will you be joining me?"

"Nye, I am not permitted to leave the premises for the next month."

"Why not?"

"Because I displeased her highness, recently and she's chosen to make my life difficult."

"I'll take care of it."

"Not necessary, my lord. I'll be released from the restrictions upon your safe and speedy return."

"If you aren't, I expect you to tell me, and I will fix this." The look he gave Charles left no room for argument.

"You have my word, my lord."

"Now that we've settled your predicament, you can send word that I should be ready to leave by dinner. I'm going to shower and take a long siesta before my journey." He turned the shower on with his elemental power and filled the freestanding tub as well.

"She won't be pleased," Charles said with an approving gleam in his eye.

"I don't give a fuck. I'm not her personal errand boy. 'Bout time she realizes that." He walked away, headed for the soothing power of scalding water awaiting him.

She might be the queen, but his dickwad of a father still outranked her, so she kept her claws sheathed most of the time around his sons. Kano was no one's lapdog, and it was about time Queen Meriel was reminded of that.

CHAPTER FORTY-NINE

Great Lakes Fire Clan

Fergus stepped out of the portal into the midst of the Great Lakes Fire Clan. He smiled as he made his way down the stairs to the place he'd called home for most of his life.

Two men in red leather uniforms made their way forward, greeting Fergus warmly.

"Ye've finally remembered where ye came from, Fergie. It's about time ye brought yer wild arse home fer a visit," said a mountain of a man with short, black hair and a long salt-and-pepper beard he'd banded every two inches. He wore small gold hoops in his ears and sported a crooked nose.

He pulled Fergus in for a bear hug, thumping him heartily on the back. "Sure be glad to see ye, lad. Been much too long."

Fergus laughed and swatted him back. "Good to see ye, too, Vulcan."

"Lad," the second man said, offering him a hand. "Been a long time since I've seen yer face." Brandell was the opposite of his twin with a lean physique, long, blond, banded hair, and a hint of a beard. He smiled widely as he squeezed Ferg's hand. He was half the size of Vulcan, but Fergus knew he was the deadlier of the two.

"Can I buy the pair of ye a drink?" Ferg asked amiably.

"Aye, we're off duty and always ready fer a drink," Vulcan said with a smile.

The three men headed down Main Street for two blocks before turning left near the docks. Another right and they entered a quaint little one-story building with cedar shakes and a crooked sign that was too faded to read.

Brandell grabbed a booth while Vulcan fetched a pitcher and three mugs. Settling his massive body at the booth, he poured them each a mug. He waited for the rotund barmaid, who was as high as she was wide. She had a big smile, straight teeth, and straight, thin hair bobbed beneath her ears. With a dirty tray in hand, she set down three shots of whiskey and a bottle to refill them.

"At'll be all fer now, lads?"

The men nodded. Ferg smiled at her, amused that she still treated them like they were much younger than her. "Thank ye, Aida," he said with a grin. "How are the bairns?"

"Doing fine, Fergus."

"How many ye got na?"

She rubbed her protruding belly and said with a weary smile, "This un makes an even dozen, he does."

"My God, woman, how do ye keep 'em all in line?"

"With a slim switch and a firm hand. All lads, too. I be cursed."

"I'm beginning to think ye jest might be, lass."

"Doan listen to her, na," Vulcan said as he slung an arm around her middle. "Me boys are decent lads, they are. Take after me."

"Aye, they do," she agreed with a glint in her eye. "What in the Mother's name was I thinking letting ye lay yer hands on me?"

"I don't think it was his hands that gotchya in trouble, lass," Brandell said with a smirk as Vulcan chuckled and pulled her in for a kiss.

"Any more sass from ye, and I'll be taking the bottle and bringing back me switch," she huffed, extricating herself from Vulcan's arms. "I've work to do and no to time fer the lot of ye." She nodded at Fergus. "Good to see ye back, laddie. Will ye be staying a bit?"

"Unfortunately, this shall be a short visit, but I promise to come back soon and take a peek at yer new bairn."

"Ye seen one, ye seen them all," Brandell said with a laugh. "Looks just like him, minus the jewelry and the beard."

"The hell with ye, Brand. Will be the last beer ye get tonight," she hollered afore she stalked off.

Vulcan cuffed Brand upside the head. "Doan be pissing off me woman. Ye won't be the only one cut off, ye bastard."

Ferg chuckled heartily. He missed his family. Brandell and Vulcan were cousins on his mother's side. "What's this I hear of a betrothal between the Court of Tears and the Court of Luminosity?"

"Oh, that bullshit," Vulcan said. "Da's marrying off Elyana to one of the Tyde princes."

"Whatever for?" Fergus asked. "He always said that he would allow her to choose her mate. Why the sudden change of heart?"

A look passed between Vulcan and Brandell that Fergus was unable to translate. "All right, ye two oafs, what the feck's going on?" His tone had a bite in it, and they glanced at him, surprised.

"Since when do ye give two shites about court policy?" Vulcan asked with a lifted brow. "What do ye ken that yer not sharing?"

"Ye first."

Vulcan drained his mug and then refilled it, graciously topping off theirs as well. "Rumor has it that it's a trade agreement." He stared Fergus in the eye, all humor gone. "Thing is, the Court of Tears ain't got anything we need that we can't find elsewhere, so it makes no fecking sense. Yer right, he did promise Elyana she could choose her future, and she is devastated. Won't talk to any of us or come out of her rooms. Wouldn't put it past her to tunnel out." He smirked. "Kinda hoping she does jest to piss the old man off."

Brandell traced the condensation on the outside of his mug. "Other rumors say that he's being blackmailed and hasn't got a choice." He sighed heavily. "Elyana has always been his favorite, and it's unlike him to break her heart."

A look passed between the two men, and Vulcan gave a short nod, so Brandell continued. "One of the Tyde men is supposed to escort her to court, but we're taking bets on her running off before he arrives. So do ye think he'll take her to court, or will she be leading him on a merry little chase?"

"I'd choose option B," Vulcan said with a laugh. "The girl is smart and quick and will do whatever she can to escape from this betrothal. I wouldn't put it past her to cut off her nose to spite her face."

"So, no one knows where she is at the moment?"

"Nye," they both said in unison.

"Yer turn," Vulcan said.

"Rumor has it that the Tyde prince she is supposed to marry is in love with someone else and as opposed to this as much as she is."

"Mayhap she'll take him on a merry little chase," Brandell said with a smile. "I hope the lass gets away with it. She deserves to be happy."

"I agree," said Vulcan.

"What do you think Queen Meriel has on the King?" Fergus muttered.

"Couldn't be about a woman. Da was never indiscreet," Brandell said.

"Ye, but yer ma passed near two decades ago. What would it matter now? Ferg wondered.

"Doan ken what it is, but it's bad enough to break his only daughter's heart over." Vulcan smiled at Ferg in a way that made his skin crawl. "Me thinks an official visit from the representative of the Heart Island Sanctuary is overdue in questioning the King of Luminosity."

"I was afraid you would say that," Fergus said. "You ken the man doesn't like me as a representative?"

"Aye," they said in unison again, reminding Fergus that they were fraternal twins.

"But," Brandell said deviously, "he won't be able to ignore a Sanctuary missive. I'm sure yer carrying one, ain't ye?"

Ferg nodded at him wearily. "I'll visit him in the morning, but tonight…"

"We drink!" the three of them said, raising their mugs and clinking them together. slopping beer over the side. Fergus nearly spit his out at the glare Aida was giving them.

They drank for hours, getting louder by the mug. Ferg finally sat there alone after the other two called it a night, needing to report for guard duty in the morning. He didn't envy the hangover they would be sporting in the morning. He'd come prepared and been drinking a lot less than it appeared he had. He was aware of their ability to drink him under the table.

He sat there enjoying the near silence as the place emptied out when he overheard a little man in the back who appeared to be talking to himself.

Fergus turned in the booth, stretching his long legs out and looking at the bar while listening to the man two tables over bitching to the occupant in the seat across from him about how he'd been taken advantage of. A mirror in the bar reflected the table, and he saw the man did have a companion, he just wasn't visible.

"Goddamn, Jonahhhh," he slurred to the man sleeping with his head on the table. "Only paid me less n half of what that new girl was worth. She was unspoiled and a pretty little thing I found near the Sanctuary." He tipped his mug and managed to only get half of his beer into his mouth.

Fergus used a glamour to slightly alter his appearance. He added ten years and changed the flaming red color of his hair to a drab brown that was straight and a little greasy. Grabbing what was left of his bottle, he approached the wily little man. "Might I join ye, sir? I likes a tale at the end of the night." He made sure the man saw the illusion of a nearly full bottle and took the chair the man pushed out for him.

"Name's Hamish, and I was robbed of a fine treasure I put a full day's work into. Bastards took the girl, threw pennies at me, then threatened me." He spat on the floor before continuing his woebegone tale. "They thinks they've seen the last of me. Wait til I burn them down in their sleep."

Fergus refilled their shot glasses, and putting a mild compulsion into his voice he asked, "Who robbed ye, man?"

"Fecking Jonah and that whore who controls him, Pearl."

The hair on Fergus's arms stood up. He'd heard these names before.

"I'm done working fer them. Next girl I take will go to another ship on the dark market. They'll pay better and be grateful for me find without any of the bullshit."

"Aye, I don't blame ye," Ferg said, commiserating with him. "Jonah's a fecking prick. Thinks he's a badass. Rarely treats suppliers right from what I've heard." He poured them each a shot.

"That's what I be talking about, me man." He clinked his glass on the table and eyed the bottle Fergus was keeping a tight hold on. "Thinks that fecking scar makes him scary. Jest makes the fecker ugly, is all."

"Aye, it does. Where's the best place in this area to find ships sailing the dark tides, mate? Been looking fer work meself." He smiled at the man. "Didna plan on being stuck here this long. But I met a woman..." They both laughed at that.

"Got ye by the balls, lad?" Hamish asked with a sneer.

"Not anymore," Fergus said, reaching down and cupping them. "Don't need a wench whining all the time. Rather travel on me own."

Hamish nodded in agreement. "Never had no use for a lass more than a quick tumble. Get what I need and get the feck out." He gave Fergus a wink. "Ifn I'se lucky, I escape before I pays em."

Fergus laughed like the man was sly and took another shot before he cold-cocked the bastard. The lil bastard had information he needed, and he needed to earn his trust.

"I'm used to the eastern routes. I'm looking fer the darker gambling dens. I make sure the house wins more oft than not, and I've worked security during the private auctions."

Hamish watched him with cautious eyes. It wasn't safe to talk to the wrong people about his line of work. If he weren't careful, he'd end up on the wrong end of island justice.

"I'll keep ye in mind next time I make the rounds. Where can I find ye?"

"Jest leave a message here fer me, an I'll get it."

Hamish studied him carefully before reaching out a hand and shaking on it. "All right, what's the name I'll be leaving it for?"

Ferg smiled broadly and said, "Me name be Cyrus, and I look forward to working with ye. I've got some scores to settle of me own—mayhap we can work together. I help ye, ye help me."

Hamish studied him through bleary eyes, calculating the risk of working with someone versus the benefits of help. "Meet me here tomorrow at midnight, and we'll see what yer worth."

"Deal," Fergus said as he joined the man in a drink.

CHAPTER FIFTY

Kai

Kai stepped from the portal into the Caribbean sun on a privately owned island. Shielded from outsiders, only a handful of people were allowed to access this destination. The power of Neptune's protection could be felt as soon as your feet hit the white sand. Invisible barriers surrounded the tropical paradise, creating a haven for one of the most beloved members of the Court of Tears.

Kai left his boots and jacket at the portal and walked barefoot through the sand to the pavilion on the beach. Long silk curtains enclosed three sides of the structure while the front faced the water. He headed for the stairs leading to the open platform above him. A smile crossed his face as he anticipated her surprise at his visit.

The former Queen Yareli of the Court of Tears turned as he stepped into the enormous room. "Kai!" she screeched before dropping her palette of paints and running to him with arms outstretched.

He opened his arms and picked her up, twirling her around. "Mama, it's been too long."

"Set me down, you oaf," she said, laughing. "May the Mother help us. Look at you! My baby, and you're bigger than all your brothers, and I doubt that you've stopped growing yet."

Her hands lovingly traced his features. Her dark chestnut hair gleamed with auburn highlights from the sun and was piled in a messy bun on top of her head. The wind had pulled strands loose that hung to her waist, and there were streaks of paint through them where she kept pushing it out of her way. High cheekbones set off her mahogany eyes as they traced his features and teared up at the changes she found. "You're no longer my boy, Kai. You've become a man."

He blushed at the compliment. "I'm trying to become a man you'll be proud of, Mama."

"I've never had any doubt about that, my child." She shook her head as she laughed. "Now, your brothers, on the other hand…I don't think they'll ever settle down with one woman." They both laughed, and she took his hand, dragging him along.

"Come, come. Sit with me and tell me everything I've missed." She pulled him to large silk cushions and pillows arranged on an oriental rug in the center of the room.

Handmaidens appeared silently with trays of tropical fruit, cheese, and wine. They left the offerings, then disappeared just as silently, although Kai could feel their eyes lingering on him as they made their way out.

"I had breakfast with my brothers yesterday; they're all doing well," he said as he took a piece of mango and ate it before licking the sticky juices from his fingers.

"Here," his mama said as she tossed him a napkin.

"Why waste it?"

She laughed at him as she nibbled on a piece of cheese.

"So, what really brings you here, Kai?" Her eyes challenged him to deny he needed something. "I rarely see any of my boys anymore unless they need a favor."

Kai sighed as guilt made him flush. "I'm sorry, mama." He tried to formulate an excuse and failed. "I don't blame you for being upset with us."

"I know you have lives, and I'm just jealous I can't be a bigger part of them." Her voice was soft and held a longing he'd never heard before. "When I agreed to the King's requirements for the dissolution of our union, I never knew how difficult it would be to maintain my distance from my children for this long. Now that you are all old enough to be released from mandatory visits, I struggle to keep my end of our bargain as the years pass."

Kai took her hand and stroked his thumb over the back of it softly. "I'm so sorry you've had to do this. Why don't you come back with me?"

She laughed ruefully. "No, Kai. I can't. If I leave this island, I will set events into motion that cannot be undone, and I'm not sure I am willing to do that yet."

"Mama, we need you." His tone was urgent, and his eyes beseeched her. "Kyran needs you. He's in love, yet he is being forced into a marriage with someone he doesn't even know for a trade agreement with the Great Lakes Fire Clan. You wouldn't recognize the man he's become, but you'd be pleased by it. He's finally ready to settle down with the woman he loves, but he's going to lose her if nothing changes. Won't you help him?"

Yareli listened to Kai with a somber expression. "I'm not sure how much help I can be to anyone at court, my child. My authority there has long since expired, and I don't know that I can stand to see your father with that woman again."

Kai nodded in understanding. "I can only imagine how painful it would be for you to see him again, and I know that Kyran will kick my ass for coming to you for help. I just can't stand to see him forced to spend the rest of his life miserable with a stranger."

Yareli listened to him seeking her help for Kyran and silently screamed inside. Tethered to this place that once offered her protection and peace, her exile now felt like a leash she couldn't shake.

Sighing, she reached out and took his hand. "Give me some time to think on how best I can be of assistance. When is the wedding?"

"In a fortnight."

She gasped at the short amount of time she had to help fix this. "They seem to have forgotten to send my invitation."

Her voice was sharp, and Kai could sense the anger buried beneath it.

"I'm sorry to be the bearer of unwelcome news, Mama."

"You have nothing to be sorry about, my child. I am proud of you for risking both your father and your brother's wrath by coming to me." She smiled at him. "Enough of this for now. Come walk with me and tell me all about you."

She pulled him up and headed for the path to the beach. The sun burned away her anger and her fears, for a little while at least, while she listened to her son's hopes and dreams and laughed at the way he interacted with his siblings.

"Where is Klaree?" Kai asked, looking around expectantly. By this time, she has usually appeared with a list of books she wants me to bring her next time I visit."

Yareli laughed. "She looks forward to your visits, Kai. She's closer to you than your brothers. They visit so rarely; she hardly knows them."

"I enjoy her company, too. She's smart, sassy, and likes to challenge me. She can nearly beat me with a sword or at chess. I've taught her everything I know. Not sure what I have left to offer her on my next visit."

His mother smiled up at him. "Just the pleasure of your company will be enough. She's off visiting friends on the mainland for the week, but she'll be back tomorrow night if you can stick around."

"Unfortunately, I have commitments I must return to." He gave her a hug and a kiss on the cheek. "I'd much rather spend my week here. I miss the time I spent on this island with you." His voice held a hint of nostalgia.

"I miss having you here, but I understand commitments." They'd circled back to the portal. Kai donned his boots and coat and nodded at the beautiful woman who had brought him into this world. "I promise to return soon."

"I eagerly await your return, Kai." She smiled as her eyes filled with tears. "Until then, my son."

"Until then." He waved to her as the portal door closed, then selected the Court of Tears and left her behind once again. He hated leaving her there. He hated his father even more for the conditions he forced her to live in. Yes, she lived in paradise, but what good was paradise when you had no one to share it with? Trapped alone with only her attendants and her daughter to entertain her, Yareli existed, but she didn't live life to its fullest. Kai knew exactly where to lay the blame for that, and he would dedicate his life to trying to gain his mother's freedom even at the expense of his own.

CHAPTER FIFTY-ONE

Take Care Who You Trod On

Kano stood under the water for a long time, trying to wash the dirt from his soul. He knew he was a bastard and didn't pretend otherwise. Most days, he couldn't stand himself, but he didn't care enough to try and change.

After washing off his latest conquest, he shaved the sides of his head and stepped out of the shower and into the deep soaking tub. Special ordered to fit his height, the back supported his head while allowing his long legs to fully extend in front of him. Few things in life brought him joy, but this did.

He sucked a deep breath in as his legs adjusted to the temperature. Scalding, like his shower, his body cringed at the heat. It was his penance, and one day, he hoped it would heat the deepest, coldest core of his soul. He doubted that day would ever arrive. There were too many sins for him to atone for and too many people he'd disappointed.

Three centuries he'd existed, and in that time, he'd never loved a woman. Hell, there were very few people he liked. Never needed it, didn't want it, and sure the fuck wasn't looking for it now. Love destroyed his family. His mother loved his father to the point of obsession. When his father failed to keep his promise of fidelity, their love turned to devastation, and he'd never seen either of them happy again. He would never allow himself to commit to someone, handing them the power to destroy him. His heart was surrounded by a metal lockbox, and he'd be damned if he ever allowed himself to get close enough for any woman to trap him in that nightmare.

Acclimating to the heat, he took the plunge and submerged himself. His scrotum was screaming, and his cock turtled into his spine, but the heat felt amazing on his muscles. Reclining, he sank in until the water was up to his chin.

The hot water relaxed him, and he allowed his mind to wander. Drifting on the edge of unconsciousness, his mind traipsed back through time to the last visit he had with his mother. Over a century ago, he had arrived for his court-mandated visit to check on her safety. He was surprised to find her happy in her isolation. She appeared so young and beautiful. It was hard to believe she had birthed four strapping boys and one lovely daughter when she appeared no older than his sister Klaree.

Overjoyed by his visit, she walked with him on the beach for miles. When they returned, she fed him his favorites, and they sat and talked in her pavilion as she sketched him with charcoal. Multiple prints of him at different angles, smiling, scowling, and a rare one she caught of him laughing. He hardly recognized himself when she showed the sketch to him. Happy and full of life, it reminded him of Kyran or Kai more than it did the face reflected at him from the mirror every morning.

She sketched him repeatedly while they visited. He was barely aware of her doing it. Even as a child, he could remember her with a sketchpad in one hand and a thin pointed charcoal stick in the other. Her fingers were always smudged gray. She was nothing like the other women at court. Never immaculate, she was real and approachable, and he missed her.

Kano wondered if that was his father's initial attraction to her. How different she must have been compared to every other woman he'd known. She wanted nothing from him—not his money, or his jewels, not his titles or the status she gained by marrying him. Yareli simply loved Varan and wanted to make him happy.

Varan loved her just as deeply for a long time, allowing her the whimsical life she wanted, not making her participate in the usual court duties his queen should share. He'd promised to give her whatever she needed to be happy. All she asked for was the ability to raise his children in her way and for him to love her exclusively.

It was a promise he was bound to break. The men in his line weren't made for exclusivity, and Varan didn't realize how difficult it would be to keep his vow after centuries passed. He tried, truly he did. Then one drunken night with a young courtier named Meriel changed all their lives forever.

Meriel seduced the king with wine and drugs—many believed. She also arranged for the queen to find them together in Yareli's bed. It was the final insult. Yareli left Varan. He set her aside and married Meriel who claimed to be pregnant at the time. The pregnancy, like everything else, was well-orchestrated and disappeared after the official ceremony. Their marriage was a loveless one, built on pain and mistrust. Varan returned to sulk in the rooms he once shared with Yareli, and the new queen Meriel reinstated the king's harem—for her pleasure as much as for his.

Kano, more than any of his siblings, knew how much Varan regretted the loss of Yareli. Another drunken night spent reminiscing with his son revealed how deeply he loved the woman he lost. He confessed to Kano that he would have gladly given up intimacy altogether just to have Yareli back in his life—in any capacity. Her loss devastated him, and he hadn't been the same since. Varan's loyal supporters at court still believed the king was drugged by Queen Meriel at all times, making him malleable and apathetic.

Sliding under the water, he let his parents' failed relationship fade away in his mind, and he examined his own apathetic behavior towards women. Emerging, he wiped the water from his face and sat back once again. His life held an endless line of women he had taken for sport. He was a cold bastard, and he owned that shit. They didn't make him feel anything but lust. Not one of them even sparked the desire to learn their name. Yeah, he was fucked up. Any wonder with the example he had from his father?

Closing his eyes, his mind drifted, wondering what was wrong with him. No one—no that wasn't entirely true. There had been one female who had caught his attention for a short while. She had been exquisite.

They met in a tavern near the foothills of the Alps. She was researching the elemental clans, creating a genealogical profile of each one. The work she was doing fascinated him, but not nearly as much as her pixie-like face had—high cheekbones and a narrow chin he'd traced over and over with his fingers, entranced by the delicate shape of them. She was petite, with an hourglass shape his hands had lovingly learned.

They spent a week trapped in the last cabin available as a blizzard raged outside. Wide hazel eyes, set in a heart-shaped frame, watched him with wonder and trust as he made love to her, gently taking her virginity from her. He taught her the pleasures of the flesh, and she taught him the ecstasy one could find by slowing down and savoring the joining of their bodies. Wavy, red hair fell to her hips, cocooning him as she sat astride, taking her time making love to him. She was the only woman he'd ever made love to.

The only woman he'd ever been tender with, and he never even learned her name. The intimacy he found with her was a gift. He only took it out on rare occasions and replayed it to remind himself that he did indeed have the capacity for more. He needed the right woman to find it in him. If only he'd known her name, he would have hunted her down and claimed her as his. But when he awoke on their last day, she was gone.

The game started the first night they met. She refused to give him her name, and he agreed they would remain nameless for their time together. Kano cooked for her, and she read to him. They played games and laughed together. After making angels in the fresh snow—naked, they returned to bed, warming up all the cold areas they had created.

Without realizing it, he was hard again. His body responded to her memory as much as it had every time he'd glanced at her during their time together. After the first night, they made love ravenously, coming up for brief periods to eat and laugh until one of them touched the other and they were at it again.

Kano searched for her for years. He even had his mother create a sketch for him from his description of his little fire-haired lass. Months turned into years, and still no sign of her. The sketch was in his wallet, always with him when he traveled, in the hopes he might find a lead or, at the very least, learn her name.

The water was cooling rapidly, yanking him out of his reverie. He could no longer put off his meeting with the evil bitch upstairs. He dried himself off, trimmed his soul patch, and returned to the bedroom. Charles had laid out his formal court colors. Turquoise—God, he hated the color, even if it brought out the deep blue green of his eyes.

He dressed quickly in the tight breeches and matching split tail jacket. A lighter blue silk shirt softened the dark jacket. Three large pearls trailed up his forearms from the cuffs. He ran his hand through his unruly curls, making them stand up haphazardly. He smiled, knowing Meriel would hate the look. It was the one way of giving her the finger without losing the aforementioned finger.

Charles met him in the hall as he exited his suite. "You'll be needing this, my lord," he said, extending a long, leather duster in the same nauseating color. "It's cool where you're headed."

"And just where the fuck is this location?" Kano snarled at him, getting more irritated by the minute as they headed for the queen's suite.

"I'm not to say, my lord, only to prepare you for what you will need." He coughed into his hand while saying, "Somewhere on the Great Lakes."

Kano smiled broadly at him. "Charles, I love you, man. How the hell do you put up with me?"

"I've been known to drink heavily in the evening, my lord," he said without any inflection. "It helps."

Kano laughed heartily. "Have one for me tonight. Make it a double."

They reached their destination, and Kano glared at the door in disgust. "Guess I may as well get it over with."

"Best of luck, my lord."

"Gonna need it." He knocked on the door and then entered without waiting for a response.

"Rude as usual," Queen Meriel said as she glared at him from her vanity mirror.

"You demanded my presence, and here I am, ready to serve."

"Hmm, I'll believe that when pigs fly."

Meriel swiveled on her seat and, look at that, her robe caught, exposing her legs and much more than he ever hoped to see again. His bland expression prevented her from further embarrassing herself or pissing him off.

Kano had done his duty by the queen—once. She had never requested him again. He made sure of it. She didn't like ending up as battered as her subjects. The agreement had been that he was in charge. She didn't want a rerun of his performance.

"How may I be of assistance, Meriel?" He never called her his queen because she would never be his queen. His mother, Yareli, was the only queen he would recognize at the Court of Tears because she would be on the damn throne if it weren't for this crazy whore.

"You know I hate when you don't address me properly," she admonished.

"Yes, Meriel, and you know I will never call you by that title, so let's move on. Where do you need me to represent the court, and what for?"

She glared at him but let the slight go, aware that he was never going to change. None of Varan's boys would refer to her as their queen. She had earned their animosity, and she honestly didn't blame them but insisted on reminding them they were with their betters every time she saw them.

"The Fire Princess, Elyana, will stay with us until the ceremony. I want you to retrieve her from Laird Killam's and return with her posthaste. I hear she is not happy about the betrothal, and I don't want any chances of the brat running away. Collect her and return with or without her belongings if she gives you any problems."

"Is Laird Killam on board with this plan, or will I be executed by the court of Luminosity for an attempted kidnapping?" He didn't trust Meriel not to set him up to take the fall and toss him out of the way.

"You have his blessing. Honestly, I think he's relieved we are taking the hellion off his hands. She's been quite destructive lately, showing her displeasure."

"Can't hardly blame her, or Kyran, now, can you?" His disgusted look showed her exactly what he thought of her plan. "Keep in mind, Meriel, I'll fucking kill you if you ever pull that shit with me. Kyran is too much of a gentleman, but you are pushing him to extreme measures as well. Take care who you trod on." *"You evil bitch,"* he added silently.

Ignoring him, she handed him a sheaf of papers. Writs of safe passage for the court and a map of where he would be going. "If all goes well, we'll see you for dinner."

"If not, I'll see you when I return. Might have to take a side trip along the way."

"Kano, do not cross me on this. You won't like the results." She turned back to her vanity. "Before I forget, be a bit gentler with my girls. They're not much good to anyone else when they aren't able to walk afterward."

"Not my fucking problem. She earned her rank through me, and I gave her every opportunity to leave. If they've survived your sadistic playroom, they should be able to handle anything I can dish out because you sure the hell don't go easy on them."

Not waiting for an answer, he headed for the door, slamming it on his way out. Donning his coat, he headed for the portal, wanting to get this assignment the fuck over with. Stepping inside, he studied the map, seeing the portal he was looking for along the northern edge of the lakes and grimaced. Great. Spring would have barely made an appearance yet. Placing his palm on the wall, he waited for the map to appear and then selected his destination.

Kano took a deep breath as the door closed, preparing himself for the sense of falling. He loved traveling by portal because it was one of the few things he couldn't control, and for a few seconds, he could let go of everything and just be.

Moments passed, and the doors opened. He opened his eyes in time to see a green-cloaked figure come barreling in with guards yelling and running behind. The figure knocked him over before slapping their hand on the map, picking another location, and closing the doors in a matter of seconds.

Seriously pissed off, Kano picked himself up and grabbed the back of the cloak, swinging the figure around as he pulled back his hand to punch them. He was supposed to make a good impression, and the fucker managed to rip his monkey suit in multiple places.

As he swung the idiot around, he didn't have time to compensate for the knee connecting with his crotch at full throttle and the portal activating. The last thing he remembered as he collapsed to the floor, cupping his family jewels, were startled hazel eyes in a pale face looking up at him before he started retching. Could this day get any worse?

CHAPTER FIFTY-TWO

The Laird

Fergus Emberz, a son of the Great Lakes Fire Clan, entered the main hall of the white marble complex housing the Court of Luminosity. Situated on the shores of Lake Gichi-Gami, The Great Lakes Clan was the dominant clan in the Court of Luminosity's hierarchy. Unlike the Water Court's monarchy, the fire court was more of a democracy. Lairds were chosen for life unless a challenge was issued to their rule. The title was often handed down through a family line after a supporting vote from the people confirmed the appointment.

Fergus was on his way to pay his respects to Laird McKay. Dressed in his finest kilt, a yellow-and-red plaid—McKay colors—he made his way to the laird's office. His fist knocked lightly on the partially open door as he waited to be acknowledged.

"'Tis open," a voice full of gravel bellowed. "Why must they all knock on an open fecking door?" he muttered, irritated.

With his teeth clenched to stifle a laugh, Fergus entered the spacious office. Burnished walnut bookcases, heavily carved with scenes of fire drakes and their larger cousins, dragons, lined the walls. Overstuffed with ledgers, scrolls, and books on farming and sailing, the laird's office had the comfy feel of an old estate library.

"Laird McKay," Fergus said on his best behavior, "I be here as a representative of the Heart Island Sanctuary to beseech thy help." He handed a letter sealed with wax from Madylyn to the laird.

The man finally looked up at him, bemused. "Fergus, ye done with the posturing yet?"

Fergus gave him a wide grin. "Aye, Uncle Killam. We've got the formal bullshit out of the way." He laughed as the barrel-chested man stepped out from behind the desk and gave him a bear hug.

Killam framed his face between his beefy hands and gave him a long look. "Yer too thin. Don't the feckers feed ye out there?"

"I never stop eating; just can't put any weight on."

"Whiskey?"

"Ye ever known me to say no?"

"That's me boy." Killam led the way to two worn leather chairs in front of an unlit stone fireplace. A decanter and crystal-cut glasses sat on a table, between them. Pouring them both four fingers of the best Irish whiskey available, he raised his glass, and they both took healthy swigs.

"Damn, that's good." Fergus said, "Been a bit since I'se had the good stuff."

"What kind of swill you been settling for?"

"Whatever I can find—usually the cheap shite."

"I'll send a case home with ye." The glass tipped back again, and the man gave him his full attention. "So, out with it, lad. This a personal visit, or ye here on Sanctuary business?"

"A bit of both," Fergus said solemnly. "Which do ye want first?"

"Let's get the bullshite out of the way, then we can enjoy the rest of the day."

"All right, then. Ye asked for it. Madylyn SkyDancer is asking for yer help with a problem affecting the St. Lawrence. Folks are disappearing at alarming rates. One of our allies is searching for his sixteen-year-old sister, who was snatched from her boat a few months ago. We're beginning to suspect a human trafficking ring is using the river to abduct and transfer victims. Some heavy magic is involved because we can't locate any of these vessels, yet we've indications that they are running the river nights."

"Ye think they're ending up here for the sales and distribution of their newly acquired property?" He coughed deeply as he reached for his cigars. Cutting the end off, he puffed lightly as he lit the stogie, heavy smoke filling the air between them. "Have one. This is the good shite, too." He offered the wooden box housing them to Fergus.

"Think it's a possibility, or the dark circles are setting up camp somewhere new for their illegal gaming and whoring," Ferg said. Inhaling deeply, he let the nicotine hit his system, chasing away the dregs of last night's hangover. "Will ye let us know if ye hear of anything?"

"Aye. I've had reports of missing here as well—up about five percent the last year or so. Haven't had any luck tracking them down, and we've tried to."

"Same. Found a shipwrecked lot of girls, half of them drowned in the hull. Three survivors told us their tales, and it's fecking horrific. We need to stop the bastards doing this. Maddy's filling ye in and formally requesting yer assistance if needed." His eyes traveled to the table her letter now sat on.

"Aye, I'll have a message to send back to her as well. The little information I can offer. Not sure it'll be any help at all." Puffing heartily, he gazed out the window for a long time. "That all the business end of this?"

"Almost." Fergus took a deep drag, knowing the next part was going to be awkward.

"Need to ask ye something, Uncle."

"Now, I'm yer uncle?" Killam's amber eyes squinted at him suspiciously as his left eyebrow arched.

"Yer me uncle all the time, me clan leader as long as I've been breathing, and me laird when we deal with political bullshite or yer taking me to task fer the drunken exploits in me youth—which, I might add, typically involved yer twins. I'se led astray by them boys many a time."

Killam roared with laughter. "I think ye did yer share of leading those antics, ye lil pissant." His laughter turned into a coughing jag that lasted until his face turned purple, and Fergus thought he might need assistance. "Get on with the rest of it, lad," he gasped as he refilled his glass and topped off Fergus's even though it was barely ten in the morning. "Stop pussy-footing around with pleasantries."

"I need to understand the agreement yer making with the Court of Tears. This union has far-reaching implications and is tearing apart a couple I care about who are deeply in love." A pause while he took a sip of his whiskey helped him to phrase the rest of his question. "And why in the feck are ye doing this to Elyana after all the promises ye made her?"

"As yer laird, I don't answer to ye." Killam's eyes were flashing flames in the amber depths.

"Nye, as me laird, ye need to answer Mistress Skydancer the first half of that question, and as me uncle, ye owe me an answer to the second." Fergus was done playing safe, and his tone was sharp. "Elyana has always been so proud of ye for not making her a bargaining chip, and ye swore—with me standing witness—that ye would never do this to her."

The glass in Killam's hand shook as his arm trembled. His eyes were still flashing dangerously, and his fire drakes had emerged, eagerly absorbing the rage emanating from him. "Ye might be a favored nephew, but don't push yer fecking luck with me, Fergus. I still have the power to make yer life a living hell." His fingers ran through his crazy red hair, making the curls stick out in every direction.

"Ye have the power to try, me laird," Fergus dared him with the power in his voice vibrating through the room. "I answer to a higher authority than ye, and yer well aware of that. If it makes ye feel better to threaten me, have at it." A slow blink waited for his uncle's posturing to begin, but the man deflated right in front of him. "If ye tell me what's wrong and what that woman is holding against ye, I may be able to help ye."

Killam set the wobbly glass on the table before he dropped it. Gnarled hands clasped the arms of his chair as he tried to figure out how to tell his nephew what a fecking mess he was in. "The Court of Tears ain't got nothing we need. Designed to appear as a trade agreement, this is all manufactured shite from that whore sitting at the helm of the mighty Tears."

Head shaking back and forth, he said, "If Varan would pull his head out of his ass long enough to run his kingdom, this would've never happened." A meaty palm wiped over his ruddy face as he stared at the floor and said, "I don't even fecking know where to begin, Ferg."

"At the beginning, and leave nothing out." Fergus leaned forward, elbows resting on his knees, giving the man his full attention.

"Ye ken Elyana is me heart. Ye ken that?"

"Aye. That's why what yer doing to her makes no fecking sense."

"Ye'll never see me the same way, Ferg, once ye ken why." Amber eyes bored into his, pleading with him for another way. "Ye'll never respect me after this."

"I'll na respect ye at all if ye don't make me understand how ye would destroy yer daughter's chances of happiness, Uncle," he snapped. Fergus met his gaze, and his eyes softened. "No matter what ye tell me, I will always love ye. Ye was like a second father ta me, and I'll never forget that." Grasping the hand on the chair next to him, he squeezed it tightly. "I can't help ye if ye don't talk to me."

"'Tis advice I once would've given ye, lad." Sad eyes closed, and his shoulders slumped. "'Twas the year they voted me in as laird." Voice barely above a whisper, he told his tale. "I'd nearly clinched the election unanimously. Yer aunt and I were set to be pledged immediately after the ceremony." A ghost of a smile graced his face, and some of his furrows eased at the memory.

"I fell in love with yer Auntie Meghan Murphy the first time I laid eyes on her. Beautiful like a spring morning and sweet like honey. Woman never had a bad thing to say 'bout anyone," a scowl crossed his face, "unlike her da and five brothers. Miserable lot of men—liked to fight, rough up the women, and none dared to call them on their behavior. The bastards ran illegal drugs and women. Made a fortune off the shite. Always had the laird in their back pocket."

"Some believed I might reign them in, and I might have held that delusion for a short while. The Murphy family was instrumental in me gaining the leadership of me clan with the peoples' vote. Me da was ill, and they could smell the shift of power in our house. The vote was forced early, and many thought the Murphys would challenge me for the position, but I was the strongest shifter in the Water Clan, and they knew they couldn't take me one on one." The glass in his hand was empty, but he tipped it to his lips. Fergus took the decanter and refilled it for him, topping off his own in the process.

"I'd already asked fer permission to take Meghan as me wife and been granted it." A long sigh escaped his parted lips as his eyes glazed, and he traveled back to the past. "Never anticipated how far they'd go to control the laird.

"I'se to be crowned, and we were to be pledged on the same day. "Twas to be the happiest day of me life." A wry grin crossed his face. "I'se cocky and never could have anticipated the way that day would turn out." The grin faded, and he continued in a hollow voice. "Meghan and I had waited to consummate our love, wanting to wait for our special day." He swallowed hard, then cleared his throat, trying to clear the past choking him, waiting to come out. "Night afore, her four brothers show up to take me out for one last bender. I protested, not wanting to have a throbbing head the next day. I got completely pissed, no two ways about that, and could barely see by the time I stumbled back to me bed. Lights were out, and I fell into me bed jest wanting to fecking sleep and praying that I could function by dawn.

"I'd almost passed out when I realized I wasn't alone in that bed. Meghan was there waiting for me, without a stitch of clothing on. I may have been three sheets to the wind, but when she put her fingers to me lips and shushed me, my brain stopped functioning, and me cock took over. Being drunk and all didn't make me the most patient of lovers, and I'm fairly sure I hurt her more than I should have in my rush to finally have her under me. Her tears only lasted a moment, and as I kissed her, her body responded, and I enjoyed every fecking moment of our first time until the door popped open, and her father appeared, dragging Meghan in with tears running down her face. 'Twas dark in me room, but by the light shining in from the hall, I realized, to me horror, that I was balls deep inside of her sister, Rowan, and had just released me seed into her." His head hung as the horror of his words hung heavily in the room.

Fergus said nothing. What the feck was there to say? He took a drink and waited, realizing there had to be much more to this tale. Infidelity was embarrassing, but it wasn't worth all the bullshite he was putting Elyana through. Meriel wouldn't be able to blackmail him with that. He opened another bottle from the bottom shelf of the table and refilled both of their glasses. Killam barely seemed to notice.

"The girls were nearly identical, even in height. Rowan was tall for her age, and Meghan petite. I thought she was more reserved when I kissed her—more timid than usual. I should've fecking known it wasn't her, and sober, I would've. The lass always had a crush on me, following me around with these big, dark, puppy dog eyes." His eyes snapped to Fergus. "I never encouraged her, mind ye." Another drink wet his lips but couldn't parch the desert in his throat. "Seems her father and brothers set the whole thing up as a way to control me, never caring what it did to Meghan and I." Silence filled the small space, heavy and ominous. "Or to Rowan...

"It was a fecking nightmare for both of us, and I hated meself for not standing up to the man. Every time I tried to argue with her father, his eyes would cut to Rowan, and I ken he would've told the entire clan about what he found. I could've taken that, and I would've gladly renounced the position and prayed I could've fixed things with the woman I loved, but I would've ruined Rowan in the process. Meghan begged me not to do that. The girl would've been shunned by many in our small village. She begged me to continue with the ceremony, not because she wanted to be mine anymore, but because she loved her sister and was aware that Rowan had no idea what the consequences of her actions would be.

"Devastated, Meghan was forced to pledge herself to me even though she hated me for what I'd done to her with her much younger sister. She sure the feck didn't want me to touch her, and I couldn't fecking blame her. Her father, the prick that he was, insisted on consummation witnesses, and he made sure he was one of them, not giving us the opportunity to talk even once or the time to work through what had happened. With four elders standing there, I took Meghan's virginity without a word between us and with her hatred glaring back at me the entire time." A tear rolled down his cheek.

"Neither of us enjoyed our first night together. When they left, she left me bed, and it took me months of begging and wooing for her to return to me." A cough interrupted him, making him reach for another cigar as if that would help the situation.

"When she finally returned to me, it was her choice. Her eldest brother, Davydd, confessed to her what they had done. They had gotten Rowan drunk as well, so she didn't think to protest to anything I was doing to her. I was her first crush, and she was getting what she wanted—so she thought."

Ferg cleared his throat, lost in the sad tale. One question kept burning through his brain and he had to ask, "How old was Rowan?"

Another tear fell. "Jest turned thirteen the week before her brothers whored her out."

"Feck me." Fergus ken how the clan would've felt about that. Killam would have been labeled a pedophile—a man nearing thirty with a *young* girl in his bed and with witnesses no one would refute.

"Not even the worst of it, Ferg." The man finally turned his head and met his eyes. "I killed that sweet child."

"What the feck do you mean, ye fecking killed her?" Fergus's eyes drew together, blazing. His fire drakes rolled through his hair and down his arms, hissing at Killam. Usually, they would have soaked up his sorrow, but today they were giving him a wide berth, and now Fergus understood their aversion to him. They thrived on pain and anger, but self-loathing and guilt repulsed them. "This gets fecking worse?"

Killam paled beneath his gaze, his cigar nearly falling from his mouth. "And ye wondered why I didn't want to share this." Sucking the stogie more firmly between his lips, he continued his tale. "Me and Rowan took some time to figure things out, but we managed to salvage our relationship, and she was expecting our lads. We finally managed to regain a little piece of that happiness we'd started with.

"Rowan had been sent away to be fostered by another aunt on Lake Huron. The constant reminder of our mistake was too hard on Meghan, and I wouldn't allow it. Her father and I nearly came to blows on that one, but he finally gave in when Meghan was the one asking. She never spoke to Rowan again after that awful day, even though it wasn't truly that child's fault." Smoke billowed around his head as he puffed like a chimney. Eyes closed, he leaned his head against the high back of the chair, working his way up to the rest of his tale.

"Three seasons passed before we heard anything of Rowan again. But me one mistake was bound to continue to haunt us." The man Fergus had always looked up to stared out the window for a long time, lost in the rainy day, the weather matching his mood and his tale.

"A messenger arrived on the winter solstice with a letter for Meghan and a gift for me. Rowan gave birth to a wee lass a month earlier. The child was early, and the birth was difficult on Rowan's immature body and mind. The lass always was a little behind other children her age, making all of this even harder. The month following the birth was difficult on her. The guilt over what she'd done to her sister was eating away at her, and once the bairn came, she couldn't live with herself any longer. They found…"

A hiccupping breath escaped him as he tried to finish his tale. Clearing his throat, he tried to finish. "They found her hanging from the rafters of the barn with the letter to Meghan pinned to her dress. The bairn was out by the wide-open doors, nearly frozen to death. The stable hands found them, but it was too late for Rowan." His head turned, and he waited for Fergus to condemn him. His nephew waited patiently for the story to conclude, and Killam was surprised to find his eyes filled with compassion. Not one ounce of blame stared back at him, giving him the strength to finish.

"Meghan nearly joined her when she read the letter Rowan had written, begging for her forgiveness, apologizing for the harm she'd done to us. The only thing that kept me Meg from her grave was a favor Rowan asked for. She begged us to take the child and raise it as our own because she was in no shape to do so, and she wanted her to be loved by the two people Rowan loved the most. She didn't want their family to have anything to do with our child. The past year made her understand what the men in her family had done to her for power. Her child would not end up as another one of her family's bargaining chips. Elyana was Rowan's middle name. We honored her daughter with it so that we would never forget the price that she paid for our happiness."

A bittersweet smile crossed his lips. "Meghan struggled with the guilt of hating her sister for an awfully long time, knowing her abandonment and inability to forgive the girl ultimately led to her death. The only thing she found joy in was Elyana until the boys arrived." A sad smile crossed his face as he remembered that period of their life.

"Rowan's death was the final blow to our physical relationship. Neither of us was able to move past Rowan's ghost in our bed. We became lifelong friends and partners but never again were we anything more. Even though that was all we had left, I never stopped loving her, and to this day—I've never strayed. When me Meghan left me years ago, I knew it was from a broken heart, and I've always wondered if the price of being the laird was worth it in the end."

"Her family, where are they now, and why aren't ye afraid of them anymore?"

A cold smile crossed the older man's face, his eyes growing hard. "I was under their thumb for centuries, but I eliminated them one at a time— slowly. They paid the ultimate price for trying to control me and for ruining me life with Meghan." The smile faded, and his eyes filled once more. "They didn't suffer nearly enough for what they took from us. Meriel's the only other one who kens the truth."

Fergus stared into his glass, looking for something to say after absorbing Killam's heartbreaking story. "I'm sorry for what ye've endured over the years, Uncle Killam, truly I be," Fergus said, looking him in the eye. "I don't ken why ye would've allowed her to blackmail ye over this. Why not jest tell Elyana the truth?"

Rheumy eyes looked up at him, near to overflowing. "Someday, Fergus, when ye have a wee lass who thinks the sun rises and sets on yer command and makes ye feel ten feet tall, ask yerself if ye would ever want her seeing ye like ye'se nothing but a piece of shite on the bottom of her shoes because I can guarantee ye that's how Elyana's gonna see me once she knows. That young woman's all I've got left of the women I loved—the one who owned me heart and soul and the one who created another piece of it by birthing me child."

"Ye said Rowan didn't want Elyana to end up as a bargaining chip." Fergus examined the ceiling for a long time before turning his head and meeting his uncle's glare. "Isn't that exactly what yer doing to her now?" Fergus asked. "That girl adores ye, Uncle. She's smart, fierce, and logical. If ye tell her the entire thing start to finish, jest like ye did me, she'll need time to process, but in the end, she'll come 'round and most likely forgive ye. Forcing this betrothal will guarantee ye lose her forever."

Tears freely flowed down the man's face. "I can't cancel now, Ferg. 'Tis nearly time, and Elyana's there already. The cunt has a larger bargaining chip with me daughter's life."

"Give me some time to think on it, and we'll figure this fecking mess out. I don't want to lose ye both over this, and Meriel doesn't get to win this round."

Both men stood. Fergus clamped a hand on his uncle's shoulder, knowing the man felt like he'd lost his respect. "I still love ye the same way I did when I walked in that door. Elyana may need some time to adjust to everything, but she's yer daughter, and she loves ye. The only way ye'll lose her is if ye force this bullshite wedding to Kyran. I'll help ye. Ye have me word." His hand clamped on his uncle's neck, and he pulled him in for a hug.

Killam accepted the hug, then leaned his forehead against Fergus's shoulder and wept for everything he'd lost and everything he had left to lose.

CHAPTER FIFTY-THREE

Illusions

Rhy entered Madylyn's office after a courtesy knock as she passed the door.

"Have ye heard anything from the Court of Tears or from Kyran?" she asked breathlessly. "I haven't been able to reach him. Maybe Kai's heard something…" The look on Maddy's face brought her up short.

Maddy's expression bordered between indignation and dread as her eyes met the emerald gaze of one of her closest friends. She knew the information she was going to give Rhy would devastate her.

Rhy was struggling to keep her emotions in check as Maddy handed her a missive from the Elemental High Court.

"I'm so sorry, Rhy," Maddy said, acknowledging the heartbreak that was inside.

Rhy opened the missive that Maddy had already read.

Mistress SkyDancer,

Once again, we are contacting you to intervene on behalf of the Court of Tears. King Varan and Queen Meriel insist that any contact between Mistress Cairn and Kyran Tyde cease immediately, including telepathic links.

Kyran has been fitted with a collar that mutes any transmissions—at his request. Please see that your warden respects the boundaries that he has set forth. I've attached a written request—signed by Kyran in front of witnesses—as proof of his intentions. I thank you for giving a copy to Mistress Cairn and request that she respect their wishes.

A small envelope was enclosed with her name written on the front. Rhyanna recognized his handwriting from the message he left on her bed only days before.

With shaky hands, she held the smaller missive needing to read what was enclosed, but not wanting to. Rhyanna glanced at Maddy with tear-filled eyes. With her back straight, she held herself together with an iron will and turned away before she broke down in the middle of the office. As she left, she felt the love and compassion flowing from Maddy to her on their link and was grateful for the strength and support it offered.

Rhy barely made it to her suite without hyperventilating. The envelope was wrinkled in her tight palm, and she carefully laid it on a small end table in her sitting room. Collapsing into a nearby chair, a sob escaped her. With trembling hands, she tried to smooth out the creases her clenched hand had made in the paper.

She opened it carefully as if the act of kindness might change the soul-wrenching news within. She knew it was bad by the energetic feel where he'd touched the paper—and it was Kyran's; she would know his energy anywhere. She also knew without a doubt that King Varan had not authorized this correspondence because he was still here on Heart Island.

Sliding a finger under the turquoise wax sealing the paper, she broke the seal. The crack running jaggedly across it felt like the one that was crawling across her heart. She unfolded the paper and forced her eyes to focus on the carefully written words gracing the small sheet of paper.

Mistress Rhyanna,

I have had the unexpected luxury of much time to think over the past few days, and I have spent an excessive amount of said time reflecting on our failed attempt of a relationship.

Even though at one point I may have mistakenly thought my feelings for you were more than a casual encounter, I have come to realize that any illusion of a future together is exactly that—an illusion. The events that transpired the last time we were together proved to me that we are not compatible.

I don't want to wonder who I am competing with when I leave you alone, and I don't believe we are sexually compatible. You require something from me that I am not willing to give. The violence that exploded between us is not something I wish to repeat. It is not the relationship I envisioned nor want with you.

I will do my best by my family and perform my duty to my court by pledging myself to the Princess Elyana anon. I have accepted the path that I will be taking and intend to make the most of my future with her.

Our dalliance over the past few months has been exactly that—a dalliance. I release you from any commitments you have made to me, and I will sever my connections to you as well. I am researching ways to undo the hastily and ill-thought-out bridge we created, and the lamp posts lighting our way are slowly dimming one by one.

I intend to create a relationship that I will find some happiness in, and I encourage you to let go of this fantasy you have of me and find your own.

I thank you in advance for accepting my choices and respecting them by not contacting me in any manner. I wish you only the best and will look back fondly on our time, if I look back at all.

Have a blessed life.

Prince Kyran Tyde
Court of Tears

Rhyanna was in a state of shock after reading the correspondence the first time. By the third time, the lines were blurring, and she was trying to sort out the insanity in her head. Refusing to cry, she tried to focus on what was wrong about the letter, but there were so many things that she couldn't begin to know where to start.

Finally, she decided to approach it like she would an injury or an illness—find out where the most damage was and then proceed with a course of action. The fact that he not only mentioned their bridge but specifically the lamp posts seemed odd. Deciding to pursue her misgivings, she settled on the floor with two large pieces of rose quartz on either side of her to help calm her heart chakra and see clearly what was meant to deceive.

Slowing her breathing, she grounded herself and allowed her mind to drift inward. While she looked for the peace and courage to approach the bridge she and Kyran built on the ethereal plane, she allowed herself to drift back and remember how they originally created the work of art.

Kyran twined the heavy roots of night-blooming water lilies together, braiding a thick rope with leaves draped over the sides until it reached his feet. As the rope touched the ground, it grew wider and stronger, the thick plaits becoming a woven path stretching out in front of him.

He stepped onto the bridge, and every step he took left a wake of small, pale yellow-and-white water lilies behind him. Scattered amongst the pale blooms were large sapphire blue ones that beckoned her soul closer to him.

Rhyanna gazed at him, fascinated by the beautiful bridge he was building for them.

He watched her step out from her side of the ethereal plane and start braiding links of her own to meet him.

Every step Kyran took brought him closer to her inner self shining softly in the distance. He continued along the bridge until they met in the middle, and he took her hands in his.

"It's absolutely beautiful," she said in wonder.

"Wait until we're finished, my lady. We've only begun. This is the foundation of our basic link. Now, together, we'll create a lover's bridge. Add what you will to make it feel like yours, too."

Rhy thought for a moment before leaning down and touching a lily pad. A post sprung up, and a lantern hung at the top. She cast soft blue light into it. "A light for our darkest days," she said. "I want them to go all the way across the bridge on both sides."

"As you wish, my lady," Kyran said as lantern posts sprung up in front of them.

With each step they took, large fresh water pearls appeared, scattered over the lily pads glowing softly. "The pearls represent your purity, our loyalty, and they symbolize your inner beauty. They also offer protection from nightmares," he said.

Rhyanna looked at the stunning work of art they created. "We have something representing every element but mine," she said. Quickly, she laid rectangular steppingstones of moonstone in the center of the bridge. "They come from the earth and represent water and new beginnings. May they give us clarity and nothing but truth betwixt us."

Rhyanna gasped, reliving her vision. Kyran buried clues in the letter he sent her. "Light for our darkest days…and clarity and nothing but truth betwixt us" reminded her of the pledges they had made to each other.

Every other one of the lamp posts was dark. She walked out onto the bridge to the first one and opened the side of the glass to see why it had gone out. Inside was a small piece of paper that had the letter *"I"* on it. She hurried to the next one and found *"will always."* The third made her smile, and her heart found her normal rhythm. *"Love you."* She ran to the next. *"My lady."* A few steps to the final one and she found a bigger ray of hope. *"Don't give up on us. The ceremony will occur this coming Sunday. Seek any help you can find. I'm doing what I can. Trust nothing they tell you."*

Tears of joy filled her eyes. Rhy knew the cruel letter she read earlier couldn't possibly relay his true feelings, not after the last night they'd spent together and the way he'd cared for her. She needed to find a way to let him know that she'd found his clues and understood.

Rhyanna moved to the first lit lantern and dimmed the light to a mere spark then altered the blue light with a hint of purple and left her own notes along the way. She left him pieces with the words, *"I love you, too. Don't give up. I have help and will do what I can. Have faith, me laird."*

Hopeful that he would find her messages, she returned to her physical body. She sat there and let the tears of relief roll down her face for a moment. Pulling herself together, she wrote down his messages from the lanterns, gathered the false letter, and ran out the door.

Rhyanna needed to speak to the one person who could help her find a way out of this, and she needed to do it now. King Varan hadn't arrived early by chance. Destiny sent them assistance, and she damn well planned to use every weapon at her disposal to free the man she loved from this insanity.

CHAPTER FIFTY-FOUR

Self-Preservation

Ronan tossed in his sleep, his dreams dark and ominous. His past often came to revisit him at night. Reuniting with Maddy and finding out about his son Landon chased away the shadows for a while, but the happier and more complacent he was becoming during the day, the easier it was for the dark demons of his past to come knocking at night.

The dreams he had of the two hundred plus years spent in captivity were horrifying reminders of the lengths he went to just to survive. There were so many things he was ashamed of doing. He was terrified they would come into the light and ruin the happiness they'd only recently found.

Madylyn was draped over his chest, clinging tightly to him with her hand in his hair. Ronan often found her like this, and he wondered if his dreams woke her, and she was trying to calm him back to sleep. Whatever reason, he loved having her beautiful body and long hair tangled over the top of him.

His hand went to her slightly rounded belly, and he smiled, thinking of the little girl their love created. Maddy lost a daughter of theirs when he was in captivity and unaware of the gift he left behind. This child was their miracle, a bridge between their past and their future. Every day Ronan spent with this beautiful woman beside him was even more of a miracle because she was willing to look past the devastation he caused her in his youth and give him another chance to prove his love to her.

Pressing a kiss to her forehead, his hand slid down to cup her heavy breast. He stroked his thumb over the tip, and, ever sensitive to his desire, she arched towards him in her sleep. His groin throbbed, and he debated continuing his ministrations, knowing she always welcomed his advances no matter the time of day or night. A hint of shadows under her eyes prevented him from following through, though. Might not just be his sleep that was getting disrupted by his nightmares. He would have to see Rhy and request a sleeping draft. Drugs were something he hated to use after being forced to use them during his captivity, but he didn't want to disrupt her, and he wasn't sure he could sleep away from her anymore.

Slipping out of bed, he pulled on a pair of leather breeches before heading down to the kitchen and getting a glass of milk. He stood looking out the window as the hell-hound pack roamed by on their way back to the stables. The animals were given free rein of the island at night—allowed to hunt animals that were not protected by the Sanctuary. Deer herds were thick near the lake, and small game was plentiful on their island, so they were given the right to roam under the moon. Ronan understood their need to be free. Living in a cage killed a part of your soul, and the only reason he caged any animal in his stable was to protect them or to protect others from them.

"Want to talk about it, my son?" a deep voice rasped behind him. He turned and smiled at the tall, dark-skinned man leaning against the doorway, with his long, black braids hanging heavily over each shoulder.

Cheveyo was a Hopi shaman. His daughter Kaia found Ronan when he escaped his imprisonment after killing his captors. Their relationship was casual, and his son was the product of their time together. Kaia always knew his heart belonged to another and encouraged him to find Maddy and reconcile. Ronan did so, never knowing when he left, she was pregnant. Killed in a flash flood a year ago, her father brought their son, Landon, to Ronan to raise. Cheveyo was their guest as he helped Landon with the transition to his new family.

Ronan was incredibly grateful and relieved when Maddy welcomed them both with open arms. Cheveyo was one of his mentors, and it was nice having one of his best friends nearby. More importantly, he was able to get to know his son and try to be the father the boy deserved.

"Couldn't sleep's all."

"Why do you hide the truth from me when you know that I see it so clearly?" His fathomless dark eyes peered deeply into the windows of Ronan's soul. "I thought we were past all of this nonsense."

Ronan wiped a hand over his face and, with a sigh, sat down at the small kitchen table. "Forgive me, old friend. Nothing has changed. Same demons, calling my name." His hand tangled in his hair as he tried to continue. "Some nights I don't understand how I'm allowed to be this fucking happy after the things I've done and the pain I've caused to others." Tormented eyes stared out at the man who looked closer to the age of his brother than his father. "I worry that my past will seek out the present and destroy everything I've finally found."

"To fear losing what you love is a natural response, my son."

A hand clamped down on Ronan's shoulder in support. "Facing your fear is the only way you can outrun it. Pull out all the cards, lay them on the table for all to see, then nothing can come along and surprise you. You did what was necessary to survive and nothing more. Joy was not found in the deeds you were forced to perform."

"Fuck no." Ronan grunted. Not wanting to continue this conversation, he stood and headed for the door. "I'm going to get dressed and work with that falcon. Any suggestions on how to force him back to his human form?"

"Limit his options and don't give him a choice." Cheveyo followed him into the hall. "At some point, you're going to need to come clean with Maddy about all of it. Better that you be the one to do it, than a stranger."

"I know," he said with a sigh. "I just wanted to take a little time to enjoy the happiness we've found before I burst our bubble." He took the stairs two at a time and entered their bedroom. Maddy looked so beautiful laying there that his body responded strongly to the vision she presented. Ignoring his discomfort, he grabbed a shirt and his boots before leaning down and brushing his lips over her forehead. Silently, he headed back out. If he couldn't sleep, he might as well work.

Dawn was kissing the night goodbye when he entered the stables. A light on told him one of the hands beat him to work. It was rare that they were able to get the drop on him, but the Romani boys were good workers and not afraid to start early.

The lights leading into the eyrie flickered as he walked in to check on his most recent project. One of the largest peregrine falcons he'd ever seen sat in a cage in the corner by itself. The creature didn't do well with the other falcons, and it wasn't because of his predatory behavior. The energy he emitted alerted his fellow flyers that he was more powerful and deadlier than any of the other avian residents.

Ronan pulled up the stool he used when he sat with the falcon. Most peregrines were about the size of an enormous crow, but this one was closer to the size of a small eagle.

Peregrine falcons are known for their grace and speed, often reaching speeds of over two hundred miles per hour. This made them wonderful hunters and perfect for taking smaller prey by surprise as they dive-bombed them.

The falcon Ronan watched had been trapped in this cage for far too long, in his opinion.

Records confirmed Ronan's suspicions that he was much older than the other birds, and Ronan could feel the shifter's magic around him.

Fergus filled him in on the creature's history, confirming that he was once a powerful shifter who stayed in his favorite form for too long and no longer remembered how to return to his human shape. The shifter's magic contributed to the unnatural lifespan of the bird. Kerrygan was his name, and he had once been a valuable member of the sanctuary.

Ronan sat in front of the cage, watching him for quite a while. Lately, he'd sought solace with the winged creature. Kerrygan became his own private therapist and one who offered no judgment at the end of the session. Ronan confided in him regularly. He'd pause, waiting for answers he never received, but he always gave Kerrygan an opportunity to respond every time he spoke to him.

He reached out telepathically first. "Morning. You willing to talk yet?"

"Well, I'll share. I can't fucking sleep. I'm terrified my past will come back to haunt me." His eyes met the bird's, challenging him to say something, anything. Once again, nothing. He ran his hand through his hair as he softly chuckled to himself. "Why do I talk to you like it will help?"

He waited, giving the creature a chance to communicate telepathically. Hell, even a squawk would've felt like progress. When no answer was forthcoming, he said, "Then again, why the fuck not? You can't argue with me or tell me I am being an ass. You'll never tell my secrets or my fears. I guess you're the safest bet."

"Back to my story," he said as his stomach soured. "I'm having nightmares of my time in captivity—of the horrific things I did just to survive. I'm fucking terrified that someone from my past will wander through and share the things I was forced to do to others."

A long sigh escaped him. "I'll tell her eventually. I wasn't sure it was best to tell her while she's pregnant." He ran his fingers through his hair watching the caged shifter.

Inspiration made an appearance as Ronan watched the critter. Cheveyo's voice echoed in his head. *"Limit his options and don't give him a choice."* He walked over and opened the door, reaching in to pet the falcon.

Kerrygan backed into a corner and shied away from Ronan, or maybe it was the rage emanating from him that made the shifter realize he was dealing with a bigger predator. Ronan finally snatched him up and placed him on a stoop after tying the leads on his feet to the perch.

He stroked his hands down over the falcon's head and back, trying to soothe him as he danced to the side in an effort to avoid Ronan's hands. Ronan placed both hands on either side of his head, holding the unwilling prisoner still on the rough piece of wood.

Peering into his prey's dark eyes, he stared deeply into the fathomless depths looking out at him. "You must hate being stuck in this body, don't you?" he asked as he increased the pressure on the sides of the bird's neck.

"I can't imagine all that intelligence wasted in this form." He increased the pressure again, feeling the muscles straining through the feathers. The falcon's feet danced nervously, and his wings beat against his arms as he tried to get away from Ronan.

"Talk to me, you little bastard. Tell me if you want to live." He applied more pressure, nearly suffocating the poor creature. "If you don't answer, I'll assume you prefer death than to a lifetime in that cage. I know I would."

The eyrie was unusually silent as all eyes focused on the drama playing out between the two of them. "I guess I'm doing you a favor, huh?"

Ronan squeezed harder before he was knocked flat on the floor as the falcon transformed into a tall man who sprawled on top of him. Ronan lay there, stunned that his ploy worked. He wouldn't have killed him, but he wanted Kerrygan's self-preservation skills to kick in.

Tall and lanky with long dark hair and wild dark eyes that still looked more like a falcon's than a man's, he struggled to gain his bearings and make his limbs move. As he finally managed to pull himself up, he pulled his arm back and started punching Ronan in the face repeatedly.

"Motherfucker, ye were going to kill me, weren't ye?" His voice was hoarse with disuse, and the crazy in his eyes should have been a warning.

Ronan couldn't help himself as he started laughing. He was relieved that the man wasn't trapped but was also keenly aware that he now knew many of Ronan's secrets. Ronan's hands came up around the other man's throat, and he started squeezing as the other man flailed on top of him.

The mystery man knocked his arms away easily before falling to his side and breathing raggedly. "Ever occur to ye, asshole, that I was in the form I wanted to be in?"

Ronan chuckled loudly, and this time it wasn't with deadly intent. The sound was pure and clear. "So much for our therapy time, huh?"

"I'se getting really tired of all yer fecking whining."

Ronan stood and offered the man a hand. "Well, you know who I am. You mind telling me who the fuck are you?"

The other man allowed Ronan to pull him to standing. He leaned heavily on him as they slowly moved towards the door.

The mystery man chuckled ruefully. "Name's Kerrygan, and I've had me eye on Maddy fer years. Aren't ye glad ye brought me back now?" His laughter bordered on madness for a moment, and Ronan knew how he must feel.

"Well, my crazy friend, I'm not worried about your scrawny ass as competition. Let's find you some pants before we confront Madylyn, shall we?"

Their laughter rang out, and for a moment, it was hard to tell which voice had the sound of crazy ringing through because, honestly, they both sounded pretty much the same.

Their laughter was telling fate to fuck off because we're back, and you can't keep us hidden or down for long.

CHAPTER FIFTY-FIVE

Who do Ye Trust?

Rhyanna burst into the clinic, anxious to speak with King Varan. Her hopes were dashed when she heard him retching in the bathroom. Grabbing a damp cloth, she handed it to him as he exited. He was pale and shaky as he returned to his bed. He sat on the edge, elbows on his knees and head supported in his hands.

"Have ye been able to keep anything down, me laird?"

Varan shook his head, reaching for a glass of water on the side table next to him. His hands were shaking so badly that water sloshed over the side as he took a tentative sip.

Rhyanna steadied the glass for him and observed him through a healer's eyes. His color was chalky and his eyes sunken from dehydration. "Try and take another sip, me laird," she encouraged.

He managed a small one and wiped his hand over his mouth, trying to force his body to accept the small, desperately needed offering. "How much longer can I anticipate this reaction?" he asked pitifully.

"Not much longer, sire," she said as she gently wiped his face of the cold sweat clinging to it. "Yer through the worst of it." Rinsing the cloth, she wiped his bare arms and chest, then stood to reach his back from the other side of the bed. "Lie down, and I will work on you some more."

Rhy helped him recline, then covered him with a light blanket before settling on a stool near his head. Grounding herself and protecting herself in a white energy bubble, she laid her hands on either side of his head and examined him.

The muddy colors of his aura had nearly cleared, and with today's session they should reach optimal healing. Some extra attention in his heart chakra and solar plexus would clear up the nausea and help him to crave healthy, healing foods.

Pulling healing energy through her feet and root chakra, she called on the Earth Mother to help her heal this man. The king had suffered enough and had much to atone for. His healing was required for the sake of his people, and he didn't have time to do it gradually. The brutal pace he insisted on had been very difficult on his body, and it would take him weeks to be up to full speed.

Rhy prayed he had enough strength to get him through the coming week because it would be difficult physically and emotionally on all of them, and they needed him thinking and reacting as clearly as possible. All their futures depended on his actions and reactions.

His muscles relaxed, and his breathing was slow and steady. A smile crossed her face, and she was grateful that he'd finally fallen into the deep sleep his body required to complete the healing. Rhy knew that, like Kyran, he pulled negative emotions from the island's residents to aid in his swift healing, but he could only harness what he had the strength to manipulate.

The afternoon light faded as evening rolled in. Her stomach grumbling made her sit back and stretch as she decided to take a break for her dinner. Varan mumbled in his sleep, and she traced a pattern over his forehead, helping to relax him so that he could continue sleeping until she returned.

Tristan sat silently in a corner, watching her for hours without a word. His eyes followed her now as she headed toward him.

"I be needing to fuel up afore I can help him anymore," she said with a tight smile. "Would ye like me to bring ye something whence I return?"

His dark eyes watched her for a long moment before responding. "I wouldn't mind something simple, my lady," he said in a quiet voice.

"I shall return as quickly as I am able."

"Can ye help him find his way back to us, my lady?"

"Aye, I believe I can, but he needs to do the work, and he hasn't shirked in any aspect so far. Ye've been friends for a long time, I take it?"

"Aye, since we were wee lads."

"He's lucky to have ye." She started to turn away but hesitated for a moment.

"What is it, Mistress Rhyanna?"

"Who do ye trust at court? If I were able to get a message to Kyran, what allies does he have there?"

"Dashiel, first and foremost. Some of the others who have been abused and punished by the queen, and his brothers, of course, are all loyal to the Tyde family."

A smile of relief and gratitude eased across her face. "Ye have our gratitude fer yer help, Tristan. Yer assistance shan't be forgotten."

"Our court deserves better than what that woman is offering. I know King Varan, in his right mind, never would've allowed what's happening to continue, and I've no doubt that he will put an end to it as soon as he is able."

"I pray it is so, for I don't ken what will happen to any of us if he doesn't follow through. He'll lose his sons and any respect his people might still have for him."

"Aye, may the mother make it so," he agreed. "Because I can't stomach the thought of living under her rule any longer. I will take my chances and get my family out of there, no matter the consequences I may face." Tristan's fierce gaze pierced hers. "I'll die before I take the chance of that woman touching a member of my family, and so will many others." He glanced at the sleeping monarch. "We need our king to come back to us. He's our only chance at surviving."

Rhyanna nodded sadly as her gaze followed his. "Aye, we will all lose someone we love if he fails, and I don't think his sons will ever forgive him...I don't think he'll be able to forgive himself."

CHAPTER FIFTY-SIX

Remember My Touch

Elyana Drake couldn't believe her luck. Could this day possibly get any worse? She had finally managed to slip away from her personal guard and jump into the portal as the door opened. Not giving the occupant a chance to exit, she went into full defense mode, needing to escape from here. The unfortunate soul she bowled over would be able to return as soon as she exited.

Racing to the controls, she sealed the door and pulled up a map of Europe. She reached out to select the port in Italy, but before she pressed the button, the man behind her grabbed her by the back of the cloak. She felt the fury radiating off him as he swung her around. The closed fist decided it for her. She took advantage of her small stature and used the arm holding her as a pivot point, swinging her knee up as hard as possible towards the tall man's gonads.

Her knee connected with the soft, ultra-sensitive tissue at the same time she finally got a good look at him. For a moment, she thought she might pass out from the surprise, but the shock wasn't enough to stop her from her original plan. Turning back to the controls, she changed her destination and headed for the Amazon first. Europe held too many memories.

The man behind her was dry heaving and groaning in agony. She regretted any damage she might have caused and hoped it wasn't permanent. Knowing she couldn't avoid him…or could she? The portal would open in less than a minute. This was the man she fantasized about for decades and prayed he would care enough to come find her when the time together was over. They didn't exchange names or clans, wanting their time together to be unencumbered by their past, their families, and their everyday lives. Everyone deserved a fantasy week with a stranger before they settled down.

Sadly, after the week ended, he was all she could think about, and every man she met afterwards was a disappointment. They lacked his humor, his eyes, his laughter…and dear God, his magnificent body, and the things he did to her with it. The memory made her blush thinking about it.

The heat in her cheeks faded as she remembered how disappointed she was when he hadn't sought her out. She gave him a clue the day she left in case he was interested in finding her. Their time together had been magical—at least to her it had been. Elyana gave herself to him willingly. She was inexperienced, but the way he touched her and treated her seemed special and not the way you would care for a stranger.

The memories bombarding her brought a rush of heat to her core, and she didn't know how to face him and leave again. She had been unencumbered when they met. If he had wanted a relationship with her then, they might have had a chance at a future. Now, her future was out of her control. Her clan's well-being was now in her hands. Her father had agreed to a trade agreement with the Court of Tears. A union between the clans was part of the pact he made. This betrothal offered her up like a sacrificial lamb to seal the deal.

Fury rolled through her at the idea of her father making this bargain with the she-devil without giving Elyana the consideration of a conversation about it first. The king had always given her free reign over her time and educational endeavors. He was so proud of her when she became a historian and made it her mission to preserve the stories and genealogy of all the clans. This was the first decision he had made for her that didn't make any sense.

Elyana was devastated and horrified to be betrothed to a stranger with no thoughts to her happiness. She always believed she would have a love match like her parents or remain single. Never in her wildest nightmares did she see a future she had no say in.

Groaning behind her snapped her out of her reverie as the doors opened in the rainforest. She headed for the door, looking over her shoulder as she reached the safety of it. Her former lover was on his knees with his hand outstretched to her. His face was pale—a result of all the blood rushing south, she was sure.

His voice rolled over her like a caress as he finally managed to speak. "Don't go. Please wait a moment." His eyes begged her to give him a chance to speak with her.

Elyana peeked at the leather watch on her left wrist. "I can't," she said, sadly. "They'll be following me in a few moments. I have to keep moving." She stepped out of the portal saying, "I wish things were different, truly, I do." With one last look of longing, she left him there on the floor and headed into the heat of the rainforest.

She removed her cloak as she ran down the gravel path, tying it around her waist to keep it out of the way. Her boots were sensible, and she thanked all her lucky stars that she loved to run every morning. The terrain was flat, and she would be able to cover the twenty miles to the next portal in no time flat. Her tightly braided hair slapped against her back with every step.

The mystery man plagued her. She would have at least liked to have known his name. He hadn't changed much since she'd met him. His hair was cropped tighter on the sides now, and he seemed leaner. His eyes were different. The ice blue had changed. Where she had once seen only a warm, welcoming light, now they offered a hard, dangerous glint that she didn't recognize. It was best that she hadn't spoken to him. More likely than not, he was nothing like the man she had given her virginity to. She once believed he had been the one she wanted to give her heart to.

With a burst of speed, she tried to outrun her memories and nearly succeeded until she was tackled to the ground from behind. The gravel came up fast and embedded in her hands and her knees. Fortunately, her arms cushioned her face. The breath was knocked from her chest by the weight of a large body covering hers. Panicking, she started thrashing beneath him even though she still couldn't breathe.

Kano effectively caged her in beneath him. As she struggled feebly, this time for oxygen, he rubbed his cheek against hers and finally spoke, "Don't even think about running or kneeing me in the balls again. I promise you won't like the repercussions if you do." His voice was cold and threatening.

Elyana gasped, trying to speak. "Can't...get...off...breathe..."

Kano finally realized what was happening and released her immediately. Watching her lying flat with her torso barely moving as she gasped, trying to suck air into her lungs, he realized she was having a panic attack. Feeling like a shit for scaring the hell out of her, he pulled her upright and sat with her between his legs. Her back was against his chest as he ran his hands up and down her arms gently.

He spoke to her in a soothing voice like you would to a child. "I'm not going to hurt you. You know my voice. Remember my touch."

His hands continued tracing her arms as he rocked her gently. He moved his arm between her breasts so that his large palm rested on her collarbone while his voice soothed her. "Baby, I need you to breathe with me. Feel my chest rising and falling against your back. Feel the heat of me behind you. My hand is grounding you to me. Breathe in with me now," he commanded. His chest rose, and she tried to take a small breath. "That's good, baby doll. Let's try to inhale again." He took a deep breath with his palm pressing slightly against her skin to remind her body to join him.

This time she partially succeeded. His other hand kept rubbing her arm, encouraging her. His voice in her ear entranced her. His lips brushed the outer edge, sending shivers through her. He rubbed his cheek softly next to hers, and the subtle stubble that was appearing on his skin was an erotic caress. The sensation of his skin so sensually rubbing against hers—even if that wasn't his intention—helped her to finally take a deep breath.

"That's it, baby. That's perfect."

His voice, damn the things it did to her. With a shudder, she exhaled in a throaty moan, unable to stop the pure female sound of satisfaction that escaped her.

His hand pulled her closer, snugging her into his body, where there was no mistaking the hard length she was leaning against. "God damn, I've missed that sound," he said in a gravelly voice. He hesitated, then thought, "Fuck it." He might not have another chance to see her, or make her listen to him, the way she was hell-bent on running away. He rubbed his cheek against hers again, unable to miss the way she arched her back to snuggle closer to his face. "I've missed the soft touch of your body, your laugh, and that beautiful smile. Hell, I miss everything about you, and I haven't been able to stop thinking about you since you ran away from me."

Elyana was so focused on the sound of his voice to simply breathe that it took a moment for her mind to catch up with the implications of the confession he was making. "You don't have to say that. I promise, I'll live," she said in a whisper. "Don't feel like you have to be nice to me after all this time."

He turned her sideways to look into her eyes. Her legs were over his, and his arm supported her back while he cupped her cheek. "I wouldn't say anything I didn't mean. I never lie, and I rarely can be accused of doing anything nice. Just once, I wanted you to know that you made a hell of an impression on me and that no one else has ever come close to making me experience what you did." His mind was screaming at him to shut the hell up, but his heart needed to get this out before he lost her again. For all he knew she might already belong to someone else, and then he would look like an idiot, but at this point he didn't give a fuck what anyone thought, only what she thought.

Her large, hazel eyes were wide as they stared at him in shock and disbelief. Then to his horror, they filled with tears, and she tried to turn away.

"I'm sorry. For fucks sake, I didn't mean to make you cry," he said as his hands framed her face. "Say something."

Elyana tried to rein in her emotions before looking at him. Finally working up the courage, she gave him her full attention. "That's hard to believe when you never followed up on the information I left you. You never once tried to contact me." The confusion on his face stopped her.

"What information?"

"I left word for you at the desk. I left you a letter, telling you how to find me, should you choose to. When I didn't hear from you, I decided my inexperience mistakenly led me to believe what we shared was nothing more than common sex."

"I never got the information. He leaned back and pulled out his wallet. Unfolding a piece of paper, he gave it to her.

Her eyes filled as her fingers outlined the crude likeness of her. "Did you draw this?"

"No, I described you to my mother—she's the artist in the family." His eyes traced her features repeatedly, still unable to believe that she was sitting right in front of him. "I went crazy for months trying to find you. For years, anytime I met someone new, I would show them your picture hoping to learn your name. I started to believe that you never existed and that I was losing my mind."

His fingers wiped the moisture under her eyes. "There are a lot of adjectives that I would use to describe the time we spent together. Common is the farthest thing from what we created together. These are a few of my favorites..." He placed a kiss on her forehead, then whispered, "beautiful," moved on to her eyes, where he sighed, "sensual." Brushing his nose against hers, he said, "amazing." His lips skimmed her chin before hovering over her lips. "But the most important way I can describe our time together was," he captured her bottom lip between his before finishing with, "life-changing."

Elyana once again struggled to catch her breath as he said the words she dreamed of hearing from him. His lips played with hers for a minute before he gazed into her eyes, seeking, and finding permission, then kissing her properly. She moaned long and low at the taste of him on her lips again. Self-doubt had been hounding her, with recent events nearly convincing her that she had imagined their time together.

Kano matched her moan with a deep one of his own. He pulled her around on his lap so that she could wrap her arms around him as tightly as he was holding her. He kept the kiss gentle, afraid if he weren't careful, he would take her right here in the open. Her tongue caressed his tentatively, and he was surprised that she still seemed shy for all the years between them.

His lips reminded her how in sync they had been together, and she was glad that the knowledge came back to her as if they had never been apart.

She hoped he never stopped because then she wouldn't have to face the future without him in it after finally finding him again.

He finally pulled away and stared at her. A broad smile crossed his face as he said, "God, I have missed you." His lips found hers again as his hands started to familiarize him with her gorgeous curves. "And I'm never letting you go again."

His words were like a splash of reality that made her pull away, trying to put space between them. "Stop! We must stop. I can't do this; we can't do this."

She tried to leave his arms, but he pulled her in close and started rocking her to soothe her again. "Shh," he said, whispering in her ear. "Whatever is wrong, baby, I promise we can make this work. There is nothing that can keep us apart this time."

Elyana wrenched herself back and gazed at him with such sorrow that his heart tightened as fear made its first appearance in his life. Her voice was barely audible. "We can't make this work. You can't fix this. No matter how badly I might want to, this will never happen."

Kano was stunned by her words. "If you feel absolutely nothing for me, tell me now, but I'll have a tough time believing you after the way you just reacted to me. Tell me what is standing between us. You don't know this about me, but I have a lot of power and influence that can help us to make this work." He saw the color drain from her face as she examined his clothing, noticing the colors and cut of his clothes for the first time.

She put a hand up to stop him. Tears fell, and she wiped them quickly away. "Why were you in the portal today?"

He stared at her, stunned. "What does it matter? All that matters is that we finally found each other again."

"Please, just answer my question." Her voice was raw, but there was a hint of command mixed in with it as she glared at him.

He cleared his throat. "I was sent as an emissary from my court to collect Princess Elyana from the Court of Luminosity to return with me until her betrothal."

Horror crossed her face, and she wrenched herself away from him, sobbing. "No, this can't be happening. Who are you? Give me your name and position. Now."

The imperial command was in her voice, and he felt nauseous as a niggling suspicion in the back of his mind formed, warning him that today was about to turn into one of the worst days of his life. "Why were you running away?" he countered, his unease turning into straight-up pissed-off.

"Your name, damn you."

He stood to his full height and gave her a bow that would make his father proud. "I am Kano, third son of King Varan and a prince of the

Court of Tears. I was assigned to escort Princess Elyana from her home to the home of her future husband." His eyes glared at her as he stalked towards her. "Your turn to answer my question. Why were you running away?" When he thought her face couldn't become any paler, she lost all color, and her hair was a stark contrast to the pallor of her face.

Her breathing was shallow as she faced him. Pain-filled eyes gazed at him with such sorrow that he knew the next words out of her mouth would break his heart. Curtsying deeply, she spoke in a barely audible voice. "I am the Princess Elyana, and I am betrothed to your brother Kyran. I was running away because I would rather dishonor myself and my family than spend a lifetime in a loveless marriage with a stranger. You arrived to escort me to my own personal hell." She gave a maniacal laugh. "This is the definition of irony."

Kano watched her as the happiness he thought he'd regained turned to ash in his hands. He took a slow step towards her carefully as he tried to think of a way out of their predicament and saw the moment her mind dealt with too much. Her eyes rolled back in her head, and she fainted.

Somehow, he caught her before she hit the dirt. She was light in his arms, much lighter than she used to be. He smiled as a plan formed. They needed more time together, and he knew right where they were going to spend that time.

As far as the Court of Tears was concerned, she was leading him on a merry chase, and he would return with her when she was recaptured.

He sent a missive to his valet with the message, knowing Meriel would be furious. Then, he smiled as he glanced down at the woman who had haunted his nights for years. He didn't give a shit what the queen wanted. With a little more compassion for Kyran's situation, Kano fully intended to do everything in his power to stop this betrothal and keep Elyana for his own.

CHAPTER FIFTY-SEVEN

Handle With Care

Pearl returned in a foul mood. The woman had always remained calm, cool, and collected the entire time Rosella had been on board this steel prison. Today was the first time she'd seen the madam lose her composure.

The lessons about releasing control had continued in her absence. Thankfully, Braden hadn't appeared again to torment her dreams with his handsome body. The girls had just finished with the men before them, and she was finding it easier to relax and let them take their pleasure from her. After Braden, they weren't much of a challenge, and she found herself bored throughout the encounter, waiting for it to be over.

The experience with him had made her feel powerful and sultry. The man in front of her today had taken no time to start thrusting violently into her mouth, and she missed the gentleness Braden had shown her.

As the men filed out, Pearl walked down the row before the young women with a riding crop in her hand. She made two circuits before she called Gemma and another, Tessa, forward. Tessa was tall and wore her chestnut hair in a bob with bangs. The cut framed her delicate face beautifully, and Rosella was jealous of her straight locks.

"On your knees, hands out, palms up." Pearl waited until the two girls complied. "The rings are on the floor to prevent you from touching the man in front of you. 'Tis especially important to remember to not intervene."

Tears ran down both girls' faces, and Rosella understood why they had been singled out. Both girls had reached up, trying to slow the men down who were choking them with their cocks.

With a vicious swing, Pearl brought the crop down and across both girls' hands. "Keep them there," she shouted as she brought it down twice more. Welts instantly welled up across their hands, and the room was silent except for the hiccupping sobs of the young women.

Pearl's eyes glinted dangerously as she glared at the girls before her. "When I send you to perform a service, you are a reflection of me. You exhibit what I have taught you, and your failures will reflect on me. Should I receive complaints about your performances, you will not like the consequences.

"You will do whatever is required of you with a smile. No matter how painful, how immoral, or how debased it may seem, you will do it with a smile on your face because when you are returned, I receive either compliments or complaints about my services. Any complaints I receive jeopardize my reputation. I promise you do not want to fuck with my reputation, or I will make you rue the day you were born."

A piece of paper was produced, and she rattled off six names that Rosella wasn't familiar with yet. The girls stood before her trembling, afraid they were next to be punished.

Pearl attempted a smile, even though she was breathing hard. "You were highlighted at our last auction. You will be auctioned off to the highest bidder for the weekend. You are only expected to be proficient in that which you have been trained. First sales are of interest to one type of client only. These men relish breaking maidens." She paused, letting that sink in. "Some men will be gentle with you, and others will do so in a manner to cause you as much pain as possible. You will survive your virginity being taken. Do so with grace and dignity, and I will reward you richly."

"Karyn, Tryna, and Ella will be showcased." She headed for the door. "You're dismissed. Girls, have the healer treat your hands. By this evening, you'll barely have a mark, only the memory of the pain to remind you."

The color drained out of Rosella's face. Time was running out for her family to find her or for her to escape. One by one, they filed out and returned to their respective rooms.

Shaelyn began chattering with her when she walked in, but Ella couldn't focus on the words streaming from her. Her hands were ice cold, and her breathing sounded harsh to her own ears. She paced from wall to wall, trying to wrap her mind around the way events were barreling forward.

"Please go fetch me something to snack on." Her voice was terse and short. "I'm sorry, Shaelyn, but I'm being showcased this weekend, and I can't focus on you right now." Tears filled Ella's eyes, and before she knew it, the young woman had come over and hugged her tightly.

"I ken, and I'll give ye some time. Braden must stay, or he will be punished."

Ella nodded and then collapsed on the settee, ripping at her bodice trying to loosen her corset. A moment later, the door shut, and Braden was kneeling before her. He took her cold hands in his, rubbing them vigorously as she sat there in shock.

Large tears rolled down Ella's cheeks. "I'm not ready. It's too soon." Her voice was shrill as she continued, "I can't do this." Sobs welled up with the panic.

"Hush, Ella," Braden said softly. "Hush, now."

"I'm not ready for some stranger to touch my body, Braden." His hands squeezed hers tightly, trying to ground her, but it wasn't working. "I can't do this..." Ella's wails filled the small room, and she struggled to pull in enough air to continue.

His calloused hands framed her face as his eyes met hers. "You are stronger than you realize, Ella. I've studied you since the night you arrived, and I've never known anyone with your strength to walk these halls, and I've been here a while. You refused to give in, and I respect you so much for that." He kissed her forehead; his lips dry against her skin. "You are a survivor. You CAN do this, and you will." His fingers brushed away her tears. "When you return...after, Shaelyn and I will be here to help you through the aftermath. "I promise we'll be here for you."

Ella threw herself into his arms, needing the illusion of safety just for a few moments. He hesitated for a moment, then his arms wrapped around her tightly, rocking her back and forth as he comforted her. Ella's sobs faded, and she stayed there, not wanting to leave the temporary security he offered.

Braden released her. A shaky hand pushed the hair back off her face as he wiped the last of the tears away. His eyes searched hers, and the way he gazed at her made her feel special—cared for.

In a voice full of gravel, he said, "I need you to survive for me. You are the only joy I find in this place. Every day is a struggle for me to remain here, but one glance across the room at you is enough to get me through another day."

The way he sounded saying those words took Ella away from her misery. Her eyes widened as their faces were close enough to kiss. Their breaths mingled, and she wanted him to kiss her, but didn't ask him to. The naked desire in his eyes told her what he wanted, but he was too worried about the consequences to ask her. They stayed like that until the door flew open and Shaelyn rushed in with a tray.

Setting the tray on a small table next to the settee, she sat next to Ella, rubbing her back. "I be so sorry, mistress."

Ella leaned her head against Shaelyn's and said in a weary voice, "I'm not your mistress, Shaelyn. I'd never force you to be my maid. I would very much like you to be my friend; I need that so much more."

Shaelyn's eyes filled as she peered into Ella's. "Aye, I would like that, too." She glanced down at their clasped hands then back to Ella. "The three of us need to stick together. We're all we've got. I'm but a mistake away from being in yer position." Placing her hand on top of theirs, she whispered, "You have me word that anything that happens in this room is between the three of us."

"You have mine as well," Braden adds.

"You have mine," Ella said, meeting both of their eyes. "I will do everything I can to protect you from this as long as I can, but I need your help to try and communicate with someone. Are you willing to help me?"

The color leeched out of her new friends' faces. "You'll get us all killed," Shaelyn gasped. "It's happened before,"

"No, I don't need you to risk anything," Ella said quickly. "I just need time to reach out to my maman." She blew out a breath and decided to take a chance on the two of them. "She managed to come to me when I was locked in that cell. I need to try and tell her I'm running out of time." Her eyes pleaded with them. "I promise you, if they come to rescue me, I will take all of you with me."

"What do we need to do?"

"Just watch over my body while I attempt to astral travel to her." Her voice grew stronger now that she had a plan.

Shaelyn and Braden exchange a glance. "We'll help you," Braden said. "What do you need from us?"

"Time without interruptions, candles—any color—white chalk, and salt."

"I can find those by tonight," Shaelyn said with certainty.

"I'm putting my life in your hands," Ella whispered. "Please handle it with care."

Their solemn nods were all she had to go by, but it felt like enough. Rosella leaned her head against Shaelyn's and gazed at Braden. The turmoil in his eyes mirrored hers, and she knew that his betrayal would put his sisters in danger if this failed. "I promise I'll handle both of you with the same care."

CHAPTER FIFTY-EIGHT

Thick as Thieves

Glamor firmly in place, Fergus leaned against the outside wall of the tavern, nonchalantly waiting for Hamish to appear. The drunk man had been hell-bent on getting even with Jonah when they parted last night and agreed to meet up today to formulate a plan.

Lips pursed, he drew hard on the joint between his lips, needing to mellow out and fit in with the river rat he could see sauntering down the lane towards him. Hamish slowed to a stop in front of him, wearing the same filthy clothes he had on last night and looking like something the cat had drug in. Ferg made certain the man drank enough last night that the old boozer was still hurting today.

"Wadn't sure ye'd show," Hamish said with a sneer. His eyes stared pointedly at the butt in his hand, so Fergus handed it over, grudgingly sacrificing his favorite blend.

"I'se having the same reservations meself." Fergus met his gaze, never flinching from the man's glare. "Buy ye a drink?"

"Aye, but na here," Hamish said with a grimace. "The laird's lads own the place, and ye can't trust the bastards."

"Ye sure were spouting off some hostile shite last night for not trusting the place."

"Too much in me cups last night. Usually, I be smarter than that." He hocked phlegm and spit a chunk into the street. "There's a place down the road a bit I feel safer in."

"Lead the way."

Hamish took Fergus on a merry chase through alleys and driveways, doubling back more than once. Ferg bit back a smile. The little man was trying to confuse him, not realizing he'd run these streets as a lad and could walk them blindfolded. He knew exactly where they were. Finally satisfied that he was covering his tracks, Hamish led him through the swinging doors of a brothel.

A shadowed table in the corner was the one Hamish headed for, calling to the wench for a bottle of the good stuff on the way. Fergus sat carefully, avoiding a splotch of something on the seat he didn't want to contemplate and thanking his lucky stars that he chose to wear breeches today. The Mother knew what diseases he might have picked up off the chair in his kilt. A shudder ran through him, thinking about it.

A buxom brunette with dark eyes set the bottle on the table and waited expectantly to be compensated. "He's buying," Hamish said, waving an arm at Fergus.

"As ye wish," Ferg said, giving the woman enough for the bottle and a damn good tip. "So, what's yer master plan to hit Jonah where it hurts?"

"I'se thought about scuttling his ship," he said with a grin, "but 'tis a massive fecker and would take too much work, even if the cargo would be worth the resale value."

"What kind a cargo we talking about?" Fergus asked nonchalantly, taking a sip and grateful at least the glasses were clean. He lit a cigar and waited patiently.

An oily smile crossed the man's face, and his eyes sparkled delightedly. "Pretty young things," he said in a raspy whisper.

Fergus returned his smile, although inside, he alternated between wanting to puke and wanting to kill the man. Needing to convince the man he was a safe bet, he donned a personality so completely different from his own that he barely recognized himself.

A lecherous look appeared in his eyes as he asked Hamish, "Boys or girls?"

"Hard to say; often both."

"Where do they bring them in from?"

"That's where I'se usually helpful to the lightning-scarred fecker," he said with a chuckle. "Jonah thinks that scar on his face makes him scary. Jest makes him ugly, so's he can't convince them to come willingly." Taking a slug of the amber liquid, he wiped his chin with the back of his hand where some missed his mouth, then continued.

"As an old man, I coax them in by convincing 'em I'm near to drowning. Kill anyone who might challenge me and take the others to Jonah to be trained fer the next auction." His eyes sparkled as he looked at Fergus, proud of his accomplishments.

"How long ye been running this gig?"

"Decades. Usually, I'se no problem selling me finds. If not Jonah, then someone else'll take them off me hands. Lots of fish in the pond looking for unspoiled things."

"Is it worth the risk? Do ye pull enough in to make it worth Island Law if n ye get caught?"

"The feckers'll never catch me." A dark chuckle erupted from behind his stained crooked teeth. "I'm protected."

"How the feck do ye manage that?" Ferg asked incredulously, seriously wondering how this little pissant had been able to afford the kind of protection he was referring to.

"Same way they keep their ships hidden from the Romani river patrols. Friends in the right places."

"Must have some fecking powerful mages on their payroll."

"Don't ken about all that, just know they gives me a glamor and charms to make me less noticeable—easier to blend in. I can do nearly anything I'se want as long as I keep the untouched ones coming in."

"Ye do this all by yerself?" Fergus arched an eyebrow, surprised the little bastard could manage to do so much damage to so many.

"Na, there's a whole slew of us. Never put all yer eggs in one basket, he always says."

"He?"

"The man with the purse."

"So, what's yer grand plan?" Ferg asked, trying to put them back on track and not raise the man's suspicions with too many questions.

"I'se gonna wait for him to drop anchor fer the next auction. When they're off peddling their wares, their ship will be vulnerable. I fully intend to sink it to the bottom of the river."

"Ye give me an in with yer network, and I'll help ye take that fecker's ship down."

Suspicion swirled in his eyes, and Fergus wondered if he'd overplayed his hand. "Why ye so interested in helping me with this? It be dangerous, and ye ain't got no horse in this race."

Fergus's flinty eyes nailed Hamish as he lazily swirled the whiskey in his glass. "I'se has me own predilections, if ye ken what I mean." Dark promises swirled between them, and he saw the moment suspicion turned into greed and unholy desire of his own.

"I'se never had an unsoiled one meself. Worth too much to waste it on a quick feck."

"Ye help me get into the game, and I give ye me word to bring ye something I promise ye'll want to take the time to enjoy. Find me work in the dark circles, and I'll make enough to keep ye in the finest young pussy ye can imagine…unless your preferences swing in the other direction."

"Either one works fine for me. Not terribly picky, I ain't."

Hamish's eyes glittered with a sexual heat that made Fergus want to kill him where he sat, but he needed the disgusting little fecker to enter the dark world calling to him. He was certain if the man stood, he'd be tenting the breeches hanging from his slim hips. "What do we need to do first?"

"New moon's coming up; that's when the auctions and showcases take place—under cover of the darkest part of the month."

"How far do we need to go to get there?"

"Ye ain't fecking going nowhere until I ken I can trust ye."

"What do ye need me to do to prove meself?"

"Cross the way be two little girls playing. Their mam works upstairs. I want ye to bring me one out back and keep her quiet for me."

Fergus kept his gaze neutral, trying not to let his hatred of this man show. "Busy time a night to try and make that happen. Lots of folks in and out right now. I'm not willing to put me neck on the line for either of us, no matter how badly I be wanting that job."

"I'se only fecking with ye, but ye should've seen the look on yer face." Hamish laughed. "At least I ken now that ye gots a few brains in yer head afore ye get both of us killed with all yer questions. Ye only talk to me. Ye understand me, lad?"

"Aye, I'll keep me mouth shut," Fergus said, looking him in the eye. *"Until I put ye in yer grave ye perverted motherfecker,"* he thought to himself, wondering how he was going to work with this imbecile. "Jest let me know when the games begin."

"Soon, me new friend. Very soon." Hamish finished his drink. Scratching his crotch like he had crabs, he perused the women hawking their wares. I'll be in touch whens I gets the details. Will leave a message fer ye at the other place."

"I look forward to hearing from ye," Fergus said, with a smile that should have been a warning, and meaning it because he was already thinking of the most vicious ways to kill the evil little fecker.

CHAPTER FIFTY-NINE

May the Gods Afford Me the Opportunity

Rhyanna sat, cupping the king's head in her hands. The monarch was in better spirits mentally and physically. His aura was free of the poison that had trapped him in a fugue state for years. The color of his skin was much healthier, and his eyes were clear. The nausea had faded, and he was able to consume tiny amounts of food. His appetite was returning, but Rhyanna cautioned him against eating too much at once.

He was sleeping deeply as she worked on him. The best remedy for him at this point was to allow his body the rest it needed to regain his physical strength and the mental acuity to retake his throne and redeem himself in the eyes of his people and his children.

She'd seen Kai in passing over the past few days and couldn't help but compare the Tyde men. Kai had his father's coloring, but his features were softer, less defined. His face bordered on pretty until you paired that with his massive, defined body. He was always courteous, and she restrained herself from asking about Kyran and from mentioning that his father was in the clinic.

She lived by strict rules regarding the privacy of her patients, and she wouldn't break them even for the rest of the Tyde clan, Kyran and Kai included—although she couldn't have told him even if she wanted to since their ability to communicate had been disabled.

She missed the ever-present feel of him on her link. Even when she was angry with him, he had always been only a thought away. Knowing she couldn't reach him was a horrible feeling, and she realized that she never wanted to lose the bridge they had built because she couldn't imagine living with this missing piece of her soul.

Humming an old tune, she worked with Tristan's ever-constant gaze locked on her. They'd grown accustomed to each other over the past week, and she felt a grudging respect forming between them. His loyalty to the man under her care couldn't be questioned. Rhy's willingness to help the monarch and her ability to return him to health earned his approval.

They had taken to playing cards in between her healing sessions, and though he was a seasoned poker player, she won three out of five rounds as a rule.

Genny, a young woman Rhyanna recently treated, had begun working with her in the shoppe. She was a dainty girl with auburn hair and haunted, hazel eyes. Petite, with less than five feet of height to lay claim to and not enough meat on her bones to keep a strong wind from blowing her away, she was fragile. Terrified of returning home and reliving the same cycle she'd recently escaped, she begged to stay at the sanctuary.

Rhy gave her a position helping in the apothecary shoppe and clinic, and she was slowly learning to stand on her own two feet again. She endured a horrible ordeal and tended to jump at her own shadow, but Rhy was happy to find her beginning to relax in their presence.

Tristan and Varan both sensed her fragility and were quiet and kind around her. She made them tea and did some light cleaning as she built up her endurance physically and mentally. They had been teaching her how to play poker and were hopeful that someday soon she might win a hand.

Finishing with Varan, Rhy joined them at the small card table where Genny was playing solitaire.

"Deal me in, lass," Rhy said, "and we'll practice again."

Genny looked silently at Tristan, asking him without a word if he would join them.

"Aye, someone needs to keep the two of you out of trouble," he said with a wink.

Genny dealt the hand, and the three of them examined their cards.

"I'll take two, lass," Rhy said, laying her discards down.

"Give me three," Tristan said with a shake of his head at his hand.

Genny took one, and for the first time, she raised the bet, pushing a colored pebble that they were using for poker chips into the center. She sat solemnly while the others matched it.

Rhy laid down two pairs with a smile. "See if ye can beat that."

Tristan laughed. "I can and will," he said, laying down a full house.

They both waited patiently for Genny to reveal her hand.

The lass studied her cards closely before laying them down. She glanced up shyly at Tristan and said, "A full house may beat two pairs, sir, but I believe my straight beats your full house." She hunched her shoulders as if afraid he would be angry.

Tristan gave her a look of surprise, then grinned at the girl like she'd won a prize. "It sure does, lass. Congrats on your first win."

Genny rewarded him with a rare smile that lit up her whole face. The smile transformed her, turning her into a beautiful young woman without a care in the world. The simple pleasure of winning a hand made her glow, and they all smiled with her.

"Don't forget to take your treasure," Tristan said as he pushed the colored stones towards her. "Now that you know what you're doing, lass, we won't be going easy on you."

"I wouldn't know what to do if someone took it easy on me, sir," she said, looking down at the cards she was shuffling, unable to meet his eyes.

Tristan glanced at Rhy across the table, and she felt his sorrow for the girl the same way that it was running through her. Genny had never known anything kind in this world. She had been taken advantage of by her family and by the slavers who purchased her from them. The young woman deserved so much better than what this life had granted her so far.

The bell in the shoppe rang as the door opened. Rhy started to get up, but Genny laid the cards down and said in a small voice, "Let me, Mistress Rhyanna. It's time for me to start carrying my weight around here."

Rhy nearly stopped her until she saw Tristan subtly shake his head at her. She let her go, listening for any sound of distress.

"Let her feel like she's worth something, Rhy. She needs a purpose, and you've given her one, along with a great deal of kindness and self-worth." He drained a glass of water and wiped his lips on the back of his hand. "She reminds me of my youngest daughter. A tiny thing, too, but a scrapper at heart. I think they would get on well. My Jade would talk enough for both of them and lighten things up a bit."

"I think that would be lovely. We'll set it upon your return."

Minutes passed, and the young woman didn't reappear. Worried, Rhy stood and headed for the front of the building. "Jest gonna check on the lass," she said over her shoulder.

She reached the clinic door and spied Kai standing in the doorway with Genny shaking in front of him. Rhy started to enter until she heard his soft, melodic voice rumble through the empty room.

"I'm sorry, lass, to have startled you," he said gently. "And I know my size is intimidating, but I mean you no harm."

Genny's body trembled as she was caught in a flashback.

Rhy came forward and stepped in front of Genny, blocking her view of the gentle giant. She snapped her fingers and said, "Look at me, Genny."

The girl glanced at Rhy fearfully and whispered, "I'm so sorry, it's not him. My apologies, my lord." She curtsied deeply, looking down, unable to face him.

Rhyanna looked at Kai, pleading with her eyes for him to move from in front of the door. He immediately moved to the side, allowing the sun to come back in.

"Genny, why don't ye go feed the lazy cat that's taken up residence on me porch. Getting to be dinner time, and she's bound to be a begging."

"Aye, Mistress," she said in a relieved voice and dashed out the door.

Rhy closed it behind her and turned to apologize to Kai.

His gaze was fixed on the window and by Genny outside stroking the cat. "I didn't mean to startle her. It's a curse sometimes—my size."

"Oh, Kai, tis not ye. That wee thing has not had an easy life, nor a pleasant one. I think she's been taken advantage of by those stronger than her. It's a pattern she is trying to break, but I fear it will take some time." She smiled at him as she said, "Don't take it personally, lad. Genny still reacts to me that way half the time."

"I'll try not to, but it's a reaction I get much too often," he said in a sad voice.

The door to the clinic opened, and Tristan stepped out. "Is the wee thing all right?"

Kai's head snapped up and he looked at Tristan suspiciously. "Why are you here?" he asked, raising a brow. "You rarely leave my father's side, and if you think you are going to make me return, you'll need some help to force me to go."

Tristan looked at Rhy helplessly. Before he could respond, Varan stumbled through the door. "Kai, my son, is that you?" he asked incredulously.

Kai's eyes were wide as his father acknowledged him for the first time in years. "Why? Like you even care?" His entire body tensed as he turned to leave.

Rhy grabbed his arm and spoke to him quietly. "Kai, I ken there are a lot of hard feelings towards yer father, but I would like the chance to give ye some facts to ponder afore ye judge him anymore." Her emerald gaze pleaded with him to listen to her. "Please wait outside fer me." She could sense the anger and disappointment he felt for the man behind her. "Please, jest a few moments."

Kai nodded and ignored the other two men in the room as he walked outside, slamming the door behind him. His fists were clenched, and he stood there strung so tightly he thought he might snap. He reclined against a post, trying to sort through the emotional turbulence he was experiencing.

A shadow moved out of the corner of his eye, and he turned, surprised to see the timid little thing he had frightened inside. She clutched a large calico cat, who didn't seem too enthused by the attention. Shyly she approached him, her hazel eyes meeting his as she approached.

Two steps from him, she stopped and glanced away. A flush stained her face as she struggled to speak. "Sir, I just wanted to apologize," she stammered, "for my behavior inside." Her foot scuffed at a rough piece of the wood in front of her. "T'was nothing you did. I struggle sometimes to be around men, is all." She peeked back up at him and asked, "Forgive me?"

Kai waited for her to finish, then said in a soft voice, "There is nothing to forgive, my lady. I'm sorry that I startled you." His blue eyes traveled over the delicate features of her face, and he fought the urge to trace the same path with his fingertips. "I'm Kai," he said, offering a hand. "I've just arrived and don't know many people here." He smiled at her, the action displaying the deep dimples in his cheeks. "It would be nice to have a friend on the island."

The young woman watched him carefully before offering a slender hand that trembled slightly. "Genevieve at your service, but my friends call me Genny."

Kai took her hand and pressed a light kiss to the back as he bowed over it.

"Genevieve, it's truly a pleasure to meet you."

She stroked the cat, the motion soothing her. "This creature needs a name if he's determined to stay."

Kai sat down on the deck, leaning his back to the post so that he wouldn't intimidate her as much. Genny joined him there, settling the content animal between them.

"I've never had a cat," Kai said.

"Me neither. We weren't allowed pets," she said. "Would you like to pet him? It helps me when I'm not feeling well or when I'm afraid."

"Do you think he'll let me?" he asked as he presented a massive hand to the animal to peruse. The cat leaned into him and started purring loudly. Kai smiled at the soft fur rumbling beneath his hand. "He likes me."

Genny smiled up at him, lighting up his entire day. "Yes, I think he does."

They laughed and settled into a comfortable silence, enjoying the fading afternoon light and the critter that had crawled into his lap and gone to sleep.

"Would ye look at that?" Rhyanna said as she looked out the window at the two of them chatting together. Tristan joined her and looked out.

"Who would've thought?" Tristan agreed. "He's always been good with fragile things. He'll be good for her if she gives him a chance."

"Twill be a long time til she's ready for much more than what she's offering right now," Rhy said sadly.

"Kai is nothing like his older brothers, Mistress. He's considerate, thoughtful, and careful with those he is interested in. He'll take what she offers and be grateful for what she is able to give him. Unlike most men, he won't push her for more until she is ready."

"You're both reading a lot into her sharing a cat with him, aren't you?" Varan asked, trying to peer around them.

"Well, I think someone is feeling better today," Rhy said with a smile. She reached up to touch his forehead.

"You're cool, and your eyes are clear." Dropping her hand, she asked, "How is your stomach?"

"I'm starving. What have you got to eat? And don't give me any more tea or broth, for God's sake. I need a real meal."

Rhy and Tristan laughed, grateful for the change in his condition. "I'll see what I can do," Tristan said, heading for the door.

Varan glanced outside once more before heading back into the clinic. "And then I would like to see my youngest son, if he will permit me to." His voice was sad and held a longing to reconnect with his child.

Rhy gazed at him with sympathy and said, "If he's willing to meet with you, my lord, I'll make it so."

"I have many things to be grateful for today and many to make up for. May the gods afford me the opportunity to be a better father than the one they've had." His voice faded off as he turned and walked back with an exhausted sigh.

Rhy's eyes followed Varan as he retreated. She glanced out at Kai and was relieved to see the two sitting in a comfortable silence. Kai stroked the cat on his lap while glancing at Genny occasionally. Genny sat with her back against a post a few feet away from him, and for the first time since Rhy had met her, she didn't seem terrified.

Mayhap the large man who had startled her at first now offered her an illusion of safety.

Hating to interrupt the two, she joined them on the porch. She smiled at Genny and said, "Would ye make us a spot of tea, lass?"

"Aye, Mistress," she replied quickly, coming to her feet and leaving them alone.

Rhy sat next to Kai, trying to figure out how to approach his father's request.

He beat her to it, saying, "Why is he here? I don't want to leave Heart Island." His voice was quiet, but there was a defiant tone to it.

"Aye, lad, I understand yer misgivings with his arrival, but alas, he's come to see me, not thee." She fiddled with a piece of her hair as she worked her way around to asking him if he would be willing to see his father. "I ken he's not been himself of late…"

"He hasn't been himself since I was a boy," he said bitterly.

"Be that as it may," Rhy said in a cautious voice, "yer father has been drugged for a very long time. It doesn't excuse his behavior, but it goes a long way to explaining it na."

Kai looked at her suspiciously. "So, I'm just supposed to forgive and forget because of a poor decision he made that affected all of our futures?"

"Well, I'm not sure how much of that poor choice long ago was his to make and how much of it was influenced by the drugs he was unknowingly given."

"What does he want? You wouldn't be out here defending him if he didn't want something from me." He quirked an eyebrow at her. "If anyone should understand how I feel about him, I would think it would be you due to the situation you are trapped in with Kyran."

Rhy nodded her head in understanding. "I'll not make ye do anything ye don't want to, Kai, but you might want to think about it at least."

The orange tabby stretched and jumped from his lap, sensing his irritation. Kai stood and reached down a hand to help her up. "I appreciate your concern, and I hear what you are saying, but I just can't do this today."

He left her on the porch with the task of telling a king his request had been denied. She sighed and walked back in to face the monarch inside and tell him that the gods hadn't afforded him the privilege today.

CHAPTER SIXTY

You're Safe Here With Me

Kano exited the portal with an unconscious Elyana in his arms. He headed for the pavilion on the beach, hoping his mother was nearby.

Elyana stirred as her head nestled closer to his shoulder, and her fingers stroked his neck. "Am I still dreaming?"

He glanced down at her, a rare smile crossing his face. "If we are, I don't want to wake up." He brushed his lips against her forehead.

"Put me down. I am capable of walking."

"And deprive me the pleasure of holding you?" The right side of his lip quirked up. "I don't think so."

With a sigh, she settled against him, letting the steady beat of his heart beneath her soothe her worries for a moment.

Kano headed up the stairs to the wooden structure his mother spent most of her days in. Shame swamped him as he realized he hadn't been to see her in over a year. She deserved better from all her sons. The situation she was currently in hadn't been of her making, yet she suffered the most for it.

The pavilion, surprisingly, was empty. He made his way to the corner sitting area with its oversized pillows and chaise lounges. Gently, he sat down with her still in his arms, not willing to let her go yet. His eyes traced her features longingly, remembering the nights he had fantasized about her, trying to keep the details sharp in his mind.

Elyana sat there quietly, barely moving except for the gentle rise and fall of her chest. Her eyes were closed, but Kano could see her pulse racing wildly on her neck. His thumb stroked the throbbing skin as he said, "Baby, talk to me."

Her lashes lifted, and her eyes met his. The uncertainty in her gaze gutted him. "What is left to say, Kano?" Her voice trembled as she spoke, and her eyes filled. "We are cursed to never be together; it's not meant to be."

"Bullshit," he said in a tone she had never heard him use. "I'm not willing to give up on us. Tell me you felt nothing when I kissed you. Tell me that you've never thought of me since the morning that you left. Tell me that this doesn't feel right." His monologue ended as his lips captured hers, taking what he wanted without permission or apology.

Elyana moaned as he reminded her what they were like together. His touch was like an ember laid to kindling, and her body responded to the heat, her fire drakes dancing up and down her arms, craving the energy they created together. The unruly drakes danced in the heat of their passion—a myriad of sensuous movements in scarlet, terra cotta, and golden hues.

"Don't move!" a soft feminine voice came from behind them. "Stay just like that, Kano. I need my sketchbook."

Elyana tried to pull away, her cheeks flushing at being caught in his embrace. Kano held her tightly, whispering to her, "You heard the woman, hold still." His lips brushed over hers again, making her nearly forget they had an audience.

A petite, dark-haired beauty appeared in front of them with a large sketch pad and a charcoal pencil. She worked quickly, sketching in the bare hint of an outline in her book. Elyana was mortified but intrigued that the woman was so fascinated by them that she'd want a visual reminder of their guilt.

"Enough!" Elyana said harshly, uncomfortable by being put on display. Her breeding came through in the imperial tone she used, causing the woman to drop her pencil.

"I'm sorry to have caused you any distress, my lady," the unknown woman said, closing the book and settling on a large cushion opposite them. "Perhaps you won't mind telling me what you are doing on my restricted island." Her tone matched the one she had just received.

Kano sighed, rubbing his hand over his face, still holding Elyana tightly against him. He could feel the tension in her body and knew she would flee the second she had a chance. He just needed a chance to talk to her.

"Mama, I want to introduce you to Princess Elyana Drake from the Great Lakes Fire Clan." He glanced down at Elyana's shocked face and said, "This isn't how I imagined it, but I would like you to meet my mother, Queen Yareli from the Court of Tears."

Elyana's jaw dropped as she stared at the casually dressed woman in front of her. She stammered, trying to form words. "Forgive me, Your Majesty, but I thought you were dead."

Yareli laughed aloud. "Oh, child, that's what I want everyone to believe. I will bind you to your silence, or you will remain here with me. The choice is yours."

"You have my word that none shall hear of it from my lips, Your Majesty."

"Stop. I am no longer the queen, nor do I wish to be. I am simply Yareli. Now, will one of you please tell me why you're here?"

She glanced at Kano with an irritated look. "I haven't seen nor heard from you in nearly two years." Tipping her head, she scrutinized Elyana for a moment. Her eyes flew to his, and a smile crossed her face. "You found her."

He grinned broadly. "Yeah, today, actually. That's why I'm here. I know I haven't been around, but I need your help if you would be willing to give it after my extended absence."

Yareli shook her head at him in disappointment. "It doesn't matter how long it's been; I will always help you—if it's within my power to grant, my child."

"Have any of my brothers been by recently?"

"Kai made an appearance a few days ago."

"Did he fill you in on the mess Kyran's in?"

"I heard he's found true love and an unwanted betrothal contract with a complete stranger." A huge grin crossed her face. "He always was an overachiever."

Kano laughed then, the sound so foreign to him that he cut it off quickly. "Have you considered helping him?"

"I am contemplating the consequences of any actions I may determine to make." Her answer was cool and noncommittal.

Elyana could feel Kano tense beneath her. Her hand clutched the fabric of his shirt while her eyes stayed locked on the woman in front of them. This woman might be their only ally—the only one who could make a difference. But would she step out of her comfort zone to do so?

Yareli watched the reaction of the pair in front of her. The fear that crossed over Elyana's face chased away her fire drakes as tears filled her eyes. Kano was as tight as a bowstring and ready to explode. He had always been the most volatile of her boys, but she had never seen him show the care he was giving to Elyana to anyone other than his siblings.

"I take it the woman you have longed for and scoured the earth for," she waved her hands at Elyana before continuing, "is the woman Kyran is betrothed to?"

Kano's arms tightened around Elyana as he nodded his head, and his eyes pleaded with his mother, saying things he couldn't force himself to speak.

Yareli laughed a bitter, brittle sound. "You would think the gods have played with my life enough by now that they would be bored with the way my heart keeps on breaking."

Kano opened his mouth but, not knowing what to say, shut it again.

"I know, my son, what it is to only love one person for your entire life. No matter how much they continue to hurt you, the heart longs for the comfort and the compatibility of your soul mate." With a sigh, she stood and called for her attendants.

"Mama..." Kano said, willing to beg if necessary. "Please, I never beg anyone, but I will beg for your help if that's what it will take for you to forgive me and help us."

Yareli's eyes locked on his anguished ones. "You never have to beg me. There is nothing to forgive, Kano. I have missed you, my child, and I will always love you and be in your corner."

Yareli glanced at the beautiful woman in his arms and spoke to Elyana, "You must be exhausted, my lady."

Elyana nodded, not sure what had just transpired.

Attendants entered the tent in brightly colored caftans, bearing trays of tropical fruits, fresh coconut, cheeses, and beverages. A large platter held roasted pork and poached salmon.

"Come now, let us eat and visit. I would like to learn more about you, Lady Elyana."

"So would I," Kano thought with a wry smile.

As the last of her retainers was leaving, Yareli spoke to her in a language Elyana didn't understand. With a nod and a quick glance at the couple, she left them.

"A bungalow will be prepared for the two of you for later. I am sure it has been a taxing day for you both." A smile flitted over her face as her eyes took in the panicked look on Elyana's face and the satisfaction on her son's.

Elyana tried to eat and respond appropriately to the comment. But the thought of being alone with Kano for the night made her stomach uneasy in anticipation. She remembered the pleasure he had given her and was sure that he had been with many women since she left him. It was different for her. She had been with no one since then, and she was terrified he would find her performance lacking after so long without practice.

She dropped the mango she'd lifted to her lips as he leaned towards her and whispered, "Relax. You're safe here—you're safe with me."

Was she? He would protect her and try to keep her, but was her heart safe from the potential loss she would suffer when he tired of her? She wasn't the kind of woman he was used to, and he didn't really know her. Would he like the woman she was, or would it have been better to remain the perfect stranger he had secluded with during the perfect storm in perfect anonymity? She was a lot of things, but perfect wasn't one of them.

CHAPTER SIXTY-ONE

My Debt to Pay

Two days after Kyran's homecoming, Satish dragged him through the entirety of the Court of Tears, making sure everyone would bear witness his acquiescence to the queen's request to have him in her bed. The collar was brutal as Satish kept a quick pace, leading him like an animal through a market.

Kyran met the eyes of everyone he saw, letting them see the rage brewing and the tempest about to let loose. The weather was becoming treacherous outside as the elements reflected his emotions. He held his head high, refusing to let them shame him publicly.

Dash caught his eyes as he passed and quirked an eyebrow asking silently if he wanted him to intervene. Kyran shook his head, not wanting to involve him any more than he already had.

Satish paraded him through the casino, where Kai and Kenn were settled around a poker table. He smirked at them as he paused with Kyran. "Which one of ye spoiled arseholes will be next?"

Kenn kicked his chair back as he stood with fists clenched, about to incite an altercation until Kai stepped in front of him asking, "What's going on, Kyr?"

"Nothing I didn't sign up for, Kai." Kyran gave them a pitiful attempt at a smile. "Don't worry about it; I will be fine."

"This is fucking wrong, bro, and you know it," Kenn said through clenched teeth. "You don't want to be doing this."

"Want has nothing to do with it," Kyran said. "This is my debt to pay."

"Well, if you're going into the pit with that viper, I'm gonna join the party, too," Kenn snarled at Satish.

"No, lad, ye won't be. This party is by invitation only, and yer not on the guest list," Satish growled.

"She'll accept me," Kai said softly, "so I'll be joining you."

"No, fucking way," Kyran shouted as he strained against his collar. "You're not even supposed to be here." His eyes begged Kenn as he shouted, "Don't you let him move from this room. I don't care if you have to knock his ass out and tie him down, he will not follow through on that. You take him back to Heart Island and make sure Madylyn keeps him there."

Kenn slapped a hand on Kai's shoulder, holding him in place. "I got this." He glared at Satish and, in a deadly voice, said, "He best return unharmed."

"Ye ken as well as I do, the condition he's likely to return in, so keep yer threats to yerself. She won't kill him, and I doubt she'll do any permanent damage. Thought ye pretty boys were built of stronger stuff than that." His cocky tone dared Kenn to challenge him. "Come any closer, and I'll make sure that collar will do some damage. I'd rethink the crazy rolling through yer eyes, lad."

"Kai, tell her I'm indisposed when you return, please."

"I will, Kyr. I'll make sure she knows you aren't forgetting her."

"Tell her I love her; nothing will change that."

"Enough of the hearts and flowers, ye feckers. Move it along, got a way to go afore they begin preparing ye fer the festivities, me laird."

Kyran watched his brothers until they exited the room, making sure Kai didn't join the procession. He would do this every night if it kept her sights off his youngest brother. Meriel would destroy him if she were allowed to touch him.

Satish took way too much pleasure dragging Kyran through the halls, and Kyran started to imagine creative ways to get back at the bastard when this ordeal was over. Finished with the display, he hauled him off to the queen's private baths. His clothes were cut off him, and he was led into the hottest of the three stone bathing chambers. He was shackled spread eagle with his hands and legs attached to iron rings mounted to the white marble walls.

Naked courtiers joined the party and took immense pleasure in soaping him up, shaving him, and rinsing him off. The bitch who had sent Rhyanna running days before dropped to her knees in front of him. She picked up a marble bowl with soap and a brush which she used to lather his pubic area.

Kyran flinched as she picked up a straight razor and looked up at him. "I'd stay very still, my lord," she said with an evil smile. "You wouldn't want me to slip."

She started high and worked her way down his genitals, carefully removing the curls that were there. On the second stroke, with the razor firmly against him, she spoke again. "I don't know what you see in your little healer, my lord." Kyran flinched as her hand completed its downward stroke. "She's not much physically to look at, her hips are too wide, and her speech is deplorable. One would think that hundreds of years living with civilized folk would cure her of that."

Kyran bit his tongue as she slammed Rhyanna, not wanting to give her a reason to slip with the razor. He tried not to wince as she grabbed his flaccid cock and pulled it harshly to the side as she focused on his balls.

"She insinuated in front of most of the court that I was afflicted with the pox. Can you believe that?"

Kyran could well imagine that and struggled not to laugh outright. He realized he must have given some indication to his amusement as he felt the razor nick him just enough to burn. Refusing to show his discomfort, he ignored her and stared straight ahead.

"The wench running the Sanctuary sent us on some ridiculous scavenger hunt while the king was playing with your little healer. You could hear her screams of pleasure outside of the clinic she runs. I know you Tyde boys don't mind sharing, but I'm not sure Daddy is going to be done with her for a while. He hadn't come out of there even once the two days I was there." She smiled up at him innocently, the gleam in her eyes as she saw his clenched jaw acknowledged that she had his full attention.

"If I were you, my lord, I would enjoy the next few days because I guarantee that she will be well taken care of while you are gone."

Kyran's tried to rationalize why Rhy wouldn't have told him Varan was there, and he couldn't find a reason. He wanted to trust her, and his father for that matter, but recent events made it difficult on both accounts. Refusing to let her bait him anymore, he looked down his nose at her and said, "Are you finally finished? The longer you touch me, the more my cock shrinks. I doubt that is the reaction the queen wants from me."

Her fake smile fell, and the hatred behind her mask gave him pause. She reached for an amber jar of ointment and opened it. The scent hit him, and he groaned, knowing what was about to happen. "I'm only supposed to use a little bit of this to prepare you, but since you are struggling to perform, we'll make sure we use enough to have you perking right up, Prince Kyran."

Kyran couldn't help but jerk back as she reached for him. He'd never used the herbs she was about to slather on him, but he'd heard about their effects from his siblings and others who had experienced them. The cool ointment surrounded his cock as she applied it liberally before also coating his balls. The nick in his skin stung as the oils penetrated. His skin tingled in a pleasant way as the oils soaked into him. Through no will of his own, his cock responded to the stimulation, swelling and throbbing against his skin. His hips thrust forward as her hand stroked him with another application. The sensation of her skin against his painfully aroused cock was pure pleasure, and he could only imagine how incredible it would be when he thrust inside of someone else.

He moaned and was instantly ashamed of his reaction. This kind of pleasure should be reserved for Rhy and no one else, but his body was reacting on a purely primal level with no way for him to prevent what was happening.

"Hurry up, Brisa, the queen's waiting." Satish chuckled. "I believe ye had a chance at him a bit ago. Yer own damn fault if ye didna take what ye wanted from him."

Brisa stood and leaned into Kyran, the texture of her clothing tormenting him. She placed her still tacky fingers on his lips and smeared the last of the oil onto them, knowing he would eventually lick them off. "This is only the beginning of what you will experience. In a quarter of an hour, you will be begging to fuck anything she'll let you." An evil grin crossed her face. "It will be a long time before she will let you take your own pleasure, so make your peace with the fact that you will be in agony for quite a while. Enjoy your weekend. I'll be stopping by to check in on you so I can update your lil plaything on how things are going."

"Ouch!" she said as he snapped at the fingers still lingering on his lips. He'd managed to catch the tips of them hard with his teeth, leaving a reminder that he didn't like being tormented.

Brisa reached down with her other hand and grabbed his scrotum, twisting it as much as she dared. Sweat popped out on his head at the pain she was causing and sadly at the waves of pleasure he also received from the touch of her hand on his sensitive skin. Remembering Fergus's advice, he gazed at her with a lazy smile before saying, "Give me more."

She released him with a disgusted sound, then dragged her long nails along his throbbing cock. Pleasure and pain burst through his nerve endings again as she turned towards Satish. "He's all yours. Enjoy."

Satish let out a throaty chuckle. "We fully intend to, don't we, boys?"

Kyran could hear their agreement and tried not to cringe at what was awaiting him over the next few days. Satish released his limbs, then jerked the chain attached to the collar, forcing him to follow in his wake. Kyran used everything in his mental arsenal to prevent himself from reaching down and stroking himself, settling for the friction caused by moving to mildly sooth the burning need between his legs.

CHAPTER SIXTY-TWO

He's Finally Come Back to Me

Danyka tied off the boat as Jameson gathered the supplies they picked up on the mainland. They were tired and filthy after a long day and night tromping through the woods looking for evidence of a unicorn locals spotted on Deer Island.

They walked for miles and found signs that may have been from the mythical beast or from the deer herd that roamed freely on the island. The Sanctuary already had one unicorn in their stables. He would have enjoyed the company had they successfully located the other one. Unicorns weren't dangerous to the population; it was the poachers that were dangerous to them and the reason the Sanctuary tried to protect them.

Rumors of the healing property of their horns abounded, and the black market was always looking for mythical items to sell. When the Sanctuary heard of the creature, they wanted to find it and offer it safety.

Danyka slung a heavy messenger bag cross body so that she could carry something else. "I know I saw the freaking thing, Jamey. It was beautiful. There one moment and gone the next. I got a glimpse of it twice from the sky and then nearly touched it before it disappeared from right in front of me."

Jameson shouldered the majority of the load they had returned with. His shoulders heaved as he carried bags of feed and salt blocks that Ronan had requested. "Damn, wish I had caught a glimpse of it. Only one I've ever seen is that miserable one we have. He might be pretty, but he hisses and spits every time I go near him. Thought Ferg was going to turn him to stone last time we were there, and the little beast took a bite out of his favorite kilt."

Danny laughed. "Which one? I would have given him a treat if it was that god-awful pink one."

"No, we couldn't be so lucky. This was one of the five lime green ones he seems to love."

The unicorn that lived at the Sanctuary was various shades of blue. Pale blue started at his head and grew darker until it was nearly a midnight shade on his legs. The creature was absolutely beautiful but ornery as hell.

"Any chance it's a female?" Jameson asked.

"Couldn't get close enough to tell, but man, they would make some pretty offspring. This beauty was a dark burgundy color with white socks and small bits of white spotting it like an appaloosa."

"Sounds beautiful," Jameson said as they cleared the top of the hill. He tried to think of another question to keep her chattering because he loved the sound of her voice, and it kept him distracted from her other attributes he was falling more in love with. He stumbled as the thought sank in. But the more he thought about it, he couldn't backtrack and negate it. It was the truth about how he felt, and he wouldn't change it. He might not be ready to admit it out loud and scare her away yet, but he could keep it and cherish it until he was—or more importantly, until he thought she was ready to hear it.

They cleared the rise near the stables as Ronan and another man walked outside. The mystery man was taller than Ronan and seemed unsure on his feet, like he'd been incapacitated for a long while. Jamey watched him, trying to place him from this distance. Danny was still chattering next to him. She was looking to her left and hadn't noticed the men yet.

Out of nowhere, her hand cuffed him upside the head, for God's sake, like he was Fergus. "What?" he asked in shock.

"Are you listening to a word I said, Jamey?" she asked in a long-suffering voice.

"I am, I swear. Just got distracted by the man ahead of us. Do you recognize him?"

Danny turned her extra perceptive vision on the pair, and Jamey heard her shocked gasp.

"It can't be..." she said in an unsteady voice. "How did he come back? He's been trapped for over a century in that goddamn cage?"

"Who, Danny?" Jamey asked, not following her. "Who the hell is it? I can't see him clear enough."

Danyka started dropping the bags she'd been carrying at his feet as a rare and beautiful smile crossed her face. A sheen of tears in her eyes confused him even more. "It's Kerrygan, Jamey. He's finally come back to me."

Jameson stood there stunned as he watched the woman he'd been falling in love with takeoff at a dead run towards the man leaning on Ronan.

Ronan and Kerrygan turned as they heard Danny's approach. Danny flung herself into Kerrygan's arms, nearly knocking him down. Ronan barely managed to keep the two of them upright. Kerrygan's face lit up at the sight of her, and his hands framed her face. "Danny, is it really you, sweet thing?"

She clung to him like a tick, her legs around his waist in an embrace that was damn near obscene. "Don't you ever fucking leave me like that again, you asshole. I've missed rescuing your ass more than you can know. Has Maddy seen you yet?"

"No, lass, I've been in this form for less than an hour," he said in a ragged voice.

Jamey finally joined them, carrying his load and hers. He nodded at Kerrygan who watched him warily. Ronan reached out to take the feed from him, and Jamey followed him inside with the salt blocks. He heard Danny and Kerry laughing outside as they headed for the castle.

"Put them against the wall, Jamey," Ronan said as he dumped the grain into a feed bin.

Jamey did, then leaned against the wall as he watched the door closing behind the two wardens.

Ronan watched him from a distance, seeing the disappointment and frustration cross his face. Jamey was the happy-go-lucky one in their band of misfits, so catching him at odds was rare.

"Everything all right?" Ronan asked.

"Yeah, everything's just fine," Jamey said in a monotone. "How the hell did he finally make his way back to us after centuries trapped like that?" What he didn't say was, "Why now, of all times?"

"I gave him a choice," Ronan said with a hint of chagrin. "I started choking the life out of him, trying to convince his sense of self-preservation to come to the forefront."

Jamey looked closely at Ronan. "Guessing that's where you got the shiner?"

Ronan laughed. "Yeah, he got a few good hits in before I stopped laughing long enough to defend myself."

"What took him so long to come back."

"He was in too small of an area to shift into his true size." Ronan shook his head. "Can you imagine being trapped like that because someone accidentally threw you in a cage? Might be a point worth mentioning in Danny's shifting classes. I've never heard of it before."

"Neither have I," Jamey said. "Glad he's back, though. He's been missed by many."

Ronan wasn't sure, but something in the tone of his voice told him that Jamey wasn't one of the ones who had really missed him.

"You mean that?" he asked.

"Of course, I do, Ronan," Jamey said. "Why wouldn't I?"

Ronan wasn't buying it, but it really wasn't any of his business. He'd watched Danny and Jamey together. He wasn't a psychic like Fergus or Rhy, and he didn't get premonitions like Maddy, but he was definitely able to hear when someone wasn't being honest. The things Jamey wasn't verbalizing said as much as the ones he did.

"Nearly time for dinner. I'm heading in. You coming?" Ronan asked.

"Go ahead. I'll be right behind you. Have a few things I need to drop in the weapons locker before I head in.

Ronan gave him a long look but left without saying anything else. Jamey knew how perceptive the man was, and he was grateful that Ronan dropped it for now.

Jamey headed towards the pit and the wooden building adjacent to it. As he unpacked the new daggers he was adding to the collection, he turned and flung one at the target at the other end of the room without even looking. The steel vibrated from the force it hit the target with, but like all his shots, it was dead center.

He walked the length of the building to retrieve it, testing the balance across the flat of his palm as he returned and placed the dagger in an empty slot in the cabinet. Danny picked this one out—said she liked the feel of it.

They'd had a great day off the island together, and he'd been looking forward to an evening at the Rusty Tap with her and Ferg. Kerrygan's reappearance changed the dynamics of their little band, and Jamey wasn't sure how to feel about it. He knew how he felt about his little hellion. That hadn't changed for him. But if there was one thing other than Danny's stubborn streak that could prevent Jameson from having a chance with her, Kerrygan was it. The two of them had been nearly inseparable when Jamey arrived at the Sanctuary. He'd nearly forgotten about the man until today.

Jameson ran his hands over his face, trying to get his shit together because he needed to go in there and give the performance of his life. He would laugh at the jokes and appear truly happy to see the man returned to the fold. His only hope was that the people who knew him best would buy his act because he sure the fuck didn't want to talk to anyone about it.

CHAPTER SIXTY-THREE

A Long Time Coming

Dashiel carried a tray to Kyran's suite. Four guards outside the door looked down their noses at him in disgust. He had been their friend once until he crossed the queen, and she turned him into her whore and whipping boy.

"Asslicker," the tall man to the right of the door sneered at him before he spit on him.

"Whoreson," came from behind him before he took a hit to his right kidney. The pain was sharp and, at one time, would have knocked him to his knees, but the past six months had trained him to take pain in nearly any form without flinching.

Dash stared straight ahead, knowing that if he looked at the men, he would kill them all with nothing more than the tray in his hands. He was much more skilled and creative than they had ever been in battle, and if they forced his hand, they wouldn't live to regret it. But there was more at stake than his wounded pride, so he stood there quietly and took it.

The man to the left of the door opened it and ushered him in, kicking the back of his left knee as he passed. His balance lost, he struggled to stay upright until he regained his footing. Thankfully, he'd had a lot of practice and didn't spill a drop of tea from the pot balanced precariously in front of him.

With a false cheerfulness in his voice, he tossed a "Thank you!" over his shoulder when he really wanted to scream and let the berserker inside loose.

Dash found Kyran glowering in an overstuffed velvet chair. Both arms dangled over the sides of the chair, cuffed to an iron chain that looped tightly under the chair, keeping both arms at his sides with very limited mobility.

"My lord," Dash said as he set the tray down, "a spot of tea?" he asked with mock concern and humor dancing in his eyes as he wiped the spittle off his face with Kyran's linen napkin.

"You're enjoying that role a little too much, Dash," Kyran snarled.

"No, my lord," he said through gritted teeth. "I am doing what I must to keep us both alive, and nothing more." Pouring the tea, he continued, "One day, you will release me from this nightmare, and I will repay every unkindness that has been done to us tenfold."

"God help us when you do," Kyran said. He'd witnessed Dash when his berserker made an appearance, and he was fucking terrifying, even if he was on your side. He had no urge to ever witness Dash losing control again.

"What news have you?" Kyran asked, squirming uncomfortably in the chair. He was beginning to feel desperate as the hours until his evening appointment passed much too slowly to relieve his discomfort.

His movements had Dash reexamining him in the chair. Kyran's wrists were rubbed raw, and his ankles were bound to the legs of the chair. A swath of silk was tented over his groin, doing little to hide the massive erection beneath the fabric.

"Oh, fuck, Kyran," Dash said sympathetically. "They didn't."

"They did."

"How long ago?"

"At least an hour ago." Involuntarily, his hips moved again.

"You're good and fucked, man. She'll leave you like that for a while to punish you for denying her this long."

"I know. Satish promised me that this will be a night from hell."

"He'll be the worst. There are others bigger, but he's one of the meanest that she allows to join her. That man will bring you to your knees and enjoy every moment of it so that he can throw it in your face later."

Kyran's head kicked back against the chair, his hips trying to thrust forward. Unable to move, the only thing he managed to do was dig the manacles deeper into his skin. Blood trickled from his wrist to his fingers.

Dash let out a sigh. "Close your eyes, Kyr."

"Why?"

"Just do what I say and close your fucking eyes!"

Kyran glared at him for a moment until Dash's raised eyebrow made him realize he had little choice. Afraid of where this was going, he closed his eyes.

The feel of Dash's hands on his thighs had him opening them again in shock.

"Dash, you don't have to…"

Dash's eyes bore into his. "Shut the fuck up and close your eyes before I fucking leave you like this. There are things we need to discuss, and you aren't going to be able to focus with that." His hand waved at the angry purple cock jutting from between his legs.

Kyran shook his head, opening his mouth to argue, but Dash beat him to it.

"You gave me a gift when you returned, Kyr. You allowed me to touch the woman I love. I got to make love to her with no one watching or threatening either of us. Neither of us thought we would get the opportunity to be together. You gave us the most beautiful night of our lives. Unless your father pulls his head out of his ass, you're the only hope this court has left."

Dash ran a hand through his hair. "I know what you are experiencing right now; Meriel's used that shit on me dozens of times, and it's fucking cruel and will drive you fucking mad. I'm going to take the edge off for you whether you like it or not. You can't stop me, and if you don't shut the fuck up about it, I will gag you."

Kyran looked at him with a mixture of gratitude and horror. "I just don't want you to ever think that I would require this of you. You are one of my oldest friends."

"And it's only because you are my friend and that you don't expect this that I will even consider doing it. Since that whore put this diamond on my forehead, I've blown most of the guards. Some say I've gotten pretty good at it, even though it takes all I've got not to bite the fuckers."

His eyes glittered dangerously. "There will be a reckoning someday, and I will call in what's due. This," he nodded at Kyran's lap, "is a favor for a friend, a gift to repay what you gave me. Trust me, you will thank me later. We're running out of time. Close your fucking eyes and think of your woman."

Kyran stared at him for a long time and realized it was a losing battle of wills. With a defeated sigh, he leaned his head back and closed his eyes as Dash's hand stroked his painfully hard cock. The sensation of his rough palm made him moan, and rather than examine those feelings, he pulled up the image of Rhy on her knees to get him through the next few moments.

Dash stroked him with a firm grip, twisting as he came up over the head of him. A dozen strokes, and Kyran was grateful for the touch, but his orgasm was well out of reach. As over-sensitized as he was, the cream also numbed him to a certain degree. Dash's grip tightened, and he swore creatively. "The cream she chose will need more than my touch for you to come." Before Kyran could respond, Dash sucked his cock into his mouth, deep throating him.

"No! You don't have to…FUCK—please don't stop."

With the suction added, it only took a half dozen strokes for Kyran to finally come, and he did so with a loud moan.

Dash stood up, picked up the cup of tea he had poured earlier, and downed it.

"Dash," Kyran said in a voice full of regret, unable to meet his eyes.

Dash squatted down in front of him, grabbed his chin, and forced him to meet his eyes. "You stop that shit, right now. You fucking hear me? Nothing ever happened, and it will never change the relationship you and I have unless you let it. We good?"

Kyran's lip quirked up, and he nodded. "We're good." This humiliation was just one more item to add to the long list of crimes that Meriel would need to pay for. His body was still ready to perform, but the pain and desperation had eased to a bearable level

"To answer your earlier question, I have at least a dozen men who swear they will back you in a coup," Dash said softly.

"That's all?" Kyran asked, disappointed. "What about Tristan?"

"Tristan is your father's lap dog and will always be. He's a wild card and one dog you can't count on in this fight." Dash sipped at his tea, then added, "The king and his guard have not been seen for days, and speculation is running through the halls as quickly as pox through the harem."

"I'm not sure I want to stage a coup, Dash," Kyran said as he ran a hand through his hair. "I just want control over my own life; I don't want to run everyone else's."

"How the fuck do you think you are going to accomplish this without removing her from the throne?" Dash slammed his cup down, sloshing liquid over the side as he looked at Kyran in disbelief. "For fucks sake, Kyran, you were always the least selfish of the princes. Are you seriously implying that as soon as you get what you want, you will leave the rest of us here to rot in this hellhole? Because, if that is the case, you're on your own. I won't encourage nor help you in this foolishness unless you give me your word that you will change this court for the better. I don't care how the fuck you do it, but you don't leave that whore in charge, or I will burn this place to the ground." His eyes bordered on crazy as they glared at Kyran. "I thought we were friends, and I believed you actually gave a shit about your people." His voice was laced with disappointment and, worse than that, disgust.

Kyran faced his verbal assault, absorbing the accusations and denying nothing. Clearing his throat, he said, "Thank you for helping me find clarity. I will not abandon my people, and I will not leave her in place to ruin any more lives, but I need more help than the dirty dozen you've found." His eyes glared back at Dash. "I won't lead you all to a slaughter. We need better odds than this."

Dash's eyes cleared, and he nodded in agreement. "I will do what I can, and you need to survive the next two days with enough left to help us. She will be drunk on her victory over finally humiliating you in her bed."

Kyran nodded regretfully. "I need you to do something for me tonight," he said.

"Anything I can."

"Can you use the portal without supervision?"

"I am not monitored. They know I will never leave permanently and let my family suffer in my place."

"Good. I need you to deliver a message for me to Heart Island. It's in the right-hand drawer of my desk."

Dash walked to the desk and removed the letter. The parchment was sealed with teal colored wax holding the edges together and exhibiting the image of crashing waves from Kyran's signet ring.

"Take this to Mistress Rhyanna Cairn. She runs the Apothecary Clinic. Look for her there first, and then go to the castle and ask for her. If she is not available, request an audience with Madylyn Skydancer and place this in her hands. She will see Rhy gets this. Leave it with no one else."

Dash tucked the letter into an inner pocket of his shirt. "I will see Mistress Cairn receives your letter." He grabbed the prince by the neck and leaned his forehead against Kyran's. "Meriel finds pleasure in your pain and your fear. She will rejoice in your agony. Don't show her any. If she thinks you enjoy everything she does to you, then she will grow bored much quicker. Walk in there with a smile on your face and your cock ready to perform. Releasing him, he reached into his pocket and pulled out a small amber vial. Take this right before you leave. It will lower your inhibitions and make you hard as steel for the entire night."

Kyran shook his head. "I hate taking drugs of any kind."

Dash glared at him. "I can promise you're going to hate what's going to happen this evening much more. Don't be a fool. Trust me. Use this and let the herbs relax you. You are going to need it, I guarantee it." He bent down and placed it in the palm of Kyran's hand. "Don't drop it."

Kyran closed his eyes in defeat. "I will use it. You have my word."

Dash's eyes filled with sorrow. "I'm sorry that I can't stop what is about to happen to you."

"This has been a long time coming. I'm surprised I've been given a pass for this long."

"Don't you fucking die on me, you bastard," Dash said vehemently as he hugged him fiercely. "I'll be back as soon as I can." Without another word or a glance back, he left the chamber, ignoring the abuse from the guards outside. He stumbled through the halls, knowing the only thing he could do was to deliver the message Kyran entrusted him with.

RIVER OF REMORSE

CHAPTER SIXTY-FOUR

Finally Alone

The sun was low in the sky, nearly kissing the ocean when Kano kissed his mother goodnight. Elyana was pleased to see the tenderness he exhibited with her. The week she had spent with him so long ago had shown her a carefree young man who enjoyed a good time. He'd made her laugh and loved her until she screamed his name, but what did she really know about him as a man—as an individual? What she knew about him would fit into a walnut shell, and that wasn't nearly enough to make decisions by.

Taking her hand, Kano led her down the steps of the pavilion to a wooden walkway that ran parallel to the beach. They walked silently until she could no longer see the lights behind them. Lost in her own thoughts and the beauty before her, she stumbled into him when he stopped abruptly.

Wrapping his arm around her waist to stabilize her, he leaned into her and whispered, "Look," into her ear, sending shivers down her spine. Her eyes darted to where he pointed over the rail as her breath caught from his nearness. Dozens of sea turtles were heading back to the water after laying their eggs, while others were just beginning to dig or were flinging dirt to cover any trace of their nests as they finished.

"There are so many of them," she whispered in awe.

"Each of them will lay nearly a hundred eggs in the hope that a few will survive."

"So many at one time?"

"Yes. Then she will leave the nest untended, and her children will push their way into this world, fighting to survive from the second they emerge."

"Tough world for them."

"That it is," he agreed. The wind was picking up as she shivered next to him. He began to walk again, holding her hand as if it were the most natural thing in the world for her to be at his side.

Lights in the distance beckoned. The sound of the waves crashing not far from them and the wind in her hair brought her to a halt. "Can we stop for a moment?" she asked in a whisper.

"Of course."

"This may be something you see every day, but I live far from the ocean. She kicked off her shoes, closed her eyes, and tipped her head back, letting her hair whip around her face. Tugging her hand free, she stepped off the walkway and walked towards the water, raising both of her hands at her sides with her palms up.

Kano's breath caught as he looked at her. The sun was nearly gone, its final rays reflecting on the water, and the moon was emerging behind them. Her red hair glowed in the light, and she looked ethereal with her hair whipping around her. Fire drakes wove in and out the strands of her hair and down her shoulders as the sun faded before her. A wide smile crossed her face, and he had to restrain himself from taking her into his arms and loving her right here.

She was at peace. Today had given her little to enjoy, so he waited silently, enjoying the view she presented while she took what she needed from the elements flowing around her.

Elyana lowered her arms and turned to Kano with that huge grin on her face. "Thank you for taking the time." Her smile faded as reality crashed back in. "I'm sure there are other official things you need to be doing. I'm sorry to keep you."

"Since you were my only assignment today," he said somberly, "I have all the time in the world to spend with you." Even with night settling heavily around them, he could see the blush staining her cheeks.

"I think I derailed your assignment."

"Thank the gods for that," he said softly as he moved closer. His hand came up and brushed the hair back from her face before tracing her cheekbone and trailing down to her jaw. He watched her eyes widen as her breath hissed in softly when his thumb came up to trace her lower lip. "I want to kiss you again," he said. His arm wrapped around her waist as he continued tracing her lips. His heart was hammering in his chest. Kano wanted her permission this time. No, he needed it. He wanted no doubts that the next time his lips touched hers was mutual.

Elyana watched him as her breath came quickly. The heat radiating from him warmed her body and her soul. She had dreamt of being with him again—repeatedly. Now that he was here, she was nervous and unsure, having nothing to compare her reaction to. Her life had been that of a scholar, with her nose buried in books and ancient records, trying to trace the elemental branches of the tree of life as far back as she could. She never allowed herself time for distractions. He was the one and only man she had allowed herself to enjoy, and there wasn't a moment of the week they spent together that she didn't fantasize about repeatedly over the years.

Looking into his turbulent eyes, she knew he was restraining himself and allowing her to control the situation. He licked his lips, and she tried not to moan. There was no doubt that she wanted the taste of him on her lips and the touch of his arms banding her close. Reality came crashing in as her fingers touched his formal silk shirt, reminding her why he was dressed this way. She looked down and said, "Kyran..."

"Is not here. You don't belong to him—you don't even know him. If you don't want me, just say so, but please don't use that sham of a betrothal to hide from me," he said in a gravelly voice. His finger hooked under her chin, tipping her head back up, forcing her to meet his eyes. "What do you want, Elyana? What do you want for yourself?"

The way her name rolled off his tongue was like a purr against her skin. Her life was on the verge of changing very rapidly in the coming days, but this was one choice she could make and take something for herself in the process. With her eyes still on his, she stretched up and looped her arms around his neck, whispering in his ear, "I want you to kiss me, Kano."

He groaned, this time in relief. His eyes devoured her features as he pulled her closer, tugging her hips snug against his. "I've missed you," he whispered against her lips before taking his time reacquainting himself with the taste of her. He kissed her gently, appreciating the texture and shape of her lips before sliding his tongue against hers. His hands traveled up to cup the back of her head as her silken strands threaded between his fingers, and he kissed her thoroughly.

Elyana sighed as his lips traveled over her face and back to her lips, stealing the breath from her once again. His hands were large and made her feel protected and cared for as he gently cradled her head. She kissed him back until they both were breathless.

Kano stepped away before he was unable to. Reclaiming her hand, he led her down the path until they reached a small bungalow far from his family and the threats of the world they had left this afternoon. He pulled her up the steps leading to the door, then leaned her against it, kissing her again. She clung to him, moaning eagerly against his lips. His hands grasped her hips, then moved around to lovingly cup her ass and lift her against him. She hooked her feet around his waist as he fumbled with the door.

Finally managing to open it, he walked in, kicking it closed behind him as he made his way to the king size bed in the middle of the room. It was covered in light fabrics with a thin down comforter on the top looking like a cloud. Gently, he laid her down. She was a vision with her scarlet hair spread around her like a halo and her chest heaving as she looked up at him in anticipation.

Kano kissed her again as he ran his hands under the shirt she wore, covering her waist with his palms while his thumbs stroked her nipples through her corset. His lips captured her gasp as her torso raised towards him, seeking more attention. He knelt over her, pulling the shirt over her head and reaching for the ties at the waist of her pants.

Elyana was lost, drowning in his kisses as his hands teased her body. Sitting up, she reached for the hem of his shirt. "I need to touch you," she said desperately. She leaned back on her elbows as he removed it and pressed her back.

"Touch me, baby." He kissed her again and reached for her hand, guiding it to his waist. "I've imagined your hands on me so many times." Her touch was hesitant as she traced his abdomen and worked her way up the muscles of his chest. It was his turn to suck in a breath when she traced the pads of her fingers lightly over his nipples. His hands trapped hers there as he bent down and whispered against her lips, "Harder."

Elyana applied more pressure as her fingers clamped down and squeezed steadily, the way she remembered he liked it. His head kicked back, and he tangled his hands in her hair as she took it in her mouth and raked her teeth over the tip.

Kano's eyes rolled into the back of his head as his torso arced towards her. He pressed her tightly against him as she sucked lightly, hissing at the pleasure she was giving him. Leaning back, he pushed his hand down the front of her pants, wanting to make her feel just as good as he was.

At the first stroke of his fingers against her clit, she detonated. It had been building since he had first kissed her that morning, and her body was instantly ready. Sobbing his name, she came, leaning her head against his chest as she tried to catch her breath.

"Again," Kano said as his fingers worked their magic once more.

"Stop…" Elyana sobbed as her body once more followed his direction. "We need to slow down. I need to think."

"Talk to me, baby," he whispered against her lips. "Please talk to me. Don't push me away." His hands framed her face as he rested his forehead against hers.

"I'm still not free, Kano," she said sadly. "We can't do this until I am officially released from my betrothal."

"How can you believe that, Elyana?" He looked at her as his fingers traced her cheekbones. "You never agreed to this in the first place. How can you be expected to honor a deal that was brokered on your behalf without your permission?" His lips found hers once again, soft and sweet, offering to take her away from the confusion she was trapped in.

Returning his kiss, Elyana melted into him. Every time he touched her made her believe she was exactly where she belonged. How could wanting him be wrong? But her integrity crawled back front and center, and she gasped as she pushed him away and crawled back by the headboard. Pulling a pillow across her lap as if it would protect her, she banded her arms around her knees and stared at him sorrowfully as she said, "Kano, I can't."

He stared at her, stunned, as his hands dropped to his lap. His breathing was ragged, and his cock was straining painfully against his breeches. "Elyana..." he said, peering at her through half-closed eyes and trying to be patient. "Tell me why you can't." His eyes pleaded with her before he managed to say, "Please." It was a word he seldom used and seemed foreign on his tongue.

Sitting in front of her, he grabbed a pillow and reached for her ankle. Pulling her leg towards him, he started massaging the arch of her foot to distract her from the heat arcing between them.

Her emerald gaze was tormented as she looked at him. "It seems wrong, forbidden..." Her eyes begged him to understand. "Pick a word, but it feels inappropriate, no matter how much I might want it to feel differently, and no matter how logical you sound."

His hands continued manipulating her foot. She sighed in pleasure and scooted down a little more in the bed. "I'm sorry to disappoint you. I didn't mean to get you all worked up and..." her hands made a gesture to the pillow on his lap.

"Leave me with a case of blue balls?" He winked at her and gave a smirk. "Don't worry about it, baby. I'll live." His smirk faded, and he looked much too serious as his eyes never left her face. "I want you to think about something before you sleep. I'm not gonna lie to you and tell you I've been celibate since I was with you because I'll never bullshit you, but I have never stopped looking for you. I made it my mission for many years, but you're not very well known, princess."

"Why?" she asked as her brow furrowed, trying to answer the question on her own. "We spent one week together. Why did you spend so much time looking for me when you could be with anyone you wanted?"

"I'm not trying to be cocky," he said, unable to meet her eyes, "but I've been able to have anyone for most of my life." He cleared his throat, and she could tell he was uncomfortable talking about this. "But no one has ever made me want anything more until I found you." His eyes snapped to hers, and she could see his sincerity. He reached for her other foot pulling her closer still. "I loved waking up to you in my arms and wondering how we would entertain ourselves for the day. Your smile lit up the whole room, and I still miss the sound of you laughing. I haven't stopped thinking of you since the day you left, but I started to believe that I had fantasized you when I could no longer find you.

"I'm sorry," she said softly. "I never should have left the way that I did." Glancing down, her fingers picked at the pillow nervously. "I didn't want to assume you wanted more than the time we had."

"I understand why you might have thought that way," he said, looking at the foot he was working on. He needed to find a way to convince her to give them a chance. "Let me be clear now. I want to get to know you better. I want to spend time with you." A sensuous smile crossed his face as she blushed. "Yes, I desperately want to make love to you, but I also want to see what makes you laugh, what makes you happy or mad. What are your favorite foods and books? Are you ticklish?" As he said that, his fingers attacked the bottom of her feet in a different manner, making her squeal in laughter.

"Yes, I am," she gasped between laughing and trying to pull away from him. "I'm ticklish." Catching her breath, she asked, "Is that all you want to know to see if I am fit to date?"

He pulled her down until they were facing each other, then kissed the tip of her nose. "I want to know everything about you, and I want to be more than your boyfriend."

"How can you be so sure?"

Kano laughed. "Because even when you kicked my balls into my throat, I couldn't get up fast enough to run after you. I'm not willing to let you walk away from me this time, not without a fight." He sobered considerably as he said, "Promise me you won't take off when I leave tomorrow. I'm going to try and fix this."

She looked down, not wanting to promise something she couldn't follow through on. "I'm not sure I can give you that."

He lifted her chin with a finger. "If you don't feel the same way I do, be honest with me." His eyes searched hers, and finding only sorrow there, he kissed her softly, not looking for anything else.

Elyana returned the kiss, knowing it would lead only to more heartbreak for both of them. "Unlike you," she whispered, "I haven't been with anyone else because I couldn't imagine anyone else touching me but you." Her cheeks heated, and she looked away, embarrassed by her admission.

Her confession stunned and humbled him. Kano looked at her in awe. "I don't know what to say."

She shook her head, trying to dismiss it. "I shouldn't have said anything."

He pinched her chin between his thumb and forefinger, forcing her to meet his eyes. "I'm glad you told me." His eyes traced her face, and he realized another reason she had put the brakes on. "I was going too fast, wasn't I?"

Elyana gave him a slow nod. "I'm afraid I don't have the experience to keep up with you."

Kano groaned. "I don't want you to keep up with me. I'm glad you're nothing like me because I am ashamed of the way I've been and the way I've treated women since you left. I have used them and dismissed them because they weren't you." Brushing his lips over hers, he said, "You took a piece of my soul with you when you left, and I haven't been the same since. I missed you."

He kissed her on the forehead, then pulled her against his chest. "You must be exhausted. It's been a long day."

"I am very tired."

"Get some sleep, baby. I'll be here when you wake."

Large emerald orbs stared up at him. "Promise?"

"Yeah, baby. I promise." His hands rubbed her back soothingly as she settled against him, wondering how the hell he was going to convince her to stay.

Elyana's fingers were tracing patterns on his chest as her breathing slowed and her sleepy eyes shut for the night. Her body relaxed into the heat radiating from him and the strength of his arms banding around her, both making her feel like she had come home and was safe.

Kano brushed a kiss to the top of her head. As much as he had wanted to make love to her earlier, he was content to simply hold her while she slept, breathing in the scent of her and trying to figure out a way to make her his permanently. He drifted off to dreams of battling with Kyran for her. The outcome was cloudy, and all he remembered when he woke was that he was holding a bloody sword and he couldn't find his brother or the woman sleeping in his arms. Pulling her in tighter, he buried his head in her neck and tried to sleep once again, hoping for a few hours more before he needed to return to court and face the repercussions for disobeying the queen.

CHAPTER SIXTY-FIVE

A Change in Dynamics

Kerrygan leaned heavily on Danyka as she guided him into a suite in the East Wing. Carefully, he lowered his scrawny ass into a chair by the fire. Excellent choice, he thought because using all his energy trying to remember how to shift left him freezing his bollocks off.

"Do you need help getting into the shower?" she asked.

"Nye, I just need some time to regain the use of my legs and some food—heavy on the protein."

"I'm on it," she said. On impulse, she threw her arms around his neck. "It's so fucking awesome to have you back again. I've missed you."

He clung to her tightly, in desperate need of the reconnection. "Missed you too, sprite."

Danny left him alone, on a mission to find him food and drink. Head feeling heavy, he rested it in his hands as he tried to reacclimate to the structure of his human body. The love of soaring high above the ground was like a drug to him, and he'd spent way too much time gliding through the currents high above the earth.

One of the first shifting lessons he'd learned as a teen was that you needed to spend more time in your human form than in any form you transformed into. Your cell memory needed to remember its original form to return to it. Kerry had broken that rule and lost a century paying for it.

His body was struggling to stay in this form. He could sense the shifter energy wanting to flip back to the familiar. His body needed fuel to strengthen his muscles and help his metabolic system stabilize. As the heat soaked into his muscles, he focused on the tactile feel of the chair beneath his legs, and the floor beneath his feet. Fingers clenched the wooden arms of the captain's chair he sat in. Flexing them one at a time, he stretched the ligaments and tendons in his metatarsals, realizing as he did that his little fingers sported claws instead of nails.

Fear made an appearance as he wondered what other parts of his body were fucked up from a partial transition. Hands clenching the wood, he tried to stand and fell back into the chair, weak from the effort. Laser-sharp focus on his task made the second attempt successful and he lurched towards the bath, clinging to the furniture as he went. Four steps separated him from the wall and the sink. He took tentative lumbering steps, hoping he wouldn't end up on the tile floor with something broken.

The last step nearly keeled him over when his ankle twisted, but he was close enough to the sink to grab onto the vanity. Fear gripped him as he sought the courage to gaze in the mirror, terrified of what he would find staring back at him. The pulse in his neck raced, and he counted thirteen heartbeats before forcing himself to look. Never a coward in his other life, he wasn't about to remain one today.

Shock greeted him as his eyes took in his haggard appearance. Sunken eyes stared out at him from a skeletal face. Thick, black hair had once covered his head. Longer now, it was coarser, and he thought he caught hints of blue-gray streaks running throughout the layers framing his face. Dark brown eyes were now ringed with yellow. His eyes hadn't successfully changed with the rest of him.

The hair didn't faze him, but the eyes were an adjustment and would announce him to anyone he met as a failed shifter. Fuck. Horror crossed his skeletal features as he wondered what else hadn't made the transition. He'd been too fucking overwhelmed earlier to even worry about it, but as his hands went to the button on the pants he was wearing, his motions were frantic as he let the oversized breeches hit the ground. Closing his eyes, he used his hand to reacquaint himself with the family jewels and blew out a sigh of relief when all the bits and bobs seemed to be in the right place. Cock in his hand, his mind wandered back to the moment Danny had nearly bowled him over, remembering the tight fit of her hips against his groin. With a shout of triumph, his cock properly inflated.

A delicate cough in the doorway had his brows shooting into his hairline as he turned and caught a beet-red Rhyanna turning back to the bedroom. "I'll jest wait out here," her voice squeaked out.

"Oh, fuck, I'm sorry, Rhy darling." Somehow, he managed to regain his drawers without bashing his head on the vanity. Clutching the wall, he made his way back to the sitting room and gave her a smile to ward off the awkwardness. "Hey there, sweetness."

Rhy smiled at him broadly and moved in for a long hug. With a step back, she clasped his face in her hands and scolded him. "I told ye, ye stubborn shite, that ye was spending too much time as a fecking bird. Did ye listen?" Tears formed in her eyes as she thought of the years he had been lost to them. "I missed ye, Kerry. We've all missed ye."

"Come here, darling," he said, pulling her back in for another hug. "I ken I be a stubborn shite, ye got that part right, and I'm sorry to have put all of us through this, but I be back, and I gots no plans of returning to the skies anytime soon."

Her hand smacked the side of his head and fuck did that hurt. "Ye best not, or I'll make sure yer sorry." Eyes flashing, she blinked and stepped into her healer's role in an instant. "Let me look at ye." A strong pull on his hand had him following her to the bed and taking a seat on the edge.

Emerald eyes traveled over his features. Supple hands pushed through his lank hair, examining the color and texture. Lips pursed when she stared into his new eyes, and he couldn't miss the hint of sorrow when she did. Opening his mouth, he allowed her to study the state of his teeth and tongue. Her hands caressed the side of his neck, checking for swollen glands and who-the-fuck-knew what else. Maybe he came back with gills, too.

A giggle escaped him. A fecking giggle. What the hell kind of sound was that to escape his manly body. She picked up his weak arms and pinched the skin between her fingers, finding no body fat. He might seriously need to rethink that description.

"So, what I walked in on in the bathroom..." A delicate blush colored her cheeks, but she didn't glance away.

"I was checking for further defects." Cheeks flamed as mortification flared through him, knowing she'd seen him stroking his cock.

"And the results?"

"Inconclusive, seeings how ye interrupted me." A huge grin crossed his face as her eyes widened. "Only joking, little sister. Take it easy with the slaps. Me ears still ringing from the last one."

Rhy glared at him. "Would've served ye right if ye returned with one the size of yer birds." Sniffing haughtily, she continued, "Ye ken that every time ye change in the future, ye risk the chance of not returning, or shifting with even less of yer humanity intact."

A somber nod spoke volumes. "Or I might get it right next time." His hand caught hers as she prepared to wallop him once again. "I'se joking, Rhy. Don't fecking brain me again."

"Don't fecking make me, ye stupid arse." Her eyes dared him to make one more smart-ass comment, then began to fill. "Don't ye ever leave us like that again! Nothing was the same after ye left." A sniffle from her, and then she pulled herself together. "Maddy's gonna be so happy to welcome ye back."

"I don't think young Jameson was so happy to find me out of me cage, lass."

"What makes ye think that?"

"Danny nearly knocked me over when she saw me, wrapping herself around me and all. If his glare didn't give it away, his shifter energy was off the charts, but he kept it under control." He ran a hand through his bizarre hair. "Are they together."

"Nye, not yet anyways."

"Mutual?"

"I believe so, but she's too blind to see it—or too afraid."

"Most likely the second scenario."

"Aye." Her brow furrowed, and she was playing with his hand, examining the claw on his little finger. A nail traced the edges of the claw, trying to figure out how it was attached to the muscles and skin. "The two of you ever...?"

"Feck no," he said sharply. "She be like me little sister and best friend all rolled into one."

"So, there be no conflict, then."

"I didna say that, darling."

"What are ye about?"

"Might do the boy good to think he's got some competition."

"Or he might shift into his grizzly and eat you."

"There is that. A change in the dynamics of things isn't always a bad thing. He and I might end up as friends when it's all said and done."

Laughter rang out, and she put a hand to the side of his face. "'Tis so nice to have ye back Kerry, love. Doubt ye'll end up friends. Yer too much of an instigator to let this go, and yer guaranteed to stir up trouble between them." Emerald eyes grew sober as she said, "I believe Jameson is precisely what Danny needs, and ye should consider that before ye go lighting fires ye can't put out."

Kerrygan absorbed her words, then kissed her gently on the cheek. "I promise to tread carefully, Rhy. I wouldn't do anything to harm her, ye ken that."

"I hope not." Her voice was soft and thoughtful. "I'd be mighty disappointed in ye if ye did." She left him with that thought and some more advice, "Eat as much as ye can stomach to fuel yer body. Yer metabolism will still be running high for a few days until ye fully transition back to yer human genes."

"Will do. And Rhy?" He waited for her to look back at him. "Thank you for everything. I've missed ye, too."

RIVER OF REMORSE

CHAPTER SIXTY-SIX

Until You Walk in My Shoes

Movement woke Kano, and for a moment, he wondered who had been stupid enough to crawl into his bed. Anger flared, but then her scent hit him, and the past twenty-four hours came rushing back to him. Elyana was in his bed, and he was spooned around her. Her hips were tucked into his, and she was moving closer to him in her sleep.

His head was tucked into her neck, and his left hand was tangled in her hair while his right held her tightly around the waist. Allowing himself the luxury of enjoying her in his arms, he nuzzled her neck. A soft sigh escaped her lips as his thumb lazily stroked from her waist to the bottom of her breasts. He kept his touch light, teasing, not wanting to wake her yet. She needed him to go slow, and he didn't want to push for more than she was comfortable with, but his raging hard-on was cradled in the crease of her ass and every inhale subtly shifted her against him, doing some teasing of her own.

As his thumb stroked, his mind wandered through the possible ways to extricate her from the fucking betrothal about to destroy two of the Tyde men for life. There was no way Meriel would have known about his weekend with Elyana, but she sure had managed to fuck them both with this situation. Kyran was a conquest she couldn't make, and if he wouldn't come to her willingly, she would see he would never be happy. Kano's constant disrespect was enough to throw him in the trajectory of her hatred, and he had no one to blame but himself.

Question was—what the fuck were they going to do about it? What the fuck could they do about it? He and Kyran would manage to avoid her, even if it meant leaving court and being on the run, but Kyran would never leave his little hedge witch. In their absence, Meriel would find a way to recall Kai and make his life an ever-loving hell. Kai might be the largest of the Tyde boys, but he was also the most empathic and gentle of them. Dragging him into her fucked up sexual nightmare would break something vital in him, and they all knew it. Kai thought he would be able to manage her, but it had been all Kano could do to tolerate her, and he was only able to do so because he turned the tables on her and took control of their encounter.

"Kano, are you awake?" His mother's voice came through telepathically on the link they had formed when he was a child.

"Barely."

"You want to share whatever you're planning with me? I can sense the wheels turning from here."

He fought back a chuckle and smiled into Elyana's neck. *"You make it sound like anything I plan will be a bad thing. Mother, do you have so little faith in me?"*

"No, but I know you, and whatever it is might end up catastrophic if you don't keep your temper reigned in."

"You're right on that count, and she's bound to push every one of my buttons."

"So, are you ready to get down on your knees and give her the respect and adoration she wants from you?"

"How do you know what she wants from me?"

"I may not be at court, but I'm not dead." He sensed her amusement coming through their bond. *"I still have some connections. They are my eyes and ears so that I can have some concept of what my children are enduring in my absence, especially when they can't be bothered to visit more than once or twice every decade."* The censure in her tone was light. She never pulled guilt trips on her boys but delivered the truth as she saw it without emotion. If guilt found you, then it was usually earned, and her boys tried to change their behavior accordingly. *"You're never lonely for long, Kano. What makes you think she will keep your attention any longer than any of the others have? You're going to a hell of a lot of effort for a woman you haven't seen in centuries. Be sure you know what you are doing before you make a bigger mess of her life than it is currently in. She deserves better from you, and if you're not ready..."*

Kano groaned inwardly at her comments. He never claimed to be a saint, but for fucks sake, he wouldn't want his mother to hear what a man-whore he had been. Discretion was never his strong point—a point he was now regretting. His temper flared at her insinuation that he wouldn't be good for Elyana.

"Damn it, don't you think I understand that? She's the only one for me. You know I've looked for her for years. Yes, I have done my share of whoring around. I'll own that shit, but no one has interested me for more than a tumble. I go to bed every night thinking

of her. Every woman I have been with has been nothing but a shallow substitute for who I really want—and I realize I haven't been fair to them or me by doing that." The line was silent for a moment as they both thought about the situation. Disappointed that she wouldn't support him made him say, *"After the way you fell so quickly for my father, I thought you, of all people, would understand how I felt about her."*

"Oh, Kano, I do—I truly do. It's because of the mistakes I've made with your father that I voice my concerns, and only because of our history. I don't want any of my children to end up where I am now."

"You mean hurt and hiding from their children, the rest of the world, and their responsibilities to the people they swore to protect?" He heard the sharp hiss of breath she took and felt the hurt radiating through their link, but he couldn't stop himself from adding, *"Don't worry, I won't ever fucking be like either of you. I won't turn to drugs, and I won't tuck tail and hide."*

"I'm sorry that is how you've interpreted our failed relationship. Someday, when you find the person who is your entire world entwined with someone else, mayhap you can judge my reactions and decisions, but until you walk in my shoes, you have no right."

Her tone changed from hurt to angry in a second, and he didn't blame her. None of his brothers would have spoken to her like this, and all of them would have kicked his ass for doing so. She wasn't the reason he was in this situation, and she didn't deserve to have him act like this.

"Mama, I'm sorry. Please forgive me. I can't stand the thought of you angry with me, and you're correct—I have absolutely no right to judge the heartbreak he put you through. You weren't the only one who was heartbroken. You lost a partner. We lost a happy family, two parents who adored each other, and a mother who was always there along with our way of life. We missed you."

"There's nothing to forgive, Kano. I lost a partner, that's true, but I also lost my family and way of life, too. I lost my boys, which was the price for me to leave court. I was only permitted short court-sanctioned visits with you, and I've regretted it every single day that I was forced to be away from all of you. I lost the relationships I might have had with you as adults."

"That's on us as much as it is on you. It wasn't solely your job to maintain our relationship. We need to meet you halfway."

"Will you trust her here with me while you return to court?"

"I will, but I'm not sure you can make her stay once I'm gone. She's like a skittish foal."

"Let me worry about keeping her here."

Elyana shifted in his arms, her hand coming up to run over his cheek. "What's wrong?"

"I've got to go. We'll see you soon."

His mother said nothing, but he felt the warmth of her love radiating through to him.

Kano turned his head and kissed the center of her palm. "What makes you think something is wrong?"

Her lips tipped up in a partial smile. "Maybe the way you were beginning to squeeze me so tightly was a hint."

He brushed a gentle kiss over her forehead. "I'm sorry. I didn't mean to wake you. You looked so peaceful lying there."

"I am very peaceful, but I have the feeling something you're about to say will change how I'm feeling."

"Then I refuse to speak for the next few minutes." He traced her lips with his fingers, laughing when she snapped at him, then replacing them with his lips. His lips lingered, gently moving against hers until a whisper of breath escaped her, and she joined him.

Elyana was breathless with him kissing the daylights out of her. Her hands tangled in his short hair, anchoring herself to him and the wild emotions running through her. Finally, she pulled away, looked him in the eye, and demanded, "Tell me why you're uneasy."

Kano met her eyes as he said, "I need you to stay here for me. Will you please remain here without question?"

His sweet innocent woman snorted at him. "Nope. Now tell me where you're going and why, then convince me to stay willingly."

He sighed, knowing it was a losing battle. "I need to return to court and face Queen Meriel. She sent me to escort you, and I am long overdue. People I care about will be in danger if I don't return soon with a full report."

"Those same people will be in danger if you return without me. Won't they?"

"I have a proposition for Meriel. I am hoping she will consider what I offer, but I need you safely out of the crossfire until I'm sure it's going to work."

"Will you tell me about your proposition?"

"Not until I know if it's successful or not. Can you accept that?"

"I'll have to trust you."

"Do you trust me?" he asked gravely.

"I'm still here, aren't I?"

He smiled down at her. "Yeah, I'm not quite sure why you are, but I'm glad you didn't run away in the night."

"Kind of hard with the death grip you had on me," she teased.

He laughed with her. "Good, that's settled." He gave her a swift kiss before getting up and pulling on his shirt. "Hungry?"

"Famished."

Tossing her a quick grin along with her clothes, he said, "Get dressed."

CHAPTER SIXTY-SEVEN

Rosella Diaries
Sixth Entry

Somehow, Rosella managed to get through the evening meal with a soft smile and the ability to communicate adequately when spoken to. Many of the girls were somber tonight, knowing that their world was about to change and there wasn't a damn thing they could do about it.

Braden led her back to her room, her silent companion. When the door closed and locked behind them, they scurried to set up what was needed.

Rosella stared at the two people who were coming to mean more to her than she wanted to admit. Trust was a precious thing to give, but she couldn't waste any more time second-guessing it. "Do either of you have any clue as to where we are right now or where we might have been recently?"

Disappointment filled her as they both shook their heads no. "We're rarely allowed above deck," Braden said.

"I understand."

Ella drew a wide chalk circle around herself near the glass windows of the deck. With a glance at Braden, she instructed, "Create a second circle of salt outside the first."

Shaelyn placed the candles where she directed, one for each of the cardinal directions and one for her in the center.

When everything was ready, she pointed toward the circles surrounding her. "No matter what you hear or see in here, you stay outside the circle. Promise me!" She waited until they nodded their assent. "It may appear that I've collapsed, but I'm fine. You will do me more harm trying to pull me back unexpectedly. Until I blow out the candle inside, do not attempt to reach me."

Grim nods met her decree. Neither of them was going to do anything to mess with this unfamiliar ritual she was performing. She thought Shaelyn used the sign to ward off evil and tried not to laugh.

What she was doing wasn't evil. She was simply going to allow her soul to vacate her body and travel on the ethers. Maman did this many times and taught her when she was a child. Rosella loved listening to her explain why they used the chalk to provide boundaries and the salt for protection outside those boundaries. A fifth candle would be inside the circle with her. It would be her beacon on her return trip back to her physical form.

Thrice she walked around the circle, casting it with protection and burning a sprig of lavender to purify the site.

With a careful step over the lines, she moved through the protective energy. The spell recognized her as she walked the inner perimeter, carrying items representing the corresponding elements.

Stopping by the candle facing east, she laid down a feather and struck a match, setting it alight.

"Watch Tower of the East, I beseech thee,
Fill me with knowledge, my maman I seek"

Moving to the one in the south, she laid down a gold button she'd taken from one of her gowns and lit the candle.

"Watch Tower of the South, I call to thee,
Help me take action to set me free."

The west received a mirror to represent water and a flame to the wick.

"Watch Tower of the West, come to me,
May the intentions of my heart carry me."

Finally, in the north, she laid down the palm full of earth and created light.

"Watch Tower of the North balance me,
May your wisdom help to guide me."

The hair on Rosella's arms stood straight up. The shock on Braden's face and Shaelyn's eyebrows climbing into her hairline told her that they sensed the energy, too.

With her legs crossed, she settled on the floor in the middle of the circle. As she lit the final candle in front of her, she sent all her intentions into it as the flame caught.

"Let my spirit roam tonight,
Set it free, take the flight.

"Like an arrow, straight and true,

373

Help me fly and return to you.

"My maman, I hope to find,
I leave this body, clear my mind.

"My return when its time is due,
Will be safe, clear, and true.

"Watch Towers on the corners,
Salt on the floor

"Light against shadows,
Locks on the door.

"Safety first and always sees
As I will, so mote it be."

A sweet smile crossed her lips before she closed her eyes and tipped her head back. A release of the breath she didn't remember holding helped her to refocus on her mission and toss off the fears. She needed to release her ties to her physical body by giving in to the flow of the air around her and the hum of the engine below.

Deep breaths in and slow breaths out helped to quiet the chatter in her mind as she searched for the inner part of herself she'd ignored for much too long. Peace settled into her soul as she imagined roots beneath her growing through the ship hull and riverbed, digging deep into the earth.

Imagining herself as a piece of dandelion fluff, she allowed her spirit to rise slowly until she exited her body. As she slowly rose towards the ceiling, she glanced down and observed her body slumped in the circle. On either side of the circle, her two friends sat as sentinels. Shaelyn was chewing on her fingernails nervously, while Braden sat still as stone, watching her physical body. His head tilted, and he gazed up near where she was hovering. Somber, he nodded at her, making her heart sing that he sensed her spirit.

A moment was needed for her to acclimate once again to this form of travel. A silver cord trailed behind her, connecting her astral form to her physical one. The cord was her tether, and were she to damage or sever it, the consequences would be dire. Her body would never wake, eventually wasting away, and her soul would be trapped in the ether, unable to return or reincarnate.

Rosella embraced the weightlessness of her soul's form and allowed herself to travel through the ceiling into the rooms above her. As her confidence returned, she did this repeatedly, moving through multiple levels of the vessel they traveled on. The final level she passed through seemed different to her. The energy was sludgy and heavy. She moved through it as quickly as possible, sighing in relief when she reached the moonlit night.

The elation she found at seeing the sky lit up with so many stars was priceless. She flew over the river, traveling a few miles in each direction, trying to gain some perspective as to where she was being held. None of the landmarks seemed familiar to her. Frustrated, she paused as she returned to the ship. A wide circle around it told her nothing. Unlabeled, it was nondescript. A massive black vessel with three center masts, it could have been any of a hundred she had seen. No numbers or letters were visible.

The more frustrated she was, the heavier her body became, and she felt herself being pulled back. Although she didn't need to breathe here, she thought about the deep breaths she had taken and took a few moments to settle her soul. Calmer, she pictured her maman. A wide smile came to mind with flashing, dark eyes and long, caramel-colored hair. Her maman was a beautiful woman in her prime—sweet and sassy all rolled into one with a bit of her Cajun roots coming through her melodic voice.

The connection they shared as mother and child called to her, and she allowed herself to float until a gentle tug in her chest pulled her in the direction she needed to go. The landscape went by too quickly to pay attention to anything. Before she could comprehend how far she traveled, she was floating outside of the house she had been born in.

Heart clenching simultaneously in pain and joy, she allowed herself to float through the roof down through the many levels until she hovered in her mother's dining room.

The entire family was there, and it made her so homesick that she almost lost the link. Roarke was at the head of the table. His dirty blond hair was longer, his beard was growing in, and the dark circles under his eyes aged him.

Both of her sisters and their families piled around the table, trying to keep on top of their broods. The littlest Gallagher was finally walking, and Sasha, her oldest sister, appeared to be pregnant again with number four. A stranger joined them. A man with skin dark as night and brilliant sapphire eyes.

Maman sat at the end opposite Roarke. The time Rosella had been gone had been hard on her also. Her hair was limp, and her cheeks hollowed. Rosella wondered how much of this was because of her attempt to communicate with her missing daughter a few weeks ago.

Exhaustion was claiming her physical body, and Rosella was aware her time on this plane was limited. She hadn't practiced this skill in a long time, and she needed to maximize her impact during this trip.

Hovering next to her maman, she reached over and tried to place a hand on her shoulder to let her know she was near. Caterina Gallagher glanced over her shoulder with a frown but didn't find Rosella. Frustrated, she tried to remember how her maman had gotten her attention.

Focusing all her attention she screamed, *"Maman, I'm here!"* as loud as she could imagine in her head.

Caterina's fork hit the table with a loud clang, and Roarke's head shot up as well. He stared at his mother and said, *"Did you hear her, too?"*

Her maman's eyes welled up as her gaze flitted from corner to corner. *"We sense yooo 'ere chile. Try again, mon cher,"* she said in a hoarse whisper, afraid to believe this was real.

"Maman, I'm running out of time. Please find me soon. I will be up for bid at the next auction. Please hurry. I love you, but I'm not sure how much time I have left…"

"Goddamn it, NO!" Roarke roared as he received her message. "I will find you, Rosie. You stay alive, honey. No matter what. Don't give them a reason to kill you. Stay alive! I will find you."

"I'm trying, but it's getting harder…"

"We love you, mon bebe." The sound of her maman's choked voice and her sister's tears followed her as she was sucked back to her body so quickly it made her dry heave when she opened her eyes.

Sobs welled up in her chest as she remembered the cozy feel of home and how close she had been to all of them. "I can't do this," she sobbed. "I miss them so much, and I don't know if I will ever be with any of them again."

Braden's heart broke seeing her curled into a ball on the floor. "Ella, let me in," he said quietly, reaching for her. The protective energy of the circle tingled painfully along his arm. "Please, Ella, open the circle and let us in."

Ella witnessed the pain in his eyes for her and somehow managed to reach out and pinch the candle between her fingers, uncaring that she burned the skin. Her hand fell lifelessly along the chalk line, and she managed to wipe away part of the line.

A moment later, Braden had her in his lap, cradled against his chest. "Hush. I've got you, Ella." His lips brushed against her temple as she clung to his neck, weeping despondently.

"My entire family sat around my maman's dining room table, but I couldn't join them. I had to come back here to hell." Tears fell harder as she struggled to speak. "I didn't think it would be so hard to view them and then have to come back here…"

Shaelyn took her hand, squeezing lightly. "You're not alone, Ella. We're here."

Ella gazed at her with such despair that Shaelyn's heart broke for her. "I'm glad I have the two of you, but what if we're all cursed and never get out of here? Why are the gods punishing us? Where's the Mother's mercy when we need it? Where's Her vengeance now?"

The sobbing changed to maniacal laughter, and Braden wasn't sure which was more chilling. His eyes met Shaelyn's, and he realized they all had tears streaming down their faces for the families they lost along the way and the unknown horrors ahead of them because their journey was just beginning.

As her exhausted mind began to drift off in his arms, she pulled up her diary in her mind.

Dear Diary,

I successfully was able to astral travel home, and both maman and Roarke knew I was there. The moment was bittersweet as I could see all, but not participate. Even more bitter was knowing that I had no choice but to return to my prison.

Shaelyn and Braden are the only saving graces that I have in this hell hole. He is holding my exhausted body as I write this, offering me his compassion and his strength. I will be sold soon and am struggling to contain my revulsion and choke back the fears of what is yet to come.

My emotional state is fragile at best, and I pray something changes soon, for I know not how much of this I will be able to endure. Roarke told me to survive. The question I wonder in my darkest hours is...do I still want to survive?

Rosella

CHAPTER SIXTY-EIGHT

The Cost of Indifference

Dashiel made his way to the portal without notice and headed for Heart Island. As he stepped out of the portal under the stag gate, he couldn't help but notice the difference in the feel of the place as he stepped onto the island. Opening his senses, he wasn't bombarded with any of the ongoing fear or rage the Court of Tears was steeped in, and he couldn't help wondering what it would be like to live every day without fear of pain or humiliation. His people knew that once, but now he wasn't sure they could imagine what it felt like anymore.

He remembered life when Yareli was their queen. As Kyran's friend, he often spent time with the royal family. They were more down-to-earth than any of the other nobles he'd interacted with. He missed the tranquility of his childhood and longed to see a permanent change for personal reasons and for many others who remained trapped in the nightmare of service to the Court of Tears.

Exiting the portal, he made his way up the hill towards the castle-like structure that was the Sanctuary on Heart Island. It had been many years since he'd made his way to this island, but he remembered the apothecary shoppe was in front of the main building.

"Dash!" a voice called from behind him. He turned, surprised to find Kyran's youngest brother jogging toward him.

"Good to see you, Kai," Dash said, reaching out a hand to the young man. "What on earth are you doing here?"

Kai's smile dimmed. "Kyran thinks I need to be protected, so he convinced Madylyn SkyDancer to grant me political asylum." He grimaced before continuing, "I hate that he has tucked me out of the way and doesn't trust me to help him."

"It's not about trust, lad," Dash said. "The root of his concern is fear. Take it from one who has been in her service for much too long; I would do anything to get my family out of her grasp. Unlike Kyran, I don't have powerful allies to call favors in for."

"You know we would help you in any way we could, Dash," Kai said without hesitation. "I still consider you one of my older brothers by association."

Dash smiled, happy to hear Kai hadn't forgotten him. "At one time, that was true. Currently, your name doesn't carry much weight with the only ruler we can access at the moment."

A shadow passed over Kai's face so quickly that Dash thought it was a trick of the light. "What are you here for?"

"I've a message from Kyran that he wants me to give to Mistress Cairn directly."

"You know your way?" Kai asked, looking relieved.

"Aye, I've been there before." He placed a hand on the massive young man's shoulder. "What's troubling you?"

"Nothing," Kai said much too quickly. "I have to go; I was heading towards the bay to help with some wounded river otters. I best be going."

Dash watched him hurry off, thinking it odd that he had approached him coming from the opposite direction from the one he was currently heading—maybe he misunderstood him. A ten-minute walk brought him to the quaint stone building used as an apothecary. A sign on the door said open, so he entered without knocking as was customary. His eyes adjusted to the dimmer light as he entered, and he nearly fell over in shock as he heard a sword leave its sheath.

Sitting before him was the missing monarch from the Court of Tears. King Varan sat at a small, well-used table, sipping tea. Tristan stood in front of him, sword ready. For the first time in years, King Varan's eyes were clear, and his color seemed healthy.

Dash's temper flared as he found the only man who could make a difference in their world sipping tea like he hadn't a care in the world. "What the fuck are you doing here, Your Highness?" he sneered at the man. "Do you have any idea what you have left Kyran to deal with?"

Tristan took a menacing step toward him, and Dash met him in the middle of the room, ready and spoiling for a fight. Toes nearly touching, Tristan said in a deadly tone, "Regardless of your personal feelings, he still rules the Court of Tears and all the subjects under it, including you. He has the power to destroy you, boy. Choose your next words very carefully." His voice was cold and clear, leaving no doubt of the violence that would be incited if Dash didn't stand down.

A door shutting behind them made both men tense and glance over their shoulders at the incensed woman headed their way. Rhyanna approached them, emerald eyes flashing green fire as she said, "Not in this room or this place will ye spill blood, or I'll bloody both of ye imbeciles." She glared at Tristan before speaking. "Put it away this instant." Turning her full fury to the stranger standing in her shoppe and causing a disturbance, she snapped, "Now would be a suitable time to introduce yerself and tell me why yer here afore ye get on the bad side of me."

Dash stood there stunned when the captain of the guard sheathed his sword and looked ashamed. The woman's full attention on him calmed the berserker clamoring in his head and amused the hell out of him. He couldn't help the laugh that burst out as he said, "You must be Mistress Rhyanna Cairn." He took her in from head to toe before chuckling again. "Kyran said you were feisty. I see now, he wasn't kidding."

Rhy's anger evaporated at the mention of Kyran's name. "How is he? I haven't heard from him…" Remembering where she was and how many others were in the room, her voice faded off.

His amusement evaporated as he witnessed the sorrow crossing her face. "Mistress, he wanted you to have this." He held out the letter to her, meeting her eyes and the questions lingering in them. "He misses you, my lady, and he has been blocked from using telepathic communication until the ceremony." Dash felt like a heel as her eyes welled with tears.

"If ye'll excuse me, gentlemen." She walked to the clinic door and was nearly through it when she glanced back at the three men, fierce once more. "Ye best not shed any blood while I'm gone. I'll not be tending new wounds born of stupidity."

The three men waited until the door closed, then turned towards each other again as the tension ratcheted up another notch.

King Varan stood and approached the man who had been like a son to him for many years. "I believe you had a question for me before we were interrupted," he said in a tone that demanded a reply. "Speak freely, Dashiel."

Dash met the eyes of the man he had known all his life. Once a good monarch and a father figure to him as well as all his boys, he took a moment, remembering who the man had once been to him. A moment was all he was able to manage as the past decade came rushing back to him. The pain, humiliation, and horrors of the time since Queen Meriel's arrival washed away any pleasant memories he might have tried to rekindle.

"Why have you abandoned your people?" he asked simply. "My lord," he sneered, "do you have any idea how your people are suffering? Can you even pretend to care that your eldest son is losing the only woman he has ever cared about?" Shadows passed over the monarch's face as he spoke. "Kyran loves Rhyanna like you once loved Queen Yareli. Would you deny him the chance to be happy? Will you turn your back on his pain and let him be forced into an unnecessary arrangement? Will you continue to allow her to abuse your people and eliminate anyone who threatens to change things?"

Varan listened to the questions and absorbed the accusations in silence, taking the blows because he knew he deserved no less. He paled as he realized the extent of the damage and the cost of his indifference. Yes, the drugs had altered his ability to make rational decisions, but his apathy after losing the woman he loved had also shaped the course of events that had continued for far too long.

Varan dropped to his knees before Dash and bowed his head. "I don't have the right to ask this, but I would like to beg for your forgiveness and for the forgiveness of my people. I have made many mistakes and have much to atone for. I would like the opportunity to change things for the better and to save my people and my son. Can you forgive me? Will you help me reclaim my throne?"

Dash looked at the man kneeling before him and stumbled back. This man had been one of his heroes, and he would have never imagined an outcome that would have him begging for help. "Your Majesty," he stammered, reaching down and placing a hand on Varan's shoulder, "if you've finally decided to reclaim your balls along with your throne by eliminating that evil bitch, then yes, you have my full support and assistance."

Tristan moved towards them as he said, "Boy, you are overstepping..." he trailed off as Varan raised a hand and silenced him.

"Leave it be, Tristan," Varan said, glancing up at him. He accepted the hand Dash offered him and stood up. "We have much to do, and I believe we can overlook propriety for the time being."

"Are you truly yourself, Your Majesty?" Dash asked suspiciously. "Lately, I haven't recognized who the hell you had become, and I sure as hell haven't liked or trusted you."

Turning to Dash, Varan said, "I haven't been myself in an awfully long time, but thanks to Mistress Cairn, I have been returned to health. We don't have the time to get into all of it now. How can we help Kyran, and who else can we count on to back our play for the throne?"

Tristan and Dash both began to speak. Dash stopped and with a nod at Tristan, encouraged him to go first. He listened to the man, respecting his position and his knowledge, and then he prayed they could make a difference quickly enough to affect Kyran's future.

CHAPTER SIXTY-NINE

My Little Enemy

Rhyanna shut the door to the shoppe and stumbled through the clinic simply by feel rather than sight. Her eyes filled as she pushed through the screen door going to the back porch.

She glared down at the letter in her hand as if it might bite her, then closed her eyes, trying to regain some semblance of control before she opened it. Sitting down in a wooden rocker with seats she had lovingly woven, her fingers traced the edges of the seat where the reeds slid over the wood, back and forth, pressing harder so the reeds dug into her fingers.

There were times she hated her empathic gifts, and this was one of those times. Sorrow leached from the paper into her as Kyran's emotions telegraphed to her from the paper he had touched. Her name was neatly written on the front, and when she turned the letter over, brushing her hand against his seal in the wax, the first tear rolled down her cheek.

"Ye've never been a coward, lass. Don't be starting now," her inner voice scolded. She wiped the tear away and took a deep breath as her fingers slid beneath the wax, breaking the seal. The pop as it released seemed loud to her enhanced emotions as she bravely unfolded the edges. The message was short, and as she read it a second time, and then a third, she didn't feel the tears flowing steadily down her face until she felt a silk handkerchief pressed into her hand.

"I could sense your distress, my lady," King Varan said as he knelt in front of her. "Is there anything I can do to help?"

"I don't ken, me laird." The look she gave him was equal parts hope mixed with hatred. "What power 'ave ye left in yer own court to stop this?" She flapped the hand holding the letter towards him.

"May I?"

"May as well. Everyone else will witness our humiliation, why not ye?"

Varan's face paled at her words and the monotone in which she spoke to him. He reached out for the letter, regretting the need to pry into their privacy and only doing it to try to be of assistance and repay the debt he owed to her and to his son.

It fell from her fingers before he could touch it as she leaned back and closed her eyes, going very still beside him. With the drugs fully out of his system he sensed her anguish, her loss, and her hatred for his queen. He also felt her fury with him for allowing the situation to occur in the first place. Bracing himself for what he would find inside, he read the message enclosed.

Rhyanna,

It is with a heavy heart and a change in circumstances that I'm forced to send this news to you. I almost lost you once trying to protect you, and I gave you my word I would not do so again. With this in mind, please remember how much I adore you before you continue reading this.

We knew your visit to court and your altercation with the queen would result in consequences—consequences I arranged to take in your stead, allowing you to leave. You know of what I speak, and I will not give it any more power by writing it down here. I gladly take on the repercussions and would do it repeatedly if it meant your safety was ensured. The blame for this does not lie with you, and I demand that you not take this to heart. I have long avoided this rendezvous with our queen, but my debt has been called due.

I gave you my word—something I don't do lightly—that I would come to you the night before and the night following my duty. Circumstances as they currently are do not allow me to honor my promise to you. Please know I deeply regret the pain I know this will cause you and the damage I understand my actions will cause us.

I am barred from using telepathy at all and unable to leave my suite, or I would have come to you immediately with this news, prepared to follow through on our original agreement. Dashiel is one of my oldest friends, and you can trust him should you decide to reply. I completely understand if you choose not to and will harbor no ill feelings towards you should you decide to end your relationship with me.

My lady, you were never just a dalliance to me. You will always be the woman who stole my heart at first glance and the woman my soul will always be bound to. If you are no longer able to stomach the thought of me after…her, I understand and wish you nothing but happiness in the future. You deserve to be happy, and you are worth so much more than I can give you at this time. I longed for the future where I could spend every day showing you how much you meant to me. If you choose to no longer tread this path with me, I will do my best to dissolve the bond between us, leaving you free to follow your heart wherever it may lead you.

I will always love and long for you. Thank you for the time you have allowed me to spend with you. I hope you can remember me fondly if you think of me at all.

Always yours,
Kyran

Varan read the letter twice before looking up at the pale woman beside him. "Mistress Rhyanna, please explain to me the price he is referring to and the consequences of which he speaks."

Rhyanna cleared her throat, trying to find the words to explain the indignation the queen had caused her, the fury she had unleashed, and the pact his son made with his wife.

Her glazed eyes looked at him sorrowfully for a long time before she was able to speak. Her voice was barely a whisper, and it cracked as she said, "The Elemental High Court requested me presence to address your poor health at court. I was ushered," she gave a harsh laugh, "by Tristan, no less, to Her Majesty's suite. He left me there, telling me everything would be all right…" her voice faded off as she remembered the day she had arrived.

"Queen Meriel paralyzed, then nearly assaulted me sexually, provoking a side of me nature rarely seen. In self-defense, I nearly killed her and would've gleefully done so to prevent her from assaulting anyone else in a similar manner. Kyran arrived and prevented me from finishing my task. He purchased me release from Court with the agreement to spend a weekend in her bed, me laird."

Varan's face blanched as she spoke.

"He will be used, abused, and violated in every way possible. That is the cost he is paying for preventing me from having to endure the same."

Rhyanna glared at him accusingly. "These are the games *yer wife*," she sneered, "be playing with the members of yer family and yer court, my lord."

Varan looked at her, unable to speak. He swallowed, visibly trying to process what she was telling him.

"Kai remains here under the guise of an apprenticeship through the Elemental Court to protect him from her games," Rhy said in a tone dripping with disdain. "These be the lives your children are living as a result of yer poor choices, me laird." Her emerald gaze locked on his troubled blue one as she said, "Will ye do nothing to help them? Ye've the power to affect change. Will ye sit back and watch the havoc yer queen is set on creating, or will ye find yer backbone, yer balls, and some of yer notorious diplomacy and fix this."

Still silent, he never looked away, but Rhy could sense his determination as he gazed at her. His fury was also building at an alarming rate. *It's about fecking time,* she thought to herself. "Ye'll have the full support of the Sanctuary if ye choose to take out the trash, me laird."

Massive cumulonimbus clouds rolled overhead as the king's rage affected the local weather. Dark and ominous, with lightning arcing back and forth between them, they circled overhead in a threatening manner.

Rhyanna reached out and put a hand on Varan's shoulder. "Glad, I am to see ye finally willing to fight for yer throne, Yer Highness. But let's not level this island in the process." Varan's eyes matched the storm brewing, but the clouds slowly dissipated as he fought for control of his rage.

The screen door slammed shut behind Tristan as he rushed to his king's aid, recognizing the signs of his distress. Varan held up a hand, requesting silence as he reached up and cupped Rhyanna's cheek in the other. "Mistress Rhyanna, you have been nothing but kind to me, even when I'm sure it's the last thing you've wanted to be. I am grateful for everything you have done to save my sanity, and I'm more grateful for the kick in the ass to protect my children's futures."

Standing, he offered her his hand. "I need to speak with Mistress SkyDancer at once. I harbor no delusions that I can reclaim my throne alone, so I will take any allies I can find in this endeavor."

"I'll arrange a meeting, me laird," Rhyanna said, offering him a hint of a curtsy before she hurried from the room with hope peeking up its bowed head for the first time in the past week. She wanted to believe he could fix this, but she remembered what they were going up against. Queen Meriel might be an evil bitch, but she was a powerful evil bitch. Good thing Rhyanna had some powerful friends of her own.

A children's rhyme ran through her mind as an evil smile of her own crossed her face. *My little enemy, come out and play with me…*" She continued humming the tune as she swiftly made her way to the granite castle across from her shoppe. If Meriel wanted to persist with her debauchery, then they were going to bring the full force of their little army with a pissed-off king at the helm into the picture. May the Mother be merciful.

CHAPTER SEVENTY

Gallaghers Never Give Up

Roarke slammed out of the front door of his maman's home, roaring his pain to the sky. His body vibrated with helpless rage. Rosie, his sweet little sister, had taken a chance to reach out for their help, and he was no more able to do anything than he was a month ago.

Fists clenched, he paced, wanting to hit something or someone and needing somewhere to dump this fury running through him. Long legs covered the distance to the woodshed, and he picked up the axe they used for splitting wood. If he was going to hit something, he might as well do something useful in the process. With a shout, he lifted the ax overhead and let the well-worn handle slide through his palms until the recoil with the wood trembled through his hands. On autopilot, he continued until his shirt was soaked and his voice was hoarse. The blisters on his hands were a surprise when he carefully placed the ax back on the wall.

The shirt came off, and he used it to wipe the sweat dripping down his face. A short walk brought him to the dock, where he kicked off his boots. After quickly glancing around to make sure none of the littles were around, he stripped off his pants and dove into the cool embrace of the river. With the moon overhead to keep him company, he floated on his back, allowing his tormented mind to drift like the waves carrying him.

The progress in locating Rosie stalled after following his last lead. Fergus was due back soon, and Roarke prayed that his trip would bring something new they could follow. When the rational part of his brain took over once again, he returned to shore, dried, and dressed himself. Silently, he entered the dark house.

A plate on the counter was covered with a tea towel. Maman always left him food when he was out late, knowing well how ravenous he was late at night. Without tasting anything, he cleared the plate, then washed, dried, and returned it to the cabinet it belonged in. Maman made sure her children learned early on how to clean up after themselves. Old habits die hard.

The partially finished bottle of wine left over from dinner called his name, as did the full one sitting next to it. A glass in one hand and bottles dangling from the other, he walked silently through the house, heading for the full front porch where his mother waited for him.

Catalina Gallagher would be waiting for him to come to his senses before attempting to speak to him. Roarke dreaded this chat and the disappointment he knew would be in her eyes because he had nothing new to offer her. No use waiting any longer; she wouldn't move until he made an appearance, so he opened the screen door and stepped outside.

His maman was settled on the porch in a wide swing that hung from the rafters. This, he expected. The part he didn't anticipate was the fact that she sat sideways with her legs over Samson's and her head tucked against his shoulder. Samson's arm was around her shoulders, and his thumb stroked back and forth over her skin in a light caress. Tears were in his mother's eyes, but she appeared more peaceful than he had seen her in a while. The contrast between his ebony skin and her light caramel was beautiful, and Roarke wondered how fucking long this had been going on.

Roarke stood there like a dumbass, fully aware that his face was giving them the *"What in the ever-loving fuck?"* look, but he kept his shit together by squeezing the necks of the bottles tighter into his blisters. Eyes shifting between his maman's nervous ones and Samson's challenging blue orbs, he paused and considered his maman's state of mind recently. If this man—temporary though he might be in their lives—made her happy, he didn't give a shit.

From what he'd ascertained about the man so far, he was honorable and brave, and he didn't whore around. His maman had been lonely for years since his pa passed. The woman in her deserved whatever it was she needed to carry her through this ordeal. Guilt wasn't an emotion he was willing to use as a weapon against her, especially when she had been so instrumental in helping him resolve his guilt about failing Rosella.

The cork came out easily, and he dumped the rest of the open bottle into the glass before handing it to her. "You can share that, I assume?" His eyebrow quirked at them.

A shy smile passed over his maman's face as she glanced up at the man next to her. Samson smiled back at her. With Roarke watching, he leaned down and kissed her forehead, snuggling her closer. He took the glass from her, taking a long sip while his eyes met Roarke's, staking a claim. "Aye, mon, we'll share dis." His voice lilted with a hint of the islands, and Roarke wondered if that was part of the attraction for her. He sounded like the people and places of her youth.

Roarke popped the cork on the other bottle and took a healthy swig, processing the situation before him.

"Thank you, mon chéri, for your civility. I know dis comes as a shock."

"Does he make you happy?"

"He does. He's become a welcome source of comfort to me."

"You deserve to be happy, Maman. I'd never stand in the way of that. Do the others know?"

"Not yet. I wanted to see yer reaction afore I told dem."

Roarke chuckled. "So, I'm your trial run."

"You could say dat."

"I knew you were too young to stay single forever. You have my blessing, but if he hurts you…they'll never find his body."

"Counting on it, mon chéri."

"Ya all done talking 'bout me?" Samson asked with a wide grin.

"For now," Roarke said as he pointed a finger at him. "But you and I will be talking later, you feel me?"

"I expected ya to beat de shit out of me—or try to at da very least, so ya, I feel ya, podna."

"I want to try to reach her again," Catalina said in a quiet voice.

"Nearly killed you the last time. There must be another way," Roarke said vehemently.

"'Twas not so bad. I be merely fatigued, no more dan usual."

"Bullshit."

"Language!" she scolded. It didn't help that Sampson's deep chuckle erupted.

"Maman, you can't be sleeping with a man my age and still scold me on my language. We both curse like the sailors we are, and just because he's behaving to get on your good side, he ain't no different."

"Fair enough," Catalina said, laughing. "Who says we have any time left ta sleep?" Her fingers played with the blue beads in his long, thin braids.

"STOP!" Roarke groaned. "I can accept this," he waved an arm at them on the swing. "But I can't hear the details." His eyes drilled into Samson's twinkling gaze. "You hear me, podna?"

Giving his maman a smoldering glance first, he said, "I don kiss and tell, ma chérie." Catalina blushed, gazing up at him.

"Moving on to plan B," Roarke said with a cough. "Ferg will be back tomorrow, and we'll see what he found first. Please wait until he contacts me before you do anything else." His dark chocolate eyes begged her to consider this.

"You have my word, Roarke."

"Thank you, Maman." The constriction in his chest eased for the first time since dinner. Her impulsiveness on hold, he had one less thing to worry about.

His mind turned to Rosie and the fear in her voice tonight. What lay ahead of her was too horrific for her brother to even consider, but consider it he must. "At least we know she's alive. That's a good thing. She has a difficult path ahead of her, but she's a Gallagher, and Gallaghers never give up."

Catalina Gallagher studied her son's profile in the dark where he sat on the steps. His jaw was clenched, as were his fists. The abduction of the youngest Gallagher was transforming him into more of a man and less of a carefree young adult. The only thing she wasn't sure of was the kind of man this situation was turning him into. The laugh lines around his eyes were seldom used anymore, he was leaner, and his temper was quicker to flare.

Roarke was right; Gallaghers never gave up, but what this journey was doing to all of them wasn't healthy. Roarke was her oldest child, but he'd always been light-hearted and fun to be around despite the mantle of responsibility he'd donned. The colder, darker, willing-to-do-anything Gallagher in front of her made a shiver run down her spine. Catalina would move heaven and earth to reach her daughter. But her son, he would burn it all to the ground to reach her. And when the dust cleared, he would care nothing about the carnage he left behind or the people he trampled over to accomplish this.

May the gods have mercy on them all if they couldn't find Rosella. Failure to do so would result in Roarke's detonation, and Catalina didn't know if any of them would survive the repercussions when her oldest child exploded.

CHAPTER SEVENTY-ONE

No Coincidences

The portal door opened much too quickly for Kano's liking. He sent a brief prayer to the water gods he could remember that the meeting he needed to have would go in his favor, even though he couldn't think of more than a handful after his grandfather Neptune. Yeah, guess he should have paid more attention to that part of his education.

Satish and his goons approached him. "Queen Meriel requests your presence immediately, Prince Kano."

Kano quirked an eyebrow. Satish was in a mellow mood today. It was a sign that didn't bode well. "I am headed there directly," he said as he pushed by the arrogant little fuck. "No need for an escort. I know my way."

Satish made as if to follow when an approaching soldier called his name. Kano took the opportunity and headed inside without him. Looking behind him when he reached the end of the corridor and finding no one following, he turned left instead of right, heading for Kyran's suite.

The guards outside his brother's door made no attempt to stop him as he reached for the handle. He entered and found Kyran handcuffed to a chair. "Big brother, you're only supposed to get tied up when you have someone to play with. Have I taught you nothing?" he asked in a long-suffering tone.

Kyran glowered at him as Kano perched on the edge of the bed. "What do you want?"

"Seriously," Kano said with a glare worthy of the glower, "is that any way to greet someone who may have the answer to your prayers?" He raised an eyebrow at him and nodded towards his hands shackled under the chair. "Care to explain?"

A frustrated sigh escaped Kyran as he scowled at his brother. "Meriel doesn't trust me to follow through tonight, so she has ensured that I can't leave my quarters. What, pray tell, are you up to?"

"Well, our luck being what it is, I was sent to escort your future wife to the palace for safekeeping as well. Seems she is not keen to join you either."

Kano looked down at his hands and began picking at his nails. His silence was more surprising than the fact that he had come for a visit. Loud and boisterous, he was nearly always the center of attention at any gathering, even amongst his family.

Kyran knew something was seriously askew if this was his brother's reaction. "For fuck's sake, out with it already!" His temper was on a short leash since he had acquired his new bracelets, was unable to communicate telepathically, and just had his cock sucked by someone with a penis. His frustration was reaching the boiling point.

"Do you remember my trip to the Alps?"

Kyran's brow furrowed as he tried to recall something from a century ago. "Vaguely."

"I met someone there and have been unsuccessfully looking for her." The blank look on Kyran's face made him groan. "C'mon, you've seen the sketch Mother drew for me."

"Yes, your mystery woman who never existed. What about her."

Kano cleared his throat. "She does exist, asshole, and she is the Princess Elyana Drake."

Kyran's eyes grew wide, and his mouth formed an O. "Are you fucking kidding me? How could Meriel know about her? It's no coincidence that she can screw both of us over with one blow. This can't be that random." The tendons on the side of his neck stuck out as he processed the fact that he was supposed to marry the only woman his brother had ever shown interest in. The queen was destroying their family from the inside out, and he was trapped here, unable to do anything about it.

Struggling against his restraints, he almost knocked the chair over as he tried dislodging the chains keeping him in place. As he seethed, Kano reached out and cuffed him upside the head, helping him to focus. Kyran glared at him and growled.

"Are you done with your temper tantrum?" Kano asked.

Kyran blinked and then nodded his head as he slumped defeatedly in his chair. "What's your brilliant idea?"

"I'm going to offer to take your place without telling her what Elyana means to me. She'll still have her alliance with the Fire Clan, and you should be able to have your little healer."

Kyran laughed then, a harsh sound steeped in irony. "You really think it's going to be that easy? What are you willing to pay to get your way? You know that Meriel does nothing without extracting a price."

Kano glared at Kyran. "I'm not a fucking idiot, asshole. Have you got a better idea—or any ideas for that matter?" Kyran's silence greeted him. "Well, in that case, shut the fuck up and at least let me try to do something." Heading for the door, he paused when his brother spoke softly.

"I'm grateful for what you are trying to do, Kano," Kyran said. "Be careful you don't make our situation worse."

Kano looked over his shoulder at Kyran and gave him a sad smile. "I'm not sure it can get any worse." Without another word, he left the suite, slamming the door on his way out and calling Kyran all kinds of foul names. He wanted the guards to wonder what the argument had been about and why they were so angry with each other.

As he walked towards the queen's private quarters, he sent a message to Kenn. "Phase one complete. Moving on to phase two. How are you making out on your end?"

"Not coming up with the numbers I want, but still working on it. Good luck with groveling. It's never been your strong suit."

"Fuck you. I can grovel with the best of them, just need something worth getting on my knees for, and this is."

"I'm on site if you get arrested. Might be able to take the time to haul your ass out of there."

"See, that's why you're my favorite brother."

"The others would have ignored your pleas for help completely, and who could blame them."

"Piss off. Any sighting of Tristan or Varan?"

"Well, that's where things are getting interesting… Sorry, gotta run. Will be in touch."

Kano stopped in front of the ornate doors leading to the queen's chambers, waiting to be announced. Breathing deeply, he tried to slow his racing heart, knowing she would sense any nervousness on his part. The doors slowly opened, allowing him a glimpse of the inner world of their reigning queen. Nauseous, he stepped inside and tried not to cringe when the door shut behind him. He prayed for the words to convince Meriel to let them change places and still maintain the trade agreements, their women, and their sanity.

CHAPTER SEVENTY-TWO

Elemental Powerhouses

Grateful that her home was a sentient being and capable of expanding as needed, Madylyn smiled as she noticed the conference table was longer and additional chairs were available surrounding it. Wardens were already seated around the conference table, and the empty seats were filling in steadily. Roarke Gallagher and his new partner in crime, Samson, took seats as Lachlan Quinn and Damian Pathfinder walked through the door laughing.

Behind them, King Varan and his shadow, Tristan, entered, both men wearing solemn expressions. Kai continued ignoring the man until he sat directly across from him. Varan's cocked eyebrow challenged him to continue doing so with him staring him down. Tristan sat to Varan's left, and Fergus sauntered in, taking the one to his right.

Rhyanna and Danyka flanked Madylyn at one end of the table, while Jameson and Kerrygan flanked Ronan at the other. The tension between the two men was palpable as they stared each other down. The air was thick with unspoken challenges. Maddy was getting closer to calling the both of them on their posturing. They had enough drama to deal with; she didn't need any fighting amongst her team members.

A noise in the hallway alerted her to the extra guests she had invited to join in this conclave. Kaniatarowanenneh—or Kani, as she was known—stepped into the room with two of her rivermen at her side for guards. Fergus smiled broadly at her and stood up to properly greet her. He settled her at the table next to him, chatting amiably with a woman who was a dear friend and, at one time, his lover.

Cheveyo, the Hopi shaman—who was also Ronan's son Landon's grandfather—took the seat across from Kani, bowing deeply to the ancient gatekeeper before he did. His hands stroked his long, black braids trailing over his shoulders as the woman named for their river gave him a nod. Her eyes traveled over his chiseled features and copper skin with a female appreciation that was apparent to everyone watching. A faint blush stained her cheeks as he gave her the same appreciation.

Madylyn sat back and enjoyed the show, never having seen either of these ancient elementals at a loss of words. The sexual tension between them centered in her core and throbbed. Ronan's voice came across their link, *"You need to turn that down, darling, before I need to escort you from the room for a quickie. Their energy and your hormones are affecting everyone in this room. Try and bring it down a notch."* Madylyn's eyes locked on his as she listened to him and tried to control the hormonal assault on her libido.

Dashiel, their informant from the Court of Tears, wandered in next, taking the seat across from Tristan. The man's gaze traveled around the table, full of curiosity and wonder at the dynamic rulers and elemental beings he was joining. The berserker in him cataloged strengths, weaknesses, and enemies, always ready to emerge.

One seat remained, and Maddy wasn't sure that it would be filled. The invitation had been extended, but no reply received. She was going to give him five more minutes before beginning. Heavy steps on the treads of the stairs carried to her, and she let a sigh of relief out, grateful that this guest had chosen to join them. Laird Killam took the vacant seat across from his nephew Fergus, giving the younger man a nod.

Madylyn felt a chill go through her as she took in this capable group of friends and family who had answered her call for the common good. A deep breath settled her nerves as she prepared to chair this conclave of gatekeepers, court heads, wardens, and lawgivers. Introductions were quickly made, and she moved forward with their agenda.

"Welcome, everyone. You have my sincerest gratitude for taking the time and blessing us with your presence today. We all have a common enemy in Queen Meriel and need to find a way to help thwart this union she is so hell-bent on. King Varan did not agree to this trade agreement and betrothal, and Laird Killam was extorted into it. Kyran and Elyana do not want this, and both are currently under house arrest at the Court of Tears. We need to find a way to peacefully extricate them from this predicament, then allow Varan to renounce Meriel and make the necessary changes to his court."

"If ye kept yer woman in line and yer head outta yer cups, this wouldna be happening," Laird Killam snapped unceremoniously.

"You're a fine one to be talking about staying out of your cups, Killam. Since Meghan passed, ye've been drowning in them. Why the fuck do you think it was any easier for me to lose the woman I loved by being manipulated by that whore?"

Killam's face paled as he realized that Varan's situation held echoes of his own treacherous past. Unclenching his fists, he conceded, "Yer right, Varan. Ye've me apologies. I be at me wits end with all of this. Elyana's all I've got left. I can't stand for her to hate me over this, and I can't find a fecking window out of it."

Madylyn quickly interceded before the two men could backtrack at all. "Lachlan, did you find anything that could help us? A loophole of any sort?"

Lachlan's jaw was clenched as he shook his head. "I've reviewed the formal agreement between the courts, and I'm sorry, but the contract is ironclad. Afraid I missed something, I took it to the Elemental High Court's Barristers, and they concurred with my findings." His gaze shifted to Killam. "Should you back out of the agreement, you will bankrupt your clan for reparations. I wish you'd had a law guardian advise you before you signed the betrothal contract. Legally, you have no recourse. I'm truly sorry."

Killam sighed heavily, not surprised by the news but disappointed, nonetheless.

Fergus met his uncle's eyes and waited for a nod, allowing him to speak on his behalf. The man was still his laird, and Ferg would show him the respect due his position without hesitation. He still loved the man and would treat him no differently after learning his secrets.

"So, a ceremony must be performed, and with the High Court's permission, I will be the mage brokering this betrothal. I can tweak some of the wording to reflect more of a contractual ceremony than a traditional pledge ceremony, and I don't think that anyone will take issue with this modification. I think we can use this to our advantage, and in the spirit of authenticity, I need to ask you all to trust me on how I will achieve this."

His eyes traveled around, meeting each of the members seated. "The less people expect what I'm going to do, the better the authenticity of the ceremony and less suspicion aroused. This is imperative. If Meriel even has one whiff of something off, the gig is up." Fingers raking through his wild hair didn't help the state of his appearance. "We'll only have one chance to pull this off or, to be completely honest, we're fecked. The only alternative if that happens is to go through with what she wants, destroying both Rhyanna, Kyran, and Elyana."

Killam's face fell, and he appeared to be holding himself together by the slightest of threads. "I'm begging all of ye to please help me save me daughter. I've fecked this up good, ain't no two ways about that, and I own the damage I've done. But I'd like the opportunity to fix it for all involved." His gazed turned to Madylyn. "Whatever ye need from me clan, we'll provide—funding, manpower, magic. Name it, and it's yers."

A tight smile crossed Maddy's face. "I appreciate your offer, Laird Killam, and we'll let you know."

Varan spoke to Dashiel, "How many can we count on?"

The handsome man met his king's eyes without flinching. "No more than a dozen I'd trust with my life."

Disappointment crossed Varan's face, and it was all he could do to rein it in.

"I'm sorry, Your Majesty, but Meriel has managed to control nearly every major family at court. Threats keep everyone in line and keep us from trusting each other. I'd rather have a handful I know will protect you with their lives than dozens who will stab you in the back."

"I agree completely," Tristan said. "The fewer aware of what we're up to, less chances of leaks." He addressed Dash, "Make sure you tell Kyran who you do trust in case you're not able to make it back."

"Will do."

Kani cleared her throat and then spoke, her musical voice lilting softly in the heavy air. "Have we any more leads on the parasites using the river to steal our young people?"

Cheveyo spoke up. "I've been spending time with the river patrols at night. Any time we get within a tenth of a mile to something we suspect might be what we are searching for, the sensation fades. It's almost as if we've been compelled to forget what we've seen." His hand stroked his long braids, playing with the tie on the end before he continued. "I'm no stranger to powerful magic or to dark magic. This is something entirely different, and I can't begin to guess what that may be."

Kani met his concerned gaze. "I've been sensing the same thing, and it troubles me because this is unfamiliar and so very dark in nature."

A solemn nod agreed with her. "I'll continue searching for them as long as you want me to, Madylyn."

"Thank you, Cheveyo." Maddy glanced at Ferg.

"I think I've found a way onto Jonah's vessel. I've found a man with a grudge against Jonah and Pearl. I be waiting for the right timing so that we can get as much intel as possible before arresting him." Fergus waited for a nod from Maddy and then turned his attention to Roarke. "I believe he be the man responsible for Rosella's abduction. He doesn't trust me yet, and I be working slowly to earn the slimy bastard's trust even when I'd rather shank the fecker I be trying to find out everything I can from him so that we can come one step closer to ending this nightmare forever. When I get the information we need, I will let ye in on the plan. I think we finally have a concrete lead to locate your sister"

Roarke's nostrils flared, and his eyes drilled into Maddy. "You gave me your word, Mistress Skydancer."

Midnight blue eyes met his hostile dark ones, acknowledging his accusation. "I did, Roarke, and I fully intend to keep it. I don't believe you would ever intend to allow other women to suffer the same fate in our haste for vengeance. Would you?"

Aggression fading, he dropped his gaze. "My apologies. This has been very difficult on my family. Rosella managed to contact us last night, and…" Choking on what he needed to say, he cleared his throat, not wanting to voice the horror awaiting her. "There will be an exhibition this weekend and she'll be auctioned off next month. She's running out of time for us to save her."

You could have heard a pin drop in the silence that ensued. Not a word was spoken because what was there to say? Well aware of the price of failure, Rosella's future was in their hands like sand sifting through their fingers, as they tried to decide which trail to follow. No one faulted him for his anger, and they all would have reacted the same way were it their daughter, sister, or cousin they sought.

Samson spoke into the silence. "I've worked on Jonah's ship before. A long dime ago. De mon drusts very few, and he'll slit your droat widout hesitation if he dinks you're a dreat. I've watched him do it." His sapphire eyes locked on Roarke's. "I understand how badly you want at dis mon, but de intel he can provide will be invaluable. You're not de only one wid a sistah to save."

Roarke nodded, then closed his eyes, trying to hold in the rage and the pain of doing nothing. Fists clenched on the table, he attempted to control his banked rage.

Rhyanna reached over and placed her hand on top of his, squeezing lightly. Roarke's tormented eyes stared into hers, wanting so badly to lean on her. Sitting next to him, she could feel his devastation and his banked desire. The need she had to comfort him bordered on a compulsion. The empathetic side of her wanted to help make it better any way that she could, but there was nothing she could offer him to make this situation better.

"I will honor my word to you, Roarke. As soon as we understand how this network operates and save as many as we can from this life, I will hand him over to you for whatever brand of justice you choose to take. You have a brother's right to whatever version of Island Law you determine. I'll not stand in your way."

Ronan's voice drifted to him from the end of the table. "Even in my captivity, I would have wanted them to save the masses if there was a possibility, even if it meant it would take longer to save me. I wouldn't want another living soul to experience what I did."

Roarke's hand opened, engulfing Rhy's tightly in his grip. "Rosie would be the same way," he said in a whisper. "Excuse me, please." Releasing her hand, he pushed his chair back and exited the room.

Rhyanna's eyes followed him, and she gave Maddy an apologetic glance before following him.

"Is there anything else anyone would like to add?"

Kai's voice rose hesitantly from the end of the table. "Have you bothered reaching out to our grandfather for help?" The question was addressed to his father, and Maddy wasn't sure if it was truly a question or more of an accusation.

Varan's shock showed on his face. Maddy wasn't sure if it was because Kai finally acknowledged him or because he hadn't thought of this himself. "I wasn't sure he would answer me," he said in a sad admission.

"Won't know until you try," Kai replied.

Varan nodded, accepting the criticism. "I'll see what I can do."

"That old fart won't refuse my request," Kani piped in with a sly smile. "Bastard owes me a visit."

The shock on everyone's faces was laughable, especially the look on Ferg's face as he realized the implications of the favor he owed her. Neptune would be serious competition for the River Queen. Good thing they only had a relationship based on mutual pleasure.

"Students will begin arriving too soon for my liking. Let's hope we can have most of this wrapped up in a suitable way by then." Maddy looked at her gathering of fellow elementals. "Thank you for coming and for any assistance you provide any of us in the near future. You've earned the Sanctuary's gratitude and the gratitude of the Court of Tears and the Court of Luminosity."

Maddy stood up and moved towards her desk as her guests mingled and chatted amongst themselves. Sighing heavily, she sat in her chair, glad this meeting was over and that no one had come to blows. There were so many powerful egos vying to run the show. She was impressed they had all taken a backseat to the problems they faced. Now, if they could continue to keep those problems first and foremost as a team, they might be able to make a huge difference to the people who relied on them for protection and leadership.

CHAPTER SEVENTY THREE

Happiness Not Required

Kano headed down the corridor to Queen Meriel's suites. Yes, he was thinking of her with the title attached because he knew damn well he would have to grovel and use the proper title. His feet hit the floor in a strong forward gait, and the short journey was both the longest and the shortest walk he'd ever taken. The distance was too short to calm his uneasiness and too long when all he wanted was to get this over with.

Two guards stood in front of the door with massive, curved swords strapped to both sides of their bodies. The teal leather crisscrossed on their chest, ending in a scabbard on both sides of their hip. The teal was a nice contrast to the white jackets and crisp white shirts worn beneath. Tall stovetop hats adorned them with a strap keeping them in place under their chins. They stared straight ahead, barely acknowledging the fact that he had stepped into their line of sight.

Kano cleared his throat, awaiting entry. The guard on the left about-faced and walked inside the chamber. Kano waited, listening as the man announced, "Prince Kano to see Your Majesty."

Kyran heard a cork pop, then a long-winded sigh. "Send him in. He has much to answer for."

Kano gritted his teeth to keep any snarkiness from escaping. Nearly cracking a tooth, he stepped in and bowed deeply in front of the plush velvet chair the woman settled into. "Queen Meriel," he said even though it nearly choked him to call her by her title. "I wanted to report to you directly that my mission to return with the Princess Elyana has been a failure."

A vassal stood to the queen's right, pouring a glass of champagne. Handing the delicate flute to Meriel, the young boy stepped back and waited for further instruction. Meriel took a long sip and looked Kano up and down. "Would you like a glass?" she asked much too politely.

Kano was torn, knowing that either decision would be the wrong one. "If it pleases you, my queen."

She motioned for the vassal to provide and glanced at Kano over her glass. Licking her lips, she asked, "The princess was problematic?"

Kano nodded, taking a sip of the fine bubbly. He hated the feel of the bubbles up his nose, but he managed to drink the beverage without gagging. "She managed to kick my balls up into my throat before I could step out of the portal, redirected us to the jungle, and ran off before I could climb to my feet."

"You recaptured her?" Meriel asked with a bite in her voice.

Kano paused, debating his options—stick as closely to the truth as he could without telling her where she was or lie through his teeth. The options were limited. He went with his first. "I did, but she was injured when I caught her."

"Our finest healers will see to her as soon as you produce her," Meriel said as if the matter was settled. "Retrieve her and return post-haste."

Kyran wandered to the window with his glass awkwardly dangling between his fingers. "I was hoping," he said, "that we might be able to come to terms that would benefit us both."

"What could you possibly have that would benefit me?"

"I want to pledge myself to the princess. You will have your trade agreement, and I will get the little spitfire to break. Leave Kyran to whatever games he is playing with his little hedge witch. There's no harm in letting him be with the woman he loves."

Meriel stood and walked over to stand next to him. "You're honestly willing to give up your future for this woman you've just met? You would give up your daily whores, not in service of your brother but to have one woman who said no to you?"

He turned towards her, afraid he had overplayed his hand and trying not to show it. "Yes, I would give up everything to see my brother happy."

Meriel's hand shot up so quickly that he never saw it coming. The champagne flute smashed against the side of his face, cutting him from his temple to his jawline. His vision blurred for a moment as blood ran freely down the side of his face, but he stood where he was without flinching or wiping the blood away.

"Do you think I'm an idiot?" she fumed at him. "You really want me to believe that your week in the Alps with the little fire whore had nothing to do with your offer?" She walked away from him, vibrating with fury.

Tossing the broken glass on the floor, she turned back and sneered, "Every one of you Tyde men thinks that you can do what you want, when, where, and with whomever you want, and there will be no repercussions. Do you honestly think that I haven't considered every possibility and covered every angle a hundred times before I do something?"

Kano stood mutely, listening to her rambling, and tried to follow her logic while his blood dripped steadily onto her Persian rugs. His cheek hurt like a motherfucker, but he refused to show any pain or discomfort of any kind.

"Your happiness is not required, Prince Kano. Neither is Prince Kyran's, Kai's, or Kano's. Happiness is nothing but an illusion as you go about your daily life with the shimmer of something waiting in the wings. A future wavering before you like heat shimmering off hot stones—fleeting, and useless. I learned that long ago from a man of your line, and I will no longer be used for someone else's whims."

Queen Meriel stepped into his space and seemed to grow even larger and more maniacal as her rant ran its course. "Your happiness may not be required, Kano, but your obedience is. You have thirty-six hours to return the little bitch to me before I set into motion events that cannot be undone."

Kano glared back at her. The only sound in the room was from the red drops dripping onto the floor as she waited for him to back down. His rage coiled inside of him—a living, breathing entity wanting to break free. Outside, lightning danced through the dark swirling clouds, mirroring his inner turmoil. He wanted to dare her to do her best, but he held himself in check as Elyana's face flashed through his mind. Right behind the woman he wanted came Kyran's visage, concerned his offer would make things worse. Slowly, he unclenched his fists and waited as the storm slowly began to break up. "I will do my best, my queen," he said in a monotone.

"No, Kano. You will do better than that, or you risk losing your little firebrand and your mother." Her voice was smug as she walked away from him towards a large, clear quartz gazing ball at least three feet in circumference. Perched on a cast iron stand four feet tall with intricate designs carved around the base, she placed her hands on either side and gazed into the ball like looking through a window.

Kano knew of the scrying balls but had never seen one used. He was trying not to scream. How the fuck could Meriel know where his mother's residence was located? One of the conditions of her exile was complete privacy. As he tried to puzzle out how this was possible, she trailed her long fingernails over the ball, then tapped them impatiently.

"To answer your unspoken question, I have allies and even more powerful trackers at my disposal."

As she spoke, he saw fog swirl in the middle of the globe. The island his mother was exiled on appeared in the fog, surrounded by the deep blue of the Caribbean. As he watched, layers formed around the image, showing all the hidden dimensions surrounding the earth. Fascinated, he focused on half a dozen hellhounds circling around the island. They were exhausted and panted heavily. He could hear their whines as they gazed intently at the island.

"What's holding them back?" he asked, knowing they didn't linger there for fun. A sick feeling was forming in the pit of his stomach. One last thick drop of blood fell from his chin, the dripping finally slowing as his blood clotted. His head whipped towards her, waiting to hear what new form of torment she had devised.

An evil smile crossed her face as she reached down and picked up a soft fuzzy ball, squeezing the sphere until it made a wheezing sound. "Fluffy," she called.

All the color drained from Kano's face as he beheld a tiny hellhound pup bounding across the room. Fluffy was tiny for a hellhound, which made her the size of a large black lab with wiry fur, glowing red eyes, razor-sharp nails, and drool able to kill you in six hours without an antidote. "How did you get her?" he asked, knowing how insanely the family protected their young.

"I borrowed her in exchange for their help."

"You stole a fucking hellhound pup," he repeated, his voice rising as shock settled on his face. "You obviously have a death wish."

"No, I have too much to live for, but I'm not sure how much you'll have to live for if you don't return here with the red-haired princess before I give the hounds permission to attack any and all at will." Her hand stroked the crystal ball lovingly as she observed those inside like a child playing with an animated dollhouse.

An hourglass appeared next to the globe. Meriel flipped the glass over and the sand drizzled through to the bottom. "You're wasting time, Kano." When time runs out, it will take my pets seconds to reach the residents and minutes to kill or maim them all." She gave him an innocent smile. "I wonder if Klaree is coming home to visit tomorrow like she does every Friday?" She threw the ball and waited for Fluffy to return with the drenched item. She reached down and retrieved it from the pup, ignoring the drool surrounding it.

He looked at her puzzled as she willingly touched the soggy ball without any concern.

Meriel laughed at his confusion. "I can't tell you all my secrets, now, can I? A woman must keep a few mysteries to herself." She turned her back to him and waved a hand imperiously. "You may leave, Kano." She looked back over her shoulder at him and gave him one last hit. "Don't return empty-handed this time, prince. The pledge ceremony has been moved up to Sunday. She'll need the twenty-four hours prior to prepare for the big day."

A smile crossed her face as she yelled at his retreating back. "Send your mother my regards while you're there!" The look he gave her when he reached the door would have shriveled a lesser woman, but she met his glare with an innocent smile, then winced as he slammed the door on his way out.

Dropping her glamor, she settled at her vanity. Picking up her ivory-handled brush, she ran the bristles through her long hair. She looked so much like her mother now, they could have been sisters. She thought of the woman who birthed her. As a child, she watched her doing the same thing and envied how beautiful she was. She had wished upon a fallen star that one day she would be just as beautiful, and look at that, she was. But the other wish she made that cold December night also came true, and her beauty hid a heart that was long past feeling anything but a need for revenge.

Revenge might be a cold bed partner, but the purpose prevented you from being a devastated one. No man would ever destroy her the way her mother had been destroyed because she gave her heart to the wrong man. Her daughter, Meriel, suffered endlessly because of her mother's obsession with a man she couldn't have, but in her suffering, Meriel found a purpose, and that purpose was coming to fruition. Every day she was one step closer to destroying the Tyde men from the inside out, and when she was finished, none of them would ever find true happiness in this lifetime—not while she still lived.

CHAPTER SEVENTY-FOUR

Heartbreak Yet to Come

Rhyanna went after Roarke needing to see him. They hadn't spoken since the night she had gotten drunk. If nothing else, she'd owed him an apology and a thank you.

He was heading down the front steps when she caught up with him—the tall man's strides were difficult for her to keep up with. As they neared her shoppe, she grabbed his hand, forcing him to stop. Dangerous eyes flew to hers as he tried to reclaim his hand. "Leave me be, Rhy. I need to be alone."

"Please, Roarke, give me five minutes of yer time. 'Tis all I ask for."

The "please" and her rapidly filling emerald gaze did him in. He needed to get over this fucking hold she had on him. There was no future for them and only heartbreak lurking.

Pulling him into the shoppe, she lit the lanterns with a thought, then shut the door behind them. "I need to apologize for what happened between us, Roarke." She twisted her hands nervously in front of her. "I never should have used ye that way. T'wasn't fair to ye, and I'm sorry."

Roarke looked down into her tormented gaze and closed his eyes, praying for the courage to keep his hands at his sides. "That night wasn't fair to either of us for different reasons, Rhy."

A blush stained her cheeks, knowing he'd witnessed her poor behavior. "I'm not proud of the way I acted, nor the way I led ye on."

"Led me on?" Fury swept through him at her interpretation of the events that transpired. "You didn't lead me on, Rhy. If you want to apologize, then apologize for lying to yourself about what really happened." He stepped closer to her, backing her up against the wall opposite the door. "You wanted me that night as much as I wanted you, and you would have given yourself to me easily. Now, you're on good terms with Kyran again, and you're ridden with guilt because if he hadn't shown up when he did, I would've been balls deep in you moments later because *you* wanted *me* to be."

Rhy's breath hitched, and a tear rolled down her cheek as she faced his truth and the fact that he was right. "I shouldn't have followed, but I was worried about ye when ye left the meeting. I jest needed to make sure ye were gonna be all right. I be sorry to have bothered ye, Roarke," she said, ignoring his accusations, unable to acknowledge the truth of them with everything else in her life falling apart.

Her dismissal and the single tear falling cooled his temper like nothing else would have, and his dark eyes softened. His hand cupped her cheek, and his thumb wiped the tear away.

"You've never been a bother, mistress. You're just an ache in my chest that won't go away. You're the person I want to come to every time I receive another piece of bad news. And you're the woman I'll never call mine because I refuse to be nothing but a substitute for who you really want." His voice was heartbreakingly gentle—a whisper of an apology without taking anything back.

If eyes were the windows to the soul, Roarke's dark chocolate ones were windows into pits of despair. "Kyran loves you in all the ways I've fantasized about. It would have been an honor to have you look at me like you do him." A harsh laugh erupted from his chest. "I fucking hate him for that some days and envy him on others. As much as I care about you and want you to be happy, I'm not sure how much longer I can be your friend."

Rhy sucked in a breath at his admission, and a piece of her heart with his name on it shredded in her chest.

He leaned down and brushed his lips against hers softly in goodbye. "I can't be there for you because it hurts too fucking much to not have my hands and lips on you again when I so desperately need to, and I won't put either of us in a position to compromise your honor again."

He dropped his hand and backed up a step, her eyes haunting him. When he took another, she surprised him by following and wrapping her arms around his middle, laying her head on his chest. "I be deeply sorry I've hurt ye and more grateful for the friendship ye granted me than ye'll ever know. Ye ken where to find me if ever I can be of assistance. I'll not trouble ye again. I understand how painful it is to watch someone ye care about from a distance. Thank ye for the affection ye've given me and the patience."

Roarke wrapped his arms around her automatically as she hugged him. Her words told him she was saying goodbye. Belatedly, he realized he'd broken something vital between them as her body shook in his arms. Tomorrow he would pull this scene out and regret his harsh words. He allowed himself to hold her for a few moments more, knowing this would be the last time. Pressing a soft kiss to the top of her head, he released her while tears streamed down her face, then walked out without another word.

Rhy watched him go, his shoulders slumped as if he carried the weight of the world on his shoulders. Closing the door behind him, she put her back to it and slid down to the floor. With her knees clasped to her chest, she hung her head and cried for the pain she was in, the pain she was causing, and the heartbreak yet to come.

CHAPTER SEVENTY FIVE

I Can Only See so Far

Kenn sauntered into the Rusty Tap and perched on the first available stool. A buxom blond came his way and asked what she could do for him. One glance down her voluptuous cleavage gave him quite a few ideas, but when he met her eyes, he found a woman who was used to being ogled by the men she served and not in the mood for another.

He gave her a shit-eating grin and offered, "My humblest apologies for not remembering where your eyes were, sweetness."

His groveling seemed to be working as a sweet smile slowly crossed her face, and she quirked an eyebrow, waiting for his order. "Whiskey—top-shelf—neat, and a pint of your best ale, please," he requested. Within seconds, she reappeared with his beverages and tossed a basket of roasted nuts in front of him as well. He placed coins on the bar for his tab and held up an additional one worth more than she probably made in the whole week. "This one's for info, should you be interested."

She held out a hand, took the coin, and bit gently on it to assess the metal's worth. Setting it back on the bar, she looked him in the eye. "Depends on who yer asking 'bout, watchya need to know, and how much harm ye intend to do with the knowledge."

He gave her a broad grin, impressed with the integrity she was exhibiting even though the coin was tempting her. "I need to find Fergus Emberz. Have I come to the right establishment?"

She gave him an odd look. "A year ago, I'se a said yes without hesitation. Past month, he's been scarce." She wiped the bar around him with a stained rag, then her eyes glanced over his head. "Seems like this be yer lucky night. He just staggered in."

"Must be yer lucky night too, sweetie." With a smile, he pushed the coin towards her. Her startled expression made his night. Helping the common man was one of his hobbies, and he used his father's treasury as often as possible to help those who truly needed it.

The pretty maid gaped at him as she picked up the coin. "I didn't earn this? Ye don't require a tumble or nothing of the sort?"

"As much as I would've enjoyed your company," he said with a wink, "that's all I need, lass." Fergus settled on the only empty stool at the bar. As luck would have it, it was the one next to Kenn.

"I see's yer slumming it tonight, lad," Ferg said, rubbing his hand over his face in a tired fashion. The barmaid served him his usual glass of whiskey the same way that Kenn asked for it. "Thanks, Syn."

"I spend as much time with the common man as you do, my friend." Kenn said, tossing his drink back and setting it on the bar for another. "She's made for sin isn't she?" he asked Ferg softly as Carsyn returned.

"I seriously doubt that, unless yer talking about the time ye spend in bed with them." Ferg nodded at Carsyn. "This one's on me." He waited until she went for change and then glared at Kenn. "She might be made for it, but ye'll leave her be jest the same. She's a friend."

"Does it really matter if I enjoy being around commoners more than the parasites at court?" Kenn asked, knocking back another whiskey and signaling for a refill and one for his companion. "You got a few minutes to talk in my office?" He tipped his head back, indicating the small table secluded in the back. The table sat in a small alcove with a door for added privacy.

"Yer office?" He cackled at that one. "Like ye've done a day's work in yer entire life." He motioned to the barmaid. "Keep 'em coming, lass."

"Be right over with a bottle, pitcher, and some glasses."

Ferg stood and walked slowly over to where Kenn waited for him. He settled on the bench across from him and waited until their beverages had been provided and the door shut firmly behind Carsyn. Silently, he studied his companion. He and Kenn had stumbled across each other on rare occasions. Usually, they were good nights—the ones he could remember. Kenn had never sought him out intentionally, and Ferg felt the hair rising on his arms. All his senses were on full alert as he sat across from the young man with a reputation for an alternate lifestyle and a short temper.

"Yer in an awfully good mood." Surrounding the room with a cushion of air to prevent eavesdropping, Ferg steepled his fingers against his chin and said, "What do ye need from me, Kenn?"

"You assume I need something, wise one."

"Don't feck with me, lad." His tone was sharp, and Kenn raised an eyebrow at him as he continued. "Ye want something from me, out with it. I've had a long goddamn week, and I not be in the mood fer games."

"Meriel moved the ceremony up by two weeks. This shit show is going down on Sunday."

"Feck me." Ferg rubbed his eyes, thinking of how he was going to break the news to Rhyanna. She would be devastated, of that, there was no doubt. He couldn't even begin to think of what to say.

"Kano offered to take Kyran's place. Apparently, the Princess Elyana is the woman he had a life-changing week with and then lost for nearly a century." Kenn tossed back another shot. "So, she's managing to fuck them both with one stroke. Doesn't seem so random to me. Appears pretty fucking intentional." He ticked off reasons on his fingers. "The old man's health, Kyran's betrothal, Kano in love with the betrothed… this shit show is being orchestrated."

"Aye, I ken ye've got the rights of it there." Ferg traced the condensation on his mug as his brows furrowed over his deep-set gray eyes. "Question be—who the feck is the true grandmaster behind the scenes. This fiasco is a wee bit ambitious for our little Meriel to pull off on her own."

"Is it possible that she possesses more power than we give her credit for?"

"I don't believe so," Ferg mused. "She's a strong air element with a minor fire and water elements competing, making her volatile and dangerous. She's flighty, to begin with, and then ye toss in a bit of unreasonable, unpredictable, and unkind, and you get…"

"A fucking wild card is what you get," Kenn said with resignation. "You and I both know they are the most dangerous combinations of unstable elements."

Ferg pulled out a cigar and lit the foul-smelling thing. "Aye, but what the feck is her motivation? She's not after power or money—already got those. She's after devastation, total destruction…"

"The annihilation of the Tyde family through the men in the line," Kenn said in shock and horror. "She's throwing a one-two punch and hoping we're looking left while she strikes right. Kyran and Kano aren't the only ones she will go after." His voice choked up as he realized his entire family was on the brink of destruction.

"I'd put money on the fact that while the ceremony is going down, she will go after yer mother and yer sister if she knows their whereabouts, and she'll target Kai, too, if an opportunity presents itself."

"Motherfucker! I've got to warn them."

"Sit down, asshole. What makes you think she won't come for ye too?" Ferg held up a hand, wishing for silence. "Hush. Give me a minute to fecking think, already." He motioned to the glasses as he sat back and closed his eyes. "Keep 'em coming."

An hour later, after they killed the first and nearly the second bottle Kenn went for, Ferg leaned forward and said, "This is what we need to do, and when we're finished, there's a lot of people that are going to be mighty pissed at us." Squeezing the bridge of his nose, he mused, "I don't think Rhy will ever forgive me, but the union will go forth on Sunday, and I will be the one performing the pledge ceremony. Kyran will be bound to Elyana. This is the way it must be, and so it shall be."

Kenn sat back with a big "what-the-fuck" crawling across his features as Fergus outlined their plan. That was quickly followed by rage and disbelief, then finally by acceptance. "This is the only way we can keep everyone safe?"

"The only way I can see, lad." Ferg shook his head as he pulled deeply on the lit butt. "I can only see so far, but the visions I keep having are of Kyran and Elyana bound together. It must be done."

"How are we going to tell them?"

"I'll tell Rhy." Fergus closed his eyes in defeat. "Kyran and Kano are on you."

Kenn's eyes were tormented as he looked at the scarred table beneath his hands. The lives of four people were about to be destroyed, and he was going to help make this happen. It didn't matter that it was for the greater good. All that mattered tonight was that he was going to destroy his brothers with this news, and he wasn't sure they would ever forgive him. And he didn't blame them.

CHAPTER SEVENTY-SIX

Let Me hand Ye Me Heart

Fergus stood outside of the apothecary, watching as Rhyanna tidied up the room. The past few weeks had been difficult for her, and she was showing the stress. Dark circles under her eyes told him how tired she was and not just from taking care of King Varan. Too many sleepless nights found the lass of late, and she was struggling to keep her emotions dammed up. He sensed something happened earlier in the week, but she studiously avoided talking to anyone about it.

Even the pixie snarked about it at dinner last night. Danyka bitched that she hadn't talked to her in weeks and was getting pretty damn tired of it. Fergus was afraid she would go looking for Kyran to take her frustrations out on. He talked her out of it and sent her to the bar with instructions to take advantage of his tab for a change. Cheered her up like a pint of ice cream did for other women.

He wondered idly if he would ever understand women. Oh, he had no problem pleasing the ladies in the short term; it was the morning after and the week following that staggered him. One minute they were happy and languorous, and then they were crying and bitchy, or clingy and whiny. He couldn't deal with the emotional shite, so he typically bailed while the getting was still good, never promising anything more than the pleasure they'd just received. He pleased them as well as they pleased him, and that was enough in his opinion. Too many lasses and too little time was his motto—well, it had been once. Lately, he hadn't much interest in the lasses, nor in the tavern crowd that usually amused him. No, finding the wee lasses chained and drowned in a boat off Grindstone last month sent his libido for a long-needed vacation.

Movement in the window brought his attention back to the present. "Focus on the mission in front of ye, ye daft twit," he muttered under his breath as he reached for the doorknob. He opened the door while knocking lightly on the dark wood. "Hey lass," he said with a pitiful attempt at a smile. "Have time for a cuppa?"

Rhy smiled at him, but the attempt fell short of her eyes. He could see the strain of having a visitor in her expression, but there was no help for his visit. They needed to have this conversation.

Shaking her head, she said in a soft, sad voice, "Na, Ferg, I've no time fer a cuppa with ye." She turned away from the kettle and opened a cabinet door behind her. Turning, she produced two frosted shot glasses and a bottle of proper Irish whiskey. "But seeings how ye look like I feel, and I be pretty sure yer here to deliver me some unwelcome news, we'll drink to a shitty day."

"It's a curse, lass, isn't it?" he asked with a quirk of his eyebrow. "Being empathic."

"At times. At others knowing's a godsend." Rhy poured them a healthy shot and downed hers. "So, go on then...hit me with whatever 'tis makes ye look like yer gonna heave all over me clean floor."

"Aww, Rhy, darling, I appreciate ye making this easy on me, I do, but lets me get around to what I need to share in a minute or two." He tossed his back. "How's yer king?"

"He ain't mine any more than his boy be," she said with a pitiful attempt at humor.

"Kyran's still yers, lass. Ye ken as well as I do that being away from ye is killing him."

"On the contrary, I think this weekend the queen's pleasure will be killing him."

"Whatcya going on about?" he asked, refilling his shot glass. He moved the bottle to the far side of him so that she didn't start something she'd likely regret later. Whiskey wasn't always Rhy's friend, no matter how much she liked to down the amber liquid.

Glaring at him, she got up and brought back a bottle of bourbon. Pouring herself another one of less volatile emotions, she looked at the bottle as she picked at the paper label, avoiding his probing eyes.

"He's fulfilling his part of a contract agreed to so that I was allowed to leave the island."

"The feck he is," Fergus fumed. Rhy looked at him with large eyes. "That bitch promised to keep her hands off him."

He stood quickly, knocking his chair over in the process. "Meriel made an agreement with me, and Kyran was freed of his contract. Don't ye worry about anything, Rhy darling. I will take care of this."

"Not sure that's possible, but what did ye want to speak with me about?" Rhy asked, confused by his outburst.

Fergus seemed to diminish once again as he reclaimed his seat and turned towards her. Taking her calloused hands in his enormous ones, he stroked his thumb over the back, trying to find the words.

"I can protect him from Meriel, lass," Fergus said in a tight voice. His voice caught as he continued, "But I canna prevent the ceremony from happening this Sunday. I've no way to stop this. Their union must happen, and that's not the worst of my news."

Rhy's eyes filled, and her emerald orbs shimmered as her face blanched. Her voice wobbled as she asked, "How could it possibly be any worse, Ferg?" She blinked, and twin trails ran down her cheeks as her pain overflowed like a too-full glass of water.

Fergus hated himself for what he was about to say, but there was no way around the truth. "Yer presence is required as a witness. The High Court requires yer attendance to be sure that there is no confusion as to where his loyalties lie, and that's not with ye, lass."

"The High Court, my ass. We ken who wants me in attendance. Meriel wants to rub in the fact that she won, Ferg. This whole charade is to put the Tyde men in their place and to repay the fact that I nearly killed her. My penance is to watch the man I love pledge himself to another."

The trails were still streaming as she pushed herself back from the table. She reached up and unhooked the gold chain holding the large teardrop emerald Kyran gave her. She held the pendant in her palm, looking at the stone through bleary eyes before glancing at Ferg. "Here, let me hand ye me heart." She held out the necklace. "Return this to him for me. I may have to attend, but I don't have to speak to him. This symbolized a future that doesn't exist anymore. Tell him my heart will always belong to him, but I can no longer pretend we have hope. His new wife deserves his full adoration."

A lump formed and stuck in Fergus's throat as Rhy picked up the bourbon and turned for the clinic door.

"Lock up for me, will ye?" she asked over her shoulder. "I'm gonna sit outside with my pain for a while. Time's come we get to know one another better." Her voice trailed off as she opened and shut the door so softly one wouldn't have known she passed through at all.

Ferg held the pendant so tightly in his hand that he feared he might break the beautiful piece. Swiping his hands over his eyes, he tried to curb his wild emotions. This was one of the hardest conversations he'd ever experienced, and his heart broke for her.

Rhy waited forever for Kyran to arrive in her life, allowed herself to love him, and now he needed her to allow herself to watch him pledge his life to another. He slammed his fist down on the table in frustration. There was no other way he could see to make this happen. Her pain was the only way through this mess, and he fecking hated himself for causing her anguish. He only prayed when it was all said and done that she didn't hate him forever, too.

CHAPTER SEVENTY-SEVEN

At Least I Have Tonight

Kano staggered out of Meriel's chamber like a man on death row. He shouldn't be surprised by the woman's lack of empathy, but still, she managed to shatter him. Shaking with fury, he headed for the closest exit, needing to be away from this place as soon as he could before he tried to kill her and ended up getting them all killed in the process.

He rounded the corner and nearly knocked Kenn to the ground. Kenn steadied him, and judging by the look on his face, he was already aware of how totally fucked Kano was.

"I need to talk to you, little brother," he said in an unusually sober and somber manner.

"Have you and Fergus come up with anything yet?" Kano asked hopefully.

"No, bro. As far as the mage can 'see,' this has to go down this way. There is no alternative for it. The fates, gods, or whomever you wanna fucking blame for this shit show are unhappy with the two of you at the moment because no one seems to be ready to step up and help you out of this cluster fuck."

Kano slammed open the door leading outside with a vicious push. How the fuck was he supposed to go back and tell Elyana that he was trading her future for his family's safety? Looking at Kenn for an answer, he asked, "How do I tell her that she has to suck it up and bed my brother for the rest of her life?"

Kenn winced as Kano ranted. "I don't know, bro, how you're going to tell her. Have you thought of running away with her? No princess—no ceremony."

"I've just left Meriel. I have thirty-six hours to return Elyana to Meriel's custody or…" he couldn't say the words.

Kenn knew the news had to be bad for Kano to be speechless. "Or what?" he asked, needing to comprehend what they were up against. Ferg's plan might completely end up in the shitter, depending on Meriel's move. He loved games and maneuvering people in ways they didn't anticipate, but the see-you-next-Tuesday was blocking them at every fucking exit, and he needed to understand how bad this threat was. He watched Kano rubbing the shaved sides of his head with both hands. A soothing motion when he was agitated, he was rubbing harder now as if to keep his brains inside or his temper from exploding.

His tormented eyes locked on Kenn's. "She stole a fucking hellhound pup, Kenn. Who the fuck does that?" Pacing a hole in the stone path, he moved exactly six steps one way and six back the other—repeatedly.

"And…that affects you how?" Kenn fought off the urge to shake Kano and get him to hurry up the story so he'd stop piecemealing him clues.

"The pup's clan are surrounding our favorite Caribbean hideaway where I've stashed Elyana."

"Fuck me."

"Twice," Kano managed to reply. "If Elyana is not returned by tomorrow night, they will destroy everything and everyone on our island. 'Fluffy' is her collateral."

Swearing creatively, Kenn wanted to punch something. He clasped Kano's neck and pulled him towards him. Hugging his brother, he said, "We'll find a way to fix this. Just bring her back tomorrow night, and we'll fucking figure something out." Kano leaned his head against his shoulder for a second. It was the only sign of weakness Kenn had ever seen from him. Kano came into this world a scrapper, and he clawed and fought his way through life from day fucking one. Defeated wasn't a good look on him. "I need to reconvene with Fergus. I'll be back tomorrow when you return. This ain't fucking over yet, little brother. You have my word, it ain't a done deal yet."

Kano gave a rueful grunt, and his eyes when he glanced at Kenn were pools of misery. "At least I have tonight with her." A cynical laugh erupted from him. "You know what the worst part is?"

"Not seeing any part that doesn't appear pretty fucking bad right now," Kenn said, rubbing a large hand over his face.

"If it were anyone else but the two of them, I could still be with her. I've been with my share of attached females—not saying I'm proud of my past behavior, but I've been there." He closed his eyes and took a deep breath. "Kyran can be an uptight asshole, but he's got fucking morals, and that would never work, for him or for me. As much as I can't stand him sometimes, I couldn't do that to him." The cynical laugh returned. "And, Elyana, well, she's got him beat in spades. She wouldn't let me do any more than kiss her last night because she feels committed by this fucking betrothal—she's never even met him, and she wouldn't even consider sleeping with me. That woman is better than any of us. She has a heart of gold and a mind that is unfucking believable. Can you imagine me with a fucking scholar?" He laughed loudly at the implication. "But that's who I fell for. A moral scholar who will be officially bedding my brother two days from now." He turned away. "I'm not dissing you, brother, but I am not wasting another minute away from her. The next thirty-six hours need to last me a lifetime." He walked away with a muttered, "Fuck me."

Kenn said nothing because, really, what was there left to say? He was right; they were all fucked because when this was over and Kano lost her, he would go off the rails, and may the Mother help them when he did. Kenn feared he would lose both of his siblings, one to misery and the other to just plain giving up.

Turning around, he headed back inside, needing to ruin Kyran's night as well and fucking hating himself for being the messenger from hell. As he opened the door, Kano sent him a message.

"Forgot to mention, the hag has a fucking powerful crystal ball. Make sure whatever you're scheming with Fergus is well protected before you do it because she never should have been able to find that island, and she showed it to me with the hellhounds circling like fucking sharks in the outer dimensions. And she seems to be immune from hellhound drool."

Kenn slammed the fucking door, then turned and punched the wall to his right repeatedly, leaving a massive gaping hole adorning the wallpaper. His knuckles streaming, he headed for Kyran, needing this over so that he could see Ferg, find a bottle, and if he was lucky, someone willing to let him play with them tonight. He needed to take the edge off before he went nuclear and lost his shit because if he did, it would make Kano's rage seem like a toddler's temper tantrum.

CHAPTER SEVENTY-EIGHT

Keep Yer Hands to Yerself

Fergus left Rhy to her pain and headed back to his office. Grabbing a quill, he ripped a piece of paper from the nearby sheaf and drafted a letter.

Queen Meriel,

Please accept me apologies for short notice on my unannounced arrival, but I couldn't stay away. I am commandeering the two suites on either side of Kyran's for Heart Island's use while at court. Make them ready for our arrival within the hour.

I appreciate your thoughtfulness in keeping Kyran bound, but under me supervision, cuffs will not be necessary. Remove them immediately. I will see that he stays in his quarters until the ceremony.

It's been brought to me attention that yer weekend's entertainment revolves around Kyran Tyde. Let me remind ye that our agreement was fer ye to leave Kyran and his siblings be—until after the ceremony. Should any harm come to him—even if the attempt is at pleasure—I shall bring the full force of our arrangement to bear. If ye take the time to read the fine print, ye'll remember the clause reminding ye to keep yer hands to yerself until after the treaty ye instigated has been fulfilled.

Should ye wish to ignore our treaty, I shall bring the full force of the Fire Clan against ye. Ye might feel like ye control our king with yer extortion schemes, but do not forget that I'm the strongest Fire Mage to walk the earth in hundreds of years, and I will destroy the throne ye sit on, and ye with it, should ye ignore me warning.

This is yer final warning—find yer pleasure with someone else and leave the Tyde boys alone.

I look forward to joining ye this evening, Yer Majesty."

Have a pleasant evening.

Fergus Emberz
Warden of the Elemental High Court
High Mage of the Great Lakes Fire Clan
Fire Mage to Heart Island Sanctuary
Yer worst fecking nightmare should ye try me

Sealing the letter with wax, he sat back and poured himself a drink. Taking a big swallow, he reached out telepathically. *"Jamey?"*

"What?" came Jameson's surly reply.

"I need ye to come with me to the Court of Tears."

"When?"

"Right fecking now! Why? Am I interrupting something?"

"Nada. Jest tying on a good one. Happy for the distraction."

"Move yer ass. Pack enough for the night and meet me at Rhy's shoppe."

"On, my way."

Fergus hot-footed it down the stairs. He exited the building and walked towards the apothecary. Shifting nervously while waiting for Jamey, he wondered if his thinly veiled threat would be enough to keep the woman's hands from wandering.

"Maddy."

"Ferg?"

"I need to head back to the Court of Tears. Did ye receive a formal notification?"

"I did. The ceremony has been moved up to Sunday."

"Aye, I want to return to court and make sure Meriel behaves herself over the weekend, and I want to take Rhy and Jamey with me if it's possible. She must be present on Sunday. I want to try and give them some time alone prior to then."

"Won't that make it harder for her in the long run?"

"I'm not sure anything can make it harder. I'm jest having a strong pull to take her with me. I need to follow through on this."

"Do it. We'll all be there on Sunday for the ceremony."

"Aye, ye all need to be. It's imperative."

"Ferg…"

"What is it, Maddy?"

"Be careful with her. I don't know how much more she can take."

"I ken how close she be to her breaking point. Tis why I'm doing this."

"Good luck on all fronts."

"Thanks, love. Gonna need it."

Jameson arrived moments behind him. "What do you need me to do?"

Fergus handed him the letter. "Head to the Court of Tears. Make sure to hand deliver it immediately to the queen." He clamped a hand on Jamey's shoulder. "Thank ye for yer help. Rooms should be prepared next to Kyran's suite. We'll be right behind ye."

"I'd do anything to help her, Ferg. You know that."

"I do. We all would. Jest pray we can make this right, lad." Ferg gave him a grin. "Try not to get into any trouble til I get there. We'll be right behind ye."

Walking around the perimeter of the building, he found Rhy sitting in a rocking chair, clasping the bottle of bourbon tightly by the neck as she stared straight ahead. The bottle was still almost full, and he said a quick prayer of relief that she hadn't overindulged while he was gone.

Kneeling in front of her, he took the bottle from her hands. "Rhy, love. I needs be talking to ye about something."

She looked at him, confused for a moment. "I thought ye left, Ferg," she said in a whisper.

"Aye, darling, I did." He took her hands in his. The cold from them leached into him. Briskly rubbing her arms, he spoke. "I've sent a warning to Meriel to keep her grubby lil hands from Kyran."

Her head popped up, and she stared at him in shock. "Do ye think she'll listen?"

"Not at all, lass," he said in disgust. "So, we're going to court tonight. Yer going to pull yerself together and gather a few things. Jameson will be joining us. Ye will have our protection this time, Rhy."

"Why do we have to leave so soon? Sunday is going to come fast enough. I can't stand to have to pretend to be happy for that long."

"I don't want ye to pretend, Rhy." He reached up and cupped her cheek as he looked deeply into her eyes. "Would ye like to have some time alone with Kyran?" he asked softly."

Her eyes lit up at the opportunity. "Aye, I would, more than ye can imagine."

"Sunday will still come, Rhy," Fergus said in the most serious voice she'd ever heard him use. "Will this make it harder?"

She shook her head vehemently. "I would take the chance to say goodbye privately even knowing how difficult it will be for both of us. I need to see him, Ferg. I just didn't trust her enough to go by meself."

"Well, go gather yer things, lass, and we'll head off. Jamey's gone ahead."

He started to stand, but Rhy held tightly to his hand and pulled him back down.

"I don't ken what ye got up yer sleeve, Ferg, but I trust ye with it. Even if it ends up breaking me heart, I trust ye did yer best." She leaned forward and framed his face. "Thank ye." She placed a chaste kiss on his lips, then threw her arms around him quickly.

Fergus reached up and pinched the bridge of his nose to stop his eyes from watering as he held her. He hoped he would be able to make this work. If his plan backfired, he was going to devastate her, and he didn't think he could stand to witness the look of betrayal on her face if he did. He wondered how much help he might get from King Varan should he need it.

"Where's Varan?" he asked as she extricated herself from his embrace.

"He and Tristan left this morning." She started moving towards the castle. "I don't know when or if he'll be back here."

"Let's hope the bastard has an ace up his sleeve. We're going to need it."

"Aye, by the Mother's grace, may he come up with something to remove the evil residing on his throne."

"May she honor us with some help," Ferg said, wondering if the Earth Mother listened to them at all. His communion with the gods had been sketchy at best lately. He was angry with them for some of the things he sensed ahead on the timeline for the people he cared about.

Fergus was supposed to be an observer for the Gods, but these were his people, his family, and he was damn sure not going to sit back and watch them be destroyed if he could do anything to help or change the outcome. A time would come when a price would be due for his disobedience, and he would pay the price. Until then, he was gonna do his best to help the underdogs. Any price would be worth saving them the pain he knew was looming in their future.

CHAPTER SEVENTY-NINE

Sometimes It Wears My Face

Kenn stopped in the parlor and grabbed a bottle of whiskey and a glass. He'd already destroyed one of his brothers tonight, and he needed something before he went and devastated the other. Pouring three fingers, he tossed it back neat and let the burn roll through him, slowly filling his belly with heat and the promise of numbness to come. This was the first drink he'd had today, and, for fuck's sake, it was already dark out.

Refilling it, he repeated the sequence until the bottle was half empty, but his nerves were rock steady. Leaving the mess on the table, he headed off to find Kyran, which, considering he was limited to his suite, shouldn't be that hard to do.

He moved quickly, traversing the maze of corridors until nearly running into Satish at the intersection of hallways.

"Watch where the fuck you're going!" the cocky little guard said, thrusting out his chest as if he were any match for Kenn. Lacking a foot in height and about a hundred pounds, the scrawny little shit had balls, if nothing else.

Kenn shouldered him aside and sneered, "I might say the same, you ass-kissing little fucker." Something hit his back hard as he passed the man, and Kenn smiled, hoping he would throw a punch. Pain was something he needed after this fucking day, and he honestly didn't care if it was his own or someone else's.

Kenn turned and whatever Satish saw on his face made him back down. He pointed towards the ground at a set of cast iron keys on the floor.

"Unlock your brother. No chance of escaping now that your mother's at risk, is there?"

The evil glint in his eyes made Kenn want to wipe the floor with him for exalting in the fact that their mother's safety was at stake, but Kyran had been trapped for days now in that room and deserved to have what little freedom he was able to obtain before his upcoming entrapment ceremony.

Kenn gave Satish a smile that made his balls shrink up. "One day, you and me," he pointed at the man and back to himself, "we're going to meet, and there will be a reckoning for everything you've enjoyed doing to my family." The smile took on an evil edge. "I can promise you, only one of us will be walking away from that confrontation. "Hell isn't in the other world, mother fucker. It walks in the daylight, and sometimes…" he stepped into the other man's space, "sometimes, it wears my face." Turning to leave, he grinned, knowing the little man wouldn't be able to keep his mouth shut.

"And someday before then, someone might put you down, like the rabid dog you are."

Satish never saw it coming. For a big man, Kenn moved like lightning, and the little man was eating the carpet and spitting teeth moments later. When he picked himself up, neither Kenn nor the keys were anywhere to be found. "I'll kill that fucker, if it's the last thing I do," he growled as he walked away, holding his jaw. He needed booze, ice, and maybe the surgeon—in that order.

Kenn rounded the corner and waited for the man to come at his back. Surprisingly, he didn't. Hmm, maybe he knocked some sense into him after all. A few more turns, and he reached the family's wing. He knocked on Kyran's door and listened for permission to enter, not that Kyran could've stopped him, being tied up, but ye know, manners and all. Kenn was nothing if not polite—yeah, right—NOT. He was through the door before he finished knocking, glad that his older brother wasn't doing something inappropriate, although being chained to a chair might be considered inappropriate to some.

"I always knew you'd look good in chains, brother. Decide to join me on the dark side?"

"Fuck off," Kyran sneered at him with a dark look. "You just come to gloat?"

"Nope. Actually, came to release your sorry ass, but if that's how you're gonna be…forget it." He twirled the ring of keys on his finger and turned back to the door. His fingers had just reached the knob when Kyran's growled at him.

"Don't you dare leave me here like this, asshole." He glared at Kenn, who stared back patiently until he mumbled an angry, 'Please."

"Well, if you're gonna be a dick about it," he strode to Kyran and tossed the keys on his lap, " you can figure it out for yourself."

"Not possible. C'mon man, release me."

Feeling sorry for him, Kenn fumbled with the keys as he squatted, trying to reach the lock.

"Do you have the right fucking keys?" Kyran snarled impatiently.

"How the fuck do I know? You typically see me with a ring of keys outside of my dungeon?" His eyes jumped to Kyran's waiting for the next snarky comment. Wisely his brother kept his mouth shut.

Kenn finally managed to release his hands. He grabbed Kyran's arm, looking at the bruises and cuts on his wrist. "What did she do to you?"

Drawing in a deep breath, he pulled in the smell of the oils Bresia had used on him. His eyes flared as he looked up at Kyran, but he didn't say a word, recognizing the silent plea in his brother's gaze. Knees popping, he stood and went to work on releasing the collar around his neck.

"Alls you had to do was ask nicely." Kenn was enjoying the shit out of ribbing him, trying to lighten things up. Kyran was stuck in a really shitty situation, and a little humor couldn't hurt the day, considering the news he was about to deliver.

Kyran shook his arms as the blood rushed through them, causing pins and needles to run from his shoulders to his fingertips. Wincing he said, "I need a shower and then I need to get the hell off this island and see Rhyanna."

"Well, now, that's going to be a little trickier," Kenn said as he took a seat in one of the froufrou chairs decorating his room.

"I'm still a fucking prisoner?"

Kyran's fists clenched like he was gonna punch something, and Kenn was glad he was sitting and out of the way. Kyran was one of the few who could best him. Kai was one of the others but only due to sheer size, not skill.

"Sadly, brother, yes, you are still trapped into the betrothal. I spoke with Fergus, looking for some magical loophole, charm, or fucking miracle, but it's no use. Fucker says as far as he can 'see,' it goes through. You and Elyana pledged-hitched-trapped for life with a stranger—however you want to look at it, it's gonna happen." He ran a hand through his hair and glanced at his brother with compassion. "I'm truly sorry, Kyran. I wish I had better news."

Kyran held his head in his hands, utterly defeated. How had this become his future? How would he stomach someone else in his bed? He looked up at his brother and asked forlornly, "How the fuck am I supposed to do this, Kenn? They still hold the archaic practice of consummation witnesses for betrothal contracts that aren't a love match to prevent annulments. I must have sex with a woman who doesn't want me any more than I want her for the first time with someone ogling us." He shook his head vehemently. "I can't go through with this. I love Rhyanna. She's it for me. I don't think I can get it up for anyone else."

Kenn cleared his throat, hating to be the bearer of more bad news. "Well, there's something else, Kyran, that I need to mention. You've been released from your vanilla bondage because she has a failsafe. She knows where mom and Klaree are, and she's threatening them."

Kyran was utterly defeated as he stared at his brother. Standing, he shuffled by Kenn, looking like he'd aged in the last ten minutes. "Excuse me, I need to be alone right now."

Kenn said nothing as he witnessed the dejected way that Kyran trudged into the bathroom. When he heard him become violently ill, he let himself out, knowing there was nothing left to say. Might not be anything to say, but he was damn sure going to find out what he could do to make this right before time ran out.

CHAPTER EIGHTY

Take Me Away…

Kano stepped back into the blinding sun and tropical heat, yet the sultry air did nothing to warm the ice forming around his heart. How the fuck was he supposed to do this? How the fuck was he supposed to hand Elyana over to Kyran and wish them well? There was no fucking way he could do this and maintain his sanity. Dark clouds came in quickly, shielding him from the glare, and he was so distracted with the mess he was in that he didn't sense his mother's approach.

Placing a hand on his arm, she asked in a voice laced with sorrow, "I take it things didn't go the way you had planned?"

"No. They didn't. I have thirty-six hours to return Elyana, or all hell breaks loose."

"You are welcome to stay here as long as you want. I'm protected here."

The torment in his eyes explained everything he didn't voice. "She dared to threaten me in this place?"

"Not just you, mama. Everyone in this place is at risk if I don't do what she wants."

"She's bluffing."

"I wish she were." He gave a harsh sound, which might have been an attempt at a chuckle, but it came out all wrong. "She knows Klaree returns tomorrow and how many people live here." He hung his head. "This isn't an idle threat. She showed me the island. Your exile is no longer safe." His breath hitched. "I'm sorry I brought this to your door. It wasn't fair to you."

"Enough!" his mother snapped, sounding like a queen once again. "This has nothing to do with you being here. I have been living on borrowed time here, and it's time I realize that I can't hide forever." She stepped into his arms, hugging him tightly. He rested his head on her shoulder as he struggled with the hand fate had dealt him. She stroked his head, making soothing sounds. "I know it doesn't appear that there is a light in the darkness, but I promise you I will do what I can to help change the course she has set for both you and Kyran."

He glanced at her with little hope in his eyes. The ceremony has been moved up. It's Sunday."

"Sweet Mother," she gasped. "Go, now. Elyana is waiting for you. Enjoy the time you have left. Let me know if you need anything." She hugged him tightly and kissed his cheek before releasing him.

He walked slowly back to the bungalow he shared with Elyana and stood on the beach, watching her standing in the water. She wore a flowing skirt his mother must have provided and one of the shirts he had left on his last visit. It was partially buttoned, and the tails tied under her breasts, leaving her abdomen showing. She seemed so happy walking along the shoreline as she gathered shells. Turning towards him, she shaded her eyes from the sun and waved at him with a wide smile.

Slowly, she made her way back to him, the smile dimming as she came closer. She stopped in front of him, staring into his eyes and saying nothing. He reached out and brushed a stray piece of hair the wind kept blowing across her face. His thumb caressed her as he tried unsuccessfully to tuck it behind her ear.

"Good luck," she said. "It's always unruly."

"Stands to reason, you're not exactly the easiest woman to tame," he said with a sad smile.

"You want to tame me?" She quirked an eyebrow at him in question.

"No, baby. I like you just the way you are. Wouldn't change a thing."

"Liar."

"Want to watch the sunset?"

"What are my other options?" She sounded nervous, and he wondered if she was afraid to be alone with him.

Kano closed the distance between them and looked down into her beautiful face. He threaded his hand into her hair and tipped her head up. "Come inside with me."

"Tell me what happened today first."

Hating to disappoint her, he shook his head. "I failed. I failed to gain your freedom, and I failed to protect my family. If I don't return with you Sunday morning, she will rain down hell on this island. My mother and my sister, friends I've known since I was a boy…"

"Shhhh," she said, moving into him, wrapping her arms around his middle, and laying her head against his chest. "Just hold me for a minute."

Kano wrapped his arms around her, gathering her tightly to him. He kissed the top of her head, and she sighed against him. They stood that way until he whispered, "You won't want to miss the sunset." She turned away from him, and he circled her waist with his hands, stroking the exposed skin softly as she leaned back against him.

Kano rested his chin on her head, and they enjoyed the yellow and orange hues shifting to pinks and purples as the light reflected off the clouds. As day said good night in pastels, night made way in rich tones of midnight blue and velvet black with pinpricks of light shining down on them. With the crash of the waves and the cool night air surrounding them, they stayed there, lost in the beauty of it all.

Elyana shivered in his arms, so he hugged her tighter and rubbed his hands up and down her arms to warm her.

"Do you want me to get you a blanket?" he asked.

Turning, she linked her fingers in his and tugged him back up the beach to the small hut. As he closed the door behind them, she turned towards him. Somberly, while looking him in the eye, she untied the shirt bound beneath her breasts, then released the buttons keeping it together.

Kyran stood there in a trance, watching her. He didn't say a word, not wanting to break the spell he was under. She pulled the shirt over her shoulders, letting the fabric drop to the ground. Her breath was coming quickly, and her chest was flushed. He was afraid she might have another panic attack as she reached for the tie on her skirt.

His hand reached out and clamped on her wrist, stopping her. "You don't have to do this, Elyana, if you don't want to. I'm happy just to be here with you."

Her hands continued to the tie on her skirt. With sure movements, she pulled the strings and let the material fall to the floor. Stepping forward, she reached for his shirt and pulled it from his breeches, divesting him of the garment. She reached for the tie on his breeches, but before she could release his throbbing cock, he was kissing her fiercely, his hands cupping her face.

"What do you want from me?" he asked in a hoarse voice. "Tell me what you need from me," he begged. "I promise, I won't take more than you are willing to give."

"I want you to take me away, Kano. Take me away from the future I have no control over, with a man I don't know. Take me away from the hurt and hate I feel towards my father for doing this to me. Take me away from the pain of finding you again, only to lose you days later. Please make me feel something other than this ache inside that is threatening to engulf me. Take me away from it all."

The second she finished speaking, his lips were on hers as his hands stroked her back. Reaching lower, he grabbed her ass and lifted her slightly against him, leaving no doubt to what her request was doing to him. Still, he kissed her, taking his time, gently distracting her with his lips.

Elyana gasped as he kicked off his breeches and backed her against one of the narrow bedposts.

"Put your hands around it, and don't let go," he ordered. He dropped to his knees in front of her and rubbed his face right above her red curls, scenting how much she wanted him. He pulled her slightly forward and widened her stance so that she was leaning back against the post. His hands were firm as they stroked up the inside of her thighs. With one hand, he supported her ass while he used the thumb of the other to trace a path between her lips, checking to see if she was ready for him.

She arched her back as he found her soaked and gently buried his thumb in her pussy, circling it around and thrusting gently. Her eyes were locked on his as he worked her slowly, letting her hips meet his thrusts. Removing his thumb, he used it to spread moisture around her clit. His circles were large, teasing her sensitive body while evading the sensitive nub.

Elyana moaned as he toyed with her. She remembered how well he played her body, eliciting the most pleasure he could before taking any for himself. She moved her hips forward, trying to force him to at least graze her throbbing skin, but he gave her a smile, backing off before she came too close.

"Hang on, baby doll, don't let go." It was the only warning he gave her before he slung her legs over his shoulder and sucked her clit into his mouth. The suction mixed with strokes from his tongue made her scream his name. Just as she started to come back down, he started again. He lapped at the juices flowing from her body, knowing she was ready for him now.

"Please, Kano. I can't hold on much longer." Her arms were shaking to match the tremors moving through the rest of her body.

"Let go, baby. I've got you." He gently pulled her legs around his waist as he lowered her to his lap. Her arms draped limply over him as she relaxed against him.

After catching her breath, she turned her face up to kiss him, catching the taste of her pleasure on his tongue and making her writhe against him once more. "I need you inside of me."

He groaned in relief. Still on his knees, he raised her high enough to put her legs around his hips. Grasping her hips tightly, he slid her over the length of him, moaning at the slick sensation of her gliding against his sensitive skin. On the next pass, he tipped his hips, and the head of his cock entered her. She paused for a moment with her head on his chest, adapting to his size.

"Baby, it's your turn to take me away."

When she stared up at him with a brow lifted, he squeezed her ass cheeks, pulling her against him and lifting her up until he nearly exited her body.

"I want to watch you use my body to make us come. Take me away from thoughts of a life without you. I want you to be in total control. Set the pace and rhythm you need and take me away."

"But what about you?" she asked, knowing from past experience that he was always in control when they were together.

He chuckled darkly, capturing her lips once again. "There's nothing you're going to do that I won't enjoy." He moved her slightly again as he whispered against her lips, "Make love to me, Elyana."

She loved the way he said her name, drawing out the syllables and making it sound exotic. This was the first time he'd called what they had done in the Alps making love. Her inexperience led her to believe that's what it was, but since then, she'd second-guessed their encounter so many times; she had been certain it had meant little to him. When he found her again, she realized how wrong she had been.

His hands held her poised over his cock. She captured his face in her hands, and as she kissed him, she slid down slowly, taking every inch he had to offer deep within her. Her head kicked back, and she gasped as he found the end of her. With a purr of pure pleasure, she took a moment to enjoy the way he filled her. It had been so long for her; she had nearly forgotten how wonderful he felt inside of her. Biting her lip, she tipped her head back and found his arms surrounding her, giving her something to lean against.

"Oh, fuck, baby," Kano said against her throat as she engulfed him in her heat. He found himself shaking from the pleasure and the restraint it was taking to let her take the lead. He didn't know why the hell he had offered, but holy fuck was it hot. The way she leaned back over his arms forced his cock deeper into her. The long strands of her hair were tickling his thighs, driving him fucking crazy with the erotic tease. Her torso was arched, giving him a view of the beautiful line of her neck on display. He leaned forward and brushed his lips over the length of it, sucking gently, leaving his mark on her.

Eyes closed, she settled there for a moment with a flush rising through her body as her inner muscles squeezed him tightly, making him moan. Instead of bobbing up and down on him, he felt her pelvis shift ever so slightly back, and he groaned at the sensation it produced. How did she fucking know what that would do to him?

"Oh," she whispered as her eyes popped open and locked on him in surprise. Moving slowly again, she rotated her hips and gasped as the head of his cock bumped the sensitive spot on the upper wall of her channel. "Yes, right there…" she whimpered as she continued her erotic dance on his cock. She reached up and massaged her breasts, pinching her nipples.

"Baby, allow me," Kano said as he bent down and took the right peak into his mouth, needing the distraction so that he didn't come right then and there. This was already the most erotic thing he had ever done, and he wasn't sure if he would survive, giving her control.

Elyana threaded her fingers through the short hair on top of his head and gasped at the sensations he was causing with his mouth. Her subtle movements picked up speed, although she still held him deeply inside of her, not wanting this to be over too soon.

Kano wrapped his hands around her back, holding her tightly to him. A thin sheen of perspiration covered them. Her eyes were partially shut as she moaned, and her walls started rippling around him as an orgasm rolled through her.

"You're so fucking beautiful, Elyana. Eyes on me baby while you come, I want to see it all."

His words turned her on as much as his body did, and her hips started bucking rapidly within his arms as a much more powerful climax exploded from deep within. She sobbed with pleasure as every nerve ending in her body lit up with an intensity she had never experienced. The first one had been soft and sweet, but this one was nearly overpowering in its intensity, and as it detonated within, it set off ripples of aftershocks that triggered multiple orgasms for her.

Kano moaned as she came around him, soaking him in her pleasure and triggering his own to follow. As she continued coming, he held on for the ride as his oversensitive cock followed suit, flooding him with wave after wave of bliss.

They rocked together gently as they both came down from their sexual high, gasping and trembling in each other's arms.

When they could finally breathe, she reached up and pushed an unruly lock of his hair off his forehead. "Is it always like that for you?"

"Never." His lips found hers. "I've never known anything like you, Elyana." He took her hand and placed it over his heart. "You need to know that you claimed a part of me when we first met, and now," he cleared his throat, "this belongs to you and only you. No one else will ever have a piece of me. You take my heart with you when you leave tomorrow."

As his words sank in and she witnessed the anguish crossing his face, the tears came unbidden. She wrapped herself around him, this time with her head tucked in his neck, sobbing out her grief for what they were losing.

431

Kano held her, rubbing her back and whispering sweet words while he could. He stroked her hair as his eyes burned and his chest tightened.

His legs were numb, but he managed to make them work as he stood with her and made his way unsteadily to the bed. He lost count of the number of times and ways that they made love, but when dawn came and she drifted off sprawled over his torso, he stared sightlessly at the ceiling as his hand stroked her hair. Unable to sleep, afraid he would miss a minute of the magic that was Elyana, he memorized every feature, every freckle, every lash resting on her cheek. He'd need every piece of her that he could remember to survive the rest of his life without her.

CHAPTER EIGHTY-ONE

Love Me

Fergus whistled as Rhy walked towards him. She had taken the time to change and fix her hair. A low-cut dress, the color of her emerald eyes, clung to her curves, and Ferg knew she must have used a glamour to reduce the puffiness around her eyes. "Ye look stunning, love."

Rhy blushed and looked away. "Jest didn't want to look like I'd been crying all day."

"Ye succeeded," he said in a sincere voice. He extended an arm to her. "Shall we, Mistress Rhyanna?"

"We most definitely shall," she said as she placed her hand on his arm and let him lead her to the portal.

"When we exit, lass, let me do all the talking."

"Of course. Ye do it so well."

He smiled at her, pleased that she found a little humor in the situation.

The trip through the portal took only seconds, and they were stepping out onto the drawbridge. They crossed and were met on the other side by the queen's guards—different ones than she'd encountered on her first visit.

Fergus embellished their reason for visiting, and Rhy knew the moment he lightly compelled the poor sods to let them pass. Thankfully, they made their way through the corridors without meeting anyone else. Ferg stopped in front of a large set of double doors, then turned to her.

"These are Kyran's rooms. He has been confined here for the past few days." He patted the hand still resting on his arm. "Are ye ready to see him na, lass, or would you like to go to our rooms?"

433

Her hand tightened on his arm. She looked up at him as uncertainty made a brief appearance. "Am I doing the right thing by being here?"

"Do ye need to see him, lass?"

"I do, Ferg."

"Then it's the right thing. Do ye want me to stay for a few moments with ye?"

"Nye." She gave him a wobbly smile. "I think I can manage from here."

Ferg leaned down and kissed her forehead. "I ken ye'll do jest fine, lass. Now, go see yer man." Before she thought about it any further, he reached out and knocked on the door firmly. "I'm right next door, love, if ye need me."

Kyran's voice came through the door with a muffled, "Come in."

Rhy nodded, then turned the knob and walked in. She closed it behind her as Kyran's voice came from the bathroom.

"Leave the tray on the table, please."

Rhy said nothing as she waited for him to exit. She twisted her hands anxiously, suddenly doubting her decision to appear in his room. He walked from the bath wearing nothing but black silk lounge pants. Towel drying his hair, he didn't notice her at first. He walked towards the small table, obviously looking for his meal. When he didn't find it, he turned towards her and stopped abruptly as if he'd been turned to stone.

Rhy stood there self-consciously, not realizing she was holding her breath. The sight of him without his shirt had her fingers itching to touch him. Water still clung to him in places, dripping from the ends of his hair. As she saw a drop roll down his chest, she wanted to trace the path it left with her tongue. She licked her lips as she imagined it.

Kyran stood there, barely able to breathe, convinced that Meriel had drugged him because he knew he was hallucinating. The woman behind every one of his hopes, dreams, and gods yes, his fantasies, had magically appeared in his bedroom. As he stood there, stunned stupid, his eyes traveled hungrily over her face, then down her gorgeous body. As he perused her, he noticed she was wringing her hands, and somehow, that gesture snapped him out of his fugue state.

"What are you doing here, my lady?" he asked, his voice a whisper of disbelief.

"Did I make a mistake in coming?" she asked, her brow furrowing as she took a step back towards the door.

"It's still not safe for you here."

Rhy gave him a tremulous smile then as she said, "Ferg and Jamey are with me. I be safe. I didn't come alone."

He floundered, not knowing what to do with her now that she was here. "How long do we have?"

"Until yer ceremony on Sunday," she said in a sad voice.

"Is that enough for you, my lady?" His voice was as tormented as hers.

"I'll gratefully take whatever time I've been granted with ye, Kyran."

Those words were all he needed to hear. He tossed the towel to the side and stalked towards her. His eyes bore into hers, and the passion glowing in her sultry gaze made his cock swell. As he reached her, his hands went to her ass, and he lifted her against him until their eyes met. Her legs naturally wrapped around his hips, and he took two steps until she was backed against the door. Her fingers dug into his shoulders as he held her easily with the heat of his cock teasing her core.

Rhyanna couldn't look away from him. The heat of him radiated through her, and the tension in his shoulders where she clung to him eased as his eyes traveled over her features. Her exhale was slow and steady as he slowly leaned into her, and his lips brushed against hers ever so softly. At the mere touch of them, she moaned. Her hands moved to tangle in his damp hair as he kissed her. Taking his time, he teased her lips, coaxing them to open for him. She did, stroking his tongue with hers and wondering how she had managed so long without this in her life—without him in her life.

His hips pinned her to the door, and his hands wandered over her dress, softly stroking her breasts. Rhy sighed against his lips, rubbing her hips closer to his, needing to be closer.

Kyran groaned as the kiss heated. His fingers brushed over the emerald silk, teasing her erect nipples.

Her back arched towards him. "Love me, Kyran," she said between kisses. "Please…" her voice trailed off as his lips captured hers.

Carrying her to the bed, he set her on the edge, then kneeled and removed her shoes. His hands traced up her long legs, and his lips followed the trail they left as he moved slowly up to her hips. Standing once again, he helped yank the dress over her head. His breath left him in a rush as he took his time and gazed at her, lying there on his bed, waiting for him. His hands traced intricate patterns on her thighs, raising the flesh and making her whimper.

Rhy lay there naked except for the corset she wore and a thin wispy pair of panties that left little to the imagination. The first time they had come together had been overshadowed by their fury. This time, they would come together slowly, sweetly, and she wanted him more than she ever imagined possible.

His large hands circled her waist, stroking her skin softly. He straddled her hips as her hands found his chest and she did some stroking of her own. Fascinated by his nipples, she sat up and stroked her tongue over a pert tip. Kyran sucked in a breath and cupped the back of her head, pulling her closer to him, encouraging her. She continued playing with him as her other hand teased his neglected one. Her teeth tentatively bit the tip to gauge his reaction.

Kyran moaned and cursed creatively. Tangled in her hair, his hands pulled her closer. He looked down at her with half-mast eyes, the cerulean blue turning darker with desire as she suckled him. Every pull felt like her lips were sucking on his cock, and he couldn't wait for her innocent explorations to attempt something more daring.

He pulled her head back as his lips met hers, moving closer and laying her back down so that his sensitized nipples brushed against her soft chest. Coming up for air, his hands moved to the ribbons on her corset, and, eyes on hers, he slowly unlaced it and freed her straining breasts. She gasped as he filled his hands with her generous offerings, gently massaging them. Leaning down, his lips swept over the tips with a hint of pressure. He licked and kissed every inch of them until she was writhing beneath him. When he finally engulfed one with his mouth, she nearly sobbed beneath him.

"Kyran, please…" she begged.

"Please what, my lady?"

"Don't tease me; we've waited so long."

Kyran gave her a wicked smile. "This time, my lady, we do this at my pace."

Rhy blushed at the reminder of the first time. "I'm sorry…" she started to say, but his lips cut her off.

"No apologies, Rhyanna." He framed her face and kissed her gently. "Just let me love you, my way." Eyes luminous, she nodded, and he kissed his way down her neck and through the valley of her breasts. What he didn't kiss, his tongue traced, or his fingers massaged. He could feel her hips trying to move between his knees, but he wouldn't let her. Not yet. He wanted her dripping and begging before he even came close to her core.

Rhy was struggling not to burst into flames. His hands, oh and sweet Mother, his mouth, was driving her crazy. Her hands tangled in his sun-kissed waves as he descended to her belly button, kissing it sweetly. He rubbed his cheeks back and forth over the skin below it, his stubble making her gasp and move closer, wanting more. His chuckle rumbled through her belly as he slid back and peered up at her.

Kyran took a moment to gaze at her, lying with her hair surrounding her. Her hands stroked his cheeks as he paused and took her in. He turned his head to the side and kissed her palm before looking back at her flushed cheeks and parted lips. Color stained her breasts from the full flush staining her torso, and he could smell her desire as her core wept. With his eyes locked on hers, he pushed her knees wide and settled between them. Kissing the inside of her thigh and rubbing his cheek against it, he used his hands to gently stroke from her knees to the edges of her delicate panties.

Close enough to tease but not close enough to please. Her back arched as he moved closer to where she wanted him. He smiled against her, knowing she was growing impatient. Tonight, he wouldn't be rushed in any way. He fully intended to ply numerous orgasms out of her before he joined her.

His lips traced the path from her knee to her panty line, alternating kisses with little love nips. Her body jumped beneath him as his nips elicited long moans from her. Moving to the other side, he slowed down even more until her fingers threatened to snatch him bald.

Rhyanna peered at Kyran through heavy eyes. Her body was spiraling up to a heavy crescendo, and she wasn't sure if she would survive much more. He'd been playing with her for a while, and while she was about to spontaneously combust, he looked calm and cool while he teased her. She let him have his fun because he was bringing her immense pleasure, and he deserved to take his time. Without a doubt, the man would leave her well satiated when they were through, but right now she was easing towards frustration.

Kyran met her eyes as his hands ripped the lace hiding her from him. He blew gently on her core, and his sweet little healer hissed at him as her hips tried to move closer. But he'd anchored his hands around her legs, effectively pinning her in place. Looking at the delicate folds that made up the most sacred part of her body, he licked his lips. She was beautifully formed. Delicate folds of skin curled like exotic petals, covering her sweet spot. Moisture glistened along her edges and pooled at her entrance. His body had been ready for her the moment he saw her. As the scent of her surrounded him, his cock twitched, throbbing steadily as blood rushed in, swelling it even more.

Rhyanna sensed the cool air on her in places unused to experiencing it. His soft pants of heated breath against her were an agonizing contrast, and she wanted to squeeze her knees shut so that she could at least rub her legs together and ease some of the ache between her legs. His eyes glittered at her, threatening her without a word to try and move closer and see how long he could hold out on her. She closed her eyes, remembering their bond. Ripping their link wide open, she threw all her sensations at him, wanting to meet him in this game they were playing. His sharp intake of breath told her she had been successful, and when she peeked at him, his eyes glared at her with retribution.

"I know how badly you want this, my little nymph, but I will not be rushed. Perhaps I'll make you wait until morning to finish this."

Her shocked gasp rang through the room. "You wouldn't," she whispered.

The hurt in her voice staggered him. He quirked an eyebrow at her as if challenging her to try him, and then without another word, he licked right up her center, flattening his tongue at the small throbbing mass of nerves at the top. He applied pressure, then manipulated her with the tip of his tongue until she screamed his name.

"Kyran, yes, oh gods, yes," she sobbed as he continued.

Her legs shook beneath his hands, and he witnessed the tremors work their way up and down her abdomen. As he pressed harder, she nearly came off the bed. He slowed his strokes, taking longer ones and barely flicking the top before he descended again, circling around her dripping opening. Her knees tried to close around his head to ride out the tremors, but still, he kept her open, taking his time.

Rhyanna had been impatient before, but now she honestly didn't know how much more pleasure she could take. Her body was exploding with little bursts of ecstasy through all her nerve endings as her muscles were contracting. She had experienced pleasure through him, from a distance, and unexpectedly when they came together that one drunken evening, but she hadn't been prepared for the extent of the magic he performed with his tongue. Not even close.

Kyran kept feasting on her, wanting to watch her do it all over again. On the next stroke, he dove his tongue into her, lapping up the juices flowing from her. He heard his name from a distance, but he was enjoying this too much to stop. The taste of her was addicting, and as he coated his tongue with more, his hands clasped her hips, lifting her closer to him. He speared his tongue into her, moaning as her inner walls squeezed it tightly.

Rhyanna screamed as her vision blurred and her body trembled. His thumb stroked her clit, and she spasmed as he released her hips and slowly slid a finger inside her. "Look at me, Rhyanna."

Hearing her name, she opened her eyes and loved seeing the desire in Kyran's eyes and the way he clenched his jaw as he looked at her. He wasn't as unaffected as he'd appeared moments before.

"My lady," he said in a husky voice as his finger stroked in and out once more, "have you had enough?" As he waited for her answer, he pushed the pants he wore down and fisted his thick cock.

Rhyanna licked her lips as he stroked himself, wanting him inside her, but also wanting to spend some time doing some teasing of her own.

Kyran groaned as her eyes followed his hand and she wet her lips. He closed his eyes, imaging those lips on him, but right now, he needed to sink into the velvety softness his finger was drenched in. Standing, he kicked off his pants, continuing to stroke himself as her emerald gaze followed his every move. He returned to bed, kneeling between her spread legs.

Letting go of his throbbing member, he braced himself over her and kissed her. The gentle kiss was nothing like the heat in his eyes. As she kissed him back, the head of his cock pressed against her core. Involuntarily her muscles tensed, anticipating pain. Kyran stiffened over her, and when she looked up at him, she saw the guilt written all over his face. Knowing how they had reached this destination the last time they were together was partly her responsibility, she reached up and framed his face between her palms. Her eyes held his as her thumb stroked his lips, and with a tremulous smile she whispered, "There's nothing but pleasure in this bed tonight, Kyran." His eyes searched hers for any doubts, but as he leaned in to kiss her, she murmured, "Please, show me more."

Kyran took his time kissing her, knowing this was a turning point for them and wanting her to know that she controlled every aspect of this experience. He slid his cock gently against her crease, bumping her clit gently with the tip. When she arched to meet him, he grasped her hips, holding her still, and slowly slid the tip into her dripping sheath. Still, he kissed her reverently, showing her how much he cherished this moment with her and how much he treasured her. As she demanded more with her lips and with her hips, he slid his cock slowly inside of her, pausing to let her acclimate to him.

Rhyanna gasped at the slow slide of his member inside of her. She sighed as he seated himself all the way and arched her back, wanting more. He filled her, stretched her, and the friction when he slowly began to move in her was divine. "Yes, Kyran..." she chanted as his thrusts came faster. His hands settled under her hips, changing the angle, and as he thrust inside again, a tightening began in her core, radiating once again throughout her body. She thrashed beneath him, meeting his thrusts and trying to close in on that elusive sensation rolling through her veins. As another orgasm rolled through her, he roared above her, and her body tightened around him as tides of pleasure flooded her entire system. Wave after wave rolled through her, and when she thought it was finally finished—it wasn't.

Kyran groaned as Rhy tightened around his cock, milking him. He wasn't ready for it to be over, but the sound of her screaming his name as her body clenched around him took him over the edge. Unable to stop pumping into her, he chased the last dredges of pleasure because he was unwilling to finish this quickly. Her body twitched again, clenching tightly around him as she whimpered. He tried and failed to catch his breath before collapsing on her chest.

They laid there, sweat-slicked, gasping and perfectly content. He rolled to his side, taking her with him, her hair tangling around his arms and covering her face. Gently, he brushed the long honey-colored strands away from her face and kissed the tip of her nose. He examined her for any signs of discomfort and found nothing but a pleasant glow surrounding her. The pleasure he received through their bridge kept rebounding, sending more shock waves through them. He was still lodged inside of her, and when she laughed as he playfully traced patterns on her skin, he felt her muscles contract pleasantly around him.

Rhy was trying to catch her breath. This had been beyond anything she'd anticipated. She smiled shyly at him and loved the satisfied grin he gave her. "Me laird, that was…there are no words."

"I wanted you to have something beautiful after our last encounter and before…" His grin slipped.

She stroked the side of his face with her palm. "Kyran, that's behind us and where it needs to stay. Can we please leave it there? We can't have the ghost of both of our mistakes popping up every time we be together."

Kyran nodded and kissed her, but his eyes were somber as he said, "We don't know what's in our future, my lady. I don't have the right to offer you any promises, and I have to be honest, any hope I was clinging to is dwindling."

"Shush," she chided. "Our future be out of our hands now, but while I be with ye, might I request that we not speak of it? I wants to spend my time loving and laughing with ye, Kyran. I want happy memories to keep fer as long as I needs them to get me through what's coming."

"That much I can promise you, Rhyanna." Pulling her tightly to him, his hand trailed over her side and down her hip, reaching around to lovingly cup her ass and pull her tighter in line with him. Ready for round two, he pulled out and thrust back into her. "This what you have in mind?"

"Exactly what I have in mind," she said with a throaty laugh that turned into a moan as he moved faster. A warning ran through head as she lost herself in his touch. *"Guard your heart, child."*

But she wasn't listening to anything but the thrumming of the blood in her ears, the slide of their bodies against one another, and the way that he said her name as he told her he loved her. This was all she needed to listen to tonight—all she was willing to listen to.

CHAPTER EIGHTY-TWO

Best Laid Plans of Fate and Friends

Madylyn scowled at Fergus as he paced the length of her office. It took him precisely nineteen steps from one side of her room to the other, pivot, and then return. While he paced, he muttered to himself. Not loud enough to be heard, but just loud enough to irritate the living hell out of her.

After leaving Rhyanna with Kyran, Ferg sent him a message, letting him know that he and Jamey needed to return to Heart Island briefly. From the wards on the room warning off visitors, he doubted either of them would be emerging before morning.

Jameson lounged on the sofa, looking distant. Since Ronan and Maddy had spoken with him on Wellesely, he had been quiet and kept more to himself. He rarely joined the others at the tavern, and he and Danny seemed off as well. He was sullen and sharper with everyone, it seemed, especially Kerrygan since his return. Maddy knew what the problem was, but she didn't know how to make it better for him.

Danyka, Kerrygan, and Ronan's voices could be heard bantering down the hall.

"Who else are we waiting for?" Maddy asked Ferg.

"King Varan, Tristan, Kai and Roarke."

Kerrygan entered first and sat on the other end of the sofa from Jamey. Danny plopped down in the middle between the two men, oblivious to the look Maddy gave her.

"Where you been?" she asked Jamey.

"Cleaning out the weapons storeroom."

"I could've helped."

441

"I'm sure the man is perfectly capable of handling it on his own," Kerry said.

"It's done." His amber eyes were backlit as his grizzly prowled in the background of his control when he turned to Kerry and said, "Thanks, but don't need you defending me."

Kerry's strange eyes, reminiscent of his falcon, locked on him. "We need to speak."

"Think I'll pass." Jamey studiously ignored the other man.

Danny looked at him quizzically for a moment, then shrugged and turned back to Kerry.

Maddy watched the flash in Jamey's eyes and the undercurrent in his tone and made a note to speak with him soon. This powder keg was bound to blow up soon, and she'd rather it not be during the summer session.

Ronan sat on the window seat behind her desk so that he was near. She glanced over her shoulder at him and smiled. He grinned back at her.

"You're looking beautiful, darling," he said with a wink.

"Not looking so bad, yourself." She sent a healthy shot of lust with her words that made his eyes smolder.

"For the sake of everyone else in the room, dial down the hormones, Maddy," Danny sent with a glare.

Maddy shot her a stern look as King Varan and Tristan arrived.

Varan claimed a leather captain's chair at the table while Tristan stood behind him like a shadow, and finally, Roarke sauntered in, leaning against the door frame.

"We've news that Kyran's ceremony has been moved up to Sunday. We're running out of time to change the course of action Meriel has put into play." She looked at Ferg. "What news have you from the Fire Clan?"

Uncle Killam will be arriving early Sunday morning for the ceremony. The man's willing to do anything he can on his end to prevent this and earn his daughter's forgiveness. He will attend with his sons and a large show of force representing the Court of Luminosity."

King Varan rubbed a hand through his hair. "We don't have much time for me to clean house prior to Sunday. How can I be of assistance?"

"Ye can't return through the portal, else she'll ken immediately that ye've arrived," Ferg said as he turned towards Roarke. "Can ye make it to the Court of Tears by boat in that amount of time?"

Roarke cocked his head as he thought for a moment, calculating the distance. "It will be tight, but with a little help from someone who controls the tides, I don't see a problem."

Varan nodded and said, "I can be of use getting us there in record time."

"Meriel has too much riding on this agreement not to have a failsafe in place," Ferg cautioned. Ye can't jest go storming in and think she won't have already planned for ye to make an appearance. Ye gotta admit, the woman has outwitted the best of ye. Don't underestimate her."

"You talk like you admire her, even after all the havoc she's caused," Jamey said.

"Not admire, lad. Respect. If ye don't respect what yer up against, ye get sloppy, and someone's likely to pay the price for yer arrogance. I won't allow her to destroy people we care about, but we can't go in there all cocksure, or Rhy and Elyana will be the ones to pay for it. I guarantee it."

"He's right," Varan said grudgingly. "I believed the lies she put in my head and allowed her to use my weakness for alcohol to set me up to lose the woman I loved. I never cheated on her, no matter how drunk I was." His voice broke, and he cleared his throat. "I have much to make up for, and I need to start with Kyran before I can reclaim my throne and try and make it up to my people." His face fell, and it didn't go unnoticed that he didn't believe he had a chance with Queen Yareli. Eyes closed, he pinched the bridge of his nose, trying to compose himself.

A somber silence fell over the room until a deep voice from the hall spoke. "You have much to be sorry for, but I have seen how hard you are trying since you've arrived. I think the opportunity to repent will open more doors than you realize if you keep working at it." Kai stepped into the room and stood by his father. "As long as you continue on this path, I will stand by your side."

Varan's eyes misted at the chance his youngest son was giving him. It was a far cry from the bitter boy he had encountered at the shoppe with a kitten. He wondered what Rhyanna had said to him for him to give him a chance.

"So, we've got Varan's arrival covered, Fire court in attendance, Rhy and Kano ordered to bear witness, and the Mother only knows who the feck else will turn up. Meriel has her personal hit squad surrounding her at all times, so I'm not sure how close we can get to her. I've been thinking about this for days, and I think I've found a way to beat her at her own game."

They spent the next hour going through the intricacies of his brainstorm. Questions were asked, objections raised, and modifications made. By the time they started filtering out of the room, they had hammered out a sound plan to try and change the fate of all involved.

But you know what they say about best laid plans....Fate was a funny thing; just when you thought you'd accounted for all the ways she could fuck you, she found a backdoor and did it again. Fergus hoped they weren't tempting fate one too many times because a hell of a lot was riding on this— the happiness of four people, the control of two kingdoms, and the sanity of one fire mage. Because if they failed, Ferg wasn't sure he could ever forgive himself for not making this right.

CHAPTER EIGHTY-THREE

Broken Beyond All Measure

Elyana Drake officially arrived at the Court of Tears five minutes before midnight on Saturday night by herself. Her body was present, but her mind kept replaying the day she had just completed.

After sleeping in with Kano after their late evening, they spent most of the day walking the beach, laughing, and loving each other. She kissed him goodbye with the sun setting behind him. With one last glance over her shoulder, she could see the colors changing, illuminating him with a golden halo. Quickly turning away before she was unable to leave, she ran for the portal and headed home without another word to him. They had said their goodbyes enough times already, and there was nothing left to say.

Arriving at the Fire Clan's Court, she headed for her rooms and dressed in a manner befitting a princess of the court. She did this not to make her family proud, but to establish herself in the kingdom she would be residing in. Her father wanted to see her before she left, but she refused his invitation to dine with him, unable to stomach food or the fact that he had betrayed her so easily with this betrothal. Insisting on seeing her before she left, he had come to her and begged her to forgive him before laying out the true reasons for this unholy pact.

Meriel found out one of her father's past indiscretions and threatened to expose him to his people. The man's honor was the one thing that mattered to him more than his daughter, and rather than face the embarrassment, public ridicule, and possibility of his clan losing their standing in the elemental world, he agreed to Meriel's terms. Meriel had been insistent on a union between Elyana and one of Varan's sons. It

445

mattered not to him which son she married, but Meriel was firm that it was to be Kyran and only Kyran.

Stepping from the portal, she crossed the bridge and was greeted by the queen's guard. The somber-looking guards escorted her through the court, using the longest route possible to showcase her to the nobles, the courtiers, and finally, Queen Meriel.

Entertaining in her favorite gaming parlor, the queen was surrounded by the parasites looking for her favor. The guard entered first, announcing her presence. Queen Meriel stepped away from her entourage and approached, looking down her nose at Elyana.

"Cutting your arrival, a little bit close, aren't you, child?" Meriel asked, looking out the window at the setting sun.

With the briefest attempt at a curtsy, Elyana replied, "As far as I can tell, I'm right on time to an event I want no part in."

"Now, Elyana, it's not all that bad. Kyran is a handsome man, well – liked, and if the rumors are anything to go by, a spectacular lover. This is a good match for you if you allow yourself to give him a chance."

"I wasn't looking for, nor do I care for, a match," she said sullenly, refusing to pretend she wanted to be here. "May I retire? I would like to rest before tomorrow's events."

"Of course. I would want to rest up, too. I know you will be uncomfortable having to have your first night together in front of witnesses, but nobody will judge your performance or his."

Elyana gaped at her, stunned beyond words. She was unaware of the practice and couldn't even summon a proper response. Foolishly, she had hoped for a period of time to get to know her husband before being forced to the marital bed.

Stumbling out the door, she followed her guard without seeing anyone or anything she passed on the long walk to her new hell.

Locking the door behind her, she managed to walk halfway across the room before her legs gave out and she collapsed crying on the floor, wondering how her life had become this and if she would even survive the next few weeks.

Finally, when she had cried so much her eyes had run dry, she managed to pull herself up and enter the changing room. She pulled off the clothes she hated wearing and stood looking at herself in the mirror. Thinner than when she had run away from home, she wasn't bad to look at, but she was no great beauty. Her hair and her eyes made her unique. The scarlet color and length of her hair were stunning. Her eyes were startling in her too-pale face. Red rimmed and puffy, they weren't currently a feature worth noticing.

Finding her trunks still packed, she opened the largest one and took out a wrinkled button-down shirt. She pulled the fabric to her nose and inhaled

Kano's scent as tears began to fill her eyes once more. Pulling it around her naked body, she covered herself, not wanting to be reminded of the bruises his fingers made or the brush burns on her thighs.

The sun would rise again, and tomorrow would arrive. This was a fact, and there was nothing she could do to stop the coming day. Tired of fighting the inevitable and unable to face anyone else, she crawled into the oversized bed and buried her face in the soft fabric of his shirt, taking his scent into her lungs as she drifted off, physically and emotionally exhausted and broken beyond measure.

CHAPTER EIGHTY-FOUR

Uninvited Guests

Yareli waited at the water's edge for the first hint of dawn, trying to decide what she should do. So much depended on the decisions she would make today. Consequences would come into play, and destiny's course would be forever changed.

Heartbroken by her husband's infidelity, she had been a coward and ran away instead of facing the ridicule at court. What did it say that her pride was of more importance than her family's welfare? She beseeched the powerful god who had been her father-in-law to help her dissolve their union. Unable to deny her request because of the fidelity clause in their vows, he gave her a way out, but nothing the gods did ever came without a price.

Because she was abandoning not only her husband, but her title and position at court, she was allowed to leave the Court of Tears. At a location she chose, she was allowed her exile, with stipulations. A custodial agreement for her younger children was agreed upon, and she could have any visitors and or servants she chose join her there. A small local village provided all she needed, and she treated them like family. Her location was given only to those she chose to share it with.

Yareli never anticipated how lonely exile would become after a century. Having no interest in men, she kept to herself, enjoying the beautiful scenery, the peace and quiet, and the ability to indulge in all her creative outlets with no boundaries. Painting and sketching were like breathing to her, and she drowned herself in her work to cover the ache in her chest because once the sting of betrayal passed, she missed her husband.

Varan tried to contact her incessantly at first, wanting to explain, but what was there to explain when she had seen him with her own eyes? He claimed nothing had happened between them. He had fallen asleep drunk—alone. She might have come to believe him eventually, but then Meriel became pregnant, and he made her his queen. Yareli built up intricate walls of air resembling quilted featherbeds to silence the bridge they had once used to communicate because unless it involved their children, she had nothing left to say. The man had broken her heart and shattered any trust existing between them. The worse part was, he made her doubt her own judgment, and she was unwilling to get involved with anyone else because of him.

Movement on her left caught her eye, and she turned to find Kano moving towards her. He was disheveled, and she doubted he had slept much. Carrying a bottle of tequila bordering on empty, he stood, waiting for day to break with her.

"I must return for the ceremony. Meriel decided it's not enough to ruin my life, she needs to rub my face in it as well, and I need to pledge myself to the happy couple."

"You don't have to go, Kano," she said, placing a hand on his arm. "Kyran will understand why you can't be there."

A harsh laugh erupted from him. "Wish I had the luxury of running away and avoiding everything causing me pain, but unfortunately, my absence will only cause pain for my other brothers. I don't have the choice to hide away."

Her hand fell from his arm as she felt his unguarded rage at her. This was what her boys thought of her, and she couldn't blame them.

Kano sensed her pain at his words and instantly regretted it. "Mama, I didn't mean it. I just don't have anything nice to say right now. This is not your fault, but I have to go." He wrapped his arms around her, hugging her tighter than he ever had.

"I'm so sorry, Kano," she said.

"Nah, don't waste sympathy on me. I'll drink my way through it." He stepped back as she cupped his cheek.

"You're better than that."

"Am I?" His pain-filled eyes looked at her with defeat. "We all have our ways of dealing with pain and disappointment. Some people go into exile. My coping mechanisms are to drink and fuck it away. I own my faults. Only one of those even mildly appeals right now, so if you'll excuse me, I need to be completely shit-faced before I get there."

Yareli realized as he stumbled to the portal how much pain her choices had caused Kano. She never explained to her boys why she left. They were too young at the time, but she was beginning to realize her older boys believed she'd abandoned them as well as their father. Yes, they visited her, but it was never for long. Most of their formative years were spent on their own in a court known for its depravity.

How could she fault them for their beliefs when she never did anything to dispel them? Well, she couldn't change the past choices she had made, but as the light on the horizon began to change, she realized she stood on a precipice, and she had the opportunity to make a different choice.

Wading into the water until she was waist-deep, she opened herself up to the gentle sway of the waves. They soothed her as she stood there under the dawn sky. She reached out on a link she had only used once before.

"Neptune, I beseech an audience with you. Your grandsons have need of you. Appear before me, Mighty God of the Deep." When nothing happened, she opened her mouth to verbally request his presence when she heard a laugh.

Opening her eyes, she saw the form of a man rising before her. Handsome and in the prime of his life, he looked so much like Varan, she stumbled back.

He reached out to steady her, grasping both arms fully. "Steady now, sweetheart. Remember, you called me here. I'm sorry if my image holds too many painful memories for you."

Yareli yanked herself away from his hands, so that he would stop picking up on her emotions. "Stop! You have no right to intrude on my inner thoughts."

"You might be right, but you weren't shielding very well, and you implied my descendants needed help. I just saved you the time of having to explain it all to me." He chuckled at the outrage still on her face. "Question is, sweet cakes, what are you willing to do about it?"

She glared at him, then remembered something Kano said. "Is our conversation private? There are rumors I'm being watched?"

Neptune snapped his fingers, and fog lifted off the water, surrounding them completely. "No one will hear a thing we say, and look at the privacy it will afford us." He offered her a sultry smile.

"Never going to happen, so get over yourself."

So much of the irritating god reminded her of the man she still—God help her—longed for in the darkest hours of the night. Neptune's features—sharp cheekbones, chiseled jaw, and a dimple in his chin, although his was harder to see with the goatee he sported—were mirrored in his son. His darkly tanned skin, heavily muscled physique, and even his laugh had been passed down. The only difference was Neptune's shoulder-length hair was chestnut-colored with sun-kissed highlights producing amber tones in the right light. His sense of humor, fortunately, hadn't been passed down because Varan was much more grounded than this lighthearted, fun-loving figure in front of her.

Unbidden, she thought of a box beside her bed where a sketch pad of nothing but her husband's expressions existed. Smiling, laughing, somber, sleeping, loving her, every variation of Varan she could imagine at the time. Tucked in the back were sketches she'd made of him while he slept, fully aroused. Occasionally when she drank too much, she would pull out her visual reminder of all the things about him she was grateful for before...but the similarities ended there. Neptune was like a dog in heat, with a reputation for never bedding anyone more than once—apparently, Kano hadn't come by his libido anywhere strange.

"So, sweet thing, got your panties in a twist because you weren't invited to the party?" He grinned broadly at the outrage on her face. "I know you don't really wanna slap me with the palm you've raised, so let's just put it down, wontchya?"

Yareli dropped her palm and looked at him in disgust. "Why did I bother calling on you? You haven't bothered with anyone in your line for generations. Why would you care if your grandsons' hearts are being broken by the same evil woman who ruined my marriage? I was delusional to think you would give a shit. Never mind, I'll do this on my own"

Disgusted, she turned and started walking up the beach, tossing one last thought into the wind as she kept moving. "Maybe, you ought to be considering why you, as their grandsire, wasn't invited to such a monumental event. A marriage clenching a treaty with the Great Lakes Fire Clan should be something you were included in."

Before she could take a breath and continue her tirade, Neptune appeared right in front of her, causing her to slam into his well-formed chest. Her hands came out to steady herself as he grabbed her hips. "All right, sweet cheeks, now you've got my attention." He pinched her chin between his thumb and forefinger. "You recall the repercussions you will be subject to upon leaving this island?" he asked in a surprisingly somber tone.

"I do," she said softly, knowing once she set foot off this place, her exile would be canceled. She would no longer be off the grid. "I willingly accept the consequences and responsibilities I will incur with my decision."

"Alright then, let's do this." He raised an eyebrow at her island outfit. "Sweetness, you're not properly attired." He sighed heavily and muttered, "I guess I have to do everything myself if I want it done right," under his breath.

More mist formed around her, and a moment later, she stood in fine silks and pearls in her court's colors—various shades of turquoise and teal. Her hair was carefully coiffed, and seashells and pearls were woven amongst the braids. Placing her hands on her waist, she was uncomfortably aware of how much she hated wearing a corset.

451

A mirror of water formed in front of her, reflecting her image. Yareli gasped at how beautiful she appeared with the heart-shaped, plunging neckline, tiny waist, and intricately embroidered silks, also embellished with shells and pearls. "Thank you, sire." She tried unsuccessfully to bow, but the corset made it impossible.

"I'll accept your thanks, but the cost for this little adventure, my lady, is a kiss."

Her eyes flashed dangerously at him. "You always were so easy to rile up." He presented his cheek. "This will be adequate."

Yareli brushed her lips against his stubble and asked, "Why are you helping me?"

"You were the only good match any of my spawn made, and I detest the fact you were devastated in the process. I truly wish I had been able to prevent my son from hurting you. Regardless of your relationship with him, my lady, you will always be my daughter in spirit." For all his frivolity and foolishness, his words held substance and sincerity, for which she was eternally grateful.

Looking down at himself, he snapped his fingers and was instantly clothed in a formal outfit complimenting hers. Extending his arm in a courtly fashion, he asked with a gleam in his eye, "Shall we go crash a party, sweetie? Because there's nothing like the excitement of uninvited guests!"

Yareli moved in closer with a smile as her hand reached down faster than he would have imagined, clamped on his testicles, and twisted far enough to bring tears to his eyes. "Yes, let's go crash that party. But if you call me sweet anything one more time, I will remove your party favors with my fingernails." Smiling sweetly at his purple face, she asked, "Do we understand each other?"

Somehow, Neptune managed a nod, and when she released his family jewels, it was all he could do to not puke his guts up. When his breathing regulated and the boys stopped throbbing, he stood, looked her in the eye and said, "Queen Yareli, are you ready to depart?" His eyes twinkled and held a newfound respect for her as he offered her his arm.

With a curtsy, she accepted it, and as they made their way to the portal, she heard him whisper under his breath, "Varan was a fool to let you go. I would have done anything to have kept a woman like you."

A ghost of a whisper floated her answer on the wind. "I'm starting to believe we were both fools."

CHAPTER EIGHTY-FIVE

Stand Down!

Madylyn finished dressing as Ronan entered the room. Handsome in his midnight blue formal wear, Maddy wished they had some time to appreciate taking it off him for a bit

Ronan walked towards her slowly, recognizing the desire in her eyes and feeling it coursing through their link like a livewire. Taking the necklace from her hands, he turned her around and hooked the clasp as his lips grazed the side of her neck.

"Don't you dare tease me; you know we don't have time to play." She pouted at him, but her cheeks flushed at the thought.

"I'm not so sure about that, Maddy," he said with a sultry smile. He backed her up against her desk, pulled the front of her skirt up, and slipped his hand under her panties, stroking her clit firmly.

Gasping, Maddy clung to the desk as his fingers worked their magic, and in a matter of minutes, she was sobbing his name.

Ronan kissed her gently, helping her to calm down from her intense orgasm before putting her clothes to rights and offering his arm. "Do you think you can walk?" With his other hand, he stroked her gently rounded belly.

"My legs are trembling, but I don't believe you'll let me fall down the stairs."

"Do you want me to carry you?"

"No, I don't need everyone knowing what we just did."

"If you're worried about that, maybe next time we should close the door first." Somehow, he managed to keep a straight face as she cursed creatively.

"That is your job from now on," she said in a huff. "If you're going to attack me in my office, make sure the damn door is shut."

The laughter he was trying to hold back escaped, and though he tried to harness it, he struggled with the glare she was giving him. Hugging her, he said, "At least now you can relax and enjoy the ceremony."

"I might be able to relax, but I'm not sure how much any of us will enjoy the ceremony."

Ronan sobered up as he nodded at her. "I hope for Rhy's sake, Fergus can come up with something to turn the tables on this fiasco."

"Me, too, because what he is suggesting will have far-reaching consequences for all of us if it fails."

Raised voices made them head for the hall. The noise was coming from Jameson's wing.

"What the fuck is your problem lately?" Danyka shouted at Jameson.

"Not aware I had one." He scowled down at her.

"You have been fucking miserable to be around, you never hang out with us anymore…" Her voice trailed off as he avoided her eyes. "What the fuck did I do wrong, Jamey?"

His features softened at the hurt in her voice. "Ah, Danny, you haven't done a damn thing wrong." Reaching out, he grabbed the nape of her neck and pulled her into him. Resting his forehead against hers, they stood there silently for a moment. *"I have some things I need to work out on my own. Sorry if I've been taking it out on you lately."*

"Did I do something to trigger this?" She couldn't help but think everything had changed between them after the night outside the Rusty Tap, but she sure as hell didn't want to remind him of what they did or the memories that she erased.

"No, honey, you didn't."

"No, Danny you didn't do anything," a voice came from beside them. "I did. I rejoined the living and have been taking up too much of your time. Me thinks Jameson has a bit of a green twinge around the edges," Kerrygan piped up, as if he needed to be adding his two cents to the fucking show.

Jamey released her as if she were on fire and turned to the lanky man standing next to him with eyes like a falcon and the freaky ability to hear everything telepathically said.

"You stay the fuck out of our business and out of our private conversations. Do you fucking hear me?" He drilled a finger into Kerrygan's chest to emphasize his point.

"Take your hands off of me," Kerrygan hissed at him as his fingers elongated into claws.

"You gonna put your shifter into play, Kerry?" he sneered as he began unbuttoning his shirt. "I'll be happy to work with that."

"Whoa, STAND DOWN immediately," Maddy shouted, moving between the two men beating their chests. "Don't you dare throw down in my house. Today isn't about either one of your egos. Rhyanna is going to have her heart ripped out in front of an entire court full of witnesses, and I don't need the people showing up to support her looking like they just arrived from a tavern brawl. Pull your heads out of your asses and wait downstairs for us."

Danny stood there, lost, as two of her closest friends left before they beat the shit out of each other. "I don't understand?"

"I think Jamey feels threatened by your bond with Kerry," Ronan said.

"That makes no fucking sense. I've been friends with both of them forever. Why is Jamey being such a dick?"

"You were friends with them at different times, and they didn't have to compete for your attention. I don't think he trusts Kerry, and he cares about you, Danny."

"Well, I care about him, too, but I didn't threaten to beat the shit out of Carsyn when I ran into the pair of them outside the back door." She wouldn't admit out loud how seeing his hands all over the barmaid had made her feel

Maddy shook her head, unable to believe Danny was truly so clueless. "We'll deal with this later. Rhy is waiting for us."

Danny nodded. "I'm sorry, Maddy, for this mess." She turned and made her way down the stairs, her head bowed.

"This is going to boil over if nothing changes between the two of them," Ronan said.

"I know, and I'm not sure what to do about it."

"Send Kerry and Jamey on a mission together. Then if they need to beat the shit out of each other to get it out of their system, there will be no witnesses or guilt trips."

"That's a damn good idea."

"Yeah, I'm full of them. And Maddy, I've got one more for you."

She raised an eyebrow at him and said, "Don't stop now."

"Don't *ever* step between two shifters ready to tear each other apart, please."

Even though he tacked the "please" on so that she didn't get her panties twisted over him telling her what to do, she could still feel the fear and anger that briefly flared when she chose to intervene close to the surface.

"Not my smartest move to date."

"No, darling, it wasn't."

Maddy peered down at the hand rubbing her belly, then glanced back up at him. "I will try to remember I put more than myself at risk in the future, I promise."

"Darling, even if it is *only* you at stake, don't do it."

"Yes, Ronan," she said with a sigh. "Can we go now?"

They reconvened with the sullen threesome outside. Maddy gave them all a cool look before saying, "We are a family in this sanctuary. If you need to work something out, do it on your own time. We work as a cohesive unit, or we don't work at all. We stand for each other, celebrate our victories, and support each other in our disappointments and defeats. If any of you can't make that work, come see me, and we will discuss your options." Her glare landed on each of them in turn.

Danny glanced away, Kerry met her boldly, and Jamey couldn't look at any of them.

"Let's deal with one problem at a time, darling. Today is Rhy and Kyran's turn," Ronan said.

"What did I miss?" Kai asked Ronan as he joined them.

"Nothing you want any part of."

Maddy headed for the portal with a trail of wardens who looked like whipped puppies following behind. Ronan took her hand, squeezing it lightly as they walked slowly towards the next problem they needed to witness.

CHAPTER EIGTHY-SIX

The Price of Love

Rhyanna recognized the heat cocooning her in the massive bed as her eyes struggled to open. The sheets were tangled around her feet, and Kyran's arm draped heavily over her side. Facing him, she didn't move, wanting to watch him while he slept. The lines that usually formed on his brow were relaxed. At ease, his features were calm, exhausted, and well sated.

Happy to have given him some peace before the coming storm, she memorized every angle of his face. The sharp cheekbones framed his straight nose. His full lips had curved into a sultry, satisfied smile as he glanced up at her from between her legs one of many times last night. When they weren't smiling at her, they were brushing softly against her skin or kissing her tenderly.

Dark blond hair shaped his brows, and although she couldn't view his blue eyes at the moment, she would always remember how they sparkled at her with laughter, then changed to a darker, deeper blue with desire. And at the end, during the last time they came together fiercely and desperately, knowing it would be the final time they touched each other this way, they became nearly midnight with hints of dark gray storm clouds wisping across them as he pounded into her, chasing one last memory before he said goodbye to her.

Their loving was spectacular, and his version of slow and sweet made her nearly weep from the tenderness and slow buildup of their energy mingling together for what turned into multiple orgasms for both of them as they gazed into each other's eyes.

457

The last time had been her favorite memory and the one she would revisit the most. They both held on and held out for an eternity. He started out gently, and their passion built like the waves making love to a beach as high tide slowly rolled in. Building in intensity and battering against one another as wave upon wave of pleasure washed over them, she watched him above her and under her. And when his hands gripped her hips tightly as his cock thrust fiercely into her, claiming her body, and marking it as his forevermore, she begged for more. Finally, he'd lifted her in his arms and held her while thrusting into her fiercely. When they reached their pinnacle this time, he staggered back against the wall trying to keep his balance. Laughing, he slid down the wall until they were laughing so hard tears coursed down her face. And as she gazed at him, realizing she would never know him like this again, the tears transformed into tears of loss and grief.

Kyran gathered her close and held her as his eyes misted, too. He held her as tightly as possible without hurting her, and they eventually made it to the bed. They lie there with the scent of their pleasure in the air and the devastation in their souls, eased only by the way they wrapped around each other, kissing and stroking—this time to soothe.

The dark stubble appearing on his face made her want to run her hand over it, but she didn't want to wake him. She slid from under his arm and was grateful when, exhausted, he rolled onto his back without waking. Even asleep, he was partially erect, and she wondered if he was reliving their evening in his dreams.

Quickly, she found her dress, and drawing it on, she picked up her shoes and left without a backward glance, for she knew that if she were to peer back at him once more, she would rejoin him again, and she would not survive saying goodbye this morning.

Slipping from the room, she ignored the lascivious looks from the guards and walked two doors down to her room. Fergus was housed in the suite in between them.

Leaning back against the door after closing it, she gazed at the opulent surroundings and tried to focus on just one thing. Her eyes kept traveling around the room, from item to item, landing for a second and flitting to the next like a drunk honeybee.

Running for the French doors leading to her balcony, she flung them open and ran down into the gardens below. The soft grass beneath her bare feet instantly soothed her as she felt the earth's magic work through her. She tried to still her ragged breathing and racing heart enough so she was able to listen to the voice of the Earth Mother for guidance. Throwing her arms out to the side and closing her eyes, she reached for her inner link that ran straight through her body and down through the earth with roots spreading tree-like beneath her feet as she imagined them going deeper and growing stronger. Finally well-grounded, she steadied herself and found the inner silence she sought.

"Why did you send me such a monumental love, only to take it away?" She projected her thoughts into the silence, waiting and expecting an answer because, goddamn it, she deserved one.

"WHY?" she fiercely threw out into the ethers.

In her dark place, a soft light approached her from a distance. As it grew brighter, the Earth Mother, creator of all, stood in front of her. Her form wavered, shimmering from maiden, to lover, to crone and back again, exhibiting all the forms a woman could take.

"You are all the same, child. Everyone wants a perfect love, but no one realizes that true love always comes with a price. Sometimes, the cost is a piece of your soul, or a piece of your heart, or the joining and creating of something new that you will also have to give up eventually." Her melodic voice soothed the ache in Rhyanna's chest and stilled the screaming in her soul. *"Sometimes, the price is the willingness to let go for the greater good of all."* Her young hand became arthritic as she reached out to push the hair back from Rhy's face. *"Are you willing to pay the price for your true love, child? Are you willing to sacrifice yourself for the happiness of others?"*

Rhyanna heard her words and understood what she was asking. Her answer would have always been yes because she had always been a self-sacrificing person, but this request was nearly more than she could bear. Could she willingly let him go, stop fighting the inevitable, and give him/them her blessing and her pledge?

With tears streaming down her face, she glared at the Earth Mother. *"I will pay the price and willingly sacrifice my happiness."*

The hand, now that of a young woman, reached up and wiped the tears from her eyes. *"You have chosen well, child. Return, witness this union without the anger you arrived carrying. Give them your blessing from your whole heart, and make sure you mean it."*

"Thank you, Mother, for your counsel," Rhy managed to say before the visage of the Earth Mother faded from her view.

Even though she no longer saw her, one last whisper in the dark carried to her, *"I am proud of you, earth child, prouder than you can imagine."*

Rhy opened her eyes to find the sun still streaming and her eyes now dry. Her breathing was normal, and her heart beat slow and steady in her chest. When she thought of Kyran, the pain was a dull ache, like a wound that was slowly healing. Part of her was grateful for the reprieve, and another part felt cheated without it because no matter how much pain there would have been, it only proved how much she truly loved him, and she wasn't sure she ever wanted to lose the sharp edge of grief that she'd earned.

CHAPTER-EIGHTY-SEVEN

About Fecking Time

Kyran woke slowly when he finally realized that the pounding in his head was actually somebody pounding on his door.

"Go the fuck away," he hollered at them, just wanting to sleep up until the time he had to sell his soul into a commitment with a stranger.

"Kyran, let me in." Kano's voice dripped with sorrow and slurred from the alcohol he must have consumed last night.

Knowing Kano was probably the only person at court who understood what he was going through made Kyran claw his way free of the covers. As he stood, it hit him. She was gone. There had been no warm spot in the bed, and her dress was no longer strewn across his floor. She left him while he slept, not even giving him one last kiss goodbye. Pain filled his chest because even though the parting would have been difficult for them both, he never would have wasted time sleeping while she lay beside him.

Kyran turned the lock, and Kano staggered in. He must have been leaning against the door and almost ended up on his ass because of it.

Clasping Kyran's shoulder, he said in a loud whisper, "Ye gotta promise me something, Kyr."

The alcohol on his breath made Kyran want to heave. "What do you want from me?"

"Promise me you won't fuck her." Kano's eyes were crazy as he looked at him. "Please, it's making me fucking nuts imagining the two of you going at it like rabbits."

Kyran laughed at him. Pinching his nose between his fingers, he tried to calm the headache lack of sleep was causing him. "Believe me, the last thing

I want to do is fuck anyone. Rhyanna is the only woman I want in my bed; I don't even think I can perform with anyone else."

"Speaking of performance, cover that little fucker up—way too fucking early to be seeing your junk."

Kyran looked down, forgetting he was nude. "I wasn't thinking about it when you banged on my door sounding all forlorn and shit."

"Well, cover yourself, for fuck's sake."

Kyran found the black silk pants he had quickly abandoned after Rhy arrived in his room. His heart ached, thinking of what was about to happen at high tide. "I don't know how to do this." He looked at Kano for support, a snide comment, anything to help him make sense of this nightmare. "How is Elyana?"

"Bout the same, last I saw her. We said our goodbyes yesterday when she was mandated to appear here, or Kai would take the brunt of the consequences." He flopped down in a chair and put his head in his hands. "How the fuck am I supposed to sit there and watch you do this, man? How many men has Dash come up with?"

"I don't know. Haven't seen him since I was excused from the weekend entertainment. I'm afraid he may have taken my place to punish us both."

"She needs to fucking go."

"You boys are absolutely right." A deep voice came from behind them. Neither of them had heard the man enter, and both stood there with their mouths hanging open as their father took a seat near the fireplace.

Varan sat there in a servant's livery, looking the clearest he had been in years. "I know I have a lot to atone for, but I'm starting with the two of you. Kyran, do you love Mistress Rhyanna?"

"Yes, I do."

"Kano, do you love Elyana?"

"I've never been in love, but I believe I do."

"You both fell for your true loves as quickly as I did for your mother. She was the best thing to happen to me, and I fucked it up. Let's see what we can do to fix this fiasco before I get to work on mine." Varan said with storm clouds rolling through his eyes. "Meriel has a lot to answer for, and the payment begins tonight."

Fergus rushed through the door like a teal-colored whirlwind.

"Are you wearing a fucking sheet?" Kano asked as his eyes traveled up and down the fabric knotted on his shoulder. Silver markings swirled around the fabric, making the material glitter in the light. Ferg wore matching bells in his beard and dangling from his ears. Every time he moved his head, they tinkled.

"Don't ye worry, lad, about what I be wearing. All's ye need to ken is that this sheet-wearing mofo is trying to save yer relationships and yer father's kingdom."

He opened his palms and offered a medallion to each man. Wear this under yer clothes where it will not be seen but is touching yer skin."

Kyran and Kano each picked up the strange lump of dark metal formed into intricate knots and swirls.

"What does this do?" Kyran asked suspiciously.

"Well, partly, it prevents others from listening in or influencing ye in any way. Any transmissions ye make will remain private. There are other attributes, but it'll be better if ye don't ken how they work. Ye'll have a more genuine reaction to events as they unfold if yer not anticipating them."

Kano quirked an eyebrow at him suspiciously. "You're not going to turn us into frogs or anything are you?"

"Depends on how much of a dick ye are," Ferg deadpanned.

"Your reputation precedes you, brother," Kyran said, trying not to laugh.

"Only way this will work, lads," he said somberly, "is if ye can trust me implicitly." He waited for them to process his words. "When I tell ye to do something, ye feckers best do it. Don't look at me like I'm bat shit crazy, which at times I might be, jest fecking do it. If I tell ye to hold hands and dance a jig, get to it, not one bit of sass or bull shite, or this will never go down, and four of ye will pay for it."

The two men nodded at him, accepting the direction and the consequences without any further questions.

"One more thing I forgot to mention...ignore any change in temperature. They may become warm or freezing cold on your skin, but you mustn't show any discomfort."

"As long as we don't spontaneously combust," Kano said.

"If ye can handle a fire princess, I think ye'll survive," Ferg said with a chuckle as Kano glared at him.

Kyran glanced at his father and asked, "Where do you come to play in this master plan."

A slow smile crossed his face as Varan said, "There's nothing like a fox in the hen house. I'll be out of sight and out of mind until the right time." He stood and walked towards them. "I know I've a lot of years to make up for and a lot of problems to fix, but you have my word—I will do everything possible to change our world for the better."

"About fucking time," Kano said with a sneer, turning away from him.

Kyran looked at him, saying nothing, but the rage brewing just below the surface was easy to read and needed no confirmation.

"Kano, escort Elyana to the front of the room and wait there with her until I arrive. Ye mustn't speak to her or anyone else until I arrive." His gaze drilled into Kano. "If ye can't do this, speak now. Ye must follow my directions to the letter, or all of this is a fecking waste of our time."

"I will," Kano said as the metal against his chest heated uncomfortably. "You have my word."

"Kyran, ye'll escort Rhyanna to her seat and sit next to her until I call ye forward. Ye'll not leave her side until I command ye to, nor will ye speak to her aloud."

Kyran watched him shrewdly, wondering what the sneaky little fucker was up to. As he contemplated their accomplice, his pendant chilled against his chest. "Are you compelling us, Ferg? I sense the weight of compulsion through this item."

"Not compulsion, Kyran," he said somberly. "I swear 'tis a reminder only, should ye forget. Will provide other benefits as well, but I canna tell ye them na." He regarded the suspicion in Kyran's eyes and said in a huff, "Ye ken, Rhyanna be like me sister. Didchya honestly think I would pull something that would aim to harm her, Kyran? For fecks sake, ye ought to know me better by now."

Kyran stared at the floor as Ferg put him in his place. "We've had no hope for days, and I find this hard to believe. You've finally showed up with a miracle to save us?" He met Ferg's eyes and said, "Forgive me if it's taking a little getting used to."

"Done. Now go escort the ladies to where I told ye. Speak to no one, and try not to get us all killed before the ceremony begins."

Kyran dressed quickly, and the two Tyde brothers exited the room, still not looking convinced whatever plan Ferg hatched up would work.

Fergus joined Varan in front of the fire and poured himself a water glass of whiskey. Offering the bottle to Varan, he drank the entire glass without coming up for air.

The king lifted a brow, impressed, as he tried to suppress his concern. If their only hope for the day was three sheets to the wind before they started, they would be doomed to fail. He took the bottle, more to keep Ferg from finishing the damn thing than because he wanted any himself.

"What are our chances of succeeding?"

"Slim to none, jest the kinds of odds I prefer." Fergus grinned at him. "Always love when the underdog wins."

"I have a fondness for the underdog living to fight another day," Varan said dryly.

"Aye, I see yer point, but I'm at me best when shit's deep and I be near to drowning in it." Standing, he asked, "Shall we go reunite young lovers and stage a coup before dinner?"

Varan stood, stepping into his space and meeting his eyes. "Fergus Emberz, I'll follow you without question. If I lose anyone I love in the process, including my kingdom, I'll fucking kill you when we're done. We clear?"

"As a glacier-fed lake, me laird." He pulled the door open and held it for the man. "About fecking time the real king made his appearance, and good to have ye back."

Varan laughed as they headed down the hall, and his laughter held an edge of darkness that made the hair on Ferg's arms stand up. He was glad he had never crossed this man because the fury rolling off him and the vengeance riding fury's coat tails were about to be unleashed. God help whoever got in Varan's way. Ferg would be happy to stand on the sidelines and help, but when this day was over, he doubted Varan unleashed would need very much help to reclaim his kingdom. The king's power had been growing every day since the drugs had cleared his system. Varan had been banking that power and nursing his rage, and the time for action had finally come, giving him the opportunity to unleash all of it. May the mother be merciful, and may the Court of Tears still be standing when this demigod was done.

CHAPTER EIGHTY-EIGHT

My Blessing

Elyana stood in front of the full-length mirror, gazing at the mirrored reflection of a woman looking out at her. Was this really her? Dark scarlet curls tumbled over her shoulders, while part of her hair was arranged on the top of her head in intricate twists and turns, then adorned with pieces of golden vines that gave the illusion of flames when the light caught her hair.

Her fire drakes were in evidence, also adding to the flame illusion. Movement of golden and amber hues danced through the strands, soaking in her battered emotions and growing as her anxiety increased. Her time with Kano, and her meltdown, had sated the little beasts for quite a while, and they had subsided and slept most of the morning unnoticed.

Pulling herself out of bed this morning, she soaked in the tub for a long time, letting the lavender-scented water soothe her battered soul. When she was finished, she stood on her balcony and watched a beautiful blond earth element communing two doors down. Her hands were held out in supplication, her head kicked back, soaking up the sun. As tears rolled down the woman's face, Elyana could see the emotional maelstrom she was trying to balance and wondered if this was the woman Kyran loved trying to come to terms with the hand destiny dealt her. The woman was stunning, and when she finally opened her eyes, they locked on Elyana. The acceptance in her eyes was at odds with the sorrow still surrounding her aura. Elyana had given her a deep curtsy honoring her pain and the fact that she was going to be the one causing it.

Elyana stayed that way until she felt a hand on her shoulder.

A sweet melodic voice emerged from the heartbroken nymph. "This isna yer fault, and I donna hold ye responsible any more than I can blame him. I ken where yer heart lies and sense the anguish this is causing ye as well. If naught else, we be sisters in sorrow, milady, and I'll mourn with ye today whence yer freedom is taken away and placed in the hands of a man ye barely ken." Rhyanna took a deep, shuddering breath.

"Kyran be a good man, one of the best I've had the privilege to ken. He'll be good to ye and try his best to be true to ye. Ye've me permission and blessing to be happy with him, if ye are able to, milady. He has too much honor to stray from ye, not even for me. Not sure if I respect him more fer that or resent him." Clearing her throat, she said, "There's nothing worse than being trapped with a stranger with no hope for affection or a future of love." When the woman stared at Rhyanna in shock, Rhyanna bowed and said, "I wish you many blessings on both. Might ye find affection together and eventually love." As tears threatened once again, she whispered, "If ye'll excuse me, milady, I be sorry if I spoke out of turn and will take me leave na."

"Mistress Rhyanna, please wait a moment." Elyana waited until Rhyanna met her eyes. "You're quite right, this was neither of our choices, and pleasure and affection between us will be one hell of a long time in coming. I, too, love someone else, and the horror of what we will put on display this evening makes me ill. Were he a less honorable man, I would send him to you, and this would be a union in name only. Unfortunately, I, too, suffer from the inability to not live by my word, and I don't think Kano will ever forgive me for my decision."

Pausing, she twisted her hands in front of her. "I vow to someday bring him some form of joy, knowing that he will only ever truly love you, and I hope you, too, may find someone to ease your burden of loneliness with."

"Thank ye, milady." Rhyanna tried and failed at a smile and backing up, nearly ran as she said, "If ye'll excuse me na."

As Elyana's emotional grid lit up again, her drakes cooed to her, wanting to follow the Lady Rhyanna and ease some of her burden. "Nye, little ones, she is not for you. Earth elements heal differently than we do, and what she needs, you cannot provide. Come now, for soon I will have much need of what you can provide me."

Walking back into her room, she pulled a rope by the side of her bed, summoning a lass. Rarely using personal help, she hated to bother the woman. Unfortunately, the intricacy of the dress she would be wearing would require her assistance.

As a knock came on the door, she bid them enter and untied the robe covering her. A young cousin of hers from her mother's side of the family was chosen to be by her side today. As McKenna entered, she dropped the robe to her bed and stood nude as she waited for the layers of clothing she needed to wear.

An intricate pair of lace panties with garters came first in scarlet. Elyana pulled them on and attached the lace stockings to them. A scarlet corset with a sweetheart neckline was next, with gold hooks and eyes in the front and gold ribbons to cinch up the back. McKenna yanked her in tight, making sure she would not be able to draw forth a full breath to protest this injustice at the last minute.

The young girl looked at her and said, "I'm so sorry, Ely. You deserve better than this, and I know not what to say."

Elyana attempted to smile. "Nothing to say, love. Hand me the skirts please."

McKenna nodded and handed her the full, bright golden skirts that would trail four feet behind her. Tiny rubies were sewn in a diamond pattern around the entire skirt making the jewels catch flashes of light like flames when she moved. A front panel, contrasted in fading shades of scarlet to the palest hint of orange, reminded her of a brilliant sunset or a flickering flame. Scarlet, velvet-heeled boots were hidden by the skirt. A short-sleeved bolero jacket in the same gold silk covered her shoulders, and finally an oval, pigeon blood ruby in an intricate gold setting was placed around her neck with matching chandelier earrings to complete her ensemble.

Elyana gazed at herself in the mirror. The corset accentuated her tiny waist, making it even more so. Her court colors complimented her pale skin and scarlet hair. Her fingers caressed the ruby, the only thing representing her mother's lineage today. She wished her mother had lived to see this day, and she couldn't help but wonder if she had, would Elyana be on the verge of tying herself to a stranger?

The reflection staring back at her was beautiful but for the saddest eyes she had ever seen. Deep pools of agony stared out at her, and her throat kept restricting as it struggled to contain the screams and sobs begging to burst forth. If she had become anything over the years, it was honorable. She would go through with this sham of a union because she would never dishonor her Court. There was more at stake than her happiness, and she finally recognized the peril her court was in after her father spoke with her last night before she departed, confessing that it was his indiscretions she was paying for. The treaty created today would prevent her clan from losing their status in the Elemental High Court because of a poor personal decision her father made long ago.

"You are absolutely gorgeous, Elyana," McKenna said, even though the compliment fell flat.

Elyana wondered how she would have felt if it had been Kano waiting for her at the other end of this journey. She would have been excited, preparing for the happiest day of her life and hard-pressed to keep from smiling.

A soft knock on the door made her heartbeat race in fear, knowing there was no going back now—the only path left was straight ahead through that door and into the next phase of her life as a pledged woman.

Nodding at McKenna to open the door, she turned and tried to catch her breath. Her corset was too tight, and she was struggling to draw air into her chest. Bending over at the waist, she tried sucking air in and failed. She reached back, clawing at her corset strings, trying to release them just a little so she could breathe. Spots formed in front of her eyes, and she was mortified, thinking she might pass out in front of this stranger.

McKenna's voice murmured behind her, and she heard her saying she was going to find the healer. She felt strong hands on her waist, and suddenly the cinches loosened just enough that she could draw a breath. The man behind her rubbed her back soothingly, and she felt him rest his hand on her shoulder as a voice from earlier this week floated through her mind.

"Baby, I need you to breathe with me."

Elyana knew it was a figment of her imagination, but she wanted it so badly to be Kano behind her that she stepped away and turned so she could see him.

The Tyde men were remarkably similar in appearance. This one's facial features were less harsh than Kano's, and his eyes were kind, his hair longer. Mistress Rhyanna's face flew through her mind, and she couldn't help but think what a handsome couple they would've been.

Not wanting to have a conversation, she dropped a half-assed curtsy with a muttered, "Thank you, my lord."

He bowed to her and silently offered her his arm. Knowing the time had finally come to face her future, she placed her hand through his, and they made their way down the hall. Grateful for the silence, she tried to control her galloping heart and her queasy stomach as they marched to the beat of destiny's drum into the next chapter of their lives.

CHAPTER EIGHTY-NINE

An Old Score to Settle

Fairfax McAllister was hidden in the shadows of a recessed area of the garden. Queen Meriel had contacted him a week ago with a change of plans regarding Mistress Rhyanna Cairn's fate.

A change in the timeline allowed for a change in venue and scored him an invite to the kind of party he never got to attend. Wearing the best of his shoddy outfits, he lingered along the back wall. This location gave him a full view of the guests attending the ceremony.

Mistress Cairn walked down the aisle on the arm of one of Varan's spawns. A lovely thing to look at, he salivated at her large breasts tightly bound in her dress, showing a considerable amount of cleavage. This woman would be worth the risk to obtain, and he would be paid handsomely for it. His men would have to wait for their turn because Fairfax intended to enjoy her for a long while before passing her on. Many years had passed since a woman had interested him at all. This lush piece of ass piqued his interest.

Biding his time until he could catch the woman alone, he watched the participants of this play settle into their places. The whore who ran the Sanctuary walked down the aisle on the arm of the Pathfinder man. Rumor had it, they were pledged and expecting. Fairfax would have taken her just for spite if he thought he could remove her escort. The power and rage she aimed at him in Warden's Court was the only thing holding him back because he was no match for the wench elementally.

Associates of his were scattered throughout the crowd so that Rhyanna's departure wouldn't be missed no matter which exit she chose when leaving.

Everyone knew who their target was, and they were simply waiting for the theatrics to end.

This plan appealed to him so much more than the one Meriel originally proposed. He wasn't forbidden to be at the Court of Tears, whereas his life would be forfeit if found near Heart Island. Meriel's only request was that he wait until the celebration was in full swing. Once the wine started flowing and the pitiful lass drowned out her loss, he could easily maneuver her onto his vessel and leave with no one the wiser.

Fairfax's head jerked to the left as a throaty voice and laugh caught his attention. Any color that might have been in his gray face faded as he laid eyes on a woman he hadn't seen in centuries. He'd have never known her with dark hair, but that voice made him look at the petite woman with black hair in a pixie cut that framed her startling blue eyes. 'Til the day he died; he would remember her eyes. He shuddered, remembering the sound of her screaming, and then laughing while she tore the throat out of his brother Max. Her dark laugh still haunted him, as his mind wandered back in time, and he remembered that fateful week.

A blond back then, she'd had wavy hair to her waist and those haunting pale blue eyes. Winning at cards, Fairfax decided to treat himself to something special. In a brothel specializing in young things, he'd purchased—for a discounted price, mind ye— fifteen minutes with a little spitfire. He'd taken her roughly from behind, not trusting her attempts to bite him when he approached from the front.

Fucking her while she'd been chained to the ceiling of a dungeon cell had been one of the best days of his life. Her young body had been so tight and felt so fucking good that he'd bragged to his younger brother Max about her, encouraging him to stay away from the overused whores on the docks.

Max listened to him and took a friend to join him for the allotted time. Fairfax had been two cells down trying something new, unaware that Max had already made his way into the hell cat's cell.

The only sound in the room was the slap of Fairfax's middle-aged body against the little brunette he picked tonight. He liked the smaller, younger ones. She wasn't as tight as the wild cat, but beggars couldn't be choosy.

The wild cat had already been busy when he arrived, and his cock was throbbing and ready to play, so he hadn't waited on her. As Fairfax screamed his pleasure, releasing his seed into the battered young thing he'd pinned against the wall, he thought he'd heard the wild cat's scream. The sound revived his cock, and he kept fucking the brunette harder, still holding her by the neck while his hips had slammed her lower body against the damp stone wall. Her arms were spread out by the chains in the wall, and his hold on her throat kept her from trying to head butt him or bite.

Tears ran down her face, making his second orgasm even better as he grunted his way through it. He kept thrusting until his cock was too flaccid to stay in, then kept going just because he knew he was hurting her by slamming her against the wall. Sweat dripped down his wrinkled brow, and he wiped it against her bruised chest.

Releasing her, he stumbled back, tucking his diminished cock back into his pants. A metal bat beating on the bars told him his time was up. He picked his hat up, then grabbed his threadbare jacket and headed for the cell door, oblivious to the sobbing behind him. He'd gotten what he'd paid for and didn't give two shites about the damaged girl he left behind.

Stepping into the damp corridor as screaming came from the hell cat's cell, he paused. "You've killed him you little cunt," a man's deep voice shouted. "We just wanted a little fun, that's all. Why the fuck did you have to kill him?"

Fairfax stopped in the hallway, waiting for the guards to come running. When nothing but silence echoed down the stone walkway, an uneasy feeling settled over him. Tucking himself into a closet, he left the door cracked so he could hear what was going on.

The shouting man was cut off abruptly. Fairfax could hear a woman's voice murmuring in the room, but with the door mostly closed, he couldn't hear her clearly enough to recognize her. The cell door swung open, and a woman in a long, midnight blue velvet cape with her hood up walked swiftly down the hall cradling the hellcat in her arms.

As they passed Fairfax's hiding spot, he noticed the hellcat's head falling over the woman's arm. Her face was covered in a mask of blood, and blood ran steadily down her legs, dripping onto the floor as they moved by. It was as if time stood still—everything seemed heavy and hazy until the strange woman left his line of sight.

Able to move once again, he stole out of the closet and felt a strong urge to glance in the cell where she'd been held. His eyes took in the carnage, but his mind couldn't process it. A massive iron worker lay there with his throat slit, terrified eyes peering up at him. A shudder ran through his body as his eyes moved past him and took in the brown-haired lad lying on the floor behind him. Eyes staring sightlessly at the ceiling and a chunk of flesh missing from the side of his neck, the man's face was pale from the amount of blood he'd lost.

Fairfax's stomach churned as he thought of the mask of blood on the hellcat's face. Walking woodenly into the cell, his knees cracked the stone floor. Tears fell down his weathered cheeks as he looked into the opaque eyes of his youngest brother Max. Pulling Max's head to his chest, he sobbed, hating that he'd encouraged him to seek his pleasure here. "Someday, I'll find her, Max. I swear someday I'll find her, and she'll pay for every day she's stolen from ye. Ye have me word."

All these years and Fairfax never found one hint of the woman. 'Til the day he died, he'd know that voice, and tonight, he'd recognized it. Still petite, the hair was the only difference he could see, and that was easy enough to change. His eyes tracked her as his hell cat walked down the aisle and sat behind Mistress Cairn.

His mission had just changed. He didn't give a fuck about the healer or the money Meriel promised him. He didn't give a shite if she came after him and took him off the grid.

A promise needed to be fulfilled, and he intended to fulfill it before he died. He sent a message to his team, *"Change of plans. Ignore the blond and follow the petite woman in the row behind her. The one with short dark hair. She's the target. Do not engage. I want intel only. I need to ken where to find the little cunt."*

A cruel smile crossed his face as he thought about all the things he would do to her before he even considered letting her die. He would destroy her in the most terrifying ways possible—by taking her on a trip through memory lane and making her relive her childhood over and over again.

CHAPTER NINETY

Chalices of Tears and the Feast of Broken Hearts

Rhyanna fiddled with the clasp of her necklace, nearly dropping the beautiful piece as she did. Lily helped with her hair and dress choices earlier. Gazing into the looking glass, she knew the ivy-green silk dress with the empire waist suited her figure. Swirls of lighter green and white marbled the fabric, creating an exquisite pattern. The effect was gorgeous, but she didn't care what she wore today. As long as she didn't embarrass the sanctuary, she didn't give a damn about what anyone else thought. What was the proper ensemble to give the man you loved to someone else?

Finally, she managed to hook the large moonstone around her neck. The weight of the stone between her fingers reminded her to tap into the strength the gem offered. A light knock on the door startled her. With a final glance, she answered the summons.

Expecting Fergus or Madylyn, she was surprised to find a man in the formal wear of the Court of Tears. Taller than Kyran, he reminded her of Varan. Giving her a short nod and a bow, he raised an eyebrow as if to ask if she was ready. With a nod, she waited while he held the door open and offered his arm to escort her to the ceremony.

Content with the silence, she didn't attempt to engage the man. Distracted and emotionally devastated, she lacked the patience to participate in idle chit-chat. The only thing she wanted was to survive this day, drink herself to oblivion, and remain there for the next week or more. A laugh burst from her as she thought of the last time she drank and where that got her.

Her escort gave her a confused glance, but still said nothing.

With her eyes straight ahead as the halls blurred by, she ignored the clusters of nobles whispering behind their decorative fans. They gazed at her with equal parts amusement and sympathy. What passed for entertainment in this court was appalling. Rhy couldn't understand the need to belittle someone else for personal enjoyment. Biting her tongue until the metallic copper tang of blood hit her palate, she managed to keep her temper reigned in.

Everyone they passed wore their finery, each competing like the peacocks in the gardens outside. A blond wearing excessive jewels. A ginger with too much makeup. Two brunettes over there displaying barely-there dresses. How difficult it must be to always feel the need to prove oneself, to maintain one's place in this world, Rhyanna mused. The effort needed would be exhausting, and the rewards were minimal and short-lived.

As they made their way through these halls, she was reminded of how grateful she was for the life she chose to live. She was lucky to be surrounded by people who were in her life because they wanted to be—not because they were forced to be.

The aroma of salt water, roses and despair filled the air, assaulting her senses. Rhy realized they'd arrived in the formal gardens. Her mind had wandered, and she'd missed the moment they left the palace and walked outdoors. They'd arrived in the location where the ceremony between the Court of Tears and the Court of Luminosity would be held.

Row after row of rose arbors six feet wide covered the path they walked down. The roses formed a tunnel where the vines met and intertwined between the arbors. Carefully cultivated, the effect was captivating. They slowly made their way through the whimsical lane, and Rhy wondered if he took his time for her to enjoy the experience.

Miniature white roses were in full bloom. The smell overpowered Rhy's emotionally exhausted senses. The scent of roses always elicited memories, and the memories they recalled, made her want to blush and weep alternately. The petals softly rained down, and she wondered what kind of magic made them fall so randomly. They drifted like snowflakes before them, beautifully lining the path.

Emerging from the arbors, she expected the sun to be shining on such a monumental day. Ominous storm clouds swirled overhead, and the winds were picking up, reflecting the mood of the Tyde men. Her escort led her down a flagstone path towards groupings of chairs arranged in a semi-circle near the center of the garden. The arc parted in the center to allow entry for guests and the couple being joined.

Rhyanna's eyes darted anxiously around, hoping to find a friendly face or two. No matter where her eyes fell, she saw nothing but vultures, waiting to sip from chalices of tears as the feast of broken hearts began. Refusing to face their amusement at her expense, she held her head high and maintained a mask of neutrality for her protection and her sanity. Preferring to remain anonymously in the back, she tried to head for an empty seat there. Her silent companion guided her to one with her name on a banner in the front row. Rhy's eyes flew to him in shock and horror. How could they expect her to sit this close while Kyran formed a lifelong bond with another? The man shook his head sadly as Rhyanna realized Meriel's cruelty knew no bounds. Her complete disregard for anyone else shouldn't have been a surprise, but it still stung. Just when Rhy thought the queen couldn't hurt her again, she managed to do exactly that.

Unwilling to make a scene prior to the ceremony, she took her seat without any noticeable protest, seething. The attempt to keep the rage flowing through her bottled up throughout the next hour was going to be a challenge.

Kai sat to her left. The sweet young man gave her a sad smile as she joined him. A young woman sat to his left appearing, alternately nervous and excited. Like her brothers with light hair and blue eyes, she was incredibly beautiful. A dark-haired man sat on the end. He must have been another sibling because, except for the dark hair, his features favored his brothers. Her escort— whom she assumed must be Kano—sat to her right. Rhy could sense the same anxiety and anger flowing through him that raced through her.

A hand on her shoulder made her glance up, and she managed a pitiful attempt at a true smile as her fellow wardens settled in the row of seats behind her. Jameson came first, squeezing her shoulder. Danny leaned over and hugged her. Kerrygan cupped her cheek with the palm of his hand, his shifter eyes staring into hers before he kissed her on the cheek. A sad smile crossed Ronan's face as he met her gaze. Maddy's damp eyes nearly did her in before she sent her a telepathic boost saying, *"Don't give up yet, love. 'Tis not over until it's over."*

Rhy gave her a dumbfounded stare. *"I'm certain it's over, Maddy. Are ye feeling well?"* Pregnancy hormones were bound to make the most intelligent of women daft at times. Rhy ignored her advice, knowing no miracle waited for her at the end of this horrid day.

The rows of seating filled in quickly. The side they occupied represented the Court of Tears. The right-hand side exhibited a fine showcase of the Court of Luminosity's current fashions. Exotic variations of gold dresses lined the rows. The fashions were flashy but much more conservative than the retinue from the Court of Tears.

An orchestra played softly in the background while a bard sang about love found, then lost again. Rhy giggled at the irony of his words, drawing a few concerned glances. Clearing her throat, she managed to calm herself down. The bard completed his horribly accurate ballad, and the conversations died down as the music became softer and sweeter with light notes reflecting love's expression through sound.

Movement behind her once more caught her eye, and they widened as Roarke took the last seat behind her. Gratitude filled her eyes as she turned to him, reaching out a hand. She hadn't been sure he would come after his confession the last time they'd met. He latched onto her fingers as he held her gaze, telling her without words how sorry he was. Rhy knew when she finally moved on, she wouldn't be lonely for long. He kissed the tips, then released them. The man beside her gave her a long stare of censure before glancing away and twining his hands tightly together.

"Ye don't ken anything about me or what I've been through, me lord. So don't ye dare judge anything I be doing today as I watch the man I love tied to someone else." Her words were barely above a whisper, and using small puffs of air, she made sure only he heard them. Her eyes flashed dangerously at him. He turned and gave her a soul-searching stare and a curt nod, then gazed straight ahead, still maintaining his silence. At this point, his behavior was beginning to piss her off, but before she could call him on it, Kai leaned towards her.

"What the hell does Fergus have on? Is he wearing a sheet?" he whispered, successfully distracting her and diffusing her temper. She turned to the young man beside her and wondered if this was his intention all along. His eyes twinkled, but not at Fergus, at her. Kai was shrewder than she gave him credit for.

"Aye, sadly, I ken it is." She chuckled slightly. "He doesn't possess much of a sense of style, but his formalwear brings into question if the daft man has any sense at all."

Fergus walked barefoot down the aisle in one of his ceremonial sheaths. Deep turquoise in color and knotted on one shoulder, the garment hung below his knees. Gold glyphs and elemental symbols were embroidered on the fabric. The embroidery shimmered as he moved. He'd slicked his flaming red hair back and banded the mass at the base of his neck. Fresh braids in his long beard exhibited gold bells. Uncharacteristically somber for the usually jovial soul, he stared at the ground, waiting for the rest of the participants in this farce of a play to arrive.

Meriel came next, walking regally down the center and smiling like the cat who'd claimed the canary. Dashiel and Elise were chained behind her. Dashiel sported varying shades of purple and blue bruises on his face, and Elise looked much too pale. With their chains wrapped around the wrist of one hand and the leash to a hellhound pup in the other, the queen paused as she walked in front of Rhyanna and the Tyde siblings.

Rhy tried her best to ignore her until Meriel grasped her chin firmly between her fingers and forced her to meet her eyes.

"You thought you could best me, little nymph," she whispered in a voice meant for Rhy alone. She leaned in closer, while glaring at Maddy sitting behind her. Whispering in Rhy's ear, she said, "I always win, one way or another. Just because you cock-blocked me once doesn't mean it will happen again. I control your man now, and he'll do what I want when I want because he knows if he doesn't, I'll make sure you pay for his arrogance. He might be forming an alliance today, but you, little peasant girl, will always be his weakness."

The queen turned to Kano next. "You thought you could outsmart me by running and hiding with Elyana. Wait and see how much your siblings pay for your insolence." An evil smile crossed her face. "I've made sure Klaree will be joining us at court in the fall. Time to break her in properly."

Delivering her final blow, she looked at the pup and said, "Come along, Fluffy," then sauntered off, hips swinging. Meriel took her place on a raised dais behind Fergus. Her personal guard followed and formed an arc behind her throne. With a yank of the chains, Dashiel and Elise fell to their knees beside her like pets, and Fluffy curled up on her feet. From this vantage, Meriel could witness the distress she caused to all parties involved.

The fury crossing Kano's face due to the treatment of the couple made Rhy reach over and grasp his forearm tightly. "Don't! She's counting on us breaking in front of her." She waited until he glared at her. "Don't give her the satisfaction. Her hand found his, and they held on tightly to each other. Strangers, though they were, they were each other's anchor in the storm hurtling towards them from the horizon. The clouds circled violently in the sky, mirroring his emotions. Streaks of lightning jumped between the clouds, lighting up the day eerily.

Indeed, the sky—overcast to begin with—now darkened ominously as they were about to begin. The crowd stood as a unit as Kyran and Elyana walked down the aisle together. Rhy tried not to watch them, but she couldn't follow through. The need to meet his eyes was overpowering, but her heart broke when Kyran passed by as if she weren't even there. He never even glanced her way.

Kyran stood on the right, nearly facing Rhyanna, tormenting her. His focus was solely on the woman across from him. This shouldn't have surprised her, but somehow his disregard opened a raw wound in her heart. Elyana faced forward on the left and somehow managed to keep her expression neutral. Kyran was too honorable to give his attention to anyone else once he stood with the woman destined to become his. Right now, Rhy detested his sense of honor.

This time, Kano tightened his grip on her, bringing her back to the present with his touch.

Fergus stepped forward, and his booming voice carried over those gathered. "Welcome, one and all. Today, we come together on the cusp of the Strawberry Moon to witness a union not just between two individuals, but betwixt two powerful clans.

"This is not the usual bond created from love, but a treaty allowing for better relationships between the two clans diplomatically. By creating an alliance, both houses have agreed to better trade relations and employment opportunities for their people. The Court of Tears and the Court of Luminosity will once again become strong allies, and the children of either court respectfully will be the tie that holds these two mighty houses accountable to one another, in times of peace or in times of trouble."

The crowd was silent, but the tension running through them was palpable as if they all waited for one or the other of the pair to abandon the plan. When no one fled, Fergus focused on the two people standing in front of him and began to speak.

"Prince of the Water, do ye humbly take on the commitment ye have accepted as a liaison for the Court of Tears? Do ye accept the role yer relationship will play in aforesaid commitment, willfully knowing the consequences should ye ever wish to dissolve this bond?"

Kyran took Elyana's hands, and smiling gently at her, he said, "I do, and I will."

Rhyanna sat there, devastated and speechless. Kyran never even glanced at her. Not once since he'd entered the garden had he even tried to catch her eye. How could this be the same man who loved her so fiercely last night?

The man holding her hand was stroking the top gently. A shudder ran through her as she remembered the way Kyran traced her hands when they lay in bed. He'd attempted to write letters on her hand, sending cute little messages. A stranger touching her in the same way was unnerving. Rhy gave him a hostile look and tried to pull her hand free.

Fergus's voice pulled her back to the festivities. "Princess of Fire, do you humbly take on the commitment ye have accepted as a liaison for the Court of Luminosity? Do ye accept the role yer relationship will play in aforesaid commitment, willfully knowing the consequences should ye ever wish to dissolve this bond?"

Elyana stood there trembling. A quick glance at her father showed her the tears in his eyes, and her gaze begged him to stop this from happening. Reaching out to him one last time, she sent through their parental link, *"Is there truly no other way to do this, Papa?"*

He shook his head sadly at her. *"Nye, child. I ask ye to trust me one last time, knowing I would do anything I could to see you happy. Trust me, and give him yer pledge."*

Different sections of her heart broke this time. Their relationship was always respectful of her choices, and the realization that she was nothing more than a pawn to him destroyed her. A lone tear rolled down her face. Her sorrowful eyes examined the man before her.

Kyran was handsome, no denying the truth, but his hair was too long. She loved the sensation of the stubble under her hands and on the insides of her legs when Kano…. Her face heated at the memory, and she tried to recall the question the high mage just asked her.

Elyana's eyes found Kano sitting next to the beautiful Earth Mistress. This woman was also losing everything she cared about today. Rhyanna was pale, and tears filled her eyes. Elyana's heart ached for the pain this was causing her, too.

For some reason, she expected Kano's eyes to be locked on her, wanting to catch her eye one last time. Confusion swamped her as she realized he held the hand of Mistress Rhyanna and couldn't stop stealing glances at her. He was tracing something on the top of her hand, and if Elyana was reading the other woman correctly, she was near to slapping the man. Elyana wished Kano would meet her eyes so she knew she wasn't making a horrible mistake.

The man next to her squeezed her hand in his. His hands were large and more calloused than his younger brother's. The gentle pressure on her hand reminded her they were waiting on her, and her eyes snapped to his. The way he gazed at her so reverently should have been reserved for the woman sitting devastated in the first row. Her breath started to come in soft gasps as she started to have an anxiety attack.

"Not now, dammit," she thought as her vision started to fade. *"For God's sake, not in front of all these people."*

Kano might not have been able to look at her, but he was there for her now. *"Baby, I need you to breathe for me. C'mon, baby doll, you've got this. Look at me."*

Her gaze wandered once again to the front row. The man sitting there was oblivious to what she was experiencing. The Kano she loved would have been trying to calm her down. He would have come up here in the middle of the ceremony to make sure she could breathe. Oh, crap, she was hallucinating and about to keel over.

"Look at ME!" came through once again, loud and clear as the man holding her hand squeezed her fingers tightly on the "ME!" part.

The realization came rushing in like the air suddenly flooding her lungs. "I will, and I do," she finally managed to whisper, trying not to let her feelings show on her face or in her voice. The ceremony wasn't complete, and she didn't want to chance anything stopping the proceedings from here.

The high mage wrapped strands of fine gold around their hands, binding them together in the old ways. "Because this is a contract between two clans and not a pledge between lovers, we forgo the usual pledges and ask now for the blessing of the Fire Clan."

Laird Brand stood and, meeting his daughter's eyes, said, "I speak for the Great Lakes Fire Clan and the Court of Luminosity. May you both receive many blessings you did not anticipate in this union."

Fergus continued running the cord around their hands as he said, "Water Clan, will ye offer yer blessing."

Knitting her brows together and tipping her head to the side, Queen Meriel stood and gazed down at the couple waiting for her blessing. Something was off, but she couldn't put her finger on exactly what it was. Instrumental in organizing this charade, she couldn't pull out now. Her inner senses were screaming that something unforeseen was changing her plans.

"Water Clan, will ye offer your blessing?" Fergus repeated the question, and the entire assembly held their breath as they felt the power shift.

Tears ran down Rhyanna's face as she viewed the couple in front of her. He wouldn't even turn towards her. How did she not deserve even one glance goodbye? Kai took her left hand for support, and she could sense her family behind her. The Tyde brother to her right kept tracing symbols on her hand until she wanted to punch him.

Irritated, she glared at him out of the corner of her eye and observed his fingers as he traced the letters I-T-S-M-E on the top of her hand.

Watery eyes struggled to see what he was tracing to distract herself from the pain. The letters took shape, and her overwhelmed mind finally formed the words. Now, she understood why the man up there wouldn't look at her and the one down here wouldn't stop.

"Kyran?"

Rhyanna couldn't stop watching his fingers as they traced Y-E-S out, and she needed all her willpower not to react to his revelation, knowing if Meriel figured it out, the charade would be over. Interlacing their fingers, she tightened her grip on him and let out a sigh of relief when he did the same.

Queen Meriel needed to decide and quickly. The damn mage just repeated his question. Without her crystal gazing ball, she was unable to see the whole picture—hell, she couldn't see beyond her next words. Trapped by her own machinations, she chose to save face.

"I represent the Northeast Water Clan and the Court of Tears. I bless this union between this man and woman and will seek to enforce their commitment to each other and to their clans. I will remind them of the consequences should they fail, not only to themselves, but to their people."

As she finished, Fergus chanted, reaching up to the tumultuous sky and down to the Earth.

"In front of your Courts,
And both of your Clans

I seal yer commitments
With water from her tears and gold from this land

May the God's bless this union
By entwining this couple where they now stand."

Elyana's Fire Drakes raced along the chain, binding their souls to the contract they'd just agreed upon. Fergus grabbed the gold chain and chanted over the strand until it transformed into two gold rings which he offered to the couple in front of him.

Elyana picked up the larger ring and, turning to the man who now belonged to her, said, "I claim you as mine. You belong to my clan as I do. You are committed to their welfare as well as mine. I *choose* you to be mine," Elyana said solemnly as she placed the ring on the left ring finger of the man in front of her. She gazed up at him, and on a bridge they created last night, she sent, *"My heart and soul chose you long ago. I just needed to wait for you to find me again so I can love you properly."*

The man before her took the other ring and slid the gold band on her left ring finger as he said, "I claim you as mine. You belong to my clan as I do and are committed to their welfare as well as mine. I *choose* you to be mine." He placed the ring on her finger, and gazing into her eyes, he sent, *"I've waited my whole life to be loved by you. I only hope to make you as happy as you've made me."*

Kano peered over at Fergus. "Is this official? May I remove the gift you gave me?"

Fergus's eyes twinkled as he nodded at him. "Aye, Kyran and Kano, ye may both remove them."

Rhyanna was unable to stop staring at the hand holding hers, and as Fergus's words sank in, she peered into his eyes and whispered, "Kyran, is it truly you?"

The man next to her and the Kyran before Fergus both reached under their tunic and ripped off their talismans at the same time.

A loud gasp rolled through the crowd as the Kyran standing before them transformed into Kano, and Kano once again became Kyran.

Kyran reached for Rhyanna's face and, using his thumbs, wiped her tears away before kissing her eyes and working his way down to her lips. "I'm so sorry, my lady, but we were under gag orders from Fergus. I hated seeing you in so much pain and not being able to ease it for you."

Rhyanna laughed, and the tears slipping from her eyes this time were happy ones. "I nearly brained ye when ye wouldn't release me hand." She kissed him as he leaned into her, needing the feel of him in her arms and the taste of him on her lips.

Kyran pulled her onto his lap, needing her close and unwilling to stop touching her.

Kano beamed at Elyana as he took her face in his hands and kissed her passionately. He leaned his forehead against hers and said, "Thanks for trusting me, baby. I promise, you won't regret this. I'll do everything I can to make you happy for the rest of our lives."

"I didn't think I was going to be able to go through with this. The thought of being with anyone but you made me physically ill. I swear I won't make you regret binding yourself to me." Their lips met again, and the crowd cheered behind them.

"You are so beautiful, baby," Kano whispered against her lips. "I need to get you alone."

She chuckled at him as she wrapped her arms around his neck and found his lips once more until a loud clap of thunder shook the ground beneath them.

Meriel strode down the steps towards Fergus. "You all think you're so damn clever. High Fire Mage of the Elemental Court, you are here to honor a contract I created between the Fire Clan. I did not authorize this union. I insist you remove this binding and properly tie Kyran to Elyana."

"I will na, Meriel, and ye canna force me," Fergus said, facing her wrath. "Ye authorized a union between a Prince of the Water Clan and a Princess of the Fire Clan, which is exactly what I gave ye. The gods recognize this union, and the binding shall stand, even in the face of yer temper tantrum."

"Temper tantrum?" she asked furiously. "You haven't begun to see my temper yet. I rescind my blessing. I curse thee, Elyana and Kano, to know nothing but pain and disappointment together. Thrice I curse you." She turned to Kyran and Rhyanna, who were walking towards Kano and Elyana. "I curse you two as well. May the deception which you performed today come back to bite both pairs of you harder and with more teeth than you can begin to imagine. May your wombs be inhospitable and your souls too cold and fickle to properly be true to anyone."

Lightning struck the ground between the two pairs of lovers, branching out and cracking the ground as her curse took hold. The intense light blinded everyone nearby, and no one noticed Meriel's guards making their way down the steps of the dais. With weapons unsheathed, they moved through the crowd.

Fergus strode forward in a blaze of fire, lightning crackling from his hands. "Ye think to play with fire, me queen?" His laughter was dark and still full of deep mystical power from his communion with the gods. "Ye picked the wrong mage to bet against." Lightning bolts danced between his fingers and flew from his hands as he shot them into the ground at her feet, destroying the curse she threw down. "What is done is final. Tis the way the gods want this to be, and ye shall learn to accept their decision with grace."

"With the little you know about me, Fire Mage, you should realize that I will never accept this, and I will do everything in my power to destroy both of these couples."

She glared down at the gathering of nobles and guests before stating. "I represent the Court of Tears. I speak on behalf of the king, and I rescind my blessing on this union. All promises made under the illusion of this ceremony are declared null and void."

A commotion at the back of the room made her look to the arbors. What she saw there made all the color drain from her face.

"NO ONE speaks for the king." A deep, booming voice came from the back of the garden. "I shall speak for myself."

CHAPTER NINETY-ONE

Allow Me

"Varan?" Meriel whispered, recognizing a debt had finally come due.

King Varan, Monarch of the Court of Tears, strode down the carpet leading to the dais and glared at his quivering queen. "You seem to have forgotten my invitation along with my throne, Meriel," he said with a sneer. "Did you honestly believe I wouldn't want to attend a treaty committing one of my children to another clan?"

Meriel backed up a step at the storms swirling through his eyes, and she could hear the waves crashing violently on the nearby shore as the ocean mirrored his discontent. "I simply was trying to keep your court in good standing, my love, while you were unwell."

Varan smiled at her then, and her blood ran cold. The smile promised retribution and reparation for everything she had cost him. "I was unwell because my queen was poisoning me," he snarled into her upturned face.

Meriel's pale-gray eyes widened at the fury on his face and the shocked gasps coming from the crowd. She took a step back but didn't make it far when Varan's hand shot out and grabbed her by the throat, lifting her off the ground.

"You ruined my life. You poisoned me and let the woman I loved think I was fucking a piece of trash when she found you in our bed uninvited. You faked a pregnancy so that I would commit to you because you knew it was the only way you could trap me into making you my queen, even though I had not nor have since ever slept with you. You continued to drug me near to the point of catastrophic organ failure, yet you were doing all this for the good of MY court?"

Meriel clawed at his hands, trying to take a breath. He lowered her to her knees, then released her as if touching her repulsed him. She coughed and tried to suck air into her lungs. When she finally managed to breathe, she gazed up at him through the tears coursing down her face and laughed hysterically. Instead of being remorseful, she was spiteful.

"You made it so easy. Because of your past, you never once doubted you'd fucked me, and Yareli never gave you the opportunity to deny it. A false pregnancy was easy to claim as I was pregnant—just not with a child of your line. Drink became your mistress after your old whore left you, making it easy to taint it a little at a time. I tried to supply you with all the women you could want, never thinking you would spend years celibate, mourning your shabby little artist. Must have been some magic pussy to attain that kind of loyalty from one of the Tyde men."

Varan glanced at her with disgust while his hands clenched into fists at his side. He was afraid if he touched her, he would kill her in front of all these witnesses. In a voice vibrating with barely contained rage, he said, "I renounce you, Meriel, as my queen and partner. I renounce any power you once had and maliciously used against the people in my kingdom. You shall be stripped of all titles, jewels, personal effects, retainers, and protection. I cast you out into the streets with nothing more than the clothes on your back. Your rooms have been sealed, and you shall take nothing with you once you are escorted from this garden. I foolishly fell for your antics once.

"I am aware of the demented games you have played with my sons and the intentions you have for my youngest children. I am aware of the harm you have caused Mistress Rhyanna Cairn—a guest in my home. I am aware of the members of my household you have used and abused over the years, wreaking havoc on their lives.

"The High Elemental Court will see you are held accountable for the crimes against your fellow men and women. May they have mercy on you because you shall find none here. If you are found on the grounds of the Court of Tears again, you will be struck down where you stand, without trial or warning. This is my decree." Looking out at the silent crowd watching him, he added, "And these," he motioned to the crowd, "are my witnesses.

"With these words, I renounce you, and with this deed, you are no longer a queen, but a penniless waif who will wander with my mark on you, warning all you are not to be trusted and will bring only pain. No matter how you try and cover my mark, all will see. They will recognize who you are and what you are capable of."

King Varan reached down and touched her in the middle of her forehead. A teardrop formed in the center of the skin there for all to see. "No amount of makeup or cloth will hide this mark. Only the gods themselves, should they choose to give you their blessing, may remove it."

Meriel screamed as the mark settled into her skin. She reached up, trying to wipe it off. Unsuccessful, she glared at him, then gave him an evil smile. "You think to curse me, My King? Do your best because I promise you, any curse you place on me will rebound on your family tenfold. This is my oath to you."

"Enough!" Varan thundered. "We are no longer going to live in fear of your shadow stalking these halls for prey." He was reaching for her crown when a voice stopped him.

"No, my king. Please... allow me."

Varan's head whipped around at the sound of the woman's voice who had once been his everything.

Yareli walked down the aisle with his father, Neptune, by her side. Wearing the court's colors and dressed like it was her ceremony they were attending, she moved next to him and regarded the woman on the ground before her. "You have something that belongs to me," she said in a calm voice as she reached down and yanked the crown off Meriel's head, taking clumps of hair with it.

Pulling the platinum chunks out of it with disdain, she finally turned to Varan and gazed at the man who still owned her heart, even if she wasn't ready to admit it to him. "My King," she said as she placed the crown in his hand and bowed her head.

"Are you sure this is what you want, my lady?" Varan whispered to her. "I believe it was never your intention to return to this role."

"My family needs me, and I will do what I need to, to ensure their safety and their happiness." She observed the gathering around them, waiting expectantly. Speaking so all could hear, she said, "I willingly reclaim my crown and my place in the Court of Tears as its queen, in title only."

Varan's heart sank as she tacked on the last bit. Then he realized, if she was near, he still had a chance of winning her back. "My lady," he said as he held the crown in front of him.

Yareli met his eyes as he placed the crown on her head, and the love and hope in them made her heart race.

Meriel laughed at them from the floor. In a loud voice, she called out, "Let it begin!" Her back arched, and her arms flung open. Maniacal laughter erupted from her as she called down lightning from the sky. Taking it into her body, she stood and allowed the deadly bolts to emerge from her hands and scatter throughout the crowd.

Varan knocked Yareli to the ground as a bolt narrowly missed her. His eyes locked on hers, begging her, "Please, stay down. I can't lose you again." Not knowing if either of them would survive this day, he took a kiss from her, lingering for a moment.

Yareli was too shocked to move, but her body and her heart recognized him, and in the heat of the moment, she responded, kissing him back for the same reasons. Varan was everything she remembered and still fantasized about.

Screams erupted from the crowd, and he abruptly pulled away because his people needed him, but not without looking back at her like he desperately wished to stay with her on the floor.

Meriel continued laughing as she saw her guards moving silently through the crowd, delivering her final blows. They had been provided with a list of people to dispense of should anything go wrong today. One might say things were not going in her favor.

Neptune helped Yareli up, and she searched for her children, needing to see they were safe. Kano was fighting for his life with one of Yareli's guards, and Elyana was trying to hold off another with flames. Kyran and Rhyanna joined them on the dais. Rhyanna was trying to help the injured while Kryan battled alongside Kano.

A howl rang out, and everything paused for a moment. Kyran's gaze found Dashiel racing towards Elise. One of Meriel's guards had her by the hair and was pulling a knife across her throat. Dash's eyes were turning red as his berserker finally broke loose of the chains restraining him.

Rhyanna rushed to the woman bleeding profusely on the floor, calling for Fergus to join her. She knelt before her, clamping her hands over the gaping wound and looking at the fear in the woman's eyes.

Ferg dropped next to her as she tried to slow the blood flow. "Ye need to cauterize the wound, Ferg."

"I'm not sure how much we can do, Rhy," he said, struggling to know where to begin.

"On the right side." Rhy closed her eyes and found the injury on the auric field. Very carefully, she used her powers to begin healing the severed artery. She imagined stitching the two sides of the artery closed with healing light. Proceeding carefully to still allow blood to flow through, she made tiny stitches. When she finally finished, she was dripping with sweat. "Now, Ferg. Give me a little bit of heat."

Fergus focused until a minute thread of fire was available. "Help me to focus it, Rhy, so I don't botch the whole fecking thing."

"Jest a bit on the edges to help seal where I stitched. 'Tis all we need." Grabbing his hand in her own, she maneuvered his hand where she wanted it. Stabilizing the artery, she focused on the woman's pain-glazed eyes and said, "I'm sorry, lass, this is gonna hurt, and it's gonna leave a scar. I need ye to hold still na"

The woman blinked, acknowledging her words.

Using Fergus's flame, she sealed the rest of the wound, working from the inside out.

As she carefully removed her right hand, she was pleased to view no seepage. Moving her left hand, she sighed in relief because the assassin had been stopped before he severed both sides.

"I need ye to stay still and stay here while I check on the others now." Rhy smiled at her and said, "Yer gonna be jest fine, lass."

Fergus glanced at her. "Ye ever managed that successfully before?"

Rhy smiled at him. "Nye, but I never had the most powerful fire mage, in his magic sheet, helping me afore, have I?" She managed a sarcastic laugh as she headed into the battle, trying to locate who she could save and check in on her friends, and fellow wardens.

Ronan had Maddy in his arms and was trying to make his way safely through the crowd. Jamey and Danny were engaged under the arbors, with Kerry guarding their backs. Neptune was protecting Klaree and Yareli while Varan tried to stop Meriel from doing any more damage. Kenn paired off with Satish, a confrontation long in the making, while Kai battled another of Meriel's guards coming towards them. Roarke had a man pinned to the wall with his sword. Pulling it out, his eyes met Rhyanna's. He gave her a solemn nod, then turned to the next man attacking him.

Elyana's scream shattered Rhyanna's attention, and she turned to find the woman running towards the front row where her father had been sitting.

A bolt of lightning had struck Killam in the chest. His body was in shock, and his heart was struggling to regulate. Fergus beat her to his uncle. Rhy fell to her knees, wondering if they could help him at all.

The smell of burning flesh assaulted her nostrils. His shirt melted into his flesh in a sunburst pattern where the bolt had entered him. The jolt traveled down his left arm, and the exit of all that power had taken part of his forearm and his left hand on its way out.

The blast cauterized the wound, but his heart was struggling to cope with the shock to his system and the disruption of its normal rhythm.

Ferg regarded her, desperate for something to help his kin. "What can we do, lass? There must be something we can do."

"We can try to shock him like we did Ronan when his heart stopped. Might be we can get the rhythm regulated again, and then he'll be stable enough until we can deal with the burns."

"Everyone, stand back," Fergus ordered as he stood. Placing his hand on Rhy's shoulder, he waited while she properly grounded herself by sinking one hand into the earth and then placing the other on his uncle's chest. He released a controlled current running through her and exiting into the man below them.

Nothing happened. They waited a few moments, and with no change before them, Rhy shouted, "Again!"

This time, the head of the Great Lakes Fire Clan took a shallow raspy breath, and then another. Ferg dropped to his knees beside her. "Go! I'll stay with him."

Rhyanna stood, her eyes again scanning the crowd for those she loved. Kyran turned and grinned widely at her as the fighting wound down. As he took a step in her direction, she screamed his name as she saw Meriel step behind him with a sword. Waving her hands behind him as if casting a spell, Meriel smiled at Rhy trying to reach him in time.

Rhyanna pushed people out of the way as she raced for Kyran. Screaming like a banshee, she barreled by Varan, who, seeing the horror on her face turned and screamed his son's name not far behind her.

Kyran's eyes were latched on hers as she ran for him. *Something's wrong, my lady. I can't move a muscle. From the looks on yours and my father's faces, I know it must be bad. Never forget how much I loved you, Rhy.*

Rhyanna continued screaming as she ran towards him, somehow managing to vault over a man on his knees and continue the second her feet hit the floor.

"Meriel, NOOOOOO!" Rhy screamed as she saw her knock Kyran to his knees.

Wrapping her hand in Kyran's hair, Meriel leaned down and whispered in his ear. His smile faded as he watched Rhy closing in on him.

As Rhyanna reached the stairs, Varan took the lead, and still, she knew he wouldn't make it in time. Screaming as Meriel drew the sword back and then plunged it forward towards Kyran's back, she realized the time to reach him had run out. Without another thought, Rhy teleported, landing between Kyran and Meriel, taking the blade meant for him through her abdomen.

CHAPTER NINETY-TWO

She's Everything to Me

Rhyanna collapsed to her knees. Kyran, finally freed from his paralysis, whipped around, and caught her before she hit the ground fully. His hands cupped her face as tears streamed down his. "No, my lady, you are not allowed to leave me like this. We can finally be together. I will not allow you to leave me."

Rhy gazed up at him and attempted a smile. "I love ye, Kyran." Her hand touched the side of his face, and a long sigh escaped her when he turned his head and kissed her palm.

The shock on Meriel's face as she was denied her victory was worth the pain. Before she surrendered to the darkness, Rhyanna called forth her elemental magic fully into her dying body. Screaming her fury at the circumstances, once again taking her from the man she loved, she turned her hands towards the ground and moved the earth.

Meriel fell backwards onto a small plateau rising from the ground. Barely six square feet, there was nowhere for her to run. Massive fissures on every side prevented her from leaping to safety.

Rhy made sure everyone else scampered out of the way before finishing what she had begun. Time was suspended as silence settled around the two women.

"Meriel, you have become a scourge upon this earth and no longer deserve to walk upon it. I take from you willingly and gleefully the life you have repeatedly wasted. Time and again, you have been given the opportunity to choose a gentler path. With the Earth Mother's blessing, I send you to a place you shall never return from." The smile crossing Rhy's cold face was pale and deadly. "The penalty for your crimes upon my people is death."

Meriel screamed her denial at the sentence, but Rhyanna silenced her with a thought. "Your time for penance has passed, and your soul shall be dismantled, never to walk this plane again. May hell be merciful because we shall show you none."

The voice emerging from Rhyanna's mouth and passing sentence was not her own. Ancient and filled with power transcending any of the elementals in attendance, the mother of all was claiming vengeance for one of her favored children, and her vengeance would not be denied.

Meriel's face paled, and she dropped to her knees, lowering her forehead to the ground when she realized she was facing the divine power fully capable of unmaking her. "I beg your forgiveness, Mother, and your mercy."

"I forgive you, but mercy is not mine to grant."

Her voice changed, and now it was Rhyanna's voice again speaking. "I can also forgive ye, Meriel, but I have no mercy left to offer ye." She took a pain-filled breath before trying to speak once more. "Ye nearly assaulted me, tried to separate me from the man I love, and have no consideration for anyone in this world 'cept yerself." She shook her head sadly at the woman. "I don't ken what made ye this way, but everyone has some redeeming quality, and ye've done nothing to prove ye have even one. It be negligent of me to allow ye to roam this world freely. I refuse to live always looking over me shoulder, waiting for ye to stab me back again." Rhy shook her head, even as her decision broke something fundamental inside of her—her oath to harm none. "Nye, I'll not grant ye mercy."

Her eyes shuttered, and when they opened again, it was that ancient soul who peered out at Meriel once more. "Mercy has not been found. Farewell, Meriel, Daughter of Daphne. This world bids ye farewell."

"Wait, if you will, Mother." A gasp escaped Rhyanna as Neptune, of all people, stepped forward. "Daughter of Daphne, from the southern seas?" he asked Meriel.

Meriel took a chance and peered up at the man interceding for her. "Yes, I am from the southern seas."

Neptune searched her features, and when his eyes latched onto her gray ones, they closed in resignation. He turned and knelt before the Earth Mother in Rhyanna's body.

"I believe I may be partly responsible for this child's behavior and would like to plead for mercy on her behalf. I will take full responsibility for her in the future and will bind her powers so that she may harm none." When silence greeted him, he added, "I owe a debt to her mother. Please, give me the opportunity to pay it back."

The powerful entity was silent as she conferred with Rhyanna, knowing that it would be just as much her decision to make. When her eyes popped back open, she glared down at the woman before her.

"Mercy has been temporarily granted. Meriel, you shall be given one last chance to prove your life is worth saving. Fail this test in the slightest way, and your life will be immediately forfeited."

Meriel nodded her agreement.

"However, you will spend the next fortnight in less-than-ideal conditions to remind you of the path you nearly walked today. Hell will seem like a paradise if you fail me again, child." Her voice thundered, shaking the earth as she asked, "Do you understand what you are being offered and the consequences if you fail?"

"Yes, Mother. I do." Meriel whimpered.

As her words ended, the earth shifted, and the plateau she stood on collapsed into the earth. The crevices filled in, and grass grew where the woman had once stood. Meriel, Daughter of Daphne and one-time Queen of the Court of Tears, was in Hell.

"You shall have your own consequences to pay should you be unable to tame that child and produce a decent soul out of her," the Earth Mother thundered once more. "Do you understand, Neptune?"

"I do, Mother, and I will not disappoint you."

Rhyanna's vision was fading as her lifeforce seeped from her body, soaking Kyran's lap and the ground beneath them. As she drifted off, the Earth Mother appeared before her as a young maiden, dewy-eyed, tall, and lean with dark, black hair and caramel skin. "You stand at a crossroads, my child, and need to choose which world you will walk in."

"Can me body survive the wound?" Rhy asked in a whisper. She stood now, unharmed in front of the Earth Mother in a flowing white gown, but her skin was transparent.

"Aye, if you choose life, you will be healed instantly when the weapon is removed from your body." She walked to Rhy and pushed the hair out of her eyes. "There is much damage to your womb. I can't guarantee whether you'll be able to bear children. Is that a price you are willing to pay to remain with your man?"

Around them, she could still see friends and acquaintances battling to subdue Meriel's guards. Dashiel's eyes were red as his berserker tore through many of those who had tormented Varan's people. Kyran's dark-haired brother was still combatting Satish, while Kai dealt with another man trying to get to his sister. Wardens were scattered throughout the crowd, trying to protect the innocent from the men and women who were attacking at random.

Behind her, she found Kyran cradling her body with her friends sobbing around him. The anguish on his face as he held her broke her heart. A conversation they had after the melding replayed through her mind as he reassured her that it mattered not to him whether she could bear young. Rhy was all he wanted. Returning her gaze to the Earth Mother, she said, "I choose a life with him for however long he will have me."

"As you wish, my child," her creator said with a nod, then reached out and tapped a finger on her forehead while saying, "Return."

As time lurched forward once again, the pain returned, and with it, the screams of the wounded around her and the stench of battle. Rhyanna opened her eyes slowly, looking into Kyran's devastated gaze. His hand caressed her cheek. "Welcome back, my lady." He kissed her brow. "Please don't scare me like that again."

"Find Fergus?" she rasped out, looking for him as Danny and Maddy knelt at her side. Maddy was sobbing, and Danny's face was pale with shock. Ronan supported Maddy, and Jameson wrapped his arms around Danny from behind.

Ferg appeared, pushing his way through the crowd until he could kneel beside her. His eyes filled as he studied her, but he let not a one fall. "What is it we can do to fix this, lass?"

"Not sure we can fix this, Ferg." She grimaced as pain twisted inside of her. "But I needs ye to help pull this out of me." She looked up at him, her eyes dull from the blood loss and pain.

"Are ye sure, lass?" he asked with a sniffle. "I'se afraid ye'll bleed out afore I can staunch it."

"I have it on good authority that I'll witness another sunrise, but ye have to hurry afore she leaves." Her eyes drifted shut, but she whispered, "Trust me, ye daft twit, and do it."

Fergus's eyes locked on Kyran's as he chuckled. "Yer call, lad."

They were both a mess, but Kyran nodded and asked, "Have you ever known her to be wrong?"

"Nye." He grabbed the hilt, and in one heave, drew it from her body.

Rhy's back arched, and she screamed from the agony of the metal exiting her body. Her head fell limply over Kyran's arm, and he glanced at Ferg in a panic.

Ferg reached out and touched the pulse in her neck; it was thready but getting stronger. He reached down to put pressure on the wound, but when he moved the fabric, the wound was gone, and only a faint scar remained—a thin white line the width of the sword. "Feck me, the wound's healed." The tears he'd held in fell in relief.

As her family stood there holding each other and celebrating the fact that she would live, a voice came from the ether. "Ye've all witnessed the power

I still possess. Rhyanna sacrificed herself for another and earned my favor. Pass the word that the Earth Mother's power grows. She sees and knows all. My wrath is still something to fear, and my favor something worth gaining. Be well, my children."

A chorus of "Be well, our mother" went up.

Kyran cradled Rhy in his arms as the others saw to the injured and took Meriel's co-conspirators into custody. Someone handed him a cool cloth, and he used it to wipe the blood and debris from her face. "Come back to me, Rhy," he whispered over and over. "Come back to me, my lady."

Neptune, his grandsire, knelt beside him. "May I add some of my power to heal your lady, Kyran?"

Kyran narrowed his eyes at the man suspiciously. He was unusually quiet and somber. Glancing at how pale Rhy was, he asked, "Will it harm her at all?"

"No, lad. It will only assist with the blood flow to her abdomen and help prevent any scar tissue that might form in her womb."

"Proceed."

Neptune placed both hands on her abdomen and imagined healing yellow and orange light flowing through her, clearing away anything that didn't serve her. He could sense where the damage had been done, and he used the light to remove adhesions and any risk of infection.

As he sat back and removed his hands, he smiled at his grandson. "She's quite a woman. A powerful, mystical one with a beautiful soul, she will keep you on your toes, Kyr."

Kyran kissed the side of her head as he cradled her body to his chest. "Aye, she will." Brushing the hair from her head, he whispered, "She's everything to me."

CHAPTER NINETY-THREE

Kiss Me

Danny stumbled away from the elegant garden that had exploded into a gruesome battlefield. Without knowing where she was headed, she ended up on the beach. Stumbling into the surf fully dressed, she collapsed in the chilly water, trying to process what she had just witnessed.

Tears coursed down her face, falling harder every time she blinked. Rhyanna was her sister in every way that mattered, and she'd seen her nearly die only moments before. Logically, she understood what she'd witnessed was only possible through divine intervention, but holy fuck. Rhy stopped breathing, and she stopped bleeding because her body had pumped all the blood out of her body.

The anguish on Kyran's face and the sound of his keening fucking gutted her. If Rhy hadn't made it, Danny had no doubt that Kyr would have followed her to the other side. The thought of it made her want to vomit. She never wanted anyone to have that much power over her. But as she sat there watching all the people she loved right there mourning with him, she realized how much she stood to lose because the loss of any one of them would have gutted her, too.

Yes, they were fellow wardens and fellow drinking buddies, but they were more than that to her. As pitiful as it was, they were the only family she knew—her biological family sold her into a life of prostitution. Their wheel wouldn't turn with any of the spokes missing, and Danny, try as she might, couldn't fucking face it again.

Jamey witnessed Danny running off and gave her a few minutes to gather herself before following her to the beach. His chest tightened as he crested

495

the dunes and found her on her knees in the water, pounding her hands against the sand. Her shrieks rose above the sound of the waves and the gulls screaming overhead. Kerry sidled up next to him, looking down at her.

"Go to her," the man with the falcon eyes said. "Yer who she needs. I'll never be to her what ye already are." He turned away but not before Jamey heard him say, "I doubt I'll ever be that for anyone."

Kerrygan walked away, and Jamey was surprised by the admission. The man saved his life today when he didn't have to. He'd earned his grudging respect as a man and as one hell of a swordsman.

Following the pain in his chest, he made his way over to the woman he most admired in the world. Her strength, loyalty, and commitment to the people in her life were why he was already head over heels in love with her, even though he knew he was setting himself up to be disappointed. He didn't know if she would ever be able to give herself to one man, and he wasn't sure if he could tolerate the infidelity she would use to push him away.

Right now, he didn't give a fuck about any of that. He just needed to hold her or fight with her. Whatever she fucking needed, he would provide.

His long stride ate up the short distance between them. She was curled over her knees in the surf with her hands stretched out in front of her, sobbing. Her petite body shook with the force of her sobs.

Dropping to his knees behind her, he leaned down and wrapped his massive arms around her waist, laying his chest against her back and his face in her neck. Her body stiffened and went instantly into defense mode.

"Easy, Danny," he said in a soothing voice. "It's Jamey. Let me in, Hellion. Please, let me in," he pleaded.

Danny remained on the verge of turning into a wildcat until her mind registered his voice and her body recognized his scent. He leaned forward, running his hands along her arms until he entwined his fingers with hers, grounding her. Sobs still shook her small frame.

Eventually her body relaxed, and he released her hands. His face was still buried in her neck, and he kept talking to her in the voice he used with his horses, calming and gentling them until they let him touch them. The tension released from her body, but he wasn't expecting it when she turned and threw herself into his arms so hard that she almost knocked him over. Wrapping her arms tightly around his neck, she clung to him, plastering herself against his broad chest.

Jamey banded his arms around her, rubbing her back while he held her. "I gotchya," he said. "Let it all out."

Danny shivered in his arms as her wet dress dropped her body temp.

He moved enough to untangle her arms from his neck. "Hellion, you need to take that dress off." He pulled his shirt over his head. "You can put this on; it will help you warm up."

Her pale blue eyes locked on his as they overflowed once again.

"Honey," Jamey said as he framed her face between his hands. Using his thumbs, he wiped her tears away. He couldn't look away from her eyes, even as he leaned in and brushed his lips over her forehead, then slowly skimmed them across her brows. Her eyes closed as his fingers stroked her face. Jamey kissed her eyes, then captured the tears still flowing. When he missed one and it trailed down her face, he tracked it to the corner of her mouth.

His breathing was coming raggedly as he stared into her eyes, wanting desperately to kiss her and trying to talk himself out of it before he ruined everything.

"Do you want me to turn away so you can take your dress off?"

Jamey's voice deepened and did something to Danny. It made her ache to hear it more and to have his hands on her everywhere.

She shook her head no and pulled the strapless gown over her head, throwing it to the side. God bless the man, he never looked away from her eyes, although she thought his body might have stirred beneath her.

Picking up the shirt he'd dropped between them, she pulled it on. Lost in the overwhelming scent of a rugged male, her sorrow abated. She dried her face and wiped her nose on the sleeve. Sheepishly glancing up at him, she said, "Sorry."

His drop-chocolate eyes were luminous as they looked at her, and even darker with desire, though he tried to reign it in. Unable to help herself, she placed her hands on his face and studied the man beneath her.

Tonight, she didn't think of him as Jamey, her partner. No, this was Jameson, the man who kept her safe, who was always considerate and sweet, and who she knew to be an exceptionally generous lover. She only knew the last part through secondhand experience, but she had been fantasizing about his body for months since the first time she caught him fucking Carsyn.

Her thumbs brushed over his prominent cheekbones. His eyes never left hers as she touched him. The strength of his arms around her and the heat of his body made her shudder on his lap.

The involuntary movement made him pull her closer. He rubbed her arms brusquely. With a halfhearted smile, he said, "The shifter in me is always hot; it will help you warm up, darling."

Danny didn't have the energy to smile yet—she was still too emotionally distraught to even consider it. Swallowing hard, she couldn't dislodge the lump in her throat. Her fingers ghosted over his cheeks, tracing the high bridge of the straight nose he'd inherited from his indigenous ancestors, and then slowly moving down to his full, sensual lips.

The saddest eyes he'd ever seen gazed at him quizzically, her brow quirking as she asked, "Why are you the only man who makes me feel safe? At the same time, the way you make me feel fucking terrifies me."

Not sure she was looking for answers, he remained silent.

Her brows drew together as she followed the movement of her fingers. Skimming around his lips, she went down over the strong cleft in his chin and the square edges of his jaw, running her hands back up and tangling them into his hair, pulling his head back as she controlled him with his silken strands. His hair was so soft. Her right hand ran through it repeatedly, and she didn't tangle in anything, not even once.

Jamey was mesmerized as her hands mapped out his features. The sensation of her stroking his hair made him imagine her stroking other things... He didn't dare break the spell they were under by moaning, terrified that she would stop.

Still looking perplexed, she raised up and skimmed her lips over his forehead as if testing the sensation against her skin before proceeding. She moved down over his temple and cheekbone.

Trying not to let his cock get too excited by her innocent explorations, Jameson held her tightly, afraid in a moment of lucidity she would run and escape like smoke drifting through his fingers. Her hands touching his face made him feel more vulnerable than if he was nude in front of her.

Afraid that she could see how he felt about her every time she gazed into his eyes, he swallowed hard. This was the first time she hadn't taken off like a terrified rabbit. He pushed down all his reactions physically and emotionally and let her take her time touching him without censure or fear.

As her lips moved down his cheek, she tightened her left hand in the hair at the base of his neck, holding him tightly in place. Her right hand traced his face, running along the edge of his hairline as her lips brushed the edge of his jaw near his ear. Using her handhold, she tipped his head back and continued along the edge of his jaw until she was under his chin.

Her breathing was getting more ragged the closer she came to his lips.

Danny paused as she lifted herself higher on his lap. She needed to take something for herself today, a bright light after the nightmare of events she had just witnessed. Her eyes flashed to his, and she tipped his head and asked him, "Did you know I've never willingly kissed a man?"

Jamey shook his head. He knew she never kissed her lovers. She told him so one drunken night, and he didn't want to dwell too long on the willing part of her statement.

Her fingers finally touched his lips, tracing the full upper bow and then using her thumb to trace the lush lower lip. Her eyes flew to his as his lips parted, and he sucked in a gasp. "I'm not sure if I can without hurting you, but would you be willing to let me try to kiss you, Jamey?"

Jamey was holding his breath. He'd wanted this for so long, but he could hear the soft pants coming from her and knew she was on the verge of panicking. His hand came up and cupped the side of her face, stroking her cheekbone with his thumb. "Honey, you can do anything at all you want to me. You control every aspect of this. Other than holding you and stroking your back or arms the way I am doing right now, I won't touch you or try to take over in any way."

His fingers continued stroking her skin, and when she closed her eyes and leaned into his hand, he waited for her to start purring. These were huge steps for Danny, and he didn't want to move her any faster than she wanted to go.

When she opened her eyes and stared into his again, he used his thumb to brush over her lower lip. "Kiss me, Danyka."

"I don't know what to do, Jamey." Her voice was so soft. It was rare that she would admit to anything she wasn't sure about.

"Keep following your instincts, sweetheart. You're doing great so far."

"Really?"

"Really, Danny," he said with a gentle smile.

Focusing on him once more, her hand stroked his hair as she used her lips on his jaw once again, moving slowly towards her destination. Her hand returned to his mouth, and she touched his lower lip, brushing it gently back and forth before moving to the side of his face and holding him still as her lips hovered over his.

Her eyes snapped to his one last time, and they were half closed in the anticipation of finally kissing her. The way he was looking at her with so much desire and adoration helped to shatter her fears, and she gently brought her lips to his, like a whisper on the summer wind.

Softly, sweetly she moved her lips back and forth over his. Braver and wanting more from him, she used the tip of her tongue to trace the seam of his lips. His hands tightened around her as he allowed her to kiss him, and when he parted his lips for her, she sucked on his lower lip before slipping her tongue in to stroke shyly against his.

Danny's eyes closed, and she kept moving closer to his chest like she couldn't be close enough to him. Jamey was sure that she was unaware of her hips grinding against his cock, making him harder than he'd ever been. He almost came when she stroked his tongue with hers, and it took everything he had not to respond and encourage her in the steps of this mating dance they were performing.

"Jamey..."

"Yeah, honey?" he asked as their breath mingled.

"Would you mind kissing me back?" she asked uncertainly.

The moment that she paused, he stroked her lips with his slowly, letting her acclimate to him being in control. He suckled her lower lip, and when she moaned deeply, his tongue stroked hers, needing the sugar-and-spice taste of her in his system. He kept the kiss smoldering, and when she'd gotten the hang of it, he stroked deeper and turned up the heat a little letting her lips take his for a test drive.

Danny moaned low and deep as her body responded to the things he was doing to her. She realized her lower body was grinding against his, and by the rock-solid state of his cock straining against her groin, he wasn't hating it. Every time she rocked against his cock, he stroked against a place that was giving her immense pleasure. If she could keep doing this, she was sure she could make herself come. Wondering if this was fair to him, she pulled back and asked, "Do you want me to stop?"

His hands had shifted to her hips to help her find her rhythm. "Don't you fucking dare," he said, his dark eyes flashing at her.

Her lips crashed into his again, and her hips slid back and forth, stroking her core against his cock. Their tongues collided and she took over, taking what she needed from him. The only time she pulled away was when her back arched, and shuddering in his arms, she sobbed, "Yes, yes, Jamey, yes."

He stole the words right from her mouth when he palmed her neck and pulled her lips back to his. He kept rocking her against him until he followed her, moaning. As they sat there shuddering together, he gentled the kiss, taking it back down to where they had started. As he caught his breath, he leaned his forehead against hers, holding her tightly, savoring the moment.

Danny tucked her head against his neck as they sat there silently. Her lips placed a small kiss behind his ear as she relaxed against him, exhausted.

"Do you think she'll make it, Jamey?'

"I have absolutely no doubt, honey. Rhy will be fine, and after a good night's sleep, so will we."

"Promise?"

"Promise." His hand stroked over her head, and he hoped he was right and could keep his promise.

Jamey kept stroking her skin underneath his shirt and knew the moment the mood changed. She took a hiccupping breath and whispered, "I'm sorry, Jamey."

When she pulled back to look at him with tears in her eyes, he clamped his hand over her mouth and growled at her. "Don't you fucking dare compel me to forget one of the best moments of my life, Danyka. No matter how much you try to make me forget, my soul will always remember the moment you first kissed me, and no compulsion will change that. If you do this, I promise you when I do remember…" his meaty palm slid down her bare skin to her ass, "I will blister your ass so badly you won't be able to sit for a week. I've never hit a woman; don't make me break that vow."

Wide, blue eyes snapped to his in surprise, with a hint of fear and a lot of desire ramping back up in them. "What are we doing here, Jamey?" she asked him in a breathless whisper.

"Tonight, we're comforting each other. You're not the only one who needed this. Rhy is like my sister, too. Danny, I was as torn up inside about tonight as you were."

His hand moved to cup her face again. "This will be whatever you need it to be, hellion. Nothing more and nothing less. No pressure."

Her breath hitched as she said, "This will never be enough for you, Jamey. You deserve so much more."

"You have no idea what is enough for me. Let me be the one to decide that." His thumb traced her bottom lip again, and his cock jerked when she bit it, then slowly sucked it into her mouth, making his cock rock hard again.

Danny loved the look in his eyes as desire made an appearance once again. She released his thumb, not quite sure why she had teased him because she still wasn't ready to go any further with this.

Jamey cleared his throat. His hands were clenching her hips tightly, and he forced his fingers to relax instead of sliding her back and forth over his cock again the way he wanted to.

"I need to clean up. Do you want to head back, and I'll join you in a few?" He was giving her an out, but a part of him wanted her to wait for him to return. His eyes challenged her to stay.

Danny realized he was giving her the easy way out, and as much as she wanted to run with the opportunity, she wasn't a coward—only when it came to the way he made her feel. His eyes bore into hers, double daring her, and who was she to back down from that?

"I'll walk back with you." She leaned against his forehead for a moment and stroked her hands on the sides of his face before reluctantly vacating his lap.

Jamey stood and headed into the waves up to his waist. He unlaced his breeches and dropped them to clean himself up.

Danny couldn't stop herself from watching him walk into the waves. The broad expanse of his back tapering into his narrow waist was chiseled with muscles. The graceful way he moved turned her on. Everything about him lately turned her on. When his pants fell, exposing his sculpted ass, she wanted her hands on those tight globes. Shaking herself out of it, she turned and retrieved her dress. Nearly dry, she exchanged his shirt for it, hating to give it up.

Jamey could sense her eyes on him as he cleaned himself. He wanted to turn with his still hard cock in his hand and stroke it with her watching, like he had during Maddy and Ronan's melding. The intelligent part of him that was still functioning put the damn thing away, but it was a struggle between the size and the wet pants. Lacing the pants back up, he exited, dripping. With a bit of heat and air from the minor elements he controlled, he was dry in moments.

"Why didn't you use that nifty trick to dry my dress earlier?" she taunted, handing him back his shirt.

He grasped her chin in his hand and said, "If I'd done that, I wouldn't have gotten the pleasure of holding you." He brushed a kiss on her brow and offered her his hand.

Danny glanced at it for a moment as if unsure what to do with it, then placed her small hand inside his massive paw. His thumb absently brushed the back of her hand, and she liked the soothing motion.

The garden was almost empty when they arrived. Kerrygan sat at a table with a bottle of whiskey to himself. Jamey released her and kept his shit together when she went over and plopped down in Kerry's lap, taking the bottle from his lips.

"Don't be greedy; you need to share that with us."

Jameson sat beside them, taking the bottle when she offered it and chugging back a double. He tipped the bottle at Kerry and said, "Thanks for your help this morning. Had my hands full with the one in front of me and didn't see the asshole coming from behind."

Surprise crossed his face before he said, "Happy to, brother." Kerry's attention turned to Danny. "You good, pixie?"

She gave him a half-hearted smile. "I'll be fine. How's Rhy?"

"Sleeping. Expect she will for a day or two." He took the bottle back from Jamey. "Nearly dying's exhausting work on the body."

"Ain't that the fucking truth," Danny said with a sigh. "I don't think I'll ever get the sight of that sword nearly cutting her in half out of my head."

Kerry kissed her brow when she settled against his chest and tucked his arm around her. His hand rubbed her arm soothingly. "I don't think any of us will."

Kerry peered at Jamey with a raised eyebrow asking if he was all right with her on his lap.

Jamey nodded at him but took the bottle again, nearly draining it, glad that he and Kerry seemed to have come to some sort of an unspoken agreement regarding Danny.

"Ye feckers. Ye finished it without saving me a fecking shot." Fergus's voice came at them from behind. "Damn good thing I picked up two more, ye stingy bastards." He opened the bottle and took a decent chug. "I be keeping this one; the three of ye can share that one." He let out a long sigh as he scrubbed his hands over his face. "Fecking hell, never saw that coming."

"You don't see everything, do you?" Danny asked him.

"Na, we never see the outcome, just potential pitfalls and possibilities. Usually, I have enough of a hint fer a fecking heads up at least. This motherfecker," his hands waved at the carnage around them, "never came to light, not even a hint of it."

"Who'd ye piss off on the other side, ye arrogant bastard?" Kerry asked with a grin.

Ferg shook his head, eyes going towards the twilight sky. "Beginning to wonder that meself." He tipped the bottle again.

"Don't know that I'd want to know," Jamey said. "Where's the fun in that? I'll take all the chaos and heartbreak along with the spontaneity."

"I'm still blessed with all that," Fergus said. "I rarely catch any glimpses of me role in the larger picture."

"You don't need a glimpse, Ferg," Danny said with a chuckle. "We'll keep you busy enough with our chaos that you won't have time for a life of your own."

"And that, ye lil shite," Fergus said, "is what I be most afeared of."

Laughter rang out as night trumped day, bottles emptied, and their panic faded away with the light. Rhy would be fine. They all would be fine as long as they had each other's backs. Everything was going to be all right.

CHAPTER NINETY-FOUR

Let Me Take Care for You

Kano held Elyana in his lap as they waited for the healer to come out of her father's room. Eyes swollen from her tears stared at the woman approaching them.

The healer was an elderly woman with a widow's hump and gnarled hands. Her eyes were rheumy, and Elyana doubted her ability to properly treat her father, even though Kano vouched for her repeatedly. Since Rhyanna was incapacitated, Fergus returned through the portal to the Great Lakes Clan to fetch their best healers.

Elyana assisted the healer in stripping her father's clothes from his torso. The fabric was melted into his skin in places on his chest, and they were unable to remove every bit of the melted mass. His pain-filled screams would haunt her for a long time. The stump of his arm was still seeping and would need to be debrided before cauterization.

Rivulets of his blood soaked through the beautiful gown she wore. Dried now, the fabric was stiff, and as she fixated on her hands, she found it under her nail beds and splattered on her forearms also. She rubbed her nails repeatedly against her dress, trying to get it off her skin and not scream in frustration at the failure to do so.

Kano was worried and unsure of how to help her. He linked his fingers with hers, trying to distract her from the blood. Startled eyes flew to his as if she had forgotten she was sitting on his lap. He cupped her face in his large palm and asked, "What can I do for you, baby? What do you need from me?"

"I don't know," she whispered in a choked voice. "I can't focus."

A flurry of activity at the door caught their attention, and Fergus entered, followed by half a dozen healers. He ushered them into the bedroom and settled in a chair next to theirs.

A half-hour later, a portly man came out of the room, wiping his hands on a towel. "He's stable, but he's lost a lot of blood." He wiped the towel over his dripping brow. "The damage is extensive, and it will be painful to remove the skin we need to if he's alert, so we are going to do as much as we can tonight while he's still out." A nod at Elyana acknowledged her position, and he scratched his head before speaking. "My lady, he won't be awake for a day or more. There's nothing else you can do tonight. Your father will need you more in the coming days. Please get some sleep." He waved at her dress. "I'm sure you want to change at the very least."

Elyana blinked slowly, then looked down at her dress. The horror of how much blood was there made her start fidgeting with the buttons in the back.

"I give you my word, Miss Elyana, I will send for you if anything changes. You will be the first to know."

Fergus reached for her hand, "Little cousin, trust me to stay and oversee this until yer brothers return. Ye ken he's like a father to me, too, lass, and I promise ye, I'll not leave him alone. If they need anything, or if his condition changes, I'll send word. Ye have me solemn vow."

Tears overflowed as she reached out and took the hand he offered her. "Thank you, Fergus. I'm so grateful you're here." Her skirts made it easy to slide off Kano's lap. Before her feet hit the floor, he was taking her hand and walking with her towards the door.

Hands linked, he pulled her in the right direction as they made their silent way down the hall. Kano was silent because what the fuck did you say after seeing your parent like that? A brand would be heavily scarred on his chest, and his hand...he shivered at the thought of losing a limb.

Before Elyana knew it, they stood in a spacious suite of rooms. Water began running in an adjacent bathroom. Barely registering her surroundings, she stood there mute while Kano unhooked the back of her dress and slid the blood-stained fabric from her body. Coming around to her front, he stared down into her devastated face and kissed her forehead gently. Kneeling in front of her, he lifted one foot and untied the shoe strapped on her foot, then repeated the action with the other.

Elyana's hands found his shoulders, trying to maintain her balance while he stripped off her stockings and garters next. His fingers hooked the edges of her panties and unceremoniously pulled them down. Deftly releasing the metal hooks in the front of her red corset, he released the uncomfortable contraption and looked up at the raw agony in her face.

Eyes still straight ahead, she knew Kano was concerned about her, but didn't know how she was supposed to react to the near death of her father. Papa was the only parent she had left, and she had serious doubts about his ability to pull through the injuries he sustained.

Still dressed, he stood and took her hand, leading her into the largest bathroom she had ever been in. A massive copper tub with a high back was filled with hot water. Steam rose from the surface. Kano threw a small linen bag with herbs into the water. The smell of rosemary and peppermint filled the room.

The thought of a bath was so enticing that she stepped towards the tub as Kano toed off his boots. As she bent over to step in, her eyes locked on the blood covering her torso. Backpedaling quickly, a sob escaped her, "Get it off of me, please, get it off of me."

The pitiful sound of her voice grabbed Kano's attention immediately. Eyes moving towards her, he saw her trying to wipe off the brown streaks of blood that painted her abdomen, where her father's blood soaked through the multiple layers of fabric.

Turning on the shower with a thought, he strode towards her. "Come here, baby." Her eyes stared up at him with such horror it broke his heart, and he wished he could have killed Meriel for causing her so much pain tonight. His large hands covered hers, stopping her from digging herself raw. With a gentle tug, he pulled her into the shower with him. "Let me take care of you." A brief kiss on her temple calmed her a bit as the water ran over her back.

Kano was fully dressed, but he didn't give a shit. Tonight, she needed him to give her his full attention, and he was going to be whatever she needed him to be. "Lean back so I can wash your hair." Elyana followed his instructions, closing her eyes so she didn't get soap in them. Lathering her thick hair, he massaged her scalp until a soft moan escaped her. He pulled her back to his front and continued washing her hair. Her body relaxed against him as he worked. Reaching for the shower head, he turned her away so that she could lean further back.

Rinsing, then conditioning her long hair made him feel like he was doing something important for her, and he loved that he was the one here doing it. The thought that this could have been Kyran scrubbing her body tonight flitted through his mind, and his temper flared at the reminder of how close he came to fucking losing her. Thank fucking God for Fergus's plan.

Finished with her hair, he reached for a bar of soap and ignored the washcloth. Hands rolling the soap into thick suds, he reached for her. The second his hands connected with her skin, his temper eased, and he focused on cleansing the horrors off her body and soothing her frayed nerves. A soapy fist below her chin lifted her to meet his eyes. "If you're comfortable with this, I'm going to wash your body, baby." After such a traumatic day, he didn't want to assume too much.

Her big hazel eyes stared up at him through the water dripping down her face. "Please," she managed in a whimper. With one word, she completely slayed him with her trust.

His soapy hands wiped the splatters off her cheeks, working quickly down her neck, over her shoulders, and down her arms. Dropping to his knees in front of her again, he thoroughly washed her torso, needing to do it twice to erase any evidence that lingered. In a very calm utilitarian way, his hands moved over her back, hips, and luscious ass without one inappropriate thought crossing his mind. He finished her front the same way, working his way down her long legs and sliding slippery fingers between her legs.

After hosing her off, he stripped his clothes, leaving them on the floor of the shower before stepping onto the bath mat with her. Grabbing two towels, he laid them on a bench next to the tub and stepped into the hot water. He reached for her hand and helped her over the high side. Settling down against the back, he expected her to sit with him, but she stood there trembling.

"Baby, come here. Please, let me hold you. He tugged on her hand until she stumbled back. Wrapping his arms around her hips to stabilize her, he eased her into the fragrant water. With her settled on his lap, he leaned back against the warm metal.

Elyana's slight body drifted to the top of the water. He'd never paid attention to how tiny she was until tonight. Her head barely reached the middle of his chest, but she felt so right laying against him. Arms banding under her full breasts, he bent his knees and shifted her up higher so he could brush his lips over her neck.

With a sigh, she snuggled into him. Cradled against his shoulder, she turned her head, hoping he wouldn't see the tears leaking out of her eyes. When his lips traced the damp trails, she cried harder, worrying about her Papa. "I was horrible to him last night, Kano. I said such hateful things to him. The switch wasn't a surprise to him. He knew, didn't he?"

"I think so, but we were all under gag orders from Ferg. There's no way that he could have safely told you what was going on."

"During the ceremony, he told me to trust him—that he would do anything to see me happy."

Jaw clenching, he asked, "Do you have any regrets?" The unease in his voice was hard to disguise. It would kill him if she didn't want him now.

Elyana tipped her head to gaze up at him. Her luminous gaze locked on his as she reassured him, "Not a one, and I hope you don't either. I just wish we had been able to celebrate the way we feel about each other without the secrecy." Her face paled as she had a moment of panic. "Do you think we made a mistake?"

His voice cut her off before her exhausted mind went down that road. "Absolutely not," he whispered against her skin. "You're the only woman I want to spend my life with. I'm just afraid I might be more than you bargained for."

A hand rose to cup his face, stroking the stubble on his jaw. "I don't think I'll have any problem handling all of you." His lips brushed hers in a gentle kiss. Exhausted, they let the hot water soak away the pain and fears of the day.

"If I lose him, I've hardly any family left," she said in a lonely whisper.

The hitch in her voice made his chest ache. Coming from a large family, he couldn't imagine being the last of his line. "You're wrong about that, baby," he said against her temple with a kiss. "I'm your immediate family now, and I come with a lot of branches in my family tree." A hand in her hair pulled her head back so he could meet her gaze. "They're your family now, too, and they're gonna love you, just like I do."

"Are you sure? Because every decision we've made this past week has been because of fear. Would we ever have ended up here if we hadn't been forced to do this."

"Elyana, I've loved you since the first week I spent with you, don't you ever doubt that." A finger caressed the lines in her brow. "If I'd been able to find you, we would have been right here loving each other a long time ago."

A hint of a smile crossed her face, the first one since Meriel's attack. "I love you too, Kano." A shiver ran through her as the water cooled.

"C'mon, let's get you dried off, then we both need some sleep."

Barely able to pick up her feet, she managed to dry off. She gasped as Kano picked her up and carried her to his bed. Spooning her, he buried his head in her hair, content just to hold her. "Get some sleep, baby. I'm not going anywhere."

Before he finished speaking, she gave in to the exhaustion claiming her. Safe, warm, and held by the man she loved, she let herself fall into the healing power of sleep, knowing she would never be alone again.

Kano saw her eyes close and felt her breathing slow and her body relax beside him. The sensation of her warm body beside him was heavenly, and he couldn't begin to imagine life without her. The lack of sleep the past few nights and the unsettled day caught up with him, and he drifted off quickly, knowing there was no place else he would rather be than wrapped around the woman who held his heart.

CHAPTER NINETY-FIVE

Firelight

Rhyanna slept for nearly two days after her near-death experience. Kyran barely left her side while she recovered, needing to reassure himself that she was still safe and sound. Today, Rhy finally felt up to joining everyone for the noon meal. Kyran led her into the dining room amongst applause from everyone waiting for them.

King Varan sat at the head of the long banquet table with Kyran's brothers and his sister lining the sides, interspersed with wardens from the Heart Island Sanctuary. The queen sat at the other end, looking much more casual today, wearing something Rhy herself would've been comfortable in.

Everyone stood, trying to get to her first. After the hugs and kisses, she took a seat between Kyran and his mother. Starving, she dove into the food placed before her. The bantering around the table made her smile, as did Fergus's usual antics.

Laughter from the Court of Tears's king was a welcome sound. Varan was a completely different man from the one she'd met only a month ago. Today he looked healthy and whole. The joy he exuded from having his family gathered was palpable. The glances he kept giving his queen left no doubt about the man's hopes for a reconciliation. Yareli tried to be more subtle, but Rhy caught her looking his way when his laughter rang out and when he spoke with his children. Rhy truly hoped they would find their way back together, but she knew there was a lot of water under their bridge to deal with before that had any chance of happening.

Kyran doted on her, touching her often and leaning over to take her hand in his or run his fingers over her skin. Rhy's senses were overwhelmed, and she tired more quickly than she liked to admit. In tune with her as he always was, he excused them and took her back to his suite for a long nap.

Hours later, Rhy woke alone. She wandered through the suite of rooms looking for Kyran and found their bags packed and ready to go. Hope soared that this was a sign they would be returning to the sanctuary soon.

A strong need to ground herself sent her through the French doors and down the sandy path leading to the beach. The walk in her bare feet made her body sing as she realigned her connection to the earth through the warm sand.

The tug on her heartstrings through their lover's bridge led her straight to Kyran. His energy was anxious, and Rhy couldn't help but worry about his concern when she saw him with his pants rolled to his knees, standing in the surf.

Just as the earth grounded her, the ocean calmed him, and she knew he would need this connection frequently to reset himself.

Rhy was no longer afraid of the Court of Tears. The harem had been dismantled, and reparations and healing were offered to those who had been harmed through Meriel's tyranny. The first time she attended this court, fear and lust had been the dominant emotions. Today, hope was overcoming all the negativity of the past few years, and where hope bloomed, there would come changes for a better world for these people.

Aware of her presence behind him, Kyran turned and held out a hand palm up, silently asking her to join him. Rhyanna tied her long skirt up to her knees and wandered in to take his hand. He pulled her close and kissed her gently, tucking her head under his chin when her arms went around his waist.

"How are you feeling, my lady?"

"A wee bit homesick."

"Are you up to using the portal?"

"Aye, I'll have no trouble at all."

"Would you like to leave tonight?"

She looked up at him with a smile. "If it's not too inconvenient for ye."

"Nothing's too inconvenient for me where you're concerned, Rhyanna." His lips brushed her forehead. "I have a surprise for you when we get there."

"I love surprises!" she said excitedly. "Are ye ready?"

"Let's go," he said with a wide grin as he took her hand and walked beside her. "Our bags will follow tomorrow. Is there anything you need for tonight?"

Her eyes lit on his mischievously. "Ye, Kyran. I have a strong need for ye."

Desire flashed in his eyes, and he kissed her. "Then we best be on our way."

"Take me home, me laird."

"As my lady wishes," he said with a smile as they made their way down the path to the portal.

Rhyanna saw the portal ahead of them and thought about the last time she used it, running away from Kyran. This time, she was running towards a future with him by her side, and she was eager for it to begin.

Exiting the portal on Heart Island, just in time for the sun to set on the Stag Gate, Rhyanna put her hands out and twirled in a circle. "'Tis good to be back home." He caught her when her balance failed her from the spinning. Laughing with him, she said, "And it's so good to have ye here with me, with nothing keeping us apart."

"Are you up to a walk before we turn in?"

"I'd love a walk with ye, back where it all began."

He grinned broadly. "I was hoping you'd say that because that's where my surprise is."

She pulled on his hand, trying to hurry him. "Hurry up, then."

As they crested the final hill, he turned her towards him. "I need you to keep your eyes closed for the rest of the way."

"Good thing we ain'ts got far to go."

Taking her hand, he led her the last few steps over the rise. "Keep them closed," he said as he stepped behind her, covering her eyes with his hands.

"I wasna peeking!" she protested.

"I know you weren't, my lady." He nuzzled the side of her neck, making her lean back against him to give him better access.

"Maddy and Ethelinda helped me manifest this. I hope you love it as much as I do."

He removed his hands from her eyes and heard her gasp of surprise. Moving to her side to see her expression, he saw the tears forming and wondered if he'd ruined their special place.

Rhy was speechless. In front of her was a two-story house with a large stone porch facing the lake.

"If you don't like it, we can move it, or change it however you want, Rhy," he said nervously, her silence killing him.

She flung herself at him, almost knocking him down. "I love it, Kyr," she said, kissing him. "How did ye manage it so quickly?"

He kissed her back, nuzzling her with his nose. "Ethelinda manifested the main structure. You'll need to decide how you want the floor plan inside."

Kyran pulled her up the stairs onto the front porch. Two rough-cut rocking chairs faced the lake. He sat in one and pulled her across his lap.

She tucked her head under his chin and stared out across the water, completely at peace with everything in her life.

"I've always longed for a place to stay up here," she said with a sigh.

"I thought we could stay at the Sanctuary during the summer season, but when we need some time to ourselves..." he lifted her chin, and his lips found hers. He kissed her gently, and when she returned his kiss with more heat, he stood easily with her and walked to the front door without breaking the kiss. The evening air was cooling down, and he didn't want her to catch a chill.

Kyran managed to open the door and carry her across the threshold with one hand holding her in place. As he carried her across the enormous room, she noted the windows facing the water on either side of a massive stone fireplace. He lit the fire with a thought and set her down on the bear skin rug in front of the hearth.

Rhy laid there with her hair fanning out around her head, reminding him of something he said to her the first night he found her at the lake. "You still look like an angel to me."

"Even with me devilish temperament on display at times?"

"Yes," he said as he settled between her legs and gazed down at her with a cheeky grin. "Especially then. I like my angels with a little bit of spice."

"I've got that covered and then some." Her hands traced his face. "I know it's only been a few days," she raised her hips against his, "but I've missed ye, Kyr." Her voice was sultry, and her eyes turned a darker green as they met his.

As she finished speaking, his lips met hers in a bruising kiss, needing her just as badly. The sight of a sword impaling her had destroyed him, knowing it was a killing blow. For a moment, he'd lost his mind completely as he held her bleeding body in his lap. The Earth Mother was not known for reversing death. Somehow, Rhy earned her grace, and Kyran wouldn't take a moment of the time they were allotted for granted.

His tongue stroked hers, encouraging her to dance with him as his hands traveled down to the hem of her shirt. Pushing the fabric out of his way, his fingers stroked her breasts as he swallowed her moans of pleasure. Unhooking the cinches on the front of her corset, he released her voluptuous bosoms into his large palms. His hands gently massaged them, eliciting gasps of pleasure as her fingers gripped his hair tightly.

He kissed his way down her neck, pausing to nip here and there. When he reached her waist, he removed her shirt and corset. Straddling her, he kneaded her breasts while his lips traced a path to them. His fingers grazed over the sensitive tips before he took one into his mouth.

Rhy's back arched as she moved closer to the magic his mouth was performing. Heat spread down her torso and settled in her core, making her slick and ready for him. Little shock waves radiated out from his lips, working their way down her body until they gathered in her moist heat. "Yes, Kyran. Don't stop; tis so good."

Kyran smiled around her breast, suckling harder as he pinched the neglected nipple next to it. He felt the ripples of an orgasm roll through her. The vibrations transmitted through his thighs, making his cock throb right along with her. Damn, he loved how sensitive she was to his touch.

Removing her skirt, Kyran sat back on his haunches between her legs and slowly unbuttoned his shirt. The vision of her with the firelight flickering across her body made his cock throb harder in his pants. Her chest was flushed, and her hands were stroking her breasts. Long legs fell open, exposing her wet center to him, and his gaze followed her right hand as it trailed slowly down her abdomen, dipping between her legs.

Kyran's eyes narrowed, and he sucked in a breath of pure pleasure, watching her. Tossing the shirt aside, he began untying his breeches. He loved the way her eyes were following his movements, and the moment he was finished, his cock sprang out of its confines, laying heavily across his stomach, thick and throbbing.

He stood quickly to remove them, his eyes never leaving her because he didn't want to miss one expression crossing her face. "You look so damn beautiful, Rhy," he said. "Don't stop what you're doing."

Her neck arched as her fingers teased the sensitive bundle of nerves at the top of her slit. Half closed, her eyes were luminous as she gazed up at him.

Kneeling between her legs and fisting his cock, he stroked it slowly from the base to the tip, rolling his hand over the thick head. He repeated the motion, each time slower than the last. When a pearly drop appeared on the head, he smeared it around, then, leaning over on one arm, brought his finger to her lips and nearly lost it when she sucked his finger into her mouth, cleaning him off. His grip tightened almost painfully to keep himself in control as her sensual nature enthralled him.

Rhy loved the control she had over this man. His eyes worshiped her as he touched himself. They roamed over her body, watching her hand, and then returned to her eyes, wanting to see how much it was affecting her. She was getting more turned on as he stroked himself. On the next stroke of her fingers over her clit, she slid them down further, entering her slick core. Dripping with desire, she easily inserted two fingers up to her middle knuckles and pumped them into her tight sheath. Her inner muscles tightened around her fingers, and she could only imagine how good her velvet walls felt to him when he sank his cock into her. Pulling her dripping fingers back out, she stroked her clit again with a sob. An orgasm hovered, and she wasn't sure if she should embrace it yet or wait for him.

The light flickered off her slick fingers and Kyran groaned at the sight of it. He reached down and took her hand, bringing her fingers to his mouth, and sucking them clean. Rhy gasped and writhed beneath him. His hand moved faster on his thick cock. "How do you want to come, Rhy?"

"I need ye inside of me, Kyr." He loved that she'd started using his nickname, and that was the answer he'd been hoping for. Releasing his cock, he used both hands to lift her hips off the floor and pull her closer to him. He leaned down and, using his tongue, took one deep swipe up through her cleft, making her whimper beneath him. Slowly, he eased her onto his cock—not thrusting into her—but slowly sliding her onto him.

The sight of her splayed back on her shoulders while twitching around his cock was so fucking beautiful. Rhy was clueless about what she did to him, but she was about to find out.

"You are the most beautiful thing I have ever seen, my lady," he said as he reached down and used his thumb to slowly circle her clit. She'd asked for him inside of her, but that was all the direction she'd given him. He fully intended to take full advantage and creative license in the way that he was going to make her scream. She tried to move her hips, but the angle she was at and his hand on her hip held her in her place.

The warm, wet sheath he was wrapped in was rippling up and down his length. His balls were pulling up, and he was damn near ready to cum. It was embarrassing how quickly she did him in, with her large, emerald eyes watching him and the body of a goddess undulating beneath him.

"Kyr, please, I'm so close..." she whimpered as his thumb continued to stroke her in ever-widening circles away from where she needed him to touch her. Her fingers pulled tightly on her nipples, making her sheath pulse tightly around him.

"Oh, God, Rhy..." he said in a voice hoarse with need. "As soon as you come, you're going to take me with you." He clamped down on the need to hold her down and pump as hard as possible into her because he was enjoying the game they were playing, but it was getting harder by the moment to maintain his composure.

The sight of her massaging and squeezing her breasts while she was impaled on his cock in the firelight was so fucking erotic that he was panting as he watched where they were connected. He loved the way they were joined, and when he pulled out a few inches to watch her beautiful pussy slowly swallow him again, her shuddering gasps did it for him. He gazed down at the flush on her face and her chest rising quickly. Removing his thumb, he looked her in the eye and said, "Come for me, Rhy."

Rhy watched Kyran's eyes as he inched out of her slowly. She wanted to beg him to stroke her a few times, but she, too, was enjoying the erotic game they were playing together. As he filled her again, her body shuddered from the sensation, and when he took his thumb away, she cried out in disappointment. Then he flicked her clit with his forefinger, and the brief flash of pain on her overstimulated skin made her body begin convulsing tightly around him in shuddering ripples, squeezing his cock tightly.

Kyran groaned loudly as her inner walls gripped his cock in a viselike fist. Still trying not to pump into her, he let her walls milk him dry as sweat dripped off his face onto her abdomen. Carefully laying her back down with his hard cock still buried inside of her, he reached beneath her to grab her ass. With a slow rhythm, he moved in and out of her, making their orgasm last longer. The overpowering sensations to their sensitive body parts kept him hard. He continued stroking her, picking up speed as they worked their way back up for another.

Rhy's body wept for him, her juices running down both their bodies as his strokes grew longer and harder. She loved how he made love to her, but sometimes she wished he would let the monster loose that she met the first night he'd taken her. Their first time together had been unexpected, and there were so many reasons on both their parts that it should never had happened that way, but right now, she was craving the man who lost all control with her.

She reached up and pulled his head down, kissing him ferociously. Ending the kiss with a little bite, she looked him in the eye and said, "I want ye behind me on yer knees, Kyr."

Kryan looked at her in shock. They hadn't chosen to return to that position since their first night. His cock throbbed harder at the thought of her ass in his hands. "Are you sure?" he asked, wanting no misunderstandings. "I have a hard time controlling myself behind you."

"I'm sure, Kyran." She moved her body away from his and flipped to her knees. Long hair flipped over her shoulder as her eyes sought his. "I want ye to take what ye need from me as much as ye want me to ask for what I want. Right now, I need ye deeper and harder inside of me. Will ye give me that?" She arched her back and gave him such a sultry look that it was hard to comprehend how new she was to this dance.

His cock throbbed harder at her displayed in front of him. She widened her stance, and her glistening pussy beckoned him. Without another thought, he positioned himself behind her and slid his cock through her cleft, making sure he was well lubricated before he slid inside her waiting body. This time, there would be nothing but pleasure between the two of them in this position.

Grabbing her hips and tilting her pelvis, Kyran sank his cock into her welcoming body. The movement of her ass against him was divine, and as his hips picked up speed, he fisted her hair, pulling her head back so he could watch her. The expression of nothing but pure erotic joy on her face allowed him to let his inner beast loose and he pumped into her as hard and as fast as he could, chasing his own pleasure. As he felt her body rippling around him once more, he banded his left hand around her middle, pulling her upright against him while using his right hand to stroke her clit, making her orgasm last longer.

Rhy sobbed with pleasure from the multiple orgasms he coaxed out of her body. She bucked in his arms as her body rode out the waves on his cock. Every stroke intensified what she was experiencing, and from the sound of Kyran roaring behind her, he was gaining just as much pleasure.

Spent, they collapsed to the floor, trying to catch their breath. Kyran rolled them to their sides with his head buried in her hair and his arms wrapped around her. Small shudders still traveled up and down her abdomen, and he gently rubbed her skin, bringing her down softly as his lips found the side of her neck and kissed her.

Rhy rolled over so that she could see him. Her hand pushed his sweaty hair back, and he kissed her palm when she stroked his cheek. "I love ye, Kyran.

"I love you, Rhyanna. More every day."

He gave her a soft kiss, merely brushing his lips over hers. "When we catch our breath, I'll give you a tour," he said, nuzzling her neck. "But I'm not sure I can walk quite yet."

Giggling at that, she tucked closer into him and stroked his chest. "Thank ye, me laird, for never giving up on us, even when it would've been a hell of a lot easier to do so."

"Thank you, my lady, for giving me a second chance when some wouldn't have believed I deserved one. I promise I'll never make you regret it."

Their lips met again softly and sweetly, and as he pulled a blanket over them, they spent the first night in their new home loving each other, laughing, and talking about the future they could see on the horizon.

The flickering light played over their undulating bodies as they enjoyed each other repeatedly throughout the night. Their loving was a celebration of life, knowing that they had faced death, survived, and a beautiful future awaited them. Destiny indeed had a plan for Rhyanna, and his name was Kyran.

CHAPTER NINETY-SIX

Deadly Distraction

"My office as soon as you can," came through urgently from Madylyn.

Jameson was sparring with Damian and on the verge of kicking his ass. He needed someone to spar with now that Danny was all but ignoring him again after their first kiss. He was tired of the farce he was living— pretending she had compelled him weeks ago and getting more frustrated by her ignoring him like he had done something wrong by comforting her.

"On my way," he sent back, momentarily distracted. A moment was all Damian needed, and he took full advantage of it by knocking Jamey flat on his back.

"What's up with you today?" Damian asked as he gathered their weapons and returned them to the building behind him. "You're distracted and completely off your game. It's not like you."

Jamey was in a pissy mood already, and even though he knew Damian meant it constructively, he wasn't in the mood to defend his poor performance. As Damian offered him a hand, he considered using the leverage to flip him over the top of him and continue with the hand-to-hand training.

Damian braced himself, and Jamey cursed himself again for telegraphing his intentions so easily. He seriously needed to get his shit together before he did or said something that made Danny realize she'd never compelled him weeks ago and that he desperately wanted her lips on his again. Jamey reached up and took Damian's hand graciously.

"You don't have to tell me, Jamey, but if you need someone to talk to, you know where to find me."

"Appreciate that, but I've got to go. Maddy calls."

"Well, I wouldn't keep the lady waiting then. Tomorrow?"

"Aye," Jamey said. They had been sparring most mornings since Damian's return to the Sanctuary. It was an old habit they always fell back into whenever Damian was on site. He brushed the dirt off after having his ass handed to him and headed for Maddy's office.

He crossed the lawn and headed for the front door. Danny met him where the lanes intersected. "G'morning," he said.

Danny glared at him as he held the door for her. "Not so sure what's good about it," she mumbled, looking at him from bleary eyes. She looked like she'd just rolled out of bed.

With nothing more forthcoming, they walked in silence up the stairs to the second floor. He'd like to think it was a comfortable silence; however, it was anything but. Danny had been ignoring him since the Court of Tears fiasco. If this kept up, he wasn't sure how long he could maintain his facade without blowing his cool. Every time he thought they moved ten paces forward, she retreated thirty the following day. After their latest round, she was treating him like a stranger, not like one of her best friends. If that weren't bad enough, she'd been spending all of her free time with Kerry, rubbing salt into the wound.

"Rough night?" he asked, stating the obvious.

The glare returned full force. "You could say that." And there she went back to being an ice queen again.

"Ferg and I are heading to the Tap later. You coming?"

"Probably not."

Short, terse, and really pissing him off, he found himself unable to let it go. "Got a better offer all of a sudden?" He tried to smile, but it felt wrong, and he knew he needed to back off—but couldn't.

"Maybe I'm just sick of the two of you for a change. My God, we do just about everything but sleep together…" her voice trailed off and her eyes went wide before her favorite emotion—anger—rolled in to save the day. "Maybe I just need a fucking break from all the testosterone." She stomped off into Maddy's office ahead of him.

Okaaay then. Moving on and trying really hard not to pick a fight with her with a reminder that he was fairly certain Kerrygan had a set of balls, too, he took a seat in front of Maddy's desk.

Danny stood to his right, supporting the wall.

Maddy looked at the two of them and raised a brow. "Problem?"

Danny looked at the ground, and Jamey shook his head.

"Good," Maddy said. She walked to a wall of maps and moved some aside until they looked at a topographical outline of Singer Island. "We've been notified by the River Rats River Patrol that at least one rogue hellhound has taken up residence on Singer Island. They've seen him along the docks threatening anyone who attempts to approach. The owners were off island for the winter and have been unable to return. He's already attacked two boats trying to dock and bitten three of the men on board. Thankfully, they had antivenom in a medical kit. He needs to be contained or put down."

"How the hell did he get out there?" Danny grumbled.

"Probably over the ice this past winter," Jamey said. "It freezes all the way across and wouldn't have taken much for one to be chasing deer across and then end up stuck there after it thawed. They're not fond of swimming far. Well, at least it's a nice day for an adventure," Jamey said, standing and trying to act normal. "When do you want us to leave?"

"Sooner the better," Maddy said. "While you're in the area, scout out a few of the nearby islands and see if you find anything unusual."

Jamey looked at Danny, then said tersely, "I'll meet you at the portal in thirty after I weapon up. Need me to grab anything for you?"

"Nada," she said, heading out the door, the ice queen once again.

He headed for the door, trying to rein in his temper at her dismissive tone as every inch of him wanted to call her on her bullshit.

"Jamey," Madylyn's voice interrupted the full-on pissed-off he was about to work up to. "Be careful."

Sparing a glance back at her, he wondered if she had seen something, then shook it off. Those were words she rarely said to him. He nodded and left, heading for the weapons room on the ground floor.

The weapons room was full of trunks and cabinets displaying all manner of sharp, deadly objects. Jamey strapped knives all over his body while his mind wandered back to the night Danny shared her past with him a not long ago. She shared her horrific childhood with him, then compelled him to forget the entire evening. So far, he had played the part well, he thought, but his patience was beginning to wear thin.

A heavy leather belt went through two scabbards. Sheathing a short sword on either hip, he gathered up the rest of the supplies for the journey ahead of them. He slung the leather strap of a crossbow across his chest and tucked a quarrel of bolts onto his belt, hoping they wouldn't have to fight up close with the demon hound.

With a groan, he remembered the way Danny shuddered in his arms as she climaxed with her eyes locked on his right after she took her first kiss from him. The emotions she unknowingly shared through their link had floored him—surprise that she could feel that way, an unwillingness to need to feel that way, and finally, a longing to have him inside of her the next time she found that kind of a release.

Body responding to the memory, his pants grew tighter as his cock swelled and throbbed, wanting more. His body knew what it wanted even when his mind worried about the consequences, and his heart wasn't sure it could take the rejection.

"Down boy," he muttered to himself with an adjustment. Skittish around him since Rhyanna nearly died, Danny sure the fuck didn't need to sense his body's raging desire when he was near her. The cock twitching in his pants needed him to think about something else.

Hellhounds. Jamey hated the fuckers. Not the ones housed on Sanctuary grounds; he had formed a grudging respect for them. Life had to be damn near unbearable when you were held on a choke chain, especially when your very nature pushed you to take what you wanted, when you wanted. On the plus side, the ill-mannered, mangy bastards were the best trackers he'd ever seen—better even than him—and he was one of the best. They begrudgingly collaborated with the wardens whenever it was necessary.

The rogue animals—typically younger males—sought freedom on the outlying islands. The Sanctuary tended to leave them alone— if the island was uninhabited, had a sufficient game population, and the massive beasts avoided the humans who wandered in. Most of the intelligent animals obeyed, terrified of being captured and once again penned. Once they went completely rogue, there was no reasoning with them. They were a threat to everyone.

He slung a leather pack cross-body over his shoulder. The pack contained provisions for several days and emergency medical supplies, including doses of an antivenom Rhyanna created for hellhound bites, and sedatives to knock the bastard out if they were able to subdue him.

A battle axe called his name as he headed for the door. With that swinging from his hand, he left the weapons room and headed for the portal, meeting Danyka on the way. Her body language was stiff, and she was still ignoring him.

Fuck it. Two could play that game. If he hadn't wanted some time alone with her, he would have suggested that Kerry should have taken his place. Second-guessing that choice now, as they trudged silently down the hill, didn't do him any good. However, Maddy requested him, and he never shirked his duty to the Sanctuary.

The portal took them to an island close to the coast of Singer, where they could rent a boat and get a closer look. They haggled with a River Rat over a fair price for the Sanctuary's use of a small skiff for two days until both parties were satisfied. The man's price was steep, but the boat was in beautiful condition, and he included a bagged lunch with the purchase.

They traveled the river without a word passing between them. The only sound on their passing was the light splash of the oars in the water. Danny stood at the front of the boat, facing away from him as Jameson steadily rowed them towards Singer Island. A glance at the sky confirmed his shifter's sense of smell, alerting him to a storm blowing in from the west. There would be rain. Not today, but tonight, and lots of it. The air was cool with a steady breeze across the water, but he was plenty warm as he easily moved them closer to their destination.

Singer Castle came into view, and he moved cautiously around the coastline while Danny kept watch from the bow.

"There," she said, pointing toward the southern dock.

It was the only word she had spoken today, and Jamey found he missed her chattering like a magpie at him.

Jamey could see the rogue beast roaming the dock. Red eyes watched them as they drifted by. The hound's lips pulled back, and he could hear the eerie growl emanating from behind the creature's clenched teeth. Red eyes tracked them, and Jamey wondered exactly how far they could swim. He should have asked Ronan that question before they left. It would be a nightmare trying to deal with one on the open water.

Danny removed her black leather jacket, then unbuttoned the matching black vest she wore beneath. Dropping it to the bottom of the boat, she kicked off her boots and shimmied out of her black leather pants.

Jameson memorized every inch of her skin as she undressed. This wasn't the first time he'd seen her naked. Danny often used her peregrine form to scout out situations they were entering blind. He usually looked away and gave her privacy, although she never asked for it.

Never shy about her body, the minute leather halters and vests she preferred left little to the imagination, nor did the painted-on leather breeches. This time, however, he stared at her unabashedly—hungrily.

Perhaps it was because she was facing away from him, or maybe it was because he was finally looking at her as an available female who was calling to him at a soul level, making his hands ache to stroke her and his body desperate to love her. Might have just been that he was still angry at her for compelling him, and he was feeling defiant today.

Whatever reasons he had, his eyes traced her petite form longingly. The slight curve of her neck led to strong, narrow shoulders. She was lean, but that didn't stop her from having curves in all the right places. Full breasts graced her narrow torso. Her waist was tiny—he doubted he would need two full hands to wrap around her. Tiny though her waist was, it flared into full ripe hips and a luscious ass. His eyes traced every inch of her the way he longed to do with his hands. As his body started to react once again to the visual display in front of him, her voice snapped him back to attention.

"If you're done cataloging every inch of me, can you bring the boat around to the other side and see if he follows you around the shoreline? We need a way onto the island safely."

His eyes snapped up and found her ice blue shards watching him. Tremendous willpower kept a blush from staining his cheeks as he met her eyes without flinching.

"Yes, ma'am. Anything else you want me to bring?"

"My clothes and the medical kit."

"See you on the other side," he said with a mocking salute. He wasn't sure why he was feeling so cocky, but he couldn't help himself. Tired of the charade they were playing, his temper was rising as she continued shutting him out.

Danny stared at him for a long time, and then in the blink of an eye, she vanished, and a small falcon flew into the sky with a shrill cry. The fastest bird in the sky, or animal on land, she took off like a flash—there one moment and gone the next.

Jamey envied her ability to shift easily into the small falcon. His spirit animal was a grizzly, and along with the lumbering size came the irrational temper of the animal. His animal form was a sharp contrast to Jamey's easygoing temperament. He rarely shifted because he hated losing control. In his bear form, he lacked the capacity to make rational decisions. His animal was a wonderful form of protection but much too hard to control when he transformed.

He nearly cleared the tip of the island when he lost sight of the hound. The foliage was thick and scraggly there, and it would be difficult for an animal his size to navigate through the scrubby bushes.

Danny soared above him, circling the island repeatedly as she surveyed the safest possible way to gain entrance. He floated as he waited for her report. A soft leather bag lay near her clothes, and he gathered up the discarded items and neatly folded them. He couldn't stop himself from bringing the jacket up to his face. Inhaling deeply, he took her scent into him. Sweet and spicy, just like her personality. He folded the leather before placing everything into the bag and securing it to his back so he didn't forget to take her clothes with him.

"The southern side has an easy way for you to get in, and it's hidden from the main path around the island. There's an old smugglers' cove."

"On my way." He maneuvered the craft around the island and found the cove she mentioned. Slowly, he worked his way to shore, watching the surrounding area carefully, always anticipating an attack. Stepping carefully onto shore, he attached the long strap of the emergency medical kit crossbody over his left hip. He wanted his hands free if he needed to defend himself.

A high-pitched shriek had him looking up, and Danny tipped to one side, using their prearranged signal to tell him all was clear. He headed up a steep bank, grabbing roots and vines to help pull himself up. He finally crested the top, his breath heaving from the exertion. Danny perched on a wall with a narrow expanse of lawn between them. He walked toward her and dropped the pack behind the hedge, giving her a bit of privacy to dress.

Jamey heard the falcon transform back into the woman behind him as he made his way towards the right side of the building in front of him. One of many castles on the river, this one was smaller than some of the others. A private home only used part of the year; he could see the damage the hellhound had done from here. Shattered windows on the ground floor showed where the animal had sought shelter from the winter snow, wind, and freezing temperatures.

"Jamey, wait for me. I'm almost done"

Danny's voice cautioned him, but he continued moving forward. He could sense her irritation with him and her frustration.

"He's a big bastard, Jamey," she said as she quickly pulled on her boots. *"Trust me, you don't want him to surprise you out in the open."*

"You're talking to me now?" His tone was harsh and so unlike him. *"I don't plan to stay in the open for long."* His voice was short, his frustration with her coming through loud and clear. *"This isn't the first tracking mission I've been on."*

"Good to know because that's not how you're acting right now. The first rule of survival is to wait for your partner, goddamn it. Now wait for me, you asshole." Her tone was pure bitch, matching his miserable mood.

Jameson ignored her, moving slowly ahead towards the front of the building. He was angry at the situation they seemed to be in since their intimate encounter and with himself for not letting it go until she was ready to talk to him again. Danny would talk to him when she was ready and not a moment before. Pushing her back to the wall would only make this worse, and he fucking *knew* this but couldn't seem to let it fucking go.

A twig snapped from behind him to the left, and he whirled to see the nasty-looking creature stalking toward Danny in the back. She bent over, pulling on her last boot, and didn't see him coming at her. Panic froze him in place for a moment as he realized everything he stood to lose.

Without another thought, he ran towards the enormous creature, trying to block him from Danny. This hound made a Great Dane look like a toy fucking poodle. His head nearly reached Jamey's shoulders, and he was twice the length of a domestic canine. Weighing in at an easy two-fifty, he was scrawny—starving from the long winter. The only thing left was solid muscle hell-bent on death and destruction. His long canines were bared, and the growl issuing forth came straight from the bowels of hell. Thick ropes of saliva dangled from the massive jowls of his mouth, toxic enough to kill a man easily with just a scratch. His eyes were bulging, and the fires of hell covered the black pupils with red flames.

The canine turned towards Jamey, snarling, and paced towards him eagerly. The low growl became throatier and menacing as Jamey backed up, trying to lead the demon from Danny.

"Jamey, don't make any sudden moves," Danny projected to him. *"If you can shift into your bear, it will give you a longer reach and protection from his fangs."*

"Can't do that. In the time I need to shift, he'll be on me. I left the crossbow in the boat. Couldn't climb with it. Wasn't the smartest thing to do, but I haven't been thinking clearly for the last week or so," he admitted grudgingly. *"I don't seem to be able to think clearly at all lately around you."*

"Shut the fuck up about all that. We need a plan that involves him dead and both of us alive."

"Not sure that's going to work this time, Danny," he said in a wistful tone.

"I'm using my knives on him. Be ready to pull yours and aim for his chest while I hit his head and spine."

"Danny, Hellion, you need to know…"

"Shut up and put your hands on your fucking weapons now!"

Danny pulled titanium blades from her arms and sent them sailing as the beast lunged. Jamey managed to let one sail through the air as the hound's massive jaws clamped down on his right arm between the elbow and shoulder.

The beast bellowed in pain but held on to Jamey as it shrieked. Clamped between its massive jaws, the damn thing shook him like a rag doll. Jamey punched the beast with his left hand, trying to make it release him, but the animal held on and clamped down tighter.

Danny moved closer, trying for a better head shot at the animal. She never missed when she threw sharp objects, but they were moving so damn fast, she was afraid she was going to hit Jamey in the process.

The normal caramel tone of Jamey's skin was fading quickly to a sickly gray as toxins flooded his system, and he lost copious amounts of blood. Her heart nearly thudded out of her chest as he struggled to free himself. Fighting tears of frustration, she ran at the beast, leaping high onto his back, her knees straddling his neck as she double-fisted her blades into his eyes.

The beast went stiff as the titanium reached his brain, then collapsed beneath her. She jumped clear over his head, somersaulting away from him to prevent him from rolling over her.

Unfortunately, he landed partially on Jamey, who was struggling to breathe beneath him. Danny ran to him, grateful for the overload of adrenaline allowing her to pull him from beneath the beast. She cut the strap on the medical bag hanging from his dangling arm and said a quick prayer of thanks to whoever was listening that the vials with the antivenom were intact. Filling a syringe, she injected him above the wound while she sent an urgent message to every warden in the area.

"WARDEN DOWN. HELLHOUND bite. Assistance needed immediately on Singer Island ASAP. Hurry the fuck up!"

To the Heart Island crew, she screamed, *"It's Jamey, and it's fucking BAD. He's bleeding out on me. Rhy, you need to teleport here from the closest portal. PLEASE HURRY; he doesn't have much time."* She couldn't help the sob that accompanied the next line. *"I can't lose him. Please hurry."*

Disconnecting as she felt their shock and disbelief radiating back to her, she turned all of her attention to Jamey. His breathing eased a little after the shot kicked in and his body stopped fighting the venomous bite. She cut the other end of the leather strap from the bag and used it to tie a tourniquet above the bite. As she finished tying it off, she noticed the claw marks that had scored his chest. Blood ran freely from there as well, soaking the ground beneath him. The gouges were deep, and air bubbles were appearing in the blood, showing how deeply the claws reached into his lungs. Straddling his hips, she removed the vest she had just put back on and applied pressure in a desperate bid to stop the bleeding. Her body weight on his chest would make it harder for him to breathe, but if he bled out first, it would be a moot point.

"On my way. Danny, give him a shot, stop the bleeding, and keep him awake until I arrive," Rhyanna shouted at her.

"We're coming!" Madylyn and Ronan said simultaneously.

"Don't ye let that fecker die on us, lass. I'll kick both yer asses," Ferg sent, and she could hear the concern in his voice beneath the threat.

"Almost there," said Roarke. *"I can transport him if he can't teleport out."*

"I'm coming, grabbing help on my way," Kyran answered tersely.

Danyka sobbed, seeing how pale Jamey was. His eyes were drifting shut, so she hollered at him, "Eyes up here, buddy. You stay with me, goddamn it. Rhy's on her way, and she wants you alert when she gets here. Gonna hurt like a bitch to put you back together, but don't you go to sleep, Jamey."

Jamey looked at her with unfocused eyes as he weakly moved his head. His lips moved, but nothing came out. *"I'm trying Hellion, truly, I am, but I'm tired and cold."*

Her heart was pounding in her chest and ears, and she prayed she didn't pass out from lack of oxygen. She didn't feel like she could draw a breath through the sobs emerging from her chest and the tears trailing down her face. The Sanctuary needed him, and more importantly than that, Danny just realized that she needed him so much more than she'd been willing to admit.

"Stay with me, Jamey, damn it. Don't you even think about leaving me. I need you," her voice wavered between a shout and a sob.

"You've never needed anyone, Hellion. Helluva time to change your mind now…" His eyes drifted shut as his breathing became more labored under her bloody hands.

"Jamey," she shouted, trying to make him open his eyes. "Wake up, you bastard. There's no sleeping for the damned in my world."

A sad smile crossed his face as his eyes focused for a moment and met hers. *"But what a way to be damned, Hellion, with you straddling my lap, the sun on my face, and the wind in my hair…I love you, Danny."* With that last thought, his eyes rolled back in his head. He gasped once and blacked out.

EPILOGUE

Fergus staggered into his suite and collapsed into a chair by the fireplace. Not bothering with a glass, he opened one of the bottles that Uncle Killam had gifted him and drank a fourth of it without coming up for air. Worst fucking day ever—and he'd had some doozies over the centuries.

As a lad in Scotland, he witnessed his father slain by a rival laird right in front of him, and that hadn't affected him as today had. His mam relocated them to the Great Lakes Clan to be near her family. Losing everyone and everything he knew had been a breeze next to this. Children were blessed with the gift of flexibility when their lives changed drastically. Adults didn't have that luxury.

Watching his best friend fucking dying in front of him would haunt him til the day he fucking died. He raised the bottle again, not slowing down. This shite was like mother's milk to him, and it was the good shite. He had no doubt he'd be cracking another bottle before the night was out.

Ronan had taken a devastated Madylyn away soon after they arrived, afraid the stress would affect her pregnancy. At the end of her first trimester, he wasn't taking a chance with either of them, and Fergus couldn't blame him. The amount of energy Rhyanna had to channel was completely insane, and when Maddy stepped in to add hers to the mix, Rhy's magic shoved her back hard to protect her. Thankfully, Ronan had been there to catch her.

Rhyanna was drained so badly physically and emotionally; Fergus didn't know if she was going to completely return from the energy expenditure. Such an amazing healer, she rarely lost anyone. The shock on Kyran's face as he gathered her pale body to him was nearly as bad as when she nearly died at Kano and Elyana's ceremony.

And fuck, the pixie. The anguish on her face as she finally realized what she stood to lose and the wails emerging from her would haunt his dreams. Barely able to stumble away, she'd shifted and flown away, unable to face the pain and horror in her human form.

527

Kerrygan stood there with tears streaming down his face at their devastation. With Rhyanna screaming at him not to, he changed back into his falcon form and followed her, knowing full well he might not make the transition back to human once again.

Another fourth met his belly, and he staggered to his feet, wandering into his workroom. On the shelf in front of him were hand carved pieces representing his team. He was working on a chess set, something he was compelled to do. A month ago, when he built the shelf to display them, the one of Jamey had fallen, and his arm had broken off near the shoulder.

Fergus had been horrified, sensing a harbinger of doom around the young man. He'd quickly repaired the piece and hoped his actions would be enough to counteract anything that might happen to the lad.

Looking at the display, he saw the one of Jamey was on its back again, the arm lying next to it again. Another fecking sign. Idly, he wondered how long it had lain there like that. He'd not had time to venture in here lately, and if he had seen it, would he have warned them? Or would he have made the mistake of thinking the piece was flawed, the weight just off and wouldn't stand properly? Who the feck ken?

All he did ken was that he and Jamey'd always been tight. There was nothing about the lad not to like. His drinking buddy and partner in crime with the pixie right there next to them, they had some good times. Jamey tended to be the one talking them out of stupid shite when they were wasted, too. Smart, that one was, but a lot of fecking fun.

Quick with a smile, lighthearted, loyal to a fault, fierce as fuck in battle; the man was Fergus's best friend. God help them if they were knee-deep in shite and needed him to shift into his grizzly because he was the animal equivalent of a berserker. But he managed to turn the tide for them more than once. As long as they made sure they stayed the fuck out of his way, they were safe. All 'cept the pixie. That grizzly loved the lass. She'd run up his back and settled on his shoulders, and he'd carried her around for a bit last time he was called into battle. Made perfect sense because the man in him loved her, too.

Sadly, the pixie was just coming around to that fact a little too late. Thinking of her heartbreak, he threw the bottle at the wall, watching the amber fluid paint it with sad, thin streaks running to the floor. Would've been more effective, he thought randomly, with a full bottle.

A scarred work table eight feet in length caught his eye. Covered in raw materials and partially carved pieces of new Sanctuary members, the sight of it infuriated him, and he roared as he moved forward and flipped the whole damn thing over, not caring what he broke or damaged.

Leaving the destruction behind, he headed back to his sitting room, pacing as he tried to burn off the adrenaline coursing through him. "What the feck is the point of any of this?" he roared into the empty space. The flames in the fireplace flared to the full height of the hearth, the dancing flames reflecting his anguish.

"Ye motherfeckers show me jest enough to be a cock sucking tease, then never give me any way to change or fix it. Why fecking bother showing me that at all?" His fury hadn't dimmed, and the fire blazed hotter, the temperature in the room elevating drastically. "Take yer fecking 'gifts' back because I don't fecking want them anymore! They're fecking useless if I can't do anything with them to help the people I love." He kicked out, knocking a chair to the floor where he stomped it to pieces, screaming the entire while.

The massive house shook with his fury, and fear radiated back to him from the other residents, but he didn't fecking care. Eventually, when the adrenaline rush died and the alcohol kicked in, his anguish finally brought him to his knees. Tears ran freely down his face, his vision blurred as his fire drakes—the pitiful wee things—hid in his beard. He'd scared the lil feckers. Their strength had grown with his outburst, but now they were afraid of him.

Fergus looked down at his hands resting on his knees and stared at the blood covering his hands and arms. He stumbled to his feet and barely made it to the bathroom before all that lovely Scottish whiskey came back up in a hurry. He kept at it until he was dry heaving, then stripped and stepped into the shower, letting the water clear his head of the fog, his body of his best friend's blood, and his aching heart of the anguish choking it.

Finally, as clean as he could manage, he stepped out, dried off, and donned his McKay kilt. Heat still radiating from his body, he wore nothing else as he settled in front of the fire, looking for a message in the flames of his element. Sitting there, his mind blank, waiting for some fecking hint of inspiration, explanation, or jest plain bullshite...his ass eventually went numb, and no answers came through.

His eyes were swollen and heavy when movement in the flames caught his attention. Alert, he gazed more intently and followed the movement of the NightMare, Sabbath, through the flames. The horse was one of a handful that resided in their stables.

Only allowed to roam at night, like the hellhounds, they were incredibly dangerous creatures. Feasting on pain and suffering, they managed to invade your psyche and pull out all the emotions humans tried to push down and hide. Their presence on the island initially caused numerous suicides and an increase in residents needing to be institutionalized for losing their sanity. The feckers were as dangerous as they came.

Fergus quirked a brow as he saw the shape grow larger, finally putting it together that the mare was drawn to his pain. Sabbath had projected her image into the flames to garner his attention. A half-assed chuckle emerged. He must be a fecking mess to draw that crazy bitch to him. His blood ran cold as he felt the mare picking at his links, trying to find a way in. He battened down his defenses, discouraging her, and thinking he had, figured she'd go away.

The flame mare stomped her hoof at him in the coals of his fireplace and, when he continued to ignore her, stepped out of the stone enclosure running full force at him. Only the size of a kitten, smoke rose from the rug as her hooves touched down. Stopping in front of him, she looked up at him and stomped her front hoof again.

"Let me in, Fire Mage!" The intensity of her voice thundered in his head. *"I mean you no harm."*

Fergus glared down at the little fecker, debating what to do when his drakes ran down his legs and circled the prancing fire equine in solidarity. They rejoined him, and he exhaled a long sigh, figuring if they trusted her, he might as well, too. Feck it, what else did he have to lose? His mind? Some would argue he'd already done that.

"What do ye want, Sabbath?" he asked sullenly.

"Come to me Laird of the Emberz," the words snapped out, a command not an invitation.

Puzzled because he could sense a tug in his chest drawing him downstairs, he chose to follow her instructions—at least that's what he told himself. Barefoot, he headed down the staircase and went to the front door. Exiting, he stood on the top step and couldn't believe it when the terrifyingly gorgeous animal knelt down on the ground before him.

NightMares were easily half again the size of the largest horse he'd ever seen. With smoke rising from her hooves and the ability to breathe smoke and flames from her glowing nostrils, she was a literal nightmare come to life. Red eyes glowed at him, the flames dancing within their mirrored surfaces taunting him, daring him to go for a ride.

Fergus stood there dumbfounded. He'd been around the creature before, but she'd never interacted with him before. This was an honor and one he wasn't sure he deserved or trusted.

"Why would I do such a thing as trust ye, me dark mistress?" he said aloud.

"Because I can help you burn off the horror of today and all the rest of the emotions that are blocking your communion with your puny gods. Come for a ride with me. Let me ease your burden for a bit and learn something about me you didn't know. You could share this information with your fellow wardens."

The knowledge alone tempted him, but the ability to unload the overload of depression and horror was enough to have him walking down the stairs, grabbing her mane, and slinging himself onto her back with an ease that surprised him. Barely able to balance on the breadth of her, he found a spot that was semi-comfortable, then leaned down along her neck and said, "All right, ye hell bitch, show me what ye got."

He'd barely fisted her mane when she raced off into the night, with him clinging for dear life. The sheer thrill of being on her back was beyond anything he could have imagined. Fergus's cackle of laughter floated behind them, ringing through the night. As Sabbath raced at breakneck speed, Levyathan, Maddy's stallion, joined them. His lifespan was magically enhanced, and he wasn't anywhere as big as Sabbath, but he was the father of her foals and seemed to take pleasure in her company.

As she flew through the night with him clinging to her back, she sent him a message, *"Open yourself to me emotionally, fire mage. Allow me to drain the worst of the horrors of this day and the last few weeks away from you."* She waited for an answer or a denial, and when neither came, she spoke again, *"I'll only take what you want me to have. You can close the conduit to anything you don't want me to access. The power is all yours. I can't take from you what you won't willingly give."*

Fergus contemplated the offer, and in a rare display of feck-it –isms, he opened the gates to his emotional overload and let her run through them. All the fears and heartbreak of Kyran and Rhyanna's breakup, Meriel's bullshite, Rhyanna's near-death experience…and today…Jamey. Screaming aloud, he let her have all of his anger, fears, and devastation. The louder he screamed, the faster they went as her body soaked up his energy.

"That's it, let it all out. These emotions no longer serve you or anyone you care about. Release it so that you can once again do some good when you return."

"Why are ye helping me? Why do ye care?"

"What makes you think I do? You forget I receive something from this exchange. I experience a boost of your elemental magic from your powerful line of mages. This is the closest thing to ecstasy I can achieve."

"Guess Levyathan's not doing something right." He felt more like himself, able to jest again.

"You're wrong about that; he does everything right that I need him to do. Now, open your links to the others."

"That doesn't seem right to me. It's a violation of their privacy and their trust in me."

"Is this so different than Mistress Rhyanna healing them? I'm giving them the ability to face another day. This will help Madylyn calm herself and protect the child within her. If Rhy is able to unload the pain, fear, and devastation, won't it help her to rest so that she can continue healing tomorrow?"

Sabbath gave him a moment to process everything she'd said. *"What about your little pixie? Doesn't it stand to reason that reducing her pain, removing her horror and, more than anything, the guilt that is eating her alive would be beneficial? If I could help alleviate her guilt to give her a reason to keep going on when she wakes up tomorrow to her new reality…would you deny her that?"*

"Yer not that fecking selfless, so what else are ye taking in return? There's something yer not telling me, and I won't risk anything more than my own fecking sanity until I know what the feck yer after, hell bitch."

Not liking his tone, she bucked and kicked beneath him, and Levyathan snapped at his legs. *"Where I come from, I am a queen, and you will at least treat me with a modicum of respect, you ungrateful little human."*

Fergus held on for dear life, the adrenaline rush pushing away all the cloudy haze of pain from earlier. "Me apologies, me lady. I will endeavor to treat ye with respect. What do ye seek in return for the gift of our emotions?"

"An audience with Madylyn. I want a separate place for us to exist. One that we will claim as ours, staying within preset borders, but outside of a cage during the day. Perhaps we can be rewarded by helping with your island law."

"I will speak to Maddy and present yer case. That's the best I can offer."

"'Tis all I request. You'll allow me to harvest from the others, or you won't. The decision is yours to make. Ask yourself how emotionally stable you are now compared to when I first arrived before you determine my motives."

Fergus paused, knowing she wasn't tacking on an "you ass" to her statement. Evaluating his current level of insanity, he was surprised to realize he was much more stable and able to focus. The horror of the day was still there, but it was muted, somehow easier. *"What other information will ye have access to?"* he asked because there was always a fecking loophole.

"I will have access to nothing more than you offer me, Fire Mage. You'll lead our dance."

"Better be ready to do a jig then."

The massive beast's humor came through their link, and actually made him smile, a feat he wouldn't have thought possible an hour ago. *"Rhyanna and Maddy are the only ones ye may siphon from. Rhy so she can use her healing powers immediately and Maddy to protect her child. No one else. Leave the pixie alone. The pain she is experiencing is a lesson she needs. That much I do ken."*

The surprisingly graceful animal thundered down the path into the woods that ran along the shoreline, leaving sparks along the way. Little glowing embers lined the path behind them for seconds only before fading away in the damp night air. Fergus closed his eyes and enjoyed the sensation of the wind ripping his hair off his face. Closing his eyes, he released her mane, praying she didn't toss his ass off. Stretching his arms out to his sides and sitting up straight on her back, he allowed her to take what she needed through the links he opened to her. *"Sabbath, don't take it all. They need the pain and sorrow to process the day. Jamey was special, and the pain and horror of today shouldn't be that easy to forget. There's lessons to be learned. Do ye understand what I mean?"*

"Aye, I do, and I intended to only take the raw edges off, not the brunt of it, because you're right. Nothing should fully dull the pain of someone you loved. It's a betrayal to them. I'll leave Danyka to wallow in hers unless you tell me otherwise, and I will only do this once while you are with me."

"I appreciate you respecting our personal boundaries." His body balanced on the mare, and his mind blew away the day's catastrophe as his arms fell to his sides, and he simply enjoyed the freedom she gave him from his anguish. "In case I don't think to say it later," his arms clung to her neck for a moment, "thank ye, Sabbath, for being a vital part of our team today and for helping ease our burden."

"You're welcome, Fergus Emberz. You're very welcome."

ACKNOWLEDGEMENTS

I want to thank my husband Eric for his patience and encouragement as I finished this book. Your willingness to fend for yourself while I submerged myself in this world is appreciated more than you know.

I want to thank Kassie for your help with my story bible and plotting. Your perspective is always valued and the time you make for us is always appreciated.

Lady Di, thank you for listening to my frustrations and my victories.

Cori Preston, thank you for the beautiful cover, website and your infinite patience.

Emily Hostetter at Ems Creative Pen is my editing and proofreading goddess. Any mistakes in the final copy are mine. I have loved working on this series with you. I look forward to your input along the way!

Nicki Wilber thank you for the input and final read throughs.

Miss Cin D thank you for going to that first STAR meeting at Barnes Noble so long ago.

Barbidoll, Di, Kassie, Josie, Nancy, Tania, Liz and Liane, thank you for being my biggest cheerleaders!

Chrissy H. Thank you for the Wednesday nights encouraging me to get back to writing.

ABOUT THE AUTHOR

A member of the RWA and the Southern Tier Authors of Romance, AnnaLeigh Skye loves to read and write steamy fantasy romances. She lives on a farm in the Endless Mountains with the man of her dreams, her lovely daughter, two possessed felines, and her extended family.

River of Remorse is the second novel in the Heart Island Sanctuary Series.

www.annaleighskye.com

BY ANNALEIGH SKYE

HEART ISLAND SANCTUARY SERIES

RIVER OF REDEMPTION
RIVER OF REMORSE

COMING SOON

RIVER OF REMEMBRANCE